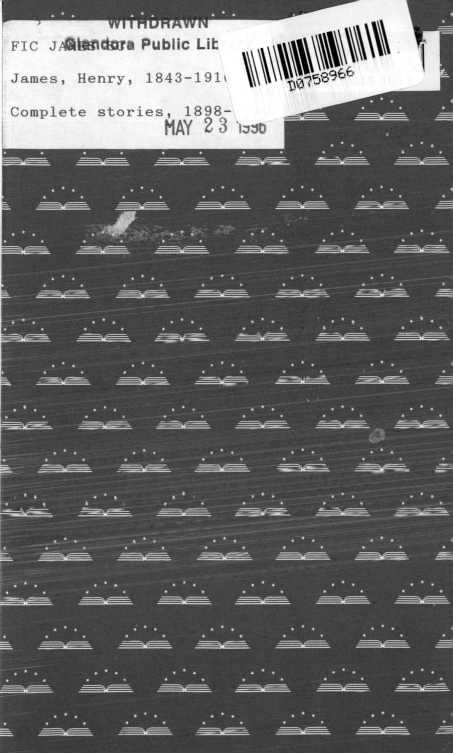

HENRY JAMES

HENRY JAMES

COMPLETE STORIES
1892–1898

THE LIBRARY OF AMERICA

Distributed to the trade in the United States
by Penguin Books USA Inc
and in Canada by Penguin Books Canada Ltd.

Library of Congress Catalog Number: 95-23463
For cataloging information, see end of Notes.
ISBN: 1–883011–09–4

First Printing
The Library of America—82

DAVID BROMWICH AND JOHN HOLLANDER
WROTE THE NOTES FOR THIS VOLUME
IN HONOR OF
IRVING HOWE (1920–1993)

Contents

Nona Vincent

"I WONDERED whether you wouldn't read it to me," said Mrs. Alsager, as they lingered a little near the fire before he took leave. She looked down at the fire sideways, drawing her dress away from it and making her proposal with a shy sincerity that added to her charm. Her charm was always great for Allan Wayworth, and the whole air of her house, which was simply a sort of distillation of herself, so soothing, so beguiling that he always made several false starts before departure. He had spent some such good hours there, had forgotten, in her warm, golden drawing-room, so much of the loneliness and so many of the worries of his life, that it had come to be the immediate answer to his longings, the cure for his aches, the harbour of refuge from his storms. His tribulations were not unprecedented, and some of his advantages, if of a usual kind, were marked in degree, inasmuch as he was very clever for one so young, and very independent for one so poor. He was eight-and-twenty, but he had lived a good deal and was full of ambitions and curiosities and disappointments. The opportunity to talk of some of these in Grosvenor Place corrected perceptibly the immense inconvenience of London. This inconvenience took for him principally the line of insensibility to Allan Wayworth's literary form. He had a literary form, or he thought he had, and her intelligent recognition of the circumstance was the sweetest consolation Mrs. Alsager could have administered. She was even more literary and more artistic than he, inasmuch as he could often work off his overflow (this was his occupation, his profession), while the generous woman, abounding in happy thoughts, but inedited and unpublished, stood there in the rising tide like the nymph of a fountain in the plash of the marble basin.

The year before, in a big newspapery house, he had found himself next her at dinner, and they had converted the intensely material hour into a feast of reason. There was no motive for her asking him to come to see her but that she liked him, which it was the more agreeable to him to perceive as he perceived at the same time that she was exquisite. She

was enviably free to act upon her likings, and it made Wayworth feel less unsuccessful to infer that for the moment he
happened to be one of them. He kept the revelation to himself, and indeed there was nothing to turn his head in the
kindness of a kind woman. Mrs. Alsager occupied so completely the ground of possession that she would have been
condemned to inaction had it not been for the principle of
giving. Her husband, who was twenty years her senior, a massive personality in the City and a heavy one at home (wherever
he stood, or even sat, he was monumental), owned half a big
newspaper and the whole of a great many other things. He
admired his wife, though she bore no children, and liked her
to have other tastes than his, as that seemed to give a greater
acreage to their life. His own appetites went so far he could
scarcely see the boundary, and his theory was to trust her to
push the limits of hers, so that between them the pair should
astound by their consumption. His ideas were prodigiously
vulgar, but some of them had the good fortune to be carried
out by a person of perfect delicacy. Her delicacy made her
play strange tricks with them, but he never found this out.
She attenuated him without his knowing it, for what he
mainly thought was that he had aggrandised *her*. Without her
he really would have been bigger still, and society, breathing
more freely, was practically under an obligation to her which,
to do it justice, it acknowledged by an attitude of mystified
respect. She felt a tremulous need to throw her liberty and
her leisure into the things of the soul—the most beautiful
things she knew. She found them, when she gave time to seeking, in a hundred places, and particularly in a dim and sacred
region—the region of active pity—over her entrance into
which she dropped curtains so thick that it would have been
an impertinence to lift them. But she cultivated other beneficent passions, and if she cherished the dream of something
fine the moments at which it most seemed to her to come
true were when she saw beauty plucked flower-like in the garden of art. She loved the perfect work—she had the artistic
chord. This chord could vibrate only to the touch of another,
so that appreciation, in her spirit, had the added intensity of
regret. She could understand the joy of creation, and she
thought it scarcely enough to be told that she herself created

happiness. She would have liked, at any rate, to choose her way; but it was just here that her liberty failed her. She had not the voice—she had only the vision. The only envy she was capable of was directed to those who, as she said, could do something.

As everything in her, however, turned to gentleness, she was admirably hospitable to such people as a class. She believed Allan Wayworth could do something, and she liked to hear him talk of the ways in which he meant to show it. He talked of them almost to no one else—she spoiled him for other listeners. With her fair bloom and her quiet grace she was indeed an ideal public, and if she had ever confided to him that she would have liked to scribble (she had in fact not mentioned it to a creature), he would have been in a perfect position for asking her why a woman whose face had so much expression should not have felt that she achieved. How in the world could she express better? There was less than that in Shakespeare and Beethoven. She had never been more generous than when, in compliance with her invitation, which I have recorded, he brought his play to read to her. He had spoken of it to her before, and one dark November afternoon, when her red fireside was more than ever an escape from the place and the season, he had broken out as he came in "I've done it, I've done it!" She made him tell her all about it—she took an interest really minute and asked questions delightfully apt. She had spoken from the first as if he were on the point of being acted, making him jump, with her participation, all sorts of dreary intervals. She liked the theatre as she liked all the arts of expression, and he had known her to go all the way to Paris for a particular performance. Once he had gone with her the time she took that stupid Mrs. Mostyn. She had been struck, when he sketched it, with the subject of his drama, and had spoken words that helped him to believe in it. As soon as he had rung down his curtain on the last act he rushed off to see her, but after that he kept the thing for repeated last touches. Finally, on Christmas day, by arrangement, she sat there and listened to it. It was in three acts and in prose, but rather of the romantic order, though dealing with contemporary English life, and he fondly believed that it showed the hand if not of the master, at least of the prize pupil.

Allan Wayworth had returned to England, at two-and-twenty, after a miscellaneous continental education; his father, the correspondent, for years, in several foreign countries successively, of a conspicuous London journal, had died just after this, leaving his mother and her two other children, portionless girls, to subsist on a very small income in a very dull German town. The young man's beginnings in London were difficult, and he had aggravated them by his dislike of journalism. His father's connection with it would have helped him, but he was (insanely, most of his friends judged—the great exception was always Mrs. Alsager) *intraitable* on the question of form. Form—in his sense—was not demanded by English newspapers, and he couldn't give it to them in *their* sense. The demand for it was not great anywhere, and Wayworth spent costly weeks in polishing little compositions for magazines that didn't pay for style. The only person who paid for it was really Mrs. Alsager: she had an infallible instinct for the perfect. She paid in her own way, and if Allan Wayworth had been a wage-earning person it would have made him feel that if he didn't receive his legal dues his palm was at least occasionally conscious of a gratuity. He had his limitations, his perversities, but the finest parts of him were the most alive, and he was restless and sincere. It is however the impression he produced on Mrs. Alsager that most concerns us: she thought him not only remarkably good-looking but altogether original. There were some usual bad things he would never do—too many prohibitive puddles for him in the short cut to success.

For himself, he had never been so happy as since he had seen his way, as he fondly believed, to some sort of mastery of the scenic idea, which struck him as a very different matter now that he looked at it from within. He had had his early days of contempt for it, when it seemed to him a jewel, dim at the best, hidden in a dunghill, a taper burning low in an air thick with vulgarity. It was hedged about with sordid approaches, it was not worth sacrifice and suffering. The man of letters, in dealing with it, would have to put off all literature, which was like asking the bearer of a noble name to forego his immemorial heritage. Aspects change, however, with the point of view: Wayworth had waked up one morning in a different bed altogether. It is needless here to trace this accident to its source; it would have been much more interesting to a spectator of the young man's life to follow some of the consequences. He had been made (as he felt) the subject of a special revelation, and he wore his hat like a man in love. An angel had taken him by the hand and guided him to the shabby door which opens, it appeared, into an interior both splendid and austere. The scenic idea was magnificent when once you had embraced it—the dramatic form had a purity which made some others look ingloriously rough. It had the high dignity of the exact sciences, it was mathematical and architectural. It was full of the refreshment of calculation and construction, the incorruptibility of line and law. It was bare, but it was erect, it was poor, but it was noble; it reminded him of some sovereign famed for justice who should have lived in a palace despoiled. There was a fearful amount of concession in it, but what you kept had a rare intensity. You were perpetually throwing over the cargo to save the ship, but what a motion you gave her when you made her ride the waves—a motion as rhythmic as the dance of a goddess! Wayworth took long London walks and thought of these things— London poured into his ears the mighty hum of its suggestion. His imagination glowed and melted down material, his intentions multiplied and made the air a golden haze. He saw not only the thing he should do, but the next and the next and the next; the future opened before him and he seemed to walk on marble slabs. The more he tried the dramatic form the more he loved it, the more he looked at it the more he perceived in it. What he perceived in it indeed he now perceived everywhere; if he stopped, in the London dusk, before some flaring shop-window, the place immediately constituted itself behind footlights, became a framed stage for his figures. He hammered at these figures in his lonely lodging, he shaped them and he shaped their tabernacle; he was like a goldsmith chiselling a casket, bent over with the passion for perfection. When he was neither roaming the streets with his vision nor worrying his problem at his table, he was exchanging ideas on the general question with Mrs. Alsager, to whom he promised details that would amuse her in later and still happier hours. Her eyes were full of tears when he

read her the last words of the finished work, and she murmured, divinely—

"And now—to get it done, to get it done!"

"Yes, indeed—to get it done!" Wayworth stared at the fire,
slowly rolling up his type-copy. "But that's a totally different
part of the business, and altogether secondary."

"But of course you want to be acted?"

"Of course I do—but it's a sudden descent. I want to intensely, but I'm sorry I want to."

"It's there indeed that the difficulties begin," said Mrs. Alsager, a little off her guard.

"How can you say that? It's there that they end!"

"Ah, wait to see where they end!"

"I mean they'll now be of a totally different order," Wayworth explained. "It seems to me there can be nothing in the
world more difficult than to write a play that will stand an all-
round test, and that in comparison with them the complications that spring up at this point are of an altogether smaller
kind."

"Yes, they're not inspiring," said Mrs. Alsager; "they're discouraging, because they're vulgar. The other problem, the
working out of the thing itself, is pure art."

"How well you understand everything!" The young man
had got up, nervously, and was leaning against the chimney-
piece with his back to the fire and his arms folded. The roll
of his copy, in his fist, was squeezed into the hollow of one
of them. He looked down at Mrs. Alsager, smiling gratefully,
and she answered him with a smile from eyes still charmed
and suffused. "Yes, the vulgarity will begin now," he presently
added.

"You'll suffer dreadfully."

"I shall suffer in a good cause."

"Yes, giving *that* to the world! You must leave it with me,
I must read it over and over," Mrs. Alsager pleaded, rising to
come nearer and draw the copy, in its cover of greenish-grey
paper, which had a generic identity now to him, out of his
grasp. "Who in the world will do it?—who in the world *can*?"
she went on, close to him, turning over the leaves. Before he
could answer she had stopped at one of the pages; she turned
the book round to him, pointing out a speech. "That's the

most beautiful place—those lines are a perfection." He glanced at the spot she indicated, and she begged him to read them again—he had read them admirably before. He knew them by heart, and, closing the book while she held the other end of it, he murmured them over to her—they had indeed a cadence that pleased him—watching, with a facetious complacency which he hoped was pardonable, the applause in her face. "Ah, who can utter such lines as *that*?" Mrs. Alsager broke out; "whom can you find to do *her*?"

"We'll find people to do them all!"

"But not people who are worthy."

"They'll be worthy enough if they're willing enough. I'll work with them—I'll grind it into them." He spoke as if he had produced twenty plays.

"Oh, it will be interesting!" she echoed.

"But I shall have to find my theatre first. I shall have to get a manager to believe in me."

"Yes—they're so stupid!"

"But fancy the patience I shall want, and how I shall have to watch and wait," said Allan Wayworth. "Do you see me hawking it about London?"

"Indeed I don't—it would be sickening."

"It's what I shall have to do. I shall be old before it's produced."

"I shall be old very soon if it isn't!" Mrs. Alsager cried. "I know one or two of them," she mused.

"Do you mean you would speak to them?"

"The thing is to get them to read it. I could do that."

"That's the utmost I ask. But it's even for that I shall have to wait."

She looked at him with kind sisterly eyes. "You sha'n't wait."

"Ah, you dear lady!" Wayworth murmured.

"That is *you* may, but *I* won't! Will you leave me your copy?" she went on, turning the pages again.

"Certainly; I have another." Standing near him she read to herself a passage here and there; then, in her sweet voice, she read some of them out. "Oh, if *you* were only an actress!" the young man exclaimed.

"That's the last thing I am. There's no comedy in *me*!"

She had never appeared to Wayworth so much his good genius. "Is there any tragedy?" he asked, with the levity of complete confidence.

She turned away from him, at this, with a strange and charming laugh and a "Perhaps that will be for you to determine!" But before he could disclaim such a responsibility she had faced him again and was talking about Nona Vincent as if she had been the most interesting of their friends and her situation at that moment an irresistible appeal to their sympathy. Nona Vincent was the heroine of the play, and Mrs. Alsager had taken a tremendous fancy to her. "I can't *tell* you how I like that woman!" she exclaimed in a pensive rapture of credulity which could only be balm to the artistic spirit.

"I'm awfully glad she lives a bit. What I feel about her is that she's a good deal like *you*," Wayworth observed.

Mrs. Alsager stared an instant and turned faintly red. This was evidently a view that failed to strike her; she didn't, however, treat it as a joke. "I'm not impressed with the resemblance. I don't see myself doing what she does."

"It isn't so much what she *does*," the young man argued, drawing out his moustache.

"But what she does is the whole point. She simply tells her love—I should never do that."

"If you repudiate such a proceeding with such energy, why do you like her for it?"

"It isn't what I like her for."

"What else, then? That's intensely characteristic."

Mrs. Alsager reflected, looking down at the fire; she had the air of having half-a-dozen reasons to choose from. But the one she produced was unexpectedly simple; it might even have been prompted by despair at not finding others. "I like her because *you* made her!" she exclaimed with a laugh, moving again away from her companion.

Wayworth laughed still louder. "You made her a little yourself. I've thought of her as looking like you."

"She ought to look much better," said Mrs. Alsager. "No, certainly, I shouldn't do what *she* does."

"Not even in the same circumstances?"

"I should never find myself in such circumstances. They're exactly your play, and have nothing in common with such a life as mine. However," Mrs. Alsager went on, "her behaviour was natural for *her*, and not only natural, but, it seems to me, thoroughly beautiful and noble. I can't sufficiently admire the talent and tact with which you make one accept it, and I tell you frankly that it's evident to me there must be a brilliant future before a young man who, at the start, has been capable of such a stroke as that. Thank heaven I can admire Nona Vincent as intensely as I feel that I don't resemble her!"

"Don't exaggerate that," said Allan Wayworth.

"My admiration?"

"Your dissimilarity. She has your face, your air, your voice, your motion; she has many elements of your being."

"Then she'll damn your play!" Mrs. Alsager replied. They joked a little over this, though it was not in the tone of pleasantry that Wayworth's hostess soon remarked: "You've got your remedy, however: have her done by the right woman."

"Oh, have her 'done'—have her 'done'!" the young man gently wailed.

"I see what you mean, my poor friend. What a pity, when it's such a magnificent part—such a chance for a clever serious girl! Nona Vincent is practically your play—it will be open to her to carry it far or to drop it at the first corner."

"It's a charming prospect," said Allan Wayworth, with sudden scepticism. They looked at each other with eyes that, for a lurid moment, saw the worst of the worst; but before they parted they had exchanged vows and confidences that were dedicated wholly to the ideal. It is not to be supposed, however, that the knowledge that Mrs. Alsager would help him made Wayworth less eager to help himself. He did what he could and felt that she, on her side, was doing no less; but at the end of a year he was obliged to recognise that their united effort had mainly produced the fine flower of discouragement. At the end of a year the lustre had, to his own eyes, quite faded from his unappreciated masterpiece, and he found himself writing for a biographical dictionary little lives of celebrities he had never heard of. To be printed, anywhere and anyhow, was a form of glory for a man so unable to be acted, and to be paid, even at encyclopædic rates, had the consequence of making one resigned and verbose. He couldn't smuggle style into a dictionary, but he could at least reflect that he had done his best to learn from the drama that it is a gross impertinence almost anywhere. He had knocked at the door of every theatre in London, and, at a ruinous expense, had multiplied type-copies of *Nona Vincent* to replace the neat transcripts that had descended into the managerial abyss. His play was not even declined—no such flattering intimation was given him that it had been read. What the managers would do for Mrs. Alsager concerned him little today; the thing that was relevant was that they would do nothing for *him*. That charming woman felt humbled to the earth, so little response had she had from the powers on which she counted. The two never talked about the play now, but he tried to show her a still finer friendship, that she might not think he felt she had failed him. He still walked about London with his dreams, but as months succeeded months and he left the year behind him they were dreams not so much of success as of revenge. Success seemed a colourless name for the reward of his patience; something fiercely florid, something sanguinolent was more to the point. His best consolation however was still in the scenic idea; it was not till now that he discovered how incurably he was in love with it. By the time a vain second year had chafed itself away he cherished his fruitless faculty the more for the obloquy it seemed to suffer. He lived, in his best hours, in a world of subjects and situations; he wrote another play and made it as different from its predecessor as such a very good thing could be. It might be a very good thing, but when he had committed it to the theatrical limbo indiscriminating fate took no account of the difference. He was at last able to leave England for three or four months; he went to Germany to pay a visit long deferred to his mother and sisters.

Shortly before the time he had fixed for his return he received from Mrs. Alsager a telegram consisting of the words: "Loder wishes see you—putting *Nona* instant rehearsal." He spent the few hours before his departure in kissing his mother and sisters, who knew enough about Mrs. Alsager to judge it lucky this respectable married lady was not there—a relief, however, accompanied with speculative glances at London and the morrow. Loder, as our young man was aware, meant the new "Renaissance," but though he reached home in the evening it was not to this convenient modern theatre that Wayworth first proceeded. He spent a late hour with Mrs. Alsager, an hour that throbbed with calculation. She told him that Mr. Loder was charming, he had simply taken up the play in its turn; he had hopes of it, moreover, that on the part of a professional pessimist might almost be qualified as ecstatic. It had been cast, with a margin for objections, and Violet Grey was to do the heroine. She had been capable, while he was away, of a good piece of work at that foggy old playhouse the "Legitimate;" the piece was a clumsy *réchauffé*, but she at least had been fresh. Wayworth remembered Violet Grey—hadn't he, for two years, on a fond policy of "looking out," kept dipping into the London theatres to pick up prospective interpreters? He had not picked up many as yet, and this young lady at all events had never wriggled in his net. She was pretty and she was odd, but he had never prefigured her as Nona Vincent, nor indeed found himself attracted by what he already felt sufficiently launched in the profession to speak of as her artistic personality. Mrs. Alsager was different—she declared that she had been struck not a little by some of her tones. The girl was interesting in the thing at the "Legitimate," and Mr. Loder, who had his eye on her, described her as ambitious and intelligent. She wanted awfully to get on— and some of those ladies were so lazy! Wayworth was sceptical—he had seen Miss Violet Grey, who was terribly itinerant, in a dozen theatres but only in one aspect. Nona Vincent had a dozen aspects, but only one theatre; yet with what a feverish curiosity the young man promised himself to watch the actress on the morrow! Talking the matter over with Mrs. Alsager now seemed the very stuff that rehearsal was made of. The near prospect of being acted laid a finger even on the lip of inquiry; he wanted to go on tiptoe till the first night, to make no condition but that they should speak his lines, and he felt that he wouldn't so much as raise an eyebrow at the scene-painter if he should give him an old oak chamber.

He became conscious, the next day, that his danger would be other than this, and yet he couldn't have expressed to himself what it would be. Danger was there, doubtless—danger was everywhere, in the world of art, and still more in the world of commerce; but what he really seemed to catch, for the hour, was the beating of the wings of victory. Nothing could undermine that, since it was victory simply to be acted. It would be victory even to be acted badly; a reflection that didn't prevent him, however, from banishing, in his politic optimism, the word "bad" from his vocabulary. It had no application, in the compromise of practice; it didn't apply even to his play, which he was conscious he had already outlived and as to which he foresaw that, in the coming weeks, frequent alarm would alternate, in his spirit, with frequent esteem. When he went down to the dusky daylit theatre (it arched over him like the temple of fame) Mr. Loder, who was as charming as Mrs. Alsager had announced, struck him as the genius of hospitality. The manager began to explain why, for so long, he had given no sign; but that was the last thing that interested Wayworth now, and he could never remember afterwards what reasons Mr. Loder had enumerated. He liked, in the whole business of discussion and preparation, even the things he had thought he should probably dislike, and he revelled in those he had thought he should like. He watched Miss Violet Grey that evening with eyes that sought to penetrate her possibilities. She certainly had a few; they were qualities of voice and face, qualities perhaps even of intelligence; he sat there at any rate with a fostering, coaxing attention, repeating over to himself as convincingly as he could that she was not common—a circumstance all the more creditable as the part she was playing seemed to him desperately so. He perceived that this was why it pleased the audience; he divined that it was the part they enjoyed rather than the actress. He had a private panic, wondering how, if they liked *that* form, they could possibly like his. His form had now become quite an ultimate idea to him. By the time the evening was over some of Miss Violet Grey's features, several of the turns of her head, a certain vibration of her voice, had taken their place in the same category. She *was* interesting, she was distinguished; at any rate he had accepted her: it came to the same thing. But he left the theatre that night without speaking to her—moved (a little even to his own mystification) by an odd procrastinating impulse. On the morrow he was to read his three acts to the company, and then he should have a good deal to say; what he felt for the moment was a vague indisposition to commit himself. Moreover he found a slight confusion of annoyance in the fact that though he had been trying all the evening to look at Nona Vincent in Violet Grey's person, what subsisted in his vision was simply Violet Grey in Nona's. He didn't wish to see the actress so directly, or even so simply as that; and it had been very fatiguing, the effort to focus Nona both through the performer and through the "Legitimate." Before he went to bed that night he posted three words to Mrs. Alsager—"She's not a bit like it, but I dare say I can make her do."

He was pleased with the way the actress listened, the next day, at the reading; he was pleased indeed with many things, at the reading, and most of all with the reading itself. The whole affair loomed large to him and he magnified it and mapped it out. He enjoyed his occupation of the big, dim, hollow theatre, full of the echoes of "effect" and of a queer smell of gas and success—it all seemed such a passive canvas for his picture. For the first time in his life he was in command of resources; he was acquainted with the phrase, but had never thought he should know the feeling. He was surprised at what Loder appeared ready to do, though he reminded himself that he must never show it. He foresaw that there would be two distinct concomitants to the artistic effort of producing a play, one consisting of a great deal of anguish and the other of a great deal of amusement. He looked back upon the reading, afterwards, as the best hour in the business, because it was then that the piece had most struck him as represented. What came later was the doing of others, but this, with its imperfections and failures, was all his own. The drama lived, at any rate, for that hour, with an intensity that it was promptly to lose in the poverty and patchiness of rehearsal; he could see its life reflected, in a way that was sweet to him, in the stillness of the little semi-circle of attentive and inscrutable, of waterproofed and muddy-booted, actors. Miss Violet Grey was the auditor he had most to say to, and he tried on the spot, across the shabby stage, to let her have the soul of her part. Her attitude was graceful, but though she appeared to listen with all her faculties her face remained perfectly blank; a fact, however, not discouraging to Wayworth, who liked her better for not being premature. Her companions gave discernible signs of recognising the passages of comedy; yet Wayworth forgave her even then for being inexpressive. She evidently wished before everything else to be simply sure of what it was all about.

He was more surprised even than at the revelation of the scale on which Mr. Loder was ready to proceed by the discovery that some of the actors didn't like their parts, and his heart sank as he asked himself what he could possibly do with them if they were going to be so stupid. This was the first of his disappointments; somehow he had expected every individual to become instantly and gratefully conscious of a rare opportunity, and from the moment such a calculation failed he was at sea, or mindful at any rate that more disappointments would come. It was impossible to make out what the manager liked or disliked; no judgment, no comment escaped him; his acceptance of the play and his views about the way it should be mounted had apparently converted him into a veiled and shrouded figure. Wayworth was able to grasp the idea that they would all move now in a higher and sharper air than that of compliment and confidence. When he talked with Violet Grey after the reading he gathered that she was really rather crude: what better proof of it could there be than her failure to break out instantly with an expression of delight about her great chance? This reserve, however, had evidently nothing to do with high pretensions; she had no wish to make him feel that a person of her eminence was superior to easy raptures. He guessed, after a little, that she was puzzled and even somewhat frightened—to a certain extent she had not understood. Nothing could appeal to him more than the opportunity to clear up her difficulties, in the course of the examination of which he quickly discovered that, so far as she *had* understood, she had understood wrong. If she was crude it was only a reason the more for talking to her; he kept saying to her "Ask me—ask me: ask me everything you can think of."

She asked him, she was perpetually asking him, and at the first rehearsals, which were without form and void to a degree that made them strike him much more as the death of an experiment than as the dawn of a success, they threshed things out immensely in a corner of the stage, with the effect of his coming to feel that at any rate she was in earnest. He felt

more and more that his heroine was the keystone of his arch,
for which indeed the actress was very ready to take her. But
when he reminded this young lady of the way the whole thing
practically depended on her she was alarmed and even slightly
scandalised: she spoke more than once as if that could scarcely
be the right way to construct a play—make it stand or fall by
one poor nervous girl. She was almost morbidly conscientious,
and in theory he liked her for this, though he lost patience
three or four times with the things she couldn't do and the
things she could. At such times the tears came to her eyes;
but they were produced by her own stupidity, she hastened
to assure him, not by the way he spoke, which was awfully
kind under the circumstances. Her sincerity made her beautiful, and he wished to heaven (and made a point of telling
her so) that she could sprinkle a little of it over Nona. Once,
however, she was so touched and troubled that the sight of it
brought the tears for an instant to his own eyes; and it so
happened that, turning at this moment, he found himself face
to face with Mr. Loder. The manager stared, glanced at the
actress, who turned in the other direction, and then smiling
at Wayworth, exclaimed, with the humour of a man who
heard the gallery laugh every night:

"I say—I say!"

"What's the matter?" Wayworth asked.

"I'm glad to see Miss Grey is taking such pains with you."

"Oh, yes—she'll turn me out!" said the young man, gaily.
He was quite aware that it was apparent he was not superficial
about Nona, and abundantly determined, into the bargain,
that the rehearsal of the piece should not sacrifice a shade of
thoroughness to any extrinsic consideration.

Mrs. Alsager, whom, late in the afternoon, he used often to
go and ask for a cup of tea, thanking her in advance for the
rest she gave him and telling her how he found that rehearsal
(as *they* were doing it—it was a caution!) took it out of one—
Mrs. Alsager, more and more his good genius and, as he repeatedly assured her, his ministering angel, confirmed him in
this superior policy and urged him on to every form of artistic
devotion. She had, naturally, never been more interested than
now in his work; she wanted to hear everything about everything. She treated him as heroically fatigued, plied him with

luxurious restoratives, made him stretch himself on cushions
and rose-leaves. They gossipped more than ever, by her fire,
about the artistic life; he confided to her, for instance, all his
hopes and fears, all his experiments and anxieties, on the subject of the representative of Nona. She was immensely interested in this young lady and showed it by taking a box again
and again (she had seen her half-a-dozen times already), to
study her capacity through the veil of her present part. Like
Allan Wayworth she found her encouraging only by fits, for
she had fine flashes of badness. She was intelligent, but she
cried aloud for training, and the training was so absent that
the intelligence had only a fraction of its effect. She was like
a knife without an edge—good steel that had never been
sharpened; she hacked away at her hard dramatic loaf, she
couldn't cut it smooth.

                                II.

"Certainly my leading lady won't make Nona much like *you*!"
Wayworth one day gloomily remarked to Mrs. Alsager. There
were days when the prospect seemed to him awful.
    "So much the better. There's no necessity for that."
    "I wish you'd train her a little—you could so easily," the
young man went on; in response to which Mrs. Alsager requested him not to make such cruel fun of her. But she was
curious about the girl, wanted to hear of her character, her
private situation, how she lived and where, seemed indeed
desirous to befriend her. Wayworth might not have known
much about the private situation of Miss Violet Grey, but, as
it happened, he was able, by the time his play had been three
weeks in rehearsal, to supply information on such points. She
was a charming, exemplary person, educated, cultivated, with
highly modern tastes, an excellent musician. She had lost her
parents and was very much alone in the world, her only two
relations being a sister, who was married to a civil servant (in
a highly responsible post) in India, and a dear little old-fashioned aunt (really a great-aunt) with whom she lived at Notting Hill, who wrote children's books and who, it appeared,
had once written a Christmas pantomime. It was quite an artistic home—not on the scale of Mrs. Alsager's (to compare

the smallest things with the greatest!) but intensely refined and honourable. Wayworth went so far as to hint that it would be rather nice and human on Mrs. Alsager's part to go there— they would take it so kindly if she should call on them. She had acted so often on his hints that he had formed a pleasant habit of expecting it: it made him feel so wisely responsible about giving them. But this one appeared to fall to the ground, so that he let the subject drop. Mrs. Alsager, however, went yet once more to the "Legitimate," as he found by her saying to him abruptly, on the morrow: "Oh, she'll be very good—she'll be very good." When they said "she," in these days, they always meant Violet Grey, though they pretended, for the most part, that they meant Nona Vincent.

"Oh yes," Wayworth assented, "she wants so to!"

Mrs. Alsager was silent a moment; then she asked, a little inconsequently, as if she had come back from a reverie: "Does she want to *very* much?"

"Tremendously—and it appears she has been fascinated by the part from the first."

"Why then didn't she say so?"

"Oh, because she's so funny."

"She *is* funny," said Mrs. Alsager, musingly; and presently she added: "She's in love with you."

Wayworth stared, blushed very red, then laughed out. "What is there funny in that?" he demanded; but before his interlocutress could satisfy him on this point he inquired, further, how she knew anything about it. After a little graceful evasion she explained that the night before, at the "Legitimate," Mrs. Beaumont, the wife of the actor-manager, had paid her a visit in her box; which had happened, in the course of their brief gossip, to lead to her remarking that she had never been "behind." Mrs. Beaumont offered on the spot to take her round, and the fancy had seized her to accept the invitation. She had been amused for the moment, and in this way it befell that her conductress, at her request, had introduced her to Miss Violet Grey, who was waiting in the wing for one of her scenes. Mrs. Beaumont had been called away for three minutes, and during this scrap of time, face to face with the actress, she had discovered the poor girl's secret. Wayworth qualified it as a senseless thing, but wished to know what had led to the discovery. She characterised this inquiry as superficial for a painter of the ways of women; and he doubtless didn't improve it by remarking profanely that a cat might look at a king and that such things were convenient to know. Even on this ground, however, he was threatened by Mrs. Alsager, who contended that it might not be a joking matter to the poor girl. To this Wayworth, who now professed to hate talking about the passions he might have inspired, could only reply that he meant it couldn't make a difference to Mrs. Alsager.

"How in the world do you know what makes a difference to *me*?" this lady asked, with incongruous coldness, with a haughtiness indeed remarkable in so gentle a spirit.

He saw Violet Grey that night at the theatre, and it was she who spoke first of her having lately met a friend of his.

"She's in love with you," the actress said, after he had made a show of ignorance; "doesn't that tell you anything?"

He blushed redder still than Mrs. Alsager had made him blush, but replied, quickly enough and very adequately, that hundreds of women were naturally dying for him.

"Oh, I don't care, for you're not in love with *her*!" the girl continued.

"Did she tell you that too?" Wayworth asked; but she had at that moment to go on.

Standing where he could see her he thought that on this occasion she threw into her scene, which was the best she had in the play, a brighter art than ever before, a talent that could play with its problem. She was perpetually doing things out of rehearsal (she did two or three to-night, in the other man's piece), that he as often wished to heaven Nona Vincent might have the benefit of. She appeared to be able to do them for every one but him—that is for every one but Nona. He was conscious, in these days, of an odd new feeling, which mixed (this was a part of its oddity) with a very natural and comparatively old one and which in its most definite form was a dull ache of regret that this young lady's unlucky star should have placed her on the stage. He wished in his worst uneasiness that, without going further, she would give it up; and yet it soothed that uneasiness to remind himself that he saw grounds to hope she would go far enough to make a marked success of Nona. There were strange and painful moments when, as the interpretress of Nona, he almost hated her; after which, however, he always assured himself that he exaggerated, inasmuch as what made this aversion seem great, when he was nervous, was simply its contrast with the growing sense that there *were* grounds—totally different—on which she pleased him. She pleased him as a charming creature—by her sincerities and her perversities, by the varieties and surprises of her character and by certain happy facts of her person. In private her eyes were sad to him and her voice was rare. He detested the idea that she should have a disappointment or an humiliation, and he wanted to rescue her altogether, to save and transplant her. One way to save her was to see to it, to the best of his ability, that the production of his play should be a triumph; and the other way—it was really too queer to express—was almost to wish that it shouldn't be. Then, for the future, there would be safety and peace, and not the peace of death—the peace of a different life. It is to be added that our young man clung to the former of these ways in proportion as the latter perversely tempted him. He was nervous at the best, increasingly and intolerably nervous; but the immediate remedy was to rehearse harder and harder, and above all to work it out with Violet Grey. Some of her comrades reproached him with working it out only with her, as if she were the whole affair; to which he replied that they could afford to be neglected, they were all so tremendously good. She was the only person concerned whom he didn't flatter.

The author and the actress stuck so to the business in hand that she had very little time to speak to him again of Mrs. Alsager, of whom indeed her imagination appeared adequately to have disposed. Wayworth once remarked to her that Nona Vincent was supposed to be a good deal like his charming friend; but she gave a blank "Supposed by whom?" in consequence of which he never returned to the subject. He confided his nervousness as freely as usual to Mrs. Alsager, who easily understood that he had a peculiar complication of anxieties. His suspense varied in degree from hour to hour, but any relief there might have been in this was made up for by its being of several different kinds. One afternoon, as the first performance drew near, Mrs. Alsager said to him, in giving him his cup of tea and on his having mentioned that he had not closed his eyes the night before:

"You must indeed be in a dreadful state. Anxiety for another is still worse than anxiety for one's self."

"For another?" Wayworth repeated, looking at her over the rim of his cup.

"My poor friend, you're nervous about Nona Vincent, but you're infinitely more nervous about Violet Grey."

"She *is* Nona Vincent!"

"No, she isn't—not a bit!" said Mrs. Alsager, abruptly.

"Do you really think so?" Wayworth cried, spilling his tea in his alarm.

"What I think doesn't signify—I mean what I think about that. What I meant to say was that great as is your suspense about your play, your suspense about your actress is greater still."

"I can only repeat that my actress *is* my play."

Mrs. Alsager looked thoughtfully into the teapot.

"Your actress is your—"

"My what?" the young man asked, with a little tremor in his voice, as his hostess paused.

"Your very dear friend. You're in love with her—at present." And with a sharp click Mrs. Alsager dropped the lid on the fragrant receptacle.

"Not yet—not yet!" laughed her visitor.

"You will be if she pulls you through."

"You declare that she *won't* pull me through."

Mrs. Alsager was silent a moment, after which she softly murmured: "I'll pray for her."

"You're the most generous of women!" Wayworth cried; then coloured as if the words had not been happy. They would have done indeed little honour to a man of tact.

The next morning he received five hurried lines from Mrs. Alsager. She had suddenly been called to Torquay, to see a relation who was seriously ill; she should be detained there several days, but she had an earnest hope of being able to return in time for his first night. In any event he had her unrestricted good wishes. He missed her extremely, for these last days were a great strain and there was little comfort to be derived from Violet Grey. She was even more nervous than

himself, and so pale and altered that he was afraid she would
be too ill to act. It was settled between them that they made
each other worse and that he had now much better leave her
alone. They had pulled Nona so to pieces that nothing seemed
left of her—she must at least have time to grow together
again. He left Violet Grey alone, to the best of his ability, but
she carried out imperfectly her own side of the bargain. She
came to him with new questions—she waited for him with old
doubts, and half an hour before the last dress-rehearsal, on
the eve of production, she proposed to him a totally fresh
rendering of his heroine. This incident gave him such a sense
of insecurity that he turned his back on her without a word,
bolted out of the theatre, dashed along the Strand and walked
as far as the Bank. Then he jumped into a hansom and came
westward, and when he reached the theatre again the business
was nearly over. It appeared, almost to his disappointment,
not bad enough to give him the consolation of the old playhouse adage that the worst dress rehearsals make the best first
nights.

The morrow, which was a Wednesday, was the dreadful day;
the theatre had been closed on the Monday and the Tuesday.
Every one, on the Wednesday, did his best to let every one
else alone, and every one signally failed in the attempt. The
day, till seven o'clock, was understood to be consecrated to
rest, but every one except Violet Grey turned up at the theatre. Wayworth looked at Mr. Loder, and Mr. Loder looked
in another direction, which was as near as they came to conversation. Wayworth was in a fidget, unable to eat or sleep or
sit still, at times almost in terror. He kept quiet by keeping,
as usual, in motion; he tried to walk away from his nervous
ness. He walked in the afternoon toward Notting Hill, but he
succeeded in not breaking the vow he had taken not to meddle with his actress. She was like an acrobat poised on a slippery ball—if he should touch her she would topple over. He
passed her door three times and he thought of her three hundred. This was the hour at which he most regretted that Mrs.
Alsager had not come back—for he had called at her house
only to learn that she was still at Torquay. This was probably
queer, and it was probably queerer still that she hadn't written
to him; but even of these things he wasn't sure, for in losing,

as he had now completely lost, his judgment of his play, he
seemed to himself to have lost his judgment of everything.
When he went home, however, he found a telegram from the
lady of Grosvenor Place—"Shall be able to come—reach town
by seven." At half-past eight o'clock, through a little aperture
in the curtain of the "Renaissance," he saw her in her box
with a cluster of friends—completely beautiful and beneficent.
The house was magnificent—too good for his play, he felt;
too good for any play. Everything now seemed too good—
the scenery, the furniture, the dresses, the very programmes.
He seized upon the idea that this was probably what was the
matter with the representative of Nona—she was only too
good. He had completely arranged with this young lady the
plan of their relations during the evening; and though they
had altered everything else that they had arranged they had
promised each other not to alter this. It was wonderful the
number of things they had promised each other. He would
start her, he would see her off—then he would quit the theatre and stay away till just before the end. She besought him
to stay away—it would make her infinitely easier. He saw that
she was exquisitely dressed—she had made one or two
changes for the better since the night before, and that seemed
something definite to turn over and over in his mind as he
rumbled foggily home in the four-wheeler in which, a few
steps from the stage-door, he had taken refuge as soon as he
knew that the curtain was up. He lived a couple of miles off,
and he had chosen a four-wheeler to drag out the time.

When he got home his fire was out, his room was cold, and
he lay down on his sofa in his overcoat. He had sent his landlady to the dress-circle, on purpose; she would overflow with
words and mistakes. The house seemed a black void, just as
the streets had done—every one was, formidably, at his play.
He was quieter at last than he had been for a fortnight, and
he felt too weak even to wonder how the thing was going.
He believed afterwards that he had slept an hour; but even if
he had he felt it to be still too early to return to the theatre.
He sat down by his lamp and tried to read—to read a little
compendious life of a great English statesman, out of a "series." It struck him as brilliantly clever, and he asked himself
whether that perhaps were not rather the sort of thing he

ought to have taken up: not the statesmanship, but the art of brief biography. Suddenly he became aware that he must hurry if he was to reach the theatre at all—it was a quarter to eleven o'clock. He scrambled out and, this time, found a hansom—he had lately spent enough money in cabs to add to his hope that the profits of his new profession would be great. His anxiety, his suspense flamed up again, and as he rattled eastward—he went fast now—he was almost sick with alternations. As he passed into the theatre the first man—some underling—who met him, cried to him, breathlessly: "You're wanted, sir—you're wanted!" He thought his tone very ominous—he devoured the man's eyes with his own, for a betrayal: did he mean that he was wanted for execution? Some one else pressed him, almost pushed him, forward; he was already on the stage. Then he became conscious of a sound more or less continuous, but seemingly faint and far, which he took at first for the voice of the actors heard through their canvas walls, the beautiful built-in room of the last act. But the actors were in the wing, they surrounded him; the curtain was down and they were coming off from before it. They had been called, and *he* was called—they all greeted him with "Go on—go on!" He was terrified—he couldn't go on—he didn't believe in the applause, which seemed to him only audible enough to sound half-hearted.

"Has it gone?—has it gone?" he gasped to the people round him; and he heard them say "Rather—rather!" perfunctorily, mendaciously too, as it struck him, and even with mocking laughter, the laughter of defeat and despair. Suddenly, though all this must have taken but a moment, Loder burst upon him from somewhere with a "For God's sake don't keep them, or they'll *stop*!" "But I can't go on for *that*!" Wayworth cried, in anguish; the sound seemed to him already to have ceased. Loder had hold of him and was shoving him; he resisted and looked round frantically for Violet Grey, who perhaps would tell him the truth. There was by this time a crowd in the wing, all with strange grimacing painted faces, but Violet was not among them and her very absence frightened him. He uttered her name with an accent that he afterwards regretted—it gave them, as he thought, both away; and while Loder hustled him before the curtain

he heard some one say "She took her call and disappeared."
She had had a call, then—this was what was most present to
the young man as he stood for an instant in the glare of the
footlights, looking blindly at the great vaguely-peopled horse-
shoe and greeted with plaudits which now seemed to him at
once louder than he deserved and feebler than he desired.
They sank to rest quickly, but he felt it to be long before he
could back away, before he could, in his turn, seize the manager by the arm and cry huskily—"Has it really gone—*really*?"

Mr. Loder looked at him hard and replied after an instant:
"The play's all right!"

Wayworth hung upon his lips. "Then what's all wrong?"

"We must do something to Miss Grey."

"What's the matter with her?"

"She isn't *in* it!"

"Do you mean she has failed?"

"Yes, damn it—she has failed."

Wayworth stared. "Then how can the play be all right?"

"Oh, we'll save it—we'll save it."

"Where's Miss Grey—where *is* she?" the young man asked.

Loder caught his arm as he was turning away again to look
for his heroine. "Never mind her now—she knows it!"

Wayworth was approached at the same moment by a gentleman he knew as one of Mrs. Alsager's friends—he had perceived him in that lady's box. Mrs. Alsager was waiting there
for the successful author; she desired very earnestly that he
would come round and speak to her. Wayworth assured himself first that Violet had left the theatre—one of the actresses
could tell him that she had seen her throw on a cloak, without
changing her dress, and had learnt afterwards that she had,
the next moment, flung herself, after flinging her aunt, into a
cab. He had wished to invite half a dozen persons, of whom
Miss Grey and her elderly relative were two, to come home
to supper with him; but she had refused to make any engagement beforehand (it would be so dreadful to have to keep it
if she shouldn't have made a hit), and this attitude had
blighted the pleasant plan, which fell to the ground. He had
called her morbid, but she was immovable. Mrs. Alsager's
messenger let him know that he was expected to supper in
Grosvenor Place, and half an hour afterwards he was seated

there among complimentary people and flowers and popping corks, eating the first orderly meal he had partaken of for a week. Mrs. Alsager had carried him off in her brougham—the other people who were coming got into things of their own. He stopped her short as soon as she began to tell him how tremendously every one had been struck by the piece; he nailed her down to the question of Violet Grey. Had she spoilt the play, had she jeopardised or compromised it—had she been utterly bad, had she been good in any degree?

"Certainly the performance would have seemed better if *she* had been better," Mrs. Alsager confessed.

"And the play would have seemed better if the performance had been better," Wayworth said, gloomily, from the corner of the brougham.

"She does what she can, and she has talent, and she looked lovely. But she doesn't *see* Nona Vincent. She doesn't see the type—she doesn't see the individual—she doesn't see the woman you meant. She's out of it—she gives you a different person."

"Oh, the woman I meant!" the young man exclaimed, looking at the London lamps as he rolled by them. "I wish to God she had known *you*!" he added, as the carriage stopped. After they had passed into the house he said to his companion: "You see she *won't* pull me through."

"Forgive her—be kind to her!" Mrs. Alsager pleaded.

"I shall only thank her. The play may go to the dogs."

"If it does—if it does," Mrs. Alsager began, with her pure eyes on him.

"Well, what if it does?"

She couldn't tell him, for the rest of her guests came in together; she only had time to say: "It *sha'n't* go to the dogs!"

He came away before the others, restless with the desire to go to Notting Hill even that night, late as it was, haunted with the sense that Violet Grey had measured her fall. When he got into the street, however, he allowed second thoughts to counsel another course; the effect of knocking her up at two o'clock in the morning would hardly be to soothe her. He looked at six newspapers the next day and found in them never a good word for her. They were well enough about the piece, but they were unanimous as to the disappointment caused by the young actress whose former efforts had excited such hopes and on whom, on this occasion, such pressing responsibilities rested. They asked in chorus what was the matter with her, and they declared in chorus that the play, which was not without promise, was handicapped (they all used the same word) by the odd want of correspondence between the heroine and her interpreter. Wayworth drove early to Notting Hill, but he didn't take the newspapers with him; Violet Grey could be trusted to have sent out for them by the peep of dawn and to have fed her anguish full. She declined to see him—she only sent down word by her aunt that she was extremely unwell and should be unable to act that night unless she were suffered to spend the day unmolested and in bed. Wayworth sat for an hour with the old lady, who understood everything and to whom he could speak frankly. She gave him a touching picture of her niece's condition, which was all the more vivid for the simple words in which it was expressed: "She feels she isn't right, you know—she feels she isn't right!"

"Tell her it doesn't matter—it doesn't matter a straw!" said Wayworth.

"And she's so proud—you know how proud she is!" the old lady went on.

"Tell her I'm more than satisfied, that I accept her gratefully as she is."

"She says she injures your play, that she ruins it," said his interlocutress.

"She'll improve, immensely—she'll grow into the part," the young man continued.

"She'd improve if she knew how—but she says she doesn't. She has given all she has got, and she doesn't know what's wanted."

"What's wanted is simply that she should go straight on and trust me."

"How can she trust you when she feels she's losing you?"

"Losing me?" Wayworth cried.

"You'll never forgive her if your play is taken off!"

"It will run six months," said the author of the piece.

The old lady laid her hand on his arm. "What will you do for her if it does?"

He looked at Violet Grey's aunt a moment. "Do you say your niece is very proud?"

"Too proud for her dreadful profession."

"Then she wouldn't wish you to ask me that," Wayworth answered, getting up.

When he reached home he was very tired, and for a person to whom it was open to consider that he had scored a success he spent a remarkably dismal day. All his restlessness had gone, and fatigue and depression possessed him. He sank into his old chair by the fire and sat there for hours with his eyes closed. His landlady came in to bring his luncheon and mend the fire, but he feigned to be asleep, so as not to be spoken to. It is to be supposed that sleep at last overtook him, for about the hour that dusk began to gather he had an extraordinary impression, a visit that, it would seem, could have belonged to no waking consciousness. Nona Vincent, in face and form, the living heroine of his play, rose before him in his little silent room, sat down with him at his dingy fireside. She was not Violet Grey, she was not Mrs. Alsager, she was not any woman he had seen upon earth, nor was it any masquerade of friendship or of penitence. Yet she was more familiar to him than the women he had known best, and she was ineffably beautiful and consoling. She filled the poor room with her presence, the effect of which was as soothing as some odour of incense. She was as quiet as an affectionate sister, and there was no surprise in her being there. Nothing more real had ever befallen him, and nothing, somehow, more reassuring. He felt her hand rest upon his own, and all his senses seemed to open to her message. She struck him, in the strangest way, both as his creation and as his inspirer, and she gave him the happiest consciousness of success. If she was so charming, in the red firelight, in her vague, clear-coloured garments, it was because he had made her so, and yet if the weight seemed lifted from his spirit it was because she drew it away. When she bent her deep eyes upon him they seemed to speak of safety and freedom and to make a green garden of the future. From time to time she smiled and said: "I live— I live—I live." How long she stayed he couldn't have told, but when his landlady blundered in with the lamp Nona Vincent was no longer there. He rubbed his eyes, but no dream had ever been so intense; and as he slowly got out of his chair it was with a deep still joy—the joy of the artist—in the thought of how right he had been, how exactly like herself he had made her. She had come to show him that. At the end of five minutes, however, he felt sufficiently mystified to call his landlady back—he wanted to ask her a question. When the good woman reappeared the question hung fire an instant; then it shaped itself as the inquiry: "Has any lady been here?"

"No, sir—no lady at all."

The woman seemed slightly scandalised.

"Not Miss Vincent?"

"Miss Vincent, sir?"

"The young lady of my play, don't you know?"

"Oh, sir, you mean Miss Violet Grey!"

"No I don't, at all. I think I mean Mrs. Alsager."

"There has been no Mrs. Alsager, sir."

"Nor anybody at all like her?"

The woman looked at him as if she wondered what had suddenly taken him. Then she asked in an injured tone: "Why shouldn't I have told you if you'd 'ad callers, sir?"

"I thought you might have thought I was asleep."

"Indeed you were, sir, when I came in with the lamp—and well you'd earned it, Mr. Wayworth!"

The landlady came back an hour later to bring him a telegram; it was just as he had begun to dress to dine at his club and go down to the theatre.

"See me to-night in front, and don't come near me till it's over."

It was in these words that Violet communicated her wishes for the evening. He obeyed them to the letter; he watched her from the depths of a box. He was in no position to say how she might have struck him the night before, but what he saw during these charmed hours filled him with admiration and gratitude. She *was* in it, this time; she had pulled herself together, she had taken possession, she was felicitous at every turn. Fresh from his revelation of Nona he was in a position to judge, and as he judged he exulted. He was thrilled and carried away, and he was moreover intensely curious to know what had happened to her, by what unfathomable art she had managed in a few hours to effect such a change of base. It was as if *she* had had a revelation of Nona, so convincing a clearness had been breathed upon the picture. He kept himself quiet in the *entr'actes*—he would speak to her only at the end; but before the play was half over the manager burst into his box.

"It's prodigious, what she's up to!" cried Mr. Loder, almost more bewildered than gratified. "She has gone in for a new reading—a blessed somersault in the air!"

"Is it quite different?" Wayworth asked, sharing his mystification.

"Different? Hyperion to a satyr! It's devilish good, my boy!"

"It's devilish good," said Wayworth, "and it's in a different key altogether from the key of her rehearsal."

"I'll run you six months!" the manager declared; and he rushed round again to the actress, leaving Wayworth with a sense that she had already pulled him through. She had with the audience an immense personal success.

When he went behind, at the end, he had to wait for her; she only showed herself when she was ready to leave the theatre. Her aunt had been in her dressing-room with her, and the two ladies appeared together. The girl passed him quickly, motioning him to say nothing till they should have got out of the place. He saw that she was immensely excited, lifted altogether above her common artistic level. The old lady said to him: "You must come home to supper with us: it has been all arranged." They had a brougham, with a little third seat, and he got into it with them. It was a long time before the actress would speak. She leaned back in her corner, giving no sign but still heaving a little, like a subsiding sea, and with all her triumph in the eyes that shone through the darkness. The old lady was hushed to awe, or at least to discretion, and Wayworth was happy enough to wait. He had really to wait till they had alighted at Notting Hill, where the elder of his companions went to see that supper had been attended to.

"I was better—I was better," said Violet Grey, throwing off her cloak in the little drawing-room.

"You were perfection. You'll be like that every night, won't you?"

She smiled at him. "Every night? There can scarcely be a miracle every day."

"What do you mean by a miracle?"

"I've had a revelation."

Wayworth stared. "At what hour?"

"The right hour—this afternoon. Just in time to save me—and to save *you*."

"At five o'clock? Do you mean you had a visit?"

"She came to me—she stayed two hours."

"Two hours? Nona Vincent?"

"Mrs. Alsager." Violet Grey smiled more deeply. "It's the same thing."

"And how did Mrs. Alsager save you?"

"By letting me look at her. By letting me hear her speak. By letting me know her."

"And what did she say to you?"

"Kind things—encouraging, intelligent things."

"Ah, the dear woman!" Wayworth cried.

"You ought to like her—she likes *you*. She was just what I wanted," the actress added.

"Do you mean she talked to you about Nona?"

"She said you thought she was like her. She *is*—she's exquisite."

"She's exquisite," Wayworth repeated. "Do you mean she tried to coach you?"

"Oh, no—she only said she would be so glad if it would help me to see her. And I felt it did help me. I don't know what took place—she only sat there, and she held my hand and smiled at me, and she had tact and grace, and she had goodness and beauty, and she soothed my nerves and lighted up my imagination. Somehow she seemed to *give* it all to me. I took it—I took it. I kept her before me, I drank her in. For the first time, in the whole study of the part, I had my model—I could make my copy. All my courage came back to me, and other things came that I hadn't felt before. She was different—she was delightful; as I've said, she was a revelation. She kissed me when she went away—and you may guess if I kissed *her*. We were awfully affectionate, but it's *you* she likes!" said Violet Grey.

Wayworth had never been more interested in his life, and he had rarely been more mystified. "Did she wear vague, clear-coloured garments?" he asked, after a moment.

Violet Grey stared, laughed, then bade him go in to supper. "*You* know how she dresses!"

He was very well pleased at supper, but he was silent and a little solemn. He said he would go to see Mrs. Alsager the next day. He did so, but he was told at her door that she had returned to Torquay. She remained there all winter, all spring, and the next time he saw her his play had run two hundred nights and he had married Violet Grey. His plays sometimes succeed, but his wife is not in them now, nor in any others. At these representations Mrs. Alsager continues frequently to be present.

The Real Thing

WHEN the porter's wife (she used to answer the house-bell), announced "A gentleman—with a lady, sir," I had, as I often had in those days, for the wish was father to the thought, an immediate vision of sitters. Sitters my visitors in this case proved to be; but not in the sense I should have preferred. However, there was nothing at first to indicate that they might not have come for a portrait. The gentleman, a man of fifty, very high and very straight, with a moustache slightly grizzled and a dark grey walking-coat admirably fitted, both of which I noted professionally—I don't mean as a barber or yet as a tailor—would have struck me as a celebrity if celebrities often were striking. It was a truth of which I had for some time been conscious that a figure with a good deal of frontage was, as one might say, almost never a public institution. A glance at the lady helped to remind me of this paradoxical law: she also looked too distinguished to be a "personality." Moreover one would scarcely come across two variations together.

Neither of the pair spoke immediately—they only prolonged the preliminary gaze which suggested that each wished to give the other a chance. They were visibly shy; they stood there letting me take them in—which, as I afterwards perceived, was the most practical thing they could have done. In this way their embarrassment served their cause. I had seen people painfully reluctant to mention that they desired anything so gross as to be represented on canvas; but the scruples of my new friends appeared almost insurmountable. Yet the gentleman might have said "I should like a portrait of my wife," and the lady might have said "I should like a portrait of my husband." Perhaps they were not husband and wife—this naturally would make the matter more delicate. Perhaps they wished to be done together—in which case they ought to have brought a third person to break the news.

"We come from Mr. Rivet," the lady said at last, with a dim smile which had the effect of a moist sponge passed over a "sunk" piece of painting, as well as of a vague allusion to

32

vanished beauty. She was as tall and straight, in her degree, as her companion, and with ten years less to carry. She looked as sad as a woman could look whose face was not charged with expression; that is her tinted oval mask showed friction as an exposed surface shows it. The hand of time had played over her freely, but only to simplify. She was slim and stiff, and so well dressed, in dark blue cloth, with lappets and pockets and buttons, that it was clear she employed the same tailor as her husband. The couple had an indefinable air of prosperous thrift—they evidently got a good deal of luxury for their money. If I was to be one of their luxuries it would behove me to consider my terms.

"Ah, Claude Rivet recommended me?" I inquired; and I added that it was very kind of him, though I could reflect that, as he only painted landscape, this was not a sacrifice.

The lady looked very hard at the gentleman, and the gentleman looked round the room. Then staring at the floor a moment and stroking his moustache, he rested his pleasant eyes on me with the remark: "He said you were the right one."

"I try to be, when people want to sit."

"Yes, we should like to," said the lady anxiously.

"Do you mean together?"

My visitors exchanged a glance. "If you could do anything with *me*, I suppose it would be double," the gentleman stammered.

"Oh yes, there's naturally a higher charge for two figures than for one."

"We should like to make it pay," the husband confessed.

"That's very good of you," I returned, appreciating so unwonted a sympathy—for I supposed he meant pay the artist.

A sense of strangeness seemed to dawn on the lady. "We mean for the illustrations—Mr. Rivet said you might put one in."

"Put one in—an illustration?" I was equally confused.

"Sketch her off, you know," said the gentleman, colouring.

It was only then that I understood the service Claude Rivet had rendered me; he had told them that I worked in black and white, for magazines, for story-books, for sketches of contemporary life, and consequently had frequent employment for models. These things were true, but it was not less true (I may confess it now—whether because the aspiration was to lead to everything or to nothing I leave the reader to guess), that I couldn't get the honours, to say nothing of the emoluments, of a great painter of portraits out of my head. My "illustrations" were my pot-boilers; I looked to a different branch of art (far and away the most interesting it had always seemed to me), to perpetuate my fame. There was no shame in looking to it also to make my fortune; but that fortune was by so much further from being made from the moment my visitors wished to be "done" for nothing. I was disappointed; for in the pictorial sense I had immediately *seen* them. I had seized their type—I had already settled what I would do with it. Something that wouldn't absolutely have pleased them, I afterwards reflected.

"Ah, you're—you're—a—?" I began, as soon as I had mastered my surprise. I couldn't bring out the dingy word "models"; it seemed to fit the case so little.

"We haven't had much practice," said the lady.

"We've got to *do* something, and we've thought that an artist in your line might perhaps make something of us," her husband threw off. He further mentioned that they didn't know many artists and that they had gone first, on the off-chance (he painted views of course, but sometimes put in figures—perhaps I remembered), to Mr. Rivet, whom they had met a few years before at a place in Norfolk where he was sketching.

"We used to sketch a little ourselves," the lady hinted.

"It's very awkward, but we absolutely *must* do something," her husband went on.

"Of course, we're not so *very* young," she admitted, with a wan smile.

With the remark that I might as well know something more about them, the husband had handed me a card extracted from a neat new pocket-book (their appurtenances were all of the freshest) and inscribed with the words "Major Monarch." Impressive as these words were they didn't carry my knowledge much further; but my visitor presently added: "I've left the army, and we've had the misfortune to lose our money. In fact our means are dreadfully small."

"It's an awful bore," said Mrs. Monarch.

They evidently wished to be discreet—to take care not to swagger because they were gentlefolks. I perceived they would have been willing to recognise this as something of a drawback, at the same time that I guessed at an underlying sense—their consolation in adversity—that they *had* their points. They certainly had; but these advantages struck me as preponderantly social; such for instance as would help to make a drawing-room look well. However, a drawing-room was always, or ought to be, a picture.

In consequence of his wife's allusion to their age Major Monarch observed: "Naturally, it's more for the figure that we thought of going in. We can still hold ourselves up." On the instant I saw that the figure was indeed their strong point. His "naturally" didn't sound vain, but it lighted up the question. "*She* has got the best," he continued, nodding at his wife, with a pleasant after-dinner absence of circumlocution. I could only reply, as if we were in fact sitting over our wine, that this didn't prevent his own from being very good; which led him in turn to rejoin: "We thought that if you ever have to do people like us, we might be something like it. *She*, particularly—for a lady in a book, you know."

I was so amused by them that, to get more of it, I did my best to take their point of view; and though it was an embarrassment to find myself appraising physically, as if they were animals on hire or useful blacks, a pair whom I should have expected to meet only in one of the relations in which criticism is tacit, I looked at Mrs. Monarch judicially enough to be able to exclaim, after a moment, with conviction: "Oh yes, a lady in a book!" She was singularly like a bad illustration.

"We'll stand up, if you like," said the Major; and he raised himself before me with a really grand air.

I could take his measure at a glance—he was six feet two and a perfect gentleman. It would have paid any club in process of formation and in want of a stamp to engage him at a salary to stand in the principal window. What struck me immediately was that in coming to me they had rather missed their vocation; they could surely have been turned to better account for advertising purposes. I couldn't of course see the thing in detail, but I could see them make someone's fortune—I don't mean their own. There was something in them for a waistcoat-maker, an hotel-keeper or a soap-vendor. I could imagine "We always use it" pinned on their bosoms with the greatest effect; I had a vision of the promptitude with which they would launch a table d'hôte.

Mrs. Monarch sat still, not from pride but from shyness, and presently her husband said to her: "Get up my dear and show how smart you are." She obeyed, but she had no need to get up to show it. She walked to the end of the studio, and then she came back blushing, with her fluttered eyes on her husband. I was reminded of an incident I had accidentally had a glimpse of in Paris—being with a friend there, a dramatist about to produce a play—when an actress came to him to ask to be intrusted with a part. She went through her paces before him, walked up and down as Mrs. Monarch was doing. Mrs. Monarch did it quite as well, but I abstained from applauding. It was very odd to see such people apply for such poor pay. She looked as if she had ten thousand a year. Her husband had used the word that described her: she was, in the London current jargon, essentially and typically "smart." Her figure was, in the same order of ideas, conspicuously and irreproachably "good." For a woman of her age her waist was surprisingly small; her elbow moreover had the orthodox crook. She held her head at the conventional angle; but why did she come to *me*? She ought to have tried on jackets at a big shop. I feared my visitors were not only destitute, but "artistic"—which would be a great complication. When she sat down again I thanked her, observing that what a draughtsman most valued in his model was the faculty of keeping quiet.

"Oh, *she* can keep quiet," said Major Monarch. Then he added, jocosely: "I've always kept her quiet."

"I'm not a nasty fidget, am I?" Mrs. Monarch appealed to her husband.

He addressed his answer to me. "Perhaps it isn't out of place to mention—because we ought to be quite business-like, oughtn't we?—that when I married her she was known as the Beautiful Statue."

"Oh dear!" said Mrs. Monarch, ruefully.

"Of course I should want a certain amount of expression," I rejoined.

"Of *course*!" they both exclaimed.

"And then I suppose you know that you'll get awfully tired."

"Oh, we *never* get tired!" they eagerly cried.

"Have you had any kind of practice?"

They hesitated—they looked at each other. "We've been photographed, *immensely*," said Mrs. Monarch.

"She means the fellows have asked us," added the Major.

"I see—because you're so good-looking."

"I don't know what they thought, but they were always after us."

"We always got our photographs for nothing," smiled Mrs. Monarch.

"We might have brought some, my dear," her husband remarked.

"I'm not sure we have any left. We've given quantities away," she explained to me.

"With our autographs and that sort of thing," said the Major.

"Are they to be got in the shops?" I inquired, as a harmless pleasantry.

"Oh, yes; *hers*—they used to be."

"Not now," said Mrs. Monarch, with her eyes on the floor.

II.

I could fancy the "sort of thing" they put on the presentation-copies of their photographs, and I was sure they wrote a beautiful hand. It was odd how quickly I was sure of everything that concerned them. If they were now so poor as to have to earn shillings and pence, they never had had much of a margin. Their good looks had been their capital, and they had good-humouredly made the most of the career that this resource marked out for them. It was in their faces, the blankness, the deep intellectual repose of the twenty years of country-house visiting which had given them pleasant intonations. I could see the sunny drawing-rooms, sprinkled with period-

icals she didn't read, in which Mrs. Monarch had continuously
sat; I could see the wet shrubberies in which she had walked,
equipped to admiration for either exercise. I could see the rich
covers the Major had helped to shoot and the wonderful garments in which, late at night, he repaired to the smoking-
room to talk about them. I could imagine their leggings and
waterproofs, their knowing tweeds and rugs, their rolls of
sticks and cases of tackle and neat umbrellas; and I could
evoke the exact appearance of their servants and the compact
variety of their luggage on the platforms of country stations.

They gave small tips, but they were liked; they didn't do
anything themselves, but they were welcome. They looked so
well everywhere; they gratified the general relish for stature,
complexion and "form." They knew it without fatuity or vulgarity, and they respected themselves in consequence. They
were not superficial; they were thorough and kept themselves
up—it had been their line. People with such a taste for activity
had to have some line. I could feel how, even in a dull house,
they could have been counted upon for cheerfulness. At present something had happened—it didn't matter what, their little income had grown less, it had grown least—and they had
to do something for pocket-money. Their friends liked them,
but didn't like to support them. There was something about
them that represented credit—their clothes, their manners,
their type; but if credit is a large empty pocket in which an
occasional chink reverberates, the chink at least must be audible. What they wanted of me was to help to make it so.
Fortunately they had no children—I soon divined that. They
would also perhaps wish our relations to be kept secret: this
was why it was "for the figure"—the reproduction of the face
would betray them.

I liked them—they were so simple; and I had no objection
to them if they would suit. But, somehow, with all their perfections I didn't easily believe in them. After all they were
amateurs, and the ruling passion of my life was the detestation
of the amateur. Combined with this was another perversity—
an innate preference for the represented subject over the real
one: the defect of the real one was so apt to be a lack of
representation. I liked things that appeared; then one was
sure. Whether they *were* or not was a subordinate and almost

always a profitless question. There were other considerations, the first of which was that I already had two or three people in use, notably a young person with big feet, in alpaca, from Kilburn, who for a couple of years had come to me regularly for my illustrations and with whom I was still—perhaps ignobly—satisfied. I frankly explained to my visitors how the case stood; but they had taken more precautions than I supposed. They had reasoned out their opportunity, for Claude Rivet had told them of the projected *édition de luxe* of one of the writers of our day—the rarest of the novelists—who, long neglected by the multitudinous vulgar and dearly prized by the attentive (need I mention Philip Vincent?) had had the happy fortune of seeing, late in life, the dawn and then the full light of a higher criticism—an estimate in which, on the part of the public, there was something really of expiation. The edition in question, planned by a publisher of taste, was practically an act of high reparation; the wood-cuts with which it was to be enriched were the homage of English art to one of the most independent representatives of English letters. Major and Mrs. Monarch confessed to me that they had hoped I might be able to work *them* into my share of the enterprise. They knew I was to do the first of the books, "Rutland Ramsay," but I had to make clear to them that my participation in the rest of the affair—this first book was to be a test—was to depend on the satisfaction I should give. If this should be limited my employers would drop me without a scruple. It was therefore a crisis for me, and naturally I was making special preparations, looking about for new people, if they should be necessary, and securing the best types. I admitted however that I should like to settle down to two or three good models who would do for everything.

"Should we have often to—a—put on special clothes?" Mrs. Monarch timidly demanded.

"Dear, yes—that's half the business."

"And should we be expected to supply our own costumes?"

"Oh, no; I've got a lot of things. A painter's models put on—or put off—anything he likes."

"And do you mean—a—the same?"

"The same?"

Mrs. Monarch looked at her husband again.

"Oh, she was just wondering," he explained, "if the costumes are in *general* use." I had to confess that they were,
and I mentioned further that some of them (I had a lot of
genuine, greasy last-century things), had served their time, a
hundred years ago, on living, world-stained men and women.
"We'll put on anything that *fits*," said the Major.

"Oh, I arrange that—they fit in the pictures."

"I'm afraid I should do better for the modern books. I
would come as you like," said Mrs. Monarch.

"She has got a lot of clothes at home: they might do for
contemporary life," her husband continued.

"Oh, I can fancy scenes in which you'd be quite natural."
And indeed I could see the slipshod rearrangements of stale
properties—the stories I tried to produce pictures for without
the exasperation of reading them—whose sandy tracts the
good lady might help to people. But I had to return to the
fact that for this sort of work—the daily mechanical grind—I
was already equipped; the people I was working with were
fully adequate.

"We only thought we might be more like *some* characters,"
said Mrs. Monarch mildly, getting up.

Her husband also rose; he stood looking at me with a dim
wistfulness that was touching in so fine a man. "Wouldn't it
be rather a pull sometimes to have—a—to have—?" He hung
fire; he wanted me to help him by phrasing what he meant.
But I couldn't—I didn't know. So he brought it out, awkwardly: "The *real* thing; a gentleman, you know, or a lady."
I was quite ready to give a general assent—I admitted that
there was a great deal in that. This encouraged Major Monarch to say, following up his appeal with an unacted gulp: "It's
awfully hard—we've tried everything." The gulp was communicative; it proved too much for his wife. Before I knew it
Mrs. Monarch had dropped again upon a divan and burst into
tears. Her husband sat down beside her, holding one of her
hands; whereupon she quickly dried her eyes with the other,
while I felt embarrassed as she looked up at me. "There isn't
a confounded job I haven't applied for—waited for—prayed
for. You can fancy we'd be pretty bad first. Secretaryships and
that sort of thing? You might as well ask for a peerage. I'd be
anything—I'm strong; a messenger or a coalheaver. I'd put

on a gold-laced cap and open carriage-doors in front of the haberdasher's; I'd hang about a station, to carry portmanteaus; I'd be a postman. But they won't *look* at you; there are thousands, as good as yourself, already on the ground. *Gentlemen*, poor beggars, who have drunk their wine, who have kept their hunters!"

I was as reassuring as I knew how to be, and my visitors were presently on their feet again while, for the experiment, we agreed on an hour. We were discussing it when the door opened and Miss Churm came in with a wet umbrella. Miss Churm had to take the omnibus to Maida Vale and then walk half a mile. She looked a trifle blowsy and slightly splashed. I scarcely ever saw her come in without thinking afresh how odd it was that, being so little in herself, she should yet be so much in others. She was a meagre little Miss Churm, but she was an ample heroine of romance. She was only a freckled cockney, but she could represent everything, from a fine lady to a shepherdess; she had the faculty, as she might have had a fine voice or long hair. She couldn't spell, and she loved beer, but she had two or three "points," and practice, and a knack, and mother-wit, and a kind of whimsical sensibility, and a love of the theatre, and seven sisters, and not an ounce of respect, especially for the *h*. The first thing my visitors saw was that her umbrella was wet, and in their spotless perfection they visibly winced at it. The rain had come on since their arrival.

"I'm all in a soak; there *was* a mess of people in the 'bus. I wish you lived near a stytion," said Miss Churm. I requested her to get ready as quickly as possible, and she passed into the room in which she always changed her dress. But before going out she asked me what she was to get into this time.

"It's the Russian princess, don't you know?" I answered; "the one with the 'golden eyes,' in black velvet, for the long thing in the *Cheapside*."

"Golden eyes? I *say*!" cried Miss Churm, while my companions watched her with intensity as she withdrew. She always arranged herself, when she was late, before I could turn round; and I kept my visitors a little, on purpose, so that they might get an idea, from seeing her, what would be expected of themselves. I mentioned that she was quite my notion of an excellent model—she was really very clever.

"Do you think she looks like a Russian princess?" Major Monarch asked, with lurking alarm.

"When I make her, yes."

"Oh, if you have to *make* her—!" he reasoned, acutely.

"That's the most you can ask. There are so many that are not makeable."

"Well now, *here's* a lady"—and with a persuasive smile he passed his arm into his wife's—"who's already made!"

"Oh, I'm not a Russian princess," Mrs. Monarch protested, a little coldly. I could see that she had known some and didn't like them. There, immediately, was a complication of a kind that I never had to fear with Miss Churm.

This young lady came back in black velvet—the gown was rather rusty and very low on her lean shoulders—and with a Japanese fan in her red hands. I reminded her that in the scene I was doing she had to look over someone's head. "I forget whose it is; but it doesn't matter. Just look over a head."

"I'd rather look over a stove," said Miss Churm; and she took her station near the fire. She fell into position, settled herself into a tall attitude, gave a certain backward inclination to her head and a certain forward droop to her fan, and looked, at least to my prejudiced sense, distinguished and charming, foreign and dangerous. We left her looking so, while I went down-stairs with Major and Mrs. Monarch.

"I think I could come about as near it as that," said Mrs. Monarch.

"Oh, you think she's shabby, but you must allow for the alchemy of art."

However, they went off with an evident increase of comfort, founded on their demonstrable advantage in being the real thing. I could fancy them shuddering over Miss Churm. She was very droll about them when I went back, for I told her what they wanted.

"Well, if *she* can sit I'll tyke to bookkeeping," said my model.

"She's very lady-like," I replied, as an innocent form of aggravation.

"So much the worse for *you*. That means she can't turn round."

"She'll do for the fashionable novels."

"Oh yes, she'll *do* for them!" my model humorously declared. "Ain't they bad enough without her?" I had often sociably denounced them to Miss Churm.

III.

It was for the elucidation of a mystery in one of these works that I first tried Mrs. Monarch. Her husband came with her, to be useful if necessary—it was sufficiently clear that as a general thing he would prefer to come with her. At first I wondered if this were for "propriety's" sake—if he were going to be jealous and meddling. The idea was too tiresome, and if it had been confirmed it would speedily have brought our acquaintance to a close. But I soon saw there was nothing in it and that if he accompanied Mrs. Monarch it was (in addition to the chance of being wanted), simply because he had nothing else to do. When she was away from him his occupation was gone—she never *had* been away from him. I judged, rightly, that in their awkward situation their close union was their main comfort and that this union had no weak spot. It was a real marriage, an encouragement to the hesitating, a nut for pessimists to crack. Their address was humble (I remember afterwards thinking it had been the only thing about them that was really professional), and I could fancy the lamentable lodgings in which the Major would have been left alone. He could bear them with his wife—he couldn't bear them without her.

He had too much tact to try and make himself agreeable when he couldn't be useful; so he simply sat and waited, when I was too absorbed in my work to talk. But I liked to make him talk—it made my work, when it didn't interrupt it, less sordid, less special. To listen to him was to combine the excitement of going out with the economy of staying at home. There was only one hindrance: that I seemed not to know any of the people he and his wife had known. I think he wondered extremely, during the term of our intercourse, whom the deuce I *did* know. He hadn't a stray sixpence of an idea to fumble for; so we didn't spin it very fine—we confined ourselves to questions of leather and even of liquor (saddlers and breeches-makers and how to get good claret cheap), and matters like "good trains" and the habits of small game. His lore on these last subjects was astonishing, he managed to interweave the station-master with the ornithologist. When he couldn't talk about greater things he could talk cheerfully about smaller, and since I couldn't accompany him into reminiscences of the fashionable world he could lower the conversation without a visible effort to my level.

So earnest a desire to please was touching in a man who could so easily have knocked one down. He looked after the fire and had an opinion on the draught of the stove, without my asking him, and I could see that he thought many of my arrangements not half clever enough. I remember telling him that if I were only rich I would offer him a salary to come and teach me how to live. Sometimes he gave a random sigh, of which the essence was: "Give me even such a bare old barrack as *this*, and I'd do something with it!" When I wanted to use him he came alone; which was an illustration of the superior courage of women. His wife could bear her solitary second floor, and she was in general more discreet; showing by various small reserves that she was alive to the propriety of keeping our relations markedly professional—not letting them slide into sociability. She wished it to remain clear that she and the Major were employed, not cultivated, and if she approved of me as a superior, who could be kept in his place, she never thought me quite good enough for an equal.

She sat with great intensity, giving the whole of her mind to it, and was capable of remaining for an hour almost as motionless as if she were before a photographer's lens. I could see she had been photographed often, but somehow the very habit that made her good for that purpose unfitted her for mine. At first I was extremely pleased with her lady-like air, and it was a satisfaction, on coming to follow her lines, to see how good they were and how far they could lead the pencil. But after a few times I began to find her too insurmountably stiff; do what I would with it my drawing looked like a photograph or a copy of a photograph. Her figure had no variety of expression—she herself had no sense of variety. You may say that this was my business, was only a question of placing her. I placed her in every conceivable position, but she managed to obliterate their differences. She was always a lady cer-

tainly, and into the bargain was always the same lady. She was
the real thing, but always the same thing. There were moments when I was oppressed by the serenity of her confidence
that she *was* the real thing. All her dealings with me and all
her husband's were an implication that this was lucky for *me*.
Meanwhile I found myself trying to invent types that approached her own, instead of making her own transform itself—in the clever way that was not impossible, for instance,
to poor Miss Churm. Arrange as I would and take the precautions I would, she always, in my pictures, came out too
tall—landing me in the dilemma of having represented a
fascinating woman as seven feet high, which, out of respect
perhaps to my own very much scantier inches, was far from
my idea of such a personage.

The case was worse with the Major—nothing I could do
would keep *him* down, so that he became useful only for the
representation of brawny giants. I adored variety and range, I
cherished human accidents, the illustrative note; I wanted to
characterise closely, and the thing in the world I most hated
was the danger of being ridden by a type. I had quarrelled
with some of my friends about it—I had parted company with
them for maintaining that one *had* to be, and that if the
type was beautiful (witness Raphael and Leonardo), the ser
vitude was only a gain. I was neither Leonardo nor Raphael;
I might only be a presumptuous young modern searcher, but
I held that everything was to be sacrificed sooner than character. When they averred that the haunting type in question
could easily *be* character, I retorted, perhaps superficially:
"Whose?" It couldn't be everybody's—it might end in being
nobody's.

After I had drawn Mrs. Monarch a dozen times I perceived
more clearly than before that the value of such a model as
Miss Churm resided precisely in the fact that she had no positive stamp, combined of course with the other fact that what
she did have was a curious and inexplicable talent for imitation. Her usual appearance was like a curtain which she could
draw up at request for a capital performance. This performance was simply suggestive; but it was a word to the wise—it
was vivid and pretty. Sometimes, even, I thought it, though
she was plain herself, too insipidly pretty; I made it a reproach

to her that the figures drawn from her were monotonously (*bêtement*, as we used to say) graceful. Nothing made her more angry: it was so much her pride to feel that she could sit for characters that had nothing in common with each other. She would accuse me at such moments of taking away her "reputytion."

It suffered a certain shrinkage, this queer quantity, from the repeated visits of my new friends. Miss Churm was greatly in demand, never in want of employment, so I had no scruple in putting her off occasionally, to try them more at my ease. It was certainly amusing at first to do the real thing—it was amusing to do Major Monarch's trousers. They *were* the real thing, even if he did come out colossal. It was amusing to do his wife's back hair (it was so mathematically neat,) and the particular "smart" tension of her tight stays. She lent herself especially to positions in which the face was somewhat averted or blurred; she abounded in lady-like back views and *profils perdus*. When she stood erect she took naturally one of the attitudes in which court-painters represent queens and princesses; so that I found myself wondering whether, to draw out this accomplishment, I couldn't get the editor of the *Cheapside* to publish a really royal romance, "A Tale of Buckingham Palace." Sometimes, however, the real thing and the make-believe came into contact; by which I mean that Miss Churm, keeping an appointment or coming to make one on days when I had much work in hand, encountered her invidious rivals. The encounter was not on their part, for they noticed her no more than if she had been the housemaid; not from intentional loftiness, but simply because, as yet, professionally, they didn't know how to fraternise, as I could guess that they would have liked—or at least that the Major would. They couldn't talk about the omnibus—they always walked; and they didn't know what else to try—she wasn't interested in good trains or cheap claret. Besides, they must have felt—in the air—that she was amused at them, secretly derisive of their ever knowing how. She was not a person to conceal her scepticism if she had had a chance to show it. On the other hand Mrs. Monarch didn't think her tidy; for why else did she take pains to say to me (it was going out of the way, for Mrs. Monarch), that she didn't like dirty women?

One day when my young lady happened to be present with my other sitters (she even dropped in, when it was convenient, for a chat), I asked her to be so good as to lend a hand in getting tea—a service with which she was familiar and which was one of a class that, living as I did in a small way, with slender domestic resources, I often appealed to my models to render. They liked to lay hands on my property, to break the sitting, and sometimes the china—I made them feel Bohemian. The next time I saw Miss Churm after this incident she surprised me greatly by making a scene about it—she accused me of having wished to humiliate her. She had not resented the outrage at the time, but had seemed obliging and amused, enjoying the comedy of asking Mrs. Monarch, who sat vague and silent, whether she would have cream and sugar, and putting an exaggerated simper into the question. She had tried intonations—as if she too wished to pass for the real thing; till I was afraid my other visitors would take offence.

Oh, *they* were determined not to do this; and their touching patience was the measure of their great need. They would sit by the hour, uncomplaining, till I was ready to use them; they would come back on the chance of being wanted and would walk away cheerfully if they were not. I used to go to the door with them to see in what magnificent order they retreated. I tried to find other employment for them—I introduced them to several artists. But they didn't "take," for reasons I could appreciate, and I became conscious, rather anxiously, that after such disappointments they fell back upon me with a heavier weight. They did me the honour to think that it was I who was most *their* form. They were not picturesque enough for the painters, and in those days there were not so many serious workers in black and white. Besides, they had an eye to the great job I had mentioned to them—they had secretly set their hearts on supplying the right essence for my pictorial vindication of our fine novelist. They knew that for this undertaking I should want no costume-effects, none of the frippery of past ages—that it was a case in which everything would be contemporary and satirical and, presumably, genteel. If I could work them into it their future would be assured, for the labour would of course be long and the occupation steady.

One day Mrs. Monarch came without her husband—she explained his absence by his having had to go to the City. While she sat there in her usual anxious stiffness there came, at the door, a knock which I immediately recognised as the subdued appeal of a model out of work. It was followed by the entrance of a young man whom I easily perceived to be a foreigner and who proved in fact an Italian acquainted with no English word but my name, which he uttered in a way that made it seem to include all others. I had not then visited his country, nor was I proficient in his tongue; but as he was not so meanly constituted—what Italian is?—as to depend only on that member for expression he conveyed to me, in familiar but graceful mimicry, that he was in search of exactly the employment in which the lady before me was engaged. I was not struck with him at first, and while I continued to draw I emitted rough sounds of discouragement and dismissal. He stood his ground, however, not importunately, but with a dumb, dog-like fidelity in his eyes which amounted to innocent impudence—the manner of a devoted servant (he might have been in the house for years), unjustly suspected. Suddenly I saw that this very attitude and expression made a picture, whereupon I told him to sit down and wait till I should be free. There was another picture in the way he obeyed me, and I observed as I worked that there were others still in the way he looked wonderingly, with his head thrown back, about the high studio. He might have been crossing himself in St. Peter's. Before I finished I said to myself: "The fellow's a bankrupt orange-monger, but he's a treasure."

When Mrs. Monarch withdrew he passed across the room like a flash to open the door for her, standing there with the rapt, pure gaze of the young Dante spellbound by the young Beatrice. As I never insisted, in such situations, on the blankness of the British domestic, I reflected that he had the making of a servant (and I needed one, but couldn't pay him to be only that), as well as of a model; in short I made up my mind to adopt my bright adventurer if he would agree to officiate in the double capacity. He jumped at my offer, and in the event my rashness (for I had known nothing about him), was not brought home to me. He proved a sympathetic though a desultory ministrant, and had in a wonderful degree the *sentiment de la pose*. It was uncultivated, instinctive; a part of the happy instinct which had guided him to my door and helped him to spell out my name on the card nailed to it. He had had no other introduction to me than a guess, from the shape of my high north window, seen outside, that my place was a studio and that as a studio it would contain an artist. He had wandered to England in search of fortune, like other itinerants, and had embarked, with a partner and a small green handcart, on the sale of penny ices. The ices had melted away and the partner had dissolved in their train. My young man wore tight yellow trousers with reddish stripes and his name was Oronte. He was sallow but fair, and when I put him into some old clothes of my own he looked like an Englishman. He was as good as Miss Churm, who could look, when required, like an Italian.

IV.

I thought Mrs. Monarch's face slightly convulsed when, on her coming back with her husband, she found Oronte installed. It was strange to have to recognise in a scrap of a lazzarone a competitor to her magnificent Major. It was she who scented danger first, for the Major was anecdotically unconscious. But Oronte gave us tea, with a hundred eager confusions (he had never seen such a queer process), and I think she thought better of me for having at last an "establishment." They saw a couple of drawings that I had made of the establishment, and Mrs. Monarch hinted that it never would have struck her that he had sat for them. "Now the drawings you make from *us,* they look exactly like us," she reminded me, smiling in triumph; and I recognised that this was indeed just their defect. When I drew the Monarchs I couldn't, somehow, get away from them—get into the character I wanted to represent; and I had not the least desire my model should be discoverable in my picture. Miss Churm never was, and Mrs. Monarch thought I hid her, very properly, because she was vulgar; whereas if she was lost it was only as the dead who go to heaven are lost—in the gain of an angel the more.

By this time I had got a certain start with "Rutland Ramsay," the first novel in the great projected series; that is I had produced a dozen drawings, several with the help of the Major and his wife, and I had sent them in for approval. My understanding with the publishers, as I have already hinted, had been that I was to be left to do my work, in this particular case, as I liked, with the whole book committed to me; but my connection with the rest of the series was only contingent. There were moments when, frankly, it *was* a comfort to have the real thing under one's hand; for there were characters in "Rutland Ramsay" that were very much like it. There were people presumably as straight as the Major and women of as good a fashion as Mrs. Monarch. There was a great deal of country-house life—treated, it is true, in a fine, fanciful, ironical, generalised way—and there was a considerable implication of knickerbockers and kilts. There were certain things I had to settle at the outset; such things for instance as the exact appearance of the hero, the particular bloom of the heroine. The author of course gave me a lead, but there was a margin for interpretation. I took the Monarchs into my confidence, I told them frankly what I was about, I mentioned my embarrassments and alternatives. "Oh, take *him*!" Mrs. Monarch murmured sweetly, looking at her husband; and "What could you want better than my wife?" the Major inquired, with the comfortable candour that now prevailed between us.

I was not obliged to answer these remarks—I was only obliged to place my sitters. I was not easy in mind, and I postponed, a little timidly perhaps, the solution of the question. The book was a large canvas, the other figures were numerous, and I worked off at first some of the episodes in which the hero and the heroine were not concerned. When once I had set *them* up I should have to stick to them—I couldn't make my young man seven feet high in one place and five feet nine in another. I inclined on the whole to the latter measurement, though the Major more than once reminded me that *he* looked about as young as anyone. It was indeed quite possible to arrange him, for the figure, so that it would have been difficult to detect his age. After the spontaneous Oronte had been with me a month, and after I had given him to understand several different times that his native exuberance would presently constitute an insurmountable barrier to our further intercourse, I waked to a sense of his heroic capacity. He was only five feet seven, but the remaining inches were latent. I tried him almost secretly at first, for I was really rather afraid of the judgment my other models would pass on such a choice. If they regarded Miss Churm as little better than a snare, what would they think of the representation by a person so little the real thing as an Italian street-vendor of a protagonist formed by a public school?

If I went a little in fear of them it was not because they bullied me, because they had got an oppressive foothold, but because in their really pathetic decorum and mysteriously permanent newness they counted on me so intensely. I was therefore very glad when Jack Hawley came home: he was always of such good counsel. He painted badly himself, but there was no one like him for putting his finger on the place. He had been absent from England for a year; he had been somewhere—I don't remember where—to get a fresh eye. I was in a good deal of dread of any such organ, but we were old friends; he had been away for months and a sense of emptiness was creeping into my life. I hadn't dodged a missile for a year.

He came back with a fresh eye, but with the same old black velvet blouse, and the first evening he spent in my studio we smoked cigarettes till the small hours. He had done no work himself, he had only got the eye; so the field was clear for the production of my little things. He wanted to see what I had done for the *Cheapside*, but he was disappointed in the exhibition. That at least seemed the meaning of two or three comprehensive groans which, as he lounged on my big divan, on a folded leg, looking at my latest drawings, issued from his lips with the smoke of the cigarette.

"What's the matter with you?" I asked.

"What's the matter with *you*?"

"Nothing save that I'm mystified."

"You are indeed. You're quite off the hinge. What's the meaning of this new fad?" And he tossed me, with visible irreverence, a drawing in which I happened to have depicted both my majestic models. I asked if he didn't think it good, and he replied that it struck him as execrable, given the sort of thing I had always represented myself to him as wishing to arrive at; but I let that pass, I was so anxious to see exactly what he meant. The two figures in the picture looked colossal, but I supposed this was *not* what he meant, inasmuch as, for aught he knew to the contrary, I might have been trying for that. I maintained that I was working exactly in the same way as when he last had done me the honour to commend me. "Well, there's a big hole somewhere," he answered; "wait a bit and I'll discover it." I depended upon him to do so: where else was the fresh eye? But he produced at last nothing more luminous than "I don't know—I don't like your types." This was lame, for a critic who had never consented to discuss with me anything but the question of execution, the direction of strokes and the mystery of values.

"In the drawings you've been looking at I think my types are very handsome."

"Oh, they won't do!"

"I've had a couple of new models."

"I see you have. *They* won't do."

"Are you very sure of that?"

"Absolutely—they're stupid."

"You mean *I* am—for I ought to get round that."

"You *can't*—with such people. Who are they?"

I told him, as far as was necessary, and he declared, heartlessly: "*Ce sont des gens qu'il faut mettre à la porte.*"

"You've never seen them; they're awfully good," I compassionately objected.

"Not seen them? Why, all this recent work of yours drops to pieces with them. It's all I want to see of them."

"No one else has said anything against it—the *Cheapside* people are pleased."

"Everyone else is an ass, and the *Cheapside* people the biggest asses of all. Come, don't pretend, at this time of day, to have pretty illusions about the public, especially about publishers and editors. It's not for *such* animals you work—it's for those who know, *coloro che sanno*; so keep straight for *me* if you can't keep straight for yourself. There's a certain sort of thing you tried for from the first—and a very good thing it is. But this twaddle isn't *in* it." When I talked with Hawley later about "Rutland Ramsay" and its possible successors he declared that I must get back into my boat again or I would go to the bottom. His voice in short was the voice of warning.

I noted the warning, but I didn't turn my friends out of doors. They bored me a good deal; but the very fact that they bored me admonished me not to sacrifice them—if there was anything to be done with them—simply to irritation. As I look back at this phase they seem to me to have pervaded my life not a little. I have a vision of them as most of the time in my studio, seated, against the wall, on an old velvet bench to be out of the way, and looking like a pair of patient courtiers in a royal ante-chamber. I am convinced that during the coldest weeks of the winter they held their ground because it saved them fire. Their newness was losing its gloss, and it was impossible not to feel that they were objects of charity. Whenever Miss Churm arrived they went away, and after I was fairly launched in "Rutland Ramsay" Miss Churm arrived pretty often. They managed to express to me tacitly that they supposed I wanted her for the low life of the book, and I let them suppose it, since they had attempted to study the work—it was lying about the studio—without discovering that it dealt only with the highest circles. They had dipped into the most brilliant of our novelists without deciphering many passages. I still took an hour from them, now and again, in spite of Jack Hawley's warning: it would be time enough to dismiss them, if dismissal should be necessary, when the rigour of the season was over. Hawley had made their acquaintance—he had met them at my fireside—and thought them a ridiculous pair. Learning that he was a painter they tried to approach him, to show him too that they were the real thing; but he looked at them, across the big room, as if they were miles away: they were a compendium of everything that he most objected to in the social system of his country. Such people as that, all convention and patent-leather, with ejaculations that stopped conversation, had no business in a studio. A studio was a place to learn to see, and how could you see through a pair of feather beds?

The main inconvenience I suffered at their hands was that, at first, I was shy of letting them discover how my artful little servant had begun to sit to me for "Rutland Ramsay." They knew that I had been odd enough (they were prepared by this time to allow oddity to artists,) to pick a foreign vagabond out of the streets, when I might have had a person with whiskers and credentials; but it was some time before they learned how high I rated his accomplishments. They found him in an attitude more than once, but they never doubted I was doing him as an organ-grinder. There were several things they never guessed, and one of them was that for a striking scene in the novel, in which a footman briefly figured, it occurred to me to make use of Major Monarch as the menial. I kept putting this off, I didn't like to ask him to don the livery—besides the difficulty of finding a livery to fit him. At last, one day late in the winter, when I was at work on the despised Oronte (he caught one's idea in an instant), and was in the glow of feeling that I was going very straight, they came in, the Major and his wife, with their society laugh about nothing (there was less and less to laugh at), like country-callers—they always reminded me of that—who have walked across the park after church and are presently persuaded to stay to luncheon. Luncheon was over, but they could stay to tea—I knew they wanted it. The fit was on me, however, and I couldn't let my ardour cool and my work wait, with the fading daylight, while my model prepared it. So I asked Mrs. Monarch if she would mind laying it out—a request which, for an instant, brought all the blood to her face. Her eyes were on her husband's for a second, and some mute telegraphy passed between them. Their folly was over the next instant; his cheerful shrewdness put an end to it. So far from pitying their wounded pride, I must add, I was moved to give it as complete a lesson as I could. They bustled about together and got out the cups and saucers and made the kettle boil. I know they felt as if they were waiting on my servant, and when the tea was prepared I said: "He'll have a cup, please— he's tired." Mrs. Monarch brought him one where he stood, and he took it from her as if he had been a gentleman at a party, squeezing a crush-hat with an elbow.

Then it came over me that she had made a great effort for me—made it with a kind of nobleness—and that I owed her a compensation. Each time I saw her after this I wondered what the compensation could be. I couldn't go on doing the wrong thing to oblige them. Oh, it *was* the wrong thing, the stamp of the work for which they sat—Hawley was not the only person to say it now. I sent in a large number of the drawings I had made for "Rutland Ramsay," and I received a warning that was more to the point than Hawley's. The artistic adviser of the house for which I was working was of opinion that many of my illustrations were not what had been looked for. Most of these illustrations were the subjects in which the Monarchs had figured. Without going into the question of what *had* been looked for, I saw at this rate I shouldn't get the other books to do. I hurled myself in despair upon Miss Churm, I put her through all her paces. I not only adopted Oronte publicly as my hero, but one morning when the Major looked in to see if I didn't require him to finish a figure for the *Cheapside*, for which he had begun to sit the week before, I told him that I had changed my mind—I would do the drawing from my man. At this my visitor turned pale and stood looking at me. "Is *he* your idea of an English gentleman?" he asked.

I was disappointed, I was nervous, I wanted to get on with my work; so I replied with irritation: "Oh, my dear Major—I can't be ruined for *you*!"

He stood another moment; then, without a word, he quitted the studio. I drew a long breath when he was gone, for I said to myself that I shouldn't see him again. I had not told him definitely that I was in danger of having my work rejected, but I was vexed at his not having felt the catastrophe in the air, read with me the moral of our fruitless collaboration, the lesson that, in the deceptive atmosphere of art, even the highest respectability may fail of being plastic.

I didn't owe my friends money, but I did see them again. They re-appeared together, three days later, and under the circumstances there was something tragic in the fact. It was a proof to me that they could find nothing else in life to do. They had threshed the matter out in a dismal conference—they had digested the bad news that they were not in for the series. If they were not useful to me even for the *Cheapside* their function seemed difficult to determine, and I could only judge at first that they had come, forgivingly, decorously, to take a last leave. This made me rejoice in secret that I had little leisure for a scene; for I had placed both my other models in position together and I was pegging away at a drawing from which I hoped to derive glory. It had been suggested by the passage in which Rutland Ramsay, drawing up a chair to Arte-misia's piano-stool, says extraordinary things to her while she ostensibly fingers out a difficult piece of music. I had done Miss Churm at the piano before—it was an attitude in which she knew how to take on an absolutely poetic grace. I wished the two figures to "compose" together, intensely, and my lit-tle Italian had entered perfectly into my conception. The pair were vividly before me, the piano had been pulled out; it was a charming picture of blended youth and murmured love, which I had only to catch and keep. My visitors stood and looked at it, and I was friendly to them over my shoulder.

They made no response, but I was used to silent company and went on with my work, only a little disconcerted (even though exhilarated by the sense that *this* was at least the ideal thing), at not having got rid of them after all. Presently I heard Mrs. Monarch's sweet voice beside, or rather above me: "I wish her hair was a little better done." I looked up and she was staring with a strange fixedness at Miss Churm, whose back was turned to her. "Do you mind my just touching it?" she went on—a question which made me spring up for an instant, as with the instinctive fear that she might do the young lady a harm. But she quieted me with a glance I shall never forget—I confess I should like to have been able to paint *that*—and went for a moment to my model. She spoke to her softly, laying a hand upon her shoulder and bending over her; and as the girl, understanding, gratefully assented, she disposed her rough curls, with a few quick passes, in such a way as to make Miss Churm's head twice as charming. It was one of the most heroic personal services I have ever seen rendered. Then Mrs. Monarch turned away with a low sigh and, looking about her as if for something to do, stooped to the floor with a noble humility and picked up a dirty rag that had dropped out of my paint-box.

The Major meanwhile had also been looking for something to do and, wandering to the other end of the studio, saw before him my breakfast things, neglected, unremoved. "I say, can't I be useful *here*?" he called out to me with an irrepress-ible quaver. I assented with a laugh that I fear was awkward and for the next ten minutes, while I worked, I heard the light clatter of china and the tinkle of spoons and glass. Mrs.

Monarch assisted her husband—they washed up my crockery, they put it away. They wandered off into my little scullery, and I afterwards found that they had cleaned my knives and that my slender stock of plate had an unprecedented surface. When it came over me, the latent eloquence of what they were doing, I confess that my drawing was blurred for a moment—the picture swam. They had accepted their failure, but they couldn't accept their fate. They had bowed their heads in bewilderment to the perverse and cruel law in virtue of which the real thing could be so much less precious than the unreal; but they didn't want to starve. If my servants were my models, my models might be my servants. They would reverse the parts—the others would sit for the ladies and gentlemen, and *they* would do the work. They would still be in the studio—it was an intense dumb appeal to me not to turn them out. "Take us on," they wanted to say—"we'll do *anything*."

When all this hung before me the *afflatus* vanished—my pencil dropped from my hand. My sitting was spoiled and I got rid of my sitters, who were also evidently rather mystified and awestruck. Then, alone with the Major and his wife, I had a most uncomfortable moment. He put their prayer into a single sentence: "I say, you know—just let *us* do for you, can't you?" I couldn't—it was dreadful to see them emptying my slops; but I pretended I could, to oblige them, for about a week. Then I gave them a sum of money to go away; and I never saw them again. I obtained the remaining books, but my friend Hawley repeats that Major and Mrs. Monarch did me a permanent harm, got me into a second-rate trick. If it be true I am content to have paid the price—for the memory.

The Private Life

W E TALKED of London, face to face with a great bristling, primeval glacier. The hour and the scene were one of those impressions which make up a little, in Switzerland, for the modern indignity of travel—the promiscuities and vulgarities, the station and the hotel, the gregarious patience, the struggle for a scrappy attention, the reduction to a numbered state. The high valley was pink with the mountain rose, the cool air as fresh as if the world were young. There was a faint flush of afternoon on undiminished snows, and the fraternizing tinkle of the unseen cattle came to us with a cropped and sun-warmed odour. The balconied inn stood on the very neck of the sweetest pass in the Oberland, and for a week we had had company and weather. This was felt to be great luck, for one would have made up for the other had either been bad.

The weather certainly would have made up for the company; but it was not subjected to this tax, for we had by a happy chance the *fleur des pois*: Lord and Lady Mellifont, Clare Vawdrey, the greatest (in the opinion of many) of our literary glories, and Blanche Adney, the greatest (in the opinion of all) of our theatrical. I mention these first, because they were just the people whom in London, at that time, people tried to "get." People endeavoured to "book" them six weeks ahead, yet on this occasion we had come in for them, we had all come in for each other, without the least wire-pulling. A turn of the game had pitched us together, the last of August, and we recognized our luck by remaining so, under protection of the barometer. When the golden days were over—that would come soon enough—we should wind down opposite sides of the pass and disappear over the crest of surrounding heights. We were of the same general communion, we participated in the same miscellaneous publicity. We met, in London, with irregular frequency; we were more or less governed by the laws and the language, the traditions and the shibboleths of the same dense social state. I think all of us, even the ladies, "did" something, though we pretended we didn't when it was mentioned. Such things are not mentioned indeed in London, but it was our innocent pleasure to be different here. There had to be some way to show the difference, inasmuch as we were under the impression that this was our annual holiday. We felt at any rate that the conditions were more human than in London, or that at least we ourselves were. We were frank about this, we talked about it: it was what we were talking about as we looked at the flushing glacier, just as some one called attention to the prolonged absence of Lord Mellifont and Mrs. Adney. We were seated on the terrace of the inn, where there were benches and little tables, and those of us who were most bent on proving that we had returned to nature were, in the queer Germanic fashion, having coffee before meat.

The remark about the absence of our two companions was not taken up, not even by Lady Mellifont, not even by little Adney, the fond composer; for it had been dropped only in the briefest intermission of Clare Vawdrey's talk. (This celebrity was "Clarence" only on the title-page.) It was just that revelation of our being after all human that was his theme. He asked the company whether, candidly, every one hadn't been tempted to say to every one else: "I had no idea you were really so nice." I had had, for my part, an idea that *he* was, and even a good deal nicer, but that was too complicated to go into then; besides it is exactly my story. There was a general understanding among us that when Vawdrey talked we should be silent, and not, oddly enough, because he at all expected it. He didn't, for of all abundant talkers he was the most unconscious, the least greedy and professional. It was rather the religion of the host, of the hostess, that prevailed among us: it was their own idea, but they always looked for a listening circle when the great novelist dined with them. On the occasion I allude to there was probably no one present with whom, in London, he had not dined, and we felt the force of this habit. He had dined even with me; and on the evening of that dinner, as on this Alpine afternoon, I had been at no pains to hold my tongue, absorbed as I inveterately was in a study of the question which always rose before me, to such a height, in his fair, square, strong stature.

This question was all the more tormenting that he never suspected himself (I am sure) of imposing it, any more than he had ever observed that every day of his life every one listened to him at dinner. He used to be called "subjective" in the weekly papers, but in society no distinguished man could have been less so. He never talked about himself; and this was a topic on which, though it would have been tremendously worthy of him, he apparently never even reflected. He had his hours and his habits, his tailor and his hatter, his hygiene and his particular wine, but all these things together never made up an attitude. Yet they constituted the only attitude he ever adopted, and it was easy for him to refer to our being "nicer" abroad than at home. *He* was exempt from variations, and not a shade either less or more nice in one place than in another. He differed from other people, but never from himself (save in the extraordinary sense which I will presently explain), and struck me as having neither moods nor sensibilities nor preferences. He might have been always in the same company, so far as he recognized any influence from age or condition or sex: he addressed himself to women exactly as he addressed himself to men, and gossiped with all men alike, talking no better to clever folk than to dull. I used to feel a despair at his way of liking one subject—so far as I could tell—precisely as much as another: there were some I hated so myself. I never found him anything but loud and cheerful and copious, and I never heard him utter a paradox or express a shade or play with an idea. That fancy about our being "human" was, in his conversation, quite an exceptional flight. His opinions were sound and second-rate, and of his perceptions it was too mystifying to think. I envied him his magnificent health.

Vawdrey had marched, with his even pace and his perfectly good conscience, into the flat country of anecdote, where stories are visible from afar like windmills and signposts; but I observed after a little that Lady Mellifont's attention wandered. I happened to be sitting next to her. I noticed that her eyes rambled a little anxiously over the lower slopes of the mountains. At last, after looking at her watch, she said to me: "Do you know where they went?"

"Do you mean Mrs. Adney and Lord Mellifont?"

"Lord Mellifont and Mrs. Adney." Her ladyship's speech seemed—unconsciously indeed—to correct me, but it didn't occur to me that this was because she was jealous. I imputed to her no such vulgar sentiment: in the first place, because I liked her, and in the second because it would always occur to one quickly that it was right, in any connection, to put Lord Mellifont first. He *was* first—extraordinarily first. I don't say greatest or wisest or most renowned, but essentially at the top of the list and the head of the table. That is a position by itself, and his wife was naturally accustomed to see him in it. My phrase had sounded as if Mrs. Adney had taken him; but it was not possible for him to be taken—he only took. No one, in the nature of things, could know this better than Lady Mellifont. I had originally been rather afraid of her, thinking her, with her stiff silences and the extreme blackness of almost everything that made up her person, somewhat hard, even a little saturnine. Her paleness seemed slightly grey, and her glossy black hair metallic, like the brooches and bands and combs with which it was inveterately adorned. She was in perpetual mourning, and wore numberless ornaments of jet and onyx, a thousand clicking chains and bugles and beads. I had heard Mrs. Adney call her the queen of night, and the term was descriptive if you understood that the night was cloudy. She had a secret, and if you didn't find it out as you knew her better you at least perceived that she was gentle and unaffected and limited, and also rather submissively sad. She was like a woman with a painless malady. I told her that I had merely seen her husband and his companion stroll down the glen together about an hour before, and suggested that Mr. Adney would perhaps know something of their intentions.

Vincent Adney, who, though he was fifty years old, looked like a good little boy on whom it had been impressed that children should not talk before company, acquitted himself with remarkable simplicity and taste of the position of husband of a great exponent of comedy. When all was said about her making it easy for him, one couldn't help admiring the charmed affection with which he took everything for granted. It is difficult for a husband who is not on the stage, or at least in the theatre, to be graceful about a wife who is; but Adney was more than graceful—he was exquisite, he was inspired. He set his beloved to music; and you remember how genuine his music could be—the only English compositions I ever saw a foreigner take an interest in. His wife was in them, somewhere, always; they were like a free, rich translation of the impression she produced. She seemed, as one listened, to pass laughing, with loosened hair, across the scene. He had been only a little fiddler at her theatre, always in his place during the acts; but she had made him something rare and misunderstood. Their superiority had become a kind of partnership, and their happiness was a part of the happiness of their friends. Adney's one discomfort was that he couldn't write a play for his wife, and the only way he meddled with her affairs was by asking impossible people if *they* couldn't.

Lady Mellifont, after looking across at him a moment, remarked to me that she would rather not put any question to him. She added the next minute: "I had rather people shouldn't see I'm nervous."

"*Are* you nervous?"

"I always become so if my husband is away from me for any time."

"Do you imagine something has happened to him?"

"Yes, always. Of course I'm used to it."

"Do you mean his tumbling over precipices—that sort of thing?"

"I don't know exactly what it is: it's the general sense that he'll never come back."

She said so much and kept back so much that the only way to treat the condition she referred to seemed the jocular. "Surely he'll never forsake you!" I laughed.

She looked at the ground a moment. "Oh, at bottom I'm easy."

"Nothing can ever happen to a man so accomplished, so infallible, so armed at all points," I went on, encouragingly.

"Oh, you don't know how he's armed!" she exclaimed, with such an odd quaver that I could account for it only by her being nervous. This idea was confirmed by her moving just afterwards, changing her seat rather pointlessly, not as if to cut our conversation short, but because she was in a fidget. I couldn't know what was the matter with her, but I was presently relieved to see Mrs. Adney come toward us. She had in her hand a big bunch of wild flowers, but she was not closely attended by Lord Mellifont. I quickly saw, however, that she had no disaster to announce; yet as I knew there was a question Lady Mellifont would like to hear answered, but did not wish to ask, I expressed to her immediately the hope that his lordship had not remained in a crevasse.

"Oh, no; he left me but three minutes ago. He has gone into the house." Blanche Adney rested her eyes on mine an instant—a mode of intercourse to which no man, for himself, could ever object. The interest, on this occasion, was quickened by the particular thing the eyes happened to say. What they usually said was only: "Oh, yes, I'm charming, I know, but don't make a fuss about it. I only want a new part—I do, I do!" At present they added, dimly, surreptitiously, and of course sweetly—for that was the way they did everything: "It's all right, but something did happen. Perhaps I'll tell you later." She turned to Lady Mellifont, and the transition to simple gaiety suggested her mastery of her profession. "I've brought him safe. We had a charming walk."

"I'm so very glad," returned Lady Mellifont, with her faint smile; continuing vaguely, as she got up: "He must have gone to dress for dinner. Isn't it rather near?" She moved away, to the hotel, in her leave-taking, simplifying fashion, and the rest of us, at the mention of dinner, looked at each other's watches, as if to shift the responsibility of such grossness. The head-waiter, essentially, like all head-waiters, a man of the world, allowed us hours and places of our own, so that in the evening, apart under the lamp, we formed a compact, an indulged little circle. But it was only the Mellifonts who "dressed" and as to whom it was recognized that they naturally *would* dress: she in exactly the same manner as on any other evening of her ceremonious existence (she was not a woman whose habits could take account of anything so mutable as fitness); and he, on the other hand, with remarkable adjustment and suitability. He was almost as much a man of the world as the head-waiter, and spoke almost as many languages; but he abstained from courting a comparison of dress-coats and white waistcoats, analyzing the occasion in a much finer way—into black velvet and blue velvet and brown velvet, for instance, into delicate harmonies of necktie and subtle informalities of shirt. He had a costume for every function and a moral for every costume; and his functions and costumes and morals were ever a part of the amusement of life—a part at any rate of its beauty and romance—for an immense circle of spectators. For his particular friends indeed these things were more than an amusement; they were a topic, a social support and of course, in addition, a subject of perpetual suspense. If his wife had not been present before dinner they were what the rest of us probably would have been putting our heads together about.

Clare Vawdrey had a fund of anecdote on the whole question: he had known Lord Mellifont almost from the beginning. It was a peculiarity of this nobleman that there could be no conversation about him that didn't instantly take the form of anecdote, and a still further distinction that there could apparently be no anecdote that was not on the whole to his honour. If he had come into a room at any moment, people might have said frankly: "Of course we were telling stories about you!" As consciences go, in London, the general conscience would have been good. Moreover it would have been impossible to imagine his taking such a tribute otherwise than amiably, for he was always as unperturbed as an actor with the right cue. He had never in his life needed the prompter—his very embarrassments had been rehearsed. For myself, when he was talked about I always had an odd impression that we were speaking of the dead—it was with that peculiar accumulation of relish. His reputation was a kind of gilded obelisk, as if he had been buried beneath it; the body of legend and reminiscence of which he was to be the subject had crystallized in advance.

This ambiguity sprang, I suppose, from the fact that the mere sound of his name and air of his person, the general expectation he created, were, somehow, too exalted to be verified. The experience of his urbanity always came later; the prefigurement, the legend paled before the reality. I remember that on the evening I refer to the reality was particularly operative. The handsomest man of his period could never have looked better, and he sat among us like a bland conductor controlling by an harmonious play of arm an orchestra still a little rough. He directed the conversation by gestures as irresistible as they were vague; one felt as if without him it wouldn't have had anything to call a tone. This was essentially what he contributed to any occasion—what he contributed above all to English public life. He pervaded it, he coloured it, he embellished it, and without him it would scarcely have had a vocabulary. Certainly it would not have had a style; for a style was what it had in having Lord Mellifont. He *was* a style. I was freshly struck with it as, in the *salle à manger* of the little Swiss inn, we resigned ourselves to inevitable veal. Confronted with his form (I must parenthesize that it was not confronted much), Clare Vawdrey's talk suggested the reporter contrasted with the bard. It was interesting to watch the shock of characters from which, of an evening, so much would be expected. There was however no concussion—it was all muffled and minimized in Lord Mellifont's tact. It was rudimentary with him to find the solution of such a problem in playing the host, assuming responsibilities which carried with them their sacrifice. He had indeed never been a guest in his life; he was the host, the patron, the moderator at every board. If there was a defect in his manner (and I suggest it under my breath), it was that he had a little more art than any conjunction—even the most complicated—could possibly require. At any rate one made one's reflections in noticing how the accomplished peer handled the situation and how the sturdy man of letters was unconscious that the situation (and least of all he himself as part of it), was handled. Lord Mellifont poured forth treasures of tact, and Clare Vawdrey never dreamed he was doing it.

Vawdrey had no suspicion of any such precaution even when Blanche Adney asked him if he saw yet their third act—an inquiry into which she introduced a subtlety of her own. She had a theory that he was to write her a play and that the heroine, if he would only do his duty, would be the part for which she had immemorially longed. She was forty years old (this could be no secret to those who had admired her from the first), and she could now reach out her hand and touch her uttermost goal. This gave a kind of tragic passion—perfect actress of comedy as she was—to her desire not to miss the great thing. The years had passed, and still she had missed it; none of the things she had done was the thing she had dreamed of, so that at present there was no more time to lose. This was the canker in the rose, the ache beneath the smile. It made her touching—made her sadness even sweeter than her laughter. She had done the old English and the new French, and had charmed her generation; but she was haunted by the vision of a bigger chance, of something truer to the conditions that lay near her. She was tired of Sheridan and she hated Bowdler; she called for a canvas of a finer grain. The worst of it, to my sense, was that she would never extract her modern comedy from the great mature novelist, who was as incapable of producing it as he was of threading a needle. She coddled him, she talked to him, she made love to him, as she frankly proclaimed; but she dwelt in illusions—she would have to live and die with Bowdler.

It is difficult to be cursory over this charming woman, who was beautiful without beauty and complete with a dozen deficiencies. The perspective of the stage made her over, and in society she was like the model off the pedestal. She was the picture walking about, which to the artless social mind was a perpetual surprise—a miracle. People thought she told them the secrets of the pictorial nature, in return for which they gave her relaxation and tea. She told them nothing and she drank the tea; but they had, all the same, the best of the bargain. Vawdrey was really at work on a play; but if he had begun it because he liked her I think he let it drag for the same reason. He secretly felt the atrocious difficulty—knew that from his hand the finished piece would have received no active life. At the same time nothing could be more agreeable than to have such a question open with Blanche Adney, and from time to time he put something very good into the play. If he deceived Mrs. Adney it was only because in her despair she was determined to be deceived. To her question about their third act he replied that, before dinner, he had written a magnificent passage.

"Before dinner?" I said. "Why, *cher maître*, before dinner you were holding us all spellbound on the terrace."

My words were a joke, because I thought his had been; but for the first time that I could remember I perceived a certain confusion in his face. He looked at me hard, throwing back his head quickly, the least bit like a horse who has been pulled up short. "Oh, it was before that," he replied, naturally enough.

"Before that you were playing billiards with *me*," Lord Mellifont intimated.

"Then it must have been yesterday," said Vawdrey.

But he was in a tight place. "You told me this morning you did nothing yesterday," the actress objected.

"I don't think I really know when I do things." Vawdrey looked vaguely, without helping himself, at a dish that was offered him.

"It's enough if *we* know," smiled Lord Mellifont.

"I don't believe you've written a line," said Blanche Adney.

"I think I could repeat you the scene." Vawdrey helped himself to *haricots verts*.

"Oh, do—oh, do!" two or three of us cried.

"After dinner, in the salon; it will be an immense *régal*," Lord Mellifont declared.

"I'm not sure, but I'll try," Vawdrey went on.

"Oh, you lovely man!" exclaimed the actress, who was practising Americanisms, being resigned even to an American comedy.

"But there must be this condition," said Vawdrey: "you must make your husband play."

"Play while you're reading? Never!"

"I've too much vanity," said Adney.

Lord Mellifont distinguished him. "You must give us the overture, before the curtain rises. That's a peculiarly delightful moment."

"I sha'n't read—I shall just speak," said Vawdrey.

"Better still, let me go and get your manuscript," the actress suggested.

Vawdrey replied that the manuscript didn't matter; but an hour later, in the salon, we wished he might have had it. We sat expectant, still under the spell of Adney's violin. His wife, in the foreground, on an ottoman, was all impatience and profile, and Lord Mellifont, in the chair—it was always *the* chair, Lord Mellifont's—made our grateful little group feel like a social science congress or a distribution of prizes. Suddenly, instead of beginning, our tame lion began to roar out of tune—he had clean forgotten every word. He was very sorry, but the lines absolutely wouldn't come to him; he was utterly ashamed, but his memory was a blank. He didn't look in the least ashamed—Vawdrey had never looked ashamed in his life; he was only imperturbably and merrily natural. He protested that he had never expected to make such a fool of himself, but we felt that this wouldn't prevent the incident from taking its place among his jolliest reminiscences. It was only *we* who were humiliated, as if he had played us a premeditated trick. This was an occasion, if ever, for Lord Mellifont's tact, which descended on us all like balm: he told us, in his charming artistic way, his way of bridging over arid intervals (he had a *débit*—there was nothing to approach it in England—like the actors of the Comédie Française), of his own collapse on a momentous occasion, the delivery of an address to a mighty multitude, when, finding he had forgotten his memoranda, he fumbled, on the terrible platform, the cynosure of every eye, fumbled vainly in irreproachable pockets for indispensable notes. But the point of his story was finer than that of Vawdrey's pleasantry; for he sketched with a few light gestures the brilliancy of a performance which had risen superior to embarrassment, had resolved itself, we were left to divine, into an effort recognised at the moment as not absolutely a blot on what the public was so good as to call his reputation.

"Play up—play up!" cried Blanche Adney, tapping her husband and remembering how, on the stage, a *contretemps* is always drowned in music. Adney threw himself upon his fiddle, and I said to Clare Vawdrey that his mistake could easily be corrected by his sending for the manuscript. If he would tell me where it was I would immediately fetch it from his room. To this he replied: "My dear fellow, I'm afraid there *is* no manuscript."

"Then you've not written anything?"

"I'll write it to-morrow."

"Ah, you trifle with us," I said, in much mystification.

Vawdrey hesitated an instant. "If there *is* anything, you'll find it on my table."

At this moment one of the others spoke to him, and Lady Mellifont remarked audibly, as if to correct gently our want of consideration, that Mr. Adney was playing something very beautiful. I had noticed before that she appeared extremely fond of music; she always listened to it in a hushed transport. Vawdrey's attention was drawn away, but it didn't seem to me that the words he had just dropped constituted a definite permission to go to his room. Moreover I wanted to speak to Blanche Adney; I had something to ask her. I had to await my chance, however, as we remained silent awhile for her husband, after which the conversation became general. It was our habit to go to bed early, but there was still a little of the evening left. Before it quite waned I found an opportunity to tell the actress that Vawdrey had given me leave to put my hand on his manuscript. She adjured me, by all I held sacred, to bring it immediately, to give it to her; and her insistence was proof against my suggestion that it would now be too late for him to begin to read: besides which the charm was broken—the others wouldn't care. It was not too late for *her* to begin; therefore I was to possess myself, without more delay, of the precious pages. I told her she should be obeyed in a moment, but I wanted her first to satisfy my just curiosity. What had happened before dinner, while she was on the hills with Lord Mellifont?

"How do you know anything happened?"

"I saw it in your face when you came back."

"And they call me an actress!" cried Mrs. Adney.

"What do they call *me*?" I inquired.

"You're a searcher of hearts—that frivolous thing an observer."

"I wish you'd let an observer write you a play!" I broke out.

"People don't care for what you write: you'd break any run of luck."

"Well, I see plays all round me," I declared; "the air is full of them to-night."

"The air? Thank you for nothing! I only wish my table-drawers were."

"Did he make love to you on the glacier?" I went on.

She stared; then broke into the graduated ecstasy of her laugh. "Lord Mellifont, poor dear? What a funny place! It would indeed be the place for *our* love!"

"Did he fall into a crevasse?" I continued.

Blanche Adney looked at me again as she had done for an instant when she came up, before dinner, with her hands full of flowers. "I don't know into what he fell. I'll tell you to-morrow."

"He did come down, then?"

"Perhaps he went up," she laughed. "It's really strange."

"All the more reason you should tell me to-night."

"I must think it over; I must puzzle it out."

"Oh, if you want conundrums I'll throw in another," I said. "What's the matter with the master?"

"The master of what?"

"Of every form of dissimulation. Vawdrey hasn't written a line."

"Go and get his papers and we'll see."

"I don't like to expose him," I said.

"Why not, if I expose Lord Mellifont?"

"Oh, I'd do anything for that," I conceded. "But why should Vawdrey have made a false statement? It's very curious."

"It's very curious," Blanche Adney repeated, with a musing air and her eyes on Lord Mellifont. Then, rousing herself, she added: "Go and look in his room."

"In Lord Mellifont's?"

She turned to me quickly. "*That* would be a way!"

"A way to what?"

"To find out—to find out!" She spoke gaily and excitedly, but suddenly checked herself. "We're talking nonsense," she said.

"We're mixing things up, but I'm struck with your idea. Get Lady Mellifont to let you."

"Oh, *she* has looked!" Mrs. Adney murmured, with the oddest dramatic expression. Then, after a movement of her beautiful uplifted hand, as if to brush away a fantastic vision, she exclaimed imperiously: "Bring me the scene—bring me the scene!"

"I go for it," I answered; "but don't tell me I can't write a play."

She left me, but my errand was arrested by the approach of a lady who had produced a birthday-book—we had been threatened with it for several evenings—and who did me the honour to solicit my autograph. She had been asking the others, and she couldn't decently leave me out. I could usually remember my name, but it always took me some time to recall my date, and even when I had done so I was never very sure. I hesitated between two days and I remarked to my petitioner that I would sign on both if it would give her any satisfaction. She said that surely I had been born only once; and I replied of course that on the day I made her acquaintance I had been born again. I mention the feeble joke only to show that, with the obligatory inspection of the other autographs, we gave some minutes to this transaction. The lady departed with her book, and then I became aware that the company had dispersed. I was alone in the little salon that had been appropriated to our use. My first impression was one of disappointment: if Vawdrey had gone to bed I didn't wish to disturb him. While I hesitated, however, I recognised that Vawdrey had not gone to bed. A window was open, and the sound of voices outside came in to me: Blanche was on the terrace with her dramatist, and they were talking about the stars. I went to the window for a glimpse—the Alpine night was splendid. My friends had stepped out together; the actress had picked up a cloak; she looked as I had seen her look in the wing of the theatre. They were silent awhile, and I heard the roar of a neighbouring torrent. I turned back into the room, and its quiet lamplight gave me an idea. Our companions had dispersed—it was late for a pastoral country—and we three should have the place to ourselves. Clare Vawdrey had written his scene—it was magnificent; and his reading it to us there, at such an hour, would be an episode intensely memorable. I would bring down his manuscript and meet the two with it as they came in.

I quitted the salon for this purpose; I had been in Vawdrey's room and knew it was on the second floor, the last in a long corridor. A minute later my hand was on the knob of his door, which I naturally pushed open without knocking. It was equally natural that in the absence of its occupant the room should be dark; the more so as, the end of the corridor being at that hour unlighted, the obscurity was not immediately diminished by the opening of the door. I was only aware at first that I had made no mistake and that, the window-curtains not being drawn, I was confronted with a couple of vague star-lighted apertures. Their aid, however, was not sufficient to enable me to find what I had come for, and my hand, in my pocket, was already on the little box of matches that I always carried for cigarettes. Suddenly I withdrew it with a start, uttering an ejaculation, an apology. I had entered the wrong room; a glance prolonged for three seconds showed me a figure seated at a table near one of the windows—a figure I had at first taken for a travelling-rug thrown over a chair. I retreated, with a sense of intrusion; but as I did so I became aware, more rapidly than it takes me to express it, in the first place that this was Vawdrey's room and in the second that, most singularly, Vawdrey himself sat before me. Checking myself on the threshold I had a momentary feeling of bewilderment, but before I knew it I had exclaimed: "Hullo! is that you, Vawdrey?"

He neither turned nor answered me, but my question received an immediate and practical reply in the opening of a door on the other side of the passage. A servant, with a candle, had come out of the opposite room, and in this flitting illumination I definitely recognised the man whom, an instant before, I had to the best of my belief left below in conversation with Mrs. Adney. His back was half turned to me, and he bent over the table in the attitude of writing, but I was conscious that I was in no sort of error about his identity. "I beg your pardon—I thought you were downstairs," I said; and as the personage gave no sign of hearing me I added: "If you're busy I won't disturb you." I backed out, closing the door—I had been in the place, I suppose, less than a minute. I had a sense of mystification, which however deepened infinitely the next instant. I stood there with my hand still on the knob of the door, overtaken by the oddest impression of my life. Vawdrey was at his table, writing, and it was a very natural place for him to be; but why was he writing in the dark and why hadn't he answered me? I waited a few seconds for the sound of some movement, to see if he wouldn't rouse himself from his abstraction—a fit conceivable in a great writer—and call out: "Oh, my dear fellow, is it you?" But I heard only the stillness, I felt only the starlighted dusk of the room, with the unexpected presence it enclosed. I turned away, slowly retracing my steps, and came confusedly downstairs. The lamp was still burning in the salon, but the room was empty. I passed round to the door of the hotel and stepped out. Empty too was the terrace. Blanche Adney and the gentleman with her had apparently come in. I hung about five minutes; then I went to bed.

I slept badly, for I was agitated. On looking back at these queer occurrences (you will see presently that they were queer), I perhaps suppose myself more agitated than I was; for great anomalies are never so great at first as after we have reflected upon them. It takes us some time to exhaust explanations. I was vaguely nervous—I had been sharply startled; but there was nothing I could not clear up by asking Blanche Adney, the first thing in the morning, who had been with her on the terrace. Oddly enough, however, when the morning dawned—it dawned admirably—I felt less desire to satisfy myself on this point than to escape, to brush away the shadow of my stupefaction. I saw the day would be splendid, and the fancy took me to spend it, as I had spent happy days of youth, in a lonely mountain ramble. I dressed early, partook of conventional coffee, put a big roll into one pocket and a small flask into the other, and, with a stout stick in my hand, went forth into the high places. My story is not closely concerned with the charming hours I passed there—hours of the kind that make intense memories. If I roamed away half of them on the shoulders of the hills, I lay on the sloping grass for the other half and, with my cap pulled over my eyes (save a peep for immensities of view), listened, in the bright stillness, to the mountain bee and felt most things sink and dwindle. Clare Vawdrey grew small, Blanche Adney grew dim, Lord Mellifont grew old, and before the day was over I forgot that I had ever been puzzled. When in the late afternoon I made my way down to the inn there was nothing I wanted so much to find out as whether dinner would not soon be ready. To-night I dressed, in a manner, and by the time I was presentable they were all at table.

In their company again my little problem came back to me, so that I was curious to see if Vawdrey wouldn't look at me the least bit queerly. But he didn't look at me at all; which gave me a chance both to be patient and to wonder why I should hesitate to ask him my question across the table. I did hesitate, and with the consciousness of doing so came back a little of the agitation I had left behind me, or below me, during the day. I wasn't ashamed of my scruple, however: it was only a fine discretion. What I vaguely felt was that a public inquiry wouldn't have been fair. Lord Mellifont was there, of course, to mitigate with his perfect manner all consequences; but I think it was present to me that with these particular elements his lordship would not be at home. The moment we got up, therefore, I approached Mrs. Adney, asking her whether, as the evening was lovely, she wouldn't take a turn with me outside.

"You've walked a hundred miles; had you not better be quiet?" she replied.

"I'd walk a hundred miles more to get you to tell me something."

She looked at me an instant, with a little of the queerness that I had sought, but had not found, in Clare Vawdrey's eyes. "Do you mean what became of Lord Mellifont?"

"Of Lord Mellifont?" With my new speculation I had lost that thread.

"Where's your memory, foolish man? We talked of it last evening."

"Ah, yes!" I cried, recalling; "we shall have lots to discuss." I drew her out to the terrace, and before we had gone three steps I said to her: "Who was with you here last night?"

"Last night?" she repeated, as wide of the mark as I had been.

"At ten o'clock—just after our company broke up. You came out here with a gentleman; you talked about the stars."

She stared a moment; then she gave her laugh. "Are you jealous of dear Vawdrey?"

"Then it was he?"

"Certainly it was."

"And how long did he stay?"

"You have it badly. He stayed about a quarter of an hour— perhaps rather more. We walked some distance; he talked about his play. There you have it all; that is the only witchcraft I have used."

"And what did Vawdrey do afterwards?"

"I haven't the least idea. I left him and went to bed."

"At what time did you go to bed?"

"At what time did *you*? I happen to remember that I parted from Mr. Vawdrey at ten twenty-five," said Mrs. Adney. "I came back into the salon to pick up a book, and I noticed the clock."

"In other words you and Vawdrey distinctly lingered here from about five minutes past ten till the hour you mention?"

"I don't know how distinct we were, but we were very jolly. *Où voulez-vous en venir?*" Blanche Adney asked.

"Simply to this, dear lady: that at the time your companion was occupied in the manner you describe, he was also engaged in literary composition in his own room."

She stopped short at this, and her eyes had an expression in the darkness. She wanted to know if I challenged her veracity; and I replied that, on the contrary, I backed it up—it made the case so interesting. She returned that this would only be if she should back up mine; which, however, I had no difficulty in persuading her to do, after I had related to her circumstantially the incident of my quest of the manuscript—the manuscript which, at the time, for a reason I could now understand, appeared to have passed so completely out of her own head.

"His talk made me forget it—I forgot I sent you for it. He made up for his fiasco in the salon: he declaimed me the scene," said my companion. She had dropped on a bench to listen to me and, as we sat there, had briefly cross-examined me. Then she broke out into fresh laughter. "Oh, the eccentricities of genius!"

"They seem greater even than I supposed."

"Oh, the mysteries of greatness!"

"You ought to know all about them, but they take me by surprise."

"Are you absolutely certain it was Mr. Vawdrey?" my companion asked.

"If it wasn't he, who in the world was it? That a strange gentleman, looking exactly like him, should be sitting in his room at that hour of the night and writing at his table *in the dark*," I insisted, "would be practically as wonderful as my own contention."

"Yes, why in the dark?" mused Mrs. Adney.

"Cats can see in the dark," I said.

She smiled at me dimly. "Did it look like a cat?"

"No, dear lady, but I'll tell you what it did look like—it looked like the author of Vawdrey's admirable works. It looked infinitely more like him than our friend does himself," I declared.

"Do you mean it was somebody he gets to do them?"

"Yes, while he dines out and disappoints you."

"Disappoints me?" murmured Mrs. Adney artlessly.

"Disappoints *me*—disappoints every one who looks in him for the genius that created the pages they adore. Where is it in his talk?"

"Ah, last night he was splendid," said the actress.

"He's always splendid, as your morning bath is splendid, or a sirloin of beef, or the railway service to Brighton. But he's never rare."

"I see what you mean."

"That's what makes you such a comfort to talk to. I've often wondered—now I know. There are two of them."

"What a delightful idea!"

"One goes out, the other stays at home. One is the genius, the other's the bourgeois, and it's only the bourgeois whom we personally know. He talks, he circulates, he's awfully popular, he flirts with you—"

"Whereas it's the genius *you* are privileged to see!" Mrs. Adney broke in. "I'm much obliged to you for the distinction."

I laid my hand on her arm. "See him yourself. Try it, test it, go to his room."

"Go to his room? It wouldn't be proper!" she exclaimed, in the tone of her best comedy.

"Anything is proper in such an inquiry. If you see him, it settles it."

"How charming—to settle it!" She thought a moment, then she sprang up. "Do you mean *now*?"

"Whenever you like."

"But suppose I should find the wrong one?" said Blanche Adney, with an exquisite effect.

"The wrong one? Which one do you call the right?"

"The wrong one for a lady to go and see. Suppose I shouldn't find—the genius?"

"Oh, I'll look after the other," I replied. Then, as I had happened to glance about me, I added: "Take care—here comes Lord Mellifont."

"I wish you'd look after *him*," my interlocutress murmured.

"What's the matter with him?"

"That's just what I was going to tell you."

"Tell me now; he's not coming."

Blanche Adney looked a moment. Lord Mellifont, who appeared to have emerged from the hotel to smoke a meditative cigar, had paused, at a distance from us, and stood admiring the wonders of the prospect, discernible even in the dusk. We strolled slowly in another direction, and she presently said: "My idea is almost as droll as yours."

"I don't call mine droll: it's beautiful."

"There's nothing so beautiful as the droll," Mrs. Adney declared.

"You take a professional view. But I'm all ears." My curiosity was indeed alive again.

"Well then, my dear friend, if Clare Vawdrey is double (and I'm bound to say I think that the more of him the better), his lordship there has the opposite complaint: he isn't even whole."

We stopped once more, simultaneously. "I don't understand."

"No more do I. But I have a fancy that if there are two of Mr. Vawdrey, there isn't so much as one, all told, of Lord Mellifont."

I considered a moment, then I laughed out. "I think I see what you mean!"

"That's what makes *you* a comfort. Did you ever see him alone?"

I tried to remember. "Oh, yes; he has been to see me."

"Ah, then he wasn't alone."

"And I've been to see him, in his study."

"Did he know you were there?"

"Naturally—I was announced."

Blanche Adney glanced at me like a lovely conspirator. "You mustn't be announced!" With this she walked on.

I rejoined her, breathless. "Do you mean one must come upon him when he doesn't know it?"

"You must take him unawares. You must go to his room— that's what you must do."

If I was elated by the way our mystery opened out, I was

also, pardonably, a little confused. "When I know he's not there?"

"When you know he *is*."

"And what shall I see?"

"You won't see anything!" Mrs. Adney cried as we turned round.

We had reached the end of the terrace, and our movement brought us face to face with Lord Mellifont, who, resuming his walk, had now, without indiscretion, overtaken us. The sight of him at that moment was illuminating, and it kindled a great backward train, connecting itself with one's general impression of the personage. As he stood there smiling at us and waving a practised hand into the transparent night (he introduced the view as if it had been a candidate and "supported" the very Alps), as he rose before us in the delicate fragrance of his cigar and all his other delicacies and fragrances, with more perfections, somehow, heaped upon his handsome head than one had ever seen accumulated before, he struck me as so essentially, so conspicuously and uniformly the public character that I read in a flash the answer to Blanche Adney's riddle. He was all public and had no corresponding private life, just as Clare Vawdrey was all private and had no corresponding public one. I had heard only half my companion's story, yet as we joined Lord Mellifont (he had followed us—he liked Mrs. Adney; but it was always to be conceived of him that he accepted society rather than sought it), as we participated for half an hour in the distributed wealth of his conversation, I felt with unabashed duplicity that we had, as it were, found him out. I was even more deeply diverted by that whisk of the curtain to which the actress had just treated me than I had been by my own discovery; and if I was not ashamed of my share of her secret any more than of having divided my own with her (though my own was, of the two mysteries, the more glorious for the personage involved), this was because there was no cruelty in my advantage, but on the contrary an extreme tenderness and a positive compassion. Oh, he was safe with me, and I felt moreover rich and enlightened, as if I had suddenly put the universe into my pocket. I had learned what an affair of the spot and the moment a great appearance may be. It would doubtless be too much to say that I had always suspected the possibility, in the background of his lordship's being, of some such beautiful instance; but it is at least a fact that, patronising as it sounds, I had been conscious of a certain reserve of indulgence for him. I had secretly pitied him for the perfection of his performance, had wondered what blank face such a mask had to cover, what was left to him for the immitigable hours in which a man sits down with himself, or, more serious still, with that intenser self, his lawful wife. How was he at home and what did he do when he was alone? There was something in Lady Mellifont that gave a point to these researches—something that suggested that even to her he was still the public character and that she was haunted by similar questionings. She had never cleared them up: that was her eternal trouble. We therefore knew more than she did, Blanche Adney and I; but we wouldn't tell her for the world, nor would she probably thank us for doing so. She preferred the relative grandeur of uncertainty. She was not at home with him, so she couldn't say; and with her he was not alone, so he couldn't show her. He represented to his wife and he was a hero to his servants, and what one wanted to arrive at was what really became of him when no eye could see. He rested, presumably; but what form of rest could repair such a plenitude of presence? Lady Mellifont was too proud to pry, and as she had never looked through a keyhole she remained dignified and unassuaged.

It may have been a fancy of mine that Blanche Adney drew out our companion, or it may be that the practical irony of our relation to him at such a moment made me see him more vividly: at any rate he never had struck me as so dissimilar from what he would have been if we had not offered him a reflection of his image. We were only a concourse of two, but he had never been more public. His perfect manner had never been more perfect, his remarkable tact had never been more remarkable. I had a tacit sense that it would all be in the morning papers, with a leader, and also a secretly exhilarating one that I knew something that wouldn't be, that never could be, though any enterprising journal would give one a fortune for it. I must add, however, that in spite of my enjoyment— it was almost sensual, like that of a consummate dish—I was eager to be alone again with Mrs. Adney, who owed me an anecdote. It proved impossible, that evening, for some of the others came out to see what we found so absorbing; and then Lord Mellifont bespoke a little music from the fiddler, who produced his violin and played to us divinely, on our platform of echoes, face to face with the ghosts of the mountains. Before the concert was over I missed our actress and, glancing into the window of the salon, saw that she was established with Vawdrey, who was reading to her from a manuscript. The great scene had apparently been achieved and was doubtless the more interesting to Blanche from the new lights she had gathered about its author. I judged it discreet not to disturb them, and I went to bed without seeing her again. I looked out for her betimes the next morning and, as the promise of the day was fair, proposed to her that we should take to the hills, reminding her of the high obligation she had incurred. She recognised the obligation and gratified me with her company; but before we had strolled ten yards up the pass she broke out with intensity: "My dear friend, you've no idea how it works in me! I can think of nothing else."

"Than your theory about Lord Mellifont?"

"Oh, bother Lord Mellifont! I allude to yours about Mr. Vawdrey, who is much the more interesting person of the two. I'm fascinated by that vision of his—what-do-you-call-it?"

"His alternative identity?"

"His other self: that's easier to say."

"You accept it, then, you adopt it?"

"Adopt it? I rejoice in it! It became tremendously vivid to me last evening."

"While he read to you there?"

"Yes, as I listened to him, watched him. It simplified everything, explained everything."

"That's indeed the blessing of it. Is the scene very fine?"

"Magnificent, and he reads beautifully."

"Almost as well as the other one writes!" I laughed.

This made my companion stop a moment, laying her hand on my arm. "You utter my very impression. I felt that he was reading me the work of another man."

"What a service to the other man!"

"Such a totally different person," said Mrs. Adney. We

talked of this difference as we went on, and of what a wealth it constituted, what a resource for life, such a duplication of character.

"It ought to make him live twice as long as other people," I observed.

"Ought to make which of them?"

"Well, both; for after all they're members of a firm, and one of them couldn't carry on the business without the other. Moreover mere survival would be dreadful for either."

Blanche Adney was silent a little; then she exclaimed: "I don't know—I wish he *would* survive!"

"May I, on my side, inquire which?"

"If you can't guess I won't tell you."

"I know the heart of woman. You always prefer the other."

She halted again, looking round her. "Off here, away from my husband, I *can* tell you. I'm in love with him!"

"Unhappy woman, he has no passions," I answered.

"That's exactly why I adore him. Doesn't a woman with my history know that the passions of others are insupportable? An actress, poor thing, can't care for any love that's not all on *her* side; she can't afford to be repaid. My marriage proves that: marriage is ruinous. Do you know what was in my mind last night, all the while Mr. Vawdrey was reading me those beautiful speeches? An insane desire to see the author." And dramatically, as if to hide her shame, Blanche Adney passed on.

"We'll manage that," I returned. "I want another glimpse of him myself. But meanwhile please remember that I've been waiting more than forty-eight hours for the evidence that supports your sketch, intensely suggestive and plausible, of Lord Mellifont's private life."

"Oh, Lord Mellifont doesn't interest me."

"He did yesterday," I said.

"Yes, but that was before I fell in love. You blotted him out with your story."

"You'll make me sorry I told it. Come," I pleaded, "if you don't let me know how your idea came into your head I shall imagine you simply made it up."

"Let me recollect then, while we wander in this grassy valley."

We stood at the entrance of a charming crooked gorge, a portion of whose level floor formed the bed of a stream that was smooth with swiftness. We turned into it, and the soft walk beside the clear torrent drew us on and on; till suddenly, as we continued and I waited for my companion to remember, a bend of the valley showed us Lady Mellifont coming toward us. She was alone, under the canopy of her parasol, drawing her sable train over the turf; and in this form, on the devious ways, she was a sufficiently rare apparition. She usually took a footman, who marched behind her on the highroads and whose livery was strange to the mountaineers. She blushed on seeing us, as if she ought somehow to justify herself; she laughed vaguely and said she had come out for a little early stroll. We stood together a moment, exchanging platitudes, and then she remarked that she had thought she might find her husband.

"Is he in this quarter?" I inquired.

"I supposed he would be. He came out an hour ago to sketch."

"Have you been looking for him?" Mrs. Adney asked.

"A little; not very much," said Lady Mellifont.

Each of the women rested her eyes with some intensity, as it seemed to me, on the eyes of the other.

"We'll look for him *for* you, if you like," said Mrs. Adney.

"Oh, it doesn't matter. I thought I'd join him."

"He won't make his sketch if you don't," my companion hinted.

"Perhaps he will if *you* do," said Lady Mellifont.

"Oh, I dare say he'll turn up," I interposed.

"He certainly will if he knows we're here!" Blanche Adney retorted.

"Will you wait while we search?" I asked of Lady Mellifont.

She repeated that it was of no consequence; upon which Mrs. Adney went on: "We'll go into the matter for our own pleasure."

"I wish you a pleasant expedition," said her ladyship, and was turning away when I sought to know if we should inform her husband that she had followed him. She hesitated a moment; then she jerked out oddly: "I think you had better not." With this she took leave of us, floating a little stiffly down the gorge.

My companion and I watched her retreat, then we exchanged a stare, while a little ghost of a laugh rippled from the actress's lips. "She might be walking in the shrubberies at Mellifont!"

"She suspects it, you know," I replied.

"And she doesn't want him to know it. There won't be any sketch."

"Unless we overtake him," I subjoined. "In that case we shall find him producing one, in the most graceful attitude, and the queer thing is that it will be brilliant."

"Let us leave him alone—he'll have to come home without it."

"He'd rather never come home. Oh, he'll find a public!"

"Perhaps he'll do it for the cows," Blanche Adney suggested; and as I was on the point of rebuking her profanity she went on: "That's simply what I happened to discover."

"What are you speaking of?"

"The incident of day before yesterday."

"Ah, let's have it at last!"

"That's all it was—that I was like Lady Mellifont: I couldn't find him."

"Did you lose him?"

"He lost *me*—that appears to be the way of it. He thought I was gone."

"But you did find him, since you came home with him."

"It was he who found *me*. That again is what must happen. He's there from the moment he knows somebody else is."

"I understand his intermissions," I said after a short reflection, "but I don't quite seize the law that governs them."

"Oh, it's a fine shade, but I caught it at that moment. I had started to come home. I was tired, and I had insisted on his not coming back with me. We had found some rare flowers—those I brought home—and it was he who had discovered almost all of them. It amused him very much, and I knew he wanted to get more; but I was weary and I quitted him. He let me go—where else would have been his tact?—and I was too stupid then to have guessed that from the moment I was not there no flower would be gathered. I started homeward, but at the end of three minutes I found I had brought away his penknife—he had lent it to me to trim a branch—and I knew he would need it. I turned back a few steps, to call him, but before I spoke I looked about for him. You can't understand what happened then without having the place before you."

"You must take me there," I said.

"We may see the wonder here. The place was simply one that offered no chance for concealment—a great gradual hillside, without obstructions or trees. There were some rocks below me, behind which I myself had disappeared, but from which on coming back I immediately emerged again."

"Then he must have seen you."

"He was too utterly gone, for some reason best known to himself. It was probably some moment of fatigue—he's getting on, you know, so that, with the sense of returning solitude, the reaction had been proportionately great, the extinction proportionately complete. At any rate the stage was as bare as your hand."

"Could he have been somewhere else?"

"He couldn't have been, in the time, anywhere but where I had left him. Yet the place was utterly empty—as empty as this stretch of valley before us. He had vanished—he had ceased to be. But as soon as my voice rang out (I uttered his name), he rose before me like the rising sun."

"And where did the sun rise?"

"Just where it ought to—just where he would have been and where I should have seen him had he been like other people."

I had listened with the deepest interest, but it was my duty to think of objections. "How long a time elapsed between the moment you perceived his absence and the moment you called?"

"Oh, only an instant. I don't pretend it was long."

"Long enough for you to be sure?" I said.

"Sure he wasn't there?"

"Yes, and that you were not mistaken, not the victim of some hocus-pocus of your eyesight."

"I may have been mistaken, but I don't believe it. At any rate, that's just why I want you to look in his room."

I thought a moment. "How *can* I, when even his wife doesn't dare to?"

"She *wants* to; propose it to her. It wouldn't take much to make her. She does suspect."

I thought another moment. "Did he seem to know?"

"That I had missed him? So it struck me, but he thought he had been quick enough."

"Did you speak of his disappearance?"

"Heaven forbid! It seemed to me too strange."

"Quite right. And how did he look?"

Trying to think it out again and reconstitute her miracle, Blanche Adney gazed abstractedly up the valley. Suddenly she exclaimed: "Just as he looks now!" and I saw Lord Mellifont stand before us with his sketch-block. I perceived, as we met him, that he looked neither suspicious nor blank: he looked simply, as he did always, everywhere, the principal feature of the scene. Naturally he had no sketch to show us, but nothing could better have rounded off our actual conception of him than the way he fell into position as we approached. He had been selecting his point of view; he took possession of it with a flourish of the pencil. He leaned against a rock; his beautiful little box of water colours reposed on a natural table beside him, a ledge of the bank which showed how inveterately nature ministered to his convenience. He painted while he talked and he talked while he painted; and if the painting was as miscellaneous as the talk, the talk would equally have graced an album. We waited while the exhibition went on, and it seemed indeed as if the conscious profiles of the peaks were interested in his success. They grew as black as silhouettes in paper, sharp against a livid sky from which, however, there would be nothing to fear till Lord Mellifont's sketch should be finished. Blanche Adney communed with me dumbly, and I could read the language of her eyes: "Oh, if *we* could only do it as well as that! He fills the stage in a way that beats us." We could no more have left him than we could have quitted the theatre till the play was over; but in due time we turned round with him and strolled back to the inn, before the door of which his lordship, glancing again at his picture, tore the fresh leaf from the block and presented it with a few happy words to Mrs. Adney. Then he went into the house; and a moment later, looking up from where we stood, we saw him, above, at the window of his sitting-room (he had the best apartments), watching the signs of the weather.

"He'll have to rest after this," Blanche said, dropping her eyes on her water-colour.

"Indeed he will!" I raised mine to the window: Lord Mellifont had vanished. "He's already reabsorbed."

"Reabsorbed?" I could see the actress was now thinking of something else.

"Into the immensity of things. He has lapsed again; there's an *entr'acte*."

"It ought to be long." Mrs. Adney looked up and down the terrace, and at that moment the head-waiter appeared in the doorway. Suddenly she turned to this functionary with the question: "Have you seen Mr. Vawdrey lately?"

The man immediately approached. "He left the house five minutes ago—for a walk, I think. He went down the pass; he had a book."

I was watching the ominous clouds. "He had better have had an umbrella."

The waiter smiled. "I recommended him to take one."

"Thank you," said Mrs. Adney; and the Oberkellner withdrew. Then she went on, abruptly: "Will you do me a favour?"

"Yes, if you'll do *me* one. Let me see if your picture is signed."

She glanced at the sketch before giving it to me. "For a wonder it isn't."

"It ought to be, for full value. May I keep it awhile?"

"Yes, if you'll do what I ask. Take an umbrella and go after Mr. Vawdrey."

"To bring him to Mrs. Adney?"

"To keep him out—as long as you can."

"I'll keep him as long as the rain holds off."

"Oh, never mind the rain!" my companion exclaimed.

"Would you have us drenched?"

"Without remorse." Then with a strange light in her eyes she added: "I'm going to try."

"To try?"

"To see the real one. Oh, if I can get at him!" she broke out with passion.

"Try, try!" I replied. "I'll keep our friend all day."

"If I can get at the one who does it"—and she paused, with shining eyes—"if I can have it out with him I shall get my part!"

"I'll keep Vawdrey for ever!" I called after her as she passed quickly into the house.

Her audacity was communicative, and I stood there in a glow of excitement. I looked at Lord Mellifont's water-colour and I looked at the gathering storm; I turned my eyes again to his lordship's windows and then I bent them on my watch. Vawdrey had so little the start of me that I should have time to overtake him—time even if I should take five minutes to go up to Lord Mellifont's sitting-room (where we had all been hospitably received), and say to him, as a messenger, that Mrs. Adney begged he would bestow upon his sketch the high consecration of his signature. As I again considered this work of art I perceived there was something it certainly did lack: what else then but so noble an autograph? It was my duty to supply the deficiency without delay, and in accordance with this conviction I instantly reentered the hotel. I went up to Lord Mellifont's apartments; I reached the door of his salon. Here, however, I was met by a difficulty of which my extravagance had not taken account. If I were to knock I should spoil everything; yet was I prepared to dispense with this ceremony? I asked myself the question, and it embarrassed me; I turned my little picture round and round, but it didn't give me the answer I wanted. I wanted it to say: "Open the door gently, gently, without a sound, yet very quickly: then you will see what you will see." I had gone so far as to lay my hand upon the knob when I became aware (having my wits so about me), that exactly in the manner I was thinking of—gently, gently, without a sound another door had moved, on the opposite side of the hall. At the same instant I found myself smiling rather constrainedly upon Lady Mellifont, who, on seeing me, had checked herself on the threshold of her room. For a moment, as she stood there, we exchanged two or three ideas that were the more singular for being unspoken. We had caught each other hovering, and we understood each other; but as I stepped over to her (so that we were separated from the sitting-room by the width of the hall), her lips formed the almost soundless entreaty: "Don't!" I could see in her conscious eyes everything that the word expressed—the confession of her own curiosity and the dread of the consequences of mine. *"Don't!"* she repeated, as I stood before her. From the moment my experiment could strike her as an act of violence I was ready to renounce it; yet I thought I detected in her frightened face a still deeper betrayal—a possibility of disappointment if I should give way. It was as if she had said: "I'll let you do it if you'll take the responsibility. Yes, with some one else I'd surprise him. But it would never do for him to think it was I."

"We soon found Lord Mellifont," I observed, in allusion to our encounter with her an hour before, "and he was so good as to give this lovely sketch to Mrs. Adney, who has asked me to come up and beg him to put in the omitted signature."

Lady Mellifont took the drawing from me, and I could guess the struggle that went on in her while she looked at it. She was silent for some time; then I felt that all her delicacies and dignities, all her old timidities and pieties were fighting against her opportunity. She turned away from me and, with the drawing, went back to her room. She was absent for a couple of minutes, and when she reappeared I could see that she had vanquished her temptation; that even, with a kind of resurgent horror, she had shrunk from it. She had deposited the sketch in the room. "If you will kindly leave the picture with me, I will see that Mrs. Adney's request is attended to," she said, with great courtesy and sweetness, but in a manner that put an end to our colloquy.

I assented, with a somewhat artificial enthusiasm perhaps, and then, to ease off our separation, remarked that we were going to have a change of weather.

"In that case we shall go—we shall go immediately," said Lady Mellifont. I was amused at the eagerness with which she made this declaration: it appeared to represent a coveted flight into safety, an escape with her threatened secret. I was the more surprised therefore when, as I was turning away, she put out her hand to take mine. She had the pretext of bidding me farewell, but as I shook hands with her on this supposition I felt that what the movement really conveyed was: "I thank you for the help you would have given me, but it's better as it is. If I should know, who would help me then?" As I went to my room to get my umbrella I said to myself: "She's sure, but she won't put it to the proof."

A quarter of an hour later I had overtaken Clare Vawdrey in the pass, and shortly after this we found ourselves looking for refuge. The storm had not only completely gathered, but it had broken at the last with extraordinary rapidity. We scrambled up a hillside to an empty cabin, a rough structure that was hardly more than a shed for the protection of cattle. It was a tolerable shelter however, and it had fissures through which we could watch the splendid spectacle of the tempest. This entertainment lasted an hour—an hour that has remained with me as full of odd disparities. While the lightning played with the thunder and the rain gushed in on our umbrellas, I said to myself that Clare Vawdrey was disappointing. I don't know exactly what I should have predicated of a great author exposed to the fury of the elements, I can't say what particular Manfred attitude I should have expected my companion to assume, but it seemed to me somehow that I shouldn't have looked to him to regale me in such a situation with stories (which I had already heard), about the celebrated Lady Ringrose. Her ladyship formed the subject of Vawdrey's conversation during this prodigious scene, though before it was quite over he had launched out on Mr. Chafer, the scarcely less notorious reviewer. It broke my heart to hear a man like Vawdrey talk of reviewers. The lightning projected a hard clearness upon the truth, familiar to me for years, to which the last day or two had added transcendent support—the irritating certitude that for personal relations this admirable genius thought his second-best good enough. It *was*, no doubt, as society was made, but there was a contempt in the distinction which could not fail to be galling to an admirer. The world was vulgar and stupid, and the real man would have been a fool to come out for it when he could gossip and dine by deputy. None the less my heart sank as I felt my companion practice this economy. I don't know exactly what I wanted; I suppose I wanted him to make an exception for *me*. I almost believed he would, if he had known how I worshipped his talent. But I had never been able to translate this to him, and his application of his principle was relentless. At any rate I was more than ever sure that at such an hour his chair at home was not empty: *there* was the Manfred attitude, *there* were the responsive flashes. I could only envy Mrs. Adney her presumable enjoyment of them.

The weather drew off at last, and the rain abated sufficiently to allow us to emerge from our asylum and make our way back to the inn, where we found on our arrival that our prolonged absence had produced some agitation. It was judged apparently that the fury of the elements might have placed us in a predicament. Several of our friends were at the door, and they seemed a little disconcerted when it was perceived that we were only drenched. Clare Vawdrey, for some reason, was wetter than I, and he took his course to his room. Blanche Adney was among the persons collected to look out for us, but as Vawdrey came toward her she shrank from him, without a greeting; with a movement that I observed as almost one of estrangement she turned her back on him and went quickly into the salon. Wet as I was I went in after her; on which she immediately flung round and faced me. The first thing I saw was that she had never been so beautiful. There was a light of inspiration in her face, and she broke out to me in the quickest whisper, which was at the same time the loudest cry, I have ever heard: "I've got my *part*!"

"You went to his room—I was right?"

"Right?" Blanche Adney repeated. "Ah, my dear fellow!" she murmured.

"He was there—you saw him?"

"He saw me. It was the hour of my life!"

"It must have been the hour of his, if you were half as lovely as you are at this moment."

"He's splendid," she pursued, as if she didn't hear me. "He *is* the one who does it!" I listened, immensely impressed, and she added: "We understood each other."

"By flashes of lightning?"

"Oh, I didn't see the lightning then!"

"How long were you there?" I asked with admiration.

"Long enough to tell him I adore him."

"Ah, that's what I've never been able to tell him!" I exclaimed ruefully.

"I shall have my part—I shall have my part!" she continued, with triumphant indifference; and she flung round the room with the joy of a girl, only checking herself to say: "Go and change your clothes."

"You shall have Lord Mellifont's signature," I said.

"Oh, bother Lord Mellifont's signature! He's far nicer than Mr. Vawdrey," she went on irrelevantly.

"Lord Mellifont?" I pretended to inquire.

"Confound Lord Mellifont!" And Blanche Adney, in her elation, brushed by me, whisking again through the open door. Just outside of it she came upon her husband; whereupon, with a charming cry of "We're talking of you, my love!" she threw herself upon him and kissed him.

I went to my room and changed my clothes, but I remained there till the evening. The violence of the storm had passed over us, but the rain had settled down to a drizzle. On descending to dinner I found that the change in the weather had already broken up our party. The Mellifonts had departed in a carriage and four, they had been followed by others, and several vehicles had been bespoken for the morning. Blanche Adney's was one of them, and on the pretext that she had preparations to make she quitted us directly after dinner. Clare Vawdrey asked me what was the matter with her—she suddenly appeared to dislike him. I forget what answer I gave, but I did my best to comfort him by driving away with him the next day. Mrs. Adney had vanished when we came down; but they made up their quarrel in London, for he finished his play, which she produced. I must add that she is still, nevertheless, in want of the great part. I have a beautiful one in my head, but she doesn't come to see me to stir me up about it. Lady Mellifont always drops me a kind word when we meet, but that doesn't console me.

Lord Beaupré

SOME reference had been made to Northerley, which was within an easy drive, and Firminger described how he had dined there the night before and had found a lot of people. Mrs. Ashbury, one of the two visitors, inquired who these people might be, and he mentioned half-a-dozen names, among which was that of young Raddle, which had been a good deal on people's lips, and even in the newspapers, on the occasion, still recent, of his stepping into the fortune, exceptionally vast even as the product of a patent-glue, left him by a father whose ugly name on all the vacant spaces of the world had exasperated generations of men.

"Oh, is he there?" asked Mrs. Ashbury, in a tone which might have been taken as a vocal rendering of the act of pricking up one's ears. She didn't hand on the information to her daughter, who was talking—if a beauty of so few phrases could have been said to talk—with Mary Gosselin, but in the course of a few moments she put down her teacup with a failure of suavity and, getting up, gave the girl a poke with her parasol. "Come, Maud, we must be stirring."

"You pay us a very short visit," said Mrs. Gosselin, intensely demure over the fine web of her knitting. Mrs. Ashbury looked hard for an instant into her bland eyes, then she gave poor Maud another poke. She alluded to a reason and expressed regrets; but she got her daughter into motion, and Guy Firminger passed through the garden with the two ladies to put them into their carriage. Mrs. Ashbury protested particularly against any further escort. While he was absent the other parent and child, sitting together on their pretty lawn in the yellow light of the August afternoon, talked of the frightful way Maud Ashbury had "gone off," and of something else as to which there was more to say when their third visitor came back.

"Don't think me grossly inquisitive if I ask you where they told the coachman to drive," said Mary Gosselin as the young man dropped, near her, into a low wicker chair, stretching his long legs as if he had been one of the family.

Firminger stared. "Upon my word I didn't particularly notice, but I think the old lady said 'Home'."

"There, mamma dear!" the girl exclaimed triumphantly.

But Mrs. Gosselin only knitted on, persisting in profundity. She replied that "Home" was a feint, that Mrs. Ashbury would already have given another order, and that it was her wish to hurry off to Northerley that had made her keep them from going with her to the carriage, in which they would have seen her take a suspected direction. Mary explained to Guy Firminger that her mother had perceived poor Mrs. Ashbury to be frantic to reach the house at which she had heard that Mr. Raddle was staying. The young man stared again and wanted to know what she desired to do with Mr. Raddle. Mary replied that her mother would tell him what Mrs. Ashbury desired to do with poor Maud.

"What all Christian mothers desire," said Mrs. Gosselin. "Only she doesn't know how."

"To marry the dear child to Mr. Raddle," Mary added, smiling.

Firminger's vagueness expanded with the subject. "Do you mean you want to marry *your* dear child to that little cad?" he asked of the elder lady.

"I speak of the general duty—not of the particular case," said Mrs. Gosselin.

"Mamma *does* know how," Mary went on.

"Then why ain't you married?"

"Because we're not acting, like the Ashburys, with injudicious precipitation. Is that correct?" the girl demanded, laughing, of her mother.

"Laugh at me, my dear, as much as you like—it's very lucky you've got me," Mrs. Gosselin declared.

"She means I can't manage for myself," said Mary to the visitor.

"What nonsense you talk!" Mrs. Gosselin murmured, counting stitches.

"I can't, mamma, I can't; I admit it," Mary continued.

"But injudicious precipitation and—what's the other thing?—creeping prudence, seem to come out in very much the same place," the young man objected.

"Do you mean since I too wither on the tree?"

"It only comes back to saying how hard it is nowadays to marry one's daughters," said the lucid Mrs. Gosselin, saving Firminger, however, the trouble of an ingenious answer. "I don't contend that, at the best, it's easy."

But Guy Firminger would not have struck you as capable of much conversational effort as he lounged there in the summer softness, with ironic familiarities, like one of the old friends who rarely deviate into sincerity. He was a robust but loose-limbed young man, with a well-shaped head and a face smooth, fair and kind. He was in knickerbockers, and his clothes, which had seen service, were composed of articles that didn't match. His laced boots were dusty—he had evidently walked a certain distance; an indication confirmed by the lingering, sociable way in which, in his basket-seat, he tilted himself towards Mary Gosselin. It pointed to a pleasant reason for a long walk. This young lady, of five-and-twenty, had black hair and blue eyes; a combination often associated with the effect of beauty. The beauty in this case, however, was dim and latent, not vulgarly obvious; and if her height and slenderness gave that impression of length of line which, as we know, is the fashion, Mary Gosselin had on the other hand too much expression to be generally admired. Every one thought her intellectual; a few of the most simple-minded even thought her plain. What Guy Firminger thought— or rather what he took for granted, for he was not built up on depths of reflection—will probably appear from this narrative.

"Yes indeed; things have come to a pass that's awful for *us*," the girl announced.

"For *us*, you mean," said Firminger. "We're hunted like the ostrich; we're trapped and stalked and run to earth. We go in fear—I assure you we do."

"Are *you* hunted, Guy?" Mrs. Gosselin asked with an inflection of her own.

"Yes, Mrs. Gosselin, even *moi qui vous parle*, the ordinary male of commerce, inconceivable as it may appear. I know something about it."

"And of whom do you go in fear?" Mary Gosselin took up an uncut book and a paper-knife which she had laid down on the advent of the other visitors.

"My dear child, of Diana and her nymphs, of the spinster at large. She's always out with her rifle. And it isn't only that; you know there's always a second gun, a walking arsenal, at her heels. I forget, for the moment, who Diana's mother was, and the genealogy of the nymphs; but not only do the old ladies know the younger ones are out, they distinctly go *with* them."

"Who was Diana's mother, my dear?" Mrs. Gosselin inquired of her daughter.

"She was a beautiful old lady with pink ribbons in her cap and a genius for knitting," the girl replied, cutting her book.

"Oh, I'm not speaking of you two dears; you're not like anyone else; you're an immense comfort," said Guy Firminger. "But they've reduced it to a science, and I assure you that if one were any one in particular, if one were not protected by one's obscurity, one's life would be a burden. Upon my honour one wouldn't escape. I've seen it, I've watched them. Look at poor Beaupré—look at little Raddle over there. I object to him, but I bleed for him."

"Lord Beaupré won't marry again," said Mrs. Gosselin with an air of conviction.

"So much the worse for him!"

"Come—that's a concession to our charms!" Mary laughed.

But the ruthless young man explained away his concession. "I mean that to be married's the only protection—or else to be engaged."

"To be permanently engaged,—wouldn't that do?" Mary Gosselin asked.

"Beautifully—I would try it if I were a *parti*."

"And how's the little boy?" Mrs. Gosselin presently inquired.

"What little boy?"

"Your little cousin—Lord Beaupré's child: isn't it a boy?"

"Oh, poor little beggar, he isn't up to much. He was awfully cut up by scarlet fever."

"You're not the rose indeed, but you're tolerably near it," the elder lady presently continued.

"What do you call near it? Not even in the same garden—not in any garden at all, alas!"

"There are three lives—but after all!"

"Dear lady, don't be homicidal!"

"What do you call the 'rose'?" Mary asked of her mother.

"The title," said Mrs. Gosselin, promptly but softly.

Something in her tone made Firminger laugh aloud. "You don't mention the property."

"Oh, I mean the whole thing."

"Is the property very large?" said Mary Gosselin.

"Fifty thousand a year," her mother responded; at which the young man laughed out again.

"Take care, mamma, or we shall be thought to be out with our guns!" the girl interposed; a recommendation that drew from Guy Firminger the just remark that there would be time enough for this when his prospects should be worth speaking of. He leaned over to pick up his hat and stick, as if it were his time to go, but he didn't go for another quarter of an hour, and during these minutes his prospects received some frank consideration. He was Lord Beaupré's first cousin, and the three intervening lives were his lordship's own, that of his little sickly son, and that of his uncle the Major, who was also Guy's uncle and with whom the young man was at present staying. It was from homely Trist, the Major's house, that he had walked over to Mrs. Gosselin's. Frank Firminger, who had married in youth a woman with something of her own and eventually left the army, had nothing but girls, but he was only of middle age and might possibly still have a son. At any rate his life was a very good one. Beaupré might marry again, and, marry or not, he was barely thirty-three and might live to a great age. The child moreover, poor little devil, would doubtless, with the growing consciousness of an incentive (there was none like feeling you were in people's way), develop a capacity for duration; so that altogether Guy professed himself, with the best will in the world, unable to take a rosy view of the disappearance of obstacles. He treated the subject with a jocularity that, in view of the remoteness of his chance, was not wholly tasteless, and the discussion, between old friends and in the light of this extravagance, was less crude than perhaps it sounds. The young man quite declined to see any latent brilliancy in his future. They had all been lashing him up, his poor dear mother, his uncle Frank, and Beaupré as well, to make that future political; but even if he should get in (he was nursing—oh, so languidly!—a possible opening), it would only be into the shallow edge of the stream. He would stand there like a tall idiot with the water up to his ankles. He didn't know how to swim—in that element; he didn't know how to do anything.

"I think you're very perverse, my dear," said Mrs. Gosselin. "I'm sure you have great dispositions."

"For what—except for sitting here and talking with you and Mary? I revel in this sort of thing, but I scarcely like anything else."

"You'd do very well if you weren't so lazy," Mary said. "I believe you're the very laziest person in the world."

"So do I—the very laziest in the world," the young man contentedly replied. "But how can I regret it, when it keeps me so quiet, when (I might even say) it makes me so amiable?"

"You'll have, one of these days, to get over your quietness, and perhaps even a little over your amiability," Mrs. Gosselin sagaciously stated.

"I devoutly hope not."

"You'll have to perform the duties of your position."

"Do you mean keep my stump of a broom in order and my crossing irreproachable?"

"You may say what you like; you will be a *parti*," Mrs. Gosselin continued.

"Well, then, if the worst comes to the worst I shall do what I said just now: I shall get some good plausible girl to see me through."

"The proper way to 'get' her will be to marry her. After you're married you won't be a *parti*."

"Dear mamma, he'll think you're already levelling your rifle!" Mary Gosselin laughingly wailed.

Guy Firminger looked at her a moment. "I say, Mary, wouldn't *you* do?"

"For the good plausible girl? Should I be plausible enough?"

"Surely—what could be more natural? Everything would seem to contribute to the suitability of our alliance. I should be known to have known you for years—from childhood's sunny hour; I should be known to have bullied you, and even to have been bullied *by* you, in the period of pinafores. My relations from a tender age with your brother, which led to our schoolroom romps in holidays and to the happy footing on which your mother has always been so good as to receive me here, would add to all the presumptions of intimacy. People would accept such a conclusion as inevitable."

"Among all your reasons you don't mention the young lady's attractions," said Mary Gosselin.

Firminger stared a moment, his clear eye lighted by his happy thought. "I don't mention the young man's. They would be so obvious, on one side and the other, as to be taken for granted."

"And is it your idea that one should pretend to be engaged to you all one's life?"

"Oh no, simply till I should have had time to look round. I'm determined not to be hustled and bewildered into matrimony—to be dragged to the shambles before I know where I am. With such an arrangement as the one I speak of I should be able to take my time, to keep my head, to make my choice."

"And how would the young lady make hers?"

"How do you mean, hers?"

"The selfishness of men is something exquisite. Suppose the young lady—if it's conceivable that you should find one idiotic enough to be a party to such a transaction—suppose the poor girl herself should happen to wish to be *really* engaged?"

Guy Firminger thought a moment, with his slow but not stupid smile. "Do you mean to *me*?"

"To you—or to some one else."

"Oh, if she'd give me notice I'd let her off."

"Let her off till you could find a substitute?"

"Yes—but I confess it would be a great inconvenience. People wouldn't take the second one so seriously."

"She would have to make a sacrifice; she would have to wait till you should know where you were," Mrs. Gosselin suggested.

"Yes, but where would *her* advantage come in?" Mary persisted.

"Only in the pleasure of charity; the moral satisfaction of doing a fellow a good turn," said Firminger.

"You must think people are keen to oblige you!"

"Ah, but surely I could count on *you*, couldn't I?" the young man asked.

Mary had finished cutting her book; she got up and flung it down on the tea-table. "What a preposterous conversation!" she exclaimed with force, tossing the words from her as she tossed her book; and, looking round her vaguely a moment, without meeting Guy Firminger's eye, she walked away to the house.

Firminger sat watching her; then he said serenely to her mother: "Why has our Mary left us?"

"She has gone to get something, I suppose."

"What has she gone to get?"

"A little stick to beat you perhaps."

"You don't mean I've been objectionable?"

"Dear, no—I'm joking. One thing is very certain," pursued Mrs. Gosselin; "that you ought to work—to try to get on exactly as if nothing could ever happen. Oughtn't you?" She threw off the question mechanically as her visitor continued silent.

"I'm sure she doesn't like it!" he exclaimed, without heeding her appeal.

"Doesn't like what?"

"My free play of mind. It's perhaps too much in the key of our old romps."

"You're very clever; she always likes *that*," said Mrs. Gosselin. "You ought to go in for something serious, for something honourable," she continued, "just as much as if you had nothing at all to look to."

"Words of wisdom, dear Mrs. Gosselin," Firminger replied, rising slowly from his relaxed attitude. "But what *have* I to look to."

She raised her mild, deep eyes to him as he stood before her—she might have been a fairy godmother. "Everything!"

"But you know I can't poison them!"

"That won't be necessary."

He looked at her an instant; then with a laugh: "One might think *you* would undertake it!"

"I almost would—for *you*. Good-bye."

"Take care,—if they *should* be carried off!" But Mrs. Gosselin only repeated her good-bye, and the young man departed before Mary had come back.

II.

Nearly two years after Guy Firminger had spent that friendly hour in Mrs. Gosselin's little garden in Hampshire this far-seeing woman was enabled (by the return of her son, who at New York, in an English bank, occupied a position they all rejoiced over—to such great things might it duly lead), to resume possession, for the season, of the little London house which her husband had left her to inhabit, but which her native thrift, in determining her to let it for a term, had converted into a source of income. Hugh Gosselin, who was thirty years old and at twenty-three, before his father's death, had been dispatched to America to exert himself, was understood to be doing very well—so well that his devotion to the interests of his employers had been rewarded, for the first time, with a real holiday. He was to remain in England from May to August, undertaking, as he said, to make it all right if during this time his mother should occupy (to contribute to his entertainment), the habitation in Chester Street. He was a small, preoccupied young man, with a sharpness as acquired as a new hat; he struck his mother and sister as intensely American. For the first few days after his arrival they were startled by his intonations, though they admitted that they had had an escape when he reminded them that he might have brought with him an accent embodied in a wife.

"When you do take one," said Mrs. Gosselin, who regarded such an accident, over there, as inevitable, "you must charge her high for it."

It was not with this question, however, that the little family in Chester Street was mainly engaged, but with the last incident in the extraordinary succession of events which, like a chapter of romance, had in the course of a few months converted their vague and impecunious friend into a personage envied and honoured. It was as if a blight had been cast on all Guy Firminger's hindrances. On the day Hugh Gosselin

sailed from New York the delicate little boy at Bosco had succumbed to an attack of diphtheria. His father had died of
typhoid the previous winter at Naples; his uncle, a few weeks
later, had had a fatal accident in the hunting-field. So
strangely, so rapidly had the situation cleared up, had his fate
and theirs worked for him. Guy had opened his eyes one
morning to an earldom which carried with it a fortune not
alone nominally but really great. Mrs. Gosselin and Mary had
not written to him, but they knew he was at Bosco; he had
remained there after the funeral of the late little lord. Mrs.
Gosselin, who heard everything, had heard somehow that he
was behaving with the greatest consideration, giving the
guardians, the trustees, whatever they were called, plenty of
time to do everything. Everything was comparatively simple;
in the absence of collaterals there were so few other people
concerned. The principal relatives were poor Frank Firminger's widow and her girls, who had seen themselves so near
to new honours and comforts. Probably the girls would expect
their cousin Guy to marry one of them, and think it the least
he could decently do; a view the young man himself (if he
were very magnanimous) might possibly embrace. The question would be whether he would be very magnanimous. These
young ladies exhausted in their three persons the numerous
varieties of plainness. On the other hand Guy Firminger—
or Lord Beaupré, as one would have to begin to call him
now—was unmistakably kind. Mrs. Gosselin appealed to her
son as to whether their noble friend were not unmistakably
kind.

"Of course I've known him always, and that time he came
out to America—when was it? four years ago—I saw him every
day. I like him awfully and all that, but since you push me, you
know," said Hugh Gosselin, "I'm bound to say that the first
thing to mention in any description of him would be—if you
wanted to be quite correct—that he's unmistakably selfish."

"I see—I see," Mrs. Gosselin unblushingly replied. "Of
course I know what you mean," she added in a moment. "But
is he any more so than any one else? Every one's unmistakably
selfish."

"Every one but you and Mary," said the young man.

"And *you*, dear!" his mother smiled. "But a person may be

kind, you know—mayn't he?—at the same time that he *is* self-ish. There are different sorts."

"Different sorts of kindness?" Hugh Gosselin asked with a laugh; and the inquiry undertaken by his mother occupied them for the moment, demanding a subtlety of treatment from which they were not conscious of shrinking, of which rather they had an idea that they were perhaps exceptionally capable. They came back to the temperate view that Guy would never put himself out, would probably never do anything great, but might show himself all the same a delightful member of society. Yes, he was probably selfish, like other people; but unlike most of them he was, somehow, amiably, attachingly, sociably, almost lovably selfish. Without doing anything great he would yet be a great success—a big, pleasant, gossiping, lounging and, in its way doubtless very splendid, presence. He would have no ambition, and it was ambition that made selfishness ugly. Hugh and his mother were sure of this last point until Mary, before whom the discussion, when it reached this stage, happened to be carried on, checked them by asking whether that, on the contrary, were not just what was supposed to make it fine.

"Oh, he only wants to be comfortable," said her brother; "but he *does* want it!"

"There'll be a tremendous rush for him," Mrs. Gosselin prophesied to her son.

"Oh, he'll never marry. It will be too much trouble."

"It's done here without any trouble—for the men. One sees how long you've been out of the country."

"There was a girl in New York whom he might have married—he really liked her. But he wouldn't turn round for her."

"Perhaps she wouldn't turn round for *him*," said Mary.

"I daresay she'll turn round *now*," Mrs. Gosselin rejoined; on which Hugh mentioned that there was nothing to be feared from her, all her revolutions had been accomplished. He added that nothing would make any difference—so intimate was his conviction that Beaupré would preserve his independence.

"Then I think he's not so selfish as you say," Mary declared; "or at any rate one will never know whether he is. Isn't married life the great chance to show it?"

"Your father never showed it," said Mrs. Gosselin; and as her children were silent in presence of this tribute to the departed she added, smiling: "Perhaps you think that *I* did!" They embraced her, to indicate what they thought, and the conversation ended, when she had remarked that Lord Beaupré was a man who would be perfectly easy to manage *after* marriage, with Hugh's exclaiming that this was doubtless exactly why he wished to keep out of it.

Such was evidently his wish, as they were able to judge in Chester Street when he came up to town. He appeared there oftener than was to have been expected, not taking himself in his new character at all too seriously to find stray half-hours for old friends. It was plain that he was going to do just as he liked, that he was not a bit excited or uplifted by his change of fortune. Mary Gosselin observed that he had no imagination—she even reproached him with the deficiency to his face, an incident which showed indeed how little seriously *she* took him. He had no idea of playing a part, and yet he would have been clever enough. He wasn't even systematic about being simple; his simplicity was a series of accidents and indifferences. Never was a man more conscientiously superficial. There were matters on which he valued Mrs. Gosselin's judgment and asked her advice—without, as usually appeared later, ever taking it; such questions, mainly, as the claims of a predecessor's servants, and those, in respect to social intercourse, of the clergyman's family. He didn't like his parson— what was a fellow to do when he didn't like his parson? What he did like was to talk with Hugh about American investments, and it was amusing to Hugh, though he tried not to show his amusement, to find himself looking at Guy Firminger in the light of capital. To Mary he addressed from the first the oddest snatches of confidential discourse, rendered in fact, however, by the levity of his tone, considerably less confidential than in intention. He had something to tell her that he joked about, yet without admitting that it was any less important for being laughable. It was neither more nor less than that Charlotte Firminger, the eldest of his late uncle's four girls, had designated to him in the clearest manner the person she considered he ought to marry. She appealed to his sense of justice, she spoke and wrote, or at any rate she looked and moved, she sighed and sang, in the name of common honesty. He had had four letters from her that week, and to his knowledge there were a series of people in London, people she could bully, whom she had got to promise to take her in for the season. She was going to be on the spot, she was going to follow him up. He took his stand on common honesty, but he had a mortal horror of Charlotte. At the same time, when a girl had a jaw like that and had marked you—really *marked* you, mind, you felt your safety oozing away. He had given them during the past three months, all those terrible girls, every sort of present that Bond Street could supply: but these demonstrations had only been held to constitute another pledge. Therefore what was a fellow to do? Besides, there were other portents; the air was thick with them, as the sky over battlefields was darkened by the flight of vultures. They were flocking, the birds of prey, from every quarter, and every girl in England, by Jove! was going to be thrown at his head. What had he done to deserve such a fate? He wanted to stop in England and see all sorts of things through; but how could he stand there and face such a charge? Yet what good would it do to bolt? Wherever he should go there would be fifty of them there first. On his honour he could say that he didn't deserve it; he had never, to his own sense, been a flirt, such a flirt at least as to have given anyone a handle. He appealed candidly to Mary Gosselin to know whether his past conduct justified such penalties. "*Have* I been a flirt?— have I given anyone a handle?" he inquired with pathetic intensity.

She met his appeal by declaring that he had been awful, committing himself right and left; and this manner of treating his affliction contributed to the sarcastic publicity (as regarded the little house in Chester Street) which presently became its natural element. Lord Beaupré's comical and yet thoroughly grounded view of his danger was soon a frequent theme among the Gosselins, who however had their own reasons for not communicating the alarm. They had no motive for concealing their interest in their old friend, but their allusions to him among their other friends may be said on the whole to have been studied. His state of mind recalled of course to Mary and her mother the queer talk about his prospects that they had had, in the country, that afternoon on which Mrs. Gosselin had been so strangely prophetic (she confessed that she had had a flash of divination: the future had been mysteriously revealed to her), and poor Guy too had seen himself quite as he was to be. He had seen his nervousness, under inevitable pressure, deepen to a panic, and he now, in intimate hours, made no attempt to disguise that a panic had become his portion. It was a fixed idea with him that he should fall a victim to woven toils, be caught in a trap constructed with superior science. The science evolved in an enterprising age by this branch of industry, the manufacture of the trap matrimonial, he had terrible anecdotes to illustrate; and what had he on his lips but a scientific term when he declared, as he perpetually did, that it was his fate to be hypnotised?

Mary Gosselin reminded him, they each in turn reminded him that his safeguard was to fall in love: were he once to put himself under that protection all the mothers and maids in Mayfair would not prevail against him. He replied that this was just the impossibility; it took leisure and calmness and opportunity and a free mind to fall in love, and never was a man less open to such experiences. He was literally fighting his way. He reminded the girl of his old fancy for pretending already to have disposed of his hand if he could put that hand on a young person who should like him well enough to be willing to participate in the fraud. She would have to place herself in rather a false position of course—have to take a certain amount of trouble; but there would after all be a good deal of fun in it (there was always fun in duping the world), between the pair themselves, the two happy comedians

"Why should they both be happy?" Mary Gosselin asked. "I understand why you should; but, frankly, I don't quite grasp the reason of *her* pleasure."

Lord Beaupré, with his sunny human eyes, thought a moment. "Why, for the lark, as they say, and that sort of thing. I should be awfully nice to her."

"She would require indeed to be in want of recreation!"

"Ah, but I should want a good sort—a quiet, reasonable one, you know!" he somewhat eagerly interposed.

"You're too delightful!" Mary Gosselin exclaimed, continuing to laugh. He thanked her for this appreciation, and she returned to her point—that she didn't really see the advantage his accomplice could hope to enjoy as her compensation for extreme disturbance.

Guy Firminger stared. "But what extreme disturbance?"

"Why, it would take a lot of time; it might become intolerable."

"You mean I ought to pay her—to hire her for the season?"

Mary Gosselin considered him a moment. "Wouldn't marriage come cheaper at once?" she asked with a quieter smile.

"You *are* chaffing me!" he sighed forgivingly. "Of course she would have to be good-natured enough to pity me."

"Pity's akin to love. If she were good-natured enough to want so to help you she'd be good-natured enough to want to marry you. That would be *her* idea of help."

"Would it be *yours*?" Lord Beaupré asked rather eagerly.

"You're too absurd! You must sail your own boat!" the girl answered, turning away.

That evening at dinner she stated to her companions that she had never seen a fatuity so dense, so serene, so preposterous as his lordship's.

"Fatuity, my dear! what do you mean?" her mother inquired.

"Oh, mamma, you know perfectly." Mary Gosselin spoke with a certain impatience.

"If you mean he's conceited I'm bound to say I don't agree with you," her brother observed. "He's too indifferent to everyone's opinion for that."

"He's not vain, he's not proud, he's not pompous," said Mrs. Gosselin.

Mary was silent a moment. "He takes more things for granted than anyone I ever saw."

"What sort of things?"

"Well, one's interest in his affairs."

"With old friends surely a gentleman may."

"Of course," said Hugh Gosselin, "old friends have in turn the right to take for granted a corresponding interest on *his* part."

"Well, who could be nicer to us than he is or come to see us oftener?" his mother asked.

"He comes exactly for the purpose I speak of—to talk about himself," said Mary.

"There are thousands of girls who would be delighted with his talk," Mrs. Gosselin returned.

"We agreed long ago that he's intensely selfish," the girl went on; "and if I speak of it to-day it's not because that in itself is anything of a novelty. What I'm freshly struck with is simply that he more shamelessly shows it "

"He shows it, exactly," said Hugh; "he shows all there is. There it is, on the surface; there are not depths of it underneath."

"He's not hard," Mrs. Gosselin contended; "he's not impervious."

"Do you mean he's soft?" Mary asked.

"I mean he's yielding." And Mrs. Gosselin, with considerable expression, looked across at her daughter. She added, before they rose from dinner, that poor Beaupré had plenty of difficulties and that she thought, for her part, they ought in common loyalty to do what they could to assist him.

For a week nothing more passed between the two ladies on the subject of their noble friend, and in the course of this week they had the amusement of receiving in Chester Street a member of Hugh's American circle, Mr. Bolton-Brown, a young man from New York. He was a person engaged in large affairs, for whom Hugh Gosselin professed the highest regard, from whom in New York he had received much hospitality, and for whose advent he had from the first prepared his companions. Mrs. Gosselin begged the amiable stranger to stay with them, and if she failed to overcome his hesitation it was because his hotel was near at hand and he should be able to see them often. It became evident that he would do so, and, to the two ladies, as the days went by, equally evident that no objection to such a relation was likely to arise. Mr. Bolton-Brown was delightfully fresh, the most usual expressions acquired on his lips a wellnigh comical novelty, the most superficial sentiments, in the look with which he accompanied them, a really touching sincerity. He was unmarried and good-looking, clever and natural, and if he was not very rich was at least very free-handed. He literally strewed the path of the ladies in

Chester Street with flowers, he choked them with French confectionery. Hugh, however, who was often rather mysterious on monetary questions, placed in a light sufficiently clear the fact that his friend had in Wall Street (they knew all about Wall Street), improved each shining hour. They introduced him to Lord Beaupré, who thought him "tremendous fun," as Hugh said, and who immediately declared that the four must spend a Sunday at Bosco a week or two later. The date of this visit was fixed—Mrs. Gosselin had uttered a comprehensive acceptance; but after Guy Firminger had taken leave of them (this had been his first appearance since the odd conversation with Mary), our young lady confided to her mother that she should not be able to join the little party. She expressed the conviction that it would be all that was essential if Mrs. Gosselin should go with the two others. On being pressed to communicate the reason of this aloofness Mary was able to give no better one than that she never had cared for Bosco.

"What makes you hate him so?" her mother presently broke out in a tone which brought the red to the girl's cheek. Mary denied that she entertained for Lord Beaupré any sentiment so intense; to which Mrs. Gosselin rejoined with some sternness and, no doubt, considerable wisdom: "Look out what you do then, or you'll be thought by everyone to be in love with him!"

III.

I know not whether it was this danger—that of appearing to be moved to extremes—that weighed with Mary Gosselin; at any rate when the day arrived she had decided to be perfectly colourless and take her share of Lord Beaupré's hospitality. On perceiving that the house, when with her companions she reached it, was full of visitors, she consoled herself with the sense that such a share would be of the smallest. She even wondered whether its smallness might not be caused in some degree by the sufficiently startling presence, in this stronghold of the single life, of Maud Ashbury and her mother. It was true that during the Saturday evening she never saw their host address an observation to them; but she was struck, as she had been struck before, with the girl's cold and magnificent beauty. It was very well to say she had "gone off"; she was still handsomer than anyone else. She had failed in everything she had tried; the campaign undertaken with so much energy against young Raddle had been conspicuously disastrous. Young Raddle had married his grandmother, or a person who might have filled such an office, and Maud was a year older, a year more disappointed and a year more ridiculous. Nevertheless one could scarcely believe that a creature with such advantages would always fail, though indeed the poor girl was stupid enough to be a warning. Perhaps it would be at Bosco, or with the master of Bosco, that fate had appointed her to succeed. Except Mary herself she was the only young unmarried woman on the scene, and Mary glowed with the generous sense of not being a competitor. She felt as much out of the question as the blooming wives, the heavy matrons, who formed the rest of the female contingent. Before the evening closed, however, her host, who, she saw, was delightful in his own house, mentioned to her that he had a couple of guests who had not been invited.

"Not invited?"

"They drove up to my door as they might have done to an inn. They asked for rooms and complained of those that were given them. Don't pretend not to know who they are."

"Do you mean the Ashburys? How amusing!"

"Don't laugh; it freezes my blood."

"Do you really mean you're afraid of them?"

"I tremble like a leaf. Some monstrous ineluctable fate seems to look at me out of their eyes."

"That's because you secretly admire Maud. How can you help it? She's extremely good-looking, and if you get rid of her mother she'll become a very nice girl."

"It's an odious thing, no doubt, to say about a young person under one's own roof, but I don't think I ever saw any one who happened to be less to my taste," said Guy Firminger. "I don't know why I don't turn them out even now."

Mary persisted in sarcasm. "Perhaps you can make her have a worse time by letting her stay."

"*Please* don't laugh," her interlocutor repeated. "Such a fact as I have mentioned to you seems to me to speak volumes—to show you what my life is."

"Oh, your life, your life!" Mary Gosselin murmured, with her mocking note.

"Don't you agree that at such a rate it may easily become impossible?"

"Many people would change with you. I don't see what there is for you to do but to bear your cross!"

"That's easy talk!" Lord Beaupré sighed.

"Especially from me, do you mean? How do you know I don't bear mine?"

"Yours?" he asked vaguely.

"How do you know that *I'm* not persecuted, that *my* footsteps are not dogged, that *my* life isn't a burden?"

They were walking in the old gardens, the proprietor of which, at this, stopped short. "Do you mean by fellows who want to marry you?"

His tone produced on his companion's part an irrepressible peal of hilarity; but she walked on as she exclaimed: "You speak as if there couldn't *be* such madmen!"

"Of course such a charming girl must be made up to," Guy Firminger conceded as he overtook her.

"I don't speak of it; I keep quiet about it."

"You realise then, at any rate, that it's all horrid when you don't care for them."

"I suffer in silence, because I know there are worse tribulations. It seems to me you ought to remember that," Mary continued. "Your cross is small compared with your crown. You've everything in the world that most people most desire, and I'm bound to say I think your life is made very comfortable for you. If you're oppressed by the quantity of interest and affection you inspire you ought simply to make up your mind to bear up and be cheerful under it."

Lord Beaupré received this admonition with perfect good humour; he professed himself able to do it full justice. He remarked that he would gladly give up some of his material advantages to be a little less badgered, and that he had been quite content with his former insignificance. No doubt, however, such annoyances were the essential drawbacks of ponderous promotions; one had to pay for everything. Mary was quite right to rebuke him; her own attitude, as a young woman much admired, was a lesson to his irritability. She cut this appreciation short, speaking of something else; but a few minutes later he broke out irrelevantly: "Why, if you are hunted as well as I, that dodge I proposed to you would be just the thing for us *both*!" He had evidently been reasoning it out.

Mary Gosselin was silent at first; she only paused gradually in their walk at a point where four long alleys met. In the centre of the circle, on a massive pedestal, rose in Italian bronze a florid, complicated image, so that the place made a charming old-world picture. The grounds of Bosco were stately without stiffness and full of marble terraces and misty avenues. The fountains in particular were royal. The girl had told her mother in London that she disliked this fine residence, but she now looked round her with a vague pleased sigh, holding up her glass (she had been condemned to wear one, with a long handle, since she was fifteen), to consider the weather-stained garden group. "What a perfect place of its kind!" she musingly exclaimed.

"Wouldn't it really be just the thing?" Lord Beaupré went on, with the eagerness of his idea.

"Wouldn't what be just the thing?"

"Why, the defensive alliance we've already talked of. You wanted to know the good it would do *you*. Now you see the good it would do you!"

"I don't like practical jokes," said Mary. "The remedy's worse than the disease," she added; and she began to follow one of the paths that took the direction of the house.

Poor Lord Beaupré was absurdly in love with his invention; he had all an inventor's importunity. He kept up his attempt to place his "dodge" in a favourable light, in spite of a further objection from his companion, who assured him that it was one of those contrivances which break down in practice in just the proportion in which they make a figure in theory. At last she said: "I was not sincere just now when I told you I'm worried. I'm *not* worried!"

"They *don't* buzz about you?" Guy Firminger asked.

She hesitated an instant. "They buzz about me; but at bottom it's flattering and I don't mind it. Now please drop the subject."

He dropped the subject, though not without congratulating her on the fact that, unlike his infirm self, she could keep her head and her temper. His infirmity found a trap laid for it before they had proceeded twenty yards, as was proved by his sudden exclamation of horror. "Good Heavens—if there isn't Lottie!"

Mary perceived, in effect, in the distance a female figure coming towards them over a stretch of lawn, and she simultaneously saw, as a gentleman passed from behind a clump of shrubbery, that it was not unattended. She recognized Charlotte Firminger, and she also distinguished the gentleman. She was moved to larger mirth at the dismay expressed by poor Firminger, but she was able to articulate: "Walking with Mr. Brown."

Lord Beaupré stopped again before they were joined by the pair. "Does *he* buzz about you?"

"Mercy, what questions you ask!" his companion exclaimed.

"Does he—*please*?" the young man repeated with odd intensity.

Mary looked at him an instant; she was puzzled by the deep annoyance that had flushed through the essential good-humour of his face. Then she saw that this annoyance had exclusive reference to poor Charlotte; so that it left her free to reply, with another laugh: "Well, yes—he does. But you know I like it!"

"I don't, then!" Before she could have asked him, even had she wished to, in what manner such a circumstance concerned him, he added with his droll agitation: "I never invited *her*, either! Don't let her get at me!"

"What can I do?" Mary demanded as the others advanced.

"Please take her away; keep her yourself! I'll take the American, I'll keep *him*," he murmured, inconsequently, as a bribe.

"But I don't object to him."

"Do you like him so much?"

"Very much indeed," the girl replied.

The reply was perhaps lost upon her interlocutor, whose eye now fixed itself gloomily on the dauntless Charlotte. As Miss Firminger came nearer he exclaimed almost loud enough for her to hear: "I think I shall *murder* her some day!"

Mary Gosselin's first impression had been that, in his panic, under the empire of that fixed idea to which he confessed himself subject, he attributed to his kinswoman machinations and aggressions of which she was incapable; an impression that might have been confirmed by this young lady's decorous placidity, her passionless eyes, her expressionless cheeks and colourless tones. She was ugly, yet she was orthodox; she was not what writers of books called intense. But after Mary, to oblige their host, had tried, successfully enough, to be crafty, had drawn her on to stroll a little in advance of the two gentlemen, she became promptly aware, by the mystical influence of propinquity, that Miss Firminger was indeed full of views, of a purpose single, simple and strong, which gave her the effect of a person carrying with a stiff, steady hand, with eyes fixed and lips compressed, a cup charged to the brim. She had driven over to lunch, driven from somewhere in the neighbourhood; she had picked up some weak woman as an escort. Mary, though she knew the neighbourhood, failed to recognize her base of operations, and, as Charlotte was not specific, ended by suspecting that, far from being entertained by friends, she had put up at an inn and hired a fly. This suspicion startled her; it gave her for the first time something of the measure of the passions engaged, and she wondered to what the insecurity complained of by Guy might lead. Charlotte, on arriving, had gone through a part of the house in quest of its master (the servants being unable to tell her where he was), and she had finally come upon Mr. Bolton-Brown, who was looking at old books in the library. He had placed himself at her service, as if he had been trained immediately to recognize in such a case his duty, and informing her that he believed Lord Beaupré to be in the grounds, had come out with her to help to find him. Lottie Firminger questioned her companion about this accommodating person; she intimated that he was rather odd but rather nice. Mary mentioned to her that Lord Beaupré thought highly of him; she believed they were going somewhere together. At this Miss Firminger turned round to look for them, but they had already disappeared, and the girl became ominously dumb.

Mary wondered afterwards what profit she could hope to derive from such proceedings; they struck her own sense, naturally, as disreputable and desperate. She was equally unable to discover the compensation they offered, in another variety,

to poor Maud Ashbury, whom Lord Beaupré, the greater part
of the day, neglected as conscientiously as he neglected his
cousin. She asked herself if he should be blamed, and replied
that the others should be blamed first. He got rid of Charlotte
somehow after tea; she had to fall back to her mysterious lines.
Mary knew this method would have been detestable to him—
he hated to force his friendly nature; she was sorry for him
and wished to lose sight of him. She wished not to be mixed
up even indirectly with his tribulations, and the fevered faces
of the Ashburys were particularly dreadful to her. She spent
as much of the long summer afternoon as possible out of the
house, which indeed on such an occasion emptied itself of
most of its inmates. Mary Gosselin asked her brother to join
her in a devious ramble; she might have had other society, but
she was in a mood to prefer his. These two were "great
chums," and they had been separated so long that they had
arrears of talk to make up. They had been at Bosco more than
once, and though Hugh Gosselin said that the land of the free
(which he had assured his sister was even more enslaved than
dear old England) made one forget there were such spots on
earth, they both remembered, a couple of miles away, a little
ancient church to which the walk across the fields would be
the right thing. They talked of other things as they went, and
among them they talked of Mr. Bolton-Brown, in regard to
whom Hugh, as scantily addicted to enthusiasm as to bursts
of song (he was determined not to be taken in), became, in
commendation, almost lyrical. Mary asked what he had done
with his paragon, and he replied that he believed him to have
gone out stealthily to sketch: they might come across him. He
was extraordinarily clever at water-colours, but haunted with
the fear that the public practice of such an art on Sunday was
viewed with disfavour in England. Mary exclaimed that this
was the respectable fact, and when her brother ridiculed the
idea she told him she had already noticed he had lost all sense
of things at home, so that Mr. Bolton-Brown was apparently
a better Englishman than he. "He is indeed—he's awfully artificial!" Hugh returned; but it must be added that in spite of
this rigour their American friend, when they reached the goal
of their walk, was to be perceived in an irregular attitude in
the very churchyard. He was perched on an old flat tomb,

with a box of colours beside him and a sketch half completed. Hugh asserted that this exercise was the only thing that Mr. Bolton-Brown really cared for, but the young man protested against the imputation in the face of an achievement so modest. He showed his sketch to Mary however, and it consoled her for not having kept up her own experiments; she never could make her trees so leafy. He had found a lovely bit on the other side of the hill, a bit he should like to come back to, and he offered to show it to his friends. They were on the point of starting with him to look at it when Hugh Gosselin, taking out his watch, remembered the hour at which he had promised to be at the house again to give his mother, who wanted a little mild exercise, his arm. His sister, at this, said she would go back with him; but Bolton-Brown interposed an earnest inquiry. Mightn't she let Hugh keep his appointment and let *him* take her over the hill and bring her home?

"Happy thought—*do* that!" said Hugh, with a crudity that showed the girl how completely he had lost his English sense. He perceived however in an instant that she was embarrassed, whereupon he went on: "My dear child, I've walked with girls so often in America that we really ought to let poor Brown walk with one in England." I know not if it was the effect of this plea or that of some further eloquence of their friend; at any rate Mary Gosselin in the course of another minute had accepted the accident of Hugh's secession, had seen him depart with an injunction to her to render it clear to poor Brown that he had made quite a monstrous request. As she went over the hill with her companion she reflected that since she had granted the request it was not in her interest to pretend she had gone out of her way. She wondered moreover whether her brother had wished to throw them together: it suddenly occurred to her that the whole incident might have been prearranged. The idea made her a little angry with Hugh; it led her however to entertain no resentment against the other party (if party Mr. Brown had been) to the transaction. He told her all the delight that certain sweet old corners of rural England excited in his mind, and she liked him for hovering near some of her own secrets.

Hugh Gosselin meanwhile, at Bosco, strolling on the terrace with his mother, who preferred walks that were as slow

as conspiracies and had had much to say to him about his
extraordinary indiscretion, repeated over and over (it ended
by irritating her), that as he himself had been out for hours
with American girls it was only fair to let their friend have a
turn with an English one.

"Pay as much as you like, but don't pay with your sister!"
Mrs. Gosselin replied; while Hugh submitted that it was just
his sister who was required to make the payment *his*. She
turned his logic to easy scorn and she waited on the terrace
till she had seen the two explorers reappear. When the ladies
went to dress for dinner she expressed to her daughter her
extreme disapproval of such conduct, and Mary did nothing
more to justify herself than to exclaim at first "Poor dear
man!" and then to say "I was afraid you wouldn't like it."
There were reservations in her silence that made Mrs. Gosselin
uneasy, and she was glad that at dinner Mr. Bolton-Brown
had to take in Mrs. Ashbury: it served him so right. This
arrangement had in Mrs. Gosselin's eyes the added merit of
serving Mrs. Ashbury right. She was more uneasy than ever
when after dinner, in the drawing-room, she saw Mary sit for
a period on the same small sofa with the culpable American.
This young couple leaned back together familiarly, and their
conversation had the air of being desultory without being in
the least difficult. At last she quitted her place and went over
to them, remarking to Mr. Bolton-Brown that she wanted him
to come and talk a bit to *her*. She conducted him to another
part of the room, which was vast and animated by scattered
groups, and held him there very persuasively, quite maternally,
till the approach of the hour at which the ladies would
exchange looks and murmur good-nights. She made him talk
about America, though he wanted to talk about England, and
she judged that she gave him an impression of the kindest
attention, though she was really thinking, in alternation, of
three important things. One of these was a circumstance of
which she had become conscious only just after sitting down
with him—the prolonged absence of Lord Beaupré from the
drawing-room; the second was the absence, equally marked
(to her imagination) of Maud Ashbury; the third was a matter
different altogether. "England gives one such a sense of immemorial continuity, something that drops like a plummet-

line into the past," said the young American, ingeniously exerting himself while Mrs. Gosselin, rigidly contemporaneous, strayed into deserts of conjecture. Had the fact that their host was out of the room any connection with the fact that the most beautiful, even though the most suicidal, of his satellites had quitted it? Yet if poor Guy was taking a turn by starlight on the terrace with the misguided girl, what had he done with his resentment at her invasion and by what inspiration of despair had Maud achieved such a triumph? The good lady studied Mrs. Ashbury's face across the room; she decided that triumph, accompanied perhaps with a shade of nervousness, looked out of her insincere eyes. An intelligent consciousness of ridicule was at any rate less present in them than ever. While Mrs. Gosselin had her infallible finger on the pulse of the occasion one of the doors opened to readmit Lord Beaupré, who struck her as pale and who immediately approached Mrs. Ashbury with a remark evidently intended for herself alone. It led this lady to rise with a movement of dismay and, after a question or two, leave the room. Lord Beaupré left it again in her company. Mr. Bolton-Brown had also noticed the incident; his conversation languished and he asked Mrs. Gosselin if she supposed anything had happened. She turned it over a moment and then she said: "Yes, something will have happened to Miss Ashbury."

"What do you suppose? Is she ill?"

"I don't know; we shall see. They're capable of anything."

"Capable of anything?"

"I've guessed it,—she wants to have a grievance."

"A grievance?" Mr. Bolton Brown was mystified.

"Of course you don't understand; how should you? Moreover it doesn't signify. But I'm so vexed with them (he's a very old friend of ours) that really, though I dare say I'm indiscreet, I can't speak civilly of them."

"Miss Ashbury's a wonderful type," said the young American.

This remark appeared to irritate his companion. "I see perfectly what has happened; she has made a scene."

"A scene?" Mr. Bolton-Brown was terribly out of it.

"She has tried to be injured—to provoke him, I mean, to some act of impatience, to some failure of temper, of courtesy.

She has asked him if he wishes her to leave the house at mid-night, and he may have answered—— But no, he wouldn't!"
Mrs. Gosselin suppressed the wild supposition.

"How you read it! She looks so quiet."

"Her mother has coached her, and (I won't pretend to say *exactly* what has happened) they've done, somehow, what they wanted; they've got him to do something to them that he'll have to make up for."

"What an evolution of ingenuity!" the young man laughed.

"It often answers."

"Will it in this case?"

Mrs. Gosselin was silent a moment. "It *may*."

"Really, you think?"

"I mean it might if it weren't for something else."

"I'm too judicious to ask what that is."

"I'll tell you when we're back in town," said Mrs. Gosselin, getting up.

Lord Beaupré was restored to them, and the ladies prepared to withdraw. Before she went to bed Mrs. Gosselin asked him if there had been anything the matter with Maud; to which he replied with abysmal blankness (she had never seen him wear just that face) that he was afraid Miss Ashbury was ill. She proved in fact in the morning too unwell to return to London: a piece of news communicated to Mrs. Gosselin at breakfast.

"She'll have to stay; I can't turn her out of the house," said Guy Firminger.

"Very well; let her stay her fill!"

"I wish you would stay too," the young man went on.

"Do you mean to nurse her?"

"No, her mother must do that. I mean to keep me company."

"*You?* You're not going up?"

"I think I had better wait over to-day, or long enough to see what's the matter."

"Don't you *know* what's the matter?"

He was silent a moment. "I may have been nasty last night."

"You have compunctions? You're too good-natured."

"I dare say I hit rather wild. It will look better for me to stop over twenty-four hours."

Mrs. Gosselin fixed her eyes on a distant object. "Let no one ever say you're selfish!"

"*Does* anyone ever say it?"

"You're too generous, you're too soft, you're too foolish. But if it will give you any pleasure Mary and I will wait till to-morrow."

"And Hugh, too, won't he, and Bolton-Brown?"

"Hugh will do as he pleases. But don't keep the American."

"Why not? He's all right."

"That's why I want him to go," said Mrs. Gosselin, who could treat a matter with candour, just as she could treat it with humour, at the right moment.

The party at Bosco broke up and there was a general retreat to town. Hugh Gosselin pleaded pressing business, he accompanied the young American to London. His mother and sister came back on the morrow, and Bolton-Brown went in to see them, as he often did, at tea-time. He found Mrs. Gosselin alone in the drawing-room, and she took such a convenient occasion to mention to him, what she had withheld on the eve of their departure from Bosco, the reason why poor Maud Ashbury's frantic assault on the master of that property would be vain. He was greatly surprised, the more so that Hugh hadn't told him. Mrs. Gosselin replied that Hugh didn't know: she had not seen him all day and it had only just come out. Hugh's friend at any rate was deeply interested, and his interest took for several minutes the form of throbbing silence. At last Mrs. Gosselin heard a sound below, on which she said quickly: "That's Hugh—I'll tell him now!" She left the room with the request that their visitor would wait for Mary, who would be down in a moment. During the instants that he spent alone the visitor lurched, as if he had been on a deck in a blow, to the window, and stood there with his hands in his pockets, staring vacantly into Chester Street; then, turning away, he gave himself, with an odd ejaculation, an impatient shake which had the effect of enabling him to meet Mary Gosselin composedly enough when she came in. It took her mother apparently some time to communicate the

news to Hugh, so that Bolton-Brown had a considerable margin for nervousness and hesitation before he could say to the
girl, abruptly, but with an attempt at a voice properly gay:
"You must let me very heartily congratulate you!"

Mary stared. "On what?"

"On your engagement."

"My engagement?"

"To Lord Beaupré."

Mary Gosselin looked strange; she coloured. "Who told
you I'm engaged?"

"Your mother—just now."

"Oh!" the girl exclaimed, turning away. She went and rang
the bell for fresh tea, rang it with noticeable force. But she
said "Thank you very much!" before the servant came.

IV.

Bolton-Brown did something that evening toward dissemi-
nating the news: he told it to the first people he met socially
after leaving Chester Street; and this although he had to do
himself a certain violence in speaking. He would have preferred to hold his peace; therefore if he resisted his inclination
it was for an urgent purpose. This purpose was to prove to
himself that he didn't mind. A perfect indifference could be
for him the only result of any understanding Mary Gosselin
might arrive at with anyone, and he wanted to be more and
more conscious of his indifference. He was aware indeed that
it required demonstration, and this was why he was almost
feverishly active. He could mentally concede at least that he
had been surprised, for he had suspected nothing at Bosco.
When a fellow was attentive in America everyone knew it, and
judged by this standard Lord Beaupré made no show: how
otherwise should *he* have achieved that sweet accompanied
ramble? Everything at any rate was lucid now, except perhaps
a certain ambiguity in Hugh Gosselin, who on coming into
the drawing-room with his mother had looked flushed and
grave and had stayed only long enough to kiss Mary and go
out again. There had been nothing effusive in the scene; but
then there was nothing effusive in any English scene. This
helped to explain why Miss Gosselin had been so blank during

the minutes she spent with him before her mother came back.

He himself wanted to cultivate tranquillity, and he felt that he did so the next day in not going again to Chester Street. He went instead to the British Museum, where he sat quite like an elderly gentleman, with his hands crossed on the top of his stick and his eyes fixed on an Assyrian bull. When he came away, however, it was with the resolution to move briskly; so that he walked westward the whole length of Oxford Street and arrived at the Marble Arch. He stared for some minutes at this monument, as in the national collection he had stared at even less intelligible ones; then brushing away the apprehension that he should meet two persons riding together, he passed into the park. He didn't care a straw whom he met. He got upon the grass and made his way to the southern expanse, and when he reached the Row he dropped into a chair, rather tired, to watch the capering procession of riders. He watched it with a lustreless eye, for what he seemed mainly to extract from it was a vivification of his disappointment. He had had a hope that he should not be forced to leave London without inducing Mary Gosselin to ride with him; but that prospect failed, for what he had accomplished in the British Museum was the determination to go to Paris. He tried to think of the attractions supposed to be evoked by that name, and while he was so engaged he recognised that a gentleman on horseback, close to the barrier of the Row, was making a sign to him. The gentleman was Lord Beaupré, who had pulled up his horse and whose sign the young American lost no time in obeying. He went forward to speak to his late host, but during the instant of the transit he was able both to observe that Mary Gosselin was not in sight and to ask himself why she was not. She rode with her brother; why then didn't she ride with her future husband? It was singular at such a moment to see her future husband disporting himself alone. This personage conversed a few moments with Bolton-Brown, said it was too hot to ride, but that he ought to be mounted (*he* would give him a mount if he liked) and was on the point of turning away when his interlocutor succumbed to the temptation to put his modesty to the test.

"Good-bye, but let me congratulate you first," said Bolton-Brown.

"Congratulate me? On what?" His look, his tone were very much what Mary Gosselin's had been.

"Why, on your engagement. Haven't you heard of it?"

Lord Beaupré stared a moment while his horse shifted uneasily. Then he laughed and said: "Which of them do you mean?"

"There's only one I know anything about. To Miss Gosselin," Brown added, after a puzzled pause.

"Oh yes, I see—thanks so much!" With this, letting his horse go, Lord Beaupré broke off, while Bolton-Brown stood looking after him and saying to himself that perhaps he *didn't* know! The chapter of English oddities was long.

But on the morrow the announcement was in "The Morning Post," and that surely made it authentic. It was doubtless only superficially singular that Guy Firminger should have found himself unable to achieve a call in Chester Street until this journal had been for several hours in circulation. He appeared there just before luncheon, and the first person who received him was Mrs. Gosselin. He had always liked her, finding her infallible on the question of behaviour; but he was on this occasion more than ever struck with her ripe astuteness, her independent wisdom.

"I knew what you wanted, I knew what you needed, I knew the subject on which you had pressed her," the good lady said; "and after Sunday I found myself really haunted with your dangers. There was danger in the air at Bosco, in your own defended house; it seemed to me too monstrous. I said to myself 'We *can* help him, poor dear, and we *must*. It's the least one can do for so old and so good a friend.' I decided what to do: I simply put this other story about. In London that always answers. I knew that Mary pitied you really as much as I do, and that what she saw at Bosco had been a revelation—had at any rate brought your situation home to her. Yet of course she would be shy about saying out for herself: 'Here I am—I'll do what you want.' The thing was for me to say it *for* her; so I said it first to that chattering American. He repeated it to several others, and there you are! I just forced her hand a little, but it's all right. All she has to do is not to contradict it. It won't be any trouble and you'll be comfortable. That will be our reward!" smiled Mrs. Gosselin.

"Yes, all she has to do is not to contradict it," Lord Beaupré replied, musing a moment. "It *won't* be any trouble," he added, "and I *hope* I shall be comfortable." He thanked Mrs. Gosselin formally and liberally, and expressed all his impatience to assure Mary herself of his deep obligation to her; upon which his hostess promised to send her daughter to him on the instant: she would go and call her, so that they might be alone. Before Mrs. Gosselin left him however she touched on one or two points that had their little importance. Guy Firminger had asked for Hugh, but Hugh had gone to the City, and his mother mentioned candidly that he didn't take part in the game. She even disclosed his reason: he thought there was a want of dignity in it. Lord Beaupré stared at this and after a moment exclaimed: "Dignity? Dignity be hanged! One must save one's life!"

"Yes, but the point poor Hugh makes is that one must save it by the use of one's *own* wits, or one's *own* arms and legs. But do you know what I said to him?" Mrs. Gosselin continued.

"Something very clever, I daresay."

"That if *we* were drowning you'd be the very first to jump in. And we may fall overboard yet!" Fidgeting there with his hands in his pockets Lord Beaupré gave a laugh at this, but assured her that there was nothing in the world for which they mightn't count upon him. None the less she just permitted herself another warning, a warning, it is true, that was in his own interest, a reminder of a peril that he ought beforehand to look in the face. Wasn't there always the chance—just the bare chance—that a girl in Mary's position would, in the event, decline to let him off, decline to release him even on the day he should wish to marry? She wasn't speaking of Mary, but there were of course girls who would play him that trick. Guy Firminger considered this contingency; then he declared that it wasn't a question of 'girls,' it was simply a question of dear old Mary! If *she* should wish to hold him, so much the better: he would do anything in the world that she wanted. "Don't let us dwell on such vulgarities; but I had it on my conscience!" Mrs. Gosselin wound up.

She left him, but at the end of three minutes Mary came in, and the first thing she said was: "Before you speak a word, please understand this, that it's wholly mamma's doing. I hadn't dreamed of it, but she suddenly began to tell people."

"It was charming of her, and it's charming of you!" the visitor cried.

"It's not charming of any one, I think," said Mary Gosselin, looking at the carpet. "It's simply idiotic."

"Don't be nasty about it. It will be tremendous fun."

"I've only consented because mamma says we owe it to you," the girl went on.

"Never mind your reason—the end justifies the means. I can never thank you enough nor tell you what a weight it lifts off my shoulders. Do you know I feel the difference already?—a peace that passeth understanding!" Mary replied that this was childish; how could such a feeble fiction last? At the very best it could live but an hour, and then he would be no better off than before. It would bristle moreover with difficulties and absurdities; it would be so much more trouble than it was worth. She reminded him that so ridiculous a service had never been asked of any girl, and at this he seemed a little struck; he said: "Ah, well, if it's positively disagreeable to you we'll instantly drop the idea. But I—I thought you really liked me enough——!" She turned away impatiently, and he went on to argue imperturbably that she had always treated him in the kindest way in the world. He added that the worst was over, the start, they were off: the thing would be in all the evening papers. Wasn't it much simpler to accept it? That was all they would have to do; and all *she* would have to do would be not to gainsay it and to smile and thank people when she was congratulated. She would have to *act* a little, but that would just be part of the fun. Oh, he hadn't the shadow of a scruple about taking the world in; the world deserved it richly, and she couldn't deny that this was what she had felt for him, that she had really been moved to compassion. He grew eloquent and charged her with having recognised in his predicament a genuine motive for charity. Their little plot would last what it could—it would be a part of their amusement to *make* it last. Even if it should be but a thing of a day there would have been always so much gained. But they would be ingenious, they would find ways, they would have no end of sport.

"*You* must be ingenious; I can't," said Mary. "If people scarcely ever see us together they'll guess we're trying to humbug them."

"But they *will* see us together. We *are* together. We've been together—I mean we've seen a lot of each other—all our lives."

"Ah, not *that* way!"

"Oh, trust me to work it right!" cried the young man, whose imagination had now evidently begun to glow in the air of their pious fraud.

"You'll find it a dreadful bore," said Mary Gosselin.

"Then I'll drop it, don't you see? And *you*'ll drop it, of course, the moment *you*'ve had enough," Lord Beaupré punctually added. "But as soon as you begin to realise what a lot of good you do me you won't *want* to drop it. That is if you're what I take you for!" laughed his lordship.

If a third person had been present at this conversation—and there was nothing in it surely that might not have been spoken before a trusty listener—that person would perhaps have thought, from the immediate expression of Mary Gosselin's face, that she was on the point of exclaiming "You take me for too big a fool!" No such ungracious words in fact however passed her lips; she only said after an instant: "What reason do you propose to give, on the day you need one, for our rupture?"

Her interlocutor stared. "To you, do you mean?"

"*I* sha'n't ask you for one. I mean to other people."

"Oh, I'll tell them you're sick of me. I'll put everything on you, and you'll put everything on me."

"You *have* worked it out!" Mary exclaimed.

"Oh, I shall be intensely considerate."

"Do you call that being considerate—publicly accusing me?"

Guy Firminger stared again. "Why, isn't that the reason *you*'ll give?"

She looked at him an instant. "I won't tell you the reason I shall give."

"Oh, I shall learn it from others."

"I hope you'll like it when you do!" said Mary, with sudden gaiety; and she added frankly though kindly the hope that he might soon light upon some young person who would really meet his requirements. He replied that he shouldn't be in a hurry—that was now just the comfort; and she, as if thinking over to the end the list of arguments against his clumsy contrivance, broke out: "And of course you mustn't dream of giving me anything—any tokens or presents."

"Then it won't look natural."

"That's exactly what I say. You can't make it deceive anybody."

"I *must* give you something—something that people can see. There must be some evidence! You can simply put my offerings away after a little and give them back." But about this Mary was visibly serious; she declared that she wouldn't touch anything that came from his hand, and she spoke in such a tone that he coloured a little and hastened to say: "Oh, all right, I shall be thoroughly careful!" This appeared to complete their understanding; so that after it was settled that for the deluded world they *were* engaged, there was obviously nothing for him to do but to go. He therefore shook hands with her very gratefully and departed.

V.

He was able promptly to assure his accomplice that their little plot was working to a charm; it already made such a difference for the better. Only a week had elapsed, but he felt quite another man; his life was no longer spent in springing to arms and he had ceased to sleep in his boots. The ghost of his great fear was laid, he could follow out his inclinations and attend to his neglected affairs. The news had been a bomb in the enemy's camp, and there were plenty of blank faces to testify to the confusion it had wrought. Every one was "sold" and every one made haste to clap him on the back. Lottie Firminger only had written in terms of which no notice could be taken, though of course he expected, every time he came in, to find her waiting in his hall. Her mother was coming up to town and he should have the family at his ears; but, taking them as a single body, he could manage them, and that was a detail. The Ashburys had remained at Bosco till that establishment was favoured with the tidings that so nearly concerned it (they were communicated to Maud's mother by the housekeeper), and then the beautiful sufferer had found in her defeat strength to seek another asylum. The two ladies had departed for a destination unknown; he didn't think they had turned up in London. Guy Firminger averred that there were precious portable objects which he was sure he should miss on returning to his country home.

He came every day to Chester Street, and was evidently much less bored than Mary had prefigured by this regular tribute to verisimilitude. It was amusement enough to see the progress of their comedy and to invent new touches for some of its scenes. The girl herself was amused; it was an opportunity like another for cleverness such as hers and had much in common with private theatricals, especially with the rehearsals, the most amusing part. Moreover she was good-natured enough to be really pleased at the service it was impossible for her not to acknowledge that she had rendered. Each of the parties to this queer contract had anecdotes and suggestions for the other, and each reminded the other duly that they must at every step keep their story straight. Except for the exercise of this care Mary Gosselin found her duties less onerous than she had feared and her part in general much more passive than active. It consisted indeed largely of murmuring thanks and smiling and looking happy and handsome; as well as perhaps also in saying in answer to many questions that nothing as yet was fixed and of trying to remain humble when people expressed without ceremony that such a match was a wonder for such a girl. Her mother on the other hand was devotedly active. She treated the situation with private humour but with public zeal and, making it both real and ideal, told so many fibs about it that there were none left for Mary. The girl had failed to understand Mrs. Gosselin's interest in this elaborate pleasantry; the good lady had seen in it from the first more than she herself had been able to see. Mary performed her task mechanically, sceptically, but Mrs. Gosselin attacked hers with conviction and had really the air at moments of thinking that their fable had crystallised into fact. Mary allowed her as little of this attitude as possible and was ironical about her duplicity; warnings which the elder lady received with gaiety until one day when repetition had made them act on her nerves. Then she begged her daughter, with sudden asperity, not to talk to her as if she were a fool. She had already had words with Hugh about some aspects of the affair—so much as this was evident in Chester Street; a smothered discussion which at the moment had determined the poor boy to go to Paris with Bolton-Brown. The young men came back together after Mary had been "engaged" three weeks, but she remained in ignorance of what passed between Hugh and his mother the night of his return. She had gone to the opera with Lady Whiteroy, after one of her invariable comments on Mrs. Gosselin's invariable remark that of course Guy Firminger would spend his evening in their box. The remedy for his trouble, Lord Beaupré's prospective bride had said, was surely worse than the disease; she was in perfect good faith when she wondered that his lordship's sacrifices, his laborious cultivation of appearances should "pay."

Hugh Gosselin dined with his mother and at dinner talked of Paris and of what he had seen and done there; he kept the conversation superficial and after he had heard how his sister, at the moment, was occupied, asked no question that might have seemed to denote an interest in the success of the experiment for which in going abroad he had declined responsibility. His mother could not help observing that he never mentioned Guy Firminger by either of his names, and it struck her as a part of the same detachment that later, up stairs (she sat with him while he smoked), he should suddenly say as he finished a cigar:

"I return to New York next week."

"Before your time? What for?" Mrs. Gosselin was horrified.

"Oh, mamma, you know what for!"

"Because you still resent poor Mary's good-nature?"

"I don't understand it, and I don't like things I don't understand; therefore I'd rather not be here to see it. Besides I really can't tell a pack of lies."

Mrs. Gosselin exclaimed and protested; she had arguments to prove that there was no call at present for the least deflection from the truth; all that any one had to reply to any question (and there could be none that was embarrassing save the ostensible determination of the date of the marriage) was that nothing was settled as yet—a form of words in which for the life of her she couldn't see any perjury. "Why, then, go in for anything in such bad taste, to culminate only in something so absurd?" Hugh demanded. "If the essential part of the matter can't be spoken of as fixed nothing is fixed, the deception becomes transparent and they give the whole idea away. It's child's play."

"That's why it's so innocent. All I can tell you is that practically their attitude answers; he's delighted with its success. Those dreadful women have given him up; they've already found some other victim."

"And how is it all to end, please?"

Mrs. Gosselin was silent a moment. "Perhaps it won't end."

"Do you mean that the engagement will become real?"

Again the good lady said nothing until she broke out: "My dear boy, can't you trust your poor old mummy?"

"Is *that* your speculation? Is that Mary's? I never heard of anything so odious!" Hugh Gosselin cried. But she defended his sister with eagerness, with a gloss of coaxing, maternal indignation, declaring that Mary's disinterestedness was complete—she had the perfect proof of it. Hugh was conscious as he lighted another cigar that the conversation was more fundamental than any that he had ever had with his mother, who however hung fire but for an instant when he asked her what this "perfect proof" might be. He didn't doubt of his sister, he admitted that; but the perfect proof would make the whole thing more luminous. It took finally the form of a confession from Mrs. Gosselin that the girl evidently liked—well, greatly liked—Mr. Bolton-Brown. Yes, the good lady had seen for herself at Bosco that the smooth young American was making up to her and that, time and opportunity aiding, something might very well happen which could not be regarded as satisfactory. She had been very frank with Mary, had besought her not to commit herself to a suitor who in the very nature of the case couldn't meet the most legitimate of their views. Mary, who pretended not to know what their "views" were, had denied that she was in danger; but Mrs. Gosselin had assured her that she had all the air of it and had said triumphantly: "Agree to what Lord Beaupré asks of you, and I'll *believe* you." Mary had wished to be believed—so she had agreed. That was all the witchcraft any one had used.

Mrs. Gosselin out-talked her son, but there were two or three plain questions that he came back to; and the first of these bore upon the ground of her aversion to poor Bolton-Brown. He told her again, as he had told her before, that his friend was that rare bird a maker of money who was also a man of culture. He was a gentleman to his finger-tips, accomplished, capable, kind, with a charming mother and two lovely sisters (she should see them!) the sort of fellow in short whom it was stupid not to appreciate.

"I believe it all, and if I had three daughters he should be very welcome to one of them."

"You might easily have had three daughters who wouldn't attract him at all! You've had the good fortune to have one who does, and I think you do wrong to interfere with it."

"My eggs are in one basket then, and that's a reason the more for preferring Lord Beaupré," said Mrs. Gosselin.

"Then it *is* your calculation—?" stammered Hugh in dismay; on which she coloured and requested that he would be a little less rough with his mother. She would rather part with him immediately, sad as that would be, than that he should attempt to undo what she had done. When Hugh replied that it was not to Mary but to Beaupré himself that he judged it important he should speak, she informed him that a rash remonstrance might do his sister a cruel wrong. Dear Guy was *most* attentive.

"If you mean that he really cares for her there's the less excuse for his taking such a liberty with her. He's either in love with her or he isn't. If he is, let him make her a serious offer; if he isn't, let him leave her alone."

Mrs. Gosselin looked at her son with a kind of patient joy. "He's in love with her, but he doesn't know it."

"He ought to know it, and if he's so idiotic I don't see that we ought to consider him."

"Don't worry—he *shall* know it!" Mrs. Gosselin cried; and, continuing to struggle with Hugh, she insisted on the delicacy of the situation. She made a certain impression on him, though on confused grounds; she spoke at one moment as if he was to forbear because the matter was a make-believe that happened to contain a convenience for a distressed friend, and at another as if one ought to strain a point because there were great possibilities at stake. She was most lucid when she pictured the social position and other advantages of a peer of the realm. What had those of an American stockbroker, however amiable and with whatever shrill belongings in the background, to compare with them? She was inconsistent, but she was diplomatic, and the result of the discussion was that Hugh Gosselin became conscious of a dread of "injuring" his sister. He became conscious at the same time of a still greater apprehension, that of seeing her arrive at the agreeable in a tortuous, a second-rate manner. He might keep the peace to please his mother, but he couldn't enjoy it, and he actually took his departure, travelling in company with Bolton-Brown, who of course before going waited on the ladies in Chester Street to thank them for the kindness they had shown him. It couldn't be kept from Guy Firminger that Hugh was not happy, though when they met, which was only once or twice before he quitted London, Mary Gosselin's brother flattered himself that he was too proud to show it. He had always liked old loafing Guy and it was disagreeable to him not to like him now; but he was aware that he must either quarrel with him definitely or not at all and that he had passed his word to his mother. Therefore his attitude was strictly negative; he took with the parties to it no notice whatever of the "engagement," and he couldn't help it if to other people he had the air of not being initiated. They doubtless thought him strangely fastidious. Perhaps he was; the tone of London struck him in some respects as very horrid; he had grown in a manner away from it. Mary was impenetrable; tender, gay, charming, but with no patience, as she said, for his premature flight. Except when Lord Beaupré was present you would not have dreamed that he existed for her. In his company—he had to be present more or less of course—she was simply like any other English girl who disliked effusiveness. They had each the same manner, that of persons of rather a shy tradition who were on their guard against public "spooning." They practised their fraud with good taste, a good taste mystifying to Bolton-Brown, who thought their precautions excessive. When he took leave of Mary Gosselin her eyes consented for

a moment to look deep down into his. He had been from the
first of the opinion that they were beautiful, and he was more
mystified than ever.

   If Guy Firminger had failed to ask Hugh Gosselin whether
he had a fault to find with what they were doing, this was, in
spite of old friendship, simply because he was too happy now
to care much whom he didn't please, to care at any rate for
criticism. He had ceased to be critical himself, and his high
prosperity could take his blamelessness for granted. His happiness would have been offensive if people generally hadn't
liked him, for it consisted of a kind of monstrous candid comfort. To take all sorts of things for granted was still his great,
his delightful characteristic; but it didn't prevent his showing
imagination and tact and taste in particular circumstances. He
made, in their little comedy, all the right jokes and none of
the wrong ones: the girl had an acute sense that there were
some jokes that would have been detestable. She gathered that
it was universally supposed she was having an unprecedented
season, and something of the glory of an enviable future
seemed indeed to hang about her. People no doubt thought
it odd that she didn't go about more with her future husband;
but those who knew anything about her knew that she had
never done exactly as other girls did. She had her own ways,
her own freedoms and her own scruples. Certainly he made
the London weeks much richer than they had ever been for a
subordinate young person; he put more things into them, so
that they grew dense and complicated. This frightened her at
moments, especially when she thought with compunction that
she was deceiving her very friends. She didn't mind taking the
vulgar world in, but there were people she hated not to enlighten, to reassure. She could undeceive no one now, and
indeed she would have been ashamed. There were hours when
she wanted to stop—she had such a dread of doing too much;
hours when she thought with dismay that the fiction of the
rupture was still to come, with its horrid train of new untrue
things. She spoke of it repeatedly to her confederate, who only
postponed and postponed, told her she would never dream of
forsaking him if she measured the good she was doing him.
She did measure it however when she met him in the great
world; she was of course always meeting him: that was the

only way appearances were kept up. There was a certain attitude she could allow him to take on these occasions; it covered and carried off their subterfuge. He could talk to her unmolested; for herself she never spoke of anything but the charming girls, everywhere present, among whom he could freely choose. He didn't protest, because to choose freely was what he wanted, and they discussed these young ladies one by one. Some she recommended, some she disparaged, but it was almost the only subject she tolerated. It was her system in short, and she wondered he didn't get tired of it; she was so tired of it herself.

She tried other things that she thought he might find wearisome, but his good-humour was magnificent. He was now really for the first time enjoying his promotion, his wealth, his insight into the terms on which the world offered itself to the happy few, and these terms made a mixture healing to irritation. Once, at some glittering ball, he asked her if she should be jealous if he were to dance again with Lady Whiteroy, with whom he had danced already, and this was the only occasion on which he had come near making a joke of the wrong sort. She showed him what she thought of it and made him feel that the way to be forgiven was to spend the rest of the evening with that lovely creature. Now that the phalanx of the pressingly nubile was held in check there was accordingly nothing to prevent his passing his time pleasantly. Before he had taken this effective way the diplomatic mother, when she spied him flirting with a married woman, felt that in urging a virgin daughter's superior claims she worked for righteousness as well as for the poor girl. But Mary Gosselin protected these scandals practically by the still greater scandal of her indifference; so that he was in the odd position of having waited to be confined to know what it was to be at large. He had in other words the maximum of security with the minimum of privation. The lovely creatures of Lady Whiteroy's order thought Mary Gosselin charming, but they were the first to see through her falsity.

All this carried our precious pair to the middle of July; but nearly a month before that, one night under the summer stars, on the deck of the steamer that was to reach New York on the morrow, something had passed between Hugh Gosselin and his brooding American friend. The night was warm and splendid; these were their last hours at sea, and Hugh, who had been playing whist in the cabin, came up very late to take an observation before turning in. It was in this way that he chanced on his companion, who was leaning over the stern of the ship and gazing off, beyond its phosphorescent track, at the muffled, moaning ocean, the backward darkness, everything he had relinquished. Hugh stood by him for a moment and then asked him what he was thinking about. Bolton-Brown gave at first no answer; after which he turned round and, with his back against the guard of the deck, looked up at the multiplied stars. "He has it badly," Hugh Gosselin mentally commented. At last his friend replied: "About something you said yesterday."

"I forget what I said yesterday."

"You spoke of your sister's intended marriage; it was the only time you had spoken of it. You seemed to intimate that it might not after all take place."

Hugh hesitated a little. "Well, it *won't* take place. They're not engaged, not really. This is a secret, a preposterous secret. I wouldn't tell any one else, but I'm willing to tell *you*. It may make a difference to you."

Bolton-Brown turned his head; he looked at Hugh a minute through the fresh darkness. "It does make a difference to me. But I don't understand," he added.

"Neither do I. I don't like it. It's a pretence, a temporary make-believe, to help Beaupré through."

"Through what?"

"He's so run after."

The young American stared, ejaculated, mused. "Oh, yes—your mother told me."

"It's a sort of invention of my mother's and a notion of his own (very absurd, I think) till he can see his way. Mary serves as a kind of escort for these first exposed months. It's ridiculous, but I don't know that it hurts her."

"Oh!" said Bolton-Brown.

"I don't know either that it does her any good."

"No!" said Bolton-Brown. Then he added: "It's certainly very kind of her."

"It's a case of old friends," Hugh explained, inadequately as he felt. "He has always been in and out of our house."

"But how will it end?"

"I haven't the least idea."

Bolton-Brown was silent; he faced about to the stern again and stared at the rush of the ship. Then shifting his position once more: "Won't the engagement, before they've done, develop into the regular thing?"

Hugh felt as if his mother were listening. "I daresay not. If there were even a remote chance of that, Mary wouldn't have consented."

"But mayn't *he* easily find that—charming as she is—he's in love with her?"

"He's too much taken up with himself."

"That's just a reason," said Bolton-Brown. "Love is selfish." He considered a moment longer, then he went on: "And mayn't *she* find—?"

"Find what?" said Hugh, as he hesitated.

"Why, that she likes him."

"She likes him of course, else she wouldn't have come to his assistance. But her certainty about herself must have been just what made her not object to lending herself to the arrangement. She could do it decently because she doesn't seriously care for him. If she did—!" Hugh suddenly stopped.

"If she did?" his friend repeated.

"It would have been odious."

"I see," said Bolton-Brown gently. "But how will they break off?"

"It will be Mary who'll break off."

"Perhaps she'll find it difficult."

"She'll require a pretext."

"I see," mused Bolton-Brown, shifting his position again.

"She'll find one," Hugh declared.

"I hope so," his companion responded.

For some minutes neither of them spoke; then Hugh asked: "Are you in love with her?"

"Oh, my dear fellow!" Bolton-Brown wailed. He instantly added: "Will it be any use for me to go back?"

Again Hugh felt as if his mother were listening. But he answered: "*Do* go back."

"It's awfully strange," said Bolton-Brown. "I'll go back."

"You had better wait a couple of months, you know."

"Mayn't I lose her then?"

"No—they'll drop it all."

"I'll go back!" the American repeated, as if he hadn't heard. He was restless, agitated; he had evidently been much affected. He fidgeted away dimly, moved up the level length of the deck. Hugh Gosselin lingered longer at the stern; he fell into the attitude in which he had found the other, leaning over it and looking back at the great vague distance they had come. He thought of his mother.

VI.

To remind her fond parent of the vanity of certain expectations which she more than suspected her of entertaining, Mary Gosselin, while she felt herself intensely watched (it had all brought about a horrid new situation at home) produced every day some fresh illustration of the fact that people were no longer imposed upon. Moreover these illustrations were not invented; the girl believed in them, and when once she had begun to note them she saw them multiply fast. Lady Whiteroy, for one, was distinctly suspicious; she had taken the liberty more than once of asking the future Lady Beaupré what in the world was the matter with her. Brilliant figure as she was and occupied with her own pleasures, which were of a very independent nature, she had nevertheless constituted herself Miss Gosselin's social sponsor: she took a particular interest in her marriage, an interest all the greater as it rested not only on a freely-professed regard for her, but on a keen sympathy with the other party to the transaction. Lady Whiteroy, who was very pretty and very clever and whom Mary secretly but profoundly mistrusted, delighted in them both in short; so much so that Mary judged herself happy to be in a false position, so certain should she have been to be jealous had she been in a true one. This charming woman threw out inquiries that made the girl not care to meet her eyes; and Mary ended by forming a theory of the sort of marriage for Lord Beaupré that Lady Whiteroy really would have appreciated. It would have been a marriage to a fool, a marriage to Maud Ashbury or to Charlotte Firminger. She would have her reasons for preferring that; and, as regarded the actual prospect, she had only discovered that Mary was even more astute than herself.

It will be understood how much our young lady was on the crest of the wave when I mention that in spite of this complicated consciousness she was one of the ornaments (Guy Firminger was of course another) of the party entertained by her zealous friend and Lord Whiteroy during the Goodwood week. She came back to town with the firm intention of putting an end to a comedy which had more than ever become odious to her; in consequence of which she had on this subject with her fellow-comedian a scene—the scene she had dreaded—half-pathetic, half-ridiculous. He appealed to her, wrestled with her, took his usual ground that she was saving his life without really lifting a finger. He denied that the public was not satisfied with their pretexts for postponement, their explanations of delay; what else was expected of a man who would wish to celebrate his nuptials on a suitable scale, but who had the misfortune to have had, one after another, three grievous bereavements? He promised not to molest her for the next three months, to go away till his "mourning" was over, to go abroad, to let her do as she liked. He wouldn't come near her, he wouldn't even write (no one would know it), if she would let him keep up the mere form of their fiction; and he would let her off the very first instant he definitely perceived that this expedient had ceased to be effective. She couldn't judge of that—she must let *him* judge; and it was a matter in which she could surely trust to his honour.

Mary Gosselin trusted to it, but she insisted on his going away. When he took such a tone as that she couldn't help being moved; he breathed with such frank, generous lips on the irritation she had stored up against him. Guy Firminger went to Homburg, and if his confederate consented not to clip the slender thread by which this particular engagement still hung, she made very short work with every other. A dozen invitations, for Cowes, for the country, for Scotland, shimmered there before her, made a pathway of flowers, but she sent barbarous excuses. When her mother, aghast, said to her "What then will you do?" she replied in a very conclusive manner "I'll go home!" Mrs. Gosselin was wise enough not to struggle; she saw that the thread was delicate, that it must dangle in quiet air. She therefore travelled back with her daughter to homely Hampshire, feeling that they were people of less importance than they had been for many a week. On the August afternoons they sat again on the little lawn on which Guy Firminger had found them the day he first became eloquent about the perils of the desirable young bachelor; and it was on this very spot that, toward the end of the month, and with some surprise, they beheld Mr. Bolton-Brown once more approach. He had come back from America; he had arrived but a few days before; he was staying, of all places in the world, at the inn in the village.

His explanation of this caprice was of all explanations the oddest: he had come three thousand miles for the love of water-colour. There was nothing more sketchable than the sketchability of Hampshire—wasn't it celebrated, classic? and he was so good as to include Mrs. Gosselin's charming premises, and even their charming occupants, in his view of the field. He fell to work with speed, with a sort of feverish eagerness; he seemed possessed indeed by the frenzy of the brush. He sketched everything on the place, and when he had represented an object once he went straight at it again. His advent was soothing to Mary Gosselin, in spite of his nervous activity; it must be admitted indeed that at the moment he arrived she had already felt herself in quieter waters. The August afternoons, the relinquishment of London, the simplified life, had rendered her a service which, if she had freely qualified it, she would have described as a restoration of her self-respect. If poor Guy found any profit in such conditions as these there was no great reason to repudiate him. She had so completely shaken off responsibility that she took scarcely more than a languid interest in the fact, communicated to her by Lady Whiteroy, that Charlotte Firminger had also, as the newspapers said, "proceeded" to Homburg. Lady Whiteroy knew, for Lady Whiteroy had "proceeded" as well; her physician had discovered in her constitution a pressing need for the comfort imbibed in dripping matutinal tumblers. She chronicled Charlotte's presence, and even to some extent her behaviour, among the haunters of the spring, but it was not till some time afterwards that Mary learned how Miss Firminger's pilgrimage had been made under her ladyship's protection. This was a further sign that, like Mrs. Gosselin, Lady Whiteroy had ceased to struggle; she had, in town, only shrugged her shoulders ambiguously on being informed that Lord Beaupré's intended was going down to her stupid home.

The fulness of Mrs. Gosselin's renunciation was apparent during the stay of the young American in the neighbourhood of that retreat. She occupied herself with her knitting, her garden and the cares of a punctilious hospitality, but she had no appearance of any other occupation. When people came to tea Bolton-Brown was always there, and she had the self-control to attempt to say nothing that could assuage their natural surprise. Mrs. Ashbury came one day with poor Maud, and the two elder ladies, as they had done more than once before, looked for some moments into each other's eyes. This time it was not a look of defiance, it was rather—or it would have been for an observer completely in the secret—a look of reciprocity, of fraternity, a look of arrangement. There was however no one completely in the secret save perhaps Mary, and Mary didn't heed. The arrangement at any rate was ineffectual; Mrs. Gosselin might mutely say, over the young American's eager, talkative shoulders, "Yes, you may have him if you can get him:" the most rudimentary experiments demonstrated that he was not to be got. Nothing passed on this subject between Mary and her mother, whom the girl none the less knew to be holding her breath and continuing to watch. She counted it more and more as one unpleasant result of her conspiracy with Guy Firminger that it almost poisoned a relation that had always been sweet. It was to show that she was independent of it that she did as she liked now, which was almost always as Bolton-Brown liked. When in the first days of September—it was in the warm, clear twilight, and they happened, amid the scent of fresh hay, to be leaning side by side on a stile—he gave her a view of the fundamental and esoteric, as distinguished from the convenient and superficial motive of his having come back to England, she of course made no allusion to a prior tie. On the other hand she insisted on his going up to London by the first train the next day. He was to wait—that was distinctly understood—for his satisfaction.

She desired meanwhile to write immediately to Guy Firminger, but as he had kept his promise of not complicating their contract with letters she was uncertain as to his actual whereabouts: she was only sure he would have left Homburg. Lady Whiteroy had become silent, so there were no more sidelights, and she was on the point of telegraphing to London for an address when she received a telegram from Bosco. The proprietor of that seat had arrived there the day before, and he found he could make trains fit if she would on the morrow allow him to come over and see her for a day or two. He had returned sooner than their agreement allowed, but she answered "Come" and she showed his missive to her mother, who at the sight of it wept with strange passion. Mary said to her "For heaven's sake, don't let him see you!" She lost no time; she told him on the morrow as soon as he entered the house that she couldn't keep it up another hour.

"All right—it *is* no use," he conceded; "they're at it again!"

"You see you've gained nothing!" she replied triumphantly. She had instantly recognised that he was different, how much had happened.

"I've gained some of the happiest days of my life."

"Oh, that was not what you tried for!"

"Indeed it was, and I got exactly what I wanted," said Guy Firminger. They were in the cool little drawing-room where the morning light was dim. Guy Firminger had a sunburnt appearance, as in England people returning from other countries are apt to have, and Mary thought he had never looked so well. It was odd, but it was noticeable, that he had grown much handsomer since he had become a personage. He paused a moment, smiling at her while her mysterious eyes rested on him, and then he added: "Nothing ever worked better. It's no use now—people see. But I've got a start. I wanted to turn round and look about, and I *have* turned round and looked about. There are things I've escaped. I'm afraid you'll never understand how deeply I'm indebted to you."

"Oh, it's all right!" said Mary Gosselin.

There was another short silence, after which he went on: "I've come back sooner than I promised, but only to be strictly fair. I began to see that we couldn't hold out and that it was my duty to let you off. From that moment I was bound to put an end to your situation. I might have done so by letter, but that seemed scarcely decent. It's all I came back for, you know, and it's why I wired to you yesterday."

Mary hesitated an instant, she reflected intensely. What had happened, what would happen, was that if she didn't take care the signal for the end of their little arrangement would not have appeared to come from herself. She particularly wished it not to come from anyone else, she had even a horror of that; so that after an instant she hastened to say: "I was on the very point of wiring to *you*—I was only waiting for your address."

"Wiring to me?" He seemed rather blank.

"To tell you that our absurd affair really, this time, can't go on another day—to put a complete stop to it."

"Oh!" said Guy Firminger.

"So it's all right."

"You've always hated it!" Guy laughed; and his laugh sounded slightly foolish to the girl.

"I found yesterday that I hated it more than ever."

Lord Beaupré showed a quickened attention. "For what reason—yesterday?"

"I would rather not tell you, please. Perhaps some time you'll find it out."

He continued to look at her brightly and fixedly with his confused cheerfulness. Then he said with a vague, courteous alacrity: "I see, I see!" She had an impression that he didn't see; but it didn't matter, she was nervous and quite preferred that he shouldn't. They both got up, and in a moment he exclaimed: "Well, I'm intensely sorry it's over! It has been so charming."

"You've been very good about it; I mean very reasonable," Mary said, to say something. Then she felt in her nervousness that this was just what she ought not to have said: it sounded ironical and provoking, whereas she had meant it as pure good-nature. "Of course you'll stay to luncheon?" she continued. She was bound in common hospitality to speak of that, and he answered that it would give him the greatest pleasure. After this her apprehension increased, and it was confirmed in particular by the manner in which he suddenly asked:

"By the way, what reason shall we give?"

"What reason?"

"For our rupture. Don't let us seem to have quarrelled."

"We can't help that," said Mary. "Nothing else will account for our behaviour."

"Well, I sha'n't say anything about *you*."

"Do you mean you'll let people think it was yourself who were tired of it?"

"I mean I sha'n't *blame* you."

"You ought to behave as if you cared!" said Mary.

Guy Firminger laughed, but he looked worried and he evidently was puzzled. "You must act as if you had jilted me."

"You're not the sort of person unfortunately that people jilt."

Lord Beaupré appeared to accept this statement as incontestable; not with elation however, but with candid regret, the slightly embarrassed recognition of a fundamental obstacle. "Well, it's no one's business, at any rate, is it?"

"No one's, and that's what I shall say if people question me. Besides," Mary added, "they'll see for themselves."

"What will they see?"

"I mean they'll understand. And now we had better join mamma."

It was his evident inclination to linger in the room after he had said this that gave her complete alarm. Mrs. Gosselin was in another room, in which she sat in the morning, and Mary moved in that direction, pausing only in the hall for him to accompany her. She wished to get him into the presence of a third person. In the hall he joined her, and in doing so laid his hand gently on her arm. Then looking into her eyes with all the pleasantness of his honesty, he said: "It will be very easy for me to appear to care—for I *shall* care. I shall care immensely!" Lord Beaupré added smiling.

Anything, it struck her, was better than that—than that he should say: "We'll keep on, if you like (*I* should!) only this time it will be serious. Hold me to it—do; don't let me go; lead me on to the altar—really!" Some such words as these, she believed, were rising to his lips, and she had an insurmountable horror of hearing them. It was as if, well enough meant on *his* part, they would do her a sort of dishonour, so that all her impulse was quickly to avert them. That was not the way she wanted to be asked in marriage. "Thank you very

much," she said, "but it doesn't in the least matter. You will
seem to have been jilted—so it's all right!"

"All right! You mean—?" He hesitated, he had coloured a
little: his eyes questioned her.

"I'm engaged to be married—in earnest."

"Oh!" said Lord Beaupré.

"You asked me just now if I had a special reason for having
been on the point of telegraphing to you, and I said I had.
That was my special reason."

"I see!" said Lord Beaupré. He looked grave for a few seconds, then he gave an awkward smile. But he behaved with
perfect tact and discretion, didn't even ask her who the gentleman in the case might be. He congratulated her in the dark,
as it were, and if the effect of this was indeed a little odd she
liked him for his quick perception of the fine fitness of pulling
up short. Besides, he extracted the name of the gentleman
soon enough from her mother, in whose company they now
immediately found themselves. Mary left Guy Firminger with
the good lady for half an hour before luncheon; and when the
girl came back it was to observe that she had been crying
again. It was dreadful—what she might have been saying.
Their guest, however, at luncheon was not lachrymose; he was
natural, but he was talkative and gay. Mary liked the way he
now behaved, and more particularly the way he departed immediately after the meal. As soon as he was gone Mrs. Gosselin broke out suppliantly: "Mary!" But her daughter replied:

"I know, mamma, perfectly what you're going to say, and
if you attempt to say it I shall leave the room." With this
threat (day after day, for the following time) she kept the terrible appeal unuttered until it was too late for an appeal to be
of use. That afternoon she wrote to Bolton-Brown that she
accepted his offer of marriage.

Guy Firminger departed altogether; he went abroad again
and to far countries. He was therefore not able to be present
at the nuptials of Miss Gosselin and the young American
whom he had entertained at Bosco, which took place in the
middle of November. Had he been in England however he
probably would have felt impelled by a due regard for past
verisimilitude to abstain from giving his countenance to such
an occasion. His absence from the country contributed to the

needed even if astonishing effect of his having been jilted; so, likewise, did the reputed vastness of Bolton-Brown's young income, which in London was grossly exaggerated. Hugh Gosselin had perhaps a little to do with this; as he had sacrificed a part of his summer holiday, he got another month and came out to his sister's wedding. He took public comfort in his brother-in-law; nevertheless he listened with attention to a curious communication made him by his mother after the young couple had started for Italy; even to the point of bringing out the inquiry (in answer to her assertion that poor Guy had been ready to place everything he had at Mary's feet): "Then why the devil didn't he do it?"

"From simple delicacy! He didn't want to make her feel as if she had lent herself to an artifice only on purpose to get hold of him—to treat her as if she too had been at bottom one of the very harpies she helped him to elude."

Hugh thought a moment. "That *was* delicate."

"He's the dearest creature in the world. He's on his guard, he's prudent, he tested himself by separation. Then he came back to England in love with her. She might have had it all!"

"I'm glad she didn't get it *that* way."

"She had only to wait—to put an end to their artifice, harmless as it was, for the present, but still wait. She might have broken off in a way that would have made it come on again better."

"That's exactly what she didn't want."

"I mean as a quite separate incident," said Mrs. Gosselin.

"*I* loathed their artifice, harmless as it was!" her son observed.

Mrs. Gosselin for a moment made no answer; then she turned away from the fire into which she had been pensively gazing with the ejaculation "Poor dear Guy!"

"I can't for the life of me see that he's to be pitied."

"He'll marry Charlotte Firminger."

"If he's such an ass as that it's his own affair."

"Bessie Whiteroy will bring it about."

"What has *she* to do with it?"

"She wants to get hold of him."

"Then why will she marry him to another woman?"

"Because in that way she can select the other—a woman he won't care for. It will keep him from taking some one that's nicer."

Hugh Gosselin stared—he laughed aloud. "Lord, mamma, you're deep!"

"Indeed I am, I see much more."

"What do you see?"

"Mary won't in the least care for America. Don't tell me she will," Mrs. Gosselin added, "for you know perfectly you don't believe it."

"She'll care for her husband, she'll care for everything that concerns him."

"He's very nice, in his little way he's delightful. But as an alternative to Lord Beaupré he's ridiculous!"

"Mary's in a position in which she has nothing to do with alternatives."

"For the present, yes, but not for ever. She'll have enough of your New York; they'll come back here. I see the future dark," Mrs. Gosselin pursued, inexorably musing.

"Tell me then all you see."

"She'll find poor Guy wretchedly married, and she'll be very sorry for him."

"Do you mean that he'll make love to her? You give a queer account of your paragon."

"He'll value her sympathy. I see life as it is."

"You give a queer account of your daughter."

"I don't give any account. She'll behave perfectly," Mrs. Gosselin somewhat inconsequently subjoined.

"Then what are you afraid of?"

"She'll be sorry for him, and it will be all a worry."

"A worry to whom?"

The good lady was silent a moment. "To me," she replied, "And to you as well."

"Then they mustn't come back."

"That will be a greater worry still."

"Surely not a greater—a smaller. We'll put up with the lesser evil."

"Nothing will prevent her coming to a sense, eventually, of what *might* have been. And when they *both* recognize it——"

"It will be very dreadful!" Hugh exclaimed, completing gaily his mother's phrase. "I don't see, however," he added, "what in all this you do with Bessie Whiteroy."

"Oh, he'll be tired of her; she's hard, she'll have become despotic. I see life as it is," the good lady repeated.

"Then all I can say is that it's not very nice! But they sha'n't come back: *I'll* attend to that!" said Hugh Gosselin, who has attended to it up to this time successfully, though the rest of his mother's prophecy is so far accomplished (it was her second hit) as that Charlotte Firminger is now, strange as it may seem, Lady Beaupré.

The Visits

THE OTHER DAY, after her death, when they were discussing her, someone said in reference to the great number of years she had lived, the people she had seen and the stories she knew: "What a pity no one ever took any notes of her talk!" For a London epitaph that was almost exhaustive, and the subject presently changed. One of the listeners had taken many notes, but he didn't confess it on the spot. The following story is a specimen of my exactitude—I took it down, *verbatim*, having that faculty, the day after I heard it. I choose it, at hazard, among those of her reminiscences that I have preserved; it's not worse than the others. I will give you some of the others too—when occasion offers—so that you may judge.

I met in town that year a dear woman whom I had scarcely seen since I was a girl; she had dropped out of the world; she came up but once in five years. We had been together as very young creatures, and then we had married and gone our ways. It was arranged between us that after I should have paid a certain visit in August in the west of England I would take her—it would be very convenient, she was just over the Cornish border—on the way to my other engagements: I would work her in, as you say nowadays. She wanted immensely to show me her home, and she wanted still more to show me her girl, who had not come up to London, choosing instead, after much deliberation, to go abroad for a month with her brother and her brother's coach—he had been cramming for something—and Mrs. Coach of course. All that Mrs. Chantry had been able to show me in town was her husband, one of those country gentlemen with a moderate property and an old place who are a part of the essence in their own neighbourhood and not a part of anything anywhere else.

A couple of days before my visit to Chantry Court the people to whom I had gone from town took me over to see some friends of theirs who lived, ten miles away, in a place that was supposed to be fine. As it was a long drive we stayed to luncheon; and then as there were gardens and other things that were more or less on show we struggled along to tea, so as to get home just in time for dinner. There were a good many other people present, and before luncheon a very pretty girl came into the drawing-room, a real maiden in her flower, less than twenty, fresh and fair and charming, with the expression of some one I knew. I asked who she was, and was told she was Miss Chantry, so that in a moment I spoke to her, mentioning that I was an old friend of her mother's and that I was coming to pay them a visit. She looked rather frightened and blank, was apparently unable to say that she had ever heard of me, and hinted at no pleasure in the idea that she was to hear of me again. But this didn't prevent my perceiving that she was lovely, for I was wise enough even then not to think it necessary to measure people by the impression that one makes on them. I saw that any I should make on Louisa Chantry would be much too clumsy a test. She had been staying at the house at which I was calling; she had come alone, as the people were old friends and to a certain extent neighbours, and was going home in a few days. It was a daughterless house, but there was inevitable young life: a couple of girls from the vicarage, a married son and his wife, a young man who had "ridden over" and another young man who was staying.

   Louisa Chantry sat opposite to me at luncheon, but too far for conversation, and before we got up I had discovered that if her manner to me had been odd it was not because she was inanimate. She was on the contrary in a state of intense though carefully muffled vibration. There was some fever in her blood, but no one perceived it, no one, that is, with an exception—an exception which was just a part of the very circumstance. This single suspicion was lodged in the breast of the young man whom I have alluded to as staying in the house. He was on the same side of the table as myself and diagonally facing the girl; therefore what I learned about him was for the moment mainly what she told me; meaning by "she" her face, her eyes, her movements, her whole perverted personality. She was extremely on her guard, and I should never have guessed her secret but for an accident. The accident was that the only time she dropped her eyes upon him during the repast I happened to notice it. It might not have been much to notice, but it led to my seeing that there was a little drama going on and that the young man would naturally be the hero. It was equally natural that in this capacity he should be the cause of my asking my left-hand neighbour, who happened to be my host, for some account of him. But "Oh, that fellow? he's my nephew," was a description which, to appear copious, required that I should know more about the uncle.

We had coffee on the terrace of the house; a terrace laid out in one quarter, oddly and charmingly, in grass where the servants who waited upon us seemed to tread, processionally, on soundless velvet. There I had a good look at my host's nephew and a longer talk with my friend's daughter, in regard to whom I had become conscious of a faint, formless anxiety. I remember saying to her, gropingly, instinctively: "My dear child, can I do anything for you? I shall perhaps see your mother before you do. Can I for instance say anything to her *from* you?" This only made her blush and turn away; and it was not till too many days had passed that I guessed that what had looked out at me unwittingly in her little gazing trepidation was something like "Oh, just take me away in spite of myself!" Superficially, conspicuously, there was nothing in the young man to take her away from. He was a person of the middle condition, and save that he didn't look at all humble might have passed for a poor relation. I mean that he had rather a seedy, shabby air, as if he were wearing out old clothes (he had on faded things that didn't match); and I formed vaguely the theory that he was a specimen of the numerous youthful class that goes to seek its fortune in the colonies, keeps strange company there and comes home without a penny. He had a brown, smooth, handsome face, a slightly swaggering, self-conscious ease, and was probably objected to in the house. He hung about, smoking cigarettes on the terrace, and nobody seemed to have much to say to him—a circumstance which, as he managed somehow to convey, left him absolutely indifferent. Louisa Chantry strolled away with one of the girls from the vicarage; the party on the terrace broke up and the nephew disappeared.

It was settled that my friends and I should take leave at half-past five, and I begged to be abandoned in the interval to my devices. I turned into the library and, mounted on ladders, I handled old books and old prints and soiled my gloves. Most of the others had gone to look at the church, and I was left in possession. I wandered into the rooms in which I knew there were pictures; and if the pictures were not good there was some interesting china which I followed from corner to corner and from cabinet to cabinet. At last I found myself on the threshold of a small room which appeared to terminate the series and in which, between the curtains draping the doorways, there appeared to be rows of rare old plates on velvet screens. I was on the point of going in when I became aware that there was something else beside, something which threw me back. Two persons were standing side by side at the window, looking out together with their backs to me—two persons as to whom I immediately felt that they believed themselves to be alone and unwatched. One of them was Louisa Chantry, the other was the young man whom my host had described as his nephew. They were so placed as not to see me, and when I recognized them I checked myself instinctively. I hesitated a moment; then I turned away altogether. I can't tell you why, except that if I had gone in I should have had somehow the air of discovering them. There was no visible reason why they should have been embarrassed by discovery, inasmuch as, so far as I could see, they were doing no harm, were only standing more or less together, without touching, and for the moment apparently saying nothing. Were they watching something out of the window? I don't know; all I know is that the observation I had made at luncheon gave me a sense of responsibility. I might have taken my responsibility the other way and broken up their communion; but I didn't feel this to be sufficiently my business. Later on I wished I had.

I passed through the rooms again, and then out of the house. The gardens were ingenious, but they made me think (I have always that conceited habit) how much cleverer *I* should have been about them. Presently I met several of the rest of the party coming back from the church; on which my hostess took possession of me, declaring there was a point of view I must absolutely be treated to. I saw she was a walking woman and that this meant half a mile in the park. But I was good for that, and we wandered off together while the others returned to the house. It was present to me that I ought to ask my companion, for Helen Chantry's sake, a question about Louisa—whether for instance she had happened to notice the way the girl seemed to be going. But it was difficult to say anything without saying too much; so that to begin with I merely risked the observation that our young friend was remarkably pretty. As the point admitted of no discussion this didn't take us very far; nor was the subject much enlarged by our unanimity as to the fact that she was also remarkably nice. I observed that I had had very little chance to talk with her, for which I was sorry, having known her mother for years. My hostess, at this, looked vaguely round, as if she had missed her for the first time. "Sure enough, she has not been about. I daresay she's been writing to her mother—she's always writing to her mother." "Not always," I mentally reflected; but I waited discreetly, admiring everything and rising to the occasion and the views, before I inquired casually who the young man might be who had sat two or three below me at luncheon—the rather good-looking young man, with the regular features and the brownish clothes—not the one with the moustache.

"Oh, poor Jack Brandon," said my companion, in a tone calculated to make him seem no one in particular.

"Is he very poor?" I asked, with a laugh.

"Oh dear, yes. There are nine of them fancy!—all boys; and there's nothing for anyone but the eldest. He's my husband's nephew—his poor mother's my sister-in-law. He sometimes turns up here when he has nothing better to do; but I don't think he likes us much." I saw she meant that they didn't like *him*; and I exposed myself to suspicion by asking if he had been with them long. But my friend was not very plastic, and she simplified my whole theory of the case by replying after she had thought a moment that she wasn't clear about it—she thought he had come only the morning before. It seemed to me I could safely feel a little further, so I inquired if he were likely to stay many days. "Oh dear, no; he'll go to-morrow!" said my hostess. There was nothing whatever to show that she saw a connection between my odd interest in Mr. Brandon and the subject of our former reference; there was only a quick lucidity on the subject of the young man's departure. It reassured me, for no great complications would have arisen in forty-eight hours.

In retracing our steps we passed again through a part of the gardens. Just after we had entered them my hostess, begging me to excuse her, called at a man who was raking leaves to ask him a question about his wife. I heard him reply "Oh, she's very bad, my lady," and I followed my course. Presently my lady turned round with him, as if to go to see his wife, who apparently was ill and on the place. I continued to look about me—there were such charming things; and at the end of five minutes I missed my way—I had not taken the direction of the house. Suddenly at the turn of a walk, the angle of a great clipped hedge, I found myself face to face with Jack Brandon. He was moving rapidly, looking down, with his hands in his pockets, and he started and stared at me a moment. I said "Oh, how d'ye do?" and I was on the point of adding "Won't you kindly show me the right way?" But with a summary salute and a queer expression of face he had already passed me. I looked after him an instant and I all but stopped him; then one of the faintest voices of the air told me that Louisa Chantry would not be far off, that in fact if I were to go on a few steps I should find her. I continued and I passed through an arched aperture of the hedge, a kind of door in the partition. This corner of the place was like an old French garden, a little inclosed apartment, with statues set into the niches of the high walls of verdure. I paused in admiration; then just opposite to me I saw poor Louisa. She was on a bench, with her hands clasped in her lap, her head bent, her eyes staring down before her. I advanced on the grass, attracting her attention; and I was close to her before she looked at me, before she sprang up and showed me a face convulsed with nameless pain. She was so pale that I thought she was ill—I had a vision of her companion's having rushed off for help. She stood gazing at me with expanded eyes and parted lips, and what I was mainly conscious of was that she had become ten years older. Whatever troubled her it was something pitiful—something that prompted me to hold out my two hands to her and exclaim tenderly "My poor child, my poor child!" She wavered a moment, as if she wanted to escape me but couldn't trust herself to run; she looked away from me, turning her head this way and that. Then as I went close to her she covered her face with her two hands, she let me lay mine upon her and draw her to my breast. As she dropped her head upon it she burst into tears, sobbing soundlessly and tragically. I asked her no question, I only held her so long as she would, letting her pour out the passion which I felt at the same time she made a tremendous effort to smother. She couldn't smother it, but she could break away violently; and this she quickly did, hurrying out of the nook where our little scene—and some other greater scene, I judged, just before it—had taken place, and leaving me infinitely mystified. I sat down on the bench a moment and thought it over; then I succeeded in discovering a path to the house.

The carriage was at the door for our drive home, but my companions, who had had tea, were waiting for our hostess, of whom they wished to take leave and who had not yet come in. I reported her as engaged with the wife of one of the gardeners, but we lingered a little in the hall, a largeish group, to give her time to arrive. Two other persons were absent, one of whom was Louisa Chantry and the other the young man whom I had just seen quitting her in the garden. While I sat there, a trifle abstracted, still somewhat agitated by the sequel to that incident and at the same time impatient of our last vague dawdle, one of the footmen presented me with a little folded note. I turned away to open it, and at the very moment our hostess fortunately came in. This diverted the attention of the others from the action of the footman, whom, after I had looked at the note, I immediately followed into the drawing-room. He led me through it and through two or three others to the door of the little retreat in which, nearly an hour before, I had come upon Louisa Chantry and Mr. Brandon. The note was from Louisa, it contained the simple words "Would you very kindly speak to me an instant before you go?" She was waiting for me in the most sequestered spot she had been able to select, and there the footman left us. The girl came straight at me and in an instant she had grasped my hands. I became aware that her condition had changed; her tears were gone, she had a concentrated purpose. I could scarcely see her beautiful young face—it was pressed, beseechingly, so close to mine. I only felt, as her dry, shining eyes almost dazzled me, that a strong light had been waved back and forth before me. Her words at first seemed to me incoherent; then I understood that she was asking me for a pledge.

"Excuse me, forgive me for bringing you here—to say something I can't say before all those people. *Do* forgive me— it was so awfully kind of you to come. I couldn't think of any other way—just for two seconds. I want you to swear to me," she went on, with her hands now raised and intensely clasped.

"To swear, dearest child?"

"I'm not your dearest child—I'm not anyone's! But *don't* tell mamma. Promise me—promise me," she insisted.

"Tell her what?—I don't understand."

"Oh, you do—you do!" she kept on; "and if you're going to Chantry you'll see her, you'll be with her, you may see her before I do. On my knees I ask you for a vow!"

She seemed on the point of throwing herself at my feet, but I stopped her, I kept her erect. "When shall *you* see your mother?"

"As soon as I can. I want to get home—I want to get home!" With this I thought she was going to cry again, but she controlled herself and only pressed me with feverish eyes.

"You have some great trouble—for heaven's sake tell me what it is."

"It isn't anything—it will pass. Only don't breathe it to mamma!"

"How can I breathe it if I don't know what it is?"

"You do know—you know what I mean." Then after an instant's pause she added: "What I did in the garden."

"*What* did you do in the garden?"

"I threw myself on your neck and I sobbed—I behaved like a maniac."

"Is that all you mean?"

"It's what I don't want mamma to know—it's what I beseech you to keep silent about. If you don't I'll never, never go home. Have *mercy* on me!" the poor child quavered.

"Dear girl, I only want to be tender to you—to be perfect. But tell me first: has anyone acted wrongly to you?"

"No one—*no* one. I speak the truth."

She looked into my eyes, and I looked far into hers. They were wild with pain and yet they were so pure that they made me confusedly believe her. I hesitated a moment; then I risked the question: "Isn't Mr. Brandon responsible for anything?"

"For nothing—for nothing! Don't blame *him*!" the girl passionately cried.

"He hasn't made love to you?"

"Not a word—before God! Oh, it was too awful!" And with this she broke away from me, flung herself on her knees before a sofa, burying her face in it and in her arms. "Promise me, promise me, promise me!" she continued to wail.

I was horribly puzzled but I was immeasurably touched. I stood looking a moment at her extravagant prostration; then I said "I'm dreadfully in the dark, but I promise."

This brought her to her feet again, and again she seized my hands. "Solemnly, sacredly?" she panted.

"Solemnly, sacredly."

"Not a syllable—not a hint?"

"Dear Louisa," I said kindly, "when I promise I perform."

"You see I don't know you. And when do you go to Chantry?"

"Day after to-morrow. And when do you?"

"To-morrow if I can."

"Then you'll see your mother first—it will be all right," I said smiling.

"All right, all right!" she repeated, with her woeful eyes. "Go, go!" she added, hearing a step in the adjoining room.

The footman had come back to announce that my friends were seated in the carriage, and I was careful to say before him in a different tone: "Then there's nothing more I can do for you?"

"Nothing—good-bye," said Louisa, tearing herself away too abruptly to take my kiss, which, to follow the servant again, I left unbestowed. I felt awkward and guilty as I took leave of the company, murmuring something to my entertainers about having had an arrangement to make with Miss Chantry. Most of the people bade us good-bye from the steps, but I didn't see Jack Brandon. On our drive home in the waning afternoon my other friends doubtless found me silent and stupid.

I went to Chantry two days later, and was disappointed to find that the daughter of the house had not returned, though indeed after parting with her I had been definitely of the opinion that she was much more likely to go to bed and be ill. Her mother however had not heard that she was ill, and my inquiry about the young lady was of course full of circumspection. It was a little difficult, for I had to talk about her, Helen being particularly delighted that we had already made acquaintance. No day had been fixed for her return, but it came over my friend that she oughtn't to be absent during too much of my visit. She was the best thing they had to show—she was the flower and the charm of the place. It had other charms as well—it was a sleepy, silvery old home, exquisitely grey and exquisitely green; a house where you could have confidence in your leisure: it would be as genuine as the butter and the claret. The very look of the pleasant, prosaic drawing-room suggested long mornings of fancy work, of Berlin wool and premeditated patterns, new stitches and mild pauses. My good Helen was always in the middle of something eternal, of which the past and the future were rolled up in oilcloth and tissue paper, and the intensest moments of conversation were when it was spread out for pensive opinions. These used to drop sometimes even from Christopher Chantry when he straddled vaguely in with muddy leggings and the raw materials of a joke. He had a mind like a large, full milk-pan, and his wit was as thick as cream.

One evening I came down to dinner a little early and, to my surprise, found my troubled maiden in possession of the drawing-room. She was evidently troubled still, and had been waiting there in the hope of seeing me alone. We were too quickly interrupted by her parents, however, and I had no conversation with her till I sat down to the piano after dinner and beckoned to her to come and stand by it. Her father had gone off to smoke; her mother dozed by one of the crackling little fires of the summer's end.

"Why didn't you come home the day you told me you meant to?"

She fixed her eyes on my hands. "I couldn't, I couldn't!"

"You look to me as if you were very ill."

"I am," the girl said simply.

"You ought to see some one. Something ought to be done."

She shook her head with quiet despair. "It would be no use—no one would know."

"What do you mean—would know?"

"No one would understand."

"You ought to make them!"

"Never—never!" she repeated. "Never!"

"I confess *I* don't," I replied, with a kind of angry renunciation. I played louder, with the passion of my uneasiness and the aggravation of my responsibility.

"No, you don't indeed," said Louisa Chantry.

I had only to accept this disadvantage, and after a moment I went on: "What became of Mr. Brandon?"

"I don't know."

"Did he go away?"

"That same evening."

"Which same evening?"

"The day you were there. I never saw him again."

I was silent a minute, then I risked: "And you never will, eh?"

"Never—never."

"Then why shouldn't you get better?"

She also hesitated, after which she answered: "Because I'm going to die."

My music ceased, in spite of me, and we sat looking at each other. Helen Chantry woke up with a little start and asked what was the matter. I rose from the piano and I couldn't help saying, "Dear Helen, I haven't the least idea." Louisa sprang up, pressing her hand to her left side, and the next instant I cried aloud "She's faint—she's ill—do come to her!" Mrs. Chantry bustled over to us, and immediately afterwards the girl had thrown herself on her mother's breast, as she had thrown herself days before on mine; only this time without tears, without cries, in the strangest, most tragic silence. She was not faint, she was only in despair—that at least is the way I really saw her. There was something in her contact that

scared poor Helen, that operated a sudden revelation: I can
see at this hour the queer frightened look she gave me over
Louisa's shoulder. The girl however in a moment disengaged
herself, declaring that she was not ill, only tired, very tired,
and wanted to go to bed. "Take her, take her—go with her,"
I said to her mother; and I pushed them, got them out of the
room, partly to conceal my own trepidation. A few moments
after they had gone Christopher Chantry came in, having finished his cigar, and I had to mention to him—to explain their
absence—that his daughter was so fatigued that she had with-
drawn under her mother's superintendence. "Didn't she seem
done up, awfully done up? What on earth, at that confounded
place, did she go in for?" the dear man asked with his pointless
kindness. I couldn't tell him this was just what I myself wanted
to know; and while I pretended to read I wondered inextin-
guishably what indeed she had "gone in" for. It had become
still more difficult to keep my vow than I had expected; it was
also very difficult that evening to converse with Christopher
Chantry. His wife's continued absence rendered some conversation necessary; yet it had the advantage of making him
remark, after it had lasted an hour, that he must go to see
what was the matter. He left me, and soon afterwards I betook
myself to my room; bed-time was elastic in the early sense at
Chantry. I knew I should only have to wait awhile for Helen
to come to me, and in fact by eleven o'clock she arrived.

"She's in a very strange state—something happened there."

"And *what* happened, pray?"

"I can't make out; she won't tell me."

"Then what makes you suppose so?"

"She has broken down utterly; she says there was something."

"Then she does tell you?"

"Not a bit. She only begins and then stops short—she says
it's too dreadful."

"Too dreadful?"

"She says it's *horrible*," my poor friend murmured, with
tears in her eyes and tragic speculation in her mild maternal
face.

"But in what way? Does she give you no facts, no clue?"

"It was something she did."

We looked at each other a moment. "Did?" I echoed. "Did to whom?"

"She won't tell me—she says she *can't*. She tries to bring it out, but it sticks in her throat."

"Nonsense. She did nothing," I said.

"What *could* she do?" Helen asked, gazing at me.

"She's ill, she's in a fever, her mind's wandering."

"So I say to her father."

"And what does *she* say to him?"

"Nothing—she won't speak to him. He's with her now, but she only lies there letting him hold her hand, with her face turned away from him and her eyes closed."

"You must send for the doctor immediately."

"I've already sent for him."

"Should you like me to sit up with her?"

"Oh, I'll do that!" Helen said. Then she asked: "But if you were there the other day, what did *you* see?"

"Nothing whatever," I resolutely answered.

"*Really* nothing?"

"Really, my dear child."

"But was there nobody there who could have made up to her?"

I hesitated a moment. "My poor Helen, you should have seen them!"

"She wouldn't look at anybody that wasn't remarkably nice," Helen mused.

"Well—I don't want to abuse your friends—but nobody was remarkably nice. Believe me, she hasn't looked at anybody, and nothing whatever has occurred. She's ill, and it's a mere morbid fancy."

"It's a mere morbid fancy——!" Mrs. Chantry gobbled down this formula. I felt that I was giving her another still more acceptable, and which she as promptly adopted, when I added that Louisa would soon get over it.

I may as well say at once that Louisa never got over it. There followed an extraordinary week, which I look back upon as one of the most uncomfortable of my life. The doctor had something to say about the action of his patient's heart—it was weak and slightly irregular, and he was anxious to learn whether she had lately been exposed to any violent shock or emotion—but he could give no name to the disorder under the influence of which she had begun unmistakably to sink. She lay on the sofa in her room—she refused to go to bed, and in the absence of complications it was not insisted on—utterly white, weak and abstracted, shaking her head at all suggestion, waving away all nourishment save the infinitesimally little that enabled her to stretch out her hand from time to time (at intervals of very unequal length) and begin "Mother, mother!" as if she were mustering courage for a supreme confession. The courage never came; she was haunted by a strange impulse to speak, which in turn was checked on her lips by some deeper horror or some stranger fear. She seemed to seek relief spasmodically from some unforgettable consciousness and then to find the greatest relief of all in impenetrable silence. I knew these things only from her mother, for before me (I went gently in and out of her room two or three times a day) she gave no sign whatever. The little local doctor, after the first day, acknowledged himself at sea and expressed a desire to consult with a colleague at Exeter. The colleague journeyed down to us and shuffled and stammered: he recommended an appeal to a high authority in London. The high authority was summoned by telegraph and paid us a flying visit. He enunciated the valuable opinion that it was a very curious case and dropped the striking remark that in so charming a home a young lady ought to bloom like a flower. The young lady's late hostess came over, but she could throw no light on anything: all that she had ever noticed was that Louisa had seemed "rather blue" for a day or two before she brought her visit to a close. Our days were dismal enough and our nights were dreadful, for I took turns with Helen in sitting up with the girl. Chantry Court itself seemed conscious of the riddle that made its chambers ache; it bowed its grey old head over the fate of its daughter. The people who had been coming were put off; dinner became a ceremony enacted mainly by the servants. I sat alone with Christopher Chantry, whose honest hair, in his mystification, stuck out as if he had been overhauling accounts. My hours with Louisa were even more intensely silent, for she almost never looked at me. In the watches of the night however I at last saw more clearly into what she was thinking of. Once when I caught her wan eyes resting upon me I took advantage of it to kneel down by her bed and speak to her with the utmost tenderness.

"If you can't say it to your mother, can you say it perhaps to *me*?"

She gazed at me for some time. "What does it matter now—if I'm dying?"

I shook my head and smiled. "You won't die if you get it off your mind."

"You'd be cruel to him," she said. "He's innocent—he's innocent."

"Do you mean *you're* guilty? What trifle are you magnifying?"

"Do you call it a trifle——?" She faltered and paused.

"Certainly I do, my dear." Then I risked a great stroke. "I've often done it myself!"

"*You*? Never, never! I was cruel to him," she added.

This puzzled me; I couldn't work it into my conception. "How were you cruel?"

"In the garden. I changed suddenly, I drove him away, I told him he filled me with horror."

"Why did you do that?"

"Because my shame came over me."

"Your shame?"

"What I had done in the house."

"And what had you done?"

She lay a few moments with her eyes closed, as if she were living it over. "I broke out to him, I told him," she began at last. But she couldn't continue, she was powerless to utter it.

"Yes, I know what you told him. Millions of girls have told young men that before."

"They've been asked, they've been asked! They didn't speak *first*! I didn't even know him, he didn't care for me, I had seen him for the first time the day before I said strange things to him, and he behaved like a gentleman."

"Well he might!"

"Then before he could turn round, when we had simply walked out of the house together and strolled in the garden— it was as if I were borne along in the air by the wonder of what I had said—it rolled over me that I was lost."

"Lost?"

"That I had been horrible—that I had been mad. Nothing could ever unsay it. I frightened him—I almost struck him."

"Poor fellow!" I smiled.

"Yes—pity him. He was kind. But he'll see me that way—always!"

I hesitated as to the answer it was best to make to this; then I produced: "Don't think he'll remember you—he'll see other girls."

"Ah, he'll *forget* me!" she softly and miserably wailed; and I saw that I had said the wrong thing. I bent over her more closely, to kiss her, and when I raised my head her mother was on the other side of the bed. She fell on her knees there for the same purpose, and when Louisa felt her lips she stretched out her arms to embrace her. She had the strength to draw her close, and I heard her begin again, for the hundredth time, "Mother, mother——"

"Yes, my own darling."

Then for the hundredth time I heard her stop. There was an intensity in her silence. It made me wildly nervous; I got up and turned away.

"Mother, mother," the girl repeated, and poor Helen replied with a sound of passionate solicitation. But her daughter only exhaled in the waiting hush, while I stood at the window where the dawn was faint, the most miserable moan in the world. "I'm dying," she said, articulately; and she died that night, after an hour, unconscious. The doctor arrived almost at the moment; this time he was sure it must have been the heart. The poor parents were in stupefaction, and I gave up half my visits and stayed with them a month. But in spite of their stupefaction I kept my vow.

Sir Dominick Ferrand

THERE ARE several objections to it, but I'll take it if you'll
alter it," Mr. Locket's rather curt note had said; and there
was no waste of words in the postscript in which he had added:
"If you'll come in and see me, I'll show you what I mean." This
communication had reached Jersey Villas by the first post, and
Peter Baron had scarcely swallowed his leathery muffin before
he got into motion to obey the editorial behest. He knew that
such precipitation looked eager, and he had no desire to look
eager—it was not in his interest; but how could he maintain a
god-like calm, principled though he was in favour of it, the first
time one of the great magazines had accepted, even with a
cruel reservation, a specimen of his ardent young genius?

It was not till, like a child with a sea-shell at his ear, he
began to be aware of the great roar of the "underground,"
that, in his third-class carriage, the cruelty of the reservation
penetrated, with the taste of acrid smoke, to his inner sense.
It was really degrading to be eager in the face of having to
"alter." Peter Baron tried to figure to himself at that moment
that he was not flying to betray the extremity of his need, but
hurrying to fight for some of those passages of superior boldness which were exactly what the conductor of the "Promiscuous Review" would be sure to be down upon. He made
believe—as if to the greasy fellow-passenger opposite—that he
felt indignant; but he saw that to the small round eye of this
still more downtrodden brother he represented selfish success.
He would have liked to linger in the conception that he had
been "approached" by the Promiscuous; but whatever might
be thought in the office of that periodical of some of his flights
of fancy, there was no want of vividness in his occasional suspicion that he passed there for a familiar bore. The only thing
that was clearly flattering was the fact that the Promiscuous
rarely published fiction. He should therefore be associated
with a deviation from a solemn habit, and that would more
than make up to him for a phrase in one of Mr. Locket's
inexorable earlier notes, a phrase which still rankled, about his
showing no symptom of the faculty really creative. "You don't

163

seem able to keep a character together," this pitiless monitor
had somewhere else remarked. Peter Baron, as he sat in his
corner while the train stopped, considered, in the befogged
gaslight, the bookstall standard of literature and asked himself
whose character had fallen to pieces now. Tormenting indeed
had always seemed to him such a fate as to have the creative
head without the creative hand.

It should be mentioned, however, that before he started on
his mission to Mr. Locket his attention had been briefly engaged by an incident occurring at Jersey Villas. On leaving the
house (he lived at No. 3, the door of which stood open to a
small front garden), he encountered the lady who, a week
before, had taken possession of the rooms on the ground
floor, the "parlours" of Mrs. Bundy's terminology. He had
heard her, and from his window, two or three times, had even
seen her pass in and out, and this observation had created in
his mind a vague prejudice in her favour. Such a prejudice, it
was true, had been subjected to a violent test; it had been
fairly apparent that she had a light step, but it was still less to
be overlooked that she had a cottage piano. She had furthermore a little boy and a very sweet voice, of which Peter Baron
had caught the accent, not from her singing (for she only
played), but from her gay admonitions to her child, whom
she occasionally allowed to amuse himself—under restrictions
very publicly enforced—in the tiny black patch which, as a
forecourt to each house, was held, in the humble row, to be
a feature. Jersey Villas stood in pairs, semi-detached, and Mrs.
Ryves—such was the name under which the new lodger presented herself—had been admitted to the house as confessedly
musical. Mrs. Bundy, the earnest proprietress of No. 3, who
considered her "parlours" (they were a dozen feet square),
even more attractive, if possible, than the second floor with
which Baron had had to content himself—Mrs. Bundy, who
reserved the drawing-room for a casual dressmaking business,
had threshed out the subject of the new lodger in advance
with our young man, reminding him that her affection for his
own person was a proof that, other things being equal, she
positively preferred tenants who were clever.

This was the case with Mrs. Ryves; she had satisfied Mrs.
Bundy that she was not a simple strummer. Mrs. Bundy ad-

mitted to Peter Baron that, for herself, she had a weakness for
a pretty tune, and Peter could honestly reply that his ear was
equally sensitive. Everything would depend on the "touch"
of their inmate. Mrs. Ryves's piano would blight his existence
if her hand should prove heavy or her selections vulgar; but
if she played agreeable things and played them in an agreeable
way she would render him rather a service while he smoked
the pipe of "form." Mrs. Bundy, who wanted to let her
rooms, guaranteed on the part of the stranger a first-class
talent, and Mrs. Ryves, who evidently knew thoroughly what
she was about, had not falsified this somewhat rash prediction.
She never played in the morning, which was Baron's working-
time, and he found himself listening with pleasure at other
hours to her discreet and melancholy strains. He really knew
little about music, and the only criticism he would have made
of Mrs. Ryves's conception of it was that she seemed devoted
to the dismal. It was not, however, that these strains were not
pleasant to him; they floated up, on the contrary, as a sort of
conscious response to some of his broodings and doubts. Harmony, therefore, would have reigned supreme had it not been
for the singularly bad taste of No. 4. Mrs. Ryves's piano was
on the free side of the house and was regarded by Mrs. Bundy
as open to no objection but that of their own gentleman, who
was so reasonable. As much, however, could not be said of
the gentleman of No. 4, who had not even Mr. Baron's excuse
of being "littery" (he kept a bull-terrier and had five hats—
the street could count them), and whom, if you had listened
to Mrs. Bundy, you would have supposed to be divided from
the obnoxious instrument by walls and corridors, obstacles
and intervals, of massive structure and fabulous extent. This
gentleman had taken up an attitude which had now passed
into the phase of correspondence and compromise; but it was
the opinion of the immediate neighbourhood that he had not
a leg to stand upon, and on whatever subject the sentiment
of Jersey Villas might have been vague, it was not so on the
rights and the wrongs of landladies.

    Mrs. Ryves's little boy was in the garden as Peter Baron
issued from the house, and his mother appeared to have come
out for a moment, bareheaded, to see that he was doing no
harm. She was discussing with him the responsibility that he

might incur by passing a piece of string round one of the iron palings and pretending he was in command of a "geegee"; but it happened that at the sight of the other lodger the child was seized with a finer perception of the drivable. He rushed at Baron with a flourish of the bridle, shouting, "Ou geegee!" in a manner productive of some refined embarrassment to his mother. Baron met his advance by mounting him on a shoulder and feigning to prance an instant, so that by the time this performance was over—it took but a few seconds—the young man felt introduced to Mrs. Ryves. Her smile struck him as charming, and such an impression shortens many steps. She said, "Oh, thank you—you mustn't let him worry you"; and then as, having put down the child and raised his hat, he was turning away, she added: "It's very good of you not to complain of my piano."

"I particularly enjoy it—you play beautifully," said Peter Baron.

"I have to play, you see—it's all I can do. But the people next door don't like it, though my room, you know, is not against their wall. Therefore I thank you for letting me tell them that you, in the house, don't find me a nuisance."

She looked gentle and bright as she spoke, and as the young man's eyes rested on her the tolerance for which she expressed herself indebted seemed to him the least indulgence she might count upon. But he only laughed and said "Oh, no, you're not a nuisance!" and felt more and more introduced.

The little boy, who was handsome, hereupon clamoured for another ride, and she took him up herself, to moderate his transports. She stood a moment with the child in her arms, and he put his fingers exuberantly into her hair, so that while she smiled at Baron she slowly, permittingly shook her head to get rid of them.

"If they really make a fuss I'm afraid I shall have to go," she went on.

"Oh, don't go!" Baron broke out, with a sudden expressiveness which made his voice, as it fell upon his ear, strike him as the voice of another. She gave a vague exclamation and, nodding slightly but not unsociably, passed back into the house. She had made an impression which remained till the other party to the conversation reached the railway-station,

when it was superseded by the thought of his prospective discussion with Mr. Locket. This was a proof of the intensity of
that interest.

The aftertaste of the later conference was also intense for
Peter Baron, who quitted his editor with his manuscript under
his arm. He had had the question out with Mr. Locket, and
he was in a flutter which ought to have been a sense of triumph and which indeed at first he succeeded in regarding in
this light. Mr. Locket had had to admit that there was an idea
in his story, and that was a tribute which Baron was in a position to make the most of. But there was also a scene which
scandalised the editorial conscience and which the young man
had promised to rewrite. The idea that Mr. Locket had been
so good as to disengage depended for clearness mainly on this
scene; so it was easy to see his objection was perverse. This
inference was probably a part of the joy in which Peter Baron
walked as he carried home a contribution it pleased him to
classify as accepted. He walked to work off his excitement and
to think in what manner he should reconstruct. He went some
distance without settling that point, and then, as it began to
worry him, he looked vaguely into shop-windows for solutions and hints. Mr. Locket lived in the depths of Chelsea, in
a little panelled, amiable house, and Baron took his way
homeward along the King's Road. There was a new amusement for him, a fresher bustle, in a London walk in the morning; these were hours that he habitually spent at his table, in
the awkward attitude engendered by the poor piece of furniture, one of the rickety features of Mrs. Bundy's second floor,
which had to serve as his altar of literary sacrifice. If by exception he went out when the day was young he noticed that
life seemed younger with it; there were livelier industries to
profit by and shopgirls, often rosy, to look at; a different air
was in the streets and a chaff of traffic for the observer of
manners to catch. Above all, it was the time when poor Baron
made his purchases, which were wholly of the wandering
mind; his extravagances, for some mysterious reason, were all
matutinal, and he had a foreknowledge that if ever he should
ruin himself it would be well before noon. He felt lavish this
morning, on the strength of what the Promiscuous would do
for him; he had lost sight for the moment of what he should

have to do for the Promiscuous. Before the old bookshops and printshops, the crowded panes of the curiosity-mongers and the desirable exhibitions of mahogany "done up," he used, by an innocent process, to commit luxurious follies. He refurnished Mrs. Bundy with a freedom that cost her nothing, and lost himself in pictures of a transfigured second floor.

On this particular occasion the King's Road proved almost unprecedentedly expensive, and indeed this occasion differed from most others in containing the germ of real danger. For once in a way he had a bad conscience—he felt himself tempted to pick his own pocket. He never saw a commodious writing-table, with elbow-room and drawers and a fair expanse of leather stamped neatly at the edge with gilt, without being freshly reminded of Mrs. Bundy's dilapidations. There were several such tables in the King's Road—they seemed indeed particularly numerous today. Peter Baron glanced at them all through the fronts of the shops, but there was one that detained him in supreme contemplation. There was a fine assurance about it which seemed a guarantee of masterpieces; but when at last he went in and, just to help himself on his way, asked the impossible price, the sum mentioned by the voluble vendor mocked at him even more than he had feared. It was far too expensive, as he hinted, and he was on the point of completing his comedy by a pensive retreat when the shopman bespoke his attention for another article of the same general character, which he described as remarkably cheap for what it was. It was an old piece, from a sale in the country, and it had been in stock some time; but it had got pushed out of sight in one of the upper rooms—they contained such a wilderness of treasures—and happened to have but just come to light. Peter suffered himself to be conducted into an interminable dusky rear, where he presently found himself bending over one of those square substantial desks of old mahogany, raised, with the aid of front legs, on a sort of retreating pedestal which is fitted with small drawers, contracted conveniences known immemorially to the knowing as davenports. This specimen had visibly seen service, but it had an old-time solidity and to Peter Baron it unexpectedly appealed.

He would have said in advance that such an article was exactly what he didn't want, but as the shopman pushed up

a chair for him and he sat down with his elbows on the gentle
slope of the large, firm lid, he felt that such a basis for literature would be half the battle. He raised the lid and looked
lovingly into the deep interior; he sat ominously silent while
his companion dropped the striking words: "Now that's an
article I personally covet!" Then when the man mentioned
the ridiculous price (they were literally giving it away), he reflected on the economy of having a literary altar on which one
could really kindle a fire. A davenport was a compromise, but
what was all life but a compromise? He could beat down the
dealer, and at Mrs. Bundy's he had to write on an insincere
cardtable. After he had sat for a minute with his nose in the
friendly desk he had a queer impression that it might tell him
a secret or two—one of the secrets of form, one of the sac-
rificial mysteries—though no doubt its career had been literary
only in the sense of its helping some old lady to write invitations to dull dinners. There was a strange, faint odour in
the receptacle, as if fragrant, hallowed things had once been
put away there. When he took his head out of it he said to
the shopman: "I don't mind meeting you halfway." He had
been told by knowing people that that was the right thing.
He felt rather vulgar, but the davenport arrived that evening
at Jersey Villas.

II.

"I daresay it will be all right; he seems quiet now," said the
poor lady of the "parlours" a few days later, in reference to
their litigious neighbour and the precarious piano. The two
lodgers had grown regularly acquainted, and the piano had
had much to do with it. Just as this instrument served, with
the gentleman at No. 4, as a theme for discussion, so between
Peter Baron and the lady of the parlours it had become a basis
of peculiar agreement, a topic, at any rate, of conversation
frequently renewed. Mrs. Ryves was so prepossessing that
Peter was sure that even if they had not had the piano he would
have found something else to thresh out with her. Fortunately
however they did have it, and he, at least, made the most of
it, knowing more now about his new friend, who when, widowed and fatigued, she held her beautiful child in her arms,

looked dimly like a modern Madonna. Mrs. Bundy, as a letter of furnished lodgings, was characterised in general by a familiar domestic severity in respect to picturesque young women, but she had the highest confidence in Mrs. Ryves. She was luminous about her being a lady, and a lady who could bring Mrs. Bundy back to a gratified recognition of one of those manifestations of mind for which she had an independent esteem. She was professional, but Jersey Villas could be proud of a profession that didn't happen to be the wrong one—they had seen something of that. Mrs. Ryves had a hundred a year (Baron wondered how Mrs. Bundy knew this; he thought it unlikely Mrs. Ryves had told her), and for the rest she depended on her lovely music. Baron judged that her music, even though lovely, was a frail dependence; it would hardly help to fill a concert-room, and he asked himself at first whether she played country-dances at children's parties or gave lessons to young ladies who studied above their station.

Very soon, indeed, he was sufficiently enlightened; it all went fast, for the little boy had been almost as great a help as the piano. Sidney haunted the doorstep of No. 3; he was eminently sociable, and had established independent relations with Peter, a frequent feature of which was an adventurous visit, upstairs, to picture books criticised for not being *all* geegees and walking sticks happily more conformable. The young man's window, too, looked out on their acquaintance; through a starched muslin curtain it kept his neighbour before him, made him almost more aware of her comings and goings than he felt he had a right to be. He was capable of a shyness of curiosity about her and of dumb little delicacies of consideration. She did give a few lessons; they were essentially local, and he ended by knowing more or less what she went out for and what she came in from. She had almost no visitors, only a decent old lady or two, and, every day, poor dingy Miss Teagle, who was also ancient and who came humbly enough to governess the infant of the parlours. Peter Baron's window had always, to his sense, looked out on a good deal of life, and one of the things it had most shown him was that there is nobody so bereft of joy as not to be able to command for twopence the services of somebody less joyous. Mrs. Ryves was a struggler (Baron scarcely liked to think of it), but she occupied a pinnacle for Miss Teagle, who had lived on—and from a noble nursery—into a period of diplomas and humiliation.

Mrs. Ryves sometimes went out, like Baron himself, with manuscripts under her arm, and, still more like Baron, she almost always came back with them. Her vain approaches were to the music-sellers; she tried to compose—to produce songs that would make a hit. A successful song was an income, she confided to Peter one of the first times he took Sidney, blasé and drowsy, back to his mother. It was not on one of these occasions, but once when he had come in on no better pretext than that of simply wanting to (she had after all virtually invited him), that she mentioned how only one song in a thousand was successful and that the terrible difficulty was in getting the right words. This rightness was just a vulgar "fluke"—there were lots of words really clever that were of no use at all. Peter said, laughing, that he supposed any words he should try to produce would be sure to be too clever; yet only three weeks after his first encounter with Mrs. Ryves he sat at his delightful davenport (well aware that he had duties more pressing), trying to string together rhymes idiotic enough to make his neighbour's fortune. He was satisfied of the fineness of her musical gift—it had the touching note. The touching note was in her person as well.

The davenport was delightful, after six months of its tottering predecessor, and such a reënforcement to the young man's style was not impaired by his sense of something lawless in the way it had been gained. He had made the purchase in anticipation of the money he expected from Mr. Locket, but Mr. Locket's liberality was to depend on the ingenuity of his contributor, who now found himself confronted with the consequence of a frivolous optimism. The fruit of his labour presented, as he stared at it with his elbows on his desk, an aspect uncompromising and incorruptible. It seemed to look up at him reproachfully and to say, with its essential finish: "How could you promise anything so base; how could you pass your word to mutilate and dishonour me?" The alterations demanded by Mr. Locket were impossible, the concessions to the platitude of his conception of the public mind were degrading. The public mind!—as if the public *had* a mind, or

any principle of perception more discoverable than the stare
of huddled sheep! Peter Baron felt that it concerned him to
determine if he were only not clever enough or if he were
simply not abject enough to rewrite his story. He might in
truth have had less pride if he had had more skill, and more
discretion if he had had more practice. Humility, in the profession of letters, was half of practice, and resignation was half
of success. Poor Peter actually flushed with pain as he recognised that this was not success, the production of gelid prose
which his editor could do nothing with on the one side and
he himself could do nothing with on the other. The truth
about his luckless tale was now the more bitter from his having managed, for some days, to taste it as sweet.

As he sat there, baffled and sombre, biting his pen and wondering what was meant by the "rewards" of literature, he generally ended by tossing away the composition deflowered by
Mr. Locket and trying his hand at the sort of twaddle that
Mrs. Ryves might be able to set to music. Success in these
experiments wouldn't be a reward of literature, but it might
very well become a labour of love. The experiments would be
pleasant enough for him if they were pleasant for his inscrutable neighbour. That was the way he thought of her now, for
he had learned enough about her, little by little, to guess how
much there was still to learn. To spend his mornings over
cheap rhymes for her was certainly to shirk the immediate
question; but there were hours when he judged this question
to be altogether too arduous, reflecting that he might quite
as well perish by the sword as by famine. Besides, he did meet
it obliquely when he considered that he shouldn't be an utter
failure if he were to produce some songs to which Mrs.
Ryves's accompaniments would give a circulation. He had not
ventured to show her anything yet, but one morning, at a
moment when her little boy was in his room, it seemed to
him that, by an inspiration, he had arrived at the happy middle
course (it was an art by itself), between sound and sense. If
the sense was not confused it was because the sound was so
familiar.

He had said to the child, to whom he had sacrificed barley-
sugar (it had no attraction for his own lips, yet in these days
there was always some of it about), he had confided to the

small Sidney that if he would wait a little he should be in-trusted with something nice to take down to his parent. Sid-ney had absorbing occupation and, while Peter copied off the song in a pretty hand, roamed, gurgling and sticky, about the room. In this manner he lurched like a little toper into the rear of the davenport, which stood a few steps out from the recess of the window, and, as he was fond of beating time to his intensest joys, began to bang on the surface of it with a paper-knife which at that spot had chanced to fall upon the floor. At the moment Sidney committed this violence his kind friend had happened to raise the lid of the desk and, with his head beneath it, was rummaging among a mass of papers for a proper envelope. "I say, I say, my boy!" he exclaimed, so-licitous for the ancient glaze of his most cherished possession. Sidney paused an instant; then, while Peter still hunted for the envelope, he administered another, and this time a distinctly disobedient, rap. Peter heard it from within and was struck with its oddity of sound—so much so that, leaving the child for a moment under a demoralising impression of impunity, he waited with quick curiosity for a repetition of the stroke. It came of course immediately, and then the young man, who had at the same instant found his envelope and ejaculated "Hallo, this thing has a false back!" jumped up and secured his visitor, whom with his left arm he held in durance on his knee while with his free hand he addressed the missive to Mrs. Ryves.

As Sidney was fond of errands he was easily got rid of, and after he had gone Baron stood a moment at the window chinking pennies and keys in pockets and wondering if the charming composer would think his song as good, or in other words as bad, as he thought it. His eyes as he turned away fell on the wooden back of the davenport, where, to his re-gret, the traces of Sidney's assault were visible in three or four ugly scratches. "Confound the little brute!" he exclaimed, feeling as if an altar had been desecrated. He was reminded, however, of the observation this outrage had led him to make, and, for further assurance, he knocked on the wood with his knuckle. It sounded from that position commonplace enough, but his suspicion was strongly confirmed when, again standing beside the desk, he put his head beneath the lifted lid and gave ear while with an extended arm he tapped sharply in the same place. The back was distinctly hollow; there was a space between the inner and the outer pieces (he could measure it), so wide that he was a fool not to have noticed it before. The depth of the receptacle from front to rear was so great that it could sacrifice a certain quantity of room without detection. The sacrifice could of course only be for a purpose, and the purpose could only be the creation of a secret compartment. Peter Baron was still boy enough to be thrilled by the idea of such a feature, the more so as every indication of it had been cleverly concealed. The people at the shop had never noticed it, else they would have called his attention to it as an enhancement of value. His legendary lore instructed him that where there was a hiding-place there was always a hidden spring, and he pried and pressed and fumbled in an eager search for the sensitive spot. The article was really a wonder of neat construction; everything fitted with a closeness that completely saved appearances.

It took Baron some minutes to pursue his inquiry, during which he reflected that the people of the shop were not such fools after all. They had admitted moreover that they had accidentally neglected this relic of gentility—it had been overlooked in the multiplicity of their treasures. He now recalled that the man had wanted to polish it up before sending it home, and that, satisfied for his own part with its honourable appearance and averse in general to shiny furniture, he had in his impatience declined to wait for such an operation, so that the object had left the place for Jersey Villas, carrying presumably its secret with it, two or three hours after his visit. This secret it seemed indeed capable of keeping; there was an absurdity in being baffled, but Peter couldn't find the spring. He thumped and sounded, he listened and measured again; he inspected every joint and crevice, with the effect of becoming surer still of the existence of a chamber and of making up his mind that his davenport was a rarity. Not only was there a compartment between the two backs, but there was distinctly something *in* the compartment! Perhaps it was a lost manuscript—a nice, safe, old-fashioned story that Mr. Locket wouldn't object to. Peter returned to the charge, for it had occurred to him that he had perhaps not sufficiently visited the small drawers, of which, in two vertical rows, there were six in number, of different sizes, inserted sideways into that portion of the structure which formed part of the support of the desk. He took them out again and examined more minutely the condition of their sockets, with the happy result of discovering at last, in the place into which the third on the left-hand row was fitted, a small sliding panel. Behind the panel was a spring, like a flat button, which yielded with a click when he pressed it and which instantly produced a loosening of one of the pieces of the shelf forming the highest part of the davenport—pieces adjusted to each other with the most deceptive closeness.

This particular piece proved to be, in its turn, a sliding panel, which, when pushed, revealed the existence of a smaller receptacle, a narrow, oblong box, in the false back. Its capacity was limited, but if it couldn't hold many things it might hold precious ones. Baron, in presence of the ingenuity with which it had been dissimulated, immediately felt that, but for the odd chance of little Sidney Ryves's having hammered on the outside at the moment he himself happened to have his head in the desk, he might have remained for years without suspicion of it. This apparently would have been a loss, for he had been right in guessing that the chamber was not empty. It contained objects which, whether precious or not, had at any rate been worth somebody's hiding. These objects were a collection of small flat parcels, of the shape of packets of letters, wrapped in white paper and neatly sealed. The seals, mechanically figured, bore the impress neither of arms nor of initials; the paper looked old—it had turned faintly sallow; the packets might have been there for ages. Baron counted them—there were nine in all, of different sizes; he turned them over and over, felt them curiously and snuffed in their vague, musty smell, which affected him with the melancholy of some smothered human accent. The little bundles were neither named nor numbered—there was not a word of writing on any of the covers; but they plainly contained old letters, sorted and matched according to dates or to authorship. They told some old, dead story—they were the ashes of fires burned out.

As Peter Baron held his discoveries successively in his hands he became conscious of a queer emotion which was not al-

together elation and yet was still less pure pain. He had made
a find, but it somehow added to his responsibility; he was in
the presence of something interesting, but (in a manner he
couldn't have defined) this circumstance suddenly constituted
a danger. It was the perception of the danger, for instance,
which caused to remain in abeyance any impulse he might
have felt to break one of the seals. He looked at them all
narrowly, but he was careful not to loosen them, and he wondered uncomfortably whether the contents of the secret compartment would be held in equity to be the property of the
people in the King's Road. He had given money for the davenport, but had he given money for these buried papers? He
paid by a growing consciousness that a nameless chill had stolen into the air the penalty, which he had many a time paid
before, of being made of sensitive stuff. It was as if an occasion
had insidiously arisen for a sacrifice—a sacrifice for the sake of
a fine superstition, something like honour or kindness or justice, something indeed perhaps even finer still—a difficult deciphering of duty, an impossible tantalising wisdom. Standing
there before his ambiguous treasure and losing himself for the
moment in the sense of a dawning complication, he was startled by a light, quick tap at the door of his sitting-room. Instinctively, before answering, he listened an instant—he was
in the attitude of a miser surprised while counting his hoard.
Then he answered "One moment, please!" and slipped the
little heap of packets into the biggest of the drawers of the
davenport, which happened to be open. The aperture of the
false back was still gaping, and he had not time to work back
the spring. He hastily laid a big book over the place and then
went and opened his door.

It offered him a sight none the less agreeable for being
unexpected—the graceful and agitated figure of Mrs. Ryves.
Her agitation was so visible that he thought at first that something dreadful had happened to her child—that she had
rushed up to ask for help, to beg him to go for the doctor.
Then he perceived that it was probably connected with the
desperate verses he had transmitted to her a quarter of an hour
before; for she had his open manuscript in one hand and was
nervously pulling it about with the other. She looked frightened and pretty, and if, in invading the privacy of a fellow-

lodger, she had been guilty of a departure from rigid custom, she was at least conscious of the enormity of the step and incapable of treating it with levity. The levity was for Peter Baron, who endeavoured, however, to clothe his familiarity with respect, pushing forward the seat of honour and repeating that he rejoiced in such a visit. The visitor came in, leaving the door ajar, and after a minute during which, to help her, he charged her with the purpose of telling him that he ought to be ashamed to send her down such rubbish, she recovered herself sufficiently to stammer out that his song was exactly what she had been looking for and that after reading it she had been seized with an extraordinary, irresistible impulse—that of thanking him for it in person and without delay.

"It was the impulse of a kind nature," he said, "and I can't tell you what pleasure you give me."

She declined to sit down, and evidently wished to appear to have come but for a few seconds. She looked confusedly at the place in which she found herself, and when her eyes met his own they struck him as anxious and appealing. She was evidently not thinking of his song, though she said three or four times over that it was beautiful. "Well, I only wanted you to know, and now I must go," she added; but on his hearthrug she lingered with such an odd helplessness that he felt almost sorry for her.

"Perhaps I can improve it if you find it doesn't go," said Baron. "I'm so delighted to do anything for you I can."

"There may be a word or two that might be changed," she answered, rather absently. "I shall have to think it over, to live with it a little. But I like it, and that's all I wanted to say."

"Charming of you. I'm not a bit busy," said Baron.

Again she looked at him with a troubled intensity, then suddenly she demanded: "Is there anything the matter with you?"

"The matter with me?"

"I mean like being ill or worried. I wondered if there might be; I had a sudden fancy; and that, I think, is really why I came up."

"There isn't, indeed; I'm all right. But your sudden fancies are inspirations."

"It's absurd. You must excuse me. Good-by!" said Mrs. Ryves.

"What are the words you want changed?" Baron asked.

"I don't want any—if you're all right. Good-by," his visitor repeated, fixing her eyes an instant on an object on his desk that had caught them. His own glanced in the same direction and he saw that in his hurry to shuffle away the packets found in the davenport he had overlooked one of them, which lay with its seals exposed. For an instant he felt found out, as if he had been concerned in something to be ashamed of, and it was only his quick second thought that told him how little the incident of which the packet was a sequel was an affair of Mrs. Ryves's. Her conscious eyes came back to his as if they were sounding them, and suddenly this instinct of keeping his discovery to himself was succeeded by a really startled inference that, with the rarest alertness, she had guessed something and that her guess (it seemed almost supernatural), had been her real motive. Some secret sympathy had made her vibrate— had touched her with the knowledge that he had brought something to light. After an instant he saw that she also divined the very reflection he was then making, and this gave him a lively desire, a grateful, happy desire, to appear to have nothing to conceal. For herself, it determined her still more to put an end to her momentary visit. But before she had passed to the door he exclaimed:

"All right? How can a fellow be anything else who has just had such a find?"

She paused at this, still looking earnest and asking: "What have you found?"

"Some ancient family papers, in a secret compartment of my writing-table." And he took up the packet he had left out, holding it before her eyes. "A lot of other things like that."

"What are they?" murmured Mrs. Ryves.

"I haven't the least idea. They're sealed."

"You haven't broken the seals?" She had come further back.

"I haven't had time; it only happened ten minutes ago."

"I knew it," said Mrs. Ryves, more gaily now.

"What did you know?"

"That you were in some predicament."

"You're extraordinary. I never heard of anything so miraculous; down two flights of stairs."

"*Are* you in a quandary?" the visitor asked.

"Yes, about giving them back." Peter Baron stood smiling at her and rapping his packet on the palm of his hand. "What do you advise?"

She herself smiled now, with her eyes on the sealed parcel. "Back to whom?"

"The man of whom I bought the table."

"Ah then, they're not from *your* family?"

"No indeed, the piece of furniture in which they were hidden is not an ancestral possession. I bought it at second hand—you see it's old—the other day in the King's Road. Obviously the man who sold it to me sold me more than he meant; he had no idea (from his own point of view it was stupid of him), that there was a hidden chamber or that mysterious documents were buried there. Ought I to go and tell him? It's rather a nice question."

"Are the papers of value?" Mrs. Ryves inquired.

"I haven't the least idea. But I can ascertain by breaking a seal."

"Don't!" said Mrs. Ryves, with much expression. She looked grave again.

"It's rather tantalising—it's a bit of a problem," Baron went on, turning his packet over.

Mrs. Ryves hesitated. "Will you show me what you have in your hand?"

He gave her the packet, and she looked at it and held it for an instant to her nose. "It has a queer, charming old fragrance," he said.

"Charming? It's horrid." She handed him back the packet, saying again more emphatically "Don't!"

"Don't break a seal?"

"Don't give back the papers."

"Is it honest to keep them?"

"Certainly. They're yours as much as the people's of the shop. They were in the hidden chamber when the table came to the shop, and the people had every opportunity to find them out. They didn't—therefore let them take the consequences."

Peter Baron reflected, diverted by her intensity. She was pale, with eyes almost ardent. "The table had been in the place for years."

"That proves the things haven't been missed."

"Let me show you how they were concealed," he rejoined; and he exhibited the ingenious recess and the working of the curious spring. She was greatly interested, she grew excited and became familiar; she appealed to him again not to do anything so foolish as to give up the papers, the rest of which, in their little blank, impenetrable covers, he placed in a row before her. "They might be traced—their history, their ownership," he argued; to which she replied that this was exactly why he ought to be quiet. He declared that women had not the smallest sense of honour, and she retorted that at any rate they have other perceptions more delicate than those of men. He admitted that the papers might be rubbish, and she conceded that nothing was more probable; yet when he offered to settle the point off-hand he caught him by the wrist, acknowledging that, absurd as it was, she was nervous. Finally she put the whole thing on the ground of his just doing her a favour. She asked him to retain the papers, to be silent about them, simply because it would please her. That would be reason enough. Baron's acquaintance, his agreeable relations with her, advanced many steps in the treatment of this question; an element of friendly candour made its way into their discussion of it.

"I can't make out why it matters to you, one way or the other, nor why you should think it worth talking about," the young man reasoned.

"Neither can I. It's just a whim."

"Certainly, if it will give you any pleasure, I'll say nothing at the shop."

"That's charming of you, and I'm very grateful. I see now that this was why the spirit moved me to come up—to save them," Mrs. Ryves went on. She added, moving away, that now she had saved them she must really go.

"To save them for what, if I mayn't break the seals?" Baron asked.

"I don't know—for a generous sacrifice."

"Why should it be generous? What's at stake?" Peter demanded, leaning against the doorpost as she stood on the landing.

"I don't know what, but I feel as if something or other were in peril. Burn them up!" she exclaimed with shining eyes.

"Ah, you ask too much—I'm so curious about them!"

"Well, I won't ask more than I ought, and I'm much obliged to you for your promise to be quiet. I trust to your discretion. Good-by."

"You ought to *reward* my discretion," said Baron, coming out to the landing.

She had partly descended the staircase and she stopped, leaning against the baluster and smiling up at him. "Surely you've had your reward in the honour of my visit."

"That's delightful as far as it goes. But what will you do for me if I burn the papers?"

Mrs. Ryves considered a moment. "Burn them first and you'll see!"

On this she went rapidly downstairs, and Baron, to whom the answer appeared inadequate and the proposition indeed in that form grossly unfair, returned to his room. The vivacity of her interest in a question in which she had discoverably nothing at stake mystified, amused and, in addition, irresistibly charmed him. She was delicate, imaginative, inflammable, quick to feel, quick to act. He didn't complain of it, it was the way he liked women to be; but he was not impelled for the hour to commit the sealed packets to the flames. He dropped them again into their secret well, and after that he went out. He felt restless and excited; another day was lost for work—the dreadful job to be performed for Mr. Locket was still further off.

III.

Ten days after Mrs. Ryves's visit he paid by appointment another call on the editor of the Promiscuous. He found him in the little wainscoted Chelsea house, which had to Peter's sense the smoky brownness of an old pipebowl, surrounded with all the emblems of his office—a litter of papers, a hedge of encyclopædias, a photographic gallery of popular contributors—and he promised at first to consume very few of the moments for which so many claims competed. It was Mr. Locket himself however who presently made the interview spacious, gave it air after discovering that poor Baron had come to tell him something more interesting than that he couldn't after all patch up his tale. Peter had begun with this, had intimated respectfully that it was a case in which both practice and principle rebelled, and then, perceiving how little Mr. Locket was affected by his audacity, had felt weak and slightly silly, left with his heroism on his hands. He had armed himself for a struggle, but the Promiscuous didn't even protest, and there would have been nothing for him but to go away with the prospect of never coming again had he not chanced to say abruptly, irrelevantly, as he got up from his chair:

"Do you happen to be at all interested in Sir Dominick Ferrand?"

Mr. Locket, who had also got up, looked over his glasses. "The late Sir Dominick?"

"The only one; you know the family's extinct."

Mr. Locket shot his young friend another sharp glance, a silent retort to the glibness of this information. "Very extinct indeed. I'm afraid the subject today would scarcely be regarded as attractive."

"Are you very sure?" Baron asked.

Mr. Locket leaned forward a little, with his finger-tips on his table, in the attitude of giving permission to retire. "I might consider the question in a special connection." He was silent a minute, in a way that relegated poor Peter to the general; but meeting the young man's eyes again he asked: "Are you—a—thinking of proposing an article upon him?"

"Not exactly proposing it—because I don't yet quite see my way; but the idea rather appeals to me."

Mr. Locket emitted the safe assertion that this eminent statesman had been a striking figure in his day; then he added: "Have you been studying him?"

"I've been dipping into him."

"I'm afraid he's scarcely a question of the hour," said Mr. Locket, shuffling papers together.

"I think I could make him one," Peter Baron declared.

Mr. Locket stared again; he was unable to repress an unattenuated "You?"

"I have some new material," said the young man, colouring a little. "That often freshens up an old story."

"It buries it sometimes. It's often only another tombstone."

"That depends upon what it is. However," Peter added, "the documents I speak of would be a crushing monument."

Mr. Locket, hesitating, shot another glance under his glasses. "Do you allude to—a—revelations?"

"Very curious ones."

Mr. Locket, still on his feet, had kept his body at the bowing angle; it was therefore easy for him after an instant to bend a little further and to sink into his chair with a movement of his hand toward the seat Baron had occupied. Baron resumed possession of this convenience, and the conversation took a fresh start on a basis which such an extension of privilege could render but little less humiliating to our young man. He had matured no plan of confiding his secret to Mr. Locket, and he had really come out to make him conscientiously that other announcement as to which it appeared that so much artistic agitation had been wasted. He had indeed during the past days—days of painful indecision—appealed in imagination to the editor of the Promiscuous, as he had appealed to other sources of comfort; but his scruples turned their face upon him from quarters high as well as low, and if on the one hand he had by no means made up his mind not to mention his strange knowledge, he had still more left to the determination of the moment the question of how he should introduce the subject. He was in fact too nervous to decide; he only felt that he needed for his peace of mind to communicate his discovery. He wanted an opinion, the impression of somebody else, and even in this intensely professional presence, five minutes after he had begun to tell his queer story, he felt relieved of half his burden. His story was very queer; he could take the measure of that himself as he spoke; but wouldn't this very circumstance qualify it for the Promiscuous?

"Of course the letters may be forgeries," said Mr. Locket at last.

"I've no doubt that's what many people will say."

"Have they been seen by any expert?"

"No indeed; they've been seen by nobody."

"Have you got any of them with you?"

"No; I felt nervous about bringing them out."

"That's a pity. I should have liked the testimony of my eyes."

"You may have it if you'll come to my rooms. If you don't care to do that without a further guarantee I'll copy you out some passages."

"Select a few of the worst!" Mr. Locket laughed. Over Baron's distressing information he had become quite human and genial. But he added in a moment more dryly: "You know they ought to be seen by an expert."

"That's exactly what I dread," said Peter.

"They'll be worth nothing to me if they're not."

Peter communed with his innermost spirit. "How much will they be worth to *me* if they *are*?"

Mr. Locket turned in his study-chair. "I should require to look at them before answering that question."

"I've been to the British museum—there are many of his letters there. I've obtained permission to see them, and I've compared everything carefully. I repudiate the possibility of forgery. No sign of genuineness is wanting; there are details, down to the very postmarks, that no forger could have invented. Besides, whose interest could it conceivably have been? A labor of unspeakable difficulty, and all for what advantage? There are so many letters, too—twenty-seven in all."

"Lord, what an ass!" Mr. Locket exclaimed.

"It will be one of the strangest post-mortem revelations of which history preserves the record."

Mr. Locket, grave now, worried with a paper-knife the crevice of a drawer. "It's very odd. But to be worth anything such documents should be subjected to a searching criticism—I mean of the historical kind."

"Certainly; that would be the task of the writer introducing them to the public."

Again Mr. Locket considered; then with a smile he looked up. "You had better give up original composition and take to buying old furniture."

"Do you mean because it will pay better?"

"For you, I should think, original composition couldn't pay worse. The creative faculty's so rare."

"I do feel tempted to turn my attention to real heroes," Peter replied.

"I'm bound to declare that Sir Dominick Ferrand was never one of mine. Flashy, crafty, second-rate—that's how I've always read him. It was never a secret, moreover, that his private life had its weak spots. He was a mere flash in the pan."

"He speaks to the people of this country," said Baron.

"He did; but his voice—the voice, I mean, of his prestige—is scarcely audible now."

"They're still proud of some of the things he did at the Foreign Office—the famous 'exchange' with Spain, in the Mediterranean, which took Europe so by surprise and by which she felt injured, especially when it became apparent how much we had the best of the bargain. Then the sudden, unexpected show of force by which he imposed on the United States our interpretation of that tiresome treaty—I could never make out what it was about. These were both matters that no one really cared a straw about, but he made every one feel as if they cared; the nation rose to the way he played his trumps—it was uncommon. He was one of the few men we've had, in our period, who took Europe, or took America, by surprise, made them jump a bit; and the country liked his doing it—it was a pleasant change. The rest of the world considered that they knew in any case exactly what we would do, which was usually nothing at all. Say what you like, he's still a high name; partly also, no doubt, on account of other things—his early success and early death, his political 'cheek' and wit; his very appearance—he certainly was handsome—and the possibilities (of future personal supremacy) which it was the fashion at the time, which it's the fashion still, to say had passed away with him. He had been twice at the Foreign Office; that alone was remarkable for a man dying at forty-four. What therefore will the country think when it learns he was venal?"

Peter Baron himself was not angry with Sir Dominick Ferrand, who had simply become to him (he had been "reading up" feverishly for a week) a very curious subject of psychological study; but he could easily put himself in the place of that portion of the public whose memory was long enough for their patriotism to receive a shock. It was some time fortunately since the conduct of public affairs had wanted for men of disinterested ability, but the extraordinary documents concealed (of all places in the world—it was as fantastic as a nightmare) in a "bargain" picked up at second-hand by an obscure scribbler, would be a calculable blow to the retrospective mind. Baron saw vividly that if these relics should be made public the scandal, the horror, the chatter would be immense. Immense would be also the contribution to truth, the rectification of history. He had felt for several days (and it was exactly what had made him so nervous) as if he held in his hand the key to public attention.

"There are too many things to explain," Mr. Locket went on, "and the singular *provenance* of your papers would count almost overwhelmingly against them even if the other objections were met. There would be a perfect and probably a very complicated pedigree to trace. How did they get into your davenport, as you call it, and how long had they been there? What hands secreted them? what hands had, so incredibly, clung to them and preserved them? Who are the persons mentioned in them? who are the correspondents, the parties to the nefarious transactions? You say the transactions appear to be of two distinct kinds—some of them connected with public business and others involving obscure personal relations."

"They all have this in common," said Peter Baron, "that they constitute evidence of uneasiness, in some instances of painful alarm, on the writer's part, in relation to exposure—the exposure in the one case, as I gather, of the fact that he had availed himself of official opportunities to promote enterprises (public works and that sort of thing) in which he had a pecuniary stake. The dread of the light in the other connection is evidently different, and these letters are the earliest in date. They are addressed to a woman, from whom he had evidently received money."

Mr. Locket wiped his glasses. "What woman?"

"I haven't the least idea. There are lots of questions I can't answer, of course; lots of identities I can't establish;

lots of gaps I can't fill. But as to two points I'm clear, and they are the essential ones. In the first place the papers in my possession are genuine; in the second place they're compromising."

With this Peter Baron rose again, rather vexed with himself for having been led on to advertise his treasure (it was his interlocutor's perfectly natural scepticism that produced this effect), for he felt that he was putting himself in a false position. He detected in Mr. Locket's studied detachment the fermentation of impulses from which, unsuccessful as he was, he himself prayed to be delivered.

Mr. Locket remained seated; he watched Baron go across the room for his hat and umbrella. "Of course, the question would come up of whose property today such documents would legally be. There are heirs, descendants, executors to consider."

"In some degree perhaps; but I've gone into that a little. Sir Dominick Ferrand had no children, and he left no brothers and no sisters. His wife survived him, but she died ten years ago. He can have had no heirs and no executors to speak of, for he left no property."

"That's to his honour and against your theory," said Mr. Locket.

"I *have* no theory. He left a largeish mass of debt," Peter Baron added. At this Mr. Locket got up, while his visitor pursued: "So far as I can ascertain, though of course my inquiries have had to be very rapid and superficial, there is no one now living, directly or indirectly related to the personage in question, who would be likely to suffer from any steps in the direction of publicity. It happens to be a rare instance of a life that had, as it were, no loose ends. At least there are none perceptible at present."

"I see, I see," said Mr. Locket. "But I don't think I should care much for your article."

"What article?"

"The one you seem to wish to write, embodying this new matter."

"Oh, I don't wish to write it!" Peter exclaimed. And then he bade his host good-by.

"Good-by," said Mr. Locket. "Mind you, I don't say that I think there's nothing in it."

"You would think there was something in it if you were to see my documents."

"I should like to see the secret compartment," the caustic editor rejoined. "Copy me out some extracts."

"To what end, if there's no question of their being of use to you?"

"I don't say that—I might like the letters themselves."

"Themselves?"

"Not as the basis of a paper, but just to publish—for a sensation."

"They'd sell your number!" Baron laughed.

"I daresay I should like to look at them," Mr. Locket conceded after a moment. "When should I find you at home?"

"Don't come," said the young man. "I make you no offer."

"I might make *you* one," the editor hinted.

"Don't trouble yourself; I shall probably destroy them." With this Peter Baron took his departure, waiting however just afterwards, in the street near the house, as if he had been looking out for a stray hansom, to which he would not have signalled had it appeared. He thought Mr. Locket might hurry after him, but Mr. Locket seemed to have other things to do, and Peter Baron returned on foot to Jersey Villas.

IV.

On the evening that succeeded this apparently pointless encounter he had an interview more conclusive with Mrs. Bundy, for whose shrewd and philosophic view of life he had several times expressed, even to the good woman herself, a considerable relish. The situation at Jersey Villas (Mrs. Ryves had suddenly flown off to Dover) was such as to create in him a desire for moral support, and there was a kind of domestic determination in Mrs. Bundy which seemed, in general, to advertise it. He had asked for her on coming in, but had been told she was absent for the hour; upon which he had addressed himself mechanically to the task of doing up his dishonoured manuscript—the ingenious fiction about which Mr. Locket had been so stupid—for further adventures and not improbable defeats. He passed a restless, ineffective afternoon, asking himself if his genius were a horrid delusion, looking out of his window for something that didn't happen, something that seemed now to be the advent of a persuasive Mr. Locket and now the return, from an absence more disappointing even than Mrs. Bundy's, of his interesting neighbour of the parlours. He was so nervous and so depressed that he was unable even to fix his mind on the composition of the note with which, on its next peregrination, it was necessary that his manuscript should be accompanied. He was too nervous to eat, and he forgot even to dine; he forgot to light his candles, he let his fire go out, and it was in the melancholy chill of the late dusk that Mrs. Bundy, arriving at last with his lamp, found him extended moodily upon his sofa. She had been informed that he wished to speak to her, and as she placed on the malodorous luminary an oily shade of green pasteboard she expressed the friendly hope that there was nothing wrong with his 'ealth.

The young man rose from his couch, pulling himself together sufficiently to reply that his health was well enough but that his spirits were down in his boots. He had a strong disposition to "draw" his landlady on the subject of Mrs. Ryves, as well as a vivid conviction that she constituted a theme as to which Mrs. Bundy would require little pressure to tell him even more than she knew. At the same time he hated to appear to pry into the secrets of his absent friend; to discuss her with their bustling hostess resembled too much for his taste a gossip with a tattling servant about an unconscious employer. He left out of account however Mrs. Bundy's knowledge of the human heart, for it was this fine principle that broke down the barriers after he had reflected reassuringly that it was not meddling with Mrs. Ryves's affairs to try and find out if she struck such an observer as happy. Crudely, abruptly, even a little blushingly, he put the direct question to Mrs. Bundy, and this led tolerably straight to another question, which, on his spirit, sat equally heavy (they were indeed but different phases of the same), and which the good woman answered with expression when she ejaculated: "Think it a liberty for you to run down for a few hours? If she do, my dear sir, just send her to me to talk to!" As regards happiness indeed she warned Baron against imposing too high a standard on a young thing who had been through so much, and before he knew it he found himself, without the responsibility of choice, in submissive receipt of Mrs. Bundy's version of this experience. It was an interesting picture, though it had its infirmities, one of them congenital and consisting of the fact that it had sprung essentially from the virginal brain of Miss Teagle. Amplified, edited, embellished by the richer genius of Mrs. Bundy, who had incorporated with it and now liberally introduced copious interleavings of Miss Teagle's own romance, it gave Peter Baron much food for meditation, at the same time that it only half relieved his curiosity about the causes of the charming woman's underlying strangeness. He sounded this note experimentally in Mrs. Bundy's ear, but it was easy to see that it didn't reverberate in her fancy. She had no idea of the picture it would have been natural for him to desire that Mrs. Ryves should present to him, and she was therefore unable to estimate the points in respect to which his actual impression was irritating. She had indeed no adequate conception of the intellectual requirements of a young man in love. She couldn't tell him why their faultless friend was so isolated, so unrelated, so nervously, shrinkingly proud. On the other hand she could tell him (he knew it already) that she had passed many years of her life in the acquisition of accomplishments at a seat of learning no less remote than Boulogne, and that Miss Teagle had been intimately acquainted with the late Mr. Everard Ryves, who was a "most rising" young man in the city, not making any year less than his clear twelve hundred. "Now that he isn't there to make them, his mourning widow can't live as she had then, can she?" Mrs. Bundy asked.

Baron was not prepared to say that she could, but he thought of another way she might live as he sat, the next day, in the train which rattled him down to Dover. The place, as he approached it, seemed bright and breezy to him; his roamings had been neither far enough nor frequent enough to make the cockneyfied coast insipid. Mrs. Bundy had of course given him the address he needed, and on emerging from the station he was on the point of asking what direction he should take. His attention however at this moment was drawn away by the bustle of the departing boat. He had been long enough shut up in London to be conscious of refreshment in the mere act of turning his face to Paris. He wandered off to the pier in company with happier tourists and, leaning on a rail, watched enviously the preparation, the agitation of foreign travel. It was for some minutes a foretaste of adventure; but, ah, when was he to have the very draught? He turned away as he dropped this interrogative sigh, and in doing so perceived that in another part of the pier two ladies and a little boy were gathered with something of the same wistfulness. The little boy indeed happened to look round for a moment, upon which, with the keenness of the predatory age, he recognised in our young man a source of pleasures from which he lately had been weaned. He bounded forward with irrepressible cries of "Geegee!" and Peter lifted him aloft for an embrace. On putting him down the pilgrim from Jersey Villas stood confronted with a sensibly severe Miss Teagle, who had followed her little charge. "What's the matter with the old woman?" he asked himself as he offered her a hand which she treated as the merest detail. Whatever it was, it was (and very properly, on the part of a loyal *suivante*) the same complaint as that of her employer, to whom, from a distance, for Mrs. Ryves had not advanced an inch, he flourished his hat as she stood looking at him with a face that he imagined rather white. Mrs. Ryves's response to this salutation was to shift her position in such a manner as to appear again absorbed in the Calais boat. Peter Baron, however, kept hold of the child, whom Miss Teagle artfully endeavoured to wrest from him—a policy in which he was aided by Sidney's own rough but instinctive loyalty; and he was thankful for the happy effect of being dragged by his jubilant friend in the very direction in which he had tended for so many hours. Mrs. Ryves turned once more as he came near, and then, from the sweet, strained smile with which she asked him if he were on his way to France, he saw that if she had been angry at his having followed her she had quickly got over it.

"No, I'm not crossing; but it came over me that you might be, and that's why I hurried down—to catch you before you were off."

"Oh, we can't go—more's the pity; but why, if we could," Mrs. Ryves inquired, "should you wish to prevent it?"

"Because I've something to ask you first, something that may take some time." He saw now that her embarrassment had really not been resentful; it had been nervous, tremulous, as the emotion of an unexpected pleasure might have been. "That's really why I determined last night, without asking your leave first to pay you this little visit—that and the intense desire for another bout of horse-play with Sidney. Oh, I've come to see you," Peter Baron went on, "and I won't make any secret of the fact that I expect you to resign yourself gracefully to the trial and give me all your time. The day's lovely, and I'm ready to declare that the place is as good as the day. Let me drink deep of these things, drain the cup like a man who hasn't been out of London for months and months. Let me walk with you and talk with you and lunch with you—I go back this afternoon. Give me all your hours in short, so that they may live in my memory as one of the sweetest occasions of life."

The emission of steam from the French packet made such an uproar that Baron could breathe his passion into the young woman's ear without scandalising the spectators; and the charm which little by little it scattered over his fleeting visit proved indeed to be the collective influence of the conditions he had put into words. "What is it you wish to ask me?" Mrs. Ryves demanded, as they stood there together; to which he replied that he would tell her all about it if she would send Miss Teagle off with Sidney. Miss Teagle, who was always anticipating her cue, had already begun ostentatiously to gaze at the distant shores of France and was easily enough induced to take an earlier start home and rise to the responsibility of stopping on her way to contend with the butcher. She had however to retire without Sidney, who clung to his recovered prey, so that the rest of the episode was seasoned, to Baron's sense, by the importunate twitch of the child's little, plump, cool hand. The friends wandered together with a conjugal air and Sidney not between them, hanging wistfully, first, over the lengthened picture of the Calais boat, till they could look after it, as it moved rumbling away, in a spell of silence which seemed to confess—especially when, a moment later, their eyes met—that it produced the same fond fancy in each. The presence of the boy moreover was no hindrance to their talking in a manner that they made believe was very frank. Peter Baron presently told his companion what it was he had taken a journey to ask, and he had time afterwards to get over his discomfiture at her appearance of having fancied it might be something greater. She seemed disappointed (but she was forgiving) on learning from him that he had only wished to know if she judged ferociously his not having complied with her request to respect certain seals.

"How ferociously do you suspect me of having judged it?" she inquired.

"Why, to the extent of leaving the house the next moment."

They were still lingering on the great granite pier when he touched on this matter, and she sat down at the end while the breeze, warmed by the sunshine, ruffled the purple sea. She coloured a little and looked troubled, and after an instant she repeated interrogatively: "The next moment?"

"As soon as I told you what I had done. I was scrupulous about this, you will remember; I went straight downstairs to confess to you. You turned away from me, saying nothing; I couldn't imagine—as I vow I can't imagine now—why such a matter should appear so closely to touch you. I went out on some business and when I returned you had quitted the house. It had all the look of my having offended you, of your wishing to get away from me. You didn't even give me time to tell you how it was that, in spite of your advice, I determined to see for myself what my discovery represented. You must do me justice and hear what determined me."

Mrs. Ryves got up from her seat and asked him, as a particular favour, not to allude again to his discovery. It was no concern of hers at all, and she had no warrant for prying into his secrets. She was very sorry to have been for a moment so absurd as to appear to do so, and she humbly begged his pardon for her meddling. Saying this she walked on with a charming colour in her cheek, while he laughed out, though he was really bewildered, at the endless capriciousness of women. Fortunately the incident didn't spoil the hour, in which there were other sources of satisfaction, and they took their course to her lodgings with such pleasant little pauses and excursions by the way as permitted her to show him the objects of interest at Dover. She let him stop at a wine-merchant's and buy a

bottle for luncheon, of which, in its order, they partook, together with a pudding invented by Miss Teagle, which, as they
hypocritically swallowed it, made them look at each other in
an intimacy of indulgence. They came out again and, while
Sidney grubbed in the gravel of the shore, sat selfishly on the
Parade, to the disappointment of Miss Teagle, who had fixed
her hopes on a fly and a ladylike visit to the castle. Baron had
his eye on his watch—he had to think of his train and the dismal return and many other melancholy things; but the sea in
the afternoon light was a more appealing picture; the wind
had gone down, the Channel was crowded, the sails of the
ships were white in the purple distance. The young man had
asked his companion (he had asked her before) when she was
to come back to Jersey Villas, and she had said that she should
probably stay at Dover another week. It was dreadfully expensive, but it was doing the child all the good in the world, and
if Miss Teagle could go up for some things she should probably be able to manage an extension. Earlier in the day she had
said that she perhaps wouldn't return to Jersey Villas at all, or
only return to wind up her connection with Mrs. Bundy. At
another moment she had spoken of an early date, an immediate reoccupation of the wonderful parlours. Baron saw that
she had no plan, no real reasons, that she was vague and, in secret, worried and nervous, waiting for something that didn't
depend on herself. A silence of several minutes had fallen upon
them while they watched the shining sails; to which Mrs.
Ryves put an end by exclaiming abruptly, but without completing her sentence: "Oh, if you had come to tell me you
had destroyed them—"

"Those terrible papers? I like the way you talk about 'de-
stroying!' You don't even know what they are."

"I don't want to know; they put me into a state."

"What sort of a state?"

"I don't know; they haunt me."

"They haunted me; that was why, early one morning, suddenly, I couldn't keep my hands off them. I had told you I
wouldn't touch them. I had deferred to your whim, your
superstition (what is it?) but at last they got the better of me.
I had lain awake all night threshing about, itching with
curiosity. It made me ill; my own nerves (as I may say) were

irritated, my capacity to work was gone. It had come over me in the small hours in the shape of an obsession, a fixed idea, that there was nothing in the ridiculous relics and that my exaggerated scruples were making a fool of me. It was ten to one they were rubbish, they were vain, they were empty; that they had been even a practical joke on the part of some weak-minded gentleman of leisure, the former possessor of the confounded davenport. The longer I hovered about them with such precautions the longer I was taken in, and the sooner I exposed their insignificance the sooner I should get back to my usual occupations. This conviction made my hand so uncontrollable that that morning before breakfast I broke one of the seals. It took me but a few minutes to perceive that the contents were not rubbish; the little bundle contained old letters—very curious old letters.''

"I know—I know; 'private and confidential.' So you broke the other seals?'' Mrs. Ryves looked at him with the strange apprehension he had seen in her eyes when she appeared at his door the moment after his discovery.

''You know, of course, because I told you an hour later, though you would let me tell you very little.''

Baron, as he met this queer gaze, smiled hard at her to prevent her guessing that he smarted with the fine reproach conveyed in the tone of her last words; but she appeared able to guess everything, for she reminded him that she had not had to wait that morning till he came downstairs to know what had happened above, but had shown him at the moment how she had been conscious of it an hour before, had passed on her side the same tormented night as he, and had had to exert extraordinary self-command not to rush up to his rooms while the study of the open packets was going on. "You're so sensitively organised and you've such mysterious powers that you're uncanny,'' Baron declared.

"I feel what takes place at a distance; that's all.''

"One would think somebody you liked was in danger.''

"I told you that that was what was present to me the day I came up to see you.''

"Oh, but you don't like me so much as that,'' Baron argued, laughing.

She hesitated. "No, I don't know that I do.''

"It must be for someone else—the other person concerned. The other day, however, you wouldn't let me tell you that person's name."

Mrs. Ryves, at this, rose quickly. "I don't want to know it; it's none of my business."

"No, fortunately, I don't think it is," Baron rejoined, walking with her along the Parade. She had Sidney by the hand now, and the young man was on the other side of her. They moved toward the station—she had offered to go part of the way. "But with your miraculous gift it's a wonder you haven't divined."

"I only divine what I want," said Mrs. Ryves.

"That's very convenient!" exclaimed Peter, to whom Sidney had presently come round again. "Only, being thus in the dark, it's difficult to see your motive for wishing the papers destroyed."

Mrs. Ryves meditated, looking fixedly at the ground. "I thought you might do it to oblige me."

"Does it strike you that such an expectation, formed in such conditions, is reasonable?"

Mrs. Ryves stopped short, and this time she turned on him the clouded clearness of her eyes. "What do you mean to do with them?"

It was Peter Baron's turn to meditate, which he did, on the empty asphalt of the Parade (the "season," at Dover, was not yet), where their shadows were long in the afternoon light. He was under such a charm as he had never known, and he wanted immensely to be able to reply: "I'll do anything you like if you'll love me." These words, however, would have represented a responsibility and have constituted what was vulgarly termed an offer. An offer of what? he quickly asked himself here, as he had already asked himself after making in spirit other awkward dashes in the same direction—of what but his poverty, his obscurity, his attempts that had come to nothing, his abilities for which there was nothing to show? Mrs. Ryves was not exactly a success, but she was a greater success than Peter Baron. Poor as he was he hated the sordid (he knew she didn't love it), and he felt small for talking of marriage. Therefore he didn't put the question in the words it would have pleased him most to hear himself utter, but he compromised, with an angry young pang, and said to her: "What will you do for me if I put an end to them?"

She shook her head sadly—it was always her prettiest movement. "I can promise nothing—oh, no, I can't promise! We must part now," she added. "You'll miss your train."

He looked at his watch, taking the hand she held out to him. She drew it away quickly, and nothing then was left him, before hurrying to the station, but to catch up Sidney and squeeze him till he uttered a little shriek. On the way back to town the situation struck him as grotesque.

v.

It tormented him so the next morning that after threshing it out a little further he felt he had something of a grievance. Mrs. Ryves's intervention had made him acutely uncomfortable, for she had taken the attitude of exerting pressure without, it appeared, recognising on his part an equal right. She had imposed herself as an influence, yet she held herself aloof as a participant; there were things she looked to him to do for her, yet she could tell him of no good that would come to him from the doing. She should either have had less to say or have been willing to say more, and he asked himself why he should be the sport of her moods and her mysteries. He perceived her knack of punctual interference to be striking, but it was just this apparent infallibility that he resented. Why didn't she set up at once as a professional clairvoyant and eke out her little income more successfully? In purely private life such a gift was disconcerting; her divinations, her evasions disturbed at any rate his own tranquillity.

What disturbed it still further was that he received early in the day a visit from Mr. Locket, who, leaving him under no illusion as to the grounds of such an honour, remarked as soon as he had got into the room or rather while he still panted on the second flight and the smudged little slavey held open Baron's door, that he had taken up his young friend's invitation to look at Sir Dominick Ferrand's letters for himself. Peter drew them forth with a promptitude intended to show that he recognised the commercial character of the call and without attenuating the inconsequence of this departure from the last determination he had expressed to Mr. Locket. He showed his visitor the davenport and the hidden recess, and he smoked a cigarette, humming softly, with a sense of unwonted advantage and triumph, while the cautious editor sat silent and handled the papers. For all his caution Mr. Locket was unable to keep a warmer light out of his judicial eye as he said to Baron at last with sociable brevity—a tone that took many things for granted: "I'll take them home with me—they require much attention."

The young man looked at him a moment. "Do you think they're genuine?" He didn't mean to be mocking, he meant not to be; but the words sounded so to his own ear, and he could see that they produced that effect on Mr. Locket.

"I can't in the least determine. I shall have to go into them at my leisure, and that's why I ask you to lend them to me." He had shuffled the papers together with a movement charged, while he spoke, with the air of being preliminary to that of thrusting them into a little black bag which he had brought with him and which, resting on the shelf of the davenport, struck Peter, who viewed it askance, as an object darkly editorial. It made our young man, somehow, suddenly apprehensive; the advantage of which he had just been conscious was about to be transferred by a quiet process of legerdemain to a person who already had advantages enough. Baron, in short, felt a deep pang of anxiety; he couldn't have said why. Mr. Locket took decidedly too many things for granted, and the explorer of Sir Dominick Ferrand's irregularities remembered afresh how clear he had been after all about his indisposition to traffic in them. He asked his visitor to what end he wished to remove the letters, since on the one hand there was no question now of the article in the Promiscuous which was to reveal their existence, and on the other he himself, as their owner, had a thousand insurmountable scruples about putting them into circulation.

Mr. Locket looked over his spectacles as over the battlements of a fortress. "I'm not thinking of the end—I'm thinking of the beginning. A few glances have assured me that such documents ought to be submitted to some competent eye."

"Oh, you mustn't show them to anyone!" Baron exclaimed.

"You may think me presumptuous, but the eye that I venture to allude to in those terms—"

"Is the eye now fixed so terribly on *me*?" Peter laughingly interrupted. "Oh, it would be interesting, I confess, to know how they strike a man of your acuteness!" It had occurred to him that by such a concession he might endear himself to a literary umpire hitherto implacable. There would be no question of his publishing Sir Dominick Ferrand, but he might, in due acknowledgment of services rendered, form the habit of publishing Peter Baron. "How long would it be your idea to retain them?" he inquired, in a manner which, he immediately became aware, was what incited Mr. Locket to begin stuffing the papers into his bag. With this perception he came quickly closer and, laying his hand on the gaping receptacle, lightly drew its two lips together. In this way the two men stood for a few seconds, touching, almost in the attitude of combat, looking hard into each other's eyes.

The tension was quickly relieved however by the surprised flush which mantled on Mr. Locket's brow. He fell back a few steps with an injured dignity that might have been a protest against physical violence. "Really, my dear young sir, your attitude is tantamount to an accusation of intended bad faith. Do you think I want to steal the confounded things?" In reply to such a challenge Peter could only hastily declare that he was guilty of no discourteous suspicion—he only wanted a limit named, a pledge of every precaution against accident. Mr. Locket admitted the justice of the demand, assured him he would restore the property within three days, and completed, with Peter's assistance, his little arrangements for removing it discreetly. When he was ready, his treacherous reticule distended with its treasures, he gave a lingering look at the inscrutable davenport. "It's how they ever got into that thing that puzzles one's brain!"

"There was some concatenation of circumstances that would doubtless seem natural enough if it were explained, but that one would have to remount the stream of time to ascertain. To one course I have definitely made up my mind: not to make any statement or any inquiry at the shop. I simply accept the mystery," said Peter, rather grandly.

"That would be thought a cheap escape if you were to put it into a story," Mr. Locket smiled.

"Yes, I shouldn't offer the story to *you*. I shall be impatient till I see my papers again," the young man called out, as his visitor hurried downstairs.

That evening, by the last delivery, he received, under the Dover postmark, a letter that was not from Miss Teagle. It was a slightly confused but altogether friendly note, written that morning after breakfast, the ostensible purpose of which was to thank him for the amiability of his visit, to express regret at any appearance the writer might have had of meddling with what didn't concern her, and to let him know that the evening before, after he had left her, she had in a moment of inspiration got hold of the tail of a really musical idea—a perfect accompaniment for the song he had so kindly given her. She had scrawled, as a specimen, a few bars at the end of her note, mystic, mocking musical signs which had no sense for her correspondent. The whole letter testified to a restless but rather pointless desire to remain in communication with him. In answering her, however, which he did that night before going to bed, it was on this bright possibility of their collaboration, its advantages for the future of each of them, that Baron principally expatiated. He spoke of this future with an eloquence of which he would have defended the sincerity, and drew of it a picture extravagantly rich. The next morning, as he was about to settle himself to tasks for some time terribly neglected, with a sense that after all it was rather a relief not to be sitting so close to Sir Dominick Ferrand, who had become dreadfully distracting; at the very moment at which he habitually addressed his preliminary invocation to the muse, he was agitated by the arrival of a telegram which proved to be an urgent request from Mr. Locket that he would immediately come down and see him. This represented, for poor Baron, whose funds were very low, another morning sacrificed, but somehow it didn't even occur to him that he might impose his own time upon the editor of the Promiscuous, the keeper of the keys of renown. He had some of the plasticity of the raw contributor. He gave the muse another holiday, feeling she was really ashamed to take it, and in course of time found himself in Mr. Locket's own chair at Mr. Locket's own table—so much nobler an expanse than the slippery slope of the davenport—considering with quick intensity, in the white flash of certain words just brought out by his host, the quantity of happiness, of emancipation that might reside in a hundred pounds.

Yes, that was what it meant: Mr. Locket, in the twenty-four hours, had discovered so much in Sir Dominick's literary remains that his visitor found him primed with an offer. A hundred pounds would be paid him that day, that minute, and no questions would be either asked or answered. "I take all the risks, I take all the risks," the editor of the Promiscuous repeated. The letters were out on the table, Mr. Locket was on the hearthrug, like an orator on a platform, and Peter, under the influence of his sudden ultimatum, had dropped, rather weakly, into the seat which happened to be nearest and which, as he became conscious it moved on a pivot, he whirled round so as to enable himself to look at his tempter with an eye intended to be cold. What surprised him most was to find Mr. Locket taking exactly the line about the expediency of publication which he would have expected Mr. Locket not to take. "Hush it all up; a barren scandal, an offence that can't be remedied, is the thing in the world that least justifies an airing—" some such line as that was the line he would have thought natural to a man whose life was spent in weighing questions of propriety and who had only the other day objected, in the light of this virtue, to a work of the most disinterested art. But the author of that incorruptible masterpiece had put his finger on the place in saying to his interlocutor on the occasion of his last visit that, if given to the world in the pages of the Promiscuous, Sir Dominick's aberrations would sell the edition. It was not necessary for Mr. Locket to reiterate to his young friend his phrase about their making a sensation. If he wished to purchase the "rights," as theatrical people said, it was not to protect a celebrated name or to lock them up in a cupboard. That formula of Baron's covered all the ground, and one edition was a low estimate of the probable performance of the magazine.

Peter left the letters behind him and, on withdrawing from the editorial presence, took a long walk on the Embankment. His impressions were at war with each other—he was flurried by possibilities of which he yet denied the existence. He had consented to trust Mr. Locket with the papers a day or two longer, till he should have thought out the terms on which he might—in the event of certain occurrences—be induced to dispose of them. A hundred pounds were not this gentleman's last word, nor perhaps was mere unreasoning intractability Peter's own. He sighed as he took no note of the pictures made by barges—sighed because it all might mean money. He needed money bitterly; he owed it in disquieting quarters. Mr. Locket had put it before him that he had a high responsi-bility—that he might vindicate the disfigured truth, contribute a chapter to the history of England. "You haven't a right to suppress such momentous facts," the hungry little editor had declared, thinking how the series (he would spread it into three numbers) would be the talk of the town. If Peter had money he might treat himself to ardour, to bliss. Mr. Locket had said, no doubt justly enough, that there were ever so many questions one would have to meet should one venture to play so daring a game. These questions, embarrassments, dangers—the danger, for instance, of the cropping-up of some lurking litigious relative—he would take over unreservedly and bear the brunt of dealing with. It was to be remembered that the papers were discredited, vitiated by their childish ped-igree; such a preposterous origin, suggesting, as he had hinted before, the feeble ingenuity of a third-rate novelist, was a thing he should have to place himself at the positive dis-advantage of being silent about. He would rather give no ac-count of the matter at all than expose himself to the ridicule that such a story would infallibly excite. Couldn't one see them in advance, the clever, taunting things the daily and weekly papers would say? Peter Baron had his guileless side, but he felt, as he worried with a stick that betrayed him the granite parapets of the Thames, that he was not such a fool as not to know how Mr. Locket would "work" the mystery of his marvellous find. Nothing could help it on better with the public than the impenetrability of the secret attached to it. If Mr. Locket should only be able to kick up dust enough over the circumstances that had guided his hand his fortune would literally be made. Peter thought a hundred pounds a low bid, yet he wondered how the Promiscuous could bring itself to offer such a sum—so large it loomed in the light of literary remuneration as hitherto revealed to our young man. The explanation of this anomaly was of course that the editor shrewdly saw a dozen ways of getting his money back. There would be in the "sensation," at a later stage, the making of a book in large type—the book of the hour; and the profits of this scandalous volume or, if one preferred the name, this re-construction, before an impartial posterity, of a great historical humbug, the sum "down," in other words, that any lively publisher would give for it, figured vividly in Mr. Locket's calculations. It was therefore altogether an opportunity of dealing at first hand with the lively publisher that Peter was invited to forego. Peter gave a masterful laugh, rejoicing in his heart that, on the spot, in the *repaire* he had lately quitted, he had not been tempted by a figure that would have ap-proximately represented the value of his property. It was a good job, he mentally added as he turned his face homeward, that there was so little likelihood of his having to struggle with that particular pressure.

VI.

When, half an hour later, he approached Jersey Villas, he noticed that the house-door was open; then, as he reached the gate, saw it make a frame for an unexpected presence. Mrs. Ryves, in her bonnet and jacket, looked out from it as if she were expecting something—as if she had been passing to and fro to watch. Yet when he had expressed to her that it was a delightful welcome she replied that she had only thought there might possibly be a cab in sight. He offered to go and look for one, upon which it appeared that after all she was not, as yet at least, in need. He went back with her into her sitting-room, where she let him know that within a couple of days she had seen clearer what was best; she had determined to quit Jersey Villas and had come up to take away her things, which she had just been packing and getting together.

"I wrote you last night a charming letter in answer to yours," Baron said. "You didn't mention in yours that you were coming up."

"It wasn't your answer that brought me. It hadn't arrived when I came away."

"You'll see when you get back that my letter is charming."

"I daresay." Baron had observed that the room was not, as she had intimated, in confusion—Mrs. Ryves's preparations for departure were not striking. She saw him look round and, standing in front of the fireless grate with her hands behind her, she suddenly asked: "Where have you come from now?"

"From an interview with a literary friend."

"What are you concocting between you?"

"Nothing at all. We've fallen out—we don't agree."

"Is he a publisher?"

"He's an editor."

"Well, I'm glad you don't agree. I don't know what he wants, but, whatever it is, don't do it."

"He must do what *I* want!" said Baron.

"And what's that?"

"Oh, I'll tell you when he has done it!" Baron begged her to let him hear the "musical idea" she had mentioned in her letter; on which she took off her hat and jacket and, seating herself at her piano, gave him, with a sentiment of which the very first notes thrilled him, the accompaniment of his song. She phrased the words with her sketchy sweetness, and he sat there as if he had been held in a velvet vise, throbbing with the emotion, irrecoverable ever after in its freshness, of the young artist in the presence for the first time of "production" —the proofs of his book, the hanging of his picture, the rehearsal of his play. When she had finished he asked again for the same delight, and then for more music and for more; it did him such a world of good, kept him quiet and safe, smoothed out the creases of his spirit. She dropped her own experiments and gave him immortal things, and he lounged there, pacified and charmed, feeling the mean little room grow large and vague and happy possibilities come back. Abruptly, at the piano, she called out to him: "Those papers of yours—the letters you found—are not in the house?"

"No, they're not in the house."

"I was sure of it! No matter—it's all right!" she added. She herself was pacified—trouble was a false note. Later he was on the point of asking her how she knew the objects she had mentioned were not in the house; but he let it pass. The subject was a profitless riddle—a puzzle that grew grotesquely bigger, like some monstrosity seen in the darkness, as one opened one's eyes to it. He closed his eyes he wanted another vision. Besides, she had shown him that she had extraordinary senses—her explanation would have been stranger than the fact. Moreover they had other things to talk about, in particular the question of her putting off her return to Dover till the morrow and dispensing meanwhile with the valuable protection of Sidney. This was indeed but another face of the question of her dining with him somewhere that evening (where else should she dine?)—accompanying him, for instance, just for an hour of Bohemia, in their deadly respectable lives, to a jolly little place in Soho. Mrs. Ryves declined to have her life abused, but in fact, at the proper moment, at the jolly little place, to which she did accompany him—it dealt in macaroni and Chianti—the pair put their elbows on the crumpled cloth and, face to face, with their little emptied coffee-cups pushed away and the young man's cigarette lighted by her command, became increasingly confidential. They went afterwards to the theatre, in cheap places, and came home in "busses" and under umbrellas.

On the way back Peter Baron turned something over in his mind as he had never turned anything before; it was the question of whether, at the end, she would let him come into her sitting-room for five minutes. He felt on this point a passion of suspense and impatience, and yet for what would it be but to tell her how poor he was? This was literally the moment to say it, so supremely depleted had the hour of Bohemia left him. Even Bohemia was too expensive, and yet in the course of the day his whole temper on the subject of certain fitnesses had changed. At Jersey Villas (it was near midnight, and Mrs. Ryves, scratching a light for her glimmering taper, had said: "Oh, yes, come in for a minute if you like!"), in her precarious parlour, which was indeed, after the brilliances of the evening, a return to ugliness and truth, she let him stand while he explained that he had certainly everything in the way of fame and fortune still to gain, but that youth and love and faith and energy—to say nothing of her supreme dearness—were all on his side. Why, if one's beginnings were rough, should one add to the hardness of the conditions by giving up the dream which, if she would only hear him out, would make just the blessed difference? Whether Mrs. Ryves heard him out or not is a circumstance as to which this chronicle happens to be silent; but after he had got possession of both her hands and breathed into her face for a moment all the intensity of his tenderness—in the relief and joy of utterance he felt it carry him like a rising flood—she checked him with better reasons, with a cold, sweet afterthought in which he felt there was something deep. Her procrastinating head-shake was prettier than ever, yet it had never meant so many fears and pains—impossibilities and memories, independences and pieties, and a sort of uncomplaining ache for the ruin of a friendship that had been happy. She had liked him—if she hadn't she wouldn't have let him think so!—but she protested that she had not, in the odious vulgar sense, "encouraged" him. Moreover she couldn't talk of such things in that place, at that hour, and she begged him not to make her regret her good-nature in staying over. There were peculiarities in her position, considerations insurmountable. She got rid of him with kind and confused words, and afterwards, in the dull, humiliated night, he felt that he had been put in his place. Women in her situation, women who after having really loved and lost, usually lived on into the new dawns in which old ghosts steal away. But there was something in his whimsical neighbour that struck him as terribly invulnerable.

VII.

"I've had time to look a little further into what we're prepared to do, and I find the case is one in which I should consider the advisability of going to an extreme length," said Mr. Locket. Jersey Villas the next morning had had the privilege of again receiving the editor of the Promiscuous, and he sat once more at the davenport, where the bone of contention, in the shape of a large, loose heap of papers that showed how much they had been handled, was placed well in view. "We shall see our way to offering you three hundred, but we shouldn't, I must positively assure you, see it a single step further."

Peter Baron, in his dressing-gown and slippers, with his hands in his pockets, crept softly about the room, repeating, below his breath and with inflections that for his own sake he endeavoured to make humorous: "Three hundred—three hundred." His state of mind was far from hilarious, for he felt poor and sore and disappointed; but he wanted to prove to himself that he was gallant—was made, in general and in particular, of undiscourageable stuff. The first thing he had been aware of on stepping into his front room was that a four-wheeled cab, with Mrs. Ryves's luggage upon it, stood at the door of No. 3. Permitting himself, behind his curtain, a pardonable peep, he saw the mistress of his thoughts come out of the house, attended by Mrs. Bundy, and take her place in the modest vehicle. After this his eyes rested for a long time on the sprigged cotton back of the landlady, who kept bobbing at the window of the cab an endlessly moralising old head. Mrs. Ryves had really taken flight—he had made Jersey Villas impossible for her—but Mrs. Bundy, with a magnanimity unprecedented in the profession, seemed to express a belief in the purity of her motives. Baron felt that his own separation had been, for the present at least, effected; every instinct of delicacy prompted him to stand back.

Mr. Locket talked a long time, and Peter Baron listened and waited. He reflected that his willingness to listen would probably excite hopes in his visitor—hopes which he himself was ready to contemplate without a scruple. He felt no pity for Mr. Locket and had no consideration for his suspense or for his possible illusions; he only felt sick and forsaken and in want of comfort and of money. Yet it was a kind of outrage to his dignity to have the knife held to his throat, and he was irritated above all by the ground on which Mr. Locket put the question—the ground of a service rendered to historical truth. It might be—he wasn't clear; it might be—the question was deep, too deep, probably, for his wisdom; at any rate he had to control himself not to interrupt angrily such dry, interested palaver, the false voice of commerce and of cant. He stared tragically out of the window and saw the stupid rain

begin to fall; the day was duller even than his own soul, and
Jersey Villas looked so sordidly hideous that it was no wonder
Mrs. Ryves couldn't endure them. Hideous as they were he
should have to tell Mrs. Bundy in the course of the day that
he was obliged to seek humbler quarters. Suddenly he interrupted Mr. Locket; he observed to him: "I take it that if I
should make you this concession the hospitality of the
Promiscuous would be by that very fact unrestrictedly secured
to me."

Mr. Locket stared. "Hospitality—secured?" He thumbed
the proposition as if it were a hard peach.

"I mean that of course you wouldn't—in courtsey, in gratitude—keep on declining my things."

"I should give them my best attention—as I've always done
in the past."

Peter Baron hesitated. It was a case in which there would
have seemed to be some chance for the ideally shrewd aspirant
in such an advantage as he possessed; but after a moment the
blood rushed into his face with the shame of the idea of pleading for his productions in the name of anything but their
merit. It was as if he had stupidly uttered evil of them. Nevertheless he added the interrogation: "Would you for instance
publish my little story?"

"The one I read (and objected to some features of) the
other day? Do you mean—a—with the alteration?" Mr.
Locket continued.

"Oh, no, I mean utterly without it. The pages you want
altered contain, as I explained to you very lucidly, I think, the
very *raison d'être* of the work, and it would therefore, it seems
to me, be an imbecility of the first magnitude to cancel them."
Peter had really renounced all hope that his critic would understand what he meant, but, under favour of circumstances,
he couldn't forbear to taste the luxury, which probably never
again would come within his reach, of being really plain, for
one wild moment, with an editor.

Mr. Locket gave a constrained smile. "Think of the scandal,
Mr. Baron."

"But isn't this other scandal just what you're going in for?"

"It will be a great public service."

"You mean it will be a big scandal, whereas my poor story would be a very small one, and that it's only out of a big one that money's to be made."

Mr. Locket got up—he too had his dignity to vindicate. "Such a sum as I offer you ought really to be an offset against all claims."

"Very good—I don't mean to make any, since you don't really care for what I write. I take note of your offer," Peter pursued, "and I engage to give you to-night (in a few words left by my own hand at your house) my absolutely definite and final reply."

Mr. Locket's movements, as he hovered near the relics of the eminent statesman, were those of some feathered parent fluttering over a threatened nest. If he had brought his huddled brood back with him this morning it was because he had felt sure enough of closing the bargain to be able to be graceful. He kept a glittering eye on the papers and remarked that he was afraid that before leaving them he must elicit some assurance that in the meanwhile Peter would not place them in any other hands. Peter, at this, gave a laugh of harsher cadence than he intended, asking, justly enough, on what privilege his visitor rested such a demand and why he himself was disqualified from offering his wares to the highest bidder. "Surely you wouldn't hawk such things about?" cried Mr. Locket; but before Baron had time to retort cynically he added: "I'll publish your little story."

"Oh, thank you!"

"I'll publish anything you'll send me," Mr. Locket continued, as he went out. Peter had before this virtually given his word that for the letters he would treat only with the Promiscuous.

The young man passed, during a portion of the rest of the day, the strangest hours of his life. Yet he thought of them afterwards not as a phase of temptation, though they had been full of the emotion that accompanies an intense vision of alternatives. The struggle was already over; it seemed to him that, poor as he was, he was not poor enough to take Mr. Locket's money. He looked at the opposed courses with the self-possession of a man who has chosen, but this self-posses-

sion was in itself the most exquisite of excitements. It was
really a high revulsion and a sort of noble pity. He seemed
indeed to have his finger upon the pulse of history and to be
in the secret of the gods. He had them all in his hand, the
tablets and the scales and the torch. He couldn't keep a character together, but he might easily pull one to pieces. That
would be "creative work" of a kind—he could reconstruct
the character less pleasingly, could show an unknown side of
it. Mr. Locket had had a good deal to say about responsibility;
and responsibility in truth sat there with him all the morning,
while he revolved in his narrow cage and, watching the crude
spring rain on the windows, thought of the dismalness to
which, at Dover, Mrs. Ryves was going back. This influence
took in fact the form, put on the physiognomy of poor Sir
Dominick Ferrand; he was at present as perceptible in it, as
coldly and strangely personal, as if he had been a haunting
ghost and had risen beside his own old hearthstone. Our
friend was accustomed to his company and indeed had spent
so many hours in it of late, following him up at the museum
and comparing his different portraits, engravings and litho-
graphs, in which there seemed to be conscious, pleading eyes
for the betrayer, that their queer intimacy had grown as close
as an embrace. Sir Dominick was very dumb, but he was terrible in his dependence, and Peter would not have encouraged
him by so much curiosity nor reassured him by so much def-
erence had it not been for the young man's complete acceptance of the impossibility of getting out of a tight place by
exposing an individual. It didn't matter that the individual was
dead; it didn't matter that he was dishonest. Peter felt him
sufficiently alive to suffer; he perceived the rectification of history so conscientiously desired by Mr. Locket to be somehow
for himself not an imperative task. It had come over him too
definitely that in a case where one's success was to hinge upon
an act of extradition it would minister most to an easy conscience to let the success go. No, no—even should he be
starving he couldn't make money out of Sir Dominick's disgrace. He was almost surprised at the violence of the horror
with which, as he shuffled mournfully about, the idea of any
such profit inspired him. What was Sir Dominick to him after
all? He wished he had never come across him.

In one of his brooding pauses at the window—the window out of which never again apparently should he see Mrs. Ryves glide across the little garden with the step for which he had liked her from the first—he became aware that the rain was about to intermit and the sun to make some grudging amends. This was a sign that he might go out; he had a vague perception that there were things to be done. He had work to look for, and a cheaper lodging, and a new idea (every idea he had ever cherished had left him), in addition to which the promised little word was to be dropped at Mr. Locket's door. He looked at his watch and was surprised at the hour, for he had nothing but a heartache to show for so much time. He would have to dress quickly, but as he passed to his bedroom his eye was caught by the little pyramid of letters which Mr. Locket had constructed on his davenport. They startled him and, staring at them, he stopped for an instant, half-amused, half-annoyed at their being still in existence. He had so completely destroyed them in spirit that he had taken the act for granted, and he was now reminded of the orderly stages of which an intention must consist to be sincere. Baron went at the papers with all his sincerity, and at his empty grate (where there lately had been no fire and he had only to remove a horrible ornament of tissue paper dear to Mrs. Bundy) he burned the collection with infinite method. It made him feel happier to watch the worst pages turn to illegible ashes—if happiness be the right word to apply to his sense, in the process, of something so crisp and crackling that it suggested the death-rustle of bank-notes.

When ten minutes later he came back into his sitting-room, he seemed to himself oddly, unexpectedly in the presence of a bigger view. It was as if some interfering mass had been so displaced that he could see more sky and more country. Yet the opposite houses were naturally still there, and if the grimy little place looked lighter it was doubtless only because the rain had indeed stopped and the sun was pouring in. Peter went to the window to open it to the altered air, and in doing so beheld at the garden gate the humble "growler" in which a few hours before he had seen Mrs. Ryves take her departure. It was unmistakable—he remembered the knock-kneed white horse; but this made the fact that his friend's luggage no longer surmounted it only the more mystifying. Perhaps the cabman had already removed the luggage—he was now on his box smoking the short pipe that derived relish from inaction paid for. As Peter turned into the room again his ears caught a knock at his own door, a knock explained, as soon as he had responded, by the hard breathing of Mrs. Bundy.

"Please, sir, it's to say she've come back."

"What has she come back for?" Baron's question sounded ungracious, but his heartache had given another throb, and he felt a dread of another wound. It was like a practical joke.

"I think it's for you, sir," said Mrs. Bundy. "She'll see you for a moment, if you'll be so good, in the old place."

Peter followed his hostess downstairs, and Mrs. Bundy ushered him, with her company flourish, into the apartment she had fondly designated.

"I went away this morning, and I've only returned for an instant," said Mrs. Ryves, as soon as Mrs. Bundy had closed the door. He saw that she was different now; something had happened that had made her indulgent.

"Have you been all the way to Dover and back?"

"No, but I've been to Victoria. I've left my luggage there—I've been driving about."

"I hope you've enjoyed it."

"Very much. I've been to see Mr. Morrish."

"Mr. Morrish?"

"The musical publisher. I showed him our song. I played it for him, and he's delighted with it. He declares it's just the thing. He has given me fifty pounds. I think he believes in us," Mrs. Ryves went on, while Baron stared at the wonder— too sweet to be safe, it seemed to him as yet—of her standing there again before him and speaking of what they had in common. "Fifty pounds! fifty pounds!" she exclaimed, fluttering at him her happy cheque. She had come back, the first thing, to tell him, and of course his share of the money would be the half. She was rosy, jubilant, natural, she chattered like a happy woman. She said they must do more, ever so much more. Mr. Morrish had practically promised he would take anything that was as good as that. She had kept her cab because she was going to Dover; she couldn't leave the others alone. It was a vehicle infirm and inert, but Baron, after a

little, appreciated its pace, for she had consented to his getting
in with her and driving, this time in earnest, to Victoria. She
had only come to tell him the good news—she repeated this
assurance more than once. They talked of it so profoundly
that it drove everything else for the time out of his head—his
duty to Mr. Locket, the remarkable sacrifice he had just
achieved, and even the odd coincidence, matching with the
oddity of all the others, of her having reverted to the house
again, as if with one of her famous divinations, at the very
moment the trumpery papers, the origin really of their intimacy, had ceased to exist. But she, on her side, also had evidently forgotten the trumpery papers: she never mentioned
them again, and Peter Baron never boasted of what he had
done with them. He was silent for a while, from curiosity to
see if her fine nerves had really given her a hint; and then
later, when it came to be a question of his permanent attitude,
he was silent, prodigiously, religiously, tremulously silent, in
consequence of an extraordinary conversation that he had
with her.

This conversation took place at Dover, when he went down
to give her the money for which, at Mr. Morrish's bank, he
had exchanged the cheque she had left with him. That
cheque, or rather certain things it represented, had made
somehow all the difference in their relations. The difference
was huge, and Baron could think of nothing but this confirmed vision of their being able to work fruitfully together
that would account for so rapid a change. She didn't talk of
impossibilities now—she didn't seem to want to stop him off;
only when, the day following his arrival at Dover with the fifty
pounds (he had after all to agree to share them with her—he
couldn't expect her to take a present of money from him), he
returned to the question over which they had had their little
scene the night they dined together on this occasion (he had
brought a portmanteau and he was staying) she mentioned
that there was something very particular she had it on her
conscience to tell him before letting him commit himself.
There dawned in her face as she approached the subject a light
of warning that frightened him; it was charged with something so strange that for an instant he held his breath. This
flash of ugly possibilities passed however, and it was with the

gesture of taking still tenderer possession of her, checked indeed by the grave, important way she held up a finger, that he answered: "Tell me everything—tell me!"

"You must know what I am—who I am; you must know especially what I'm not! There's a name for it, a hideous, cruel name. It's not my fault! Others have known, I've had to speak of it—it has made a great difference in my life. Surely you must have guessed!" she went on, with the thinnest quaver of irony, letting him now take her hand, which felt as cold as her hard duty. "Don't you see I've no belongings, no relations, no friends, nothing at all, in all the world, of my own? I was only a poor girl."

"A poor girl?" Baron was mystified, touched, distressed, piecing dimly together what she meant, but feeling, in a great surge of pity, that it was only something more to love her for.

"My mother—my poor mother," said Mrs. Ryves. She paused with this, and through gathering tears her eyes met his as if to plead with him to understand. He understood, and drew her closer, but she kept herself free still, to continue: "She was a poor girl—she was only a governess; she was alone, she thought he loved her. He did—I think it was the only happiness she ever knew. But she died of it."

"Oh, I'm so glad you tell me—it's so grand of you!" Baron murmured. "Then—your father?" He hesitated, as if with his hands on old wounds.

"He had his own troubles, but he was kind to her. It was all misery and folly—he was married. He wasn't happy—there were good reasons, I believe, for that. I know it from letters, I know it from a person who's dead. Everyone is dead now—it's too far off. That's the only good thing. He was very kind to me; I remember him, though I didn't know then, as a little girl, who he was. He put me with some very good people—he did what he could for me. I think, later, his wife knew—a lady who came to see me once after his death. I was a very little girl, but I remember many things. What he could he did—something that helped me afterwards, something that helps me now. I think of him with a strange pity—I *see* him!" said Mrs. Ryves, with the faint past in her eyes. "You mustn't say anything against him," she added, gently and gravely.

"Never—never; for he has only made it more of a rapture to care for you."

"You must wait, you must think; we must wait together," she went on. "You can't tell, and you must give me time. Now that you know, it's all right; but you had to know. Doesn't it make us better friends?" asked Mrs. Ryves, with a tired smile which had the effect of putting the whole story further and further away. The next moment, however, she added quickly, as if with the sense that it couldn't be far enough: "You don't know, you can't judge, you must let it settle. Think of it, think of it; oh you will, and leave it so. I must have time myself, oh I must! Yes, you must believe me."

She turned away from him, and he remained looking at her a moment. "Ah, how I shall work for you!" he exclaimed.

"You must work for yourself; I'll help you." Her eyes had met his eyes again, and she added, hesitating, thinking: "You had better know, perhaps, who he was."

Baron shook his head, smiling confidently. "I don't care a straw."

"I do—a little. He was a great man."

"There must indeed have been some good in him."

"He was a high celebrity. You've often heard of him."

Baron wondered an instant. "I've no doubt you're a princess!" he said with a laugh. She made him nervous.

"I'm not ashamed of him. He was Sir Dominick Ferrand."

Baron saw in her face, in a few seconds, that she had seen something in his. He knew that he stared, then turned pale; it had the effect of a powerful shock. He was cold for an instant, as he had just found her, with the sense of danger, the confused horror of having dealt a blow. But the blood rushed back to its courses with his still quicker consciousness of safety, and he could make out, as he recovered his balance, that his emotion struck her simply as a violent surprise. He gave a muffled murmur: "Ah, it's you, my beloved!" which lost itself as he drew her close and held her long, in the intensity of his embrace and the wonder of his escape. It took more than a minute for him to say over to himself often enough, with his hidden face: "Ah, she must never, never know!"

She never knew; she only learned, when she asked him casually, that he had in fact destroyed the old documents she had had such a comic caprice about. The sensibility, the curiosity they had had the queer privilege of exciting in her had lapsed with the event as irresponsibly as they had arisen, and she appeared to have forgotten, or rather to attribute now to other causes, the agitation and several of the odd incidents that accompanied them. They naturally gave Peter Baron rather more to think about, much food, indeed, for clandestine meditation, some of which, in spite of the pains he took not to be caught, was noted by his friend and interpreted, to his knowledge, as depression produced by the long probation she succeeded in imposing on him. He was more patient than she could guess, with all her guessing, for if he was put to the proof she herself was not left undissected. It came back to him again and again that if the documents he had burned proved anything they proved that Sir Dominick Ferrand's human errors were not all of one order. The woman he loved was the daughter of her father, he couldn't get over that. What was more to the point was that as he came to know her better and better—for they did work together under Mr. Morrish's protection—his affection was a quantity still less to be neglected. He sometimes wondered, in the light of her general straightness (their marriage had brought out even more than he believed there was of it) whether the relics in the davenport were genuine. That piece of furniture is still almost as useful to him as Mr. Morrish's patronage. There is a tremendous run, as this gentleman calls it, on several of their songs. Baron nevertheless still tries his hand also at prose, and his offerings are now not always declined by the magazines. But he has never approached the Promiscuous again. This periodical published in due course a highly eulogistic study of the remarkable career of Sir Dominick Ferrand.

Greville Fane

COMING IN to dress for dinner, I found a telegram: "Mrs. Stormer dying; can you give us half a column for to-morrow evening? Let her off easy, but not too easy." I was late; I was in a hurry; I had very little time to think, but at a venture I dispatched a reply: "Will do what I can." It was not till I had dressed and was rolling away to dinner that, in the hansom, I bethought myself of the difficulty of the condition attached. The difficulty was not of course in letting her off easy but in qualifying that indulgence. "I simply won't qualify it," I said to myself. I didn't admire her, but I liked her, and I had known her so long that I almost felt heartless in sitting down at such an hour to a feast of indifference. I must have seemed abstracted, for the early years of my acquaintance with her came back to me. I spoke of her to the lady I had taken down, but the lady I had taken down had never heard of Greville Fane. I tried my other neighbour, who pronounced her books "too vile." I had never thought them very good, but I should let her off easier than that.

I came away early, for the express purpose of driving to ask about her. The journey took time, for she lived in the north-west district, in the neighbourhood of Primrose Hill. My apprehension that I should be too late was justified in a fuller sense than I had attached to it—I had only feared that the house would be shut up. There were lights in the windows, and the temperate tinkle of my bell brought a servant immediately to the door, but poor Mrs. Stormer had passed into a state in which the resonance of no earthly knocker was to be feared. A lady, in the hall, hovering behind the servant, came forward when she heard my voice. I recognised Lady Luard, but she had mistaken me for the doctor.

"Excuse my appearing at such an hour," I said; "it was the first possible moment after I heard."

"It's all over," Lady Luard replied. "Dearest mamma!"

She stood there under the lamp with her eyes on me; she was very tall, very stiff, very cold, and always looked as if these things, and some others beside, in her dress, her manner and

217

even her name, were an implication that she was very admirable. I had never been able to follow the argument, but that is a detail. I expressed briefly and frankly what I felt, while the little mottled maidservant flattened herself against the wall of the narrow passage and tried to look detached without looking indifferent. It was not a moment to make a visit, and I was on the point of retreating when Lady Luard arrested me with a queer, casual, drawling "Would you—a—would you, perhaps, be *writing* something?" I felt for the instant like an interviewer, which I was not. But I pleaded guilty to this intention, on which she rejoined: "I'm so very glad—but I think my brother would like to see you." I detested her brother, but it wasn't an occasion to act this out; so I suffered myself to be inducted, to my surprise, into a small back room which I immediately recognised as the scene, during the later years, of Mrs. Stormer's imperturbable industry. Her table was there, the battered and blotted accessory to innumerable literary lapses, with its contracted space for the arms (she wrote only from the elbow down) and the confusion of scrappy, scribbled sheets which had already become literary remains. Leolin was also there, smoking a cigarette before the fire and looking impudent even in his grief, sincere as it well might have been.

To meet him, to greet him, I had to make a sharp effort; for the air that he wore to me as he stood before me was quite that of his mother's murderer. She lay silent for ever upstairs—as dead as an unsuccessful book, and his swaggering erectness was a kind of symbol of his having killed her. I wondered if he had already, with his sister, been calculating what they could get for the poor papers on the table; but I had not long to wait to learn, for in reply to the scanty words of sympathy I addressed him he puffed out: "It's miserable, miserable, yes; but she has left three books complete." His words had the oddest effect; they converted the cramped little room into a seat of trade and made the "book" wonderfully feasible. He would certainly get all that could be got for the three. Lady Luard explained to me that her husband had been with them but had had to go down to the House. To her brother she explained that I was going to write something, and to me again she made it clear that she hoped I would "do mamma justice." She added that she didn't think this had ever been done. She said to her brother: "Don't you think there are some things he ought thoroughly to understand?" and on his instantly exclaiming "Oh, thoroughly—thoroughly!" she went on, rather austerely: "I mean about mamma's birth."

"Yes, and her connections," Leolin added.

I professed every willingness, and for five minutes I listened, but it would be too much to say that I understood. I don't even now, but it is not important. My vision was of other matters than those they put before me, and while they desired there should be no mistake about their ancestors I became more and more lucid about themselves. I got away as soon as possible, and walked home through the great dusky, empty London—the best of all conditions for thought. By the time I reached my door my little article was practically composed—ready to be transferred on the morrow from the polished plate of fancy. I believe it attracted some notice, was thought "graceful" and was said to be by some one else. I had to be pointed without being lively, and it took some tact. But what I said was much less interesting than what I thought—especially during the half-hour I spent in my armchair by the fire, smoking the cigar I always light before going to bed. I went to sleep there, I believe; but I continued to moralise about Greville Fane. I am reluctant to lose that retrospect altogether, and this is a dim little memory of it, a document not to "serve." The dear woman had written a hundred stories, but none so curious as her own.

When first I knew her she had published half-a-dozen fictions, and I believe I had also perpetrated a novel. She was more than a dozen years older than I, but she was a person who always acknowledged her relativity. It was not so very long ago, but in London, amid the big waves of the present, even a near horizon gets hidden. I met her at some dinner and took her down, rather flattered at offering my arm to a celebrity. She didn't look like one, with her matronly, mild, inanimate face, but I supposed her greatness would come out in her conversation. I gave it all the opportunities I could, but I was not disappointed when I found her only a dull, kind woman. This was why I liked her—she rested me so from literature. To myself literature was an irritation, a torment; but

Greville Fane slumbered in the intellectual part of it like a
Creole in a hammock. She was not a woman of genius, but
her faculty was so special, so much a gift out of hand, that I
have often wondered why she fell below that distinction. This
was doubtless because the transaction, in her case, had remained incomplete; genius always pays for the gift, feels the
debt, and she was placidly unconscious of obligation. She
could invent stories by the yard, but she couldn't write a page
of English. She went down to her grave without suspecting
that though she had contributed volumes to the diversion of
her contemporaries she had not contributed a sentence to the
language. This had not prevented bushels of criticism from
being heaped upon her head; she was worth a couple of columns any day to the weekly papers, in which it was shown
that her pictures of life were dreadful but her style really
charming. She asked me to come and see her, and I went. She
lived then in Montpellier Square; which helped me to see how
dissociated her imagination was from her character.

An industrious widow, devoted to her daily stint, to meeting the butcher and baker and making a home for her son
and daughter, from the moment she took her pen in her hand
she became a creature of passion. She thought the English
novel deplorably wanting in that element, and the task she
had cut out for herself was to supply the deficiency. Passion
in high life was the general formula of this work, for her imagination was at home only in the most exalted circles. She
adored, in truth, the aristocracy, and they constituted for her
the romance of the world or, what is more to the point, the
prime material of fiction. Their beauty and luxury, their loves
and revenges, their temptations and surrenders, their immo-
ralities and diamonds were as familiar to her as the blots on
her writing-table. She was not a belated producer of the old
fashionable novel, she had a cleverness and a modernness of
her own, she had freshened up the fly-blown tinsel. She
turned off plots by the hundred and—so far as her flying quill
could convey her—was perpetually going abroad. Her types,
her illustrations, her tone were nothing if not cosmopolitan.
She recognised nothing less provincial than European society,
and her fine folk knew each other and made love to each other
from Doncaster to Bucharest. She had an idea that she re-

sembled Balzac, and her favourite historical characters were
Lucien de Rubempré and the Vidame de Pamiers. I must add
that when I once asked her who the latter personage was she
was unable to tell me. She was very brave and healthy and
cheerful, very abundant and innocent and wicked. She was
clever and vulgar and snobbish, and never so intensely British
as when she was particularly foreign.

This combination of qualities had brought her early success,
and I remember having heard with wonder and envy of what
she "got," in those days, for a novel. The revelation gave me
a pang: it was such a proof that, practising a totally different
style, I should never make my fortune. And yet when, as I
knew her better she told me her real tariff and I saw how
rumour had quadrupled it, I liked her enough to be sorry.
After a while I discovered too that if she got less it was not
that *I* was to get any more. My failure never had what Mrs.
Stormer would have called the banality of being relative—it
was always admirably absolute. She lived at ease however in
those days—ease is exactly the word, though she produced
three novels a year. She scorned me when I spoke of difficulty—it was the only thing that made her angry. If I hinted
that a work of art required a tremendous licking into shape
she thought it a pretension and a *pose*. She never recognised
the "torment of form"; the furthest she went was to introduce
into one of her books (in satire her hand was heavy) a young
poet who was always talking about it. I couldn't quite understand her irritation on this score, for she had nothing at stake
in the matter. She had a shrewd perception that form, in prose
at least, never recommended any one to the public we
were condemned to address, and therefore she lost nothing (putting her private humiliation aside) by not having any. She
made no pretence of producing works of art, but had comfortable tea-drinking hours in which she freely confessed herself a common pastrycook, dealing in such tarts and puddings
as would bring customers to the shop. She put in plenty of
sugar and of cochineal, or whatever it is that gives these articles a rich and attractive colour. She had a serene superiority
to observation and opportunity which constituted an inexpugnable strength and would enable her to go on indefinitely.
It is only real success that wanes, it is only solid things that

melt. Greville Fane's ignorance of life was a resource still more unfailing than the most approved receipt. On her saying once that the day would come when she should have written herself out I answered: "Ah, you look into fairyland, and the fairies love you, and *they* never change. Fairyland is always there; it always was from the beginning of time, and it always will be to the end. They've given you the key and you can always open the door. With me it's different; I try, in my clumsy way, to be in some direct relation to life." "Oh, bother your direct relation to life!" she used to reply, for she was always annoyed by the phrase—which would not in the least prevent her from using it when she wished to try for style. With no more prejudices than an old sausage-mill, she would give forth again with patient punctuality any poor verbal scrap that had been dropped into her. I cheered her with saying that the dark day, at the end, would be for the like of *me*; inasmuch as, going in our small way by experience and observation, we depended not on a revelation, but on a little tiresome process. Observation depended on opportunity, and where should we be when opportunity failed?

One day she told me that as the novelist's life was so delightful and during the good years at least such a comfortable support (she had these staggering optimisms) she meant to train up her boy to follow it. She took the ingenious view that it was a profession like another and that therefore everything was to be gained by beginning young and serving an apprenticeship. Moreover the education would be less expensive than any other special course, inasmuch as she could administer it herself. She didn't profess to keep a school, but she could at least teach her own child. It was not that she was so very clever, but (she confessed to me as if she were afraid I would laugh at her) that *he* was. I didn't laugh at her for that, for I thought the boy sharp—I had seen him at sundry times. He was well grown and good-looking and unabashed, and both he and his sister made me wonder about their defunct papa, concerning whom the little I knew was that he had been a clergyman. I explained them to myself by suppositions and imputations possibly unjust to the departed; so little were they—superficially at least—the children of their mother. There used to be, on an easel in her drawing-room, an enlarged photograph of her husband, done by some horrible posthumous "process" and draped, as to its florid frame, with a silken scarf, which testified to the candour of Greville Fane's bad taste. It made him look like an unsuccessful tragedian; but it was not a thing to trust. He may have been a successful comedian. Of the two children the girl was the elder, and struck me in all her younger years as singularly colourless. She was only very long, like an undecipherable letter. It was not till Mrs. Stormer came back from a protracted residence abroad that Ethel (which was this young lady's name) began to produce the effect, which was afterwards remarkable in her, of a certain kind of high resolution. She made one apprehend that she meant to do something for herself. She was long-necked and near-sighted and striking, and I thought I had never seen sweet seventeen in a form so hard and high and dry. She was cold and affected and ambitious, and she carried an eyeglass with a long handle, which she put up whenever she wanted not to see. She had come out, as the phrase is, immensely; and yet I felt as if she were surrounded with a spiked iron railing. What she meant to do for herself was to marry, and it was the only thing, I think, that she meant to do for any one else; yet who would be inspired to clamber over that bristling barrier? What flower of tenderness or of intimacy would such an adventurer conceive as his reward?

This was for Sir Baldwin Luard to say; but he naturally never confided to me the secret. He was a joyless, jokeless young man, with the air of having other secrets as well, and a determination to get on politically that was indicated by his never having been known to commit himself—as regards any proposition whatever—beyond an exclamatory "Oh!" His wife and he must have conversed mainly in prim ejaculations, but they understood sufficiently that they were kindred spirits. I remember being angry with Greville Fane when she announced these nuptials to me as magnificent; I remember asking her what splendour there was in the union of the daughter of a woman of genius with an irredeemable mediocrity. "Oh! he's awfully clever," she said; but she blushed for the maternal fib. What she meant was that though Sir Baldwin's estates were not vast (he had a dreary house in South Kensington and a still drearier "Hall" somewhere in Essex, which was let),

the connection was a "smarter" one than a child of hers could
have aspired to form. In spite of the social bravery of her
novels she took a very humble and dingy view of herself, so
that of all her productions "my daughter Lady Luard" was
quite the one she was proudest of. That personage thought
her mother very vulgar and was distressed and perplexed by
the occasional license of her pen, but had a complicated attitude in regard to this indirect connection with literature. So
far as it was lucrative her ladyship approved of it, and could
compound with the inferiority of the pursuit by doing practical justice to some of its advantages. I had reason to know
(my reason was simply that poor Mrs. Stormer told me) that
she suffered the inky fingers to press an occasional bank-note
into her palm. On the other hand she deplored the "peculiar
style" to which Greville Fane had devoted herself, and wondered where an author who had the convenience of so lady-
like a daughter could have picked up such views about the
best society. "She might know better, with Leolin and me,"
Lady Luard had been known to remark; but it appeared that
some of Greville Fane's superstitions were incurable. She
didn't live in Lady Luard's society, and the best was not good
enough for her—she must make it still better.

I could see that this necessity grew upon her during the
years she spent abroad, when I had glimpses of her in the
shifting sojourns that lay in the path of my annual ramble. She
betook herself from Germany to Switzerland and from Switzerland to Italy; she favoured cheap places and set up her desk
in the smaller capitals. I took a look at her whenever I could,
and I always asked how Leolin was getting on. She gave me
beautiful accounts of him, and whenever it was possible the
boy was produced for my edification. I had entered from the
first into the joke of his career—I pretended to regard him as
a consecrated child. It had been a joke for Mrs. Stormer at
first, but the boy himself had been shrewd enough to make
the matter serious. If his mother accepted the principle that
the intending novelist cannot begin too early to see life, Leolin was not interested in hanging back from the application of
it. He was eager to qualify himself, and took to cigarettes at
ten, on the highest literary grounds. His poor mother gazed
at him with extravagant envy and, like Desdemona, wished

heaven had made *her* such a man. She explained to me more than once that in her profession she had found her sex a dreadful drawback. She loved the story of Madame George Sand's early rebellion against this hindrance, and believed that if she had worn trousers she could have written as well as that lady. Leolin had for the career at least the qualification of trousers, and as he grew older he recognised its importance by laying in an immense assortment. He grew up in gorgeous apparel, which was his way of interpreting his mother's system. Whenever I met her I found her still under the impression that she was carrying this system out and that Leolin's training was bearing fruit. She was giving him experience, she was giving him impressions, she was putting a *gagne-pain* into his hand. It was another name for spoiling him with the best conscience in the world. The queerest pictures come back to me of this period of the good lady's life and of the extraordinarily virtuous, muddled, bewildering tenor of it. She had an idea that she was seeing foreign manners as well as her petticoats would allow, but, in reality she was not seeing anything, least of all fortunately how much she was laughed at. She drove her whimsical pen at Dresden and at Florence, and produced in all places and at all times the same romantic and ridiculous fictions. She carried about her box of properties and fished out promptly the familiar, tarnished old puppets. She believed in them when others couldn't, and as they were like nothing that was to be seen under the sun it was impossible to prove by comparison that they were wrong. You can't compare birds and fishes; you could only feel that, as Greville Fane's characters had the fine plumage of the former species, human beings must be of the latter.

It would have been droll if it had not been so exemplary to see her tracing the loves of the duchesses beside the innocent cribs of her children. The immoral and the maternal lived together in her diligent days on the most comfortable terms, and she stopped curling the mustaches of her Guardsmen to pat the head of her babes. She was haunted by solemn spinsters who came to tea from continental *pensions*, and by unsophisticated Americans who told her she was just loved in *their* country. "I had rather be just paid there," she usually replied; for this tribute of transatlantic opinion was the only thing that galled her. The Americans went away thinking her coarse; though as the author of so many beautiful love-stories she was disappointing to most of these pilgrims, who had not expected to find a shy, stout, ruddy lady in a cap like a crumbled pyramid. She wrote about the affections and the impossibility of controlling them, but she talked of the price of *pension* and the convenience of an English chemist. She devoted much thought and many thousands of francs to the education of her daughter, who spent three years at a very superior school at Dresden, receiving wonderful instruction in sciences, arts and tongues, and who, taking a different line from Leolin, was to be brought up wholly as a *femme du monde*. The girl was musical and philological; she made a specialty of languages and learned enough about them to be inspired with a great contempt for her mother's artless accents. Greville Fane's French and Italian were droll; the imitative faculty had been denied her, and she had an unequalled gift, especially pen in hand, of squeezing big mistakes into small opportunities. She knew it, but she didn't care; correctness was the virtue in the world that, like her heroes and heroines, she valued least. Ethel, who had perceived in her pages some remarkable lapses, undertook at one time to revise her proofs; but I remember her telling me a year after the girl had left school that this function had been very briefly exercised. "She can't read me," said Mrs. Stormer; "I offend her taste. She tells me that at Dresden—at school—I was never allowed." The good lady seemed surprised at this, having the best conscience in the world about her lucubrations. She had never meant to fly in the face of anything, and considered that she grovelled before the Rhadamanthus of the English literary tribunal, the celebrated and awful Young Person. I assured her, as a joke, that she was frightfully indecent (she hadn't in fact that reality any more than any other) my purpose being solely to prevent her from guessing that her daughter had dropped her not because she was immoral but because she was vulgar. I used to figure her children closeted together and asking each other while they exchanged a gaze of dismay: "Why should she *be* so—and so *fearfully* so—when she has the advantage of our society? Shouldn't *we* have taught her better?" Then I imagined their recognising with a blush and a shrug that she was unteachable, irreformable. Indeed she was, poor lady; but it is never fair to read by the light of taste things that were not written by it. Greville Fane had, in the topsy-turvy, a serene good faith that ought to have been safe from allusion, like a stutter or a *faux pas.*

She didn't make her son ashamed of the profession to which he was destined, however; she only made him ashamed of the way she herself exercised it. But he bore his humiliation much better than his sister, for he was ready to take for granted that he should one day restore the balance. He was a canny and far-seeing youth, with appetites and aspirations, and he had not a scruple in his composition. His mother's theory of the happy knack he could pick up deprived him of the wholesome discipline required to prevent young idlers from becoming cads. He had, abroad, a casual tutor and a snatch or two of a Swiss school, but no consecutive study, no prospect of a university or a degree. It may be imagined with what zeal, as the years went on, he entered into the pleasantry of there being no manual so important to him as the massive book of life. It was an expensive volume to peruse, but Mrs Stormer was willing to lay out a sum in what she would have called her *premiers frais.* Ethel disapproved—she thought this education far too unconventional for an English gentleman. Her voice was for Eton and Oxford, or for any public school (she would have resigned herself) with the army to follow. But Leolin never was afraid of his sister, and they visibly disliked, though they sometimes agreed to assist, each other. They could combine to work the oracle—to keep their mother at her desk.

When she came back to England, telling me she had got all the continent could give her, Leolin was a broad-shouldered, red-faced young man, with an immense wardrobe and an extraordinary assurance of manner. She was fondly obstinate about her having taken the right course with him, and proud of all that he knew and had seen. He was now quite ready to begin, and a little while later she told me he *had* begun. He had written something tremendously clever, and it was coming out in the *Cheapside.* I believe it came out; I had no time to look for it; I never heard anything about it. I took for granted that if this contribution had passed through his mother's hands it had practically become a specimen of her own genius, and it was interesting to consider Mrs. Stormer's future in the light of her having to write her son's novels as well as her own. This was not the way she looked at it herself; she took the charming ground that he would help her to write hers. She used to tell me that he supplied passages of the greatest value to her own work—all sorts of technical things, about hunting and yachting and wine—that she couldn't be expected to get very straight. It was all so much practice for him and so much alleviation for her. I was unable to identify these pages, for I had long since ceased to "keep up" with Greville Fane; but I was quite able to believe that the wine-question had been put, by Leolin's good offices, on a better footing, for the dear lady used to mix her drinks (she was perpetually serving the most splendid suppers) in the queerest fashion. I could see that he was willing enough to accept a commission to look after that department. It occurred to me indeed, when Mrs. Stormer settled in England again, that by making a shrewd use of both her children she might be able to rejuvenate her style. Ethel had come back to gratify her young ambition, and if she couldn't take her mother into society she would at least go into it herself. Silently, stiffly, almost grimly, this young lady held up her head, clenched her long teeth, squared her lean elbows and made her way up the staircases she had elected. The only communication she ever made to me, the only effusion of confidence with which she ever honoured me, was when she said: "I don't want to know the people mamma knows; I mean to know others." I took due note of the remark, for I was not one of the "others." I couldn't trace therefore the steps of her process; I could only admire it at a distance and congratulate her mother on the results. The results were that Ethel went to "big" parties and got people to take her. Some of them were people she had met abroad, and others were people whom the people she had met abroad had met. They ministered alike to Miss Ethel's convenience, and I wondered how she extracted so many favours without the expenditure of a smile. Her smile was the dimmest thing in the world, diluted lemonade, without sugar, and she had arrived precociously at social wisdom, recognising that if she was neither pretty enough nor rich enough nor clever enough, she could at least in her muscular youth be rude enough. Therefore if she was able to tell her mother what really took place in the mansions of the great, give her notes to work from, the quill could be driven at home to better purpose and precisely at a moment when it would have to be more active than ever. But if she did tell, it would appear that poor Mrs. Stormer didn't believe. As regards many points this was not a wonder; at any rate I heard nothing of Greville Fane's having developed a new manner. She had only one manner from start to finish, as Leolin would have said.

She was tired at last, but she mentioned to me that she couldn't afford to pause. She continued to speak of Leolin's work as the great hope of their future (she had saved no money) though the young man wore to my sense an aspect more and more professional if you like, but less and less literary. At the end of a couple of years there was something monstrous in the impudence with which he played his part in the comedy. When I wondered how she could play *her* part I had to perceive that her good faith was complete and that what kept it so was simply her extravagant fondness. She loved the young impostor with a simple, blind, benighted love, and of all the heroes of romance who had passed before her eyes he was by far the most brilliant. He was at any rate the most real—she could touch him, pay for him, suffer for him, worship him. He made her think of her princes and dukes, and when she wished to fix these figures in her mind's eye she thought of her boy. She had often told me she was carried away by her own creations, and she was certainly carried away by Leolin. He vivified, by potentialities at least, the whole question of youth and passion. She held, not unjustly, that the sincere novelist should feel the whole flood of life; she acknowledged with regret that she had not had time to feel it herself, and it was a joy to her that the deficiency might be supplied by the sight of the way it was rushing through this magnificent young man. She exhorted him, I suppose, to let it rush; she wrung her own flaccid little sponge into the torrent. I knew not what passed between them in her hours of tuition, but I gathered that she mainly impressed on him that the great thing was to live, because that gave you material. He asked nothing better; he collected material, and the formula served as a universal pretext. You had only to look at him to see that, with his rings and breastpins, his cross-barred jackets, his early *embonpoint*, his eyes that looked like imitation jewels, his various indications of a dense, full-blown temperament, his idea of life was singularly vulgar; but he was not so far wrong as that his response to his mother's expectations was not in a high degree practical. If she had imposed a profession on him from his tenderest years it was exactly a profession that he followed. The two were not quite the same, inasmuch as *his* was simply to live at her expense; but at least she couldn't say that he hadn't taken a line. If she insisted on believing in him he offered himself to the sacrifice. My impression is that her secret dream was that he should have a *liaison* with a countess, and he persuaded her without difficulty that he had one. I don't know what countesses are capable of, but I have a clear notion of what Leolin was.

He didn't persuade his sister, who despised him—she wished to work her mother in her own way, and I asked myself why the girl's judgment of him didn't make me like her better. It was because it didn't save her after all from a mute agreement with him to go halves. There were moments when I couldn't help looking hard into his atrocious young eyes, challenging him to confess his fantastic fraud and give it up. Not a little tacit conversation passed between us in this way, but he had always the best of it. If I said: "Oh, come now, with *me* you needn't keep it up; plead guilty, and I'll let you off," he wore the most ingenuous, the most candid expression, in the depths of which I could read: "Oh, yes, I know it exasperates you— that's just why I do it." He took the line of earnest inquiry, talked about Balzac and Flaubert, asked me if I thought Dickens *did* exaggerate and Thackeray *ought* to be called a pessimist. Once he came to see me, at his mother's suggestion he declared, on purpose to ask me how far, in my opinion, in the English novel, one really might venture to "go." He was not resigned to the usual pruderies—he suffered under them already. He struck out the brilliant idea that nobody knew how far we might go, for nobody had ever tried. Did I think *he* might safely try—would it injure his mother if he did? He would rather disgrace himself by his timidities than injure his mother, but certainly some one ought to try. Wouldn't *I* try— couldn't I be prevailed upon to look at it as a duty? Surely the ultimate point ought to be fixed—he was worried, haunted by the question. He patronised me unblushingly, made me feel like a foolish amateur, a helpless novice, inquired into my habits of work and conveyed to me that I was utterly *vieux jeu* and had not had the advantage of an early training. I had not been brought up from the germ, I knew nothing of life—didn't go at it on *his* system. He had dipped into French feuilletons and picked up plenty of phrases, and he made a much better show in talk than his poor mother, who never had time to read anything and could only be vivid with her pen. If I didn't kick him down-stairs it was because he would have alighted on her at the bottom.

When she went to live at Primrose Hill I called upon her and found her weary and wasted. It had waned a good deal, the elation caused the year before by Ethel's marriage; the foam on the cup had subsided and there was a bitterness in the draught. She had had to take a cheaper house and she had to work still harder to pay even for that. Sir Baldwin was obliged to be close; his charges were fearful, and the dream of her living with her daughter (a vision she had never mentioned to me) must be renounced. "I would have helped with things, and I could have lived perfectly in one room," she said; "I would have paid for everything, and—after all—I'm some one, ain't I? But I don't fit in, and Ethel tells me there are tiresome people she *must* receive. I can help them from here, no doubt, better than from there. She told me once, you know, what she thinks of my picture of life. 'Mamma, your picture of life is preposterous!' No doubt it is, but she's vexed with me for letting my prices go down; and I had to write three novels to pay for all her marriage cost me. I did it very well—I mean the outfit and the wedding; but that's why I'm here. At any rate she doesn't want a dingy old woman in her house. I should give it an atmosphere of literary glory, but literary glory is only the eminence of nobodies. Besides, she doubts my glory—she knows I'm glorious only at Peckham and Hackney. She doesn't want her friends to ask if I've never known nice people. She can't tell them I've never been in society. She tried to teach me better once, but I couldn't learn. It would seem too as if Peckham and Hackney had had enough of me; for (don't tell any one!) I've had to take less for my last than I ever took for anything." I asked her how little this had been, not from curiosity, but in order to upbraid her, more disinterestedly than Lady Luard had done, for such concessions. She answered "I'm ashamed to tell you," and then she began to cry.

I had never seen her break down, and I was proportionately moved; she sobbed, like a frightened child, over the extinction of her vogue and the exhaustion of her vein. Her little work-room seemed indeed a barren place to grow flowers, and I wondered, in the after years (for she continued to produce and publish) by what desperate and heroic process she dragged them out of the soil. I remember asking her on that occasion what had become of Leolin, and how much longer she intended to allow him to amuse himself at her cost. She rejoined with spirit, wiping her eyes, that he was down at Brighton hard at work—he was in the midst of a novel—and that he *felt* life so, in all its misery and mystery, that it was cruel to speak of such experiences as a pleasure. "He goes beneath the surface," she said, "and he *forces* himself to look at things from which he would rather turn away. Do you call that amusing yourself? You should see his face sometimes! And he does it for me as much as for himself. He tells me every-thing—he comes home to me with his *trouvailles*. We are art-ists together, and to the artist all things are pure. I've often heard you say so yourself." The novel that Leolin was engaged in at Brighton was never published, but a friend of mine and of Mrs. Stormer's who was staying there happened to mention to me later that he had seen the young apprentice to fiction driving, in a dogcart, a young lady with a very pink face. When I suggested that she was perhaps a woman of title with whom he was conscientiously flirting my informant replied: "She is indeed, but do you know what her title is?" He pronounced it—it was familiar and descriptive—but I won't reproduce it here. I don't know whether Leolin mentioned it to his mother: she would have needed all the purity of the artist to forgive him. I hated so to come across him that in the very last years I went rarely to see her, though I knew that she had come pretty well to the end of her rope. I didn't want her to tell me that she had fairly to give her books away—I didn't want to see her cry. She kept it up amazingly, and every few months, at my club, I saw three new volumes, in green, in crimson, in blue, on the book-table that groaned with light literature. Once I met her at the Academy soirée, where you meet people you thought were dead, and she vouchsafed the information, as if she owed it to me in candour, that Leolin had been obliged to recognise insuperable difficulties in the question of *form*, he was so fastidious; so that she had now arrived at a definite understanding with him (it was such a comfort) that *she* would do the form if he would bring home the substance. That was now his position—he foraged for her in the great world at a salary. "He's my 'devil,' don't you see? as if I were a great lawyer: he gets up the case and I argue it." She mentioned further that in addition to his salary he was paid by the piece: he got so much for a striking character, so much for a pretty name, so much for a plot, so much for an incident, and had so much promised him if he would invent a new crime.

"He *has* invented one," I said, "and he's paid every day of his life."

"What is it?" she asked, looking hard at the picture of the year, "Baby's Tub," near which we happened to be standing.

I hesitated a moment. "I myself will write a little story about it, and then you'll see."

But she never saw; she had never seen anything, and she passed away with her fine blindness unimpaired. Her son published every scrap of scribbled paper that could be extracted from her table-drawers, and his sister quarrelled with him mortally about the proceeds, which showed that she only wanted a pretext, for they cannot have been great. I don't know what Leolin lives upon, unless it be on a queer lady many years older than himself, whom he lately married. The last time I met him he said to me with his infuriating smile: "Don't you think we can go a little further still—just a little?" *He* really goes too far.

Collaboration

I DON'T KNOW how much people care for my work, but they like my studio (of which indeed I am exceedingly fond myself), as they show by their inclination to congregate there at dusky hours on winter afternoons, or on long dim evenings when the place looks well with its rich combinations and low-burning lamps and the bad pictures (my own) are not particularly visible. I won't go into the question of how many of these are purchased, but I rejoice in the distinction that my invitations are never declined. Some of my visitors have been good enough to say that on Sunday evenings in particular there is no pleasanter place in Paris—where so many places are pleasant—none friendlier to easy talk and repeated cigarettes, to the exchange of points of view and the comparison of accents. The air is as international as only Parisian air can be; women, I surmise, think they look well in it; they come also because they fancy they are doing something Bohemian, just as many of the men come because they suppose they are doing something correct. The old heraldic cushions on the divans, embossed with rusty gold, are favourable both to expansion and to contraction—that of course of contracting parties—and the Italian brocade on the walls appeals to one's highest feelings. Music makes its home there—though I confess I am not quite the master of *that* house, and when it is going on in a truly receptive hush I enjoy the way my company leans back and gazes through the thin smoke of cigarettes up at the distant Tiepolo in the almost palatial ceiling. I make sure the piano, the tobacco and the tea are all of the best.

For the conversation, I leave that mostly to take care of itself. There are discussions of course and differences—sometimes even a violent circulation of sense and sound; but I have a consciousness that beauty flourishes and that harmonies prevail in the end. I have occasionally known a visitor to be rude to me because he disliked another visitor's opinions—I had seen an old habitué slip away without bidding me good night on the arrival of some confident specimen of *les jeunes*; but as a general thing we have it out together on the spot—the place is really a chamber of justice, a temple of reconciliation: we understand each other if we only sit up late enough. Art protects her children in the long run—she only asks them to trust her. She is like the Catholic Church—she guarantees paradise to the faithful. Music moreover is a universal solvent; though I've not an infallible ear I've a sufficient sense of the matter for that. Ah, the wounds I've known it to heal—the bridges I've known it to build—the ghosts I've known it to lay! Though I've seen people stalk out I've never observed them not to steal back. My studio in short is the theatre of a cosmopolite drama, a comedy essentially "of character."

One of the liveliest scenes of the performance was the evening, last winter, on which I became aware that one of my compatriots—an American, my good friend Alfred Bonus— was engaged in a controversy somewhat acrimonious, on a literary subject, with Herman Heidenmauer, the young composer who had been playing to us divinely a short time before and whom I thought of neither as a disputant nor as an Englishman. I perceived in a moment that something had happened to present him in this combined character to poor Bonus, who was so ardent a patriot that he lived in Paris rather than in London, who had met his interlocutor for the first time on this occasion, and who apparently had been misled by the perfection with which Heidenmauer spoke English— he spoke it really better than Alfred Bonus. The young musician, a born Bavarian, had spent a few years in England, where he had a commercial step-brother planted and more or less prosperous—a helpful man who had watched over his difficult first steps, given him a temporary home, found him publishers and pupils, smoothed the way to a stupefied hearing for his first productions. He knew his London and might at a first glance have been taken for one of its products; but he had, in addition to a genius of the sort that London fosters but doesn't beget, a very German soul. He brought me a note from an old friend on the other side of the Channel, and I liked him as soon as I looked at him; so much indeed that I could forgive him for making me feel thin and empirical, conscious that *he* was one of the higher kind whom the future has looked in the face. He had met through his gold spectacles

her deep eyes, and some mutual communication had occurred. This had given him a confidence which passed for
conceit only with those who didn't know the reason.

I guessed the reason early, and, as may be imagined, he
didn't grudge me the knowledge. He was happy and various—
as little as possible the mere long-haired musicmonger. His
hair was short—it was only his legs and his laughter that were
long. He was fair and rosy, and his gold spectacles glittered
as if in response to the example set them by his beautiful
young golden beard. You would have been sure he was an
artist without going so far as to decide upon his particular
passion; for you would have been conscious that whatever this
passion might be it was acquainted with many of the others
and mixed with them to its profit. Yet these discoveries had
not been fully made by Alfred Bonus, whose occupation was
to write letters to the American journals about the way the
"boys" were coming on in Paris; for in such a case he probably would not have expected such nebulous greatness to con-
dense at a moment's notice. Bonus is clever and critical, and
a sort of self-appointed emissary or agent of the great republic.
He has it at heart to prove that the Americans in Europe *do*
get on—taking for granted on the part of the Americans at
home an interest in this subject greater, as I often assure him,
than any really felt. "Come, now, do *I* get on?" I often ask
him; and I sometimes push the inquiry so far as to stammer:
"And you, my dear Bonus, do *you* get on?" He is apt to look
a little injured on such occasions, as if he would like to say in
reply: "Don't you call it success to have Sunday evenings at
which I'm a regular attendant? And can you question for a
moment the figure I make at them?" It has even occurred to
me that he suspects me of painting badly on purpose to spite
him—that is to interfere with his favourite dogma. Therefore
to spite me in return he's in the heroic predicament of refus-
ing to admit that I'm a failure. He takes a great interest in
the plastic arts, but his intensest sympathy is for literature.
This sentiment is somewhat starved, as in that school the boys
languish as yet on a back seat. To show what they are doing
Bonus has to retreat upon the studios, but there is nothing
he enjoys so much as having, when the rare chance offers, a
good literary talk. He follows the French movement closely

and explains it profusely to our compatriots, whom he mystifies, but who guess he's rather loose.

I forget how his conversation with Heidenmauer began—it was, I think, some difference of opinion about one of the English poets that set them afloat. Heidenmauer knows the English poets, and the French, and the Italian, and the Spanish, and the Russian—he is a wonderful representative of that Germanism which consists in the negation of intellectual frontiers. It is the English poets that, if I'm not mistaken, he loves best, and probably the harm was done by his having happened to say so. At any rate Alfred Bonus let him have it, without due notice perhaps, which is rather Alfred's way, on the question (a favourite one with my compatriot) of the backward state of literature in England, for which after all Heidenmauer was not responsible. Bonus believes in responsibility—the responsibility of others, an attitude which tends to make some of his friends extremely secretive, though perhaps it would have been justified—as to this I'm not sure—had Heidenmauer been, under the circumstances, technically British. Before he had had time to explain that he was not, the other persons present had become aware that a kind of challenge had passed—that nation, in a sudden startled flurry, somehow found itself pitted against nation. There was much vagueness at first as to which of the nations were engaged and as to what their quarrel was about, the question coming presently to appear less simple than the spectacle (so easily conceivable) of a German's finding it hot for him in a French house, a house French enough at any rate to give countenance to the idea of his quick defeat.

How could the right cause fail of protection in any house of which Madame de Brindes and her charming daughter were so good as to be assiduous frequenters? I recollect perfectly the pale gleam of joy in the mother's handsome face when she gathered that what had happened was that a detested German was on his defence. She wears her eternal mourning (I admit it's immensely becoming) for a triple woe, for multiplied griefs and wrongs, all springing from the crash of the Empire, from the battlefields of 1870. Her husband fell at Sedan, her father and her brother on still darker days; both her own family and that of M. de Brindes, their general situation in life, were, as may be said, creations of the Empire, so that from one hour to the other she found herself sinking with the wreck. You won't recognise her under the name I give her, but you may none the less have admired, between their pretty lemon-coloured covers, the touching tales of Claude Lorrain. She plies an ingenious, pathetic pen and has reconciled herself to effort and privation for the sake of her daughter. I say privation, because these distinguished women are poor, receive with great modesty and have broken with a hundred of those social sanctities that are dearer to French souls than to any others. They have gone down into the market-place, and Paule de Brindes, who is three-and-twenty to-day and has a happy turn for keeping a water-colour liquid, earns a hundred francs here and there. She is not so handsome as her mother, but she has magnificent hair and what the French call a look of race, and is, or at least was till the other day, a frank and charming young woman. There is something exquisite in the way these ladies are earnestly, conscientiously modern. From the moment they accept necessities they accept them all, and poor Madame de Brindes flatters herself that she has made her dowerless daughter one of us others. The girl goes out alone, talks with young men and, although she only paints landscape, takes a free view of the *convenances*. Nothing can please either of them more than to tell them they have thrown over their superstitions. They haven't, thank heaven; and when I want to be reminded of some of the prettiest in the world—of a thousand fine scruples and pleasant forms, and of what grace can do for the sake of grace—I know where to go for it.

It was a part of this pious heresy—much more august in the way they presented it than some of the aspects of the old faith—that Paule should have become "engaged," quite like a *jeune mees*, to my brilliant friend Félix Vendemer. He is such a votary of the modern that he was inevitably interested in the girl of the future and had matched one reform with another, being ready to marry without a penny, as the clearest way of expressing his appreciation, this favourable specimen of the type. He simply fell in love with Mademoiselle de Brindes and behaved, on his side, equally like one of us others, except that he begged me to ask her mother for her hand. I was inspired to do so with eloquence, and my friends were

not insensible of such an opportunity to show that they now
lived in the world of realities. Vendemer's sole fortune is his
genius, and he and Paule, who confessed to an answering
flame, plighted their troth like a pair of young rustics or (what
comes for French people to the same thing) young Anglo-
Saxons. Madame de Brindes thinks such doings at bottom
very vulgar; but vulgar is what she tries hard to be, she is so
convinced it is the only way to make a living. Vendemer had
had at that time only the first of his successes, which was not,
as you will remember—and unfortunately for Madame de
Brindes—of this remunerative kind. Only a few people recognised the perfection of his little volume of verse: my
acquaintance with him originated in my having been one of
the few. A volume of verse was a scanty provision to marry
on, so that, still like a pair of us others, the luckless lovers had
to bide their time. Presently however came the success (again
a success only with those who care for quality, not with the
rough and ready public) of his comedy in verse at the Français.
This charming work had just been taken off (it had been
found not to make money), when the various parties to my
little drama met Heidenmauer at my studio.

Vendemer, who has, as indeed the others have, a passion
for music, was tremendously affected by hearing him play two
or three of his compositions, and I immediately saw that the
immitigable German quality was a morsel much less bitter for
him than for the two uncompromising ladies. He went so far
as to speak to Heidenmauer frankly, to thank him with effusion, an effort of which neither of the quivering women would
have been capable. Vendemer was in the room the night Alfred Bonus raised his little breeze; I saw him lean on the piano
and listen with a queer face looking however rather wonderingly at Heidenmauer. Before this I had noticed the instant
paleness (her face was admirably expressive) with which Madame de Brindes saw her prospective son-in-law make up, as
it were, to the original Teuton, whose national character was
intensified to her aching mind, as it would have been to that
of most Frenchwomen in her place, by his wash of English
colour. A German was bad enough—but a German with English aggravations! Her senses were too fine to give her the
excuse of not feeling that his compositions were interesting,

and she was capable, magnanimously, of listening to them with dropped eyes; but (much as it ever cost her not to be perfectly courteous), she couldn't have made even the most superficial speech to him about them. Marie de Brindes could never have spoken to Herman Heidenmauer. It was a narrowness if you will, but a narrowness that to my vision was enveloped in a dense atmosphere—a kind of sunset bloom—of enriching and fortifying things. Herman Heidenmauer himself, like the man of imagination and the lover of life that he was, would have entered into it delightedly, been charmed with it as a fine case of bigotry. This was conspicuous in Marie de Brindes: her loyalty to the national idea was that of a *dévote* to a form of worship. She never spoke of France, but she always made me think of it, and with an authority which the women of her race seem to me to have in the question much more than the men. I dare say I'm rather in love with her, though, being considerably younger, I've never told her so— as if she would in the least mind that! I have indeed been a little checked by a spirit of allegiance to Vendemer; suspecting always (excuse my sophistication) that in the last analysis it is the mother's charm that he feels—or originally felt—in the daughter's. He spoke of the elder lady to me in those days with the insistence with which only a Frenchman can speak of the objects of his affection. At any rate there was always something symbolic and slightly ceremonial to me in her delicate cameo-face and her general black-robed presence: she made me think of a priestess or a mourner, of revolutions and sieges, detested treaties and ugly public things. I pitied her, too, for the strife of the elements in her—for the way she must have felt a noble enjoyment mutilated. She was too good for that, and yet she was too rigid for anything else; and the sight of such dismal perversions made me hate more than ever the stupid terms on which nations have organised their intercourse.

When she gathered that one of my guests was simply cramming it down the throat of another that the English literary mind was not even literary, she turned away with a vague shrug and a pitiful look at her daughter for the taste of people who took their pleasure so poorly: the truth in question would be so obvious that it was not worth making a scene about.

Madame de Brindes evidently looked at any scene between the English and the Americans as a quarrel proceeding vaguely from below stairs—a squabble sordidly domestic. Her almost immediate departure with her daughter operated as a lucky interruption, and I caught for the first time in the straight, spare girl, as she followed her mother, a little of the air that Vendemer had told me he found in her, the still exaltation, the brown uplifted head that we attribute, or that at any rate he made it visible to me that he attributed, to the dedicated Maid. He considered that his intended bore a striking resemblance to Jeanne d'Arc, and he marched after her on this occasion like a square-shouldered armour-bearer. He reappeared, however, after he had put the ladies into a cab, and half an hour later the rest of my friends, with the sole exception of Bonus, having dispersed, he was sitting up with me in the empty studio for another *bout de causerie*. At first perhaps I was too occupied with reprimanding my compatriot to give much attention to what Vendemer might have to say; I remember at any rate that I had asked Bonus what had induced him to make so grave a blunder. He was not even yet, it appeared, aware of his blunder, so that I had to inquire by what odd chance he had taken Heidenmauer for a bigoted Briton.

"If I spoke to him as one he answered as one; that's bigoted enough," said Alfred Bonus.

"He was confused and amused at your onslaught: he wondered what fly had stung you."

"The fly of patriotism," Vendemer suggested.

"Do *you* like him—a beast of a German?" Bonus demanded.

"If he's an Englishman he isn't a German—*il faut opter*. We can hang him for the one or for the other, we can't hang him for both. I was immensely struck with those things he played."

"They had no charm for me, or doubtless I too should have been demoralised," Alfred said. "He seemed to know nothing about Miss Brownrigg. Now Miss Brownrigg's great."

"I like the things and even the people you quarrel about, you big babies of the same breast. *C'est à se tordre!*" Vendemer declared.

"I may be very abject, but I *do* take an interest in the American novel," Alfred rejoined.

"I hate such expressions: there's no such thing as the American novel."

"Is there by chance any such thing as the French?"

"*Pas davantage*—for the artist himself: how can you ask? I don't know what is meant by French art and English art and American art: those seem to me mere cataloguers' and reviewers' and tradesmen's names, representing preoccupations utterly foreign to the artist. Art is art in every country, and the novel (since Bonus mentions that) is the novel in every tongue, and hard enough work they have to live up to that privilege, without our adding another muddle to the problem. The reader, the consumer may call things as he likes, but we leave him to his little amusements." I suggested that we were all readers and consumers; which only made Vendemer continue: "Yes, and only a small handful of us have the ghost of a palate. But you and I and Bonus are of the handful."

"What do you mean by the handful?" Bonus inquired.

Vendemer hesitated a moment. "I mean the few intelligent people, and even the few people who are not——" He paused again an instant, long enough for me to request him not to say what they were "not," and then went on: "People in a word who have the honour to live in the only country worth living in."

"And pray what country is that?"

"The land of dreams—the country of art."

"Oh, the land of dreams! I live in the land of realities!" Bonus exclaimed. "What do you all mean then by chattering so about *le roman russe?*"

"It's a convenience—to identify the work of three or four, *là-bas*, because we're so far from it. But do you see them *writing* 'le roman russe?' "

"I happen to know that that's exactly what they want to do, some of them," said Bonus.

"Some of the idiots, then! There are plenty of those everywhere. Anything born under that silly star is sure not to count."

"Thank God I'm not an artist!" said Bonus.

"Dear Alfred's a critic," I explained.

"And I'm not ashamed of my country," he subjoined.

"Even a critic perhaps may be an artist," Vendemer mused.

"Then as the great American critic Bonus may be the great American artist," I went on.

"Is that what you're supposed to give us—'American' criticism?" Vendemer asked, with dismay in his expressive, ironic face. "Take care, take care, or it will be more American than critical, and then where will *you* be? However," he continued, laughing and with a change of tone, "I may see the matter in too lurid a light, for I've just been favoured with a judgment conceived in the purest spirit of our own national genius." He looked at me a moment and then he remarked: "That dear Madame de Brindes doesn't approve of my attitude."

"Your attitude?"

"Toward your German friend. She let me know it when I went down stairs with her—told me I was much too cordial, that I must observe myself."

"And what did you reply to that?"

"I answered that the things he had played were extraordinarily beautiful."

"And how did she meet that?"

"By saying that he's an enemy of our country."

"She had you there," I rejoined.

"Yes, I could only reply *'Chère madame, voyons!'*"

"That was meagre."

"Evidently, for it did no more for me than to give her a chance to declare that he can't possibly be here for any good and that he belongs to a race it's my sacred duty to loathe."

"I see what she means."

"I don't then—where artists are concerned. I said to her: *'Ah, madame, vous savez que pour moi il n'y a que l'art!'*"

"It's very exciting!" I laughed. "How could she parry that?"

"'I know it, my dear child—but for *him*?' That's the way she parried it. 'Very well, for him?' I asked. 'For him there's the insolence of the victor and a secret scorn for our incurable illusions!'"

"Heidenmauer has no insolence and no secret scorn."

Vendemer was silent a moment. "Are you very sure of that?"

"Oh, I like him! He's out of all that, and far above it. But what did Mademoiselle Paule say?" I inquired.

"She said nothing—she only looked at me."

"Happy man!"

"Not a bit. She looked at me with strange eyes, in which I could read 'Go straight, my friend—go straight!' Oh, *les femmes, les femmes!*"

"What's the matter with them now?"

"They've a mortal hatred of art!"

"It's a true, deep instinct," said Alfred Bonus.

"But what passed further with Madame de Brindes?" I went on.

"She only got into her cab, pushing her daughter first; on which I slammed the door rather hard and came up here. *Cela m'a porté sur les nerfs.*"

"I'm afraid I haven't soothed them," Bonus said, looking for his hat. When he had found it he added: "When the English have beaten us and pocketed our *milliards* I'll forgive them; but not till then!" And with this he went off, made a little uncomfortable, I think, by Vendemer's sharper alternatives, while the young Frenchman called after him: "My dear fellow, at night all cats are grey!"

Vendemer, when we were left alone together, mooned about the empty studio awhile and asked me three or four questions about Heidenmauer. I satisfied his curiosity as well as I could, but I demanded the reason of it. The reason he gave was that one of the young German's compositions had already begun to haunt his memory; but that was a reason which, to my sense, still left something unexplained. I didn't however challenge him, before he quitted me, further than to warn him against being deliberately perverse.

"What do you mean by being deliberately perverse?" He fixed me so with his intensely living French eye that I became almost blushingly conscious of a certain insincerity and, instead of telling him what I meant, tried to get off with the deplorable remark that the prejudices of Mesdames de Brindes were after all respectable. "That's exactly what makes them so odious!" cried Vendemer.

A few days after this, late in the afternoon, Herman Heidenmauer came in to see me and found the young Frenchman seated at my piano—trying to win back from the keys some echo of a passage in the *Abendlied* we had listened to on the Sunday evening. They met, naturally, as good friends, and Heidenmauer sat down with instant readiness and gave him again the page he was trying to recover. He asked him for his address, that he might send him the composition, and at Vendemer's request, as we sat in the firelight, played half-a-dozen other things. Vendemer listened in silence but to my surprise took leave of me before the lamp was brought in. I asked him to stay to dinner (I had already appealed to Heidenmauer to stay), but he explained that he was engaged to dine with Madame de Brindes—*à la maison* as he always called it. When he had gone Heidenmauer, with whom on departing he had shaken hands without a word, put to me the same questions about him that Vendemer had asked on the Sunday evening about the young German, and I replied that my visitor would find in a small volume of remarkable verse published by Lemerre, which I placed in his hands, much of the information he desired. This volume, which had just appeared, contained, beside a reprint of Vendemer's earlier productions, many of them admirable lyrics, the drama that had lately been played at the Français, and Heidenmauer took it with him when he left me. But he left me late, and before this occurred, all the evening, we had much talk about the French nation. In the foreign colony of Paris the exchange of opinions on this subject is one of the most inevitable and by no means the least interesting of distractions; it furnishes occupation to people rather conscious of the burden of leisure. Heidenmauer had been little in Paris, but he was all the more open to impressions; they evidently poured in upon him and he gave them a generous hospitality. In the diffused white light of his fine German intelligence old colours took on new tints to me, and while we spun fancies about the wonderful race around us I added to my little stock of notions about his own. I saw that his admiration for our neighbours was a very high tide, and I was struck with something bland and unconscious (noble and serene in its absence of precautions) in the way he let his doors stand open to it. It would have been exasperating to many Frenchmen; he looked at them through his clear spectacles with such an absence of suspicion that they might have anything to forgive him, such a thin metaphysical view of instincts and passions. He had the air of not allowing for recollections and nerves, and would doubtless give them occasion to make afresh some of their reflections on the tact of *ces gens-là*.

A couple of days after I had given him Vendemer's book he came back to tell me that he found great beauty in it. "It speaks to me—it speaks to me," he said with his air of happy proof. "I liked the songs—I liked the songs. Besides," he added, "I like the little romantic play—it has given me wonderful ideas; more ideas than anything has done for a long time. Yes—yes."

"What kind of ideas?"

"Well, this kind." And he sat down to the piano and struck the keys. I listened without more questions, and after a while I began to understand. Suddenly he said: "Do you know the words of *that?*" and before I could answer he was rolling out one of the lyrics of the little volume. The poem was strange and obscure, yet irresistibly beautiful, and he had translated it into music still more tantalizing than itself. He sounded the words with his German accent, barely perceptible in English but strongly marked in French. He dropped them and took them up again; he was playing with them, feeling his way. "*This* is my idea!" he broke out; he had caught it, in one of its mystic mazes, and he rendered it with a kind of solemn freshness. There was a phrase he repeated, trying it again and again, and while he did so he chanted the words of the song as if they were an illuminating flame, an inspiration. I was rather glad on the whole that Vendemer didn't hear what his pronunciation made of them, but as I was in the very act of rejoicing I became aware that the author of the verses had opened the door. He had pushed it gently, hearing the music; then hearing also his own poetry he had paused and stood looking at Heidenmauer. The young German nodded and laughed and, irreflectively, spontaneously, greeted him with a friendly *"Was sagen Sie dazu?"* I saw Vendemer change colour; he blushed red and, for an instant, as he stood wavering, I thought he was going to retreat. But I beckoned him in and, on the divan beside me, patted a place for him to sit.

He came in but didn't take this place; he went and stood before the fire to warm his feet, turning his back to us.

Heidenmauer played and played, and after a little Vendemer turned round; he looked about him for a seat, dropped into it and sat with his elbows on his knees and his head in his hands. Presently Heidenmauer called out, in French, above the music: "I like your songs—I like them immensely!" but the young Frenchman neither spoke nor moved. When however five minutes later Heidenmauer stopped he sprang up with an entreaty to him to go on, to go on for the love of God. *"Foilà—foilà!"* cried the musician, and with hands for an instant suspended he wandered off into mysterious worlds. He played Wagner and then Wagner again—a great deal of Wagner; in the midst of which, abruptly, he addressed himself again to Vendemer, who had gone still further from the piano, launching to me, however from his corner a *"Dieu, que c'est beau!"* which I saw that Heidenmauer caught. "I've a conception for an opera, you know—I'd give anything if you'd do the libretto!" Our German friend laughed out, after this, with clear good nature, and the rich appeal brought Vendemer slowly to his feet again, staring at the musician across the room and turning this time perceptibly pale.

I felt there was a drama in the air, and it made me a little nervous; to conceal which I said to Heidenmauer: "What's your conception? What's your subject?"

"My conception would be realized in the subject of M. Vendemer's play—if he'll do that for me in a great lyric manner!" And with this the young German, who had stopped playing to answer me, quitted the piano and Vendemer got up to meet him. "The subject is splendid—it has taken possession of me. Will you do it with me? Will you work with me? We shall make something great!"

"Ah, you don't know what you ask!" Vendemer answered, with his pale smile.

"I do—I do: I've thought of it. It will be bad for me in my country; I shall suffer for it. They won't like it—they'll abuse me for it—they'll say of me *pis que pendre.*" Heidenmauer pronounced it *bis que bendre.*

"They'll hate my libretto so?" Vendemer asked.

"Yes, your libretto—they'll say it's immoral and horrible. And they'll say *I'm* immoral and horrible for having worked with you," the young composer went on, with his pleasant healthy lucidity. "You'll injure my career. Oh yes, I shall suffer!" he joyously, exultingly cried.

"*Et moi donc!*" Vendemer exclaimed.

"Public opinion, yes. I shall also make *you* suffer—I shall nip your prosperity in the bud. All that's *des bêtises—tes pêtisses*," said poor Heidenmauer. "In art there are no countries."

"Yes, art is terrible, art is monstrous," Vendemer replied, looking at the fire.

"I love your songs—they have extraordinary beauty."

"And Vendemer has an equal taste for *your* compositions," I said to Heidenmauer.

"Tempter!" Vendemer murmured to me, with a strange look.

"*C'est juste!* I mustn't meddle—which will be all the easier as I'm dining out and must go and dress. You two make yourselves at home and fight it out here."

"Do you *leave* me?" asked Vendemer, still with his strange look.

"My dear fellow, I've only just time."

"We will dine together—he and I—at one of those characteristic places, and we will look at the matter in its different relations," said Heidenmauer. "Then we will come back here to finish—your studio is so good for music."

"There are some things it *isn't* good for," Vendemer remarked, looking at our companion.

"It's good for poetry—it's good for truth," smiled the composer.

"You'll stay *here* and dine together," I said; "my servant can manage that."

"No, no—we'll go out and we'll walk together. We'll talk a great deal," Heidenmauer went on. "The subject is so comprehensive," he said to Vendemer, as he lighted another cigar.

"The subject?"

"Of your drama. It's so universal."

"Ah, the universe—*il n'y a que ça!*" I laughed, to Vendemer, partly with a really amused sense of the exaggerated woe that looked out of his poetic eyes and that seemed an appeal to me not to forsake him, to throw myself into the scale of the associations he would have to stifle, and partly to encourage him, to express my conviction that two such fine minds couldn't in the long run be the worse for coming to an agreement. I might have been a more mocking Mephistopheles handing over his pure spirit to my literally German Faust.

When I came home at eleven o'clock I found him alone in my studio, where, evidently, for some time, he had been moving up and down in agitated thought. The air was thick with Bavarian fumes, with the reverberation of mighty music and great ideas, with the echoes of that "universe" to which I had so mercilessly consigned him. But I judged in a moment that Vendemer was in a very different phase of his evolution from the one in which I had left him. I had never seen his handsome, sensitive face so intensely illumined.

"*Ça y est—ça y est!*" he exclaimed, standing there with his hands in his pockets and looking at me.

"You've really agreed to do something together?"

"We've sworn a tremendous oath—we've taken a sacred engagement."

"My dear fellow, you're a hero."

"Wait and see! *C'est un très-grand esprit.*"

"So much the better!"

"*C'est un bien beau génie.* Ah, we've risen—we soar; *nous sommes dans les grandes espaces!*" my friend continued with his dilated eyes.

"It's very interesting—because it will cost you something."

"It will cost me everything!" said Félix Vendemer in a tone I seem to hear at this hour. "That's just the beauty of it. It's the chance of chances to testify for art— to affirm an indispensable truth."

"An indispensable truth?" I repeated, feeling myself soar too, but into the splendid vague.

"Do you know the greatest crime that can be perpetrated against it?"

"Against it?" I asked, still soaring.

"Against the religion of art—against the love for beauty—against the search for the Holy Grail?" The transfigured look with which he named these things, the way his warm voice filled the rich room, was a revelation of the wonderful talk that had taken place.

"Do you know—for one of *us*—the really damnable, the only unpardonable, sin?"

"Tell me, so that I may keep clear of it!"

"To profane *our* golden air with the hideous invention of patriotism."

"It was a clever invention in its time!" I laughed.

"I'm not talking about its time—I'm talking about its place. It was never anything but a fifth-rate impertinence here. In art there are no countries—no idiotic nationalities, no frontiers, nor *douanes*, nor still more idiotic fortresses and bayonets. It has the unspeakable beauty of being the region in which those abominations cease, the medium in which such vulgarities simply can't live. What therefore are we to say of the brutes who wish to drag them all in—to crush to death with them all the flowers of such a garden, to shut out all the light of such a sky?" I was far from desiring to defend the "brutes" in question, though there rose before me even at that moment a sufficiently vivid picture of the way, later on, poor Vendemer would have to face them. I quickly perceived indeed that the picture was, to his own eyes, a still more crowded canvas. Félix Vendemer, in the centre of it, was an admirable, a really sublime figure. If there had been wonderful talk after I quitted the two poets the wonder was not over yet—it went on far into the night for my benefit. We looked at the prospect in many lights, turned the subject about almost every way it would go; but I am bound to say there was one relation in which we tacitly agreed to forbear to consider it. We neither of us uttered the name of Paule de Brindes— the outlook in that direction would be too serious. And yet if Félix Vendemer, exquisite and incorruptible artist that he was, had fallen in love with the idea of "testifying," it was from that direction that the finest part of his opportunity to do so would proceed.

I was only too conscious of this when, within the week, I received a hurried note from Madame de Brindes, begging me as a particular favour to come and see her without delay. I had not seen Vendemer again, but I had had a characteristic call from Heidenmauer, who, though I could imagine him perfectly in a Prussian helmet, with a needle-gun, perfectly, on definite occasion, a sturdy, formidable soldier, gave me a renewed impression of inhabiting, in the expansion of his genius and the exercise of his intelligence, no land of red tape, no province smaller nor more pedantically administered than the totality of things. I was reminded afresh too that *he* foresaw no striking salon-picture, no *chic* of execution nor romance of martyrdom, or at any rate devoted very little time to the consideration of such objects. He doubtless did scant justice to poor Vendemer's attitude, though he said to me of him by the way, with his rosy deliberation: "He has good ideas—he has good ideas. The French mind has—for me— the taste of a very delightful *bonbon*!" He only measured the angle of convergence, as he called it, of their two projections. He was in short not preoccupied with the personal gallantry of their experiment; he was preoccupied with its "æsthetic and harmonic basis."

It was without her daughter that Madame de Brindes received me, when I obeyed her summons, in her scrap of a *quatrième* in the Rue de Miromesnil.

"Ah, *cher monsieur*, how could you have permitted such a horror—how could you have given it the countenance of your roof, of your influence?" There were tears in her eyes, and I don't think that for the moment I have ever been more touched by a reproach. But I pulled myself together sufficiently to affirm my faith as well as to disengage my responsibility. I explained that there was no horror to me in the matter, that if I was not a German neither was I a Frenchman, and that all I had before me was two young men inflamed by a great idea and nobly determined to work together to give it a great form.

"A great idea— to go over to *ces gens-là*?"

"To go over to them?"

"To put yourself on their side—to throw yourself into the arms of those who hate us—to fall into their abominable trap!"

"What do you call their abominable trap?"

"Their false *bonhomie*, the very impudence of their intrigues, their profound, scientific deceit and their determination to get the advantage of us by exploiting our generosity."

"You attribute to such a man as Heidenmauer too many motives and too many calculations. He's quite ideally superior!"

"Oh, German idealism—we know what that means! We've no use for their superiority; let them carry it elsewhere—let them leave us alone. Why do they thrust themselves in upon us and set old wounds throbbing by their detested presence? We don't go near *them*, or ever wish to hear their ugly names or behold their *visages de bois*; therefore the most rudimentary good taste, the tact one would expect even from naked savages, might suggest to them to seek their amusements elsewhere. But *their* taste, *their* tact—I can scarcely trust myself to speak!"

Madame de Brindes did speak however at considerable further length and with a sincerity of passion which left one quite without arguments. There was no argument to meet the fact that Vendemer's attitude wounded her, wounded her daughter, *jusqu'au fond de l'âme*, that it represented for them abysses of shame and suffering and that for himself it meant a whole future compromised, a whole public alienated. It was vain doubtless to talk of such things; if people didn't *feel* them, if they hadn't the fibre of loyalty, the high imagination of honour, all explanations, all supplications were but a waste of noble emotion. M. Vendemer's perversity was monstrous—she had had a sickening discussion with him. What she desired of me was to make one last appeal to him, to put the solemn truth before him, to try to bring him back to sanity. It was as if he had temporarily lost his reason. It was to be made clear to him, *par exemple*, that unless he should recover it Mademoiselle de Brindes would unhesitatingly withdraw from her engagement.

"Does she *really* feel as you do?" I asked.

"Do you think I put words into her mouth? She feels as a *fille de France* is obliged to feel!"

"Doesn't she love him then?"

"She adores him. But she won't take him without his honour."

"I don't understand such refinements!" I said.

"Oh, *vous autres*!" cried Madame de Brindes. Then with eyes glowing through her tears she demanded: "Don't you know she knows how her father died?" I was on the point of saying "What has that to do with it?" but I withheld the question, for after all I could conceive that it might have something. There was no disputing about tastes, and I could only express my sincere conviction that Vendemer was profoundly attached to Mademoiselle Paule. "Then let him prove it by making her a sacrifice!" my strenuous hostess replied; to which I rejoined that I would repeat our conversation to him and put the matter before him as strongly as I could. I delayed a little to take leave, wondering if the girl would not come in—I should have been so much more content to receive her strange recantation from her own lips. I couldn't say this to Madame de Brindes; but she guessed I meant it, and before we separated we exchanged a look in which our mutual mistrust was written—the suspicion on her side that I should not be a very passionate intercessor and the conjecture on mine that she might be misrepresenting her daughter. This slight tension, I must add, was only momentary, for I have had a chance of observing Paule de Brindes since then, and the two ladies were soon satisfied that I pitied them enough to have been eloquent.

My eloquence has been of no avail, and I have learned (it has been one of the most interesting lessons of my life) of what transcendent stuff the artist may sometimes be made. Herman Heidenmauer and Félix Vendemer are, at the hour I write, immersed in their monstrous collaboration. There were postponements and difficulties at first, and there will be more serious ones in the future, when it is a question of giving the finished work to the world. The world of Paris will stop its ears in horror, the German Empire will turn its mighty back, and the authors of what I foresee (oh, I've been treated to specimens!) as a perhaps really epoch-making musical revelation (is Heidenmauer's style rubbing off on me?) will perhaps have to beg for a hearing in communities fatally unintelligent. It may very well be that they will not obtain any hearing at all for years. I like at any rate to think that time works for them. At present they work for themselves and for each other, amid drawbacks of several kinds. Separating after the episode in Paris, they have met again on alien soil, at a little place on the Genoese Riviera where sunshine is cheap and tobacco bad, and they live (the two together) for five francs a day, which is all they can muster between them. It appears that when Heidenmauer's London step-brother was informed of the young composer's unnatural alliance he instantly withdrew his subsidy. The return of it is contingent on the rupture of the unholy union and the destruction by flame of all the manuscript. The pair are very poor and the whole thing depends on their staying power. They are so preoccupied with their opera that they have no time for pot-boilers. Vendemer is in a feverish hurry, lest perhaps he should find himself chilled. There are still other details which contribute to the interest of the episode and which, for me, help to render it a most refreshing, a really great little case. It rests me, it delights me, there is something in it that makes for civilization. In their way they are working for human happiness. The strange course taken by Vendemer (I mean his renunciation of his engagement) must moreover be judged in the light of the fact that he was really in love. Something had to be sacrificed, and what he clung to most (he's extraordinary, I admit) was the truth he had the opportunity of proclaiming. Men give up their love for advantages every day, but they rarely give it up for such discomforts.

Paule de Brindes was the less in love of the two; I see her often enough to have made up my mind about that. But she's mysterious, she's odd; there was at any rate a sufficient wrench in her life to make her often absent-minded. Does her imagination hover about Félix Vendemer? A month ago, going into their rooms one day when her mother was not at home (the *bonne* had admitted me under a wrong impression) I found her at the piano, playing one of Heidenmauer's compositions—playing it without notes and with infinite expression. How had she got hold of it? How had she learned it? This was her secret—she blushed so that I didn't pry into it. But what is she doing, under the singular circumstances, with a composition of Herman Heidenmauer's? She never met him, she never heard him play but that once. It will be a pretty complication if it shall appear that the young German genius made on that occasion more than one intense impression. This needn't appear, however, inasmuch as, being naturally in terror of the discovery by her mother of such an anomaly, she may count on me absolutely not to betray her. I hadn't fully perceived how deeply susceptible she is to music. She must have a strange confusion of feelings—a dim, haunting trouble, with a kind of ache of impatience for the wonderful opera somewhere in the depths of it. Don't we live fast after all, and doesn't the old order change? Don't say art isn't mighty! I shall give you some more illustrations of it yet.

Owen Wingrave

"UPON MY HONOUR you must be off your head!" cried Spencer Coyle, as the young man, with a white face, stood there panting a little and repeating "Really, I've quite decided," and "I assure you I've thought it all out." They were both pale, but Owen Wingrave smiled in a manner exasperating to his interlocutor, who however still discriminated sufficiently to see that his grimace (it was like an irrelevant leer) was the result of extreme and conceivable nervousness.

"It was certainly a mistake to have gone so far; but that is exactly why I feel I mustn't go further," poor Owen said, waiting mechanically, almost humbly (he wished not to swagger, and indeed he had nothing to swagger about) and carrying through the window to the stupid opposite houses the dry glitter of his eyes.

"I'm unspeakably disgusted. You've made me dreadfully ill," Mr. Coyle went on, looking thoroughly upset.

"I'm very sorry. It was the fear of the effect on you that kept me from speaking sooner."

"You should have spoken three months ago. Don't you know your mind from one day to the other?"

The young man for a moment said nothing. Then he replied with a little tremor: "You're very angry with me, and I expected it. I'm awfully obliged to you for all you've done for me. I'll do anything else for you in return, but I can't do that. Everyone else will let me have it, of course. I'm prepared for it —I'm prepared for everything. That's what has taken the time: to be sure I was prepared. I think it's your displeasure I feel most and regret most. But little by little you'll get over it."

"*You'll* get over it rather faster, I suppose!" Spencer Coyle satirically exclaimed. He was quite as agitated as his young friend, and they were evidently in no condition to prolong an encounter in which they each drew blood. Mr. Coyle was a professional "coach"; he prepared young men for the army, taking only three or four at a time, to whom he applied the irresistible stimulus of which the possession was both his secret and his fortune. He had not a great establishment; he

256

would have said himself that it was not a wholesale business. Neither his system, his health nor his temper could have accommodated itself to numbers; so he weighed and measured his pupils and turned away more applicants than he passed. He was an artist in his line, caring only for picked subjects and capable of sacrifices almost passionate for the individual. He liked ardent young men (there were kinds of capacity to which he was indifferent) and he had taken a particular fancy to Owen Wingrave. This young man's facility really fascinated him. His candidates usually did wonders, and he might have sent up a multitude. He was a person of exactly the stature of the great Napoleon, with a certain flicker of genius in his light blue eye: it had been said of him that he looked like a pianist. The tone of his favourite pupil now expressed, without intention indeed, a superior wisdom which irritated him. He had not especially suffered before from Wingrave's high opinion of himself, which had seemed justified by remarkable parts; but to-day it struck him as intolerable. He cut short the discussion, declining absolutely to regard their relations as terminated, and remarked to his pupil that he had better go off somewhere (down to Eastbourne, say; the sea would bring him round) and take a few days to find his feet and come to his senses. He could afford the time, he was so well up: when Spencer Coyle remembered how well up he was he could have boxed his ears. The tall, athletic young man was not physically a subject for simplified reasoning; but there was a troubled gentleness in his handsome face, the index of compunction mixed with pertinacity, which signified that if it could have done any good he would have turned both cheeks. He evidently didn't pretend that his wisdom was superior; he only presented it as his own. It was his own career after all that was in question. He couldn't refuse to go through the form of trying Eastbourne or at least of holding his tongue, though there was that in his manner which implied that if he should do so it would be really to give Mr. Coyle a chance to recuperate. He didn't feel a bit overworked, but there was nothing more natural than that with their tremendous pressure Mr. Coyle should be. Mr. Coyle's own intellect would derive an advantage from his pupil's holiday. Mr. Coyle saw what he meant, but he controlled himself; he only demanded, as his right, a truce of three days. Owen Wingrave granted it, though as fostering sad illusions this went visibly against his conscience; but before they separated the famous crammer remarked:

"All the same I feel as if I ought to see someone. I think you mentioned to me that your aunt had come to town?"

"Oh, yes; she's in Baker Street. Do go and see her," the boy said comfortingly.

Mr. Coyle looked at him an instant. "Have you broached this folly to her?"

"Not yet—to no one. I thought it right to speak to you first."

"Oh, what you 'think right'!" cried Spencer Coyle, outraged by his young friend's standards. He added that he would probably call on Miss Wingrave; after which the recreant youth got out of the house.

Owen Wingrave didn't however start punctually for Eastbourne; he only directed his steps to Kensington Gardens, from which Mr. Coyle's desirable residence (he was terribly expensive and had a big house) was not far removed. The famous coach "put up" his pupils, and Owen had mentioned to the butler that he would be back to dinner. The spring day was warm to his young blood, and he had a book in his pocket which, when he had passed into the gardens and, after a short stroll, dropped into a chair, he took out with the slow, soft sigh that finally ushers in a pleasure postponed. He stretched his long legs and began to read it; it was a volume of Goethe's poems. He had been for days in a state of the highest tension, and now that the cord had snapped the relief was proportionate; only it was characteristic of him that this deliverance should take the form of an intellectual pleasure. If he had thrown up the probability of a magnificent career it was not to dawdle along Bond Street nor parade his indifference in the window of a club. At any rate he had in a few moments forgotten everything—the tremendous pressure, Mr. Coyle's disappointment, and even his formidable aunt in Baker Street. If these watchers had overtaken him there would surely have been some excuse for their exasperation. There was no doubt he was perverse, for his very choice of a pastime only showed how he had got up his German.

"What the devil's the matter with him, do *you* know?" Spencer Coyle asked that afternoon of young Lechmere, who had never before observed the head of the establishment to set a fellow such an example of bad language. Young Lechmere was not only Wingrave's fellow-pupil, he was supposed to be his intimate, indeed quite his best friend, and had unconsciously performed for Mr. Coyle the office of making the promise of his great gifts more vivid by contrast. He was short and sturdy and as a general thing uninspired, and Mr. Coyle, who found no amusement in believing in him, had never thought him less exciting than as he stared now out of a face from which you could never guess whether he had caught an idea. Young Lechmere concealed such achievements as if they had been youthful indiscretions. At any rate he could evidently conceive no reason why it should be thought there was anything more than usual the matter with the companion of his studies; so Mr. Coyle had to continue:

"He declines to go up. He chucks the whole thing!"

The first thing that struck young Lechmere in the case was the freshness it had imparted to the governor's vocabulary.

"He doesn't want to go to Sandhurst?"

"He doesn't want to go anywhere. He gives up the army altogether. He objects," said Mr. Coyle, in a tone that made young Lechmere almost hold his breath, "to the military profession."

"Why, it has been the profession of all his family!"

"Their profession? It has been their religion! Do you know Miss Wingrave?"

"Oh, yes. Isn't she awful?" young Lechmere candidly ejaculated.

His instructor demurred.

"She's formidable, if you mean that, and it's right she should be; because somehow in her very person, good maiden lady as she is, she represents the might, she represents the traditions and the exploits of the British army. She represents the expansive property of the English name. I think his family can be trusted to come down on him, but every influence should be set in motion. I want to know what yours is. Can *you* do anything in the matter?"

"I can try a couple of rounds with him," said young Lechmere reflectively. "But he knows a fearful lot. He has the most extraordinary ideas."

"Then he has told you some of them—he has taken you into his confidence?"

"I've heard him jaw by the yard," smiled the honest youth. "He has told me he despises it."

"What *is* it he despises? I can't make out."

The most consecutive of Mr. Coyle's nurslings considered a moment, as if he were conscious of a responsibility.

"Why, I think, military glory. He says we take the wrong view of it."

"He oughtn't to talk to *you* that way. It's corrupting the youth of Athens. It's sowing sedition."

"Oh, I'm all right!" said young Lechmere. "And he never told me he meant to chuck it. I always thought he meant to see it through, simply because he had to. He'll argue on any side you like. It's a tremendous pity—I'm sure he'd have a big career."

"Tell him so, then; plead with him; struggle with him—for God's sake."

"I'll do what I can—I'll tell him it's a regular shame."

"Yes, strike *that* note—insist on the disgrace of it."

The young man gave Mr. Coyle a more perceptive glance. "I'm sure he wouldn't do anything dishonourable."

"Well—it won't look right. He must be made to feel *that*—work it up. Give him a comrade's point of view—that of a brother-in-arms."

"That's what I thought we were going to be!" young Lechmere mused romantically, much uplifted by the nature of the mission imposed on him. "He's an awfully good sort."

"No one will think so if he backs out!" said Spencer Coyle.

"They mustn't say it to *me*!" his pupil rejoined with a flush.

Mr. Coyle hesitated a moment, noting his tone and aware that in the perversity of things, though this young man was a born soldier, no excitement would ever attach to *his* alternatives save perhaps on the part of the nice girl to whom at an early day he was sure to be placidly united. "Do you like him very much—do you believe in him?"

Young Lechmere's life in these days was spent in answering terrible questions; but he had never been subjected to so queer an interrogation as this. "Believe in him? Rather!"

"Then *save* him!"

The poor boy was puzzled, as if it were forced upon him by this intensity that there was more in such an appeal than could appear on the surface; and he doubtless felt that he was only entering into a complex situation when after another moment, with his hands in his pockets, he replied hopefully but not pompously: "I daresay I can bring him round!"

II.

Before seeing young Lechmere Mr. Coyle had determined to telegraph an inquiry to Miss Wingrave. He had prepaid the answer, which, being promptly put into his hand, brought the interview we have just related to a close. He immediately drove off to Baker Street, where the lady had said she awaited him, and five minutes after he got there, as he sat with Owen Wingrave's remarkable aunt, he repeated over several times, in his angry sadness and with the infallibility of his experience. "He's so intelligent—he's so intelligent!" He had declared it had been a luxury to put such a fellow through.

"Of course he's intelligent, what else could he be? We've never, that I know of, had but *one* idiot in the family!" said Jane Wingrave. This was an allusion that Mr. Coyle could understand, and it brought home to him another of the reasons for the disappointment, the humiliation as it were, of the good people at Paramore, at the same time that it gave an example of the conscientious coarseness he had on former occasions observed in his interlocutress. Poor Philip Wingrave, her late brother's eldest son, was literally imbecile and banished from view; deformed, unsocial, irretrievable, he had been relegated to a private asylum and had become among the friends of the family only a little hushed lugubrious legend. All the hopes of the house, picturesque Paramore, now unintermittently old Sir Philip's rather melancholy home (his infirmities would keep him there to the last) were therefore collected on the second boy's head, which nature, as if in compunction for her

previous botch, had, in addition to making it strikingly handsome, filled with marked originalities and talents. These two
had been the only children of the old man's only son, who,
like so many of his ancestors, had given up a gallant young
life to the service of his country. Owen Wingrave the elder
had received his death-cut, in close-quarters, from an Afghan
sabre; the blow had come crashing across his skull. His wife,
at that time in India, was about to give birth to her third child;
and when the event took place, in darkness and anguish, the
baby came lifeless into the world and the mother sank under
the multiplication of her woes. The second of the little boys
in England, who was at Paramore with his grandfather, became the peculiar charge of his aunt, the only unmarried one,
and during the interesting Sunday that, by urgent invitation,
Spencer Coyle, busy as he was, had, after consenting to put
Owen through, spent under that roof, the celebrated crammer
received a vivid impression of the influence exerted at least in
intention by Miss Wingrave. Indeed the picture of this short
visit remained with the observant little man a curious one—
the vision of an impoverished Jacobean house, shabby and
remarkably "creepy," but full of character still and full of felicity as a setting for the distinguished figure of the peaceful
old soldier. Sir Philip Wingrave, a relic rather than a celebrity,
was a small brown, erect octogenarian, with smouldering eyes
and a studied courtesy. He liked to do the diminished honours
of his house, but even when with a shaky hand he lighted a
bedroom candle for a deprecating guest it was impossible not
to feel that beneath the surface he was a merciless old warrior.
The eye of the imagination could glance back into his
crowded Eastern past—back at episodes in which his scrupulous forms would only have made him more terrible.

    Mr. Coyle remembered also two other figures—a faded in-
offensive Mrs. Julian, domesticated there by a system of frequent visits as the widow of an officer and a particular friend
of Miss Wingrave, and a remarkably clever little girl of eighteen, who was this lady's daughter and who struck the speculative visitor as already formed for other relations. She was
very impertinent to Owen, and in the course of a long walk
that he had taken with the young man and the effect of which,
in much talk, had been to clinch his high opinion of him, he

had learned (for Owen chattered confidentially) that Mrs. Julian was the sister of a very gallant gentleman, Captain Hume-Walker, of the Artillery, who had fallen in the Indian Mutiny and between whom and Miss Wingrave (it had been that lady's one known concession) a passage of some delicacy, taking a tragic turn, was believed to have been enacted. They had been engaged to be married, but she had given way to the jealousy of her nature—had broken with him and sent him off to his fate, which had been horrible. A passionate sense of having wronged him, a hard eternal remorse had thereupon taken possession of her, and when his poor sister, linked also to a soldier, had by a still heavier blow been left almost without resources, she had devoted herself charitably to a long expiation. She had sought comfort in taking Mrs. Julian to live much of the time at Paramore, where she became an un-remunerated though not uncriticised housekeeper, and Spencer Coyle suspected that it was a part of this comfort that she could at her leisure trample on her. The impression of Jane Wingrave was not the faintest he had gathered on that intensifying Sunday—an occasion singularly tinged for him with the sense of bereavement and mourning and memory, of names never mentioned, of the far-away plaint of widows and the echoes of battles and bad news. It was all military indeed, and Mr. Coyle was made to shudder a little at the profession of which he helped to open the door to harmless young men. Miss Wingrave moreover might have made such a bad conscience worse—so cold and clear a good one looked at him out of her hard, fine eyes and trumpeted in her sonorous voice.

She was a high, distinguished person; angular but not awkward, with a large forehead and abundant black hair, arranged like that of a woman conceiving perhaps excusably of her head as "noble," and irregularly streaked to-day with white. If however she represented for Spencer Coyle the genius of a military race it was not that she had the step of a grenadier or the vocabulary of a camp-follower; it was only that such sympathies were vividly implied in the general fact to which her very presence and each of her actions and glances and tones were a constant and direct allusion—the paramount valour of her family. If she was military it was because she sprang from a military house and because she wouldn't for the world have been anything but what the Wingraves had been. She was almost vulgar about her ancestors, and if one had been tempted to quarrel with her one would have found a fair pretext in her defective sense of proportion. This temptation however said nothing to Spencer Coyle, for whom as a strong character revealing itself in colour and sound she was a spectacle and who was glad to regard her as a force exerted on his own side. He wished her nephew had more of her narrowness instead of being almost cursed with the tendency to look at things in their relations. He wondered why when she came up to town she always resorted to Baker Street for lodgings. He had never known nor heard of Baker Street as a residence—he associated it only with bazaars and photographers. He divined in her a rigid indifference to everything that was not the passion of her life. Nothing really mattered to her but that, and she would have occupied apartments in Whitechapel if they had been a feature in her tactics. She had received her visitor in a large, cold, faded room, furnished with slippery seats and decorated with alabaster vases and wax-flowers. The only little personal comfort for which she appeared to have looked out was a fat catalogue of the Army and Navy Stores, which reposed on a vast, desolate table-cover of false blue. Her clear forehead—it was like a porcelain slate, a receptacle for addresses and sums—had flushed when her nephew's crammer told her the extraordinary news; but he saw she was fortunately more angry than frightened. She had essentially, she would always have, too little imagination for fear, and the healthy habit moreover of facing everything had taught her that the occasion usually found her a quantity to reckon with. Mr. Coyle saw that her only fear at present could have been that of not being able to prevent her nephew from being absurd and that to such an apprehension as this she was in fact inaccessible. Practically too she was not troubled by surprise; she recognised none of the futile, none of the subtle sentiments. If Philip had for an hour made a fool of himself she was angry; disconcerted as she would have been on learning that he had confessed to debts or fallen in love with a low girl. But there remained in any annoyance the saving fact that no one could make a fool of *her*.

"I don't know when I've taken such an interest in a young man—I think I never have, since I began to handle them," Mr. Coyle said. "I like him, I believe in him—it's been a delight to see how he was going."

"Oh, I know how they go!" Miss Wingrave threw back her head with a familiar briskness, as if a rapid procession of the generations had flashed before her, rattling their scabbards and spurs. Spencer Coyle recognised the intimation that she had nothing to learn from anybody about the natural carriage of a Wingrave, and he even felt convicted by her next words of being, in her eyes, with the troubled story of his check, his weak complaint of his pupil, rather a poor creature. "If you like him," she exclaimed, "for mercy's sake keep him quiet!"

Mr. Coyle began to explain to her that this was less easy than she appeared to imagine; but he perceived that she understood very little of what he said. The more he insisted that the boy had a kind of intellectual independence, the more this struck her as a conclusive proof that her nephew was a Wingrave and a soldier. It was not till he mentioned to her that Owen had spoken of the profession of arms as of something that would be "beneath" him, it was not till her attention was arrested by this intenser light on the complexity of the problem that Miss Wingrave broke out after a moment's stupefied reflection: "Send him to see me immediately!"

"That's exactly what I wanted to ask your leave to do. But I've wanted also to prepare you for the worst, to make you understand that he strikes me as really obstinate and to suggest to you that the most powerful arguments at your command—especially if you should be able to put your hand on some intensely practical one—will be none too effective."

"I think I've got a powerful argument." Miss Wingrave looked very hard at her visitor. He didn't know in the least what it was, but he begged her to put it forward without delay. He promised that their young man should come to Baker Street that evening, mentioning however that he had already urged him to spend without delay a couple of days at Eastbourne. This led Jane Wingrave to inquire with surprise what virtue there might be in *that* expensive remedy, and to reply with decision when Mr. Coyle had said "The virtue of a little rest, a little change, a little relief to overwrought nerves," "Ah, don't coddle him—he's costing us a great deal of money! I'll talk to him and I'll take him down to Paramore; then I'll send him back to you straightened out."

Spencer Coyle hailed this pledge superficially with satisfaction, but before he quitted Miss Wingrave he became conscious that he had really taken on a new anxiety—a restlessness that made him say to himself, groaning inwardly: "Oh, she *is* a grenadier at bottom, and she'll have no tact. I don't know what her powerful argument is; I'm only afraid she'll be stupid and make him worse. The old man's better—*he's* capable of tact, though he's not quite an extinct volcano. Owen will probably put him in a rage. In short the difficulty is that the boy's the best of them."

Spencer Coyle felt afresh that evening at dinner that the boy was the best of them. Young Wingrave (who, he was pleased to observe, had not yet proceeded to the seaside) appeared at the repast as usual, looking inevitably a little self-conscious, but not too original for Bayswater. He talked very naturally to Mrs. Coyle, who had thought him from the first the most beautiful young man they had ever received; so that the person most ill at ease was poor Lechmere, who took great trouble, as if from the deepest delicacy, not to meet the eye of his misguided mate. Spencer Coyle however paid the penalty of his own profundity in feeling more and more worried; he could so easily see that there were all sorts of things in his young friend that the people of Paramore wouldn't understand. He began even already to react against the notion of his being harassed—to reflect that after all he had a right to his ideas—to remember that he was of a substance too fine to be in fairness roughly used. It was in this way that the ardent little crammer, with his whimsical perceptions and complicated sympathies, was generally condemned not to settle down comfortably either into his displeasures or into his enthusiasms. His love of the real truth never gave him a chance to enjoy them. He mentioned to Wingrave after dinner the propriety of an immediate visit to Baker Street, and the young man, looking "queer," as he thought—that is smiling again with the exaggerated glory he had shown in their recent interview—went off to face the ordeal. Spencer Coyle noted that he was scared—he was afraid of his aunt; but somehow this didn't strike him as a sign of pusillanimity. *He* should have been scared, he was well aware, in the poor boy's place, and the sight of his pupil marching up to the battery in spite of his terrors was a positive suggestion of the temperament of the soldier. Many a plucky youth would have shirked this particular peril.

"He *has* got ideas!" young Lechmere broke out to his instructor after his comrade had quitted the house. He was evidently bewildered and agitated—he had an emotion to work off. He had before dinner gone straight at his friend, as Mr. Coyle had requested, and had elicited from him that his scruples were founded on an overwhelming conviction of the stupidity—the "crass barbarism" he called it—of war. His great complaint was that people hadn't invented anything cleverer, and he was determined to show, the only way he could, that *he* wasn't such an ass.

"And he thinks all the great generals ought to have been shot, and that Napoleon Bonaparte in particular, the greatest, was a criminal, a monster for whom language has no adequate name!" Mr. Coyle rejoined, completing young Lechmere's picture. "He favoured you, I see, with exactly the same pearls of wisdom that he produced for me. But I want to know what *you* said."

"I said they were awful rot!" Young Lechmere spoke with emphasis, and he was slightly surprised to hear Mr. Coyle laugh incongruously at this just declaration and then after a moment continue:

"It's all very curious—I daresay there's something in it. But it's a pity!"

"He told me when it was that the question began to strike him in that light. Four or five years ago, when he did a lot of reading about all the great swells and their campaigns—Hannibal and Julius Cæsar, Marlborough and Frederick and Bonaparte. He *has* done a lot of reading, and he says it opened his eyes. He says that a wave of disgust rolled over him. He talked about the 'immeasurable misery' of wars, and asked me why nations don't tear to pieces the governments, the rulers that go in for them. He hates poor old Bonaparte worst of all."

"Well, poor old Bonaparte *was* a brute. He was a frightful ruffian," Mr. Coyle unexpectedly declared. "But I suppose you didn't admit that."

"Oh, I daresay he was objectionable, and I'm very glad we laid him on his back. But the point I made to Wingrave was that his own behaviour would excite no end of remark." Young Lechmere hesitated an instant, then he added: "I told him he must be prepared for the worst."

"Of course he asked you what you meant by the 'worst,' " said Spencer Coyle.

"Yes, he asked me that, and do you know what I said? I said people would say that his conscientious scruples and his wave of disgust are only a pretext. Then he asked 'A pretext for what?' "

"Ah, he rather had you there!" Mr. Coyle exclaimed with a little laugh that was mystifying to his pupil.

"Not a bit—for I told him."

"What did you tell him?"

Once more, for a few seconds, with his conscious eyes in his instructor's, the young man hung fire.

"Why, what we spoke of a few hours ago. The appearance he'd present of not having——" The honest youth faltered a moment, then brought it out: "The military temperament, don't you know? But do you know what he said to that?" young Lechmere went on.

"Damn the military temperament!" the crammer promptly replied.

Young Lechmere stared. Mr. Coyle's tone left him uncertain if he were attributing the phrase to Wingrave or uttering his own opinion, but he exclaimed:

"Those were exactly his words!"

"He doesn't care," said Mr. Coyle.

"Perhaps not. But it isn't fair for him to abuse *us* fellows. I told him it's the finest temperament in the world, and that there's nothing so splendid as pluck and heroism."

"Ah! there you had *him*."

"I told him it was unworthy of him to abuse a gallant, a magnificent profession. I told him there's no type so fine as that of the soldier doing his duty."

"That's essentially *your* type, my dear boy." Young Lechmere blushed; he couldn't make out (and the danger was naturally unexpected to him) whether at that moment he didn't exist mainly for the recreation of his friend. But he was partly reassured by the genial way this friend continued, laying a hand on his shoulder: "Keep *at* him that way! we may do something. I'm extremely obliged to you." Another doubt however remained unassuaged—a doubt which led him to exclaim to Mr. Coyle before they dropped the painful subject:

"He *doesn't* care! But it's awfully odd he shouldn't!"

"So it is, but remember what you said this afternoon—I mean about your not advising people to make insinuations to *you*."

"I believe I should knock a fellow down!" said young Lechmere. Mr. Coyle had got up; the conversation had taken place while they sat together after Mrs. Coyle's withdrawal from the dinner-table and the head of the establishment administered to his disciple, on principles that were a part of his thoroughness, a glass of excellent claret. The disciple, also on his feet, lingered an instant, not for another "go," as he would have called it, at the decanter, but to wipe his microscopic moustache with prolonged and unusual care. His companion saw he had something to bring out which required a final effort, and waited for him an instant with a hand on the knob of the door. Then as young Lechmere approached him Spencer Coyle grew conscious of an unwonted intensity in the round and ingenuous face. The boy was nervous, but he tried to behave like a man of the world. "Of course, it's between ourselves," he stammered, "and I wouldn't breathe such a word to any one who wasn't interested in poor Wingrave as you are. But do you think he funks it?"

Mr. Coyle looked at him so hard for an instant that he was visibly frightened at what he had said.

"Funks it! Funks what?"

"Why, what we're talking about—the service." Young Lechmere gave a little gulp and added with a *naïveté* almost pathetic to Spencer Coyle: "The dangers, you know!"

"Do you mean he's thinking of his skin?"

Young Lechmere's eyes expanded appealingly, and what his instructor saw in his pink face—he even thought he saw a tear—was the dread of a disappointment shocking in the degree in which the loyalty of admiration had been great.

"Is he—is he *afraid*?" repeated the honest lad, with a quaver of suspense.

"Dear no!" said Spencer Coyle, turning his back.

Young Lechmere felt a little snubbed and even a little ashamed; but he felt still more relieved.

III.

Less than a week after this Spencer Coyle received a note from Miss Wingrave, who had immediately quitted London with her nephew. She proposed that he should come down to Paramore for the following Sunday—Owen was really so tiresome. On the spot, in that house of examples and memories and in combination with her poor dear father, who was "dreadfully annoyed," it might be worth their while to make a last stand. Mr. Coyle read between the lines of this letter that the party at Paramore had got over a good deal of ground since Miss Wingrave, in Baker Street, had treated his despair as superficial. She was not an insinuating woman, but she went so far as to put the question on the ground of his conferring a particular favour on an afflicted family; and she expressed the pleasure it would give them if he should be accompanied by Mrs. Coyle, for whom she inclosed a separate invitation. She mentioned that she was also writing, subject to Mr. Coyle's approval, to young Lechmere. She thought such a nice manly boy might do her wretched nephew some good. The celebrated crammer determined to embrace this opportunity; and now it was the case not so much that he was angry as that he was anxious. As he directed his answer to Miss Wingrave's letter he caught himself smiling at the thought that at bottom he was going to defend his young friend rather than to attack him. He said to his wife, who was a fair, fresh, slow woman—a person of much more presence than himself—that she had better take Miss Wingrave at her word: it was such an extraordinary, such a fascinating specimen of an old English home. This last allusion was amicably sarcastic—he had already accused the good lady more than once of being in love with Owen Wingrave. She admitted that she was, she even gloried in her passion; which shows that the subject, between them, was treated in a liberal spirit. She carried out the joke by accepting the invitation with eagerness. Young Lechmere was delighted to do the same; his instructor had good-naturedly taken the view that the little break would freshen him up for his last spurt.

It was the fact that the occupants of Paramore did indeed take their trouble hard that struck Spencer Coyle after he had been an hour or two in that fine old house. This very short second visit, beginning on the Saturday evening, was to constitute the strangest episode of his life. As soon as he found himself in private with his wife—they had retired to dress for dinner—they called each other's attention with effusion and almost with alarm to the sinister gloom that was stamped on the place. The house was admirable with its old grey front which came forward in wings so as to form three sides of a square, but Mrs. Coyle made no scruple to declare that if she had known in advance the sort of impression she was going to receive she would never have put her foot in it. She characterized it as "uncanny," she accused her husband of not having warned her properly. He had mentioned to her in advance certain facts, but while she almost feverishly dressed she had innumerable questions to ask. He hadn't told her about the girl, the extraordinary girl, Miss Julian—that is, he hadn't told her that this young lady, who in plain terms was a mere dependent, would be in effect, and as a consequence of the way she carried herself, the most important person in the house. Mrs. Coyle was already prepared to announce that she hated Miss Julian's affectations. Her husband above all hadn't told her that they should find their young charge looking five years older.

"I couldn't imagine that," said Mr. Coyle, "nor that the character of the crisis here would be quite so perceptible. But I suggested to Miss Wingrave the other day that they should press her nephew in real earnest, and she has taken me at my word. They've cut off his supplies—they're trying to starve him out. That's not what I meant—but indeed I don't quite *know* to-day what I meant. Owen feels the pressure, but he won't yield." The strange thing was that, now that he was

there, the versatile little coach felt still more that his own spirit
had been caught up by a wave of reaction. If he was there it
was because he was on poor Owen's side. His whole impression, his whole apprehension, had on the spot become much
deeper. There was something in the dear boy's very resistance
that began to charm him. When his wife, in the intimacy of
the conference I have mentioned, threw off the mask and
commended even with extravagance the stand his pupil had
taken (he was too good to be a horrid soldier and it was noble
of him to suffer for his convictions—wasn't he as upright as
a young hero, even though as pale as a Christian martyr?) the
good lady only expressed the sympathy which, under cover of
regarding his young friend as a rare exception, he had already
recognised in his own soul.

   For, half an hour ago, after they had had superficial tea in
the brown old hall of the house, his young friend had proposed to him, before going to dress, to take a turn outside,
and had even, on the terrace, as they walked together to one
of the far ends of it, passed his hand entreatingly into his
companion's arm, permitting himself thus a familiarity unusual between pupil and master and calculated to show that
he had guessed whom he could most depend on to be kind
to him. Spencer Coyle on his own side had guessed something, so that he was not surprised at the boy's having a particular confidence to make. He had felt on arriving that each
member of the party had wished to get hold of him first, and
he knew that at that moment Jane Wingrave was peering
through the ancient blur of one of the windows (the house
had been modernised so little that the thick dim panes were
three centuries old) to see if her nephew looked as if he were
poisoning the visitor's mind. Mr. Coyle lost no time therefore
in reminding the youth (and he took care to laugh as he did
so) that he had not come down to Paramore to be corrupted.
He had come down to make, face to face, a last appeal to
him—he hoped it wouldn't be utterly vain. Owen smiled sadly
as they went, asking him if he thought he had the general air
of a fellow who was going to knock under.

   "I think you look strange—I think you look ill," Spencer
Coyle said very honestly. They had paused at the end of the
terrace.

"I've had to exercise a great power of resistance, and it rather takes it out of one."

"Ah, my dear boy, I wish your great power—for you evidently possess it—were exerted in a better cause!"

Owen Wingrave smiled down at his small instructor. "I don't believe that!" Then he added, to explain why: "Isn't what you want, if you're so good as to think well of my character, to see me exert *most* power, in whatever direction? Well, *this* is the way I exert most." Owen Wingrave went on to relate that he had had some terrible hours with his grandfather, who had denounced him in a way to make one's hair stand up on one's head. He had expected them not to like it, not a bit, but he had had no idea they would make such a row. His aunt was different, but she was equally insulting. Oh, they had made him feel they were ashamed of him; they accused him of putting a public dishonour on their name. He was the only one who had ever backed out—he was the first for three hundred years. Every one had known he was to go up, and now every one would know he was a young hypocrite who suddenly pretended to have scruples. They talked of his scruples as you wouldn't talk of a cannibal's god. His grandfather had called him outrageous names. "He called me—he called me——" Here the young man faltered, his voice failed him. He looked as haggard as was possible to a young man in such magnificent health.

"I probably know!" said Spencer Coyle, with a nervous laugh.

Owen Wingrave's clouded eyes, as if they were following the far-off consequences of things, rested for an instant on a distant object. Then they met his companion's and for another moment sounded them deeply. "It isn't true. No, it isn't. It's not *that*!"

"I don't suppose it is! But what *do* you propose instead of it?"

"Instead of what?"

"Instead of the stupid solution of war. If you take that away you should suggest at least a substitute."

"That's for the people in charge, for governments and cabinets," said Owen Wingrave. "*They*'ll arrive soon enough at a substitute, in the particular case, if they're made to understand that they'll be hung if they don't find one. Make it a capital crime—that'll quicken the wits of ministers!" His eyes brightened as he spoke, and he looked assured and exalted. Mr. Coyle gave a sigh of perplexed resignation—it was a monomania. He fancied after this for a moment that Owen was going to ask him if he too thought he was a coward; but he was relieved to observe that he either didn't suspect him of it or shrank uncomfortably from putting the question to the test. Spencer Coyle wished to show confidence, but somehow a direct assurance that he didn't doubt of his courage appeared too gross a compliment—it would be like saying he didn't doubt of his honesty. The difficulty was presently averted by Owen's continuing: "My grandfather can't break the entail, but I shall have nothing but this place, which, as you know, is small and, with the way rents are going, has quite ceased to yield an income. He has some money—not much, but such as it is he cuts me off. My aunt does the same—she has let me know her intentions. She was to have left me her six hundred a year. It was all settled; but now what's settled is that I don't get a penny of it if I give up the army. I must add in fairness that I have from my mother three hundred a year of my own. And I tell you the simple truth when I say that I don't care a rap for the loss of the money." The young man drew a long, slow breath, like a creature in pain; then he subjoined: "*That's* not what worries me!"

"What are you going to do?" asked Spencer Coyle.

"I don't know; perhaps nothing. Nothing great, at all events. Only something peaceful!"

Owen gave a weary smile, as if, worried as he was, he could yet appreciate the humorous effect of such a declaration from a Wingrave; but what it suggested to his companion, who looked up at him with a sense that he was after all not a Wingrave for nothing and had a military steadiness under fire, was the exasperation that such a programme, uttered in such a way and striking them as the last word of the inglorious, might well have engendered on the part of his grandfather and his aunt. "Perhaps nothing"—when he might carry on the great tradition! Yes, he wasn't weak, and he was interesting; but there *was* a point of view from which he was provoking. "What *is* it then that worries you?" Mr. Coyle demanded.

"Oh, the house—the very air and feeling of it. There are strange voices in it that seem to mutter at me—to say dreadful things as I pass. I mean the general consciousness and responsibility of what I'm doing. Of course it hasn't been easy for me—not a bit. I assure you I don't enjoy it." With a light in them that was like a longing for justice Owen again bent his eyes on those of the little coach; then he pursued: "I've started up all the old ghosts. The very portraits glower at me on the walls. There's one of my great-great-grandfather (the one the extraordinary story you know is about—the old fellow who hangs on the second landing of the big staircase) that fairly stirs on the canvas—just heaves a little—when I come near it. I have to go up and down stairs—it's rather awkward! It's what my aunt calls the family circle. It's all constituted here, it's a kind of indestructible presence, it stretches away into the past, and when I came back with her the other day Miss Wingrave told me I wouldn't have the impudence to stand in the midst of it and say such things. I *had* to say them to my grandfather, but now that I've said them it seems to me that the question's ended. I want to go away—I don't care if I never come back again."

"Oh, you *are* a soldier; you must fight it out!" Mr. Coyle laughed.

The young man seemed discouraged at his levity, but as they turned round, strolling back in the direction from which they had come, he himself smiled faintly after an instant and replied:

"Ah, we're tainted—all!"

They walked in silence part of the way to the old portico; then Spencer Coyle, stopping short after having assured himself that he was at a sufficient distance from the house not to be heard, suddenly put the question: "What does Miss Julian say?"

"Miss Julian?" Owen had perceptibly coloured.

"I'm sure *she* hasn't concealed her opinion."

"Oh, it's the opinion of the family circle, for she's a member of it of course. And then she has her own as well."

"Her own opinion?"

"Her own family-circle."

"Do you mean her mother—that patient lady?"

"I mean more particularly her father, who fell in battle. And her grandfather, and *his* father, and her uncles and great-uncles—they all fell in battle."

"Hasn't the sacrifice of so many lives been sufficient? Why should she sacrifice *you?*"

"Oh, she *hates* me!" Owen declared, as they resumed their walk.

"Ah, the hatred of pretty girls for fine young men!" exclaimed Spencer Coyle.

He didn't believe in it, but his wife did, it appeared perfectly, when he mentioned this conversation while, in the fashion that has been described, the visitors dressed for dinner. Mrs. Coyle had already discovered that nothing could have been nastier than Miss Julian's manner to the disgraced youth during the half-hour the party had spent in the hall; and it was this lady's judgment that one must have had no eyes in one's head not to see that she was already trying outrageously to flirt with young Lechmere. It was a pity they had brought that silly boy: he was down in the hall with her at that moment. Spencer Coyle's version was different; he thought there were finer elements involved. The girl's footing in the house was inexplicable on any ground save that of her being pre-destined to Miss Wingrave's nephew. As the niece of Miss Wingrave's own unhappy intended she had been dedicated early by this lady to the office of healing by a union with Owen the tragic breach that had separated their elders; and if in reply to this it was to be said that a girl of spirit couldn't enjoy in such a matter having her duty cut out for her, Owen's enlightened friend was ready with the argument that a young person in Miss Julian's position would never be such a fool as really to quarrel with a capital chance. She was familiar at Paramore and she felt safe; therefore she might trust herself to the amusement of pretending that she had her option. But it was all innocent coquetry. She had a curious charm, and it was vain to pretend that the heir of that house wouldn't seem good enough to a girl, clever as she might be, of eighteen. Mrs. Coyle reminded her husband that the poor young man was precisely now *not* of that house: this problem was among the questions that exercised their wits after the two men had taken the turn on the terrace. Spencer Coyle told his wife that Owen was afraid of the portrait of his great-great-grandfather. He would show it to her, since she hadn't noticed it, on their way down stairs.

"Why of his great-great-grandfather more than of any of the others?"

"Oh, because he's the most formidable. He's the one who's sometimes seen."

"Seen where?" Mrs. Coyle had turned round with a jerk.

"In the room he was found dead in—the White Room they've always called it."

"Do you mean to say the house has a *ghost*?" Mrs. Coyle almost shrieked. "You brought me here without telling me?"

"Didn't I mention it after my other visit?"

"Not a word. You only talked about Miss Wingrave."

"Oh, I was full of the story—you have simply forgotten."

"Then you should have reminded me!"

"If I had thought of it I would have held my peace, for you wouldn't have come."

"I wish, indeed, I hadn't!" cried Mrs. Coyle. "What *is* the story?"

"Oh, a deed of violence that took place here ages ago. I think it was in George the First's time. Colonel Wingrave, one of their ancestors, struck in a fit of passion one of his children, a lad just growing up, a blow on the head of which the unhappy child died. The matter was hushed up for the hour—some other explanation was put about. The poor boy was laid out in one of those rooms on the other side of the house, and amid strange smothered rumours the funeral was hurried on. The next morning, when the household assembled, Colonel Wingrave was missing; he was looked for vainly, and at last it occurred to some one that he might perhaps be in the room from which his child had been carried to burial. The seeker knocked without an answer—then opened the door. Colonel Wingrave lay dead on the floor, in his clothes, as if he had reeled and fallen back, without a wound, without a mark, without anything in his appearance to indicate that he had either struggled or suffered. He was a strong, sound man—there was nothing to account for such a catastrophe. He is supposed to have gone to the room during the night, just before going to bed, in some fit of compunction or some fascination of dread. It was only after this that the truth about the boy came out. But no one ever sleeps in the room."

Mrs. Coyle had fairly turned pale. "I hope not! Thank heaven they haven't put *us* there!"

"We're at a comfortable distance; but I've seen the gruesome chamber."

"Do you mean you've been *in* it?"

"For a few moments. They're rather proud of it and my young friend showed it to me when I was here before."

Mrs. Coyle stared. "And what is it like?"

"Simply like an empty, dull, old-fashioned bedroom, rather big, with the things of the 'period' in it. It's panelled from floor to ceiling, and the panels evidently, years and years ago, were painted white. But the paint has darkened with time and there are three or four quaint little ancient 'samplers,' framed and glazed, hung on the walls."

Mrs. Coyle looked round with a shudder. "I'm glad there are no samplers here! I never heard anything so jumpy! Come down to dinner."

On the staircase as they went down her husband showed her the portrait of Colonel Wingrave—rather a vigorous representation, for the place and period, of a gentleman with a hard, handsome face, in a red coat and a peruke. Mrs. Coyle declared that his descendant Sir Philip was wonderfully like him; and her husband could fancy, though he kept it to himself, that if one should have the courage to walk about the old corridors of Paramore at night one might meet a figure that resembled him roaming, with the restlessness of a ghost, hand in hand with the figure of a tall boy. As he proceeded to the drawing-room with his wife he found himself suddenly wishing that he had made more of a point of his pupil's going to Eastbourne. The evening however seemed to have taken upon itself to dissipate any such whimsical forebodings, for the grimness of the family-circle, as Spencer Coyle had preconceived its composition, was mitigated by an infusion of the "neighbourhood." The company at dinner was recruited by two cheerful couples—one of them the vicar and his wife, and by a silent young man who had come down to fish. This was a relief to Mr. Coyle, who had begun to wonder what was after all expected of him and why he had been such a fool as to come, and who now felt that for the first hours at least the situation would not have directly to be dealt with. Indeed he found, as he had found before, sufficient occupation for his ingenuity in reading the various symptoms of which the picture before him was an expression. He should probably have an irritating day on the morrow: he foresaw the difficulty of the long decorous Sunday and how dry Jane Wingrave's ideas, elicited in a strenuous conference, would taste. She and her father would make him feel that they depended upon him for the impossible, and if they should try to associate him with a merely stupid policy he might end by telling them what he thought of it—an accident not required to make his visit a sensible mistake. The old man's actual design was evidently to let their friends see in it a positive mark of their being all right. The presence of the great London coach was tantamount to a profession of faith in the results of the impending examination. It had clearly been obtained from Owen, rather to Spencer Coyle's surprise, that he would do nothing to interfere with the apparent harmony. He let the allusions to his hard work pass and, holding his tongue about his affairs, talked to the ladies as amicably as if he had not been "cut off." When Spencer Coyle looked at him once or twice across the table, catching his eye, which showed an indefinable passion, he saw a puzzling pathos in his laughing face: one couldn't resist a pang for a young lamb so visibly marked for sacrifice. "Hang him—what a pity he's such a fighter!" he privately sighed, with a want of logic that was only superficial.

This idea however would have absorbed him more if so much of his attention had not been given to Kate Julian, who now that he had her well before him struck him as a remarkable and even as a possibly fascinating young woman. The fascination resided not in any extraordinary prettiness, for if she was handsome, with her long Eastern eyes, her magnificent hair and her general unabashed originality, he had seen complexions rosier and features that pleased him more: it resided in a strange impression that she gave of being exactly the sort of person whom, in her position, common considerations, those of prudence and perhaps even a little those of decorum, would have enjoined on her not to be. She was what was vulgarly termed a dependant—penniless, patronized, tolerated; but something in her aspect and manner signified that if her situation was inferior, her spirit, to make up for it, was above precautions or submissions. It was not in the least that she was aggressive, she was too indifferent for that; it was only as if, having nothing either to gain or to lose, she could afford to do as she liked. It occurred to Spencer Coyle that she might really have had more at stake than her imagination appeared to take account of; whatever it was at any rate he had never seen a young woman at less pains to be on the safe side. He wondered inevitably how the peace was kept between Jane Wingrave and such an inmate as this; but those questions of course were unfathomable deeps. Perhaps Kate Julian lorded it even over her protectress. The other time he was at Paramore he had received an impression that, with Sir Philip beside her, the girl could fight with her back to the wall. She amused Sir Philip, she charmed him, and he liked people who weren't afraid; between him and his daughter moreover there was no doubt which was the higher in command. Miss Wingrave took many things for granted, and most of all the rigour of discipline and the fate of the vanquished and the captive.

But between their clever boy and so original a companion of his childhood what odd relation would have grown up? It couldn't be indifference, and yet on the part of happy, handsome, youthful creatures it was still less likely to be aversion. They weren't Paul and Virginia, but they must have had their common summer and their idyll: no nice girl could have disliked such a nice fellow for anything but not liking *her*, and no nice fellow could have resisted such propinquity. Mr. Coyle remembered indeed that Mrs. Julian had spoken to him as if the propinquity had been by no means constant, owing to her daughter's absences at school, to say nothing of Owen's; her visits to a few friends who were so kind as to "take her" from time to time; her sojourns in London—so difficult to manage, but still managed by God's help—for "advantages," for drawing and singing, especially drawing or rather painting, in oils, in which she had had immense success. But the good lady had also mentioned that the young people were quite brother and sister, which *was* a little, after all, like Paul and Virginia. Mrs.

Coyle had been right, and it was apparent that Virginia was doing her best to make the time pass agreeably for young Lechmere. There was no such whirl of conversation as to render it an effort for Mr. Coyle to reflect on these things, for the tone of the occasion, thanks principally to the other guests, was not disposed to stray—it tended to the repetition of anecdote and the discussion of rents, topics that huddled together like uneasy animals. He could judge how intensely his hosts wished the evening to pass off as if nothing had happened; and this gave him the measure of their private resentment. Before dinner was over he found himself fidgetty about his second pupil. Young Lechmere, since he began to cram, had done all that might have been expected of him; but this couldn't blind his instructor to a present perception of his being in moments of relaxation as innocent as a babe. Mr. Coyle had considered that the amusements of Paramore would probably give him a fillip, and the poor fellow's manner testified to the soundness of the forecast. The fillip had been unmistakably administered; it had come in the form of a revelation. The light on young Lechmere's brow announced with a candour that was almost an appeal for compassion, or at least a deprecation of ridicule, that he had never seen anything like Miss Julian.

IV.

In the drawing-room after dinner the girl found an occasion to approach Spencer Coyle. She stood before him a moment, smiling while she opened and shut her fan, and then she said abruptly, raising her strange eyes: "I know what you've come for, but it isn't any use."

"I've come to look after *you* a little. Isn't *that* any use?"

"It's very kind. But I'm not the question of the hour. You won't do anything with Owen."

Spencer Coyle hesitated a moment. "What will *you* do with his young friend?"

She stared, looked round her.

"Mr. Lechmere? Oh, poor little lad! We've been talking about Owen. He admires him so."

"So do I. I should tell you that."

"So do we all. That's why we're in such despair."

"Personally then you'd *like* him to be a soldier?" Spencer Coyle inquired.

"I've quite set my heart on it. I adore the army and I'm awfully fond of my old playmate," said Miss Julian.

Her interlocutor remembered the young man's own different version of her attitude; but he judged it loyal not to challenge the girl.

"It's not conceivable that your old playmate shouldn't be fond of you. He must therefore wish to please you; and I don't see why—between you—you don't set the matter right."

"Wish to please me!" Miss Julian exclaimed. "I'm sorry to say he shows no such desire. He thinks me an impudent wretch. I've told him what I think of *him*, and he simply hates me."

"But you think so highly! You just told me you admire him."

"His talents, his possibilities, yes; even his appearance, if I may allude to such a matter. But I don't admire his present behaviour."

"Have you had the question out with him?" Spencer Coyle asked.

"Oh, yes, I've ventured to be frank—the occasion seemed to excuse it. He couldn't like what I said."

"What did you say?"

Miss Julian, thinking a moment, opened and shut her fan again.

"Why, that such conduct isn't that of a gentleman!"

After she had spoken her eyes met Spencer Coyle's, who looked into their charming depths.

"Do you want then so much to send him off to be killed?"

"How odd for *you* to ask that—in such a way!" she replied with a laugh. "I don't understand your position: I thought your line was to *make* soldiers!"

"You should take my little joke. But, as regards Owen Wingrave, there's no 'making' needed," Mr. Coyle added. "To my sense"—the little crammer paused a moment, as if with a consciousness of responsibility for his paradox—"to my sense he *is*, in a high sense of the term, a fighting man."

"Ah, let him prove it!" the girl exclaimed, turning away.

Spencer Coyle let her go; there was something in her tone that annoyed and even a little shocked him. There had evidently been a violent passage between these young people, and the reflection that such a matter was after all none of his business only made him more sore. It was indeed a military house, and she was at any rate a person who placed her ideal of manhood (young persons doubtless always had their ideals of manhood) in the type of the belted warrior. It was a taste like another; but, even a quarter of an hour later, finding himself near young Lechmere, in whom this type was embodied, Spencer Coyle was still so ruffled that he addressed the innocent lad with a certain magisterial dryness. "You're not to sit up late, you know. That's not what I brought you down for." The dinner-guests were taking leave and the bedroom candles twinkled in a monitory row. Young Lechmere however was too agreeably agitated to be accessible to a snub: he had a happy pre-occupation which almost engendered a grin.

"I'm only too eager for bedtime. Do you know there's an awfully jolly room?"

"Surely they haven't put you there?"

"No indeed: no one has passed a night in it for ages. But that's exactly what I want to do—it would be tremendous fun."

"And have you been trying to get Miss Julian's permission?"

"Oh, *she* can't give leave, she says. But she believes in it, and she maintains that no man dare."

"No man *shall*! A man in your critical position in particular must have a quiet night," said Spencer Coyle.

Young Lechmere gave a disappointed but reasonable sigh.

"Oh, all right. But mayn't I sit up for a little go at Wingrave? I haven't had any yet."

Mr. Coyle looked at his watch.

"You may smoke *one* cigarette."

He felt a hand on his shoulder, and he turned round to see his wife tilting candle-grease upon his coat. The ladies were going to bed and it was Sir Philip's inveterate hour; but Mrs. Coyle confided to her husband that after the dreadful things he had told her she positively declined to be left alone, for no

matter how short an interval, in any part of the house. He
promised to follow her within three minutes, and after the
orthodox handshakes the ladies rustled away. The forms were
kept up at Paramore as bravely as if the old house had no
present heartache. The only one of which Spencer Coyle noticed the omission was some salutation to himself from Kate
Julian. She gave him neither a word nor a glance, but he saw
her look hard at Owen Wingrave. Her mother, timid and
pitying, was apparently the only person from whom this
young man caught an inclination of the head. Miss Wingrave
marshalled the three ladies—her little procession of twinkling
tapers—up the wide oaken stairs and past the watching portrait of her ill-fated ancestor. Sir Philip's servant appeared and
offered his arm to the old man, who turned a perpendicular
back on poor Owen when the boy made a vague movement
to anticipate this office. Spencer Coyle learned afterwards
that before Owen had forfeited favour it had always, when he
was at home, been his privilege at bedtime to conduct his
grandfather ceremoniously to rest. Sir Philip's habits were
contemptuously different now. His apartments were on the
lower floor and he shuffled stiffly off to them with his valet's
help, after fixing for a moment significantly on the most responsible of his visitors the thick red ray, like the glow of
stirred embers, that always made his eyes conflict oddly with
his mild manners. They seemed to say to Spencer Coyle
"We'll let the young scoundrel have it to-morrow!" One
might have gathered from them that the young scoundrel,
who had now strolled to the other end of the hall, had at
least forged a cheque. Mr. Coyle watched him an instant, saw
him drop nervously into a chair and then with a restless
movement get up. The same movement brought him back to
where his late instructor stood addressing a last injunction to
young Lechmere.

"I'm going to bed and I should like you particularly to
conform to what I said to you a short time ago. Smoke a
single cigarette with your friend here and then go to your
room. You'll have me down on you if I hear of your having,
during the night, tried any preposterous games." Young
Lechmere, looking down with his hands in his pockets, said
nothing—he only poked at the corner of a rug with his toe;

so that Spencer Coyle, dissatisfied with so tacit a pledge, pres- ently went on, to Owen: "I must request you, Wingrave, not to keep this sensitive subject sitting up—and indeed to put him to bed and turn his key in the door." As Owen stared an instant, apparently not understanding the motive of so much solicitude, he added: "Lechmere has a morbid curiosity about one of your legends—of your historic rooms. Nip it in the bud."

"Oh, the legend's rather good, but I'm afraid the room's an awful sell!" Owen laughed.

"You know you don't *believe* that, my boy!" young Lech- mere exclaimed.

"I don't think he does," said Mr. Coyle, noticing Owen's mottled flush.

"He wouldn't try a night there himself!" young Lechmere pursued.

"I know who told you that," rejoined Owen, lighting a cigarette in an embarrassed way at the candle, without offer- ing one to either of his companions.

"Well, what if she did?" asked the younger of these gentle- man, rather red. "Do you want them *all* yourself?" he con- tinued facetiously, fumbling in the cigarette-box.

Owen Wingrave only smoked quietly; then he exclaimed:

"Yes—what if she did? But she doesn't know," he added.

"She doesn't know what?"

"She doesn't know anything!—I'll tuck him in!" Owen went on gaily to Mr. Coyle, who saw that his presence, now that a certain note had been struck, made the young men uncomfortable. He was curious, but there was a kind of dis- cretion, with his pupils, that he had always pretended to prac- tise; a discretion that however didn't prevent him as he took his way upstairs from recommending them not to be donkeys.

At the top of the staircase, to his surprise, he met Miss Julian, who was apparently going down again. She had not begun to undress, nor was she perceptibly disconcerted at see- ing him. She nevertheless, in a manner slightly at variance with the rigour with which she had overlooked him ten minutes before, dropped the words: "I'm going down to look for something. I've lost a jewel."

"A jewel?"

"A rather good turquoise, out of my locket. As it's the only ornament I have the honour to possess——!" And she passed down.

"Shall I go with you and help you?" asked Spencer Coyle.

The girl paused a few steps below him, looking back with her Oriental eyes.

"Don't I hear voices in the hall?"

"Those remarkable young men are there."

"*They'll* help me." And Kate Julian descended.

Spencer Coyle was tempted to follow her, but remembering his standard of tact he rejoined his wife in their apartment. He delayed however to go to bed, and though he went into his dressing-room he couldn't bring himself even to take off his coat. He pretended for half an hour to read a novel; after which, quietly, or perhaps I should say agitatedly, he passed from the dressing-room into the corridor. He followed this passage to the door of the room which he knew to have been assigned to young Lechmere and was comforted to see that it was closed. Half an hour earlier he had seen it standing open; therefore he could take for granted that the bewildered boy had come to bed. It was of this he had wished to assure himself, and having done so he was on the point of retreating. But at the same instant he heard a sound in the room—the occupant was doing, at the window, something which showed him that he might knock without the reproach of waking his pupil up. Young Lechmere came in fact to the door in his shirt and trousers. He admitted his visitor in some surprise, and when the door was closed again Spencer Coyle said:

"I don't want to make your life a burden to you, but I had it on my conscience to see for myself that you're not exposed to undue excitement."

"Oh, there's plenty of that!" said the ingenuous youth. "Miss Julian came down again."

"To look for a turquoise?"

"So she said."

"Did she find it?"

"I don't know. I came up. I left her with poor Wingrave."

"Quite the right thing," said Spencer Coyle.

"I don't know," young Lechmere repeated uneasily. "I left them quarrelling."

"What about?"

"I don't understand. They're a quaint pair!"

Spencer Coyle hesitated. He had, fundamentally, principles and scruples, but what he had in particular just now was a curiosity, or rather, to recognise it for what it was, a sympathy, which brushed them away.

"Does it strike you that *she's* down on him?" he permitted himself to inquire.

"Rather!—when she tells him he lies!"

"What do you mean?"

"Why, before *me*. It made me leave them; it was getting too hot. I stupidly brought up the question of the haunted room again, and said how sorry I was that I had had to promise you not to try my luck with it."

"You can't pry about in that gross way in other people's houses—you can't take such liberties, you know!" Mr. Coyle interjected.

"I'm all right—see how good I am. I don't want to go *near* the place!" said young Lechmere, confidingly. "Miss Julian said to me 'Oh, I daresay *you'd* risk it, but'—and she turned and laughed at poor Owen—'that's more than we can expect of a gentleman who has taken *his* extraordinary line.' I could see that something had already passed between them on the subject—some teasing or challenging of hers. It may have been only chaff, but his chucking the profession had evidently brought up the question of his pluck."

"And what did Owen say?"

"Nothing at first; but presently he brought out very quietly: 'I spent all last night in the confounded place.' We both stared and cried out at this and I asked him what he had seen there. He said he had seen nothing, and Miss Julian replied that he ought to tell his story better than that—he ought to make something good of it. 'It's not a story—it's a simple fact,' said he; on which she jeered at him and wanted to know why, if he had done it, he hadn't told her in the morning, since he knew what she thought of him. 'I know, but I don't care,' said Wingrave. This made her angry, and she asked him quite seriously whether he would care if he should know she believed him to be trying to deceive us."

"Ah, what a brute!" cried Spencer Coyle.

"She's a most extraordinary girl—I don't know what she's up to."

"Extraordinary indeed—to be romping and bandying words at that hour of the night with fast young men!"

Young Lechmere reflected a moment. "I mean because I think she likes him."

Spencer Coyle was so struck with this unwonted symptom of subtlety that he flashed out: "And do you think he likes *her*?"

But his interlocutor only replied with a puzzled sigh and a plaintive "I don't know—I give it up!—I'm sure he *did* see something or hear something," young Lechmere added.

"In that ridiculous place? What makes you sure?"

"I don't know—he looks as if he had. He behaves as if he had."

"Why then shouldn't he mention it?"

Young Lechmere thought a moment. "Perhaps it's too gruesome!"

Spencer Coyle gave a laugh. "Aren't you glad then *you're* not in it?"

"Uncommonly!"

"Go to bed, you goose," said Spencer Coyle, with another laugh. "But before you go tell me what he said when she told him he was trying to deceive you."

" 'Take me there yourself, then, and lock me in!' "

"And *did* she take him?"

"I don't know—I came up."

Spencer Coyle exchanged a long look with his pupil. "I don't think they're in the hall now. Where's Owen's own room?"

"I haven't the least idea."

Mr. Coyle was perplexed; he was in equal ignorance, and he couldn't go about trying doors. He bade young Lechmere sink to slumber, and came out into the passage. He asked himself if he should be able to find his way to the room Owen had formerly shown him, remembering that in common with many of the others it had its ancient name painted upon it. But the corridors of Paramore were intricate; moreover some of the servants would still be up, and he didn't wish to have the appearance of roaming over the house. He went back to his own quarters, where Mrs. Coyle soon perceived that his inability to rest had not subsided. As she confessed for her own part, in the dreadful place, to an increased sense of "creepiness," they spent the early part of the night in conversation, so that a portion of their vigil was inevitably beguiled by her husband's account of his colloquy with little Lechmere and by their exchange of opinions upon it. Toward two o'clock Mrs. Coyle became so nervous about their persecuted young friend, and so possessed by the fear that that wicked girl had availed herself of his invitation to put him to an abominable test, that she begged her husband to go and look into the matter at whatever cost to his own equilibrium. But Spencer Coyle, perversely, had ended, as the perfect stillness of the night settled upon them, by charming himself into a tremulous acquiescence in Owen's readiness to face a formidable ordeal—an ordeal the more formidable to an excited imagination as the poor boy now knew from the experience of the previous night how resolute an effort he should have to make. "I hope he *is* there," he said to his wife: "it puts them all so in the wrong!" At any rate he couldn't take upon himself to explore a house he knew so little. He was inconsequent—he didn't prepare for bed. He sat in the dressing-room with his light and his novel, waiting to find himself nodding. At last however Mrs. Coyle turned over and ceased to talk, and at last too he fell asleep in his chair. How long he slept he only knew afterwards by computation; what he knew to begin with was that he had started up, in confusion, with the sense of a sudden appalling sound. His sense cleared itself quickly, helped doubtless by a confirmatory cry of horror from his wife's room. But he gave no heed to his wife; he had already bounded into the passage. There the sound was repeated—it was the "Help! help!" of a woman in agonised terror. It came from a distant quarter of the house, but the quarter was sufficiently indicated. Spencer Coyle rushed straight before him, with the sound of opening doors and alarmed voices in his ears and the faintness of the early dawn in his eyes. At a turn of one of the passages he came upon the white figure of a girl in a swoon on a bench, and in the vividness of the revelation he read as he went that Kate Julian, stricken in her pride too late with a chill of compunction for what she had mockingly done, had, after coming to release the victim of her derision, reeled away, overwhelmed, from the catastrophe that was her work—the catastrophe that the next moment he found himself aghast at on the threshold of an open door. Owen Wingrave, dressed as he had last seen him, lay dead on the spot on which his ancestor had been found. He looked like a young soldier on a battle-field.

The Wheel of Time

"And your daughter?" said Lady Greyswood; "tell me about her. She must be nice."

"Oh, yes, she's nice enough. She's a great comfort." Mrs. Knocker hesitated a moment, then she went on· "Unfortunately she's not good-looking—not a bit."

"That doesn't matter, when they're not ill-natured," rejoined, insincerely, Lady Greyswood, who had the remains of great beauty.

"Oh, but poor Fanny is quite extraordinarily plain. I assure you it does matter. She knows it herself; she suffers from it. It's the sort of thing that makes a great difference in a girl's life."

"But if she's charming, if she's clever!" said Lady Greyswood, with more benevolence than logic. "I've known plain women who were liked."

"Do you mean *me*, my dear?" her old friend straightforwardly inquired. "But I'm not so awfully liked!"

"You?" Lady Greyswood exclaimed. "Why, you're grand!"

"I'm not so repulsive as I was when I was young perhaps, but that's not saying much."

"As when you were young!" laughed Lady Greyswood. "You sweet thing, you *are* young. I thought India dried people up."

"Oh, when you're a mummy to begin with!" Mrs. Knocker returned, with her trick of self-abasement. "Of course I've not been such a fool as to keep my children there. My girl *is* clever," she continued, "but she's afraid to show it. Therefore you may judge whether, with her unfortunate appearance, she's charming."

"She shall show it to *me*! You must let me do everything for her."

"Does that include finding her a husband? I should like her to show it to someone who'll marry her."

"*I'll* marry her!" said Lady Greyswood, who was handsomer than ever when she laughed and looked capable.

"What a blessing to meet you this way on the threshold of home! I give you notice that I shall cling to you. But that's

what I meant; that's the thing the want of beauty makes so
difficult—as if it were not difficult enough at the best."

"My dear child, one meets plenty of ugly women with husbands," Lady Greyswood argued, "and often with very nice
ones."

"Yes, mine is very nice. There are men who don't mind
one's face, for whom beauty isn't indispensable, but they are
rare. I don't understand them. If I'd been a man about to
marry I should have gone in for looks. However, the poor
child will *have* something," Mrs. Knocker continued.

Lady Greyswood rested thoughtful eyes on her. "Do you
mean she'll be well off?"

"We shall do everything we can for her. We're not in such
misery as we used to be. We've managed to save in India,
strange to say, and six months ago my husband came into
money (more than we had ever dreamed of), by the death of
his poor brother. We feel quite opulent (it's rather nice!) and
we should expect to do something decent for our daughter. I
don't mind it's being known."

"It *shall* be known!" said Lady Greyswood, getting up.
"Leave the dear child to me!" The old friends embraced, for
the porter of the hotel had come in to say that the carriage
ordered for her ladyship was at the door. They had met in
Paris by the merest chance, in the court of an inn, after a
separation of years, just as Lady Greyswood was going home.
She had been to Aix-les-Bains early in the season and was
resting on her way back to England. Mrs. Knocker and the
General, bringing their eastern exile to a close, had arrived
only the night before from Marseilles and were to wait in Paris
for their children, a tall girl and two younger boys, who, inevitably dissociated from their parents, had been for the past
two years with a devoted aunt, their father's maiden sister, at
Heidelberg. The reunion of the family was to take place with
jollity in Paris, whither this good lady was now hurrying with
her drilled and demoralized charges. Mrs. Knocker had come
to England to see them two years before, and the period at
Heidelberg had been planned during this visit. With the ter-
mination of her husband's service a new life opened before
them all, and they had plans of comprehensive rejoicing for
the summer—plans involving however a continuance, for a

few months, of useful foreign opportunities, during which various questions connected with the organization of a final home in England were practically to be dealt with. There was to be a salubrious house on the continent, taken in some neighbourhood that would both yield a stimulus to plain Fanny's French (her German was much commended), and permit of frequent "running over" for the General. With these preoccupations Mrs. Knocker, after her delightful encounter with Lady Greyswood, was less keenly conscious of the variations of destiny than she had been when, at the age of twenty, that intimate friend of her youth, beautiful, loveable and about to be united to a nobleman of ancient name, was brightly, almost insolently alienated. The less attractive of the two girls had married only several years later, and her marriage had perhaps emphasised the divergence of their ways. To-day however the inequality, as Mrs. Knocker would have phrased it, rather dropped out of the impression produced by the somewhat wasted and faded dowager, exquisite still, but unexpectedly appealing, who made no secret (an attempt that in an age of such publicity would have been useless), of what she had had, in vulgar parlance, to put up with, or of her having been left badly off. She had spoken of her children—she had had no less than six—but she had evidently thought it better not to speak of her husband. That somehow made up, on Mrs. Knocker's part, for some ancient aches.

It was not till a year after this incident that, one day in London, in her little house in Queen Street, Lady Greyswood said to her third son, Maurice—the one she was fondest of, the one who on his own side had given her most signs of affection·

"I don't see what there is for you but to marry a girl of a certain fortune."

"Oh, that's not my line! I may be an idiot, but I'm not mercenary," the young man declared. He was not an idiot, but there was an examination, rather stiff indeed, to which, without success, he had gone up twice. The diplomatic service was closed to him by this catastrophe; nothing else appeared particularly open; he was terribly at leisure. There had been a theory none the less that he was the ablest of the family. Two of his brothers had been squeezed into the army and had

declared rather crudely that they would do their best to keep
Maurice out. They were not put to any trouble in this respect
however, as he professed a complete indifference to the trade
of arms. His mother, who was vague about everything except
the idea that people ought to like him, if only for his extraordinary good looks, thought it strange there shouldn't be some
opening for him in political life, or something to be picked
up even in the City. But no bustling borough solicited the
advantage of his protection, no eminent statesman in want of
a secretary took him by the hand, no great commercial house
had been keeping a stool for him. Maurice, in a word, was
not "approached" from any quarter, and meanwhile he was
as irritating as the intending traveller who allows you the
pleasure of looking out his railway-connections. Poor Lady
Greyswood fumbled the social Bradshaw in vain. The young
man had only one marked taste, with which his mother saw
no way to deal—an invincible passion for photography. He
was perpetually taking shots at his friends, but she couldn't
open premises for him in Baker Street. He smoked endless
cigarettes—she was sure they made him languid. She would
have been more displeased with him if she had not felt so
vividly that someone ought to do something for him; nevertheless she almost lost patience at his remark about not being
mercenary. She was on the point of asking him what he called
it to live on his relations, but she checked the words as she
remembered that she herself was the only one who did much
for him. Nevertheless, as she hated open professions of disinterestedness, she replied that that was a nonsensical tone.
Whatever one should get in such a way one would give quite
as much, even if it didn't happen to be money; and when he
inquired in return what it was (beyond the disgrace of his
failures) that she judged a fellow like him would bring to his
bride, she replied that he would bring himself, his personal
qualities (she didn't like to be more definite about his appearance), his name, his descent, his connections—good honest commodities all, for which any girl of proper feeling would
be glad to pay. Such a name as that of the Glanvils was surely
worth something, and she appealed to him to try what he
could do with it.

"Surely I can do something better with it than sell it," said Maurice.

"I should like then very much to hear what," she replied very calmly, waiting reasonably for his answer. She waited to no purpose; the question baffled him, like those of his examinations. She explained that she meant of course that he should care for the girl, who might easily have a worse fault than the command of bread and butter. To humour her, for he was always good-natured, he said after a moment, smiling:

"Dear mother, is she pretty?"

"Is who pretty?"

"The young lady you have in your eye. Of course I see you've picked her out."

She coloured slightly at this—she had planned a more gradual revelation. For an instant she thought of saying that she had only had a general idea, for the form of his question embarrassed her; but on reflection she determined to be frank and practical. "Well, I confess I *am* thinking of a girl—a very nice one. But she hasn't great beauty."

"Oh, then it's of no use."

"But she's delightful, and she'll have thirty thousand pounds down, to say nothing of expectations."

Maurice Glanvil looked at his mother. "She must be hideous—for you to admit it. Therefore if she's rich she becomes quite impossible; for how can a fellow have the air of having been bribed with gold to marry a monster?"

"Fanny Knocker isn't the least a monster, and I can see that she'll improve. She's tall, and she's quite strong, and there's nothing at all disagreeable about her. Remember that you can't have everything."

"I thought you contended that I could!" said Maurice, amused at his mother's description of her young friend's charms. He had never heard anyone damned, as regards that sort of thing, with fainter praise. He declared that he would be perfectly capable of marrying a poor girl, but that the prime necessity in any young person he should think of would be the possession of a face—to put it at the least—that it would give him positive pleasure to look at. "I don't ask for much, but I do ask for beauty," he went on. "My eye must be gratified—I must have a wife I can photograph."

Lady Greyswood was tempted to answer that he himself had good looks enough to make a handsome couple, but she withheld the remark as injudicious, though effective, for it was a part of her son's amiability that he appeared to have no conception of his plastic side. He would have been disgusted if she had put it forward; if he had the ideal he had just described it was not because his own profile was his standard. What she herself saw in it was a force for coercing heiresses. She had however to be patient, and she promised herself to be adroit; which was all the easier as she really liked Fanny Knocker.

The girl's parents had at last taken a house in Ennismore Gardens, and the friend of her mother's youth had been confronted with the question of redeeming the pledges uttered in Paris. This unsophisticated and united family, with relations to visit and schoolboys' holidays to outlive, had spent the winter in the country and had but lately begun to talk of itself, extravagantly of course, through Mrs. Knocker's droll lips, as open to social attentions. Lady Greyswood had not been false to her vows; she had on the contrary recognised from the first that, if he could only be made to see it, Fanny Knocker would be just the person to fill out poor Maurice's blanks. She had kept this confidence to herself, but it had made her very kind to the young lady. One of the forms of this kindness had been an ingenuity in keeping her from coming to Queen Street until Maurice should have been prepared. Was he to be regarded as prepared now that he asserted he would have nothing to do with Miss Knocker? This was a question that worried Lady Greyswood, who at any rate said to herself that she had told him the worst. Her idea had been to sound her old friend only after the young people should have met and Fanny should have fallen in love. Such a catastrophe for Fanny belonged for Lady Greyswood to that order of convenience that she could always take for granted.

She had found the girl, as she expected, ugly and awkward, but had also discovered a charm of character in her intelligent timidity. No one knew better than this observant woman how thankless a task in general it was in London to "take out" a plain girl; she had seen the nicest creatures, in the brutality of balls, participate only through wistful, almost tearful eyes; her little drawing-room, at intimate hours, had been shaken by the confidences of desperate mothers. None the less she felt sure that Fanny's path would not be rugged; thirty thousand pounds were a fine set of features, and her anxiety was rather on the score of the expectations of the young lady's parents. Mrs. Knocker had dropped remarks suggestive of a high imagination, of the conviction that there might be a real efficacy in what they were doing for their daughter. The danger, in other words, might well be that no younger son need apply—a possibility that made Lady Greyswood take all her precautions. The acceptability of her favourite child was consistent with the rejection of those of other people—on which indeed it even directly depended. She remembered on the other hand the proverb about taking your horse to the water; the crystalline spring of her young friend's homage might overflow, but she couldn't compel her boy to drink. The clever way was to break down his prejudice—to get him to consent to give poor Fanny a chance. Therefore if she was careful not to worry him she let him see her project as something patient and deeply wise; she had the air of waiting resignedly for the day on which, in the absence of other solutions, he would say to her: "Well, let me have a look at my fate!" Meanwhile moreover she was nothing if not conscientious, and as she had made up her mind about the girl's susceptibility she had a scruple against exposing her. This exposure would not be justified so long as Maurice's theoretic rigour should remain unabated.

She felt virtuous in carrying her scruple to the point of rudeness; she knew that Jane Knocker wondered why, though so attentive in a hundred ways, she had never definitely included the poor child in any invitation to Queen Street. There came a moment when it gave her pleasure to suspect that her old friend had begun to explain this omission by the idea of a positive exaggeration of good faith—an honest recognition of the detrimental character of the young man in ambush there. As Maurice, though much addicted to kissing his mother at home, never dangled about her in public, he had remained a mythical figure to Mrs. Knocker: he had been

absent (culpably—there was a touch of the inevitable incivility
in it), on each of the occasions on which, after their arrival in
London, she and her husband dined with Lady Greyswood.
This astute woman knew that her delightful Jane was whimsical enough to be excited good-humouredly by a mystery:
she might very well want to make Maurice's acquaintance in
just the degree in which she guessed that his mother's high
sense of honour kept him out of the way. Moreover she desired intensely that her daughter should have the sort of experience that would help her to take confidence. Lady
Greyswood knew that no one had as yet asked the girl to
dinner and that this particular attention was the one for which
her mother would be most grateful. No sooner had she arrived at these illuminations than, with deep diplomacy, she
requested the pleasure of the company of her dear Jane and
the General. Mrs. Knocker accepted with delight—she always
accepted with delight—so that nothing remained for Lady
Greyswood but to make sure of Maurice in advance. After this
was done she had only to wait. When the dinner, on a day
very near at hand, took place (she had jumped at the first
evening on which the Knockers were free), she had the gratification of seeing her prevision exactly fulfilled. Her whimsical
Jane had thrown the game into her hands, had been taken at
the very last moment with one of her Indian headaches and,
infinitely apologetic and explanatory, had hustled poor Fanny
off with the General. The girl, flurried and frightened by her
responsibility, sat at dinner next to Maurice, who behaved
beautifully—not in the least as the victim of a trick; and when
a fortnight later Lady Greyswood was able to divine that her
mind from that evening had been filled with a virginal ecstasy, she was also fortunately able to feel serenely, delightfully
guiltless.

II.

She knew this fact about Fanny's mind, she believed, some
time before Jane Knocker knew it; but she also had reason to
think that Jane Knocker had known it for some time before
she spoke of it. It was not till the middle of June, after a
succession of encounters between the young people, that her

old friend came one morning to discuss the circumstance. Mrs. Knocker asked her if she suspected it, and she promptly replied that it had never occurred to her. She added that she was extremely sorry and that it had probably in the first instance been the fault of that injudicious dinner.

"Ah, the day of my headache—my miserable headache?" said her visitor. "Yes, very likely that did it. He's so dreadfully good-looking."

"Poor child, he can't help that. Neither can I!" Lady Greyswood ventured to add.

"He comes by it honestly. He seems very nice."

"He's nice enough, but he hasn't a farthing, you know, and his expectations are *nil*." They considered, they turned the matter about, they wondered what they had better do. In the first place there was no room for doubt; of course Mrs. Knocker hadn't sounded the girl, but a mother, a true mother was never reduced to that. If Fanny was in every relation of life so painfully, so constitutionally awkward, the still depths of her shyness, of her dissimulation even, in such a predicament as this, might easily be imagined. She would give no sign that she could possibly smother, she would say nothing and do nothing, watching herself, poor child, with trepidation; but she would suffer, and some day when the question of her future should really come up—it might after all in the form of some good proposal—they would find themselves beating against a closed door. That was what they had to think of; that was why Mrs. Knocker had come over. Her old friend cross-examined her with a troubled face, but she was very impressive with her reasons, her intuitions.

"I'll send him away in a moment, if you'd like that," Lady Greyswood said at last. "I'll try and get him to go abroad."

Her visitor made no direct reply to this, and no reply at all for some moments. "What does he expect to do—what does he want to do?" she asked.

"Oh, poor boy, he's looking—he's trying to decide. He asks nothing of anyone. If he would only knock at a few doors! But he's too proud."

"Do you call him *very* clever?" Fanny's mother demanded.

"Yes, decidedly—and good and kind and true. But he has been unlucky."

"Of course he can't bear her!" said Mrs. Knocker with a little dry laugh.

Lady Greyswood stared; then she broke out: "Do you mean you'd be willing?——"

"He's very charming."

"Ah, but you must have great ideas."

"He's very well connected," said Mrs. Knocker, snapping the tight elastic on her umbrella.

"Oh, my dear Jane—'connected'!" Lady Greyswood gave a sigh of the sweetest irony.

"He's connected with you, to begin with."

Lady Greyswood put out her hand and held her visitor's for a moment. "Of course it isn't as if he were a different sort of person. Of course I should like it!" she added.

"Does he dislike her *very* much?"

Lady Greyswood looked at her friend with a smile. "He resembles Fanny—he doesn't tell. But what would her father say?" she went on.

"He doesn't know it."

"You've not talked with him?"

Mrs. Knocker hesitated a moment. "He thinks she's all right." Both the ladies laughed a little at the density of men; then the visitor said: "I wanted to see you first."

This circumstance gave Lady Greyswood food for thought; it suggested comprehensively that in spite of a probable deficiency of zeal on the General's part the worthy man would not be the great obstacle. She had begun so quickly to turn over in her mind the various ways in which this new phase of the business might make it possible the real obstacle should be surmounted that she scarcely heard her companion say next: "The General will only want his daughter to be happy. He has no definite ambitions for her. I dare say Maurice could make him like him." It was something more said by her companion about Maurice that sounded sharply through her reverie. "But unless the idea appeals to *him* a bit there's no use talking about it."

At this Lady Greyswood spoke with decision. "It *shall* appeal to him. Leave it to me! Kiss your dear child for me," she added as the ladies embraced and separated.

In the course of the day she made up her mind, and when she again broached the question to her son (it befell that very evening) she felt that she stood on firmer ground. She began by mentioning to him that her dear old friend had the same charming dream—for the girl—that *she* had; she sketched with a light hand a picture of their preconcerted happiness in the union of their children. When he replied that he couldn't for the life of him imagine what the Knockers could see in a poor beggar of a younger son who had publicly come a cropper, she took pains to prove that he was as good as anyone else and much better than many of the young men to whom persons of sense were often willing to confide their daughters. She had been in much tribulation over the circumstance announced to her in the morning, not knowing whether, in her present enterprise, to keep it back or put it forward. If Maurice should happen not to take it in the right way it was the sort of thing that might dish the whole experiment. He might be bored, he might be annoyed, he might be horrified— there was no limit, in such cases, to the perversity, to the possible brutality of even the most amiable man. On the other hand he might be pleased, touched, flattered—if he didn't dislike the girl too much. Lady Greyswood could indeed imagine that it might be unpleasant to know that a person who was disagreeable to you was in love with you; so that there was just that risk to run. She determined to run it only if there should be absolutely no other card to play. Meanwhile she said: "Don't you see, now, how intelligent she is, in her quiet way, and how perfect she is at home—without any nonsense or affectation or ill-nature? She's not a bit stupid, she's remarkably clever. She can do a lot of things; she has no end of talents. Many girls with a quarter of her abilities would make five times the show."

"My dear mother, she's a great swell, I freely admit it. She's far too good for me. What in the world puts it into your two heads that she would look at me?"

At this Lady Greyswood was tempted to speak; but after an instant she said instead: "She *has* looked at you, and you've seen how. You've seen her several times now, and she has been remarkably nice to you."

"Nice? Ah, poor girl, she's frightened to death!"

"Believe me—I read her," Lady Greyswood replied.

"She knows she has money and she thinks I'm after it. She thinks I'm a ravening wolf and she's scared."

"I happen to know as a fact that she's in love with you!" Before she could check herself Lady Greyswood had played her card, and though she held her breath a little after doing so she felt that it had been a good moment. "If I hadn't known it," she hastened further to declare, "I should never have said another word." Maurice burst out laughing—how in the world *did* she know it? When she put the evidence before him she had the pleasure of seeing that he listened without irritation; and this emboldened her to say: "Don't you think you could *try* to like her?"

Maurice was lounging on a sofa opposite to her; jocose but embarrassed, he had thrown back his head, and while he stretched himself his eyes wandered over the upper expanse of the room. "It's very kind of her and of her mother, and I'm much obliged and all that, though a fellow feels rather an ass in talking about such a thing. Of course also I don't pretend—before such a proof of wisdom—that I think her in the least a fool. But, oh, dear——!" And the young man broke off with laughing impatience, as if he had too much to say. His mother waited an instant, then she uttered a persuasive, interrogative sound, and he went on: "It's only a pity she's so awful!"

"So awful?" murmured Lady Greyswood.

"Dear mother, she's about as ugly a woman as ever turned round on you. If there were only just a touch or two less of it!"

Lady Greyswood got up: she stood looking in silence at the tinted shade of the lamp. She remained in this position so long that he glanced at her—he was struck with the sadness in her face. He would have been in error however if he had suspected that this sadness was assumed for the purpose of showing him that she was wounded by his resistance, for the reflection that his last words caused her to make was as disinterested as it was melancholy. Here was an excellent, a charming girl—a girl, she was sure, with a rare capacity for devotion—whose future was reduced to nothing by the mere accident, in her face, of a certain want of drawing. A man could settle her fate with a laugh, could give her away with a snap of his fingers. She seemed to see Maurice administer to poor Fanny's image the little displeased shove with which he would have disposed of an ill-seasoned dish. Moreover he greatly exaggerated. Her heart grew heavy with a sense of the hardness of the lot of women, and when she looked again at her son there were tears in her eyes that startled him. "Poor girl—poor girl!" she simply sighed, in a tone that was to reverberate in his mind and to constitute in doing so a real appeal to his imagination. After a moment she added: "We'll talk no more about her—no, no!"

All the same she went three days later to see Mrs. Knocker and say to her: "My dear creature, I think it's all right."

"Do you mean he'll take us up?"

"He'll come and see you, and you must give him plenty of chances." What Lady Greyswood would have liked to be able to say, crudely and comfortably, was: "He'll try to manage it—he promises to do what he can." What she did say, however, was: "He's greatly prepossessed in the dear child's favour."

"Then I dare say he'll be very nice."

"If I didn't think he'd behave like a gentleman I wouldn't raise a finger. The more he sees of her the more he'll be sure to like her."

"Of course with poor Fanny that's the only thing one can build on," said Mrs. Knocker. "There's so much to get over."

Lady Greyswood hesitated a moment, "Maurice *has* got over it. But I should tell you that at first he doesn't want it known."

"Doesn't want what known?"

"Why, the footing on which he comes. You see it's just the least bit experimental."

"For what do you take me?" asked Mrs. Knocker. "The child shall never dream that anything has passed between us. No more of course shall her father."

"It's too delightful of you to leave it that way," Lady Greyswood replied. "We must surround her happiness with every safeguard."

Mrs. Knocker sat pensive for some moments. "So that if nothing comes of it there's no harm done? That idea—that nothing may come of it—makes one a little nervous," she added.

"Of course I can't absolutely answer for my poor boy!" said Lady Greyswood, with just the faintest ring of impatience. "But he's much affected by what he knows—I told him. That's what moves him."

"He must of course be perfectly free."

"The great thing is for her not to know."

Mrs. Knocker considered. "Are you very sure?" She had apparently had a profounder second thought.

"Why, my dear—with the risk!"

"Isn't the risk, after all, greater the other way? Mayn't it help the matter on, mayn't it do the poor child a certain degree of good, the idea that, as you say, he's prepossessed in her favour? It would perhaps cheer her up, as it were, and encourage her, so that by the very fact of being happier about herself she may make a better impression. That's what she wants, poor thing—to be helped to hold up her head, to take herself more seriously, to believe that people can like her. And fancy, when it's a case of such a beautiful young man who's all ready to!"

"Yes, he's all ready to," Lady Greyswood conceded. "Of course it's a question for your own discretion. I can't advise you, for you know your child. But it seems to me a case for tremendous caution."

"Oh, trust me for that!" said Mrs. Knocker. "We shall be very kind to him," she smiled, as her visitor got up.

"He'll appreciate that. But it's too nice of you to leave it so."

Mrs. Knocker gave a hopeful shrug. "He has only to be civil to Blake!"

"Ah, he isn't a brute!" Lady Greyswood exclaimed, caressing her.

After this she passed a month of no little anxiety. She asked her son no question, and for two or three weeks he offered her no other information than to say two or three times that Miss Knocker really could ride; but she learned from her old friend everything she wanted to know. Immediately after the conference of the two ladies Maurice, in the Row, had taken an opportunity of making up to the girl. She rode every day with her father, and Maurice rode, though possessed of nothing in life to put a leg across; and he had been so well received that this proved the beginning of a custom. He had a canter with the young lady most days in the week, and when they parted it was usually to meet again in the evening. His relations with the household in Ennismore Gardens were indeed not left greatly to his initiative; he became on the spot the subject of perpetual invitations and arrangements, the centre of the friendliest manœuvres; so that Lady Greyswood was struck with Jane Knocker's feverish energy in the good cause—the ingenuity, the bribery, the cunning that an exemplary mother might be inspired to practise. She herself did nothing, she left it all to poor Jane, and this perhaps gave her for the moment a sense of contemplative superiority. She wondered if *she* would in any circumstances have plotted so almost fiercely for one of her children. She was glad her old friend's design had her full approbation; she held her breath a little when she said to herself: "Suppose I hadn't liked it—suppose it had been for Chumleigh!" Chumleigh was the present Lord Greyswood, whom his mother still called by his earlier designation. Fanny Knocker's thirty thousand would have been by no means enough for Chumleigh. Lady Greyswood, in spite of her suspense, was detached enough to be amused when her accomplice told her that "Blake" had said that Maurice really could ride. The two mothers thanked God for the riding—the riding would see them through. Lady Greyswood had watched Fanny narrowly in the Park, where, in the saddle, she looked no worse than lots of girls. She had no idea how Maurice got his mounts—she knew Chumleigh had none to give him; but there were directions in which she would have encouraged him to incur almost any liability. He was evidently amused and beguiled; he fell into comfortable attitudes on the soft cushions that were laid for him and partook with relish of the dainties that were served; he had his fill of the theatres, of the opera—entertainments of which he was fond. She could see he didn't care for the sort of people he met in Ennismore Gardens, but this didn't matter: so much as that she didn't ask of him. She knew that when he should have something to tell her he would speak; and meanwhile she pretended to be a thousand miles away. The only thing that worried her was that he had dropped photography. She said to Mrs. Knocker more than once: "Does he make love?—that's what I want to know!" to which this lady replied with her incongruous drollery: "My dear, how can I make out? He's so little like Blake!" But she added that she believed Fanny was intensely happy. Lady Greyswood had been struck with the girl's looking so, and she rejoiced to be able to declare in perfectly good faith that she thought her greatly improved. "Didn't I tell you?" returned Mrs. Knocker to this with a certain accent of triumph. It made Lady Greyswood nervous, for she took it to mean that Fanny had had a hint from her mother of Maurice's possible intentions. She was afraid to ask her old friend directly if this were definitely true: poor Fanny's improvement was after all not a gain sufficient to make up for the cruelty that would reside in the sense of being rejected.

One day, in Queen Street, Maurice said in an abrupt, conscientious way: "You were right about Fanny Knocker—she's a remarkably clever and a thoroughly nice girl; a fellow can really talk with her. But oh mother!"

"Well, my dear?"

The young man's face wore a strange smile. "Oh mother!" he expressively, quite tragically repeated. "But it's all right!" he presently added in a different tone, and Lady Greyswood was reassured. This confidence, however, received a shock a little later, on the evening of a day that had been intensely hot. A torrid wave had passed over London, and in the suffocating air the pleasures of the season had put on a purple face. Lady Greyswood, whose own fine lowness of tone no temperature could affect, knew, in her bedimmed drawing-room, exactly the detail of her son's engagements. She pitied him—*she* had managed to keep clear; she had in particular a vision of a distribution of prizes, by one of the princesses, at a big horticultural show; she saw the sweltering starers (and at what, after all?) under a huge glass roof, while there passed before her, in a blur of crimson, the glimpse of uncomfortable cheeks under an erratic white bonnet, together also with the sense that some of Jane Knocker's ideas of pleasure were of the oddest (she had such *lacunes*), and some of the ordeals to which she exposed poor Fanny singularly ill-chosen. Maurice came in, perspiring but pale (nothing could make *him* ugly!)

to dress for dinner, and though he was in a great hurry he found time to pant: "Oh mother, what I'm going through for you!"

"Do you mean rushing about so—in this weather? We shall have a change to-night."

"I hope so! There are people for whom it doesn't do at all; ah, not a bit!" said Maurice with a laugh that she didn't fancy. But he went upstairs before she could think of anything to reply, and after he had dressed he passed out without speaking to her again. The next morning, on entering her room, her maid mentioned as a delicate duty that Mr. Glanvil, whose door stood wide open and whose bed was untouched, had apparently not yet come in. While, however, her ladyship was in the first freshness of meditation on this singular fact the morning's letters were brought up, and as it happened that the second envelope she glanced at was addressed in Maurice's hand she was quickly in possession of an explanation still more startling than his absence. He wrote from a club, at nine o'clock the previous evening, to announce that he was taking the night train for the continent. He hadn't dressed for dinner, he had dressed otherwise, and having stuffed a few things with surreptitious haste into a Gladstone bag, had slipped unperceived out of the house and into a hansom. He had sent to Ennismore Gardens, from his club, an apology—a request he should not be waited for; and now he should just have time to get to Charing Cross. He was off he didn't know where, but he was off he did know why. "You'll know why, dear mother too, I think," this wonderful communication continued; "you'll know why, because I haven't deceived you. I've done what I could, but I've broken down. I felt to-day that it was no use; there was a moment, at that beastly exhibition, when I saw it, when the question was settled. The truth rolled over me in a stifling wave. After that I made up my mind there was nothing to do but to bolt. I meant to put it off till to-morrow, and to tell you first, but while I was dressing to-day it struck me irresistibly that my true course is to break now—never to enter the house or go near her again. I was afraid of a scene with you about this. I haven't uttered a word of 'love' to her (heaven save us!) but my position this afternoon became definitely false, and that fact prescribes the course I am taking. You shall hear from me again in a day or two. I have the greatest regard for her, but I can't bear to look at her. I don't care a bit for money, but, hang it, I *must* have beauty! Please send me twenty pounds, *poste restante*, Boulogne."

"What I want, Jane, is to get at *this*," Lady Greyswood said, later in the day, with an austerity that was sensible even through her tears. "Does the child know, or doesn't she, what was at stake?"

"She hasn't an inkling of it—how should she? I recognised that it was best not to tell her—and I didn't."

On this, as Mrs. Knocker's tears had also flowed, Lady Greyswood kissed her. But she didn't believe her. Fanny herself, however, for the rest of the season, proved inscrutable. "She's a character!" Lady Greyswood reflected with admiration. In September, in Yorkshire, the girl was taken seriously ill.

III.

After luncheon at the Crisfords'—the big Sunday banquets of twenty people and a dozen courses—the men, lingering a little in the dining-room, dawdling among displaced chairs and dropped napkins while the ladies rustled away, ended by shuffling in casual pairs up to the studio, where coffee was served and where, presently, before the cigarettes were smoked out, Mrs. Crisford always reappeared to usher in her contingent. The studio was high and handsome, and luncheon at the Crisfords' was, in the common esteem, more amusing than almost anything else in London except dinner. It was Bohemia with excellent service—Bohemia not debtor but creditor. Upstairs the pictures, finished or nearly finished, and arranged in a shining row, gave an obviousness of topic, so that conversation could easily touch bottom. Maurice Glanvil, who had never been in the house before, looked about and wondered; he was struck with the march of civilization—the rise of the social tide. There were new notes in English life, which he caught quickly with his fresh sense; during his long absence—twenty years of France and Italy—all sorts of things had happened. In his youth, in England, artists and authors and actors—

people of that general kind—were not nearly so "smart." Maurice Glanvil was forty-nine to-day, and he thought a great deal of his youth. He regretted it, he missed it, he tried to beckon it back; but the differences in London made him feel that it had gone forever. There might perhaps be some sudden compensation in being fifty, some turn of the dim telescope, some view from the brow of the hill; it was a round, gross, stupid number, which probably would make one pompous, make one think one's self venerable. Meanwhile at any rate it was odious to be forty-nine. Maurice observed the young now more than he had ever done; observed them, that is, as the young. He wished he could have had a son, to be twenty with again; his daughter was only eighteen, but fond as he was of her he couldn't live instinctively into her girlishness. It was not that there was not plenty of it, for she was simple, sweet, indefinite, without the gifts that the boy would have had, the gifts—what had become of them now?—that he himself used to have.

The youngest person present, before the ladies came in, was the young man who had sat next to Vera and whom, being on the same side of the long table, he had not had under his eye. Maurice noticed him now, noticed that he was very good-looking, fair and fresh and clean, impeccable in his straight smoothness; also that apparently knowing none of the other guests and moving by himself about the studio with visible interest in the charming things, he had the modesty of his age and of his position. He had however something more besides, which had begun to prompt this observer to speak to him in order to hear the sound of his voice—a strange, elusive resemblance, lost in the profile but flickering straight out of the full face, to someone Maurice had known. For a minute Glanvil was worried by it—he had a sense that a name would suddenly come to him if he should see the lips in motion; but as he was on the point of laying the ghost by an experiment Mrs. Crisford led in her companions. His daughter was among them, and in company, as he was constantly anxious about her appearance and her attitude, she had at moments the faculty of drawing his attention from everything else. The poor child, the only fruit of his odd, romantic union, the *coup de foudre* of his youth, with her strangely beautiful mother, whose own

mother had been a Russian and who had died in giving birth
to her—his short, colourless, insignificant Vera was excessively,
incorrigibly plain. She had been the disappointment of his life,
but he greatly pitied her. Her want of beauty, with her ante-
cedents, had been one of the strangest tricks of fate; she was
acutely conscious of it and, being good and docile, would
have liked to please. She did sometimes, to her father's
delight, in spite of everything; she had been educated abroad,
on foreign lines, near her mother's people. He had brought
her to England to take her out, to do what he could for her;
but he was not unaware that in England her manners, which
had been thought very pretty on the continent, would strike
some persons as artificial. They were exactly what her mother's
had been; they made up to a certain extent for the want of
other resemblance. An extreme solicitude at any rate as to the
impression they might make was the source of his habit, in
London, of watching her covertly. He tried to see at a given
moment how she looked, if she were happy; it was always with
an intention of encouragement, and there was a frequent
exchange between them of little invisible affectionate signs.
She wore charming clothes, but she was terribly short; in England the girls were gigantic and it was only the tallest who
were noticed. Their manners, alas, had nothing to do with
it—many of them indeed hadn't any manners. As soon as he
had got near Vera he said to her, scanning her through his
single glass from head to foot:

"Who is the young man who sat next you? the one at the
other end of the room."

"I don't know his name, papa—I didn't catch it."

"Was he civil—did he talk to you?"

"Oh, a great deal, papa—about all sorts of things."

Something in the tone of her voice made him look with
greater intensity and even with greater tenderness than usual
into her little dim green eyes. "Then you're all right—you're
getting on?"

She gave her effusive smile—the one that perhaps wouldn't
do in England. "Oh beautifully, papa—everyone's so kind."

She never complained, was a brave little optimist, full of
sweet resources; but he had detected to-day as soon as he
looked at her the particular shade of her content. It made him

continue, after an hesitation: "He didn't say anything about his relations—anything that could give you a clue?"

Vera thought a moment. "Not that I can remember—unless that Mr. Crisford is painting the portrait of his mother. Ah, there it is!" the girl exclaimed, looking across the room at a large picture on an easel, which the young man had just approached and from which their host had removed the drapery that covered it. Maurice Glanvil had observed this drapery, and as the artist unveiled the canvas with a flourish he saw that he had been waiting for the ladies to show it, to produce a surprise, a grand effect. Everyone moved toward it, and Maurice, with his daughter beside him, recognised that the production, a portrait, was striking, a great success for Crisford—the figure, down to the knees, with an extraordinary look of life, of a tall, handsome woman of middle age, in full dress, in black. Yet he saw it for the moment vaguely, through a preoccupation, that of a discovery which he had just made and which had recalled to him an incident of his youth—his juxtaposition, in London, at a dinner, to a girl, insurmountably charmless to him, who had fallen in love with him (so that she was nearly to die of it), within the first five minutes, before he had even spoken; as he had subsequently learned from a communication made him by his poor mother—a reminder uttered with a pointless bitterness that he had failed to understand and accompanied with unsuspected details, much later—too late, long after his marriage and shortly before her death. He said to himself that he must look out, and he wondered if poor Vera would also be insurmountably charmless to the good-looking young man. "But what a likeness, papa—what a likeness!" he heard her murmur at his elbow with suppressed excitement.

"How can you tell, my dear, if you haven't seen her?"

"I mean to the gentleman—the son."

Everyone was exclaiming "How wonderfully clever—how beautiful!" and under cover of the agitation and applause Maurice Glanvil had drawn nearer the picture. The movement had brought him close to the young man of whom he had been talking with Vera and who, with his happy eyes on the painted figure, seemed to smile in acknowledgment of the artist's talent and of the sitter's charm.

"Do you know who the lady is?" Maurice said to him.

He turned his bright face to his interlocutor. "She's my mother—Mrs. Tregent. Isn't it wonderful?"

His eyes, his lips, his voice flashed a light into Glanvil's uncertainty—the tormenting resemblance was simply a prolonged echo of Fanny Knocker, in whose later name, precisely, he recognised the name pronounced by the young man. Maurice Glanvil stared in some bewilderment; this stately, splendid lady, with a face so vivid that it was handsome, was what that unfortunate girl had become? The eyes, as if they picked him out, looked at him strangely from the canvas; the face, with all its difference, asserted itself, and he felt himself turning as red as if he had been in the presence of the original. Young Tregent, pleased and proud, had given way to the pressing spectators, placing himself at Vera's other side; and Maurice heard the girl exclaim to him in one of her pretty effusions: "How beautiful she must be, and how amiable!"

"She is indeed—it's not a bit flattered." And while Maurice still stared, more and more mystified—for "flattered, flattered!" was the unspoken solution in which he had instantly taken refuge—his neighbour continued: "I wish you could know her—you must; she's delightful. She couldn't come here to-day—they asked her: she has people lunching at home."

"I should be so glad; perhaps we may meet her somewhere," said Vera.

"If I ask her and if you'll let her I'm sure she'll come to see you," the young man responded. Maurice had glanced at him while the face of the portrait watched them with the oddest, the grimmest effect. He was filled with a confusion of feelings, asking himself half-a-dozen questions at once. Was young Tregent, with his attentive manner, "making up" to Vera? was he going out of his way in answering for his mother's civility? Little did he know what he was taking on himself! Above all was Fanny Knocker to-day this extraordinary figure—extraordinary in the light of the early plainness that had made him bolt? He became conscious of an extreme curiosity, an irresistible desire to see her.

"Oh, papa," said Vera, "Mr. Tregent's so kind; he's so good as to promise us a visit from his mother."

The young man's friendly eyes were still on the child's face. "I'll tell her all about you. Oh, if I ask her she'll come!" he repeated.

"Does she do everything you ask her?" the girl inquired.

"She likes to know my friends!"

Maurice hesitated, wondering if he were in the presence of a smooth young humbug to whom compliments cost nothing, or in that of an impression really made—made by his little fluttered, unpopular Vera. He had a horror of exposing his child to risks, but his curiosity was greater than his caution. "Your mother mustn't come to us—it's our duty to go to her," he said to Mr. Tregent; "I had the honour of knowing her—a long time ago. Her mother and mine were intimate friends. Be so good as to mention my name to her, that of Maurice Glanvil, and to tell her how glad I have been to make your acquaintance. And now, my dear child," he added to Vera, "we must take leave."

During the rest of that day it never occurred to him that there might be an awkwardness in his presenting himself, even after many years, before a person with whom he had broken as he had broken with Fanny Knocker. This was partly because he held, justly enough, that he had never committed himself, and partly because the intensity of his desire to measure with his own eyes the change represented—misrepresented perhaps—by the picture was a force greater than any embarrassment. His mother had told him that the poor girl had cruelly suffered, but there was no present intensity in that idea. With her expensive portrait, her grand air, her handsome son, she somehow embodied success, whereas he himself, standing for mere bereavement and disappointment, was a failure not to be surpassed. With Vera that evening he was very silent; she saw him smoke endless cigarettes and wondered what he was thinking of. She guessed indeed, but she was too subtle a little person to attempt to fall in with his thoughts or to be willing to betray her own by asking him random questions about Mrs. Tregent. She had expressed as they came away from their luncheon-party a natural surprise at the coincidence of his having known the mother of her amusing neighbour, but

the only other words that dropped from her on the subject
were contained in a question that, before she went to bed,
she put to him with abrupt gaiety, while she carefully placed
a marker in a book she had not been reading.

"When is it then that we're to call upon this wonderful old
friend?"

He looked at her through the smoke of his cigarette. "I
don't know. We must wait a little, to allow her time to give
some sign."

"Oh, I see!" And Vera took leave of him with one of her
sincere little kisses.

IV.

He had not long to wait for the sign from Mrs. Tregent; it
arrived the very next morning in the shape of an invitation to
dinner. This invitation was immediately accepted, but a fortnight was still to intervene—a trial to Maurice Glanvil's patience. The promptitude of the demonstration gave him
pleasure—it showed him no bitterness had survived. What
place was there indeed for resentment, since she had married
and given birth to children and thought so well of the face
God had conferred on her as to wish to hand it on to her
posterity? Her husband was in Parliament, or had been—that
came back to him from his mother's story. He caught himself
reverting to her with a frequency that surprised him; he was
haunted by the image of that bright, strong woman on Crisford's canvas, in whom there was just enough of Fanny
Knocker to put a sort of defiance into the difference. He
wanted to see it again, and his opportunity was at hand in the
form of a visit to Mrs. Crisford. He called on this lady, without
his daughter, four days after he had lunched with her, and,
finding her at home, he presently led the conversation to the
portrait and to his ardent desire for another glimpse of it. Mrs.
Crisford gratified this eagerness—perhaps he struck her as a
possible sitter; it was late in the afternoon and her husband
was out: she led him into the studio. Mrs. Tregent, splendid
and serene, stood there as if she had been watching for him.
There was no doubt the picture was a masterpiece. Maurice
had mentioned that he had known the original years before

and then had lost sight of her. He questioned his hostess with artful detachment.

"What sort of a person has she become—agreeable, popular?"

"Everyone adores her—she's so clever."

"Really—remarkably?"

"Extraordinarily—one of the cleverest women I've ever known, and quite one of the most charming."

Maurice looked at the portrait—at the super-subtle smile which seemed to tell him Mrs. Tregent knew they were talking about her; a kind of smile he had never expected to live to see in Fanny Knocker's eyes. Then he asked: "Has she literally become as handsome as that?"

Mrs. Crisford hesitated. "She's beautiful."

"Beautiful?" Maurice echoed.

"What shall I say? It's a peculiar charm! It's her spirit. One sees that her life has been beautiful in spite of her sorrows!" Mrs. Crisford added.

"What sorrows has she had?" Maurice coloured a little as soon as he had spoken.

"Oh, lots of deaths. She has lost her husband; she has lost several children."

"Ah, that's new to me. Was her marriage happy?"

"It must have been for Mr. Tregent. If it wasn't for her, no one ever knew."

"But she has a son," said Maurice.

"Yes, the only one—such a dear. She thinks all the world of him."

At this moment a message was brought to Mrs. Crisford, and she asked to be excused while she went to say a word to someone who was waiting. Maurice Glanvil in this way was left alone for five minutes with the intensity of the presence evoked by the artist. He found himself agitated, excited by it: the face of the portrait was so intelligent and conscious that as he stood there he felt as if some strange communication had taken place between his being and Mrs. Tregent's. The idea made him nervous: he moved about the room and ended by turning his back. Mrs. Crisford reappeared, but he soon took leave of her; and when he had got home (he had settled himself in South Kensington, in a little undiscriminated house which he had hated from the first), he learned from his daughter that she had had a visit from young Tregent. He had asked first for Mr. Glanvil and then, in the second instance, for herself, telling her when admitted, as if to attenuate his possible indiscretion, that his mother had charged him to try to see her even if he should not find her father. Vera had never before received a gentleman alone, and the incident had left traces of emotion. "Poor little thing!" Maurice said to himself: he always took a melancholy view of any happiness of his daughter's, tending to believe, in his pessimism, that it could only lead to some refinement of humiliation. He encouraged her however to talk about young Tregent, who, according to her account, had been extravagantly amusing. He had said moreover that his mother was tremendously impatient to renew such an old acquaintance. "Why in the world doesn't she, then?" Maurice asked himself; "why doesn't she come and see Vera?" He reflected afterwards that such an expectation was unreasonable, but it represented at the moment a kind of rebellion of his conscience. Then, as he had begun to be a little ashamed of his curiosity, he liked to think that Mrs. Tregent would have quite as much. On the morrow he knocked at her door—she lived in a "commodious" house in Manchester Square—and had the satisfaction, as he had chosen his time carefully, of learning that she had just come in.

Upstairs, in a high, quiet, old-fashioned drawing-room, she was before him. What he saw was a tall woman in black, in her bonnet, with a white face, smiling intensely—smiling and smiling before she spoke. He quickly perceived that she was agitated and was making an heroic effort, which would presently be successful, not to show it. But it was above all clear to him that she wasn't Fanny Knocker—was simply another person altogether. She had nothing in common with Fanny Knocker—it was impossible to meet her on the ground of any former acquaintance. What acquaintance had he ever had with this graceful, harmonious, expressive English matron, whose smile had a singular radiance? That rascal of a Crisford had done her such perfect justice that he felt as if he had before him the portrait of which the image in the studio had been the original. There were nevertheless things to be said, and they said them on either side, sinking together, with friendly exclamations and exaggerated laughs, on the sofa, where her nearness seemed the span of all the distance that separated her from the past. The phrase that hummed through everything, to his sense, was his own inarticulate "How could I have known? how could I have known?" How could he have foreseen that time and life and happiness (it was probably more than anything happiness), would transpose her into such a different key? Her whole personality revealed itself from moment to moment as something so agreeable that even after all these years he felt himself blushing for the crass stupidity of his mistake. Yes, he was turning red, and she could see it and would know why: a perception that could only constitute for her a magnificent triumph, a revenge. All his natural and acquired coolness, his experience of life, his habit of society, everything that contributed to make him a man of the world, were of no avail to cover his confusion. He took refuge from it almost angrily in trying to prove to himself that she had on a second look a likeness to the ugly girl he had not thought good enough—in trying to trace Fanny Knocker in her fair, ripe bloom, the fine irregularity of her features. To put his finger on the identity would make him feel better. Some of the facts of the girl's crooked face were still there—conventional beauty was absent; but the proportions and relations had changed, and the expression and the spirit: she had accepted herself or ceased to care—had found oblivion and activity and appreciation. What Maurice mainly discovered however in this intenser observation was an attitude of hospitality toward himself which immediately effaced the presumption of "triumph." Vulgar vanity was far from her, and the grossness of watching her effect upon him: she was watching only the lost vision that had come back, the joy that, if for a single hour, she had found again. She herself had no measure of the alteration that struck him, and there was no substitution for her in the face that her deep eyes seemed to brush with their hovering. Presently they were talking like old friends, and before long each was in possession of the principal facts concerning the other. Many things had come and gone and the common fate had pressed them hard. Her parents were dead, and her husband and her first-born children. He, on his side, had lost his mother and his wife. They matched

bereavements and compared bruises, and in the way she expressed herself there was a charm which forced him, as he
wondered, to remember that Fanny Knocker had at least been
intelligent.

"I wish I could have seen your wife—you must tell me all
about her," she said. "Haven't you some portraits?"

"Some poor little photographs. I'll show them to you. She
was very pretty and very gentle; she was also very un-English.
But she only lived a year. She wasn't clever and accomplished—like you."

"Ah, me; you don't know *me*!"

"No, but I want to—oh particularly. I'm prepared to give
a good deal of time to the study."

"We must be friends," said Mrs. Tregent. "I shall take an
extraordinary interest in your daughter."

"She'll be grateful for it. She's a good little reasonable
thing, without a scrap of beauty."

"You care greatly for that," said Mrs. Tregent.

He hesitated a moment. "Don't you?"

She smiled at him with her basking candour. "I used to.
That's my husband," she added, with an odd, though evidently accidental, inconsequence. She had reached out to a
table for a photograph in a silver frame. "He was very good
to me."

Maurice saw that Mr. Tregent had been many years older
than his wife—a prosperous, prosaic, parliamentary person
whom she couldn't impose on a man of the world. He sat an
hour, and they talked of the mutilated season of their youth:
he wondered at the things she remembered. In this little hour
he felt his situation change—something strange and important
take place: he seemed to see why he had come back to England. But there was an implication that worried him—it was
in the very air, a reverberation of that old assurance of his
mother's. He wished to clear the question up—it would matter for the beginning of a new friendship. Had she had any
sense of injury when he took to his heels, any glimpse of the
understanding on which he had begun to come to Ennismore
Gardens? He couldn't find out to-day except by asking her,
which, at their time of life, after so many years and consolations, would be legitimate and even amusing. When he took

leave of her he held her hand a moment, hesitating; then he brought out:

"Did they ever tell you—a hundred years ago—that between your mother and mine there was a great question of our marrying?"

She stared—she broke into a laugh. "*Was* there?"

"Did you ever know it? Did you ever suspect it?"

She hesitated and, for the first time since he had been in the room, ceased for an instant to look straight at him. She only answered, still laughing however: "Poor dears—they were altogether too deep!"

She evidently wished to convey that she had never known. Maurice was a little disappointed: at present he would have preferred her knowledge. But as he walked home across the park, through Kensington Gardens, he felt it impossible to believe in her ignorance.

V.

At the end of a month he broke out to her. "I can't get over it, it's so extraordinary—the difference between your youth and your maturity!"

"Did you expect me to be an eternal child?" Mrs. Tregent asked composedly.

"No, it isn't that." He stopped—it would be difficult to explain.

"What is it then?" she inquired, with her systematic refusal to acknowledge a complication. There was always, to Maurice Glanvil's ear, in her impenetrability to allusion, the faintest, softest glee, and it gave her on this occasion the appearance of recognising his difficulty and being amused at it. She would be excusable to be a little cold-blooded. He really knew however that the penalty was all in his own reflections, for it had not taken him even a month to perceive that she was supremely, almost strangely indulgent. There was nothing he was ready to say that she might not hear, and her absence of coquetry was a remarkable rest to him.

"It isn't what I expected—it's what I didn't expect. To say exactly what I mean, it's the way you've improved."

"I've improved? I'm so glad!"

"Surely you've been aware of it—you've been conscious of the transformation."

"As an improvement? I don't know. I've been conscious of changes enough—of all the stages and strains and lessons of life. I've been aware of growing old, and I hold, in dissent from the usual belief, that there's no fool like a young fool. One is never, I suppose, such a fool as one *has* been, and that may count perhaps as amelioration. But I can't flatter myself that I've had two different identities. I've had to make one, such as it is, do for everything. I think I've been happier than I originally supposed I should be—and yet I had my happiness too as a girl. At all events if you were to scratch me, as they say, you'd still find——" She paused a moment, and he really hung upon her lips: there was such a charm of tone in whatever she said. "You'd still find, underneath, the blowsy girl——" With this she again checked herself and, slightly to his surprise, gave a nervous laugh.

"The blowsy girl?" he repeated, with an artlessness of interrogation that made her laugh again.

"Whom you went with that hot day to see the princess give the prizes."

"Oh yes—that dreadful day!" he answered gravely, musingly, with the whole scene pictured by her words and without contesting the manner in which she qualified herself. It was the nearest allusion that had passed between them to that crudest conception of his boyhood, his flight from Ennismore Gardens. Almost every day for a month he had come to see her, and they had talked of a thousand things; never yet however had they made any explicit mention of this remote instance of premature wisdom. Moreover if he now felt the need of going back it was not to be apologetic, to do penance; he had nothing to explain, for his behaviour, as he considered it, still struck him, given the circumstances, as natural. It was to himself indeed that explanations were owing, for he had been the one who had been most deceived. He liked Mrs. Tregent better than he had ever liked a woman—that is he liked her for more reasons. He had liked his poor little wife only for one, which was after all no reason at all: he had been in love with her. In spite of the charm that the renewal of acquaintance with his old friend had so unexpectedly added to his life there was a vague torment in his relation with her, the sense of a revenge (oh a very kind one!) to take, a haunting idea that he couldn't pacify. He could still feel sore at the trick that had been played him. Even after a month the curiosity with which he had approached her was not assuaged; in a manner indeed it had only borrowed force from all she had insisted on doing for him. She was literally doing everything now; gently, gaily, with a touch so familiar that protestations on his part would have been pedantic, she had taken his life in hand. Rich as she was she had known how to give him lessons in economy; she had taught him how to manage in London on his means. A month ago his servants had been horrid—to-day they were the best he had ever known. For Vera she was plainly a providence—her behaviour to Vera was transcendent.

He had privately made up his mind that Vera had in truth had her *coup de foudre*—that if she had had a chance she would have laid down her little life for Arthur Tregent; yet two circumstances, he could perceive, had helped to postpone, to attenuate even somewhat, her full consciousness of what had befallen her. One of these influences had been the prompt departure of the young man from London; the other was simply the diversion produced by Mrs. Tregent's encompassing art. It had had immediate consequences for the child: it was like a drama in perpetual climaxes. This surprising benefactress rejoiced in her society, took her "out," treated her as if there were mysterious injustices to repair. Vera was agitated not a little by such a change in her life; she had English kindred enough, uncles and aunts and cousins; but she had felt herself lost in her father's family and was principally aware, among them, of their strangeness and their indifference. They affected her mainly as mere number and stature. Mrs. Tregent's was a performance unpromised and uninterrupted, and the girl desired to know if all English people took so generous a view of friendship. Maurice laughed at this question and, without meeting his daughter's eyes, answered in the negative. Vera guessed so many things that he didn't know what she would be guessing next. He saw her caught up to the blue like Ganymede, and surrendered her contentedly. She had been the occupation of his life, yet to Mrs. Tregent he was willing to part with her; this lady was the only person of whom he would not have been jealous. Even in the young man's absence moreover Vera lived with the son of the house and breathed his air; Manchester Square was full of him, his photograph was on every table. How often she spoke of him to his mother Maurice had no means of knowing, nor whether Mrs. Tregent encouraged such a topic; he had reason to believe indeed that there were reserves on either side, and he felt that he could trust his old friend's prudence as much as her liberality. The attitude of forbearance from rash allusions, which was Maurice's own, could not at any rate keep Arthur from being a presence in the little drama which had begun for them all, as the older man was more and more to recognise with nervous prefigurements, on that occasion at the Crisfords'.

Arthur Tregent had gone to Ireland to spend a few weeks with an old university friend—the gentleman indeed, at Cambridge, had been his tutor—who had lately, in a district classified as "disturbed," come into a bewildering heritage. He had chosen in short for a study of the agrarian question on the spot the moment of the year when London was most absorbing. Maurice Glanvil made no remark to his mother on this anomaly, and she offered him no explanation of it; they talked in fact of almost everything except Arthur. Mrs. Tregent had to her constant visitor the air of feeling that she owed him in relation to her son an apology which she had not the materials for making. It was certainly a high standard of courtesy that would suggest to her that he ought to have put himself out for these social specimens; but it was obvious that her standard was high. Maurice Glanvil smiled when he thought to what bare civility the young man would have deemed himself held had he known of a certain passage of private history. But he knew nothing—Maurice was sure of that; his reason for going away had been quite another matter. That Vera's brooding parent should have had such an insight into the young man's motives is a proof of the amount of reflection that he devoted to him. He had not seen much of him and in truth he found him provoking, but he was haunted by the odd analogy of which he had had a glimpse on their first encounter. The late Mr. Tregent had had "interests in the north," and the care of them had naturally devolved upon his son, who by the mother's account had shown an admirable capacity for business. The late Mr. Tregent had also been actively political, and it was fondly hoped, in Manchester Square at least, that the day was not distant when his heir would, in turn and as a representative of the same respectabilities, speak reported words in debate. Maurice himself, vague about the House of Commons, had nothing to say against his making a figure there. Accordingly if these natural gifts continued to remind him of his own fastidiously clever youth, it was with the difference that Arthur Tregent's cleverness struck him as much the greater of the two. If the changes in England were marked this indeed was in general one of them, that the sharp young men were still sharper than of yore. When they had ability at any rate they showed it all; Maurice would never have pretended that he had shown all his. He had not cared whether anyone knew it. It was not however this superior intensity which provoked him, and poor young Tregent could not be held responsible for his irritation. If the circumstance in which they most resembled each other was the disposition to escape from plain girls who aspired to them, such a characteristic, as embodied in the object of Vera's admiration, was purely interesting, was even amusing, to Vera's father; but it would have gratified him to be able to ascertain from Mrs. Tregent whether, to her knowledge, her son thought his child really repulsive, and what annoyed him was the fact that such an inquiry was practically impossible. Arthur was provoking in short because he had an advantage—an advantage residing in the fact that his mother's friend couldn't ask questions about him without appearing to indulge in hints and overtures. The idea of this officiousness was odious to Maurice Glanvil; so that he confined himself to meditating in silence on the happiness it would be for poor Vera to marry a beautiful young man with a fortune and a future.

Though the opportunity for this recreation—it engaged much of his time—should be counted as one of the pleasant results of his intimacy with Mrs. Tregent, yet the sense, perverse enough, that he had a ground of complaint against her subsisted even to the point of finally steadying him while he expressed his grievance. This happened in the course of one of those afternoon hours that had now become indispensable to him—hours of belated tea and egotistical talk in the long summer light and the chastened roar of London.

"No, it wasn't fair," he said, "and I wasn't well used—a hundred years ago. I'm sore about it now; you ought to have notified me, to have instructed me. Why didn't you, in common honesty? Why didn't my poor mother, who was so eager and shrewd? Why didn't yours? She used to talk to me. Heaven forgive me for saying it, but our mothers weren't up to the mark! You may tell me they didn't know; to which I reply that mine was universally supposed, and by me in particular, to know everything that could be known. No, it wasn't well managed, and the consequence has been this odious discovery, an awful shock to a man of my time of life and under the effect of which I now speak to you, that for a quarter of a century I've been a fool."

"What would you have wished us to do?" Mrs. Tregent asked as she gave him another cup of tea.

"Why, to have said 'Wait, wait—at any price; have patience and hold on!' They ought to have told me, *you* ought to have told me, that your conditions at that time were a temporary phase and that you would infallibly break your shell. You ought to have warned me, they ought to have warned me, that there would be wizardry in the case, that you were to be the subject, at a given moment, of a transformation absolutely miraculous. I couldn't know it by inspiration; I measured you by the common law—how could I do anything else? But it wasn't kind to leave me in error."

Maurice Glanvil treated himself without scruple to this fine ironic flight, this sophistry which eased his nerves, because though it brought him nearer than he had yet come to putting his finger, visibly to Mrs. Tregent, on the fact that he had once tried to believe he could marry her and had found her too ugly, their present relation was so extraordinary and his present appreciation so liberal as to make almost any freedom excusable, especially as his companion had the advantage of being to all intents and purposes a different person from the one he talked of, while he suffered the ignominy of being the same.

"There has been no miracle," said Mrs. Tregent after a moment. "I've never known anything but the common, ah the very common, law, and anything that I may have become only the common things have made me."

He shook his head. "You wore a disfiguring mask, a veil, a disguise. One fine day you dropped them all and showed the world the real creature."

"It wasn't one fine day—it was little by little."

"Well, one fine day I saw the result; the process doesn't matter. To arrive at a goal invisible from the starting-point is no doubt an incident in the life of a certain number of women. But what is absolutely unprecedented is to have traversed such a distance."

"Hadn't I a single redeeming point?" Mrs. Tregent demanded.

He hesitated a little, and while he hesitated she looked at him. Her look was but of an instant, but it told him everything, told him, in one misty moonbeam, all she had known of old. She had known perfectly—she had been as conscious of the conditions of his experiment as of the invincibility of his repugnance. Whether her mother had betrayed him didn't matter; she had read everything clear and had had to accept the cruel truth. He was touched as he had never been by that moment's communication; he was, unexpectedly, almost awe-struck, for there was something still more in it than he had guessed. "I was letting my fancy play just now," he answered, apologetically. "It was I who was wanting—it was I who was the idiot!"

"Don't say that. You were so kind." And hereupon Mrs. Tregent startled her visitor by bursting into tears.

She recovered herself indeed, and they forbore on that occasion, in the interest of the decorum expected of persons of their age and in their circumstances, to rake over these smouldering ashes; but such a conversation had made a difference, and from that day onward Maurice Glanvil was awake to the fact that he had been the passion of this extraordinary woman's life. He felt humiliated for an hour, but after that his pleasure was almost as great as his wonder. For wonder there was plenty of room, but little by little he saw how things had come to pass. She was not subjected to the ordeal of telling him or to the abasement of any confession, but day by day he sounded, with a purity of gratitude that renewed, in his spirit, the sources of youth, the depths of everything that her behaviour implied. Of such a studied tenderness as she showed him the roots could only be in some unspeakably sacred past. She had not to explain, she had not to clear up inconsistencies, she had only to let him be with her. She had striven, she had accepted, she had conformed, but she had thought of him every day of her life. She had taken up duties and performed them, she had banished every weakness and practised every virtue, but the still, hidden flame had never been quenched. His image had interposed, his reality had remained, and she had never denied herself the sweetness of hoping that she should see him again and that she should know him. She had never raised a little finger for it, but fortune had answered her prayer. Women were capable of these mysteries of sentiment, these intensities of fidelity and there were moments in which Maurice Glanvil's heart beat strangely before a vision really so sublime. He seemed to understand now by what miracle Fanny Knocker had been beautified—the miracle of heroic docilities and accepted pangs and vanquished egotisms. It had never come in a night, but it had come by living for others. She was living for others still; it was impossible for him to see anything else at last than that she was living for him. The time of passion was over, but the time of service was long. When all this became vivid to him he felt that he couldn't recognise it enough and yet that recognition might only be tacit and, as it were, circuitous. He couldn't say to her even humorously "It's very kind of you to be in love with such a donkey," for these words would have implied somehow that he had rights—an attitude from which his renovated delicacy shrank. He bowed his head before such charity and seemed to see moreover that Mrs. Tregent's desire to befriend him was a feeling independent of any prospect of gain and indifferent to any chance of reward. It would be described vulgarly, after so much had come and gone, as the state of being "in love"—the state of the instinctive and the simple, which they both had left far behind; so that there was a certain sort of reciprocity which would almost constitute an insult to it.

VI.

He soared on these high thoughts till, toward the end of July (Mrs. Tregent stayed late in town—she was awaiting her son's return) he made the discovery that to some persons, perhaps indeed to many, he had all the air of being in love. This image was flashed back to him from the irreverent lips of a lady who knew and admired Mrs. Tregent and who professed amusement at his surprise, at his artless declaration that he had no idea he had made himself conspicuous. She assured him that everyone was talking about him—though people after all had a tenderness for elderly romance; and she left him divided between the acute sense that he was comical (he had a horror of that) and the pale perception of something that he could "help" still less. At the end of a few hours of reflection he had sacrificed the penalty to the privilege; he was about to be fifty, and he knew Fanny Knocker's age—no one better; but he cared no straw for vulgar judgments and moreover could think of plenty of examples of unions admired even after longer delays. For three days he enjoyed the luxury of admitting to himself without reserve how indispensable she had become to him; as the third drew to a close he was more nervous than really he had ever been in his life, for this was the evening on which, after many hindrances, Mrs. Tregent had agreed to dine with him. He had planned the occasion for a month—he wanted to show her how well he had learned from her how to live on his income. Her occupations had always interposed—she was teaching him new lessons; but at last she gave him the joy of sitting at his table. At the evening's end he begged her to remain after the others, and he asked one of the ladies who had been present, and who was going to a pair of parties, to be so good as to take Vera away. This indeed had been arranged in advance, and when, in the discomposed drawing-room, of which the windows stood open to the summer night, he was alone with his old friend, he saw in her face that she knew it had been arranged. He saw more than this—that she knew what he was waiting to say and that if, after a visible reluctance, she had consented to come, it was in order to meet him, with whatever effort, on the ground he had chosen—meet him once and then leave it forever. This was why, without interrupting him, but before he had finished, putting out her hand to his own, with a strange clasp of refusal, she was ready to show him, in a woeful but beautiful headshake to which nothing could add, that it was impossible at this time of day for them to marry. She stayed only a moment, but in that moment he had to accept the knowledge that by as much as it might have been of old, by so much might it never be again. After she had gone he walked up and down the drawing-room half the night. He sent the servants to bed, he blew out the candles; the forsaken place was lighted only by the lamps in the street. He gave himself the motive of waiting for Vera to come back, but in reality he threshed about in the darkness because his cheeks had begun to burn. There was a sting for him in Mrs. Tregent's refusal, and this sting was sharper even than the disappointment of his desire. It was a reproach to his delicacy; it made him feel as if he had been an ass for the second time. When she was young and free his faith had been too poor and his perceptions too dense; he had waited to show her that he only bargained for certainties and only recognised success. He dropped into a chair at last and sat there a long time, his elbows on his knees, his face in his hands, trying to cover up his humiliation, waiting for it to ebb. As the sounds of the night died away it began to come back to him that she had given him a promise to which a rich meaning could be attached. What was it that before going away she had said about Vera, in words he had been at the moment too disconcerted to take in? Little by little he reconstructed these words with comfort; finally, when after hearing a carriage stop at the door he hastily pulled himself together and went down to admit his daughter, the sight of the child on his threshold, as the brougham that had restored her drove away, brought them all back in their generosity.

"Have you danced?" he asked.

She hesitated. "A little, papa."

He knew what that meant—she had danced once. He followed her upstairs in silence; she had not wasted her time— she had had her humiliation. Ah, clearly she was too short! Yet on the landing above, where her bedroom candle stood, she tried to be gay with him, asking him about his own party and whether the people had stayed late.

"Mrs. Tregent stayed after the others. She spoke very kindly of you."

The girl looked at her father with an anxiety that showed through her smile. "What did she say?"

He hesitated, as Vera had done a moment before. "That you must be our compensation."

His daughter's eyes, still wondering, turned away. "What did she mean?"

"That it's all right, darling!" And he supplied the deficiencies of this explanation with a long kiss for good-night.

The next day he went to see Mrs. Tregent, who wore the air of being glad to have something at once positive and pleasant to say. She announced immediately that Arthur was coming back.

"I congratulate you." Then, as they exchanged one of their looks of unreserved recognition, Maurice added: "Now it's for Vera and me to go."

"To go?"

"Without more delay. It's high time we should take ourselves off."

Mrs. Tregent was silent a moment. "Where shall you go?"

"To our old haunts, abroad. We must see some of our old friends. We shall spend six months away."

"Then what becomes of *my* months?"

"Your months?"

"Those it's all arranged she's to spend at Blankley." Blankley was Mrs. Tregent's house in Derbyshire, and she laughed as she went on: "Those that I spoke of last evening. Don't look as if we had never discussed it and settled it!"

"What shall I do without her?" Maurice Glanvil presently demanded.

"What will you do *with* her?" his hostess replied, with a world of triumphant meaning. He was not prepared to say, in the sense of her question, and he took refuge in remarking that he noted her avoidance of any suggestion that he too would be welcome in Derbyshire; which led her to continue, with unshrinking frankness: "Certainly, I don't want you a bit. Leave us alone."

"Is it safe?"

"Of course I can't absolutely answer for anything, but at least it will be safer than with *you*," said Mrs. Tregent.

Maurice Glanvil turned this over. "Does he dislike me?"

"What an idea!"

But the question had brought the colour to her face, and the sight of this, with her evasive answer, kindled in Maurice's heart a sudden relief, a delight almost, that was strange enough. Arthur was in opposition, plainly, and that was why he had so promptly quitted London, that was why Mrs. Tregent had refused Mr. Glanvil. The idea was an instant balm. "He'd be quite right, poor fellow!" Maurice declared. "I'll go abroad alone."

"Let me keep her six months," said Mrs. Tregent. "I'll try it—I'll try it!"

"I wouldn't interfere for the world."

"It's an immense responsibility; but I should like so to succeed."

"She's an angel!" Maurice said.

"That's what gives me courage."

"But she mustn't dream of any plot," he added.

"For what do you take me?" Mrs. Tregent exclaimed with a smile which lightened up for him intensely that far-away troubled past as to which she had originally baffled his inquiry.

The joy of perceiving in an aversion to himself a possible motive for Arthur's absence was so great in him that before he took leave of her he ventured to say to his old friend: "Does he like her at all?"

"He likes her very much."

Maurice remembered how much he had liked Fanny Knocker and been willing to admit it to his mother; but he presently observed: "Of course he can't think her in the least pretty."

"As you say, she's an angel," Mrs. Tregent rejoined.

"She would pass for one better if she were a few inches taller."

"It doesn't matter," said Mrs. Tregent.

"One must remember that in that respect, at her age, she won't change," Maurice pursued, wondering after he had spoken whether he had pressed upon the second pronoun.

"No, she won't change. But she's a darling!" Mrs. Tregent exclaimed; and it was in these meagre words, which were only half however of what passed between them, that an extraordinary offer was made and accepted. They were so ready to understand each other that no insistence and no professions now were necessary, and that Maurice Glanvil had not even broken into a murmur of gratitude at this quick revelation of his old friend's beautiful conception of a nobler remedy—the endeavour to place their union outside themselves, to make their children know the happiness they had missed. They had not needed to teach each other what they saw, what they guessed, what moved them with pity and hope, and there were transitions enough safely skipped in the simple conversation I have preserved. But what Mrs. Tregent was ready to do for him filled Maurice Glanvil, for days after this, with an even greater wonder, and it seemed to him that not till then had she fully shown him that she had forgiven him.

Six months, however, proved much more than sufficient for her attempt to test the plasticity of her son. Maurice Glanvil went abroad, but was nervous and restless, wandering from place to place, revisiting old scenes and old friends, reverting, with a conscious, an even amused incongruity, and yet with an effect that was momentarily soothing, to places at which he had stayed with his wife, but feeling all the while that he was really staking his child's happiness. It only half reassured him to feel that Vera would never know what poor Fanny Knocker had been condemned to know, for the daily contact was cruel from the moment the issue was uncertain; and it only half helped him to reflect that she was not so plain as Fanny, for had not Arthur Tregent given him the impression that the young man of the present was intrinsically even more difficult to please than the young man of the past? The letters he received from Blankley conveyed no information about Arthur beyond the fact that he was at home; only once Vera mentioned that he was "remarkably good" to her. Toward the end of November he found himself in Paris, submitting reluctantly to social accidents which put off from day to day his return to London, when, one morning in the Rue de Rivoli, he had to stop short to permit the passage of a vehicle which had emerged from the court of an hotel. It was an open cab—the day was mild and bright—with a small quantity of neat, leathery luggage, which Maurice vaguely recognised as English, stowed in the place beside the driver—luggage from which his eyes shifted straight to the occupant of the carriage, a young man with his face turned to the allurements of travel and the urbanity of farewell to bowing waiters still visible in it. The young man was so bright and so on his way, as it were, that Maurice, standing there to make room for him, felt for the instant that he too had taken a tip. The feeling became acute as he recognised that this humiliating obligation was to no less a person than Arthur Tregent. It was Arthur who was so much on his way—it was Arthur who was catching a train. He noticed his mother's friend as the cab passed into the street, and, with a quick demonstration, caused the driver to pull up. He jumped out, and under the arcade the two men met with every appearance of cordiality, but with conscious confusion. Each of them coloured perceptibly, and Maurice was angry with himself for blushing before a boy. Long afterwards he remembered how cold, and even how hard, was the handsome clearness of the young eyes that met his own in an artificial smile.

"You here? I thought you were at Blankley."

"I left Blankley yesterday; I'm on my way to Spain."

"To Spain? How charming!"

"To join a friend there—just for a month or two."

"Interesting country—well worth seeing. Your mother's all right?"

"Oh, yes, all right. And Miss Glanvil——" Arthur Tregent went on, cheerfully.

"Vera's all right?" interrupted Maurice, with a still gayer tone.

"Everyone, everything's all right!" Arthur laughed.

"Well, I mustn't keep you. Bon voyage!"

Maurice Glanvil, after the young man had driven on, flattered himself that in this brief interview he had suppressed every indication of surprise; but that evening he crossed the Channel, and on the morrow he went down to Blankley. "To Spain—to Spain!" the words kept repeating themselves in his ears. He, when he had taken flight in a similar conjunction, had only got, for the time, as far as Boulogne; and he was reminded afresh of the progress of the species. When he was introduced into the drawing-room at Blankley—a chintzy, flowery, friendly expanse—Mrs. Tregent rose before him alone and offered him a face that she had never shown before. She was white and she looked scared; she faltered in her movement to meet him.

"I met Arthur in Paris, so I thought I might come."

Oh, yes; there was pain in her face, and a kind of fear of him that frightened him, but their hands found each other's hands while she replied: "He went off—I didn't know it."

"But you had a letter the next morning," Maurice said.

She stared. "How did you know that?"

"Who should know better than I? He wrote from London, explaining."

"I did what I could—I believed in it!" said Mrs. Tregent. "He was charming, for a while."

"But he broke down. She's too short, eh?" Maurice asked.

"Don't laugh; she's ill."

"What's the matter with her?"

Mrs. Tregent gave the visitor a look in which there was almost a reproach for the question. "She has had a chill; she's in bed. You must see her."

She took him upstairs and he saw his child. He remembered what his mother had told him of the grievous illness of Fanny Knocker. Poor little Vera lay there in the flush of a feverish cold which had come on the evening before. She grew worse from the effect of a complication, and for three days he was anxious about her; but even more than with his alarm he held his breath before the distress, the disappointment, the humility of his old friend. Up to this hour he had not fully measured the strength of her desire to do something for him, or the intensity of passion with which she had wished to do it in the particular way that had now broken down. She had counted on her influence with her son, on his affection and on the maternal art, and there was anguish in her compunction for her failure, for her false estimate of the possible. Maurice Glanvil reminded her in vain of the consoling fact that Vera had known nothing of any plan, and he guessed indeed the reason why this theory had no comfort. No one could be better aware than Fanny Tregent of how much girls knew who knew nothing. It was doubtless this same sad wisdom that kept her sombre when he expressed a confidence that his child would promptly recover. She herself had had a terrible fight—and yet with the physical victory, had she recovered? Her apprehension for Vera was justified, for the poor girl was destined finally to forfeit even the physical victory. She got better, she got up, she quitted Blankley, she quitted England with her father, but her health had failed and a year later it gave way. Overtaken in Rome by a second illness, she succumbed; unlike Fanny Knocker she was never to have her revenge.

The Middle Years

THE April day was soft and bright, and poor Dencombe, happy in the conceit of reasserted strength, stood in the garden of the hotel, comparing, with a deliberation in which, however, there was still something of languor, the attractions of easy strolls. He liked the feeling of the south, so far as you could have it in the north, he liked the sandy cliffs and the clustered pines, he liked even the colourless sea. "Bournemouth as a health-resort" had sounded like a mere advertisement, but now he was reconciled to the prosaic. The sociable country postman, passing through the garden, had just given him a small parcel, which he took out with him, leaving the hotel to the right and creeping to a convenient bench that he knew of, a safe recess in the cliff. It looked to the south, to the tinted walls of the Island, and was protected behind by the sloping shoulder of the down. He was tired enough when he reached it, and for a moment he was disappointed; he was better, of course, but better, after all, than what? He should never again, as at one or two great moments of the past, be better than himself. The infinite of life had gone, and what was left of the dose was a small glass engraved like a thermometer by the apothecary. He sat and stared at the sea, which appeared all surface and twinkle, far shallower than the spirit of man. It was the abyss of human illusion that was the real, the tideless deep. He held his packet, which had come by book-post, unopened on his knee, liking, in the lapse of so many joys (his illness had made him feel his age), to know that it was there, but taking for granted there could be no complete renewal of the pleasure, dear to young experience, of seeing one's self "just out." Dencombe, who had a reputation, had come out too often and knew too well in advance how he should look.

His postponement associated itself vaguely, after a little, with a group of three persons, two ladies and a young man, whom, beneath him, straggling and seemingly silent, he could see move slowly together along the sands. The gentleman had his head bent over a book and was occasionally brought to a stop by the charm of this volume, which, as Dencombe could perceive even at a distance, had a cover alluringly red. Then his companions, going a little further, waited for him to come up, poking their parasols into the beach, looking around them at the sea and sky and clearly sensible of the beauty of the day. To these things the young man with the book was still more clearly indifferent; lingering, credulous, absorbed, he was an object of envy to an observer from whose connection with literature all such artlessness had faded. One of the ladies was large and mature; the other had the spareness of comparative youth and of a social situation possibly inferior. The large lady carried back Dencombe's imagination to the age of crinoline; she wore a hat of the shape of a mushroom, decorated with a blue veil, and had the air, in her aggressive amplitude, of clinging to a vanished fashion or even a lost cause. Presently her companion produced from under the folds of a mantle a limp, portable chair which she stiffened out and of which the large lady took possession. This act, and something in the movement of either party, instantly characterised the performers—they performed for Dencombe's recreation—as opulent matron and humble dependant. What, moreover, was the use of being an approved novelist if one couldn't establish a relation between such figures; the clever theory, for instance, that the young man was the son of the opulent matron, and that the humble dependant, the daughter of a clergyman or an officer, nourished a secret passion for him? Was that not visible from the way she stole behind her protectress to look back at him?—back to where he had let himself come to a full stop when his mother sat down to rest. His book was a novel; it had the catchpenny cover, and while the romance of life stood neglected at his side he lost himself in that of the circulating library. He moved mechanically to where the sand was softer, and ended by plumping down in it to finish his chapter at his ease. The humble dependant, discouraged by his remoteness, wandered, with a martyred droop of the head, in another direction, and the exorbitant lady, watching the waves, offered a confused resemblance to a flying-machine that had broken down.

When his drama began to fail Dencombe remembered that he had, after all, another pastime. Though such promptitude on the part of the publisher was rare, he was already able to draw from its wrapper his "latest," perhaps his last. The cover of "The Middle Years" was duly meretricious, the smell of the fresh pages the very odour of sanctity; but for the moment he went no further—he had become conscious of a strange alienation. He had forgotten what his book was about. Had the assault of his old ailment, which he had so fallaciously come to Bournemouth to ward off, interposed utter blankness as to what had preceded it? He had finished the revision of proof before quitting London, but his subsequent fortnight in bed had passed the sponge over colour. He couldn't have chanted to himself a single sentence, couldn't have turned with curiosity or confidence to any particular page. His subject had already gone from him, leaving scarcely a superstition behind. He uttered a low moan as he breathed the chill of this dark void, so desperately it seemed to represent the completion of a sinister process. The tears filled his mild eyes; something precious had passed away. This was the pang that had been sharpest during the last few years—the sense of ebbing time, of shrinking opportunity; and now he felt not so much that his last chance was going as that it was gone indeed. He had done all that he should ever do, and yet he had not done what he wanted. This was the laceration—that practically his career was over: it was as violent as a rough hand at his throat. He rose from his seat nervously, like a creature hunted by a dread; then he fell back in his weakness and nervously opened his book. It was a single volume; he preferred single volumes and aimed at a rare compression. He began to read, and little by little, in this occupation, he was pacified and reassured. Everything came back to him, but came back with a wonder, came back, above all, with a high and magnificent beauty. He read his own prose, he turned his own leaves, and had, as he sat there with the spring sunshine on the page, an emotion peculiar and intense. His career was over, no doubt, but it was over, after all, with *that*.

He had forgotten during his illness the work of the previous year; but what he had chiefly forgotten was that it was extraordinarily good. He lived once more into his story and was drawn down, as by a siren's hand, to where, in the dim underworld of fiction, the great glazed tank of art, strange silent subjects float. He recognised his motive and surrendered to his talent. Never, probably, had that talent, such as it was, been so fine. His difficulties were still there, but what was also there, to his perception, though probably, alas! to nobody's else, was the art that in most cases had surmounted them. In his surprised enjoyment of this ability he had a glimpse of a possible reprieve. Surely its force was not spent—there was life and service in it yet. It had not come to him easily, it had been backward and roundabout. It was the child of time, the nursling of delay; he had struggled and suffered for it, making sacrifices not to be counted, and now that it was really mature was it to cease to yield, to confess itself brutally beaten? There was an infinite charm for Dencombe in feeling as he had never felt before that diligence *vincit omnia*. The result produced in his little book was somehow a result beyond his conscious intention: it was as if he had planted his genius, had trusted his method, and they had grown up and flowered with this sweetness. If the achievement had been real, however, the process had been manful enough. What he saw so intensely to-day, what he felt as a nail driven in, was that only now, at the very last, had he come into possession. His development had been abnormally slow, almost grotesquely gradual. He had been hindered and retarded by experience, and for long periods had only groped his way. It had taken too much of his life to produce too little of his art. The art had come, but it had come after everything else. As such a rate a first existence was too short—long enough only to collect material; so that to fructify, to use the material, one must have a second age, an extension. This extension was what poor Dencombe sighed for. As he turned the last leaves of his volume he murmured: "Ah for another go!—ah for a better chance!"

The three persons he had observed on the sands had vanished and then reappeared; they had now wandered up a path, an artificial and easy ascent, which led to the top of the cliff. Dencombe's bench was half-way down, on a sheltered ledge, and the large lady, a massive, heterogeneous person, with bold black eyes and kind red cheeks, now took a few moments to rest. She wore dirty gauntlets and immense diamond ear-rings; at first she looked vulgar, but she contradicted this announcement in an agreeable off-hand tone. While her companions stood waiting for her she spread her skirts on the end of Dencombe's seat. The young man had gold spectacles, through which, with his finger still in his red-covered book, he glanced at the volume, bound in the same shade of the same colour, lying on the lap of the original occupant of the bench. After an instant Dencombe understood that he was struck with a resemblance, had recognised the gilt stamp on the crimson cloth, was reading "The Middle Years," and now perceived that somebody else had kept pace with him. The stranger was startled, possibly even a little ruffled, to find that he was not the only person who had been favoured with an early copy. The eyes of the two proprietors met for a moment, and Dencombe borrowed amusement from the expression of those of his competitor, those, it might even be inferred, of his admirer. They confessed to some resentment—they seemed to say: "Hang it, has he got it *already?*—Of course he's a brute of a reviewer!" Dencombe shuffled his copy out of sight while the opulent matron, rising from her repose, broke out: "I feel already the good of this air!"

"I can't say I do," said the angular lady. "I find myself quite let down."

"I find myself horribly hungry. At what time did you order lunch?" her protectress pursued.

The young person put the question by. "Doctor Hugh always orders it."

"I ordered nothing to-day—I'm going to make you diet," said their comrade.

"Then I shall go home and sleep. *Qui dort dîne!*"

"Can I trust you to Miss Vernham?" asked Doctor Hugh of his elder companion.

"Don't I trust *you?*" she archly inquired.

"Not too much!" Miss Vernham, with her eyes on the ground, permitted herself to declare. "You must come with us at least to the house," she went on, while the personage on whom they appeared to be in attendance began to mount higher. She had got a little out of ear-shot; nevertheless Miss Vernham became, so far as Dencombe was concerned, less distinctly audible to murmur to the young man: "I don't think you realise all you owe the Countess!"

Absently, a moment, Doctor Hugh caused his gold-rimmed spectacles to shine at her.

"Is that the way I strike you? I see—I see!"

"She's awfully good to us," continued Miss Vernham, compelled by her interlocutor's immovability to stand there in spite of his discussion of private matters. Of what use would it have been that Dencombe should be sensitive to shades had he not declared in that immovability a strange influence from the quiet old convalescent in the great tweed cape? Miss Vernham appeared suddenly to become aware of some such connection, for she added in a moment: "If you want to sun yourself here you can come back after you've seen us home."

Doctor Hugh, at this, hesitated, and Dencombe, in spite of a desire to pass for unconscious, risked a covert glance at him. What his eyes met this time, as it happened, was on the part of the young lady a queer stare, naturally vitreous, which made her aspect remind him of some figure (he couldn't name it) in a play or a novel, some sinister governess or tragic old maid. She seemed to scrutinise him, to challenge him, to say, from general spite: "What have you got to do with us?" At the same instant the rich humour of the Countess reached them from above: "Come, come, my little lambs, you should follow your old *bergère*!" Miss Vernham turned away at this, pursuing the ascent, and Doctor Hugh, after another mute appeal to Dencombe and a moment's evident demur, deposited his book on the bench, as if to keep his place or even as a sign that he would return, and bounded without difficulty up the rougher part of the cliff.

Equally innocent and infinite are the pleasures of observation and the resources engendered by the habit of analysing life. It amused poor Dencombe, as he dawdled in his tepid air-bath, to think that he was waiting for a revelation of something at the back of a fine young mind. He looked hard at the book on the end of the bench, but he wouldn't have touched it for the world. It served his purpose to have a theory which should not be exposed to refutation. He already felt better of his melancholy; he had, according to his old formula, put his head at the window. A passing Countess could draw off the fancy when, like the elder of the ladies who had just retreated, she was as obvious as the giantess of a caravan. It was indeed general views that were terrible; short ones, contrary to an opinion sometimes expressed, were the refuge, were the remedy. Doctor Hugh couldn't possibly be anything but a reviewer who had understandings for early copies with publishers or with newspapers. He reappeared in a quarter of an hour, with visible relief at finding Dencombe on the spot, and the gleam of white teeth in an embarrassed but generous smile. He was perceptibly disappointed at the eclipse of the other copy of the book; it was a pretext the less for speaking to the stranger. But he spoke notwithstanding; he held up his own copy and broke out pleadingly:

"*Do* say, if you have occasion to speak of it, that it's the best thing he has done yet!"

Dencombe responded with a laugh: "Done yet" was so amusing to him, made such a grand avenue of the future. Better still, the young man took *him* for a reviewer. He pulled out "The Middle Years" from under his cape, but instinctively concealed any tell-tale look of fatherhood. This was partly because a person was always a fool for calling attention to his work. "Is that what you're going to say yourself?" he inquired of his visitor.

"I'm not quite sure I shall write anything. I don't, as a regular thing—I enjoy in peace. But it's awfully fine."

Dencombe debated a moment. If his interlocutor had begun to abuse him he would have confessed on the spot to his identity, but there was no harm in drawing him on a little to praise. He drew him on with such success that in a few moments his new acquaintance, seated by his side, was confessing candidly that Dencombe's novels were the only ones he could read a second time. He had come the day before from London, where a friend of his, a journalist, had lent him his copy of the last—the copy sent to the office of the journal and already the subject of a "notice" which, as was pretended there (but one had to allow for "swagger") it had taken a full quarter of an hour to prepare. He intimated that he was ashamed for his friend, and in the case of a work demanding and repaying study, of such inferior manners; and, with his fresh appreciation and inexplicable wish to express it, he

speedily became for poor Dencombe a remarkable, a delightful apparition. Chance had brought the weary man of letters
face to face with the greatest admirer in the new generation
whom it was supposable he possessed. The admirer, in truth,
was mystifying, so rare a case was it to find a bristling young
doctor—he looked like a German physiologist—enamoured of
literary form. It was an accident, but happier than most accidents, so that Dencombe, exhilarated as well as confounded,
spent half an hour in making his visitor talk while he kept
himself quiet. He explained his premature possession of "The
Middle Years" by an allusion to the friendship of the publisher, who, knowing he was at Bournemouth for his health,
had paid him this graceful attention. He admitted that he had
been ill, for Doctor Hugh would infallibly have guessed it; he
even went so far as to wonder whether he mightn't look for
some hygenic "tip" from a personage combining so bright an
enthusiasm with a presumable knowledge of the remedies now
in vogue. It would shake his faith a little perhaps to have to
take a doctor seriously who could take *him* so seriously, but
he enjoyed this gushing modern youth and he felt with an
acute pang that there would still be work to do in a world in
which such odd combinations were presented. It was not true,
what he had tried for renunciation's sake to believe, that all
the combinations were exhausted. They were not, they were
not—they were infinite: the exhaustion was in the miserable
artist.

Doctor Hugh was an ardent physiologist, saturated with the
spirit of the age—in other words he had just taken his degree;
but he was independent and various, he talked like a man who
would have preferred to love literature best. He would fain
have made fine phrases, but nature had denied him the trick.
Some of the finest in "The Middle Years" had struck him
inordinately, and he took the liberty of reading them to Dencombe in support of his plea. He grew vivid, in the balmy air,
to his companion, for whose deep refreshment he seemed to
have been sent; and was particularly ingenuous in describing
how recently he had become acquainted, and how instantly
infatuated, with the only man who had put flesh between the
ribs of an art that was starving on superstitions. He had not
yet written to him—he was deterred by a sentiment of respect.

Dencombe at this moment felicitated himself more than ever on having never answered the photographers. His visitor's attitude promised him a luxury of intercourse, but he surmised that a certain security in it, for Doctor Hugh, would depend not a little on the Countess. He learned without delay with what variety of Countess they were concerned, as well as the nature of the tie that united the curious trio. The large lady, an Englishwoman by birth and the daughter of a celebrated baritone, whose taste, without his talent, she had inherited, was the widow of a French nobleman and mistress of all that remained of the handsome fortune, the fruit of her father's earnings, that had constituted her dower. Miss Vernham, an odd creature but an accomplished pianist, was attached to her person at a salary. The Countess was generous, independent, eccentric; she travelled with her minstrel and her medical man. Ignorant and passionate, she had nevertheless moments in which she was almost irresistible. Dencombe saw her sit for her portrait in Doctor Hugh's free sketch, and felt the picture of his young friend's relation to her frame itself in his mind. This young friend, for a representative of the new psychology, was himself easily hypnotised, and if he became abnormally communicative it was only a sign of his real subjection. Dencombe did accordingly what he wanted with him, even without being known as Dencombe.

Taken ill on a journey in Switzerland the Countess had picked him up at an hotel, and the accident of his happening to please her had made her offer him, with her imperious liberality, terms that couldn't fail to dazzle a practitioner without patients and whose resources had been drained dry by his studies. It was not the way he would have elected to spend his time, but it was time that would pass quickly, and meanwhile she was wonderfully kind. She exacted perpetual attention, but it was impossible not to like her. He gave details about his queer patient, a "type" if there ever was one, who had in connection with her flushed obesity and in addition to the morbid strain of a violent and aimless will a grave organic disorder; but he came back to his loved novelist, whom he was so good as to pronounce more essentially a poet than many of those who went in for verse, with a zeal excited, as all his indiscretion had been excited, by the happy chance of

Dencombe's sympathy and the coincidence of their occupation. Dencombe had confessed to a slight personal acquaintance with the author of "The Middle Years," but had not felt himself as ready as he could have wished when his companion, who had never yet encountered a being so privileged, began to be eager for particulars. He even thought that Doctor Hugh's eye at that moment emitted a glimmer of suspicion. But the young man was too inflamed to be shrewd and repeatedly caught up the book to exclaim: "Did you notice this?" or "Weren't you immensely struck with that?" "There's a beautiful passage toward the end," he broke out; and again he laid his hand upon the volume. As he turned the pages he came upon something else, while Dencombe saw him suddenly change colour. He had taken up, as it lay on the bench, Dencombe's copy instead of his own, and his neighbour immediately guessed the reason of his start. Doctor Hugh looked grave an instant; then he said: "I see you've been altering the text!" Dencombe was a passionate corrector, a fingerer of style; the last thing he ever arrived at was a form final for himself. His ideal would have been to publish secretly, and then, on the published text, treat himself to the terrified revise, sacrificing always a first edition and beginning for posterity and even for the collectors, poor dears, with a second. This morning, in "The Middle Years," his pencil had pricked a dozen lights. He was amused at the effect of the young man's reproach; for an instant it made him change colour. He stammered, at any rate, ambiguously; then, through a blur of ebbing consciousness, saw Doctor Hugh's mystified eyes. He only had time to feel he was about to be ill again—that emotion, excitement, fatigue, the heat of the sun, the solicitation of the air, had combined to play him a trick, before, stretching out a hand to his visitor with a plaintive cry, he lost his senses altogether.

Later he knew that he had fainted and that Doctor Hugh had got him home in a bath-chair, the conductor of which, prowling within hail for custom, had happened to remember seeing him in the garden of the hotel. He had recovered his perception in the transit, and had, in bed, that afternoon, a vague recollection of Doctor Hugh's young face, as they went together, bent over him in a comforting laugh and expressive of something more than a suspicion of his identity. That identity was ineffaceable now, and all the more that he was disappointed, disgusted. He had been rash, been stupid, had gone out too soon, stayed out too long. He oughtn't to have exposed himself to strangers, he ought to have taken his servant. He felt as if he had fallen into a hole too deep to descry any little patch of heaven. He was confused about the time that had elapsed—he pieced the fragments together. He had seen his doctor, the real one, the one who had treated him from the first and who had again been very kind. His servant was in and out on tiptoe, looking very wise after the fact. He said more than once something about the sharp young gentleman. The rest was vagueness, in so far as it wasn't despair. The vagueness, however, justified itself by dreams, dozing anxieties from which he finally emerged to the consciousness of a dark room and a shaded candle.

"You'll be all right again—I know all about you now," said a voice near him that he knew to be young. Then his meeting with Doctor Hugh came back. He was too discouraged to joke about it yet, but he was able to perceive, after a little, that the interest of it was intense for his visitor. "Of course I can't attend you professionally—you've got your own man, with whom I've talked and who's excellent," Doctor Hugh went on. "But you must let me come to see you as a good friend. I've just looked in before going to bed. You're doing beautifully, but it's a good job I was with you on the cliff. I shall come in early to-morrow. I want to do something for you, I want to do everything. You've done a tremendous lot for me." The young man held his hand, hanging over him, and poor Dencombe, weakly aware of this living pressure, simply lay there and accepted his devotion. He couldn't do anything less—he needed help too much.

The idea of the help he needed was very present to him that night, which he spent in a lucid stillness, an intensity of thought that constituted a reaction from his hours of stupor. He was lost, he was lost—he was lost if he couldn't be saved. He was not afraid of suffering, of death; he was not even in love with life; but he had had a deep demonstration of desire.

It came over him in the long, quiet hours that only with "The Middle Years" had he taken his flight; only on that day, visited by soundless processions, had he recognised his kingdom. He had had a revelation of his range. What he dreaded was the idea that his reputation should stand on the unfinished. It was not with his past but with his future that it should properly be concerned. Illness and age rose before him like spectres with pitiless eyes: how was he to bribe such fates to give him the second chance? He had had the one chance that all men have—he had had the chance of life. He went to sleep again very late, and when he awoke Doctor Hugh was sitting by his head. There was already, by this time, something beautifully familiar in him.

"Don't think I've turned out your physician," he said; "I'm acting with his consent. He has been here and seen you. Somehow he seems to trust me. I told him how we happened to come together yesterday, and he recognises that I've a peculiar right."

Dencombe looked at him with a calculating earnestness. "How have you squared the Countess?"

The young man blushed a little, but he laughed. "Oh, never mind the Countess!"

"You told me she was very exacting."

Doctor Hugh was silent a moment. "So she is."

"And Miss Vernham's an *intrigante*."

"How do you know that?"

"I know everything. One *has* to, to write decently!"

"I think she's mad," said limpid Doctor Hugh.

"Well, don't quarrel with the Countess—she's a present help to you."

"I don't quarrel," Doctor Hugh replied. "But I don't get on with silly women." Presently he added: "You seem very much alone."

"That often happens at my age. I've outlived, I've lost by the way."

Doctor Hugh hesitated; then surmounting a soft scruple: "Whom have you lost?"

"Every one."

"Ah, no," the young man murmured, laying a hand on his arm.

"I once had a wife—I once had a son. My wife died when my child was born, and my boy, at school, was carried off by typhoid."

"I wish I'd been there!" said Doctor Hugh simply.

"Well—if you're here!" Dencombe answered, with a smile that, in spite of dimness, showed how much he liked to be sure of his companion's whereabouts.

"You talk strangely of your age. You're not old."

"Hypocrite—so early!"

"I speak physiologically."

"That's the way I've been speaking for the last five years, and it's exactly what I've been saying to myself. It isn't till we *are* old that we begin to tell ourselves we're not!"

"Yet I know I myself am young," Doctor Hugh declared.

"Not so well as I!" laughed his patient, whose visitor indeed would have established the truth in question by the honesty with which he changed the point of view, remarking that it must be one of the charms of age—at any rate in the case of high distinction—to feel that one has laboured and achieved. Doctor Hugh employed the common phrase about earning one's rest, and it made poor Dencombe, for an instant, almost angry. He recovered himself, however, to explain, lucidly enough, that if he, ungraciously, knew nothing of such a balm, it was doubtless because he had wasted inestimable years. He had followed literature from the first, but he had taken a lifetime to get alongside of her. Only to-day, at last, had he begun to see, so that what he had hitherto done was a movement without a direction. He had ripened too late and was so clumsily constituted that he had had to teach himself by mistakes.

"I prefer your flowers, then, to other people's fruit, and your mistakes to other people's successes," said gallant Doctor Hugh. "It's for your mistakes I admire you."

"You're happy—you don't know," Dencombe answered.

Looking at his watch the young man had got up; he named the hour of the afternoon at which he would return. Dencombe warned him against committing himself too deeply, and expressed again all his dread of making him neglect the Countess—perhaps incur her displeasure.

"I want to be like you—I want to learn by mistakes!" Doctor Hugh laughed.

"Take care you don't make too grave a one! But do come back," Dencombe added, with the glimmer of a new idea.

"You should have had more vanity!" Doctor Hugh spoke as if he knew the exact amount required to make a man of letters normal.

"No, no—I only should have had more time. I want another go."

"Another go?"

"I want an extension."

"An extension?" Again Doctor Hugh repeated Dencombe's words, with which he seemed to have been struck.

"Don't you know?—I want to what they call 'live.' "

The young man, for good-bye, had taken his hand, which closed with a certain force. They looked at each other hard a moment. "You *will* live," said Doctor Hugh.

"Don't be superficial. It's too serious!"

"You *shall* live!" Dencombe's visitor declared, turning pale.

"Ah, that's better!" And as he retired the invalid, with a troubled laugh, sank gratefully back.

All that day and all the following night he wondered if it mightn't be arranged. His doctor came again, his servant was attentive, but it was to his confident young friend that he found himself mentally appealing. His collapse on the cliff was plausibly explained, and his liberation, on a better basis, promised for the morrow; meanwhile, however, the intensity of his meditations kept him tranquil and made him indifferent. The idea that occupied him was none the less absorbing because it was a morbid fancy. Here was a clever son of the age, ingenious and ardent, who happened to have set him up for connoisseurs to worship. This servant of his altar had all the new learning in science and all the old reverence in faith; wouldn't he therefore put his knowledge at the disposal of his sympathy, his craft at the disposal of his love? Couldn't he be trusted to invent a remedy for a poor artist to whose art he had paid a tribute? If he couldn't, the alternative was hard: Dencombe would have to surrender to silence, unvindicated and undivined. The rest of the day and all the next he toyed in secret with this sweet futility. Who would work the miracle for him but the young man who could combine such lucidity with such passion? He thought of the fairy-tales of science and charmed himself into forgetting that he looked for a magic that was not of this world. Doctor Hugh was an apparition, and that placed him above the law. He came and went while his patient, who sat up, followed him with supplicating eyes. The interest of knowing the great author had made the young man begin "The Middle Years" afresh, and would help him to find a deeper meaning in its pages. Dencombe had told him what he "tried for;" with all his intelligence, on a first perusal, Doctor Hugh had failed to guess it. The baffled celebrity wondered then who in the world *would* guess it: he was amused once more at the fine, full way with which an intention could be missed. Yet he wouldn't rail at the general mind to-day—consoling as that ever had been: the revelation of his own slowness had seemed to make all stupidity sacred.

Doctor Hugh, after a little, was visibly worried, confessing, on inquiry, to a source of embarrassment at home. "Stick to the Countess—don't mind me," Dencombe said, repeatedly; for his companion was frank enough about the large lady's attitude. She was so jealous that she had fallen ill—she resented such a breach of allegiance. She paid so much for his fidelity that she must have it all: she refused him the right to other sympathies, charged him with scheming to make her die alone, for it was needless to point out how little Miss Vernham was a resource in trouble. When Doctor Hugh mentioned that the Countess would already have left Bournemouth if he hadn't kept her in bed, poor Dencombe held his arm tighter and said with decision: "Take her straight away." They had gone out together, walking back to the sheltered nook in which, the other day, they had met. The young man, who had given his companion a personal support, declared with emphasis that his conscience was clear—he could ride two horses at once. Didn't he dream, for his future, of a time when he should have to ride five hundred? Longing equally for virtue, Dencombe replied that in that golden age no patient would pretend to have contracted with him for his whole attention. On the part of the Countess was not such an avidity lawful? Doctor Hugh denied it, said there was no contract but only a free understanding, and that a sordid servitude was impossible to a generous spirit; he liked moreover to talk about art, and that was the subject on which, this time, as they sat together on the sunny bench, he tried most to engage the author of "The Middle Years." Dencombe, soaring again a little on the weak wings of convalescence and still haunted by that happy notion of an organised rescue, found another strain of eloquence to plead the cause of a certain splendid "last manner," the very citadel, as it would prove, of his reputation, the stronghold into which his real treasure would be gathered. While his listener gave up the morning and the great still sea appeared to wait, he had a wonderful explanatory hour. Even for himself he was inspired as he told of what his treasure would consist—the precious metals he would dig from the mine, the jewels rare, strings of pearls, he would hang between the columns of his temple. He was wonderful for himself, so thick his convictions crowded; but he was still more wonderful for Doctor Hugh, who assured him, none the less, that the very pages he had just published were already encrusted with gems. The young man, however, panted for the combinations to come, and, before the face of the beautiful day, renewed to Dencombe his guarantee that his profession would hold itself responsible for such a life. Then he suddenly clapped his hand upon his watch-pocket and asked leave to absent himself for half an hour. Dencombe waited there for his return, but was at last recalled to the actual by the fall of a shadow across the ground. The shadow darkened into that of Miss Vernham, the young lady in attendance on the Countess; whom Dencombe, recognising her, perceived so clearly to have come to speak to him that he rose from his bench to acknowledge the civility. Miss Vernham indeed proved not particularly civil; she looked strangely agitated, and her type was now unmistakable.

"Excuse me if I inquire," she said, "whether it's too much to hope that you may be induced to leave Doctor Hugh alone." Then, before Dencombe, greatly disconcerted, could protest: "You ought to be informed that you stand in his light; that you may do him a terrible injury."

"Do you mean by causing the Countess to dispense with his services?"

"By causing her to disinherit him." Dencombe stared at this, and Miss Vernham pursued, in the gratification of seeing she could produce an impression: "It has depended on himself to come into something very handsome. He has had a magnificent prospect, but I think you've succeeded in spoiling it."

"Not intentionally, I assure you. Is there no hope the accident may be repaired?" Dencombe asked.

"She was ready to do anything for him. She takes great fancies, she lets herself go—it's her way. She has no relations, she's free to dispose of her money, and she's very ill."

"I'm very sorry to hear it," Dencombe stammered.

"Wouldn't it be possible for you to leave Bournemouth? That's what I've come to ask you."

Poor Dencombe sank down on his bench. "I'm very ill myself, but I'll try!"

Miss Vernham still stood there with her colourless eyes and the brutality of her good conscience. "Before it's too late, please!" she said; and with this she turned her back, in order, quickly, as if it had been a business to which she could spare but a precious moment, to pass out of his sight.

Oh, yes, after this Dencombe was certainly very ill. Miss Vernham had upset him with her rough, fierce news; it was the sharpest shock to him to discover what was at stake for a penniless young man of fine parts. He sat trembling on his bench, staring at the waste of waters, feeling sick with the directness of the blow. He was indeed too weak, too unsteady, too alarmed; but he would make the effort to get away, for he couldn't accept the guilt of interference, and his honour was really involved. He would hobble home, at any rate, and then he would think what was to be done. He made his way back to the hotel and, as he went, had a characteristic vision of Miss Vernham's great motive. The Countess hated women, of course; Dencombe was lucid about that; so the hungry pianist had no personal hopes and could only console herself with the bold conception of helping Doctor Hugh in order either to marry him after he should get his money or to induce him to recognise her title to compensation and buy her off. If she had befriended him at a fruitful crisis he would really, as a man of delicacy, and she knew what to think of that point, have to reckon with her.

At the hotel Dencombe's servant insisted on his going back to bed. The invalid had talked about catching a train and had begun with orders to pack; after which his humming nerves had yielded to a sense of sickness. He consented to see his physician, who immediately was sent for, but he wished it to be understood that his door was irrevocably closed to Doctor Hugh. He had his plan, which was so fine that he rejoiced in it after getting back to bed. Doctor Hugh, suddenly finding himself snubbed without mercy, would, in natural disgust and to the joy of Miss Vernham, renew his allegiance to the Countess. When his physician arrived Dencombe learned that he was feverish and that this was very wrong: he was to cultivate calmness and try, if possible, not to think. For the rest of the day he wooed stupidity; but there was an ache that kept him sentient, the probable sacrifice of his "extension," the limit of his course. His medical adviser was anything but pleased; his successive relapses were ominous. He charged this personage to put out a strong hand and take Doctor Hugh off his mind—it would contribute so much to his being quiet. The agitating name, in his room, was not mentioned again, but his security was a smothered fear, and it was not confirmed by the receipt, at ten o'clock that evening, of a telegram which his servant opened and read for him and to which, with an address in London, the signature of Miss Vernham was attached. "Beseech you to use all influence to make our friend join us here in the morning. Countess much the worse for dreadful journey, but everything may still be saved." The two ladies had gathered themselves up and had been capable in the afternoon of a spiteful revolution. They had started for the capital, and if the elder one, as Miss Vernham had announced, was very ill, she had wished to make it clear that she was proportionately reckless. Poor Dencombe, who was not reckless and who only desired that everything should indeed be "saved," sent this missive straight off to the young man's lodging and had on the morrow the pleasure of knowing that he had quitted Bournemouth by an early train.

Two days later he pressed in with a copy of a literary journal in his hand. He had returned because he was anxious and for the pleasure of flourishing the great review of "The Middle Years." Here at least was something adequate—it rose to the occasion; it was an acclamation, a reparation, a critical attempt to place the author in the niche he had fairly won. Dencombe accepted and submitted; he made neither objection nor inquiry, for old complications had returned and he had had two atrocious days. He was convinced not only that he should never again leave his bed, so that his young friend might pardonably remain, but that the demand he should make on the patience of beholders would be very moderate indeed. Doctor Hugh had been to town, and he tried to find in his eyes some confession that the Countess was pacified and his legacy clinched; but all he could see there was the light of his juvenile joy in two or three of the phrases of the newspaper. Dencombe couldn't read them, but when his visitor had insisted on repeating them more than once he was able to shake an unintoxicated head. "Ah, no; but they would have been true of what I *could* have done!"

"What people 'could have done' is mainly what they've in fact done," Doctor Hugh contended.

"Mainly, yes; but I've been an idiot!" said Dencombe.

Doctor Hugh did remain; the end was coming fast. Two days later Dencombe observed to him, by way of the feeblest of jokes, that there would now be no question whatever of a second chance. At this the young man stared; then he exclaimed: "Why, it has come to pass—it has come to pass! The second chance has been the public's—the chance to find the point of view, to pick up the pearl!"

"Oh, the pearl!" poor Dencombe uneasily sighed. A smile as cold as a winter sunset flickered on his drawn lips as he added: "The pearl is the unwritten—the pearl is the unalloyed, the *rest*, the lost!"

From that moment he was less and less present, heedless to all appearance of what went on around him. His disease was definitely mortal, of an action as relentless, after the short arrest that had enabled him to fall in with Doctor Hugh, as a leak in a great ship. Sinking steadily, though this visitor, a man of rare resources, now cordially approved by his physician, showed endless art in guarding him from pain, poor Dencombe kept no reckoning of favour or neglect, betrayed no symptom of regret or speculation. Yet toward the last he gave a sign of having noticed that for two days Doctor Hugh had not been in his room, a sign that consisted of his suddenly opening his eyes to ask of him if had spent the interval with the Countess.

"The Countess is dead," said Doctor Hugh. "I knew that in a particular contingency she wouldn't resist. I went to her grave."

Dencombe's eyes opened wider. "She left you 'something handsome'?"

The young man gave a laugh almost too light for a chamber of woe. "Never a penny. She roundly cursed me."

"Cursed you?" Dencombe murmured.

"For giving her up. I gave her up for *you*. I had to choose," his companion explained.

"You chose to let a fortune go?"

"I chose to accept, whatever they might be, the consequences of my infatuation," smiled Doctor Hugh. Then, as a larger pleasantry: "A fortune be hanged! It's your own fault if I can't get your things out of my head."

The immediate tribute to his humour was a long, bewildered moan; after which, for many hours, many days, Dencombe lay motionless and absent. A response so absolute, such a glimpse of a definite result and such a sense of credit worked together in his mind and, producing a strange commotion, slowly altered and transfigured his despair. The sense of cold submersion left him—he seemed to float without an effort. The incident was extraordinary as evidence, and it shed an intenser light. At the last he signed to Doctor Hugh to listen, and, when he was down on his knees by the pillow, brought him very near.

"You've made me think it all a delusion."

"Not your glory, my friend," stammered the young man.

"Not my glory—what there is of it! It *is* glory—to have been tested, to have had our little quality and cast our little spell. The thing is to have made somebody care. You happen to be crazy, or course, but that doesn't affect the law."

"You're a great success!" said Doctor Hugh, putting into his young voice the ring of a marriage-bell.

Dencombe lay taking this in; then he gathered strength to speak once more. "A second chance—*that's* the delusion. There never was to be but one. We work in the dark—we do what we can—we give what we have. Our doubt is our passion and our passion is our task. The rest is the madness of art."

"If you've doubted, if you've despaired, you've always 'done' it," his visitor subtly argued.

"We've done something or other," Dencombe conceded.

"Something or other is everything. It's the feasible. It's *you*!"

"Comforter!" poor Dencombe ironically sighed.

"But it's true," insisted his friend.

"It's true. It's frustration that doesn't count."

"Frustration's only life," said Doctor Hugh.

"Yes, it's what passes." Poor Dencombe was barely audible, but he had marked with the words the virtual end of his first and only chance.

The Death of the Lion

I HAD simply, I suppose, a change of heart, and it must have begun when I received my manuscript back from Mr. Pinhorn. Mr. Pinhorn was my "chief," as he was called in the office: he had accepted the high mission of bringing the paper up. This was a weekly periodical, and had been supposed to be almost past redemption when he took hold of it. It was Mr. Deedy who had let it down so dreadfully: he was never mentioned in the office now save in connection with that misdemeanour. Young as I was I had been in a manner taken over from Mr. Deedy, who had been owner as well as editor; forming part of a promiscuous lot, mainly plant and office-furniture, which poor Mrs. Deedy, in her bereavement and depression, parted with at a rough valuation. I could account for my continuity only on the supposition that I had been cheap. I rather resented the practice of fathering all flatness on my late protector, who was in his unhonoured grave; but as I had my way to make I found matter enough for complacency in being on a "staff." At the same time I was aware that I was exposed to suspicion as a product of the old lowering system. This made me feel that I was doubly bound to have ideas, and had doubtless been at the bottom of my proposing to Mr. Pinhorn that I should lay my lean hands on Neil Paraday. I remember that he looked at me first as if he had never heard of this celebrity, who indeed at that moment was by no means in the centre of the heavens; and even when I had knowingly explained he expressed but little confidence in the demand for any such matter. When I had reminded him that the great principle on which we were supposed to work was just to create the demand we required, he considered a moment and then rejoined: "I see; you want to write him up."

"Call it that if you like."

"And what's your inducement?"

"Bless my soul—my admiration!"

Mr. Pinhorn pursed up his mouth. "Is there much to be done with him?"

"Whatever there is, we should have it all to ourselves, for he hasn't been touched."

This argument was effective, and Mr. Pinhorn responded: "Very well, touch him." Then he added: "But where can you do it?"

"Under the fifth rib!"

Mr. Pinhorn stared. "Where's that?"

"You want me to go down and see him?" I inquired when I had enjoyed his visible search for this obscure suburb.

"I don't 'want' anything—the proposal's your own. But you must remember that that's the way we do things *now*," said Mr. Pinhorn, with another dig at Mr. Deedy.

Unregenerate as I was, I could read the queer implications of this speech. The present owner's superior virtue as well as his deeper craft spoke in his reference to the late editor as one of that baser sort who deal in false representations. Mr. Deedy would as soon have sent me to call on Neil Paraday as he would have published a "holiday-number;" but such scruples presented themselves as mere ignoble thrift to his successor, whose own sincerity took the form of ringing door-bells and whose definition of genius was the art of finding people at home. It was as if Mr. Deedy had published reports without his young men's having, as Pinhorn would have said, really been there. I was unregenerate, as I have hinted, and I was not concerned to straighten out the journalistic morals of my chief, feeling them indeed to be an abyss over the edge of which it was better not to peer. Really to be there this time moreover was a vision that made the idea of writing something subtle about Neil Paraday only the more inspiring. I would be as considerate as even Mr. Deedy could have wished, and yet I should be as present as only Mr. Pinhorn could conceive. My allusion to the sequestered manner in which Mr. Paraday lived (which had formed part of my explanation, though I knew of it only by hearsay) was, I could divine, very much what had made Mr. Pinhorn nibble. It struck him as inconsistent with the success of his paper that any one should be so sequestered as that. And then was not an immediate exposure of everything just what the public wanted? Mr. Pinhorn effectually called me to order by reminding me of the promptness with which I had met Miss Braby at Liverpool on her return from her fiasco in the States. Hadn't we published, while its freshness and flavour were unimpaired, Miss Braby's own version of that great international episode? I felt somewhat uneasy at this lumping of the actress and the author, and I confess that after having enlisted Mr. Pinhorn's sympathies I procrastinated a little. I had succeeded better than I wished, and I had, as it happened, work nearer at hand. A few days later I called on Lord Crouchley and carried off in triumph the most unintelligible statement that had yet appeared of his lordship's reasons for his change of front. I thus set in motion in the daily papers columns of virtuous verbiage. The following week I ran down to Brighton for a chat, as Mr. Pinhorn called it, with Mrs. Bounder, who gave me, on the subject of her divorce, many curious particulars that had not been articulated in court. If ever an article flowed from the primal fount it was that article on Mrs. Bounder. By this time, however, I became aware that Neil Paraday's new book was on the point of appearing and that its approach had been the ground of my original appeal to Mr. Pinhorn, who was now annoyed with me for having lost so many days. He bundled me off— we would at least not lose another. I have always thought his sudden alertness a remarkable example of the journalistic instinct. Nothing had occurred, since I first spoke to him, to create a visible urgency, and no enlightenment could possibly have reached him. It was a pure case of professional *flair*—he had smelt the coming glory as an animal smells its distant prey.

II

I may as well say at once that this little record pretends in no degree to be a picture either of my introduction to Mr. Paraday or of certain proximate steps and stages. The scheme of my narrative allows no space for these things, and in any case a prohibitory sentiment would be attached to my recollection of so rare an hour. These meagre notes are essentially private, so that if they see the light the insidious forces that, as my story itself shows, make at present for publicity will simply have overmastered my precautions. The curtain fell lately enough on the lamentable drama. My memory of the day I alighted at Mr. Paraday's door is a fresh memory of kindness, hospitality, compassion, and of the wonderful illuminating talk in which the welcome was conveyed. Some voice of the air had taught me the right moment, the moment of his life at which an act of unexpected young allegiance might most come home. He had recently recovered from a long, grave illness. I had gone to the neighbouring inn for the night, but I spent the evening in his company, and he insisted the next day on my sleeping under his roof. I had not an indefinite leave: Mr. Pinhorn supposed us to put our victims through on the gallop. It was later, in the office, that the dance was set to music. I fortified myself, however, as my training had taught me to do, by the conviction that nothing could be more advantageous for my article than to be written in the very atmosphere. I said nothing to Mr. Paraday about it, but in the morning, after my removal from the inn, while he was occupied in his study, as he had notified me that he should need to be, I committed to paper the quintessence of my impressions. Then thinking to commend myself to Mr. Pinhorn by my celerity, I walked out and posted my little packet before luncheon. Once my paper was written I was free to stay on, and if it was designed to divert attention from my frivolity in so doing I could reflect with satisfaction that I had never been so clever. I don't mean to deny of course that I was aware it was much too good for Mr. Pinhorn; but I was equally conscious that Mr. Pinhorn had the supreme shrewdness of recognising from time to time the cases in which an article was not too bad only because it was too good. There was nothing he loved so much as to print on the right occasion a thing he hated. I had begun my visit to Mr. Paraday on a Monday, and on the Wednesday his book came out. A copy of it arrived by the first post, and he let me go out into the garden with it immediately after breakfast. I read it from beginning to end that day, and in the evening he asked me to remain with him the rest of the week and over the Sunday.

That night my manuscript came back from Mr. Pinhorn, accompanied with a letter, of which the gist was the desire to know what I meant by sending him such stuff. That was the meaning of the question, if not exactly its form, and it made my mistake immense to me. Such as this mistake was I could now only look it in the face and accept it. I knew where I had failed, but it was exactly where I couldn't have succeeded. I had been sent down there to be personal, and in point of fact I hadn't been personal at all: what I had sent up to London was just a little finicking, feverish study of my author's talent. Anything less relevant to Mr. Pinhorn's purpose couldn't well be imagined, and he was visibly angry at my having (at his expense, with a second-class ticket) approached the object of our arrangement only to be so deucedly distant. For myself, I knew but too well what had happened, and how a miracle—as pretty as some old miracle of legend—had been wrought on the spot to save me. There had been a big brush of wings, the flash of an opaline robe, and then, with a great cool stir of the air, the sense of an angel's having swooped down and caught me to his bosom. He held me only till the danger was over, and it all took place in a minute. With my manuscript back on my hands I understood the phenomenon better, and the reflections I made on it are what I meant, at the beginning of this anecdote, by my change of heart. Mr. Pinhorn's note was not only a rebuke decidedly stern, but an invitation immediately to send him (it was the case to say so) the genuine article, the revealing and reverberating sketch to the promise of which—and of which alone—I owed my squandered privilege. A week or two later I recast my peccant paper, and giving it a particular application to Mr. Paraday's new book, obtained for it the hospitality of another journal, where, I must admit, Mr. Pinhorn was so far justified that it attracted not the least attention.

III

I was frankly, at the end of three days, a very prejudiced critic, so that one morning when, in the garden, Neil Paraday had offered to read me something I quite held my breath as I listened. It was the written scheme of another book—something he had put aside long ago, before his illness, and lately taken out again to reconsider. He had been turning it round when I came down upon him, and it had grown magnificently under this second hand. Loose, liberal, confident, it might have passed for a great gossiping, eloquent letter—the overflow into talk of an artist's amorous plan. The subject I thought singularly rich, quite the strongest he had yet treated; and this familiar statement of it, full too of fine maturities, was really, in summarised splendour, a mine of gold, a precious, independent work. I remember rather profanely wondering whether the ultimate production could possibly be so happy. His reading of the epistle, at any rate, made me feel as if I were, for the advantage of posterity, in close correspondence with him—were the distinguished person to whom it had been affectionately addressed. It was high distinction simply to be told such things. The idea he now communicated had all the freshness, the flushed fairness of the conception un-touched and untried: it was Venus rising from the sea, before the airs had blown upon her. I had never been so throbbingly present at such an unveiling. But when he had tossed the last bright word after the others, as I had seen cashiers in banks, weighing mounds of coin, drop a final sovereign into the tray, I became conscious of a sudden prudent alarm.

"My dear master, how, after all, are you going to do it?" I asked. "It's infinitely noble, but what time it will take, what patience and independence, what assured, what perfect con-ditions it will demand! Oh for a lone isle in a tepid sea!"

"Isn't this practically a lone isle, and aren't you, as an en-circling medium, tepid enough?" he replied, alluding with a laugh to the wonder of my young admiration and the narrow limits of his little provincial home. "Time isn't what I've lacked hitherto: the question hasn't been to find it, but to use it. Of course my illness made a great hole, but I daresay there would have been a hole at any rate. The earth we tread has more pockets than a billiard-table. The great thing is now to keep on my feet."

"That's exactly what I mean."

Neil Paraday looked at me with eyes—such pleasant eyes as he had—in which, as I now recall their expression, I seem to have seen a dim imagination of his fate. He was fifty years old, and his illness had been cruel, his convalescence slow. "It isn't as if I weren't all right."

"Oh, if you weren't all right I wouldn't look at you!" I tenderly said.

We had both got up, quickened by the full sound of it all, and he had lighted a cigarette. I had taken a fresh one, and, with an intenser smile, by way of answer to my exclamation, he touched it with the flame of his match. "If I weren't better I shouldn't have thought of *that*!" He flourished his epistle in his hand.

"I don't want to be discouraging, but that's not true," I returned. "I'm sure that during the months you lay here in pain you had visitations sublime. You thought of a thousand things. You think of more and more all the while. That's what makes you, if you will pardon my familiarity, so respectable. At a time when so many people are spent you come into your second wind. But, thank God, all the same, you're better! Thank God, too, you're not, as you were telling me yesterday, 'successful.' If *you* weren't a failure, what would be the use of trying? That's my one reserve on the subject of your recovery—that it makes you 'score,' as the newspapers say. It looks well in the newspapers, and almost anything that does that is horrible. 'We are happy to announce that Mr. Paraday, the celebrated author, is again in the enjoyment of excellent health.' Somehow I shouldn't like to see it."

"You won't see it; I'm not in the least celebrated—my obscurity protects me. But couldn't you bear even to see I was dying or dead?" my companion asked.

"Dead—*passe encore*; there's nothing so safe. One never knows what a living artist may do—one has mourned so many. However, one must make the worst of it; you must be as dead as you can."

"Don't I meet that condition in having just published a book?"

"Adequately, let us hope; for the book is verily a masterpiece."

At this moment the parlour-maid appeared in the door that opened into the garden: Paraday lived at no great cost, and the frisk of petticoats, with a timorous "Sherry, sir?" was about his modest mahogany. He allowed half his income to his wife, from whom he had succeeded in separating without redundancy of legend. I had a general faith in his having behaved well, and I had once, in London, taken Mrs. Paraday down to dinner. He now turned to speak to the maid, who offered him, on a tray, some card or note, while agitated, excited, I wandered to the end of the garden. The idea of his security became supremely dear to me, and I asked myself if I were the same young man who had come down a few days before to scatter him to the four winds. When I retraced my steps he had gone into the house, and the woman (the second London post had come in) had placed my letters and a newspaper on a bench. I sat down there to the letters, which were a brief business, and then, without heeding the address, took the paper from its envelope. It was the journal of highest renown, *The Empire* of that morning. It regularly came to Paraday, but I remembered that neither of us had yet looked at the copy already delivered. This one had a great mark on the "editorial" page, and, uncrumpling the wrapper, I saw it to be directed to my host and stamped with the name of his publishers. I instantly divined that *The Empire* had spoken of him, and I have not forgotten the odd little shock of the circumstance. It checked all eagerness and made me drop the paper a moment. As I sat there conscious of a palpitation I think I had a vision of what was to be. I had also a vision of the letter I would presently address to Mr. Pinhorn, breaking as it were with Mr. Pinhorn. Of course, however, the next minute the voice of *The Empire* was in my ears.

The article was not, I thanked heaven, a review; it was a "leader," the last of three, presenting Neil Paraday to the human race. His new book, the fifth from his hand, had been but a day or two out, and *The Empire*, already aware of it, fired, as if on the birth of a prince, a salute of a whole column. The guns had been booming these three hours in the house without our suspecting them. The big blundering newspaper had discovered him, and now he was proclaimed and anointed and crowned. His place was assigned him as publicly as if a fat usher with a wand had pointed to the topmost chair; he was to pass up and still up, higher and higher, between the watching faces and the envious sounds—away up to the daïs and the throne. The article was a date; he had taken rank at a bound—waked up a national glory. A national glory was needed, and it was an immense convenience he was there. What all this meant rolled over me, and I fear I grew a little faint—it meant so much more than I could say "yea" to on the spot. In a flash, somehow, all was different; the tremendous wave I speak of had swept something away. It had knocked down, I suppose, my little customary altar, my twin-kling tapers and my flowers, and had reared itself into the likeness of a temple vast and bare. When Neil Paraday should come out of the house he would come out a contemporary. That was what had happened: the poor man was to be squeezed into his horrible age. I felt as if he had been over-taken on the crest of the hill and brought back to the city. A little more and he would have dipped down the short cut to posterity and escaped.

IV

When he came out it was exactly as if he had been in custody, for beside him walked a stout man with a big black beard, who, save that he wore spectacles, might have been a police-man, and in whom at a second glance I recognised the highest contemporary enterprise.

"This is Mr. Morrow," said Paraday, looking, I thought, rather white: "he wants to publish heaven knows what about me."

I winced as I remembered that this was exactly what I my-self had wanted. "Already?" I exclaimed, with a sort of sense that my friend had fled to me for protection.

Mr. Morrow glared, agreeably, through his glasses: they suggested the electric headlights of some monstrous modern ship, and I felt as if Paraday and I were tossing terrified under his bows. I saw that his momentum was irresistible. "I was con-fident that I should be the first in the field," he declared. "A great interest is naturally felt in Mr. Paraday's surroundings."

"I hadn't the least idea of it," said Paraday, as if he had been told he had been snoring.

"I find he has not read the article in *The Empire*," Mr. Morrow remarked to me. "That's so very interesting—it's something to start with," he smiled. He had begun to pull off his gloves, which were violently new, and to look encour-agingly round the little garden. As a "surrounding" I felt that I myself had already been taken in; I was a little fish in the stomach of a bigger one. "I represent," our visitor continued, "a syndicate of influential journals, no less than thirty-seven, whose public—whose publics, I may say—are in peculiar sympathy with Mr. Paraday's line of thought. They would greatly appreciate any expression of his views on the subject of the art he so brilliantly practises. Besides my connection with the syndicate just mentioned, I hold a particular commission from *The Tatler*, whose most prominent department, 'Smatter and Chatter'—I daresay you've often enjoyed it—attracts such attention. I was honoured only last week, as a representative of *The Tatler*, with the confidence of Guy Walsingham, the author of 'Obsessions.' She expressed herself thoroughly pleased with my sketch of her method; she went so far as to say that I had made her genius more comprehensible even to herself."

Neil Paraday had dropped upon the garden-bench and sat there at once detached and confused; he looked hard at a bare spot in the lawn, as if with an anxiety that had suddenly made him grave. His movement had been interpreted by his visitor as an invitation to sink sympathetically into a wicker chair that stood hard by, and as Mr. Morrow so settled himself I felt that he had taken official possession and that there was no undoing it. One had heard of unfortunate people's having "a man in the house," and this was just what we had. There was a silence of a moment, during which we seemed to acknowledge in the only way that was possible the presence of universal fate; the sunny stillness took no pity, and my thought, as I was sure Paraday's was doing, performed within the minute a great distant revolution. I saw just how emphatic I should make my rejoinder to Mr. Pinhorn, and that having come, like Mr. Morrow, to betray, I must remain as long as possible to save. Not because I had brought my mind back, but because our visitor's last words were in my ear, I presently inquired with gloomy irrelevance if Guy Walsingham were a woman.

"Oh yes, a mere pseudonym; but convenient, you know, for a lady who goes in for the larger latitude. 'Obsessions, by Miss So-and-so,' would look a little odd, but men are more naturally indelicate. Have you peeped into 'Obsessions'?" Mr. Morrow continued sociably to our companion.

Paraday, still absent, remote, made no answer, as if he had not heard the question: a manifestation that appeared to suit the cheerful Mr. Morrow as well as any other. Imperturbably bland, he was a man of resources—he only needed to be on the spot. He had pocketed the whole poor place while Paraday and I were woolgathering, and I could imagine that he had already got his "heads." His system, at any rate, was justified by the inevitability with which I replied, to save my friend the trouble: "Dear, no; he hasn't read it. He doesn't read such things!" I unwarily added.

"Things that are *too* far over the fence, eh?" I was indeed a godsend to Mr. Morrow. It was the psychological moment; it determined the appearance of his notebook, which, however, he at first kept slightly behind him, even as the dentist, approaching his victim, keeps the horrible forceps. "Mr. Paraday holds with the good old proprieties—I see!" And thinking of the thirty-seven influential journals, I found myself, as I found poor Paraday, helplessly gazing at the promulgation of this ineptitude. "There's no point on which distinguished views are so acceptable as on this question—raised perhaps more strikingly than ever by Guy Walsingham—of the permissibility of the larger latitude. I have an appointment, precisely in connection with it, next week, with Dora Forbes, the author of 'The Other Way Round,' which everybody is talking about. Has Mr. Paraday glanced at 'The Other Way Round'?" Mr. Morrow now frankly appealed to me. I took upon myself to repudiate the supposition, while our companion, still silent, got up nervously and walked away. His visitor paid no heed to his withdrawal; he only opened out the notebook with a more motherly pat. "Dora Forbes, I gather, takes the ground, the same as Guy Walsingham's, that the larger latitude has simply got to come. He holds that it has got to be squarely faced. Of course his sex makes him a less prejudiced witness. But an authoritative word from Mr. Paraday—from the point of view of *his* sex, you know—would go right round the globe. He takes the line that we *haven't* got to face it?"

I was bewildered: it sounded somehow as if there were three sexes. My interlocutor's pencil was poised, my private responsibility great. I simply sat staring, however, and only found presence of mind to say: "Is this Miss Forbes a gentleman?"

Mr. Morrow hesitated an instant, smiling. "It wouldn't be 'Miss'—there's a wife!"

"I mean is she a man?"

"The wife?"—Mr. Morrow, for a moment, was as confused as myself. But when I explained that I alluded to Dora Forbes in person he informed me, with visible amusement at my being so out of it, that this was the "pen-name" of an indubitable male—he had a big red moustache. "He only assumes a feminine personality because the ladies are such popular favourites. A great deal of interest is felt in this assumption, and there's every prospect of its being widely imitated." Our host at this moment joined us again, and Mr. Morrow remarked invitingly that he should be happy to make a note of any observation the movement in question, the bid for success under a lady's name, might suggest to Mr. Paraday. But the poor man, without catching the allusion, excused himself, pleading that, though he was greatly honoured by his visitor's interest, he suddenly felt unwell and should have to take leave of him—have to go and lie down and keep quiet. His young friend might be trusted to answer for him, but he hoped Mr. Morrow didn't expect great things even of his young friend. His young friend, at this moment, looked at Neil Paraday with an anxious eye, greatly wondering if he were doomed to be ill again; but Paraday's own kind face met his question reassuringly, seemed to say in a glance intelligible enough: "Oh, I'm not ill, but I'm scared: get him out of the house as quietly as possible." Getting newspaper-men out of the house was odd business for an emissary of Mr. Pinhorn, and I was so exhilarated by the idea of it that I called after him as he left us:

"Read the article in *The Empire*, and you'll soon be all right!"

V

"Delicious my having come down to tell him of it!" Mr. Morrow ejaculated. "My cab was at the door twenty minutes after *The Empire* had been laid upon my breakfast table. Now what have you got for me?" he continued, dropping again into his chair, from which, however, the next moment he quickly rose. "I was shown into the drawing-room, but there must be more to see—his study, his literary sanctum, the little things he has about, or other domestic objects or features. He wouldn't be lying down on his study-table? There's a great interest always felt in the scene of an author's labours. Sometimes we're fa-voured with very delightful peeps. Dora Forbes showed me all his table-drawers, and almost jammed my hand into one into which I made a dash! I don't ask that of you, but if we could talk things over right there where he sits I feel as if I should get the keynote."

I had no wish whatever to be rude to Mr. Morrow, I was much too initiated not to prefer the safety of other ways; but I had a quick inspiration and I entertained an insurmountable, an almost superstitious objection to his crossing the threshold of my friend's little lonely, shabby, consecrated workshop. "No, no—we sha'n't get at his life that way," I said. "The way to get at his life is to— But wait a moment!" I broke off and went quickly into the house; then, in three minutes, I reappeared before Mr. Morrow with the two volumes of Par-aday's new book. "His life's here," I went on, "and I'm so full of this admirable thing that I can't talk of anything else. The artist's life's his work, and this is the place to observe him. What he has to tell us he tells us with *this* perfection. My dear sir, the best interviewer's the best reader."

Mr. Morrow good-humouredly protested. "Do you mean to say that no other source of information should be open to us?"

"None other till this particular one—by far the most co-pious—has been quite exhausted. Have you exhausted it, my dear sir? Had you exhausted it when you came down here? It seems to me in our time almost wholly neglected, and some-thing should surely be done to restore its ruined credit. It's the course to which the artist himself at every step, and with such pathetic confidence, refers us. This last book of Mr. Par-aday's is full of revelations."

"Revelations?" panted Mr. Morrow, whom I had forced again into his chair.

"The only kind that count. It tells you with a perfection that seems to me quite final all the author thinks, for instance, about the advent of the 'larger latitude.' "

"Where does it do that?" asked Mr. Morrow, who had picked up the second volume and was insincerely thumb-ing it.

"Everywhere—in the whole treatment of his case. Extract the opinion, disengage the answer—those are the real acts of homage."

Mr. Morrow, after a minute, tossed the book away. "Ah, but you mustn't take me for a reviewer."

"Heaven forbid I should take you for anything so dreadful! You came down to perform a little act of sympathy, and so, I may confide to you, did I. Let us perform our little act together. These pages overflow with the testimony we want: let us read them and taste them and interpret them. You will of course have perceived for yourself that one scarcely does read Neil Paraday till one reads him aloud; he gives out to the ear an extraordinary quality, and it's only when you expose it confidently to that test that you really get near his style. Take up your book again and let me listen, while you pay it out, to that wonderful fifteenth chapter. If you feel that you can't do it justice, compose yourself to attention while I produce for you—I think I can!—this scarcely less admirable ninth."

Mr. Morrow gave me a straight glance which was as hard as a blow between the eyes; he had turned rather red, and a question had formed itself in his mind which reached my sense as distinctly as if he had uttered it: "What sort of a damned fool are *you*?" Then he got up, gathering together his hat and gloves, buttoning his coat, projecting hungrily all over the place the big transparency of his mask. It seemed to flare over Fleet Street and somehow made the actual spot distressingly humble. There was so little for it to feed on unless he counted the blisters of our stucco or saw his way to do something with the roses. Even the poor roses were common kinds. Presently his eyes fell upon the manuscript from which Paraday had been reading to me and which still lay on the bench. As my own followed them I saw that it looked promising, looked pregnant, as if it gently throbbed with the life the reader had given it. Mr. Morrow indulged in a nod toward it and a vague thrust of his umbrella. "What's that?"

"Oh, it's a plan—a secret."

"A secret!" There was an instant's silence, and then Mr. Morrow made another movement. I may have been mistaken, but it affected me as the translated impulse of the desire to lay hands on the manuscript, and this led me to indulge in a quick anticipatory grab which may very well have seemed ungraceful, or even impertinent, and which at any rate left Mr. Paraday's two admirers very erect, glaring at each other while one of them held a bundle of papers well behind him. An instant later Mr. Morrow quitted me abruptly, as if he had really carried something off with him. To reassure myself, watching his broad back recede, I only grasped my manuscript the tighter. He went to the back-door of the house, the one he had come out from, but on trying the handle he appeared to find it fastened. So he passed round into the front garden, and by listening intently enough I could presently hear the outer gate close behind him with a bang. I thought again of the thirty-seven influential journals and wondered what would be his revenge. I hasten to add that he was magnanimous: which was just the most dreadful thing he could have been. *The Tatler* published a charming, chatty, familiar account of Mr. Paraday's "Home-life," and on the wings of the thirty-seven influential journals it went, to use Mr. Morrow's own expression, right round the globe.

VI

A week later, early in May, my glorified friend came up to town, where, it may be veraciously recorded, he was the king of the beasts of the year. No advancement was ever more rapid, no exaltation more complete, no bewilderment more teachable. His book sold but moderately, though the article in *The Empire* had done unwonted wonders for it; but he circulated in person in a manner that the libraries might well have envied. His formula had been found—he was a "revelation." His momentary terror had been real, just as mine had been—the overclouding of his passionate desire to be left to finish his work. He was far from unsociable, but he had the finest conception of being let alone that I have ever met. For the time, however, he took his profit where it seemed most to crowd upon him, having in his pocket the portable sophistries about the nature of the artist's task. Observation too was a kind of work and experience a kind of success; London dinners were all material and London ladies were fruitful toil.

"No one has the faintest conception of what I'm trying for," he said to me, "and not many have read three pages that I've written; but I must dine with them first—they'll find out why when they've time." It was rather rude justice, perhaps; but the fatigue had the merit of being a new sort, and the phantasmagoric town was probably after all less of a battlefield than the haunted study. He once told me that he had had no personal life to speak of since his fortieth year, but had had more than was good for him before. London closed the parenthesis and exhibited him in relations; one of the most inevitable of these being that in which he found himself to Mrs. Weeks Wimbush, wife of the boundless brewer and proprietress of the universal menagerie. In this establishment, as everybody knows, on occasions when the crush is great, the animals rub shoulders freely with the spectators and the lions sit down for whole evenings with the lambs.

It had been ominously clear to me from the first that in Neil Paraday this lady, who, as all the world agreed, was tremendous fun, considered that she had secured a prime attraction, a creature of almost heraldic oddity. Nothing could exceed her enthusiasm over her capture, and nothing could exceed the confused apprehensions it excited in me. I had an instinctive fear of her which I tried without effect to conceal from her victim, but which I let her perceive with perfect impunity. Paraday heeded it, but she never did, for her conscience was that of a romping child. She was a blind, violent force, to which I could attach no more idea of responsibility than to the creaking of a sign in the wind. It was difficult to say what she conduced to but to circulation. She was constructed of steel and leather, and all I asked of her for our tractable friend was not to do him to death. He had consented for a time to be of india-rubber, but my thoughts were fixed on the day he should resume his shape or at least get back into his box. It was evidently all right, but I should be glad when it was well over. I had a special fear—the impression was ineffaceable of the hour when, after Mr. Morrow's departure, I had found him on the sofa in his study. That pretext of indisposition had not in the least been meant as a snub to the envoy of *The Tatler*—he had gone to lie down in very truth. He had felt a pang of his old pain, the result of the agitation wrought in him by this forcing open of a new period. His old programme, his old ideal even had to be changed. Say what one would, success was a complication and recognition had to be reciprocal. The monastic life, the pious illumination of the missal in the convent cell were things of the gathered past. It didn't engender despair, but it at least required adjustment. Before I left him on that occasion we had passed a bargain, my part of which was that I should make it my business to take care of him. Let whoever would represent the interest in his presence (I had a mystical prevision of Mrs. Weeks Wimbush) I should represent the interest in his work—in other words in his absence. These two interests were in their essence opposed; and I doubt, as youth is fleeting, if I shall ever again know the intensity of joy with which I felt that in so good a cause I was willing to make myself odious.

One day, in Sloane Street, I found myself questioning Paraday's landlord, who had come to the door in answer to my knock. Two vehicles, a barouche and a smart hansom, were drawn up before the house.

"In the drawing-room, sir? Mrs. Weeks Wimbush."

"And in the dining-room?"

"A young lady, sir—waiting: I think a foreigner."

It was three o'clock, and on days when Paraday didn't lunch out he attached a value to these subjugated hours. On which days, however, didn't the dear man lunch out? Mrs. Wimbush, at such a crisis, would have rushed round immediately after her own repast. I went into the dining-room first, postponing the pleasure of seeing how, upstairs, the lady of the barouche would, on my arrival, point the moral of my sweet solicitude. No one took such an interest as herself in his doing only what was good for him, and she was always on the spot to see that he did it. She made appointments with him to discuss the best means of economising his time and protecting his privacy. She further made his health her special business, and had so much sympathy with my own zeal for it that she was the author of pleasing fictions on the subject of what my devotion had led me to give up. I gave up nothing (I don't count Mr. Pinhorn) because I had nothing, and all I had as yet achieved was to find myself also in the menagerie. I had dashed in to save my friend, but I had only got domesticated and wedged; so that

I could do nothing for him but exchange with him over people's heads looks of intense but futile intelligence.

VII

The young lady in the dining-room had a brave face, black hair, blue eyes, and in her lap a big volume. "I've come for his autograph," she said when I had explained to her that I was under bonds to see people for him when he was occupied. "I've been waiting half an hour, but I'm prepared to wait all day." I don't know whether it was this that told me she was American, for the propensity to wait all day is not in general characteristic of her race. I was enlightened probably not so much by the spirit of the utterance as by some quality of its sound. At any rate I saw she had an individual patience and a lovely frock, together with an expression that played among her pretty features like a breeze among flowers. Putting her book upon the table, she showed me a massive album, showily bound and full of autographs of price. The collection of faded notes, of still more faded "thoughts," of quotations, platitudes, signatures, represented a formidable purpose.

"Most people apply to Mr. Paraday by letter, you know," I said.

"Yes, but he doesn't answer. I've written three times."

"Very true," I reflected; "the sort of letter you mean goes straight into the fire."

"How do you know the sort I mean?" My interlocutress had blushed and smiled, and in a moment she added: "I don't believe he gets many like them!"

"I'm sure they're beautiful, but he burns without reading." I didn't add that I had told him he ought to.

"Isn't he then in danger of burning things of importance?"

"He would be, if distinguished men hadn't an infallible nose for nonsense."

She looked at me a moment—her face was sweet and gay. "Do *you* burn without reading, too?" she asked; in answer to which I assured her that if she would trust me with her repository I would see that Mr. Paraday should write his name in it.

She considered a little. "That's very well, but it wouldn't make me see him."

"Do you want very much to see him?" It seemed ungracious to catechise so charming a creature, but somehow I had never yet taken my duty to the great author so seriously.

"Enough to have come from America for the purpose."

I stared. "All alone?"

"I don't see that that's exactly your business; but if it will make me more appealing I'll confess that I'm quite by myself. I had to come alone or not come at all."

She was interesting; I could imagine that she had lost parents, natural protectors—could conceive even that she had inherited money. I was in a phase of my own fortune when keeping hansoms at doors seemed to me pure swagger. As a trick of this bold and sensitive girl, however, it became romantic—a part of the general romance of her freedom, her errand, her innocence. The confidence of young Americans was notorious, and I speedily arrived at a conviction that no impulse could have been more generous than the impulse that had operated here. I foresaw at that moment that it would make her my peculiar charge, just as circumstances had made Neil Paraday. She would be another person to look after, and one's honour would be concerned in guiding her straight. These things became clearer to me later; at the instant I had scepticism enough to observe to her, as I turned the pages of her volume, that her net had, all the same, caught many a big fish. She appeared to have had fruitful access to the great ones of the earth; there were people moreover whose signatures she had presumably secured without a personal interview. She couldn't have worried George Washington and Friedrich Schiller and Hannah More. She met this argument, to my surprise, by throwing up the album without a pang. It wasn't even her own; she was responsible for none of its treasures. It belonged to a girl-friend in America, a young lady in a western city. This young lady had insisted on her bringing it, to pick up more autographs: she thought they might like to see, in Europe, in what company they would be. The "girl-friend," the western city, the immortal names, the curious errand, the idyllic faith, all made a story as strange to me, and as beguiling, as some tale in the Arabian Nights. Thus it was that my informant had encumbered herself with the ponderous tome; but she hastened to assure me that this was the first time she had brought it out. For her visit to Mr. Paraday it had simply been a pretext. She didn't really care a straw that he should write his name; what she did want was to look straight into his face.

I demurred a little. "And why do you require to do that?"

"Because I just love him!" Before I could recover from the agitating effect of this crystal ring my companion had continued: "Hasn't there ever been any face that you've wanted to look into?"

How could I tell her so soon how much I appreciated the opportunity of looking into hers? I could only assent in general to the proposition that there were certainly for every one such hankerings, and even such faces; and I felt that the crisis demanded all my lucidity, all my wisdom. "Oh, yes, I'm a student of physiognomy. Do you mean," I pursued, "that you've a passion for Mr. Paraday's books?"

"They've been everything to me and a little more beside— I know them by heart. They've completely taken hold of me. There's no author about whom I feel as I do about Neil Paraday."

"Permit me to remark then," I presently rejoined, "that you're one of the right sort."

"One of the enthusiasts? Of course I am!"

"Oh, there are enthusiasts who are quite of the wrong. I mean you're one of those to whom an appeal can be made."

"An appeal?" Her face lighted as if with the chance of some great sacrifice.

If she was ready for one it was only waiting for her, and in a moment I mentioned it. "Give up this crude purpose of seeing him. Go away without it. That will be far better."

She looked mystified; then she turned visibly pale. "Why, hasn't he any personal charm?" The girl was terrible and laughable in her bright directness.

"Ah, that dreadful word 'personal!'" I exclaimed; "we're dying of it, and you women bring it out with murderous effect. When you encounter a genius as fine as this idol of ours, let him off the dreary duty of being a personality as well. Know him only by what's best in him, and spare him for the same sweet sake."

My young lady continued to look at me in confusion and mistrust, and the result of her reflection on what I had just said was to make her suddenly break out: "Look here, sir— what's the matter with him?"

"The matter with him is that, if he doesn't look out, people will eat a great hole in his life."

She considered a moment. "He hasn't any disfigurement?"

"Nothing to speak of!"

"Do you mean that social engagements interfere with his occupations?"

"That but feebly expresses it."

"So that he can't give himself up to his beautiful imagination?"

"He's badgered, bothered, overwhelmed, on the pretext of being applauded. People expect him to give them his time, his golden time, who wouldn't themselves give five shillings for one of his books."

"Five? I'd give five thousand!"

"Give your sympathy—give your forbearance. Two-thirds of those who approach him only do it to advertise themselves."

"Why, it's too bad!" the girl exclaimed with the face of an angel. "It's the first time I was ever called crude!" she laughed.

I followed up my advantage. "There's a lady with him now who's a terrible complication, and who yet hasn't read, I am sure, ten pages that he ever wrote."

My visitor's wide eyes grew tenderer. "Then how does she talk——?"

"Without ceasing. I only mention her as a single case. Do you want to know how to show a superlative consideration? Simply avoid him."

"Avoid him?" she softly wailed.

"Don't force him to have to take account of you; admire him in silence, cultivate him at a distance and secretly appropriate his message. Do you want to know," I continued, warming to my idea, "how to perform an act of homage really sublime?" Then as she hung on my words: "Succeed in never seeing him at all!"

"Never at all?" she pathetically gasped.

"The more you get into his writings the less you'll want to; and you'll be immensely sustained by the thought of the good you're doing him."

She looked at me without resentment or spite, and at the truth I had put before her with candour, credulity, pity. I was afterwards happy to remember that she must have recognised in my face the liveliness of my interest in herself. "I think I see what you mean."

"Oh, I express it badly; but I should be delighted if you would let me come to see you—to explain it better."

She made no response to this, and her thoughtful eyes fell on the big album, on which she presently laid her hands as if to take it away. "I did use to say out West that they might write a little less for autographs (to all the great poets, you know) and study the thoughts and style a little more."

"What do they care for the thoughts and style? They didn't even understand you. I'm not sure," I added, "that I do myself, and I daresay that you by no means make me out." She had got up to go, and though I wanted her to succeed in not seeing Neil Paraday I wanted her also, inconsequently, to remain in the house. I was at any rate far from desiring to hustle her off. As Mrs. Weeks Wimbush, upstairs, was still saving our friend in her own way, I asked my young lady to let me briefly relate, in illustration of my point, the little incident of my having gone down into the country for a profane purpose and been converted on the spot to holiness. Sinking again into her chair to listen, she showed a deep interest in the anecdote. Then thinking it over gravely, she exclaimed with her odd intonation:

"Yes, but you do see him!" I had to admit that this was the case; and I was not so prepared with an effective attenuation as I could have wished. She eased the situation off, however, by the charming quaintness with which she finally said: "Well, I wouldn't want him to be lonely!" This time she rose in earnest, but I persuaded her to let me keep the album to show to Mr. Paraday. I assured her I would bring it back to her myself. "Well, you'll find my address somewhere in it, on a paper!" she sighed resignedly, at the door.

VIII

I blush to confess it, but I invited Mr. Paraday that very day
to transcribe into the album one of his most characteristic
passages. I told him how I had got rid of the strange girl who
had brought it—her ominous name was Miss Hurter, and she
lived at an hotel; quite agreeing with him moreover as to the
wisdom of getting rid with equal promptitude of the book
itself. This was why I carried it to Albemarle Street no later
than on the morrow. I failed to find her at home, but she
wrote to me and I went again: she wanted so much to hear
more about Neil Paraday. I returned repeatedly, I may briefly
declare, to supply her with this information. She had been
immensely taken, the more she thought of it, with that idea
of mine about the act of homage: it had ended by filling her
with a generous rapture. She positively desired to do something sublime for him, though indeed I could see that, as this
particular flight was difficult, she appreciated the fact that my
visits kept her up. I had it on my conscience to keep her up;
I neglected nothing that would contribute to it, and her conception of our cherished author's independence became at last
as fine as his own conception. "Read him, read him," I constantly repeated; while, seeking him in his works, she represented herself as convinced that, according to my assurance,
this was the system that had, as she expressed it, weaned her.
We read him together when I could find time, and the generous creature's sacrifice was fed by our conversation. There
were twenty selfish women, about whom I told her, who
stirred her with a beautiful rage. Immediately after my first
visit her sister, Mrs. Milsom, came over from Paris, and the
two ladies began to present, as they called it, their letters. I
thanked our stars that none had been presented to Mr. Paraday. They received invitations and dined out, and some of
these occasions enabled Fanny Hurter to perform, for consistency's sake, touching feats of submission. Nothing indeed
would now have induced her even to look at the object of her
admiration. Once, hearing his name announced at a party, she
instantly left the room by another door and then straightway
quitted the house. At another time, when I was at the opera
with them (Mrs. Milsom had invited me to their box) I at-

tempted to point Mr. Paraday out to her in the stalls. On this she asked her sister to change places with her, and while that lady devoured the great man through a powerful glass, presented, all the rest of the evening, her inspired back to the house. To torment her tenderly I pressed the glass upon her, telling her how wonderfully near it brought our friend's handsome head. By way of answer she simply looked at me in charged silence, letting me see that tears had gathered in her eyes. These tears, I may remark, produced an effect on me of which the end is not yet. There was a moment when I felt it my duty to mention them to Neil Paraday; but I was deterred by the reflection that there were questions more relevant to his happiness.

These questions indeed, by the end of the season, were reduced to a single one—the question of reconstituting, so far as might be possible, the conditions under which he had produced his best work. Such conditions could never all come back, for there was a new one that took up too much place; but some perhaps were not beyond recall. I wanted above all things to see him sit down to the subject of which, on my making his acquaintance, he had read me that admirable sketch. Something told me there was no security but in his doing so before the new factor, as we used to say at Mr. Pinhorn's, should render the problem incalculable. It only half reassured me that the sketch itself was so copious and so eloquent that even at the worst there would be the making of a small but complete book, a tiny volume which, for the faithful, might well become an object of adoration. There would even not be wanting critics to declare, I foresaw, that the plan was a thing to be more thankful for than the structure to have been reared on it. My impatience for the structure, none the less, grew and grew with the interruptions. He had, on coming up to town, begun to sit for his portrait to a young painter, Mr. Rumble, whose little game, as we also used to say at Mr. Pinhorn's, was to be the first to perch on the shoulders of renown. Mr. Rumble's studio was a circus in which the man of the hour, and still more the woman, leaped through the hoops of his showy frames almost as electrically as they burst into telegrams and "specials." He pranced into the exhibitions on their back; he was the reporter on canvas, the

Vandyke up to date, and there was one roaring year in which Mrs. Bounder and Miss Braby, Guy Walsingham and Dora Forbes proclaimed in chorus from the same pictured walls that no one had yet got ahead of him.

Paraday had been promptly caught and saddled, accepting with characteristic good-humour his confidential hint that to figure in his show was not so much a consequence as a cause of immortality. From Mrs. Wimbush to the last "representative" who called to ascertain his twelve favourite dishes, it was the same ingenuous assumption that he would rejoice in the repercussion. There were moments when I fancied I might have had more patience with them if they had not been so fatally benevolent. I hated, at all events, Mr. Rumble's picture, and had my bottled resentment ready when, later on, I found my distracted friend had been stuffed by Mrs. Wimbush into the mouth of another cannon. A young artist in whom she was intensely interested, and who had no connection with Mr. Rumble, was to show how far he could make him go. Poor Paraday, in return, was naturally to write something somewhere about the young artist. She played her victims against each other with admirable ingenuity, and her establishment was a huge machine in which the tiniest and the biggest wheels went round to the same treadle. I had a scene with her in which I tried to express that the function of such a man was to exercise his genius—not to serve as a hoarding for pictorial posters. The people I was perhaps angriest with were the editors of magazines who had introduced what they called new features, so aware were they that the newest feature of all would be to make him grind their axes by contributing his views on vital topics and taking part in the periodical prattle about the future of fiction. I made sure that before I should have done with him there would scarcely be a current form of words left me to be sick of; but meanwhile I could make surer still of my animosity to bustling ladies for whom he drew the water that irrigated their social flower-beds.

I had a battle with Mrs. Wimbush over the artist she protected, and another over the question of a certain week, at the end of July, that Mr. Paraday appeared to have contracted to spend with her in the country. I protested against this visit;

I intimated that he was too unwell for hospitality without a *nuance*, for caresses without imagination; I begged he might rather take the time in some restorative way. A sultry air of promises, of ponderous parties, hung over his August, and he would greatly profit by the interval of rest. He had not told me he was ill again—that he had had a warning; but I had not needed this, and I found his reticence his worst symptom. The only thing he said to me was that he believed a comfortable attack of something or other would set him up: it would put out of the question everything but the exemptions he prized. I am afraid I shall have presented him as a martyr in a very small cause if I fail to explain that he surrendered himself much more liberally than I surrendered him. He filled his lungs, for the most part, with the comedy of his queer fate: the tragedy was in the spectacles through which I chose to look. He was conscious of inconvenience, and above all of a great renouncement; but how could he have heard a mere dirge in the bells of his accession? The sagacity and the jealousy were mine, and his the impressions and the anecdotes. Of course, as regards Mrs. Wimbush, I was worsted in my encounters, for was not the state of his health the very reason for his coming to her at Prestidge? Wasn't it precisely at Prestidge that he was to be coddled, and wasn't the dear Princess coming to help her to coddle him? The dear Princess, now on a visit to England, was of a famous foreign house, and, in her gilded cage, with her retinue of keepers and feeders, was the most expensive specimen in the good lady's collection. I don't think her august presence had had to do with Paraday's consenting to go, but it is not impossible that he had operated as a bait to the illustrious stranger. The party had been made up for him, Mrs. Wimbush averred, and every one was counting on it, the dear Princess most of all. If he was well enough he was to read them something absolutely fresh, and it was on that particular prospect the Princess had set her heart. She was so fond of genius, in *any* walk of life, and she was so used to it, and understood it so well; she was the greatest of Mr. Paraday's admirers, she devoured everything he wrote. And then he read like an angel. Mrs. Wimbush reminded me that he had again and again given her, Mrs. Wimbush, the privilege of listening to him.

it has a peculiarly exhausting effect. Every one is beginning—
at the end of two days—to sidle obsequiously away from her,
and Mrs. Wimbush pushes him again and again into the
breach. None of the uses I have yet seen him put to irritate
me quite so much. He looks very fagged, and has at last confessed to me that his condition makes him uneasy—has even
promised me that he will go straight home instead of returning to his final engagements in town. Last night I had
some talk with him about going to-day, cutting his visit
short; so sure am I that he will be better as soon as he is
shut up in his lighthouse. He told me that this is what he
would like to do; reminding me, however, that the first lesson of his greatness has been precisely that he can't do what
he likes. Mrs. Wimbush would never forgive him if he should
leave her before the Princess has received the last hand.
When I say that a violent rupture with our hostess would be
the best thing in the world for him he gives me to understand that if his reason assents to the proposition his courage
hangs wofully back. He makes no secret of being mortally
afraid of her, and when I ask what harm she can do him that
she hasn't already done he simply repeats: 'I'm afraid, I'm
afraid! Don't inquire too closely,' he said last night; 'only believe that I feel a sort of terror. It's strange, when she's so
kind! At any rate, I would as soon overturn that piece of
priceless Sèvres as tell her that I must go before my date.' It
sounds dreadfully weak, but he has some reason, and he pays
for his imagination, which puts him (I should hate it) in the
place of others and makes him feel, even against himself, their
feelings, their appetites, their motives. It's indeed inveterately
against himself that he makes his imagination act. What a pity
he has such a lot of it! He's too beastly intelligent. Besides,
the famous reading is still to come off, and it has been postponed a day, to allow Guy Walsingham to arrive. It appears
that this eminent lady is staying at a house a few miles off,
which means of course that Mrs. Wimbush has forcibly an-
nexed her. She's to come over in a day or two—Mrs. Wimbush wants her to hear Mr. Paraday.

"To-day's wet and cold, and several of the company, at the
invitation of the Duke, have driven over to luncheon at Bigwood. I saw poor Paraday wedge himself, by command, into

the little supplementary seat of a brougham in which the Princess and our hostess were already ensconced. If the front glass isn't open on his dear old back perhaps he'll survive. Bigwood, I believe, is very grand and frigid, all marble and precedence, and I wish him well out of the adventure. I can't tell you how much more and more *your* attitude to him, in the midst of all this, shines out by contrast. I never willingly talk to these people about him, but see what a comfort I find it to scribble to you! I appreciate it—it keeps me warm; there are no fires in the house. Mrs. Wimbush goes by the calendar, the temperature goes by the weather, the weather goes by God knows what, and the Princess is easily heated. I have nothing but my acrimony to warm me, and have been out under an umbrella to restore my circulation. Coming in an hour ago, I found Lady Augusta Minch rummaging about the hall. When I asked her what she was looking for she said she had mislaid something that Mr. Paraday had lent her. I ascertained in a moment that the article in question is a manuscript, and I have a foreboding that it's the noble morsel he read me six weeks ago. When I expressed my surprise that he should have bandied about anything so precious (I happen to know it's his only copy—in the most beautiful hand in all the world) Lady Augusta confessed to me that she had not had it from himself, but from Mrs. Wimbush, who had wished to give her a glimpse of it as a salve for her not being able to stay and hear it read.

" 'Is that the piece he's to read,' I asked, 'when Guy Walsingham arrives?'

" 'It's not for Guy Walsingham they're waiting now, it's for Dora Forbes,' Lady Augusta said. 'She's coming, I believe, early to-morrow. Meanwhile Mrs. Wimbush has found out about *him*, and is actively wiring to him. She says he also must hear him.'

" 'You bewilder me a little,' I replied; 'in the age we live in one gets lost among the genders and the pronouns. The clear thing is that Mrs. Wimbush doesn't guard such a treasure as jealously as she might.'

" 'Poor dear, she has the Princess to guard! Mr. Paraday lent her the manuscript to look over.'

" 'Did she speak as if it were the morning paper?'

"Lady Augusta stared—my irony was lost upon her. 'She didn't have time, so she gave me a chance first; because unfortunately I go to-morrow to Bigwood.'

"'And your chance has only proved a chance to lose it?'

"'I haven't lost it. I remember now—it was very stupid of me to have forgotten. I told my maid to give it to Lord Dorimont—or at least to his man.'

"'And Lord Dorimont went away directly after luncheon.'

"'Of course he gave it back to my maid—or else his man did,' said Lady Augusta. 'I daresay it's all right.'

"The conscience of these people is like a summer sea. They haven't time to 'look over' a priceless composition; they've only time to kick it about the house. I suggested that the 'man,' fired with a noble emulation, had perhaps kept the work for his own perusal; and her ladyship wanted to know whether, if the thing didn't turn up again in time for the session appointed by our hostess, the author wouldn't have something else to read that would do just as well. Their questions are too delightful! I declared to Lady Augusta briefly that nothing in the world can ever do so well as the thing that does best; and at this she looked a little confused and scared. But I added that if the manuscript had gone astray our little circle would have the less of an effort of attention to make. The piece in question was very long—it would keep them three hours.

"'Three hours! Oh, the Princess will get up!' said Lady Augusta.

"'I thought she was Mr. Paraday's greatest admirer.'

"'I daresay she is—she's so awfully clever. But what's the use of being a Princess——'

"'If you can't dissemble your love?' I asked, as Lady Augusta was vague. She said, at any rate, that she would question her maid; and I am hoping that when I go down to dinner I shall find the manuscript has been recovered."

X

"It has not been recovered," I wrote early the next day, "and I am moreover much troubled about our friend. He came back from Bigwood with a chill and, being allowed to have a fire in his room, lay down awhile before dinner. I tried to send him to bed, and indeed thought I had put him in the way of it; but after I had gone to dress Mrs. Wimbush came up to see him, with the inevitable result that when I returned I found him under arms and flushed and feverish, though decorated with the rare flower she had brought him for his button-hole. He came down to dinner, but Lady Augusta Minch was very shy of him. To-day he's in great pain, and the advent of *ces dames*—I mean of Guy Walsingham and Dora Forbes—doesn't at all console me. It does Mrs. Wimbush however, for she has consented to his remaining in bed, so that he may be all right to-morrow for the listening circle. Guy Walsingham is already on the scene, and the doctor, for Paraday, also arrived early. I haven't yet seen the author of 'Obsessions,' but of course I've had a moment by myself with the doctor. I tried to get him to say that our invalid must go straight home—I mean to-morrow or next day; but he quite refuses to talk about the future. Absolute quiet and warmth and the regular administration of an important remedy are the points he mainly insists on. He returns this afternoon, and I'm to go back to see the patient at one o'clock, when he next takes his medicine. It consoles me a little that he certainly won't be able to read—an exertion he was already more than unfit for. Lady Augusta went off after breakfast, assuring me that her first care would be to follow up the lost manuscript. I can see she thinks me a shocking busybody and doesn't understand my alarm, but she will do what she can, for she's a good-natured woman. 'So are they all honourable men.' That was precisely what made her give the thing to Lord Dorimont and made Lord Dorimont bag it. What use *he* has for it God only knows. I have the worst forebodings, but somehow I'm strangely without passion—desperately calm. As I consider the unconscious, the well-meaning ravages of our appreciative circle I bow my head in submission to some great natural, some universal accident; I'm rendered almost indifferent, in fact quite gay (ha-ha!) by the sense of immitigable fate. Lady Augusta promises me to trace the precious object and let me have it, through the post, by the time Paraday is well enough to play his part with it. The last evidence is that her maid did give it to his lordship's valet. One would think it was some thrilling number of *The Family Budget*. Mrs. Wimbush, who is aware of the accident, is much less agitated by it than she would doubtless be were she not for the hour inevitably engrossed with Guy Walsingham."

Later in the day I informed my correspondent, for whom indeed I kept a sort of diary of the situation, that I had made the acquaintance of this celebrity and that she was a pretty little girl who wore her hair in what used to be called a crop. She looked so juvenile and so innocent that if, as Mr. Morrow had announced, she was resigned to the larger latitude, her superiority to prejudice must have come to her early. I spent most of the day hovering about Neil Paraday's room, but it was communicated to me from below that Guy Walsingham, at Prestidge, was a success. Towards evening I became conscious somehow that her superiority was contagious, and by the time the company separated for the night I was sure that the larger latitude had been generally accepted. I thought of Dora Forbes and felt that he had no time to lose. Before dinner I received a telegram from Lady Augusta Minch. "Lord Dorimont thinks he must have left bundle in train—inquire." How could I inquire—if I was to take the word as command? I was too worried and now too alarmed about Neil Paraday. The doctor came back, and it was an immense satisfaction to me to feel that he was wise and interested. He was proud of being called to so distinguished a patient, but he admitted to me that night that my friend was gravely ill. It was really a relapse, a recrudescence of his old malady. There could be no question of moving him: we must at any rate see first, on the spot, what turn his condition would take. Meanwhile, on the morrow, he was to have a nurse. On the morrow the dear man was easier, and my spirits rose to such cheerfulness that I could almost laugh over Lady Augusta's second telegram: "Lord Dorimont's servant been to station—nothing found. Push inquiries." I did laugh, I am sure, as I remembered this to be the mystic scroll I had scarcely allowed poor Mr. Morrow to point his umbrella at. Fool that I had been: the thirty-seven influential journals wouldn't have destroyed it, they would only have printed it. Of course I said nothing to Paraday.

When the nurse arrived she turned me out of the room, on which I went downstairs. I should premise that at breakfast

the news that our brilliant friend was doing well excited universal complacency, and the Princess graciously remarked that
he was only to be commiserated for missing the society of
Miss Collop. Mrs. Wimbush, whose social gift never shone
brighter than in the dry decorum with which she accepted
this fizzle in her fireworks, mentioned to me that Guy Walsingham had made a very favourable impression on her
Imperial Highness. Indeed I think every one did so, and that,
like the money-market or the national honour, her Imperial
Highness was constitutionally sensitive. There was a certain
gladness, a perceptible bustle in the air, however, which I
thought slightly anomalous in a house where a great author
lay critically ill. *"Le roy est mort—vive le roy:"* I was reminded
that another great author had already stepped into his shoes.
When I came down again after the nurse had taken possession
I found a strange gentleman hanging about the hall and pac-
ing to and fro by the closed door of the drawing-room. This
personage was florid and bald; he had a big red moustache
and wore showy knickerbockers—characteristics all that fitted
into my conception of the identity of Dora Forbes. In a moment I saw what had happened: the author of "The Other
Way Round" had just alighted at the portals of Prestidge, but
had suffered a scruple to restrain him from penetrating further. I recognised his scruple when, pausing to listen at his
gesture of caution, I heard a shrill voice lifted in a sort of
rhythmic, uncanny chant. The famous reading had begun,
only it was the author of "Obsessions" who now furnished
the sacrifice. The new visitor whispered to me that he judged
something was going on that he oughtn't to interrupt.

"Miss Collop arrived last night," I smiled, "and the Princess has a thirst for the *inédit.*"

Dora Forbes lifted his bushy brows. "Miss Collop?"

"Guy Walsingham, your distinguished *confrère*—or shall I
say your formidable rival?"

"Oh!" growled Dora Forbes. Then he added: "Shall I spoil
it if I go in?"

"I should think nothing could spoil it!" I ambiguously
laughed.

Dora Forbes evidently felt the dilemma; he gave an irritated
crook to his moustache. "*Shall* I go in?" he presently asked.

We looked at each other hard a moment; then I expressed something bitter that was in me, expressed it in an infernal "Do!" After this I got out into the air, but not so fast as not to hear, when the door of the drawing-room opened, the disconcerted drop of Miss Collop's public manner: she must have been in the midst of the larger latitude. Producing with extreme rapidity, Guy Walsingham has just published a work in which amiable people who are not initiated have been pained to see the genius of a sister-novelist held up to unmistakable ridicule; so fresh an exhibition does it seem to them of the dreadful way men have always treated women. Dora Forbes, it is true, at the present hour, is immensely pushed by Mrs. Wimbush, and has sat for his portrait to the young artists she protects, sat for it not only in oils but in monumental alabaster.

What happened at Prestidge later in the day is of course contemporary history. If the interruption I had whimsically sanctioned was almost a scandal, what is to be said of that general dispersal of the company which, under the doctor's rule, began to take place in the evening? His rule was soothing to behold, small comfort as I was to have at the end. He decreed in the interest of his patient an absolutely soundless house and a consequent break-up of the party. Little country practitioner as he was, he literally packed off the Princess. She departed as promptly as if a revolution had broken out, and Guy Walsingham emigrated with her. I was kindly permitted to remain, and this was not denied even to Mrs. Wimbush. The privilege was withheld indeed from Dora Forbes; so Mrs. Wimbush kept her latest capture temporarily concealed. This was so little, however, her usual way of dealing with her eminent friends that a couple of days of it exhausted her patience, and she went up to town with him in great publicity. The sudden turn for the worse her afflicted guest had, after a brief improvement, taken on the third night raised an obstacle to her seeing him before her retreat; a fortunate circumstance doubtless, for she was fundamentally disappointed in him. This was not the kind of performance for which she had invited him to Prestidge, or invited the Princess. Let me hasten to add that none of the generous acts which have characterised her patronage of intellectual and other merit have done so much for her reputation as her lending Neil Paraday the most beautiful of her numerous homes to die in. He took advantage to the utmost of the singular favour. Day by day I saw him sink, and I roamed alone about the empty terraces and gardens. His wife never came near him, but I scarcely noticed it: as I paced there with rage in my heart I was too full of another wrong. In the event of his death it would fall to me perhaps to bring out in some charming form, with notes, with the tenderest editorial care, that precious heritage of his written project. But where *was* that precious heritage, and were both the author and the book to have been snatched from us? Lady Augusta wrote me that she had done all she could and that poor Lord Dorimont, who had really been worried to death, was extremely sorry. I couldn't have the matter out with Mrs. Wimbush, for I didn't want to be taunted by her with desiring to aggrandise myself by a public connection with Mr. Paraday's sweepings. She had signified her willingness to meet the expense of all advertising, as indeed she was always ready to do. The last night of the horrible series, the night before he died, I put my ear closer to his pillow.

"That thing I read you that morning, you know."

"In your garden that dreadful day? Yes!"

"Won't it do as it is?"

"It would have been a glorious book."

"It *is* a glorious book," Neil Paraday murmured. "Print it as it stands—beautifully."

"Beautifully!" I passionately promised.

It may be imagined whether, now that he is gone, the promise seems to me less sacred. I am convinced that if such pages had appeared in his lifetime the Abbey would hold him to-day. I have kept the advertising in my own hands, but the manuscript has not been recovered. It's impossible, and at any rate intolerable, to suppose it can have been wantonly destroyed. Perhaps some hazard of a blind hand, some brutal ignorance has lighted kitchen-fires with it. Every stupid and hideous accident haunts my meditations. My undiscourageable search for the lost treasure would make a long chapter. Fortunately I have a devoted associate in the person of a young lady who has every day a fresh indignation and a fresh idea, and who maintains with intensity that the prize will still turn up. Sometimes I believe her, but I have quite ceased to believe myself. The only thing for us, at all events, is to go on seeking and hoping together; and we should be closely united by this firm tie even were we not at present by another.

The Coxon Fund

"THEY'VE got him for life!" I said to myself that evening on my way back to the station; but later, alone in the compartment (from Wimbledon to Waterloo, before the glory of the District Railway) I amended this declaration in the light of the sense that my friends would probably after all not enjoy a monopoly of Mr. Saltram. I won't pretend to have taken his vast measure on that first occasion, but I think I had achieved a glimpse of what the privilege of his acquaintance might mean for many persons in the way of charges accepted. He had been a great experience, and it was this perhaps that had put me into the frame of foreseeing how we should all, sooner or later, have the honour of dealing with him as a whole. Whatever impression I then received of the amount of this total, I had a full enough vision of the patience of the Mulvilles. He was staying with them all the winter: Adelaide dropped it in a tone which drew the sting from the temporary. These excellent people might indeed have been content to give the circle of hospitality a diameter of six months; but if they didn't say that he was staying for the summer as well it was only because this was more than they ventured to hope. I remember that at dinner that evening he wore slippers, new and predominantly purple, of some queer carpet stuff; but the Mulvilles were still in the stage of supposing that he might be snatched from them by higher bidders. At a later time they grew, poor dears, to fear no snatching; but theirs was a fidelity which needed no help from competition to make them proud. Wonderful indeed as, when all was said, you inevitably pronounced Frank Saltram, it was not to be overlooked that the Kent Mulvilles were in their way still more extraordinary: as striking an instance as could easily be encountered of the familiar truth that remarkable men find remarkable conveniences.

They had sent for me from Wimbledon to come out and dine, and there had been an implication in Adelaide's note (judged by her notes alone she might have been thought silly) that it was a case in which something momentous was to be

determined or done. I had never known them not be in a
"state" about somebody, and I daresay I tried to be droll on
this point in accepting their invitation. On finding myself in
the presence of their latest revelation I had not at first felt
irreverence droop—and, thank heaven, I have never been absolutely deprived of that alternative in Mr. Saltram's company.
I saw, however (I hasten to declare it), that compared to this
specimen their other phœnixes had been birds of inconsider-
able feather, and I afterwards took credit to myself for not
having even in primal bewilderments made a mistake about
the essence of the man. He had an incomparable gift; I never
was blind to it—it dazzles me at present. It dazzles me perhaps
even more in remembrance than in fact, for I'm not unaware
that for a subject so magnificent the imagination goes to some
expense, inserting a jewel here and there or giving a twist to
a plume. How the art of portraiture would rejoice in this figure if the art of portraiture had only the canvas! Nature, in
truth, had largely rounded it, and if memory, hovering about
it, sometimes holds her breath, this is because the voice that
comes back was really golden.

Though the great man was an inmate and didn't dress, he
kept dinner on this occasion waiting, and the first words he
uttered on coming into the room were a triumphant announcement to Mulville that he had found out something.
Not catching the allusion and gaping doubtless a little at his
face, I privately asked Adelaide what he had found out. I shall
never forget the look she gave me as she replied: "Everything!" She really believed it. At that moment, at any rate, he
had found out that the mercy of the Mulvilles was infinite.
He had previously of course discovered, as I had myself for
that matter, that their dinners were *soignés*. Let me not indeed,
in saying this, neglect to declare that I shall falsify my coun-
terfeit if I seem to hint that there was in his nature any ounce
of calculation. He took whatever came, but he never plotted
for it, and no man who was so much of an absorbent can ever
have been so little of a parasite. He had a system of the universe, but he had no system of sponging—that was quite
hand-to-mouth. He had fine, gross, easy senses, but it was not
his good-natured appetite that wrought confusion. If he had
loved us for our dinners we could have paid with our dinners,

and it would have been a great economy of finer matter. I make free in these connections with the plural possessive because if I was never able to do what the Mulvilles did, and people with still bigger houses and simpler charities, I met, first and last, every demand of reflection, of emotion—particularly perhaps those of gratitude and of resentment. No one, I think, paid the tribute of giving him up so often, and if it's rendering honour to borrow wisdom I have a right to talk of my sacrifices. He yielded lessons as the sea yields fish—I lived for a while on this diet. Sometimes it almost appeared to me that his massive, monstrous failure—if failure after all it was— had been intended for my private recreation. He fairly pampered my curiosity; but the history of that experience would take me too far. This is not the large canvas I just now spoke of, and I would not have approached him with my present hand had it been a question of all the features. Frank Saltram's features, for artistic purposes, are verily the anecdotes that are to be gathered. Their name is legion, and this is only one, of which the interest is that it concerns even more closely several other persons. Such episodes, as one looks back, are the little dramas that made up the innumerable facets of the big drama—which is yet to be reported.

II

It is furthermore remarkable that though the two stories are distinct—my own, as it were, and this other—they equally began, in a manner, the first night of my acquaintance with Frank Saltram, the night I came back from Wimbledon so agitated with a new sense of life that, in London, for the very thrill of it, I could only walk home. Walking and swinging my stick, I overtook, at Buckingham Gate, George Gravener, and George Gravener's story may be said to have begun with my making him, as our paths lay together, come home with me for a talk. I duly remember, let me parenthesise, that it was still more that of another person, and also that several years were to elapse before it was to extend to a second chapter. I had much to say to him, none the less, about my visit to the Mulvilles, whom he more indifferently knew, and I was at any rate so amusing that for long afterwards he never encountered

me without asking for news of the old man of the sea. I hadn't
said Mr. Saltram was old, and it was to be seen that he was
of an age to outweather George Gravener. I had at that time
a lodging in Ebury Street, and Gravener was staying at his
brother's empty house in Eaton Square. At Cambridge, five
years before, even in our devastating set, his intellectual power
had seemed to me almost awful. Some one had once asked
me privately, with blanched cheeks, what it was then that after
all such a mind as that left standing. "It leaves itself!" I could
recollect devoutly replying. I could smile at present at this
reminiscence, for even before we got to Ebury Street I was
struck with the fact that, save in the sense of being well set
up on his legs, George Gravener had actually ceased to tower.
The universe he laid low had somehow bloomed again—the
usual eminences were visible. I wondered whether he had lost
his humour, or only, dreadful thought, had never had any—
not even when I had fancied him most Aristophanesque. What
was the need of appealing to laughter, however, I could enviously inquire, where you might appeal so confidently to
measurement? Mr. Saltram's queer figure, his thick nose and
hanging lip, were fresh to me: in the light of my old friend's
fine cold symmetry they presented mere success in amusing
as the refuge of conscious ugliness. Already, at hungry twenty-
six, Gravener looked as blank and parliamentary as if he were
fifty and popular. In my scrap of a residence (he had a world-
ling's eye for its futile conveniencies, but never a comrade's
joke) I sounded Frank Saltram in his ears; a circumstance I
mention in order to note that even then I was surprised at his
impatience of my enlivenment. As he had never before heard
of the personage, it took indeed the form of impatience of
the preposterous Mulvilles, his relation to whom, like mine,
had had its origin in an early, a childish intimacy with the
young Adelaide, the fruit of multiplied ties in the previous
generation. When she married Kent Mulville, who was older
than Gravener and I and much more amiable, I gained a
friend, but Gravener practically lost one. We were affected in
different ways by the form taken by what he called their deplorable social action—the form (the term was also his) of
nasty second-rate gush. I may have held in my *for intérieur*
that the good people at Wimbledon were beautiful fools, but

when he sniffed at them I couldn't help taking the opposite line, for I already felt that even should we happen to agree it would always be for reasons that differed. It came home to me that he was admirably British as, without so much as a sociable sneer at my bookbinder, he turned away from the serried rows of my little French library.

"Of course I've never seen the fellow, but it's clear enough he's a humbug."

"Clear 'enough' is just what it isn't," I replied; "if it only were!" That ejaculation on my part must have been the beginning of what was to be later a long ache for final frivolous rest. Gravener was profound enough to remark after a moment that in the first place he couldn't be anything but a Dissenter, and when I answered that the very note of his fascination was his extraordinary speculative breadth, my friend retorted that there was no cad like your cultivated cad and that I might depend upon discovering (since I had had the levity not already to have inquired) that my shining light proceeded, a generation back, from a Methodist cheesemonger. I confess I was struck with his insistence, and I said, after reflection: "It may be—I admit it may be; but why on earth are you so sure?"—asking the question mainly to lay him the trap of saying that it was because the poor man didn't dress for dinner. He took an instant to circumvent my trap and come blandly out the other side.

"Because the Kent Mulvilles have invented him. They've an infallible hand for frauds. All their geese are swans. They were born to be duped, they like it, they cry for it, they don't know anything from anything, and they disgust one (luckily perhaps!) with Christian charity." His vehemence was doubtless an accident, but it might have been a strange foreknowledge. I forget what protest I dropped; it was at any rate something which led him to go on after a moment: "I only ask one thing—it's perfectly simple. Is a man, in a given case, a real gentleman?"

"A real gentleman, my dear fellow—that's so soon said!"

"Not so soon when he isn't! If they've got hold of one this time he must be a great rascal!"

"I might feel injured," I answered, "if I didn't reflect that they don't rave about *me*."

"Don't be too sure! I'll grant that he's a gentleman," Gravener presently added, "if you'll admit that he's a scamp."

"I don't know which to admire most, your logic or your benevolence."

My friend coloured at this, but he didn't change the subject. "Where did they pick him up?"

"I think they were struck with something he had published."

"I can fancy the dreary thing!"

"I believe they found out he had all sorts of worries and difficulties."

"That, of course, was not to be endured, and they jumped at the privilege of paying his debts!" I replied that I knew nothing about his debts, and I reminded my visitor that though the dear Mulvilles were angels they were neither idiots nor millionaires. What they mainly aimed at was re-uniting Mr. Saltram to his wife. "I was expecting to hear that he has basely abandoned her," Gravener went on, at this, "and I'm too glad you don't disappoint me."

I tried to recall exactly what Mrs. Mulville had told me. "He didn't leave her—no. It's she who has left him."

"Left him to *us*?" Gravener asked. "The monster—many thanks! I decline to take him."

"You'll hear more about him in spite of yourself. I can't, no, I really can't resist the impression that he's a big man." I was already learning—to my shame perhaps be it said—just the tone that my old friend least liked.

"It's doubtless only a trifle," he returned, "but you haven't happened to mention what his reputation's to rest on."

"Why, on what I began by boring you with—his extraordinary mind."

"As exhibited in his writings?"

"Possibly in his writings, but certainly in his talk, which is far and away the richest I ever listened to."

"And what is it all about?"

"My dear fellow, don't ask me! About everything!" I pursued, reminding myself of poor Adelaide. "About his ideas of things," I then more charitably added. "You must have heard him to know what I mean—it's unlike anything that ever *was* heard." I coloured, I admit, I overcharged a little, for such a picture was an anticipation of Saltram's later development and still more of my fuller acquaintance with him. However, I really expressed, a little lyrically perhaps, my actual imagination of him when I proceeded to declare that, in a cloud of tradition, of legend, he might very well go down to posterity as the greatest of all great talkers. Before we parted George Gravener demanded why such a row should be made about a chatterbox the more and why he should be pampered and pensioned. The greater the wind-bag the greater the calamity. Out of proportion to everything else on earth had come to be this wagging of the tongue. We were drenched with talk— our wretched age was dying of it. I differed from him here sincerely, only going so far as to concede, and gladly, that we were drenched with sound. It was not however the mere speakers who were killing us—it was the mere stammerers. Fine talk was as rare as it was refreshing—the gift of the gods themselves, the one starry spangle on the ragged cloak of humanity. How many men were there who rose to this privilege, of how many masters of conversation could he boast the acquaintance? Dying of talk?—why, we were dying of the lack of it! Bad writing wasn't talk, as many people seemed to think, and even good wasn't always to be compared to it. From the best talk indeed the best writing had something to learn. I fancifully added that we too should peradventure be gilded by the legend, should be pointed at for having listened, for having actually heard. Gravener, who had glanced at his watch and discovered it was midnight, found to all this a response beautifully characteristic of him.

"There is one little fact to be borne in mind in the presence equally of the best talk and of the worst." He looked, in saying this, as if he meant so much that I thought he could only mean once more that neither of them mattered if a man wasn't a real gentleman. Perhaps it was what he did mean; he deprived me however of the exultation of being right by putting the truth in a slightly different way. "The only thing that really counts for one's estimate of a person is his conduct." He had his watch still in his hand, and I reproached him with unfair play in having ascertained beforehand that it was now the hour at which I always gave in. My pleasantry so far failed to mollify him that he promptly added that to the rule he had just enunciated there was absolutely no exception.

"None whatever?"

"None whatever."

"Trust me then to try to be good at any price!" I laughed as I went with him to the door. "I declare I will be, if I have to be horrible!"

III

If that first night was one of the liveliest, or at any rate was the freshest, of my exaltations, there was another, four years later, that was one of my great discomposures. Repetition, I well knew by this time, was the secret of Saltram's power to alienate, and of course one would never have seen him at his finest if one hadn't seen him in his remorses. They set in mainly at this season and were magnificent, orchestral. I was perfectly aware that something of the sort was now due; but none the less, in our arduous attempt to set him on his feet as a lecturer, it was impossible not to feel that two failures were a large order, as we said, for a short course of five. This was the second time, and it was past nine o'clock; the audience, a muster unprecedented and really encouraging, had fortunately the attitude of blandness that might have been looked for in persons whom the promise (if I am not mistaken) of an Analysis of Primary Ideas had drawn to the neighbourhood of Upper Baker Street. There was in those days in that region a petty lecture-hall to be secured on terms as moderate as the funds left at our disposal by the irrepressible question of the maintenance of five small Saltrams (I include the mother) and one large one. By the time the Saltrams, of different sizes, were all maintained, we had pretty well poured out the oil that might have lubricated the machinery for enabling the most original of men to appear to maintain them.

It was I, the other time, who had been forced into the breach, standing up there for an odious lamplit moment to explain to half a dozen thin benches, where the earnest brows were virtuously void of anything so cynical as a suspicion, that we couldn't put so much as a finger on Mr. Saltram. There

was nothing to plead but that our scouts had been out from
the early hours and that we were afraid that on one of his
walks abroad—he took one, for meditation, whenever he was
to address such a company—some accident had disabled or
delayed him. The meditative walks were a fiction, for he never,
that any one could discover, prepared anything but a magnificent prospectus; so that his circulars and programmes, of
which I possess an almost complete collection, are the solemn
ghosts of generations never born. I put the case, as it seemed
to me, at the best; but I admit I had been angry, and Kent
Mulville was shocked at my want of public optimism. This
time therefore I left the excuses to his more practised patience,
only relieving myself in response to a direct appeal from a
young lady next whom, in the hall, I found myself sitting. My
position was an accident, but if it had been calculated the
reason would scarcely have eluded an observer of the fact that
no one else in the room had an approach to an appearance.
Our philosopher's "tail" was deplorably limp. This visitor was
the only person who looked at her ease, who had come a little
in the spirit of adventure. She seemed to carry amusement in
her handsome young head, and her presence quite gave me
the sense of a sudden extension of Saltram's sphere of influence. He was doing better than we hoped, and he had chosen
such an occasion, of all occasions, to succumb to heaven knew
which of his infirmities. The young lady produced an impression of auburn hair and black velvet, and had on her other
hand a companion of obscurer type, presumably a waiting-
maid. She herself might perhaps have been a foreign countess,
and before she spoke to me I had beguiled our sorry interval
by thinking that she brought vaguely back the first page of
some novel of Madame Sand. It didn't make her more fath-
omable to perceive in a few minutes that she could only be
an American; it simply engendered depressing reflections as
to the possible check to contributions from Boston. She asked
me if, as a person apparently more initiated, I would recommend further waiting, and I replied that if she considered I
was on my honour I would privately deprecate it. Perhaps she
didn't; at any rate something passed between us that led us
to talk until she became aware that we were almost the only
people left. I presently discovered that she knew Mrs. Saltram,

and this explained in a manner the miracle. The brotherhood
of the friends of the husband was as nothing to the brotherhood, or perhaps I should say the sisterhood, of the friends
of the wife. Like the Kent Mulvilles I belonged to both fra-
ternities, and even better than they I think I had sounded the
abyss of Mrs. Saltram's wrongs. She bored me to extinction,
and I knew but too well how she had bored her husband; but
she had those who stood by her, the most efficient of whom
were indeed the handful of poor Saltram's backers. They did
her liberal justice, whereas her mere patrons and partisans had
nothing but hatred for our philosopher. I am bound to say it
was we, however—we of both camps, as it were—who had
always done most for her.

I thought my young lady looked rich—I scarcely knew why;
and I hoped she had put her hand in her pocket. But I soon
discovered that she was not a fine fanatic—she was only a
generous, irresponsible inquirer. She had come to England to
see her aunt, and it was at her aunt's she had met the dreary
lady we had all so much on our mind. I saw she would help
to pass the time when she observed that it was a pity this lady
wasn't intrinsically more interesting. That was refreshing, for
it was an article of faith in Mrs. Saltram's circle—at least
among those who scorned to know her horrid husband—that
she was attractive on her merits. She was really a very common
person, as Saltram himself would have been if he hadn't been
a prodigy. The question of vulgarity had no application to
him, but it was a measure that his wife kept challenging you
to apply. I hasten to add that the consequences of your doing
so were no sufficient reason for his having left her to starve.
"He doesn't seem to have much force of character," said my
young lady; at which I laughed out so loud that my departing
friends looked back at me over their shoulders as if I were
making a joke of their discomfiture. My joke probably cost
Saltram a subscription or two, but it helped me on with my
interlocutress. "She says he drinks like a fish," she sociably
continued, "and yet she admits that his mind is wonderfully
clear." It was amusing to converse with a pretty girl who could
talk of the clearness of Saltram's mind. I expected her next to
say that she had been assured he was awfully clever. I tried to
tell her—I had it almost on my conscience—what was the

proper way to regard him; an effort attended perhaps more than ever on this occasion with the usual effect of my feeling that I wasn't after all very sure of it. She had come to-night out of high curiosity—she had wanted to find out this proper way for herself. She had read some of his papers and hadn't understood them; but it was at home, at her aunt's, that her curiosity had been kindled—kindled mainly by his wife's remarkable stories of his want of virtue. "I suppose they ought to have kept me away," my companion dropped, "and I suppose they would have done so if I hadn't somehow got an idea that he's fascinating. In fact Mrs. Saltram herself says he is."

"So you came to see where the fascination resides? Well, you've seen!"

My young lady raised her fine eyebrows. "Do you mean in his bad faith?"

"In the extraordinary effects of it; his possession, that is, of some quality or other that condemns us in advance to forgive him the humiliation, as I may call it, to which he has subjected us."

"The humiliation?"

"Why mine, for instance, as one of his guarantors, before you as the purchaser of a ticket."

"You don't look humiliated a bit, and if you did I should let you off, disappointed as I am; for the mysterious quality you speak of is just the quality I came to see."

"Oh, you can't 'see' it!" I exclaimed.

"How then do you get at it?"

"You don't! You mustn't suppose he's good-looking," I added.

"Why, his wife says he's lovely!"

My hilarity may have struck my interlocutress as excessive, but I confess it broke out afresh. Had she acted only in obedience to this singular plea, so characteristic, on Mrs. Saltram's part, of what was irritating in the narrowness of that lady's point of view? "Mrs. Saltram," I explained, "undervalues him where he is strongest, so that, to make up for it perhaps, she overpraises him where he's weak. He's not, assuredly, superficially attractive; he's middle-aged, fat, featureless save for his great eyes."

"Yes, his great eyes," said my young lady attentively. She had evidently heard all about his great eyes—the *beaux yeux* for which alone we had really done it all.

"They're tragic and splendid—lights on a dangerous coast. But he moves badly and dresses worse, and altogether he's anything but smart."

My companion appeared to reflect on this, and after a moment she inquired: "Do you call him a real gentleman?"

I started slightly at the question, for I had a sense of recognising it: George Gravener, years before, that first flushed night, had put me face to face with it. It had embarrassed me then, but it didn't embarrass me now, for I had lived with it and overcome it and disposed of it. "A real gentleman? Emphatically not!"

My promptitude surprised her a little, but I quickly felt that it was not to Gravener I was now talking. "Do you say that because he's—what do you call it in England?—of humble extraction?"

"Not a bit. His father was a country schoolmaster and his mother the widow of a sexton, but that has nothing to do with it. I say it simply because I know him well."

"But isn't it an awful drawback?"

"Awful—quite awful."

"I mean isn't it positively fatal?"

"Fatal to what? Not to his magnificent vitality."

Again there was a meditative moment. "And is his magnificent vitality the cause of his vices?"

"Your questions are formidable, but I'm glad you put them. I was thinking of his noble intellect. His vices, as you say, have been much exaggerated: they consist mainly after all in one comprehensive defect."

"A want of will?"

"A want of dignity."

"He doesn't recognise his obligations?"

"On the contrary, he recognises them with effusion, especially in public: he smiles and bows and beckons across the street to them. But when they pass over he turns away, and he speedily loses them in the crowd. The recognition is purely spiritual—it isn't in the least social. So he leaves all his belongings to other people to take care of. He accepts favours, loans, sacrifices, with nothing more deterrent than an agony of shame. Fortunately we're a little faithful band, and we do what we can." I held my tongue about the natural children, engendered, to the number of three, in the wantonness of his youth. I only remarked that he did make efforts—often tremendous ones. "But the efforts," I said, "never come to much: the only things that come to much are the abandonments, the surrenders."

"And how much do they come to?"

"You're right to put it as if we had a big bill to pay, but, as I've told you before, your questions are rather terrible. They come, these mere exercises of genius, to a great sum total of poetry, of philosophy, a mighty mass of speculation, of notation. The genius is there, you see, to meet the surrender; but there's no genius to support the defence."

"But what is there, after all, at his age, to show?"

"In the way of achievement recognised and reputation established?" I interrupted. "To 'show' if you will, there isn't much, for his writing, mostly, isn't as fine, isn't certainly as showy, as his talk. Moreover two-thirds of his work are merely colossal projects and announcements. 'Showing' Frank Saltram is often a poor business: we endeavoured, you will have observed, to show him to-night! However, if he *had* lectured, he would have lectured divinely. It would just have been his talk."

"And what would his talk just have been?"

I was conscious of some ineffectiveness as well perhaps as of a little impatience as I replied: "The exhibition of a splendid intellect." My young lady looked not quite satisfied at this, but as I was not prepared for another question I hastily pursued: "The sight of a great suspended, swinging crystal, huge, lucid, lustrous, a block of light, flashing back every impression of life and every possibility of thought!" This gave her something to think about till we had passed out to the dusky porch of the hall, in front of which the lamps of a quiet brougham were almost the only thing Saltram's treachery hadn't extinguished. I went with her to the door of her carriage, out of which she leaned a moment after she had thanked me and taken her seat. Her smile even in the darkness was pretty. "I do want to see that crystal!"

"You've only to come to the next lecture."

"I go abroad in a day or two with my aunt."

"Wait over till next week," I suggested. "It's quite worth it."

She became grave. "Not unless he really comes!" At which the brougham started off, carrying her away too fast, fortunately for my manners, to allow me to exclaim "Ingratitude!"

                              IV

Mrs. Saltram made a great affair of her right to be informed where her husband had been the second evening he failed to meet his audience. She came to me to ascertain, but I couldn't satisfy her, for in spite of my ingenuity I remained in ignorance. It was not till much later that I found this had not been the case with Kent Mulville, whose hope for the best never twirled his thumbs more placidly than when he happened to know the worst. He had known it on the occasion I speak of—that is immediately after. He was impenetrable then, but he ultimately confessed. What he confessed was more than I shall venture to confess to-day. It was of course familiar to me that Saltram was incapable of keeping the engagements which, after their separation, he had entered into with regard to his wife, a deeply wronged, justly resentful, quite irreproachable and insufferable person. She often appeared at my chambers to talk over his lapses, for if, as she declared, she had washed her hands of him, she had carefully preserved the water of this ablution and she handed it about for inspection. She had arts of her own of exciting one's impatience, the most infallible of which was perhaps her assumption that we were kind to her because we liked her. In reality her personal fall had been a sort of social rise, for there had been a moment when, in our little conscientious circle, her desolation almost made her the fashion. Her voice was grating and her children ugly; moreover she hated the good Mulvilles, whom I more and more loved. They were the people who by doing most for her husband had in the long run done most for herself; and the warm confidence with which he had laid his length upon them was a pressure gentle compared with her stiffer persuadability. I am bound to say he didn't criticise his benefactors, though practically he got tired of them; she, however, had the highest standards about eleemosynary forms. She offered the odd spectacle of a spirit puffed up by dependence, and indeed it had introduced her to some excellent society. She pitied me for not knowing certain people who aided her and whom she doubtless patronised in turn for their luck in not knowing me. I daresay I should have got on with her better if she had had a ray of imagination—if it had occasionally seemed to occur to her to regard Saltram's manifestations in any other manner than as separate subjects of woe. They were all flowers of his nature, pearls strung on an endless thread; but she had a stubborn little way of challenging them one after the other, as if she never suspected that he *had* a nature, such as it was, or that deficiencies might be organic; the irritating effect of a mind incapable of a generalisation. One might doubtless have overdone the idea that there was a general exemption for such a man; but if this had happened it would have been through one's feeling that there could be none for such a woman.

I recognised her superiority when I asked her about the aunt of the disappointed young lady: it sounded like a sentence from a phrase-book. She triumphed in what she told me and she may have triumphed still more in what she withheld. My friend of the other evening, Miss Anvoy, had but lately come to England; Lady Coxon, the aunt, had been established here for years in consequence of her marriage with the late Sir Gregory of that ilk. She had a house in the Regent's Park, a Bath-chair and a fernery; and above all she had sympathy. Mrs. Saltram had made her acquaintance through mutual friends. This vagueness caused me to feel how much I was out of it and how large an independent circle Mrs. Saltram had at her command. I should have been glad to know more about the disappointed young lady, but I felt that I should know most by not depriving her of her advantage, as she might have mysterious means of depriving me of my knowledge. For the present, moreover, this experience was arrested, Lady Coxon having in fact gone abroad, accompanied by her niece. The niece, besides being immensely clever, was an heiress, Mrs. Saltram said; the only daughter and the light of the eyes of some great American merchant, a man, over there, of endless indulgences and dollars. She had pretty clothes and pretty

manners, and she had, what was prettier still, the great thing
of all. The great thing of all for Mrs. Saltram was always sympathy, and she spoke as if during the absence of these ladies
she might not know where to turn for it. A few months later
indeed, when they had come back, her tone perceptibly
changed: she alluded to them, on my leading her up to it,
rather as to persons in her debt for favours received. What had
happened I didn't know, but I saw it would take only a little
more or a little less to make her speak of them as thankless
subjects of social countenance—people for whom she had
vainly tried to do something. I confess I saw that it would not
be in a mere week or two that I should rid myself of the image
of Ruth Anvoy, in whose very name, when I learnt it, I found
something secretly to like. I should probably neither see her
nor hear of her again: the knight's widow (he had been mayor
of Clockborough) would pass away and the heiress would return to her inheritance. I gathered with surprise that she had
not communicated to his wife the story of her attempt to hear
Mr. Saltram, and I founded this reticence on the easy supposition that Mrs. Saltram had fatigued by over-pressure the
spring of the sympathy of which she boasted. The girl at any
rate would forget the small adventure, be distracted, take a
husband; besides which she would lack opportunity to repeat
her experiment.

We clung to the idea of the brilliant course, delivered without an accident, that, as a lecturer, would still make the paying
public aware of our great mind; but the fact remained that in
the case of an inspiration so unequal there was treachery, there
was fallacy at least, in the very conception of a series. In our
scrutiny of ways and means we were inevitably subject to the
old convention of the synopsis, the syllabus, partly of course
not to lose the advantage of his grand free hand in drawing
up such things; but for myself I laughed at our playbills even
while I stickled for them. It was indeed amusing work to be
scrupulous for Frank Saltram, who also at moments laughed
about it, so far as the comfort of a sigh so unstudied as to be
cheerful might pass for such a sound. He admitted with a
candour all his own that he was in truth only to be depended
on in the Mulvilles' drawing-room. "Yes," he suggestively
conceded, "it's there, I think, that I am at my best; quite late,

when it gets toward eleven—and if I've not been too much worried." We all knew what too much worry meant; it meant too enslaved for the hour to the superstition of sobriety. On the Saturdays I used to bring my portmanteau, so as not to have to think of eleven o'clock trains. I had a bold theory that as regards this temple of talk and its altars of cushioned chintz, its pictures and its flowers, its large fireside and clear lamp-light, we might really arrive at something if the Mulvilles would only charge for admission. But here it was that the Mulvilles shamelessly broke down; as there is a flaw in every perfection, this was the inexpugnable refuge of their egotism. They declined to make their saloon a market, so that Saltram's golden words continued to be the only coin that rang there. It can have happened to no man, however, to be paid a greater price than such an enchanted hush as surrounded him on his greatest nights. The most profane, on these occasions, felt a presence; all minor eloquence grew dumb. Adelaide Mulville, for the pride of her hospitality, anxiously watched the door or stealthily poked the fire. I used to call it the music-room, for we had anticipated Bayreuth. The very gates of the kingdom of light seemed to open and the horizon of thought to flash with the beauty of a sunrise at sea.

In the consideration of ways and means, the sittings of our little board, we were always conscious of the creak of Mrs. Saltram's shoes. She hovered, she interrupted, she almost pre-sided, the state of affairs being mostly such as to supply her with every incentive for inquiring what was to be done next. It was the pressing pursuit of this knowledge that, in concat-enations of omnibuses and usually in very wet weather, led her so often to my door. She thought us spiritless creatures with editors and publishers; but she carried matters to no great effect when she personally pushed into back-shops. She wanted all moneys to be paid to herself; they were otherwise liable to such strange adventures. They trickled away into the desert, and they were mainly at best, alas, but a slender stream. The editors and the publishers were the last people to take this remarkable thinker at the valuation that has now pretty well come to be established. The former were half distraught between the desire to "cut" him and the difficulty of finding a crevice for their shears; and when a volume on this or that

portentous subject was proposed to the latter they suggested
alternative titles which, as reported to our friend, brought into
his face the noble blank melancholy that sometimes made it
handsome. The title of an unwritten book didn't after all
much matter, but some masterpiece of Saltram's may have
died in his bosom of the shudder with which it was then convulsed. The ideal solution, failing the fee at Kent Mulville's
door, would have been some system of subscription to projected treatises with their non-appearance provided for—
provided for, I mean, by the indulgence of subscribers. The
author's real misfortune was that subscribers were so wretchedly literal. When they tastelessly inquired why publication
had not ensued I was tempted to ask who in the world had
ever been so published. Nature herself had brought him out
in voluminous form, and the money was simply a deposit on
borrowing the work.

                                V

I was doubtless often a nuisance to my friends in those years;
but there were sacrifices I declined to make, and I never
passed the hat to George Gravener. I never forgot our little
discussion in Ebury Street, and I think it stuck in my throat
to have to make to him the admission I had made so easily
to Miss Anvoy. It had cost me nothing to confide to this
charming girl, but it would have cost me much to confide to
the friend of my youth, that the character of the "real gentleman" was not an attribute of the man I took such pains for.
Was this because I had already generalised to the point of
perceiving that women are really the unfastidious sex? I knew
at any rate that Gravener, already quite in view but still hungry
and frugal, had naturally enough more ambition than charity.
He had sharp aims for stray sovereigns, being in view most
from the tall steeple of Clockborough. His immediate ambition was to wholly occupy the field of vision of that smokily-
seeing city, and all his movements and postures were
calculated for this angle. The movement of the hand to the
pocket had thus to alternate gracefully with the posture of the
hand on the heart. He talked to Clockborough in short only
less beguilingly than Frank Saltram talked to his electors; with

the difference in our favour, however, that we had already voted and that our candidate had no antagonist but himself. He had more than once been at Wimbledon—it was Mrs. Mulville's work, not mine—and, by the time the claret was served, had seen the god descend. He took more pains to swing his censer than I had expected, but on our way back to town he forestalled any little triumph I might have been so artless as to express by the observation that such a man was— a hundred times!—a man to use and never a man to be used by. I remember that this neat remark humiliated me almost as much as if virtually, in the fever of broken slumbers, I hadn't often made it myself. The difference was that on Gravener's part a force attached to it that could never attach to it on mine. He was able to use people—he had the machinery; and the irony of Saltram's being made showy at Clockborough came out to me when he said, as if he had no memory of our original talk and the idea were quite fresh to him: "I hate his type, you know, but I'll be hanged if I don't put some of those things in. I can find a place for them: we might even find a place for the fellow himself." I myself should have had some fear, not, I need scarcely say, for the "things" themselves, but for some other things very near them—in fine for the rest of my eloquence.

Later on I could see that the oracle of Wimbledon was not in this case so appropriate as he would have been had the politics of the gods only coincided more exactly with those of the party. There was a distinct moment when, without saying anything more definite to me, Gravener entertained the idea of annexing Mr. Saltram. Such a project was delusive, for the discovery of analogies between his body of doctrine and that pressed from headquarters upon Clockborough—the bottling, in a word, of the air of those lungs for convenient public uncorking in corn-exchanges—was an experiment for which no one had the leisure. The only thing would have been to carry him massively about, paid, caged, clipped; to turn him on for a particular occasion in a particular channel. Frank Saltram's channel, however, was essentially not calculable, and there was no knowing what disastrous floods might have ensued. For what there would have been to do *The Empire*, the great newspaper, was there to look to; but it was no new misfortune that there were delicate situations in which *The Empire* broke down. In fine there was an instinctive apprehension that a clever young journalist commissioned to report upon Mr. Saltram might never come back from the errand. No one knew better than George Gravener that that was a time when prompt returns counted double. If he therefore found our friend an exasperating waste of orthodoxy it was because he was, as he said, up in the clouds, not because he was down in the dust. He would have been a real enough gentleman if he could have helped to put in a real gentleman. Gravener's great objection to the actual member was that he was not one.

Lady Coxon had a fine old house, a house with "grounds," at Clockborough, which she had let; but after she returned from abroad I learned from Mrs. Saltram that the lease had fallen in and that she had gone down to resume possession. I could see the faded red livery, the big square shoulders, the high-walled garden of this decent abode. As the rumble of dissolution grew louder the suitor would have pressed his suit, and I found myself hoping that the politics of the late Mayor's widow would not be such as to enjoin upon her to ask him to dinner; perhaps indeed I went so far as to hope that they would be such as to put all countenance out of the question. I tried to focus the page, in the daily airing, as he perhaps even pushed the Bath-chair over somebody's toes. I was destined to hear, however, through Mrs. Saltram (who, I afterwards learned, was in correspondence with Lady Coxon's housekeeper) that Gravener was known to have spoken of the habitation I had in my eye as the pleasantest thing at Clockborough. On his part, I was sure, this was the voice not of envy but of experience. The vivid scene was now peopled, and I could see him in the old-time garden with Miss Anvoy, who would be certain, and very justly, to think him good-looking. It would be too much to say that I was troubled by this evocation; but I seem to remember the relief, singular enough, of feeling it suddenly brushed away by an annoyance really much greater; an annoyance the result of its happening to come over me about that time with a rush that I was simply ashamed of Frank Saltram. There were limits after all, and my mark at last had been reached.

I had had my disgusts, if I may allow myself to-day such an expression; but this was a supreme revolt. Certain things cleared up in my mind, certain values stood out. It was all very well to have an unfortunate temperament; there was nothing so unfortunate as to have, for practical purposes, nothing else. I avoided George Gravener at this moment and reflected that at such a time I should do so most effectually by leaving England. I wanted to forget Frank Saltram—that was all. I didn't want to do anything in the world to him but that. Indignation had withered on the stalk, and I felt that one could pity him as much as one ought only by never thinking of him again. It wasn't for anything he had done to me; it was for something he had done to the Mulvilles. Adelaide cried about it for a week, and her husband, profiting by the example so signally given him of the fatal effect of a want of character, left the letter unanswered. The letter, an incredible one, addressed by Saltram to Wimbledon during a stay with the Pudneys at Ramsgate, was the central feature of the incident, which, however, had many features, each more painful than whichever other we compared it with. The Pudneys had behaved shockingly, but that was no excuse. Base ingratitude, gross indecency—one had one's choice only of such formulas as that the more they fitted the less they gave one rest. These are dead aches now, and I am under no obligation, thank heaven, to be definite about the business. There are things which if I had had to tell them—well, I wouldn't have told my story.

I went abroad for the general election, and if I don't know how much, on the Continent, I forgot, I at least know how much I missed him. At a distance, in a foreign land, ignoring, abjuring, unlearning him, I discovered what he had done for me. I owed him, oh unmistakably, certain noble conceptions; I had lighted my little taper at his smoky lamp, and lo, it continued to twinkle. But the light it gave me just showed me how much more I wanted. I was pursued of course by letters from Mrs. Saltram, which I didn't scruple not to read, though I was duly conscious that her embarrassments would now be of the gravest. I sacrificed to propriety by simply putting them away, and this is how, one day as my absence drew to an end, my eye, as I rummaged in my desk for another paper, was caught by a name on a leaf that had detached itself from the packet. The allusion was to Miss Anvoy, who, it appeared, was engaged to be married to Mr. George Gravener; and the news was two months old. A direct question of Mrs. Saltram's had thus remained unanswered—she had inquired of me in a postscript what sort of man this Mr. Gravener might be. This Mr. Gravener had been triumphantly returned for Clockborough, in the interest of the party that had swept the country, so that I might easily have referred Mrs. Saltram to the journals of the day. But when I at last wrote to her that I was coming home and would discharge my accumulated burden by seeing her, I remarked in regard to her question that she must really put it to Miss Anvoy.

VI

I had almost avoided the general election, but some of its consequences, on my return, had smartly to be faced. The season, in London, began to breathe again and to flap its folded wings. Confidence, under the new Ministry, was understood to be reviving, and one of the symptoms, in the social body, was a recovery of appetite. People once more fed together, and it happened that, one Saturday night, at somebody's house, I fed with George Gravener. When the ladies left the room I moved up to where he sat and offered him my congratulation. "On my election?" he asked after a moment; whereupon I feigned, jocosely, not to have heard of his election and to be alluding to something much more important, the rumour of his engagement. I daresay I coloured, however, for his political victory had momentarily passed out of my mind. What was present to it was that he was to marry that beautiful girl; and yet his question made me conscious of some discomposure—I had not intended to put that before everything. He himself indeed ought gracefully to have done so, and I remember thinking the whole man was in this assumption that in expressing my sense of what he had won I had fixed my thoughts on his "seat." We straightened the matter out, and he was so much lighter in hand than I had lately seen him that his spirits might well have been fed from a double source. He was so good as to say that he hoped I should soon make the acquaintance of Miss Anvoy, who, with her aunt, was presently coming up to town. Lady Coxon, in the country, had been seriously unwell, and this had delayed their arrival. I told him I had heard the marriage would be a splendid one; on which, brightened and humanised by his luck, he laughed and said: "Do you mean for *her*?" When I had again explained what I meant he went on: "Oh, she's an American, but you'd scarcely know it; unless, perhaps," he added, "by her being used to more money than most girls in England, even the daughters of rich men. That wouldn't in the least do for a fellow like me, you know, if it wasn't for the great liberality of her father. He really has been most kind, and everything is quite satisfactory." He added that his eldest brother had taken a tremendous fancy to her and that during a recent visit at Coldfield she had nearly won over Lady Maddock. I gathered from something he dropped later that the free-handed gentleman beyond the seas had not made a settlement, but had given a handsome present and was apparently to be looked to, across the water, for other favours. People are simplified alike by great contentments and great yearnings, and whether or no it was Gravener's directness that begot my own I seem to recall that in some turn taken by our talk he almost imposed it on me as an act of decorum to ask if Miss Anvoy had also by chance expectations from her aunt. My inquiry drew out that Lady Coxon, who was the oddest of women, would have in any contingency to act under her late husband's will, which was odder still, saddling her with a mass of queer obligations complicated with queer loopholes. There were several dreary people, Coxon cousins, old maids, to whom she would have more or less to minister. Gravener laughed, without saying no, when I suggested that the young lady might come in through a loophole; then suddenly, as if he suspected that I had turned a lantern on him, he exclaimed quite dryly: "That's all rot—one is moved by other springs!"

A fortnight later, at Lady Coxon's own house, I understood well enough the springs one was moved by. Gravener had spoken of me there as an old friend, and I received a gracious invitation to dine. The knight's widow was again indisposed— she had succumbed at the eleventh hour; so that I found Miss Anvoy bravely playing hostess, without even Gravener's help, inasmuch as, to make matters worse, he had just sent up word that the House, the insatiable House, with which he supposed he had contracted for easier terms, positively declined to release him. I was struck with the courage, the grace and gaiety of the young lady left to deal unaided with the possibilities of the Regent's Park. I did what I could to help her to keep them down, or up, after I had recovered from the confusion of seeing her slightly disconcerted at perceiving in the guest introduced by her intended the gentleman with whom she had had that talk about Frank Saltram. I had at that moment my first glimpse of the fact that she was a person who could carry a responsibility; but I leave the reader to judge of my sense of the aggravation, for either of us, of such a burden when I heard the servant announce Mrs. Saltram. From what immediately passed between the two ladies I gathered that the latter had been sent for post-haste to fill the gap created by the absence of the mistress of the house. "Good!" I exclaimed, "she will be put by *me*;" and my apprehension was promptly justified. Mrs. Saltram taken in to dinner, and taken in as a consequence of an appeal to her amiability, was Mrs. Saltram with a vengeance. I asked myself what Miss Anvoy meant by doing such things, but the only answer I arrived at was that Gravener was verily fortunate. She had not happened to tell him of her visit to Upper Baker Street, but she would certainly tell him to-morrow; not indeed that this would make him like any better her having had the simplicity to invite such a person as Mrs. Saltram on such an occasion. I reflected that I had never seen a young woman put such ignorance into her cleverness, such freedom into her modesty; this, I think, was when, after dinner, she said to me frankly, with almost jubilant mirth: "Oh, you don't admire Mrs. Saltram?" Why should I? This was truly an innocent maiden. I had briefly to consider before I could reply that my objection to the lady in question was the objection often formulated in regard to persons met at the social board—I knew all her stories. Then, as Miss Anvoy remained momentarily vague, I added: "About her husband."

"Oh yes, but there are some new ones."

"None for me. Oh, novelty would be pleasant!"

"Doesn't it appear that of late he has been particularly horrid?"

"His fluctuations don't matter," I replied, "for at night all cats are grey. You saw the shade of this one the night we waited for him together. What will you have? He has no dignity."

Miss Anvoy, who had been introducing with her American distinctness, looked encouragingly round at some of the combinations she had risked. "It's too bad I can't see him."

"You mean Gravener won't let you?"

"I haven't asked him. He lets me do everything."

"But you know he knows him and wonders what some of us see in him."

"We haven't happened to talk of him," the girl said.

"Get him to take you some day out to see the Mulvilles."

"I thought Mr. Saltram had thrown the Mulvilles over."

"Utterly. But that won't prevent his being planted there again, to bloom like a rose, within a month or two."

Miss Anvoy thought a moment. Then, "I should like to see them," she said with her fostering smile.

"They're tremendously worth it. You mustn't miss them."

"I'll make George take me," she went on as Mrs. Saltram came up to interrupt us. The girl smiled at her as kindly as she had smiled at me and, addressing the question to her, continued: "But the chance of a lecture—one of the wonderful lectures? Isn't there another course announced?"

"Another? There are about thirty!" I exclaimed, turning away and feeling Mrs. Saltram's little eyes in my back. A few days after this I heard that Gravener's marriage was near at hand—was settled for Whitsuntide; but as I had received no invitation I doubted it, and presently there came to me in fact the report of a postponement. Something was the matter; what was the matter was supposed to be that Lady Coxon was now critically ill. I had called on her after my dinner in the Regent's Park, but I had neither seen her nor seen Miss Anvoy. I forget to-day the exact order in which, at this period, certain incidents occurred and the particular stage at which it suddenly struck me, making me catch my breath a little, that the progression, the acceleration was for all the world that of

a drama. This was probably rather late in the day, and the
exact order doesn't matter. What had already occurred was
some accident determining a more patient wait. George Gravener, whom I met again, in fact told me as much, but without
signs of perturbation. Lady Coxon had to be constantly attended to, and there were other good reasons as well. Lady
Coxon had to be so constantly attended to that on the occasion of a second attempt in the Regent's Park I equally failed
to obtain a sight of her niece. I judged it discreet under the
circumstances not to make a third; but this didn't matter, for
it was through Adelaide Mulville that the sidewind of the
comedy, though I was at first unwitting, began to reach me.
I went to Wimbledon at times because Saltram was there, and
I went at others because he was not. The Pudneys, who had
taken him to Birmingham, had already got rid of him, and we
had a horrible consciousness of his wandering roofless, in dishonour, about the smoky Midlands, almost as the injured Lear
wandered on the storm-lashed heath. His room, upstairs, had
been lately done up (I could hear the crackle of the new
chintz) and the difference only made his smirches and bruises,
his splendid tainted genius, the more tragic. If he wasn't bare-
foot in the mire he was sure to be unconventionally shod.
These were the things Adelaide and I, who were old enough
friends to stare at each other in silence, talked about when we
didn't speak. When we spoke it was only about the brilliant
girl George Gravener was to marry, whom he had brought
out the other Sunday. I could see that this presentation had
been happy, for Mrs. Mulville commemorated it in the only
way in which she ever expressed her confidence in a new relation. "She likes me—she likes me": her native humility exulted in that measure of success. We all knew for ourselves
how she liked those who liked her, and as regards Ruth Anvoy
she was more easily won over than Lady Maddock.

VII

One of the consequences, for the Mulvilles, of the sacrifices
they made for Frank Saltram was that they had to give up
their carriage. Adelaide drove gently into London in a one-
horse greenish thing, an early Victorian landau, hired, near at

hand, imaginatively, from a broken-down jobmaster whose wife was in consumption—a vehicle that made people turn round all the more when her pensioner sat beside her in a soft white hat and a shawl, one of her own. This was his position and I daresay his costume when on an afternoon in July she went to return Miss Anvoy's visit. The wheel of fate had now revolved, and amid silences deep and exhaustive, compunctions and condonations alike unutterable, Saltram was reinstated. Was it in pride or in penance that Mrs. Mulville began immediately to drive him about? If he was ashamed of his ingratitude she might have been ashamed of her forgiveness; but she was incorrigibly capable of liking him to be seen strikingly seated in the landau while she was in shops or with her acquaintance. However, if he was in the pillory for twenty minutes in the Regent's Park (I mean at Lady Coxon's door, while her companion paid her call) it was not for the further humiliation of any one concerned that she presently came out for him in person, not even to show either of them what a fool she was that she drew him in to be introduced to the clever young American. Her account of the introduction I had in its order, but before that, very late in the season, under Gravener's auspices, I met Miss Anvoy at tea at the House of Commons. The member for Clockborough had gathered a group of pretty ladies, and the Mulvilles were not of the party. On the great terrace, as I strolled off a little with her, the guest of honour immediately exclaimed to me: "I've seen him, you know —I've seen him!" She told me about Saltram's call.

"And how did you find him?"

"Oh, so strange!"

"You didn't like him?"

"I can't tell till I see him again."

"You want to do that?"

She was silent a moment. "Immensely."

We stopped; I fancied she had become aware Gravener was looking at us. She turned back toward the knot of the others, and I said: "Dislike him as much as you will—I see you are bitten."

"Bitten?" I thought she coloured a little.

"Oh, it doesn't matter!" I laughed; "one doesn't die of it."

"I hope I sha'n't die of anything before I've seen more of Mrs. Mulville." I rejoiced with her over plain Adelaide, whom she pronounced the loveliest woman she had met in England; but before we separated I remarked to her that it was an act of mere humanity to warn her that if she should see more of Frank Saltram (which would be likely to follow on any increase of acquaintance with Mrs. Mulville) she might find herself flattening her nose against the clear, hard pane of an eternal question—that of the relative importance of virtue. She replied that this was surely a subject on which one took everything for granted; whereupon I admitted that I had perhaps expressed myself ill. What I referred to was what I had referred to the night we met in Upper Baker Street—the importance relative (relative to virtue) of other gifts. She asked me if I called virtue a gift—as if it were handed to us in a parcel on our birthday; and I declared that this very inquiry showed me the problem had already caught her by the skirt. She would have help, however, help that I myself had once had, in resisting its tendency to make one cross.

"What help do you mean?"

"That of the member for Clockborough."

She stared, smiled, then exclaimed: "Why, my idea has been to help *him*!"

She *had* helped him—I had his own word for it that at Clockborough her bedevilment of the voters had really put him in. She would do so doubtless again and again, but I heard the very next month that this fine faculty had undergone a temporary eclipse. News of the catastrophe first came to me from Mrs. Saltram, and it was afterwards confirmed at Wimbledon: poor Miss Anvoy was in trouble—great disasters in America had suddenly summoned her home. Her father, in New York, had had reverses—lost so much money that it was really provoking as showing how much he had had. It was Adelaide who told me that she had gone off alone at less than a week's notice.

"Alone? Gravener has permitted that?"

"What will you have? The House of Commons!"

I'm afraid I cursed the House of Commons: I was so much interested. Of course he would follow her as soon as he was free to make her his wife; only she mightn't now be able to bring him anything like the marriage-portion of which he had begun by having the virtual promise. Mrs. Mulville let me know what was already said: she was charming, this American girl, but really these American fathers! What was a man to do? Mr. Saltram, according to Mrs. Mulville, was of opinion that a man was never to suffer his relation to money to become a spiritual relation, but was to keep it wholesomely mechanical. *"Moi pas comprendre!"* I commented on this; in rejoinder to which Adelaide, with her beautiful sympathy, explained that she supposed he simply meant that the thing was to use it, don't you know? but not to think too much about it. "To take it, but not to thank you for it?" I still more profanely inquired. For a quarter of an hour afterwards she wouldn't look at me, but this didn't prevent my asking her what had been the result, that afternoon in the Regent's Park, of her taking our friend to see Miss Anvoy.

"Oh, so charming!" she answered, brightening. "He said he recognised in her a nature he could absolutely trust."

"Yes, but I'm speaking of the effect on herself."

Mrs. Mulville was silent an instant. "It was everything one could wish."

Something in her tone made me laugh. "Do you mean she gave him something?"

"Well, since you ask me!"

"Right there—on the spot?"

Again poor Adelaide faltered. "It was to me of course she gave it."

I stared; somehow I couldn't see the scene. "Do you mean a sum of money?"

"It was very handsome." Now at last she met my eyes, though I could see it was with an effort. "Thirty pounds."

"Straight out of her pocket?"

"Out of the drawer of a table at which she had been writing. She just slipped the folded notes into my hand. He wasn't looking; it was while he was going back to the carriage. Oh," said Adelaide reassuringly, "I dole it out!" The dear practical soul thought my agitation, for I confess I was agitated, had reference to the administration of the money. Her disclosure made me for a moment muse violently, and I daresay that during that moment I wondered if anything else in the world makes people so indelicate as unselfishness. I uttered, I suppose, some vague synthetic cry, for she went on as if she had had a glimpse of my inward amaze at such episodes. "I assure you, my dear friend, he was in one of his happy hours."

But I wasn't thinking of that. "Truly, indeed, these Americans!" I said. "With her father in the very act, as it were, of swindling her betrothed!"

Mrs. Mulville stared. "Oh, I suppose Mr. Anvoy has scarcely failed on purpose. Very likely they won't be able to keep it up, but there it was, and it was a very beautiful impulse."

"You say Saltram was very fine?"

"Beyond everything. He surprised even me."

"And I know what *you've* heard." After a moment I added: "Had he peradventure caught a glimpse of the money in the table-drawer?"

At this my companion honestly flushed. "How can you be so cruel when you know how little he calculates?"

"Forgive me, I do know it. But you tell me things that act on my nerves. I'm sure he hadn't caught a glimpse of anything but some splendid idea."

Mrs. Mulville brightly concurred. "And perhaps even of her beautiful listening face."

"Perhaps even! And what was it all about?"

"His talk? It was *à propos* of her engagement, which I had told him about: the idea of marriage, the philosophy, the poetry, the sublimity of it." It was impossible wholly to restrain one's mirth at this, and some rude ripple that I emitted again caused my companion to admonish me. "It sounds a little stale, but you know his freshness."

"Of illustration? Indeed I do!"

"And how he has always been right on that great question."

"On what great question, dear lady, hasn't he been right?"

"Of what other great men can you equally say it? I mean that he has never, but *never*, had a deviation?" Mrs. Mulville exultantly demanded.

I tried to think of some other great man, but I had to give it up. "Didn't Miss Anvoy express her satisfaction in any less diffident way than by her charming present?" I was reduced to inquiring instead.

"Oh yes, she overflowed to me on the steps while he was getting into the carriage." These words somehow brushed up a picture of Saltram's big shawled back as he hoisted himself into the green landau. "She said she was not disappointed," Adelaide pursued.

I meditated a moment. "Did he wear his shawl?"

"His shawl?" She had not even noticed.

"I mean yours."

"He looked very nice, and you know he's really clean. Miss Anvoy used such a remarkable expression—she said his mind is like a crystal!"

I pricked up my ears. "A crystal?"

"Suspended in the moral world—swinging and shining and flashing there. She's monstrously clever, you know."

I reflected again. "Monstrously!"

VIII

George Gravener didn't follow her, for late in September, after the House had risen, I met him in a railway-carriage. He was coming up from Scotland, and I had just quitted the abode of a relation who lived near Durham. The current of travel back to London was not yet strong; at any rate on entering the compartment I found he had had it for some time to himself. We fared in company, and though he had a blue-book in his lap and the open jaws of his bag threatened me with the white teeth of confused papers, we inevitably, we even at last sociably conversed. I saw that things were not well with him, but I asked no question until something dropped by himself made, as it had made on another occasion, an absence of curiosity invidious. He mentioned that he was worried about his good old friend Lady Coxon, who, with her niece likely to be detained some time in America, lay seriously ill at Clockborough, much on his mind and on his hands.

"Ah, Miss Anvoy's in America?"

"Her father has got into a horrid hole, lost no end of money."

I hesitated, after expressing due concern, but I presently said: "I hope that raises no objection to your marriage."

"None whatever; moreover it's my trade to meet objections. But it may create tiresome delays, of which there have been too many, from various causes, already. Lady Coxon got very bad, then she got much better. Then Mr. Anvoy suddenly began to totter, and now he seems quite on his back. I'm afraid he's really in for some big reverse. Lady Coxon is worse again, awfully upset by the news from America, and she sends me word that she *must* have Ruth. How can I give her Ruth? I haven't got Ruth myself!"

"Surely you haven't lost her?" I smiled.

"She's everything to her wretched father. She writes me every post—telling me to smooth her aunt's pillow. I've other things to smooth; but the old lady, save for her servants, is really alone. She won't receive her Coxon relations, because she's angry at so much of her money going to them. Besides, she's hopelessly mad," said Gravener very frankly.

I don't remember whether it was this, or what it was, that made me ask if she had not such an appreciation of Mrs. Saltram as might render that active person of some use.

He gave me a cold glance, asking me what had put Mrs. Saltram into my head, and I replied that she was unfortunately never out of it. I happened to remember the wonderful accounts she had given me of the kindness Lady Coxon had shown her. Gravener declared this to be false; Lady Coxon, who didn't care for her, hadn't seen her three times. The only foundation for it was that Miss Anvoy, who used, poor girl, to chuck money about in a manner she must now regret, had for an hour seen in the miserable woman (you could never know what she would see in people) an interesting pretext for the liberality with which her nature overflowed. But even Miss Anvoy was now quite tired of her. Gravener told me more about the crash in New York and the annoyance it had been to him, and we also glanced here and there in other directions; but by the time we got to Doncaster the principal thing he had communicated was that he was keeping something back. We stopped at that station, and, at the carriage-door, some one made a movement to get in. Gravener uttered a sound of impatience, and I said to myself that but for this I should have had the secret. Then the intruder, for some reason, spared us his company; we started afresh, and my hope of the secret returned. Gravener remained silent, however, and I pretended to go to sleep; in fact, in discouragement, I really dozed. When I opened my eyes I found he was looking at me with an injured air. He tossed away with some vivacity the remnant of a cigarette and then he said: "If you're not too sleepy I want to put you a case." I answered that I would make every effort to attend, and I felt it was going to be interesting when he went on: "As I told you a while ago, Lady Coxon, poor dear, is a maniac." His tone had much behind it—was full of promise. I inquired if her ladyship's misfortune were a feature of her malady or only of her character, and he replied that it was a product of both. The case he wanted to put to me was a matter on which it would interest him to have the impression—the judgment, he might also say—of another person. "I mean of the average intelligent man," he said; "but you see I take what I can get." There would be the technical, the strictly legal view; then there would be the way the question would strike a man of the world. He had lighted another cigarette while he talked, and I saw he was glad to have it to handle when he brought out at last, with a laugh slightly artificial: "In fact it's a subject on which Miss Anvoy and I are pulling different ways."

"And you want me to pronounce between you? I pronounce in advance for Miss Anvoy."

"In advance—that's quite right. That's how I pronounced when I asked her to marry me. But my story will interest you only so far as your mind is not made up." Gravener puffed his cigarette a minute and then continued: "Are you familiar with the idea of the Endowment of Research?"

"Of Research?" I was at sea for a moment.

"I give you Lady Coxon's phrase. She has it on the brain."

"She wishes to endow ——?"

"Some earnest and disinterested seeker," Gravener said. "It was a sketchy design of her late husband's, and he handed it on to her; setting apart in his will a sum of money of which she was to enjoy the interest for life, but of which, should she eventually see her opportunity—the matter was left largely to her discretion—she would best honour his memory by determining the exemplary public use. This sum of money, no less than thirteen thousand pounds, was to be called the Coxon

Fund; and poor Sir Gregory evidently proposed to himself that the Coxon Fund should cover his name with glory—be universally desired and admired. He left his wife a full declaration of his views, so far at least as that term may be applied to views vitiated by a vagueness really infantine. A little learning is a dangerous thing, and a good citizen who happens to have been an ass is worse for a community than bad sewerage. He's worst of all when he's dead, because then he can't be stopped. However, such as they were, the poor man's aspirations are now in his wife's bosom, or fermenting rather in her foolish brain: it lies with her to carry them out. But of course she must first catch her hare."

"Her earnest, disinterested seeker?"

"The flower that blushes unseen for want of the pecuniary independence necessary to cause the light that is in it to shine upon the human race. The individual, in a word, who, having the rest of the machinery, the spiritual, the intellectual, is most hampered in his search."

"His search for what?"

"For Moral Truth. That's what Sir Gregory calls it."

I burst out laughing. "Delightful, munificent Sir Gregory! It's a charming idea."

"So Miss Anvoy thinks."

"Has she a candidate for the Fund?"

"Not that I know of; and she's perfectly reasonable about it. But Lady Coxon has put the matter before her, and we've naturally had a lot of talk."

"Talk that, as you've so interestingly intimated, has landed you in a disagreement."

"She considers there's something in it," Gravener said.

"And you consider there's nothing?"

"It seems to me a puerility fraught with consequences inevitably grotesque and possibly immoral. To begin with, fancy the idea of constituting an endowment without establishing a tribunal—a bench of competent people, of judges."

"The sole tribunal is Lady Coxon?"

"And any one she chooses to invite."

"But she has invited you."

"I'm not competent—I hate the thing. Besides, she hasn't. The real history of the matter, I take it, is that the inspiration

was originally Lady Coxon's own, that she infected him with
it, and that the flattering option left her is simply his tribute
to her beautiful, her aboriginal enthusiasm. She came to England forty years ago, a thin transcendental Bostonian, and
even her odd, happy, frumpy Clockborough marriage never
really materialised her. She feels indeed that she has become
very British—as if that, as a process, as a *Werden*, were conceivable; but it's precisely what makes her cling to the notion
of the 'Fund'—cling to it as to a link with the ideal."

"How can she cling if she's dying?"

"Do you mean how can she act in the matter?" my companion asked. "That's precisely the question. She can't! As
she has never yet caught her hare, never spied out her lucky
impostor (how should she, with the life she has led?), her
husband's intention has come very near lapsing. His idea, to
do him justice, was that it *should* lapse if exactly the right
person, the perfect mixture of genius and chill penury, should
fail to turn up. Ah! Lady Coxon's very particular—she says
there must be no mistake."

I found all this quite thrilling—I took it in with avidity. "If
she dies without doing anything, what becomes of the
money?" I demanded.

"It goes back to his family, if she hasn't made some other
disposition of it."

"She may do that, then—she may divert it?"

"Her hands are not tied. The proof is that three months
ago she offered to make it over to her niece."

"For Miss Anvoy's own use?"

"For Miss Anvoy's own use—on the occasion of her prospective marriage. She was discouraged—the earnest seeker
required so earnest a search. She was afraid of making a mistake; every one she could think of seemed either not earnest
enough or not poor enough. On the receipt of the first bad
news about Mr. Anvoy's affairs she proposed to Ruth to make
the sacrifice for her. As the situation in New York got worse
she repeated her proposal."

"Which Miss Anvoy declined?"

"Except as a formal trust."

"You mean except as committing herself legally to place the
money?"

"On the head of the deserving object, the great man frustrated," said Gravener. "She only consents to act in the spirit of Sir Gregory's scheme."

"And you blame her for that?" I asked with an excited smile.

My tone was not harsh, but he coloured a little and there was a queer light in his eye. "My dear fellow, if I 'blamed' the young lady I'm engaged to, I shouldn't immediately say so even to so old a friend as you." I saw that some deep discomfort, some restless desire to be sided with, reassuringly, approvingly mirrored, had been at the bottom of his drifting so far, and I was genuinely touched by his confidence. It was inconsistent with his habits; but being troubled about a woman was not, for him, a habit: that itself was an inconsistency. George Gravener could stand straight enough before any other combination of forces. It amused me to think that the combination he had succumbed to had an American accent, a transcendental aunt and an insolvent father; but all my old loyalty to him mustered to meet this unexpected hint that I could help him. I saw that I could from the insincere tone in which he pursued: "I've criticised her of course, I've contended with her, and it has been great fun." It clearly couldn't have been such great fun as to make it improper for me presently to ask if Miss Anvoy had nothing at all settled upon herself. To this he replied that she had only a trifle from her mother—a mere four hundred a year, which was exactly why it would be convenient to him that she shouldn't decline, in the face of this total change in her prospects, an accession of income which would distinctly help them to marry. When I inquired if there were no other way in which so rich and so affectionate an aunt could cause the weight of her benevolence to be felt, he answered that Lady Coxon was affectionate indeed, but was scarcely to be called rich. She could let her project of the Fund lapse for her niece's benefit, but she couldn't do anything else. She had been accustomed to regard her as tremendously provided for, and she was up to her eyes in promises to anxious Coxons. She was a woman of an inordinate conscience, and her conscience was now a distress to her, hovering round her bed in irreconcilable forms of resentful husbands, portionless nieces and undiscoverable philosophers.

We were by this time getting into the whirr of fleeting platforms, the multiplication of lights. "I think you'll find," I said
with a laugh, "that your predicament will disappear in the very
fact that the philosopher *is* undiscoverable."

He began to gather up his papers. "Who can set a limit to
the ingenuity of an extravagant woman?"

"Yes, after all, who indeed?" I echoed, as I recalled the
extravagance commemorated in Mrs. Mulville's ancedote of
Miss Anvoy and the thirty pounds.

IX

The thing I had been most sensible of in that talk with George
Gravener was the way Saltram's name kept out of it. It seemed
to me at the time that we were quite pointedly silent about
him; but afterwards it appeared more probable there had been
on my companion's part no conscious avoidance. Later on I
was sure of this, and for the best of reasons—the simple reason
of my perceiving more completely that, for evil as well as for
good, he said nothing to Gravener's imagination. Gravener
was not afraid of him; he was too much disgusted with him.
No more was I, doubtless, and for very much the same reason.
I treated my friend's story as an absolute confidence; but
when before Christmas, by Mrs. Saltram, I was informed of
Lady Coxon's death without having had news of Miss Anvoy's
return, I found myself taking for granted that we should hear
no more of these nuptials, in which I now recognised an element incongruous from the first. I began to ask myself how
people who suited each other so little could please each other
so much. The charm was some material charm, some affinity
exquisite doubtless, yet superficial; some surrender to youth
and beauty and passion, to force and grace and fortune, happy
accidents and easy contacts. They might dote on each other's
persons, but how could they know each other's souls? How
could they have the same prejudices, how could they have the
same horizon? Such questions, I confess, seemed quenched
but not answered when, one day in February, going out to
Wimbledon, I found our young lady in the house. A passion
that had brought her back across the wintry ocean was as
much of a passion as was necessary. No impulse equally strong

indeed had drawn George Gravener to America; a circumstance on which, however, I reflected only long enough to
remind myself that it was none of my business. Ruth Anvoy
was distinctly different, and I felt that the difference was not
simply that of her being in mourning. Mrs. Mulville told me
soon enough what it was: it was the difference between a
handsome girl with large expectations and a handsome girl
with only four hundred a year. This explanation indeed did
not wholly content me, not even when I learned that her
mourning had a double cause—learned that poor Mr. Anvoy,
giving way altogether, buried under the ruins of his fortune
and leaving next to nothing, had died a few weeks before.

"So she has come out to marry George Gravener?" I demanded. "Wouldn't it have been prettier of him to have saved
her the trouble?"

"Hasn't the House just met?" said Adelaide. Then she
added: "I gather that her having come is exactly a sign that
the marriage is a little shaky. If it were certain, a self-respecting
girl like Ruth would have waited for him over there."

I noted that they were already Ruth and Adelaide, but what
I said was: "Do you mean that she has returned to make it a
certainty?"

"No, I mean that I figure she has come out for some reason
independent of it." Adelaide could only figure as yet, and
there was more, as we found, to be revealed. Mrs. Mulville,
on hearing of her arrival, had brought the young lady out in
the green landau for the Sunday. The Coxons were in possession of the house in Regent's Park, and Miss Anvoy was in
dreary lodgings. George Gravener was with her when Adelaide called, but he had assented graciously enough to the
little visit at Wimbledon. The carriage, with Mr. Saltram in it
but not mentioned, had been sent off on some errand from
which it was to return and pick the ladies up. Gravener left
them together, and at the end of an hour, on the Saturday
afternoon, the party of three drove out to Wimbledon. This
was the girl's second glimpse of our great man, and I was
interested in asking Mrs. Mulville if the impression made by
the first appeared to have been confirmed. On her replying,
after consideration, that of course with time and opportunity
it couldn't fail to be, but as yet she was disappointed, I was

sufficiently struck with her use of this last word to question her further.

"Do you mean that you're disappointed because you judge that Miss Anvoy is?"

"Yes; I hoped for a greater effect last evening. We had two or three people, but he scarcely opened his mouth."

"He'll be all the better this evening," I added after a moment. "What particular importance do you attach to the idea of her being impressed?"

Adelaide turned her mild, pale eyes on me as if she were amazed at my levity. "Why, the importance of her being as happy as *we* are!"

I'm afraid that at this my levity increased. "Oh, that's a happiness almost too great to wish a person!" I saw she had not yet in her mind what I had in mine, and at any rate the visitor's actual bliss was limited to a walk in the garden with Kent Mulville. Later in the afternoon I also took one, and I saw nothing of Miss Anvoy till dinner, at which we were without the company of Saltram, who had caused it to be reported that he was indisposed, lying down. This made us, most of us—for there were other friends present—convey to each other in silence some of the unutterable things which in those years our eyes had inevitably acquired the art of expressing. If an American inquirer had not been there we would have expressed them otherwise, and Adelaide would have pretended not to hear. I had seen her, before the very fact, abstract herself nobly; and I knew that more than once, to keep it from the servants, managing, dissimulating cleverly, she had helped her husband to carry him bodily to his room. Just recently he had been so wise and so deep and so high that I had begun to get nervous—to wonder if by chance there were something behind it, if he were kept straight for instance by the knowledge that the hated Pudneys would have more to tell us if they chose. He was lying low, but unfortunately it was common wisdom with us that the biggest splashes took place in the quietest pools. We should have had a merry life indeed if all the splashes had sprinkled us as refreshingly as the waters we were even then to feel about our ears. Kent Mulville had been up to his room, but had come back with a face that told as few tales as I had seen it succeed in telling on the evening

I waited in the lecture-room with Miss Anvoy. I said to myself that our friend had gone out, but I was glad that the presence of a comparative stranger deprived us of the dreary duty of suggesting to each other, in respect of his errand, edifying possibilities in which we didn't ourselves believe. At ten o'clock he came into the drawing-room with his waistcoat much awry but his eyes sending out great signals. It was precisely with his entrance that I ceased to be vividly conscious of him. I saw that the crystal, as I had called it, had begun to swing, and I had need of my immediate attention for Miss Anvoy.

Even when I was told afterwards that he had, as we might have said to-day, broken the record, the manner in which that attention had been rewarded relieved me of a sense of loss. I had of course a perfect general consciousness that something great was going on: it was a little like having been etherised to hear Herr Joachim play. The old music was in the air; I felt the strong pulse of thought, the sink and swell, the flight, the poise, the plunge; but I knew something about one of the listeners that nobody else knew, and Saltram's monologue could reach me only through that medium. To this hour I'm of no use when, as a witness, I'm appealed to (for they still absurdly contend about it) as to whether or no on that historic night he was drunk; and my position is slightly ridiculous, for I have never cared to tell them what it really was I was taken up with. What I got out of it is the only morsel of the total experience that is quite my own. The others were shared, but this is incommunicable. I feel that now, I'm bound to say, in even thus roughly evoking the occasion, and it takes something from my pride of clearness. However, I shall perhaps be as clear as is absolutely necessary if I remark that she was too much given up to her own intensity of observation to be sensible of mine. It was plainly not the question of her marriage that had brought her back. I greatly enjoyed this discovery and was sure that had that question alone been involved she would have remained away. In this case doubtless Gravener would, in spite of the House of Commons, have found means to rejoin her. It afterwards made me uncomfortable for her that, alone in the lodging Mrs. Mulville had put before me as dreary, she should have in any degree the air of waiting for her fate; so that I was presently relieved at hearing of her having gone to stay at Coldfield. If she was in England at all while the engagement stood the only proper place for her was under Lady Maddock's wing. Now that she was unfortunate and relatively poor, perhaps her prospective sister-in-law would be wholly won over. There would be much to say, if I had space, about the way her behaviour, as I caught gleams of it, ministered to the image that had taken birth in my mind, to my private amusement, as I listened to George Gravener in the railway-carriage. I watched her in the light of this queer possibility—a formidable thing certainly to meet—and I was aware that it coloured, extravagantly perhaps, my interpretation of her very looks and tones. At Wimbledon for instance it had seemed to me that she was literally afraid of Saltram, in dread of a coercion that she had begun already to feel. I had come up to town with her the next day and had been convinced that, though deeply interested, she was immensely on her guard. She would show as little as possible before she should be ready to show everything. What this final exhibition might be on the part of a girl perceptibly so able to think things out I found it great sport to forecast. It would have been exciting to be approached by her, appealed to by her for advice; but I prayed to heaven I mightn't find myself in such a predicament. If there was really a present rigour in the situation of which Gravener had sketched for me the elements she would have to get out of her difficulty by herself. It was not I who had launched her and it was not I who could help her. I didn't fail to ask myself why, since I couldn't help her, I should think so much about her. It was in part my suspense that was responsible for this; I waited impatiently to see whether she wouldn't have told Mrs. Mulville a portion at least of what I had learned from Gravener. But I saw Mrs. Mulville was still reduced to wonder what she had come out again for if she hadn't come as a conciliatory bride. That she had come in some other character was the only thing that fitted all the appearances. Having for family reasons to spend some time that spring in the west of England, I was in a manner out of earshot of the great oceanic rumble (I mean of the continuous hum of Saltram's thought) and my uneasiness tended to keep me quiet. There was something I wanted so little to have to say that my prudence surmounted my curiosity. I only wondered if Ruth Anvoy talked over the idea of the Coxon Fund with Lady Maddock, and also somewhat why I didn't hear from Wimbledon. I had a reproachful note about something or other from Mrs. Saltram, but it contained no mention of Lady Coxon's niece, on whom her eyes had been much less fixed since the recent untoward events.

X

Adelaide's silence was fully explained later; it was practically explained when in June, returning to London, I was honoured by this admirable woman with an early visit. As soon as she appeared I guessed everything, and as soon as she told me that darling Ruth had been in her house nearly a month I exclaimed: "What in the name of maidenly modesty is she staying in England for?"

"Because she loves me so!" cried Adelaide gaily. But she had not come to see me only to tell me Miss Anvoy loved her: that was now sufficiently established, and what was much more to the point was that Mr. Gravener had now raised an objection to it. That is he had protested against her being at Wimbledon, where in the innocence of his heart he had originally brought her himself; in short he wanted her to put an end to their engagement in the only proper, the only happy manner.

"And why in the world doesn't she do so?" I inquired.

Adelaide hesitated. "She says you know." Then on my also hesitating she added: "A condition he makes."

"The Coxon Fund?" I cried.

"He has mentioned to her his having told you about it."

"Ah, but so little! Do you mean she has accepted the trust?"

"In the most splendid spirit—as a duty about which there can be no two opinions." Then said Adelaide after an instant: "Of course she's thinking of Mr. Saltram."

I gave a quick cry at this, which, in its violence, made my visitor turn pale. "How very awful!"

"Awful?"

"Why, to have anything to do with such an idea oneself."

"I'm sure you needn't!" Mrs. Mulville gave a slight toss of her head.

"He isn't good enough!" I went on; to which she responded with an ejaculation almost as lively as mine had been. This made me, with genuine, immediate horror, exclaim: "You haven't influenced her, I hope!" and my emphasis brought back the blood with a rush to poor Adelaide's face. She declared while she blushed (for I had frightened her again) that she had never influenced anybody and that the girl had only seen and heard and judged for herself. *He* had influenced her, if I would, as he did every one who had a soul: that word, as we knew, even expressed feebly the power of the things he said to haunt the mind. How could she, Adelaide, help it if Miss Anvoy's mind was haunted? I demanded with a groan what right a pretty girl engaged to a rising M.P. had to *have* a mind; but the only explanation my bewildered friend could give me was that she was so clever. She regarded Mr. Saltram naturally as a tremendous force for good. She was intelligent enough to understand him and generous enough to admire.

"She's many things enough, but is she, among them, rich enough?" I demanded. "Rich enough, I mean, to sacrifice such a lot of good money?"

"That's for herself to judge. Besides, it's not her own money; she doesn't in the least consider it so."

"And Gravener does, if not *his* own; and that's the whole difficulty?"

"The difficulty that brought her back, yes: she had absolutely to see her poor aunt's solicitor. It's clear that by Lady Coxon's will she may have the money, but it's still clearer to her conscience that the original condition, definite, intensely implied on her uncle's part, is attached to the use of it. She can only take one view of it. It's for the Endowment or it's for nothing."

"The Endowment is a conception superficially sublime, but fundamentally ridiculous."

"Are you repeating Mr. Gravener's words?" Adelaide asked.

"Possibly, though I've not seen him for months. It's simply the way it strikes me too. It's an old wife's tale. Gravener made some reference to the legal aspect, but such an absurdly loose arrangement has no legal aspect."

"Ruth doesn't insist on that," said Mrs. Mulville; "and it's, for her, exactly this technical weakness that constitutes the force of the moral obligation."

"Are you repeating her words?" I inquired. I forget what else Adelaide said, but she said she was magnificent. I thought of George Gravener confronted with such magnificence as that, and I asked what could have made two such people ever suppose they understood each other. Mrs. Mulville assured me the girl loved him as such a woman could love and that she suffered as such a woman could suffer. Nevertheless she wanted to see me. At this I sprang up with a groan. "Oh, I'm so sorry!—when?" Small though her sense of humour, I think Adelaide laughed at my tone. We discussed the day, the nearest it would be convenient I should come out; but before she went I asked my visitor how long she had been acquainted with these prodigies.

"For several weeks, but I was pledged to secrecy."

"And that's why you didn't write?"

"I couldn't very well tell you she was with me without telling you that no time had even yet been fixed for her marriage. And I couldn't very well tell you as much as that without telling you what I knew of the reason of it. It was not till a day or two ago," Mrs. Mulville went on, "that she asked me to ask you if you wouldn't come and see her. Then at last she said that you knew about the idea of the Endowment."

I considered a little. "Why on earth does she want to see me?"

"To talk with you, naturally, about Mr. Saltram."

"As a subject for the prize?" This was hugely obvious, and I presently exclaimed: "I think I'll sail to-morrow for Australia."

"Well then—sail!" said Mrs. Mulville, getting up.

"On Thursday at five, we said?" I frivolously continued. The appointment was made definite and I inquired how, all this time, the unconscious candidate had carried himself.

"In perfection, really, by the happiest of chances: he has been a dear. And then, as to what we revere him for, in the most wonderful form. His very highest—pure celestial light. You *won't* do him an ill turn?" Adelaide pleaded at the door.

"What danger can equal for him the danger to which he

is exposed from himself?" I asked. "Look out sharp, if he has lately been decorous. He'll presently take a day off, treat us to some exhibition that will make an Endowment a scandal."

"A scandal?" Mrs. Mulville dolorously echoed.

"Is Miss Anvoy prepared for that?"

My visitor, for a moment, screwed her parasol into my carpet. "He grows bigger every day."

"So do you!" I laughed as she went off.

That girl at Wimbledon, on the Thursday afternoon, more than justified my apprehensions. I recognised fully now the cause of the agitation she had produced in me from the first— the faint foreknowledge that there was something very stiff I should have to do for her. I felt more than ever committed to my fate as, standing before her in the big drawing-room where they had tactfully left us to ourselves, I tried with a smile to string together the pearls of lucidity which, from her chair, she successively tossed me. Pale and bright, in her monotonous mourning, she was an image of intelligent purpose, of the passion of duty; but I asked myself whether any girl had ever had so charming an instinct as that which permitted her to laugh out, as it in the joy of her difficulty, into the priggish old room. This remarkable young woman could be earnest without being solemn, and at moments when I ought doubtless to have cursed her obstinacy I found myself watching the unstudied play of her eyebrows or the recurrence of a singularly intense whiteness produced by the parting of her lips. These aberrations, I hasten to add, didn't prevent my learning soon enough why she had wished to see me. Her reason for this was as distinct as her beauty: it was to make me explain what I had meant, on the occasion of our first meeting, by Mr. Saltram's want of dignity. It wasn't that she couldn't imagine, but she desired it there from my lips. What she really desired of course was to know whether there was worse about him than what she had found out for herself. She hadn't been a month in the house with him, that way, without discovering that he wasn't a man of monumental bronze. He was like a jelly without a mould, he had to be embanked; and that was precisely the source of her interest in him and the ground of her project. She put her project boldly before me: there it stood in its preposterous beauty. She was as willing to take the humorous view of it as I could be: the only difference was that for her the humorous view of a thing was not nec-essarily prohibitive, was not paralysing.

Moreover she professed that she couldn't discuss with me the primary question—the moral obligation: that was in her own breast. There were things she couldn't go into—injunc-tions, impressions she had received. They were a part of the closest intimacy of her intercourse with her aunt, they were absolutely clear to her; and on questions of delicacy, the in-terpretation of a fidelity, of a promise, one had always in the last resort to make up one's mind for oneself. It was the idea of the application to the particular case, such a splendid one at last, that troubled her, and she admitted that it stirred very deep things. She didn't pretend that such a responsibility was a simple matter; if it had been she wouldn't have attempted to saddle me with any portion of it. The Mulvilles were sym-pathy itself; but were they absolutely candid? Could they in-deed be, in their position—would it even have been to be desired? Yes, she had sent for me to ask no less than that of me—whether there was anything dreadful kept back. She made no allusion whatever to George Gravener—I thought her silence the only good taste and her gaiety perhaps a part of the very anxiety of that discretion, the effect of a deter-mination that people shouldn't know from herself that her relations with the man she was to marry were strained. All the weight, however, that she left me to throw was a sufficient implication of the weight that he had thrown in vain. Oh, she knew the question of character was immense, and that one couldn't entertain any plan for making merit comfortable without running the gauntlet of that terrible procession of interrogation-points which, like a young ladies' school out for a walk, hooked their uniform noses at the tail of governess Conduct. But were we absolutely to hold that there was never, never, never an exception, never, never, never an occasion for liberal acceptance, for clever charity, for suspended pedantry—for letting one side, in short, outbalance another? When Miss Anvoy threw off this inquiry I could have embraced her for so delightfully emphasising her unlikeness to Mrs. Saltram. "Why not have the courage of one's forgiveness," she asked, "as well as the enthusiasm of one's adhesion?"

"Seeing how wonderfully you have threshed the whole thing out," I evasively replied, "gives me an extraordinary notion of the point your enthusiasm has reached."

She considered this remark an instant with her eyes on mine, and I divined that it struck her I might possibly intend it as a reference to some personal subjection to our fat philosopher, to some aberration of sensibility, some perversion of taste. At least I couldn't interpret otherwise the sudden flush that came into her face. Such a manifestation, as the result of any word of mine, embarrassed me; but while I was thinking how to reassure her the flush passed away in a smile of exquisite good-nature. "Oh, you see, one forgets so wonderfully how one dislikes him!" she said; and if her tone simply extinguished his strange figure with the brush of its compassion, it also rings in my ear to-day as the purest of all our praises. But with what quick response of compassion such a relegation of the man himself made me privately sigh, "Ah, poor Saltram!" She instantly, with this, took the measure of all I didn't believe, and it enabled her to go on: "What can one do when a person has given such a lift to one's interest in life?"

"Yes, what can one do?" If I struck her as a little vague it was because I was thinking of another person. I indulged in another inarticulate murmur—"Poor George Gravener!" What had become of the lift *he* had given that interest? Later on I made up my mind that she was sore and stricken at the appearance he presented of wanting the miserable money. This was the hidden reason of her alienation. The probable sincerity, in spite of the illiberality, of his scruples about the particular use of it under discussion didn't efface the ugliness of his demand that they should buy a good house with it. Then, as for *his* alienation, he didn't, pardonably enough, grasp the lift Frank Saltram had given her interest in life. If a mere spectator could ask that last question, with what rage in his heart the man himself might! He was not, like her, I was to see, too proud to show me why he was disappointed.

XI

I was unable, this time, to stay to dinner: such, at any rate, was the plea on which I took leave. I desired in truth to get away from my young lady, for that obviously helped me not to pretend to satisfy her. How *could* I satisfy her? I asked myself—how could I tell her how much had been kept back? I didn't even know, and I certainly didn't desire to know. My own policy had ever been to learn the least about poor Saltram's weaknesses—not to learn the most. A great deal that I had in fact learned had been forced upon me by his wife. There was something even irritating in Miss Anvoy's crude conscientiousness, and I wondered why, after all, she couldn't have let him alone and been content to entrust George Gravener with the purchase of the good house. I was sure he would have driven a bargain, got something excellent and cheap. I laughed louder even than she, I temporised, I failed her; I told her I must think over her case. I professed a horror of responsibilities and twitted her with her own extravagant passion for them. It was not really that I was afraid of the scandal, the moral discredit for the Fund; what troubled me most was a feeling of a different order. Of course, as the beneficiary of the Fund was to enjoy a simple life-interest, as it was hoped that new beneficiaries would arise and come up to new standards, it would not be a trifle that the first of these worthies should not have been a striking example of the domestic virtues. The Fund would start badly, as it were, and the laurel would, in some respects at least, scarcely be greener from the brows of the original wearer. That idea, however, was at that hour, as I have hinted, not the source of anxiety it ought perhaps to have been, for I felt less the irregularity of Saltram's getting the money than that of this exalted young woman's giving it up. I wanted her to have it for herself, and I told her so before I went away. She looked graver at this than she had looked at all, saying she hoped such a preference wouldn't make me dishonest.

It made me, to begin with, very restless—made me, instead of going straight to the station, fidget a little about that many-coloured Common which gives Wimbledon horizons. There was a worry for me to work off, or rather keep at a distance, for I declined even to admit to myself that I had, in Miss Anvoy's phrase, been saddled with it. What could have been clearer indeed than the attitude of recognising perfectly what a world of trouble the Coxon Fund would in future save us, and of yet liking better to face a continuance of that trouble than see, and in fact contribute to, a deviation from attainable bliss in the life of two other persons in whom I was deeply interested? Suddenly, at the end of twenty minutes, there was projected across this clearness the image of a massive, middle-aged man seated on a bench, under a tree, with sad, far-wandering eyes and plump white hands folded on the head of a stick—a stick I recognised, a stout gold-headed staff that I had given him in throbbing days. I stopped short as he turned his face to me, and it happened that for some reason or other I took in as I had perhaps never done before the beauty of his rich blank gaze. It was charged with experience as the sky is charged with light, and I felt on the instant as if we had been overspanned and conjoined by the great arch of a bridge or the great dome of a temple. Doubtless I was rendered peculiarly sensitive to it by something in the way I had been giving him up and sinking him. While I met it I stood there smitten, and I felt myself responding to it with a sort of guilty grimace. This brought back his attention in a smile which expressed for me a cheerful, weary patience, a bruised, noble gentleness. I had told Miss Anvoy that he had no dignity, but what did he seem to me, all unbuttoned and fatigued as he waited for me to come up, if he didn't seem unconcerned with small things, didn't seem in short majestic? There was majesty in his mere unconsciousness of our little conferences and puzzlements over his maintenance and his reward.

After I had sat by him a few minutes I passed my arm over his big soft shoulder (wherever you touched him you found equally little firmness) and said in a tone of which the suppliance fell oddly on my own ear: "Come back to town with me, old friend—come back and spend the evening." I wanted to hold him, I wanted to keep him, and at Waterloo, an hour later, I telegraphed possessively to the Mulvilles. When he objected, as regards staying all night, that he had no things, I asked him if he hadn't everything of mine. I had abstained from ordering dinner, and it was too late for preliminaries at a club; so we were reduced to tea and fried fish at my rooms—reduced also to the transcendent. Something had come up which made me want him to feel at peace with me, which was all the dear man himself wanted on any occasion. I had too often had to press upon him considerations irrelevant, but it gives me pleasure now to think that on that particular evening I didn't even mention Mrs. Saltram and the children. Late into the night we smoked and talked; old shames and old rigours fell away from us; I only let him see that I was conscious of what I owed him. He was as mild as contrition and as abundant as faith; he was never so fine as on a shy return, and even better at forgiving than at being forgiven. I daresay it was a smaller matter than that famous night at Wimbledon, the night of the problematical sobriety and of Miss Anvoy's initiation; but I was as much in it on this occasion as I had been out of it then. At about 1.30 he was sublime.

He never, under any circumstances, rose till all other risings were over, and his breakfasts, at Wimbledon, had always been the principal reason mentioned by departing cooks. The coast was therefore clear for me to receive her when, early the next morning, to my surprise, it was announced to me that his wife had called. I hesitated, after she had come up, about telling her Saltram was in the house, but she herself settled the question, kept me reticent by drawing forth a sealed letter which, looking at me very hard in the eyes, she placed, with a pregnant absence of comment, in my hand. For a single moment there glimmered before me the fond hope that Mrs. Saltram had tendered me, as it were, her resignation and desired to embody the act in an unsparing form. To bring this about I would have feigned any humiliation; but after my eyes had caught the superscription I heard myself say with a flatness that betrayed a sense of something very different from relief: "Oh, the Pudneys!" I knew their envelopes though they didn't know mine. They always used the kind sold at post-offices with the stamp affixed, and as this letter had not been posted they had wasted a penny on me. I had seen their horrid missives to the Mulvilles, but had not been in direct correspondence with them.

"They enclosed it to me, to be delivered. They doubtless explain to you that they hadn't your address."

I turned the thing over without opening it. "Why in the world should they write to me?"

"Because they have something to tell you. The worst," Mrs. Saltram dryly added.

It was another chapter, I felt, of the history of their lamentable quarrel with her husband, the episode in which, vindictively, disingenuously as they themselves had behaved, one had to admit that he had put himself more grossly in the wrong than at any moment of his life. He had begun by insulting the matchless Mulvilles for these more specious protectors, and then, according to his wont at the end of a few months, had dug a still deeper ditch for his aberration than the chasm left yawning behind. The chasm at Wimbledon was now blessedly closed; but the Pudneys, across their persistent gulf, kept up the nastiest fire. I never doubted they had a strong case, and I had been from the first for not defending him—reasoning that if they were not contradicted they would perhaps subside. This was above all what I wanted, and I so far prevailed that I did arrest the correspondence in time to save our little circle an infliction heavier than it perhaps would have borne. I knew, that is I divined, that their allegations had gone as yet only as far as their courage, conscious as they were in their own virtue of an exposed place in which Saltram could have planted a blow. It was a question with them whether a man who had himself so much to cover up would dare his blow; so that these vessels of rancour were in a manner afraid of each other. I judged that on the day the Pudneys should cease for some reason or other to be afraid they would treat us to some revelation more disconcerting than any of its predecessors. As I held Mrs. Saltram's letter in my hand it was distinctly communicated to me that the day had come—they had ceased to be afraid. "I don't want to know the worst," I presently declared.

"You'll have to open the letter. It also contains an enclosure."

I felt it—it was fat and uncanny. "Wheels within wheels!" I exclaimed. "There is something for me too to deliver."

"So they tell me—to Miss Anvoy."

I stared; I felt a certain thrill. "Why don't they send it to her directly?"

Mrs. Saltram hesitated. "Because she's staying with Mr. and Mrs. Mulville."

"And why should that prevent?"

Again my visitor faltered, and I began to reflect on the grotesque, the unconscious perversity of her action. I was the only person save George Gravener and the Mulvilles who was aware of Sir Gregory Coxon's and of Miss Anvoy's strange bounty. Where could there have been a more signal illustration of the clumsiness of human affairs than her having complacently selected this moment to fly in the face of it? "There's the chance of their seeing her letters. They know Mr. Pudney's hand."

Still I didn't understand; then it flashed upon me. "You mean they might intercept it? How can you imply anything so base?" I indignantly demanded.

"It's not I; it's Mr. Pudney!" cried Mrs. Saltram with a flush. "It's his own idea."

"Then why couldn't he send the letter to *you* to be delivered?"

Mrs. Saltram's embarrassment increased; she gave me another hard look. "You must make that out for yourself."

I made it out quickly enough. "It's a denunciation?"

"A real lady doesn't betray her husband!" this virtuous woman exclaimed.

I burst out laughing, and I fear my laugh may have had an effect of impertinence.

"Especially to Miss Anvoy, who's so easily shocked? Why do such things concern *her*?" I asked, much at a loss.

"Because she's there, exposed to all his craft. Mr. and Mrs. Pudney have been watching this: they feel she may be taken in."

"Thank you for all the rest of us! What difference can it make when she has lost her power to contribute?"

Again Mrs. Saltram considered; then very nobly, "There are other things in the world than money," she remarked. This hadn't occurred to her so long as the young lady had any; but she now added, with a glance at my letter, that Mr. and Mrs. Pudney doubtless explained their motives. "It's all in kindness," she continued as she got up.

"Kindness to Miss Anvoy? You took, on the whole, another view of kindness before her reverses."

My companion smiled with some acidity. "Perhaps you're no safer than the Mulvilles!"

I didn't want her to think that, nor that she should report

to the Pudneys that they had not been happy in their agent; and I well remember that this was the moment at which I began, with considerable emotion, to promise myself to enjoin upon Miss Anvoy never to open any letter that should come to her in one of those penny envelopes. My emotion and I fear I must add my confusion quickly deepened; I presently should have been as glad to frighten Mrs. Saltram as to think I might by some diplomacy restore the Pudneys to a quieter vigilance.

"It's best you should take *my* view of my safety," I at any rate soon responded. When I saw she didn't know what I meant by this I added: "You may turn out to have done, in bringing me this letter, a thing you will profoundly regret." My tone had a significance which, I could see, did make her uneasy, and there was a moment, after I had made two or three more remarks of studiously bewildering effect, at which her eyes followed so hungrily the little flourish of the letter with which I emphasised them that I instinctively slipped Mr. Pudney's communication into my pocket. She looked, in her embarrassed annoyance, as if she might grab it and send it back to him. I felt, after she had gone, as if I had almost given her my word I wouldn't deliver the enclosure. The passionate movement, at any rate, with which, in solitude, I transferred the whole thing, unopened, from my pocket to a drawer which I double-locked would have amounted for an initiated observer to some such promise.

XII

Mrs. Saltram left me drawing my breath more quickly and indeed almost in pain—as if I had just perilously grazed the loss of something precious. I didn't quite know what it was it had a shocking resemblance to my honour. The emotion was the livelier doubtless in that my pulses were still shaken with the rejoicing with which, the night before, I had rallied to the rare analyst, the great intellectual adventurer and path-finder. What had dropped from me like a cumbersome garment as Saltram appeared before me in the afternoon on the heath was the disposition to haggle over his value. Hang it, one had to choose, one had to put that value somewhere; so I would put it really high and have done with it. Mrs. Mulville drove in for him at a discreet hour—the earliest she could suppose him to have got up; and I learned that Miss Anvoy would also have come had she not been expecting a visit from Mr. Gravener. I was perfectly mindful that I was under bonds to see this young lady, and also that I had a letter to deliver to her; but I took my time, I waited from day to day. I left Mrs. Saltram to deal as her apprehensions should prompt with the Pudneys. I knew at last what I meant—I had ceased to wince at my responsibility. I gave this supreme impression of Saltram time to fade if it would; but it didn't fade, and, individually, it has not faded even now. During the month that I thus invited myself to stiffen again, Adelaide Mulville, perplexed by my absence, wrote to me to ask why I *was* so stiff. At that season of the year I was usually oftener with them. She also wrote that she feared a real estrangement had set in between Mr. Gravener and her sweet young friend—a state of things only partly satisfactory to her so long as the advantage accruing to Mr. Saltram failed to disengage itself from the merely nebulous state. She intimated that her sweet young friend was, if anything, a trifle too reserved; she also intimated that there might now be an opening for another clever young man. There never was the slightest opening, I may here parenthesise, and of course the question can't come up to-day. These are old frustrations now. Ruth Anvoy has not married, I hear, and neither have I. During the month, toward the end, I wrote to George Gravener to ask if, on a special errand, I might come to see him, and his answer was to knock the very next day at my door. I saw he had immediately connected my inquiry with the talk we had had in the railway carriage, and his promptitude showed that the ashes of his eagerness were not yet cold. I told him there was something I thought I ought in candour to let him know—I recognised the obligation his friendly confidence had laid upon me.

"You mean that Miss Anvoy has talked to you? She has told me so herself," he said.

"It was not to tell you so that I wanted to see you," I replied; "for it seemed to me that such a communication would rest wholly with herself. If however she did speak to you of our conversation she probably told you I was discouraging."

"Discouraging?"

"On the subject of a present application of the Coxon Fund."

"To the case of Mr. Saltram? My dear fellow, I don't know what you call discouraging!" Gravener exclaimed.

"Well I thought I was, and I thought she thought I was."

"I believe she did, but such a thing is measured by the effect. She's not discouraged."

"That's her own affair. The reason I asked you to see me was that it appeared to me I ought to tell you frankly that decidedly I can't undertake to produce that effect. In fact I don't want to!"

"It's very good of you, damn you!" my visitor laughed, red and really grave. Then he said: "You would like to see that fellow publicly glorified—perched on the pedestal of a great complimentary fortune?"

"Taking one form of public recognition with another, it seems to me on the whole I could bear it. When I see the compliments that *are* paid right and left, I ask myself why this one shouldn't take its course. This therefore is what you're entitled to have looked to me to mention to you. I have some evidence that perhaps would be really dissuasive, but I propose to invite Miss Anvoy to remain in ignorance of it."

"And to invite me to do the same?"

"Oh, you don't require it—you've evidence enough. I speak of a sealed letter which I've been requested to deliver to her."

"And you don't mean to?"

"There's only one consideration that would make me."

Gravener's clear, handsome eyes plunged into mine a minute, but evidently without fishing up a clue to this motive—a failure by which I was almost wounded. "What does the letter contain?"

"It's sealed, as I tell you, and I don't know what it contains."

"Why is it sent through you?"

"Rather than you?" I hesitated a moment. "The only explanation I can think of is that the person sending it may have

imagined your relations with Miss Anvoy to be at an end—
may have been told this is the case by Mrs. Saltram."

"My relations with Miss Anvoy are not at an end," poor
Gravener stammered.

Again, for an instant, I deliberated. "The offer I propose
to make you gives me the right to put you a question remarkably direct. Are you still engaged to Miss Anvoy?"

"No, I'm not," he slowly brought out. "But we're perfectly
good friends."

"Such good friends that you will again become prospective
husband and wife if the obstacle in your path be removed?"

"Removed?" Gravener anxiously repeated.

"If I give Miss Anvoy the letter I speak of she may drop
her project."

"Then for God's sake give it!"

"I'll do so if you're ready to assure me that her dropping
it would now presumably bring about your marriage."

"I'd marry her the next day!" my visitor cried.

"Yes, but would she marry you? What I ask of you of course
is nothing less than your word of honour as to your conviction
of this. If you give it me," I said, "I'll engage to hand her
the letter before night."

Gravener took up his hat; turning it mechanically round,
he stood looking a moment hard at its unruffled perfection.
Then, very angrily, honestly and gallantly: "Hand it to the
devil!" he broke out; with which he clapped the hat on his
head and left me.

"Will you read it or not?" I said to Ruth Anvoy, at Wimbledon, when I had told her the story of Mrs. Saltram's visit.

She reflected for a period which was probably of the briefest, but which was long enough to make me nervous. "Have
you brought it with you?"

"No indeed. It's at home, locked up."

There was another great silence, and then she said: "Go
back and destroy it."

I went back, but I didn't destroy it till after Saltram's death,
when I burnt it unread. The Pudneys approached her again
pressingly, but, prompt as they were, the Coxon Fund had
already become an operative benefit and a general amaze: Mr.
Saltram, while we gathered about, as it were, to watch the

manna descend, was already drawing the magnificent income. He drew it as he had always drawn everything, with a grand abstracted gesture. Its magnificence, alas, as all the world now knows, quite quenched him; it was the beginning of his decline. It was also naturally a new grievance for his wife, who began to believe in him as soon as he was blighted, and who at this hour accuses us of having bribed him, on the whim of a meddlesome American, to renounce his glorious office, to become, as she says, like everybody else. The very day he found himself able to publish he wholly ceased to produce. This deprived us, as may easily be imagined, of much of our occupation, and especially deprived the Mulvilles, whose want of self-support I never measured till they lost their great inmate. They have no one to live on now. Adelaide's most frequent reference to their destitution is embodied in the remark that dear far-away Ruth's intentions were doubtless good. She and Kent are even yet looking for another prop, but no one presents a true sphere of usefulness. They complain that people are self-sufficing. With Saltram the fine type of the child of adoption was scattered, the grander, the elder style. They have got their carriage back, but what's an empty carriage? In short I think we were all happier as well as poorer before; even including George Gravener, who, by the deaths of his brother and his nephew, has lately become Lord Maddock. His wife, whose fortune clears the property, is criminally dull; he hates being in the upper House, and he has not yet had high office. But what are these accidents, which I should perhaps apologise for mentioning, in the light of the great eventual boon promised the patient by the rate at which the Coxon Fund must be rolling up?

The Altar of the Dead

H E HAD a mortal dislike, poor Stransom, to lean anniversaries, and he disliked them still more when they made a pretence of a figure. Celebrations and suppressions were equally painful to him, and there was only one of the former that found a place in his life. Again and again he had kept in his own fashion the day of the year on which Mary Antrim died. It would be more to the point perhaps to say that the day kept *him*: it kept him at least, effectually, from doing anything else. It took hold of him year after year with a hand of which time had softened but had never loosened the touch. He waked up to this feast of memory as consciously as he would have waked up to his marriage-morn. Marriage had had, of old, but too little to say to the matter: for the girl who was to have been his bride there had been no bridal embrace. She had died of a malignant fever after the wedding-day had been fixed, and he had lost, before fairly tasting it, an affection that promised to fill his life to the brim.

Of that benediction, however, it would have been false to say this life could really be emptied: it was still ruled by a pale ghost, it was still ordered by a sovereign presence. He had not been a man of numerous passions, and even in all these years no sense had grown stronger with him than the sense of being bereft. He had needed no priest and no altar to make him for ever widowed. He had done many things in the world—he had done almost all things but one: he had never forgotten. He had tried to put into his existence whatever else might take up room in it, but he had never made it anything but a house of which the mistress was eternally absent. She was most absent of all on the recurrent December day that his tenacity set apart. He had no designed observance of it, but his nerves made it all their own. They always drove him forth on a long walk, for the goal of his pilgrimage was far. She had been buried in a London suburb, in a place then almost natural, but which he had seen lose one after another every feature of freshness. It was in truth during the moments he stood there that his eyes beheld the place least. They looked at another image, they opened to another light. Was it a credible future? Was it an incredible past? Whatever it was, it was an immense escape from the actual.

It is true that if there were not other dates than this there were other memories; and by the time George Stransom was fifty-five such memories had greatly multiplied. There were other ghosts in his life than the ghost of Mary Antrim. He had perhaps not had more losses than most men, but he had counted his losses more; he had not seen death more closely, but he had, in a manner, felt it more deeply. He had formed little by little the habit of numbering his Dead: it had come to him tolerably early in life that there was something one had to do for them. They were there in their simplified, intensified essence, their conscious absence and expressive patience, as personally there as if they had only been stricken dumb. When all sense of them failed, all sound of them ceased, it was as if their purgatory were really still on earth: they asked so little that they got, poor things, even less, and died again, died every day, of the hard usage of life. They had no organised service, no reserved place, no honour, no shelter, no safety. Even ungenerous people provided for the living, but even those who were called most generous did nothing for the others. So, on George Stransom's part, there grew up with the years a determination that he at least would do something, do it, that is, for his own, and perform the great charity without reproach. Every man had his own, and every man had, to meet this charity, the ample resources of the soul.

It was doubtless the voice of Mary Antrim that spoke for them best; at any rate, as the years went on, he found himself in regular communion with these alternative associates, with those whom indeed he always called in his thoughts the Others. He spared them the moments, he organised the charity. How it grew up he probably never could have told you, but what came to pass was that an altar, such as was after all within everybody's compass, lighted with perpetual candles and dedicated to these secret rites, reared itself in his spiritual spaces. He had wondered of old, in some embarrassment, whether he had a religion; being very sure, and not a little content, that he had not at all events the religion some of the people he had known wanted him to have. Gradually this question

452   THE ALTAR OF THE DEAD

was straightened out for him: it became clear to him that the
religion instilled by his earliest consciousness had been simply
the religion of the Dead. It suited his inclination, it satisfied
his spirit, it gave employment to his piety. It answered his love
of great offices, of a solemn and splendid ritual, for no shrine
could be more bedecked and no ceremonial more stately than
those to which his worship was attached. He had no imagination about these things save that they were accessible to
every one who should ever feel the need of them. The poorest
could build such temples of the spirit—could make them blaze
with candles and smoke with incense, make them flush with
pictures and flowers. The cost, in the common phrase, of
keeping them up fell entirely on the liberal heart.

II

He had this year, on the eve of his anniversary, as it happened,
an emotion not unconnected with that range of feeling. Walking home at the close of a busy day, he was arrested in the
London street by the particular effect of a shop-front which
lighted the dull brown air with its mercenary grin and before
which several persons were gathered. It was the window of a
jeweller whose diamonds and sapphires seemed to laugh, in
flashes like high notes of sound, with the mere joy of knowing
how much more they were "worth" than most of the dingy
pedestrians staring at them from the other side of the pane.
Stransom lingered long enough to suspend, in a vision, a
string of pearls about the white neck of Mary Antrim, and
then was kept an instant longer by the sound of a voice he
knew. Next him was a mumbling old woman, and beyond the
old woman a gentleman with a lady on his arm. It was from
him, from Paul Creston, the voice had proceeded: he was talking with the lady of some previous object in the window.
Stransom had no sooner recognised him than the old woman
turned away; but simultaneously with this increase of opportunity he became aware of a strangeness which stayed him in
the very act of laying his hand on his friend's arm. It lasted
only a few seconds, but a few seconds were long enough for
the flash of a wild question. Was *not* Mrs. Creston dead?—the
ambiguity met him there in the short drop of her husband's

voice, the drop conjugal, if it ever was, and in the way the two figures leaned to each other. Creston, making a step to look at something else, came nearer, glanced at him, started and exclaimed—a circumstance the effect of which was at first only to leave Stransom staring, staring back across the months at the different face, the wholly other face the poor man had shown him last, the blurred, ravaged mask bent over the open grave by which they had stood together. Creston was not in mourning now; he detached his arm from his companion's to grasp the hand of the older friend. He coloured as well as smiled in the strong light of the shop when Stransom raised a tentative hat to the lady. Stransom had just time to see that she was pretty before he found himself gaping at a fact more portentous. "My dear fellow, let me make you acquainted with my wife."

Creston had blushed and stammered over it, but in half a minute, at the rate we live in polite society, it had practically become, for Stransom, the mere memory of a shock. They stood there and laughed and talked; Stransom had instantly whisked the shock out of the way, to keep it for private consumption. He felt himself grimacing, he heard himself exaggerating the usual, but he was conscious that he had turned slightly faint. That new woman, that hired performer, Mrs. Creston? Mrs. Creston had been more living for him than any woman but one. This lady had a face that shone as publicly as the jeweller's window, and in the happy candour with which she wore her monstrous character there was an effect of gross immodesty. The character of Hugh Creston's wife thus attributed to her was monstrous for reasons which Stransom could see that his friend perfectly knew that he knew. The happy pair had just arrived from America, and Stransom had not needed to be told this to divine the nationality of the lady. Somehow it deepened the foolish air that her husband's confused cordiality was unable to conceal. Stransom recalled that he had heard of poor Creston's having, while his bereavement was still fresh, gone to the United States for what people in such predicaments call a little change. He had found the little change indeed, he had brought the little change back; it was the little change that stood there and that, do what he would, he couldn't, while he showed those high front-teeth of his, look like anything but a conscious ass about. They were going into the shop Mrs. Creston said, and she begged Mr. Stransom to come with them and help to decide. He thanked her, opening his watch and pleading an engagement for which he was already late, and they parted while she shrieked into the fog, "Mind now you come to see me right away!" Creston had had the delicacy not to suggest that, and Stransom hoped it hurt him somewhere to hear her scream it to all the echoes.

He felt quite determined, as he walked away, never in his life to go near her. She was perhaps a human being, but Creston oughtn't to have shown her without precautions, oughtn't indeed to have shown her at all. His precautions should have been those of a forger or a murderer, and the people at home would never have mentioned extradition. This was a wife for foreign service or purely external use; a decent consideration would have spared her the injury of comparisons. Such were the first reflections of George Stransom's amazement; but as he sat alone that night—there were particular hours that he always passed alone—the harshness dropped from them and left only the pity. *He* could spend an evening with Kate Creston, if the man to whom she had given everything couldn't. He had known her twenty years, and she was the only woman for whom he might perhaps have been unfaithful. She was all cleverness and sympathy and charm; her house had been the very easiest in all the world and her friendship the very firmest. Without accidents he had loved her, without accidents every one had loved her: she had made the passions about her as regular as the moon makes the tides. She had been also of course far too good for her husband, but he never suspected it, and in nothing had she been more admirable than in the exquisite art with which she tried to keep every one else (keeping Creston was no trouble) from finding it out. Here was a man to whom she had devoted her life and for whom she had given it up—dying to bring into the world a child of his bed; and she had had only to submit to her fate to have, ere the grass was green on her grave, no more existence for him than a domestic servant he had re-placed. The frivolity, the indecency of it made Stransom's eyes fill; and he had that evening a rich, almost happy sense that he alone, in a world without delicacy, had a right to hold up his head. While he smoked, after dinner, he had a book in his lap, but he had no eyes for his page: his eyes, in the swarming void of things, seemed to have caught Kate Creston's, and it was into their sad silences he looked. It was to him her sentient spirit had turned, knowing that it was of her he would think. He thought, for a long time, of how the closed eyes of dead women could still live—how they could open again, in a quiet lamplit room, long after they had looked their last. They had looks that remained, as great poets had quoted lines.

The newspaper lay by his chair—the thing that came in the afternoon and the servants thought one wanted; without sense for what was in it he had mechanically unfolded and then dropped it. Before he went to bed he took it up, and this time, at the top of a paragraph, he was caught by five words that made him start. He stood staring, before the fire, at the "Death of Sir Acton Hague, K.C.B.," the man who, ten years earlier, had been the nearest of his friends and whose deposition from this eminence had practically left it without an occupant. He had seen him after that catastrophe, but he had not seen him for years. Standing there before the fire he turned cold as he read what had befallen him. Promoted a short time previous to the governorship of the Westward Islands, Acton Hague had died, in the bleak honour of this exile, of an illness consequent on the bite of a poisonous snake. His career was compressed by the newspaper into a dozen lines, the perusal of which excited on George Stransom's part no warmer feeling than one of relief at the absence of any mention of their quarrel, an incident accidentally tainted at the time, thanks to their joint immersion in large affairs, with a horrible publicity. Public indeed was the wrong Stransom had, to his own sense, suffered, the insult he had blankly taken from the only man with whom he had ever been intimate; the friend, almost adored, of his University years, the subject, later, of his passionate loyalty: so public that he had never spoken of it to a human creature, so public that he had completely overlooked it. It had made the difference for him that friendship too was all over, but it had only made just that one. The shock of interests had been private, intensely so; but the action taken by Hague had been in the face of men. To-day it all seemed to have occurred merely to the end that George Stransom should think of him as "Hague" and measure exactly how much he himself could feel like a stone. He went cold, suddenly and horribly cold, to bed.

III

The next day, in the afternoon, in the great grey suburb, he felt that his long walk had tired him. In the dreadful cemetery alone he had been on his feet an hour. Instinctively, coming back, they had taken him a devious course, and it was a desert in which no circling cabman hovered over possible prey. He paused on a corner and measured the dreariness; then he became aware in the gathered dusk that he was in one of those tracts of London which are less gloomy by night than by day, because, in the former case, of the civil gift of light. By day there was nothing, but by night there were lamps, and George Stransom was in a mood which made lamps good in themselves. It wasn't that they could show him anything; it was only that they could burn clear. To his surprise, however, after a while, they did show him something: the arch of a high doorway approached by a low terrace of steps, in the depth of which—it formed a dim vestibule—the raising of a curtain, at the moment he passed, gave him a glimpse of an avenue of gloom with a glow of tapers at the end. He stopped and looked up, making out that the place was a church. The thought quickly came to him that since he was tired he might rest there; so that after a moment he had in turn pushed up the leathern curtain and gone in. It was a temple of the old persuasion, and there had evidently been a function—perhaps a service for the dead; the high altar was still a blaze of candles. This was an exhibition he always liked, and he dropped into a seat with relief. More than it had ever yet come home to him it struck him as good that there should be churches.

This one was almost empty and the other altars were dim; a verger shuffled about, an old woman coughed, but it seemed to Stransom there was hospitality in the thick sweet air. Was it only the savour of the incense, or was it something larger and more guaranteed? He had at any rate quitted the great grey suburb and come nearer to the warm centre. He presently ceased to feel an intruder—he gained at last even a sense

of community with the only worshipper in his neighbourhood, the sombre presence of a woman, in mourning unre-
lieved, whose back was all he could see of her and who had
sunk deep into prayer at no great distance from him. He
wished he could sink, like her, to the very bottom, be as motionless, as rapt in prostration. After a few moments he shifted
his seat; it was almost indelicate to be so aware of her. But
Stransom subsequently lost himself altogether; he floated away
on the sea of light. If occasions like this had been more frequent in his life he would have been more frequently conscious of the great original type, set up in a myriad temples,
of the unapproachable shrine he had erected in his mind. That
shrine had begun as a reflection of ecclesiastical pomps, but
the echo had ended by growing more distinct than the sound.
The sound now rang out, the type blazed at him with all its
fires and with a mystery of radiance in which endless meanings
could glow. The thing became, as he sat there, his appropriate
altar, and each starry candle an appropriate vow. He numbered
them, he named them, he grouped them—it was the silent
roll-call of his Dead. They made together a brightness vast
and intense, a brightness in which the mere chapel of his
thoughts grew so dim that as it faded away he asked himself
if he shouldn't find his real comfort in some material act, some
outward worship.

This idea took possession of him while, at a distance, the
black-robed lady continued prostrate; he was quietly thrilled
with his conception, which at last brought him to his feet in
the sudden excitement of a plan. He wandered softly about
the church, pausing in the different chapels, which were all,
save one, applied to a special devotion. It was in this one, dark
and ungarnished, that he stood longest—the length of time
it took him fully to grasp the conception of gilding it with his
bounty. He should snatch it from no other rites and associate
it with nothing profane; he would simply take it as it should
be given up to him and make it a masterpiece of splendour
and a mountain of fire. Tended sacredly all the year, with the
sanctifying church around it, it would always be ready for his
offices. There would be difficulties, but from the first they
presented themselves only as difficulties surmounted. Even for
a person so little affiliated the thing would be a matter of

arrangement. He saw it all in advance, and how bright in especial the place would become to him in the intermissions of
toil and the dusk of afternoons; how rich in assurance at all
times, but especially in the indifferent world. Before withdrawing he drew nearer again to the spot where he had first
sat down, and in the movement he met the lady whom he
had seen praying and who was now on her way to the door.
She passed him quickly, and he had only a glimpse of her pale
face and her unconscious, almost sightless eyes. For that instant she looked faded and handsome.

This was the origin of the rites more public, yet certainly
esoteric, that he at last found himself able to establish. It took
a long time, it took a year, and both the process and the result
would have been—for any who knew—a vivid picture of his
good faith. No one did know, in fact—no one but the bland
ecclesiastics whose acquaintance he had promptly sought,
whose objections he had softly overridden, whose curiosity
and sympathy he had artfully charmed, whose assent to his
eccentric munificence he had eventually won, and who had
asked for concessions in exchange for indulgences. Stransom
had of course at an early stage of his inquiry been referred to
the Bishop, and the Bishop had been delightfully human, the
Bishop had been almost amused. Success was within sight, at
any rate, from the moment the attitude of those whom it
concerned became liberal in response to liberality. The altar
and the small chapel that enclosed it, consecrated to an ostensible and customary worship, were to be splendidly maintained; all that Stransom reserved to himself was the number
of his lights and the free enjoyment of his intention. When the
intention had taken complete effect the enjoyment became
even greater than he had ventured to hope. He liked to think of
this effect when he was far from it—he liked to convince himself of it yet again when he was near. He was not often, indeed,
so near as that a visit to it had not perforce something of the
patience of a pilgrimage; but the time he gave to his devotion
came to seem to him more a contribution to his other interests than a betrayal of them. Even a loaded life might be easier
when one had added a new necessity to it.

How much easier was probably never guessed by those who
simply knew that there were hours when he disappeared and

for many of whom there was a vulgar reading of what they used to call his plunges. These plunges were into depths quieter than the deep sea-caves, and the habit, at the end of a year or two, had become the one it would have cost him most to relinquish. Now they had really, his Dead, something that was indefeasibly theirs; and he liked to think that they might, in cases, be the Dead of others, as well as that the Dead of others might be invoked there under the protection of what he had done. Whoever bent a knee on the carpet he had laid down appeared to him to act in the spirit of his intention. Each of his lights had a name for him, and from time to time a new light was kindled. This was what he had fundamentally agreed for, that there should always be room for them all. What those who passed or lingered saw was simply the most resplendent of the altars, called suddenly into vivid usefulness, with a quiet elderly man, for whom it evidently had a fascination, often seated there in a maze or a doze; but half the satisfaction of the spot for this mysterious and fitful worshipper was that he found the years of his life there, and the ties, the affections, the struggles, the submissions, the conquests, if there had been such, a record of that adventurous journey in which the beginnings and the endings of human relations are the lettered mile-stones. He had in general little taste for the past as a part of his own history; at other times and in other places it mostly seemed to him pitiful to consider and impossible to repair; but on these occasions he accepted it with something of that positive gladness with which one adjusts one's self to an ache that is beginning to succumb to treatment. To the treatment of time the malady of life begins at a given moment to succumb; and these were doubtless the hours at which that truth most came home to him. The day was written for him there on which he had first become acquainted with death, and the successive phases of the acquaintance were each marked with a flame.

The flames were gathering thick at present, for Stransom had entered that dark defile of our earthly descent in which some one dies every day. It was only yesterday that Kate Creston had flashed out her white fire; yet already there were younger stars ablaze on the tips of the tapers. Various persons in whom his interest had not been intense drew closer to him by entering this company. He went over it, head by head, till he felt like the shepherd of a huddled flock, with all a shepherd's vision of differences imperceptible. He knew his candles apart, up to the colour of the flame, and would still have known them had their positions all been changed. To other imaginations they might stand for other things—that they should stand for something to be hushed before was all he desired; but he was intensely conscious of the personal note of each and of the distinguishable way it contributed to the concert. There were hours at which he almost caught himself wishing that certain of his friends would now die, that he might establish with them in this manner a connection more charming than, as it happened, it was possible to enjoy with them in life. In regard to those from whom one was separated by the long curves of the globe such a connection could only be an improvement: it brought them instantly within reach. Of course there were gaps in the constellation, for Stransom knew he could only pretend to act for his own, and it was not every figure passing before his eyes into the great obscure that was entitled to a memorial. There was a strange sanctification in death, but some characters were more sanctified by being forgotten than by being remembered. The greatest blank in the shining page was the memory of Acton Hague, of which he inveterately tried to rid himself. For Acton Hague no flame could ever rise on any altar of his.

IV

Every year, the day he walked back from the great graveyard, he went to church as he had done the day his idea was born. It was on this occasion, as it happened, after a year had passed, that he began to observe his altar to be haunted by a worshipper at least as frequent as himself. Others of the faithful, and in the rest of the church, came and went, appealing sometimes, when they disappeared, to a vague or to a particular recognition; but this unfailing presence was always to be observed when he arrived and still in possession when he departed. He was surprised, the first time, at the promptitude with which it assumed an identity for him—the identity of the lady whom, two years before, on his anniversary, he had seen

so intensely bowed, and of whose tragic face he had had so
flitting a vision. Given the time that had elapsed, his recollection of her was fresh enough to make him wonder. Of himself
she had of course no impression, or rather she had none at
first: the time came when her manner of transacting her business suggested to him that she had gradually guessed his call
to be of the same order. She used his altar for her own purpose—he could only hope that, sad and solitary as she always
struck him, she used it for her own Dead. There were interruptions, infidelities, all on his part, calls to other associations
and duties; but as the months went on he found her whenever
he returned, and he ended by taking pleasure in the thought
that he had given her almost the contentment he had given
himself. They worshipped side by side so often that there were
moments when he wished he might be sure, so straight did
their prospect stretch away of growing old together in their
rites. She was younger than he, but she looked as if her Dead
were at least as numerous as his candles. She had no colour,
no sound, no fault, and another of the things about which he
had made up his mind was that she had no fortune. She was
always black-robed, as if she had had a succession of sorrows.
People were not poor, after all, whom so many losses could
overtake; they were positively rich when they had so much to
give up. But the air of this devoted and indifferent woman,
who always made, in any attitude, a beautiful, accidental line,
conveyed somehow to Stransom that she had known more
kinds of trouble than one.

He had a great love of music and little time for the joy of
it; but occasionally, when workaday noises were muffled by
Saturday afternoons, it used to come back to him that there
were glories. There were moreover friends who reminded him
of this and side by side with whom he found himself sitting
out concerts. On one of these winter evenings, in St. James's
Hall, he became aware after he had seated himself that the
lady he had so often seen at church was in the place next him
and was evidently alone, as he also this time happened to be.
She was at first too absorbed in the consideration of the programme to heed him, but when she at last glanced at him he
took advantage of the movement to speak to her, greeting her
with the remark that he felt as if he already knew her. She

smiled as she said "Oh yes, I recognise you;" yet in spite of
this admission of their long acquaintance it was the first time he
had ever seen her smile. The effect of it was suddenly to contribute more to that acquaintance than all the previous meetings had done. He hadn't "taken in," he said to himself, that
she was so pretty. Later, that evening (it was while he rolled
along in a hansom on his way to dine out) he added that he
hadn't taken in that she was so interesting. The next morning,
in the midst of his work, he quite suddenly and irrelevantly
reflected that his impression of her, beginning so far back, was
like a winding river that had at last reached the sea.

His work was indeed blurred a little, all that day, by the
sense of what had now passed between them. It wasn't much,
but it had just made the difference. They had listened together
to Beethoven and Schumann; they had talked in the pauses
and at the end, when at the door, to which they moved together, he had asked her if he could help her in the matter of
getting away. She had thanked him and put up her umbrella,
slipping into the crowd without an allusion to their meeting
yet again and leaving him to remember at leisure that not a
word had been exchanged about the place in which they frequently met. This circumstance seemed to him at one moment
natural enough and at another perverse. She mightn't in the
least have recognised his warrant for speaking to her; and yet
if she hadn't he would have judged her an underbred woman.
It was odd that when nothing had really ever brought them
together he should have been able successfully to assume that
they were in a manner old friends—that this negative quantity
was somehow more than they could express. His success, it
was true, had been qualified by her quick escape, so that there
grew up in him an absurd desire to put it to some better test.
Save in so far as some other improbable accident might assist
him, such a test could be only to meet her afresh at church.
Left to himself he would have gone to church the very next
afternoon, just for the curiosity of seeing if he should find her
there. But he was not left to himself, a fact he discovered quite
at the last, after he had virtually made up his mind to go. The
influence that kept him away really revealed to him how little
to himself his Dead ever left him. They reminded him that he
went only for them—for nothing else in the world.

The force of this reminder kept him away ten days: he hated to connect the place with anything but his offices or to give a glimpse of the curiosity that had been on the point of moving him. It was absurd to weave a tangle about a matter so simple as a custom of devotion that might so easily have been daily or hourly; yet the tangle got itself woven. He was sorry, he was disappointed: it was as if a long, happy spell had been broken and he had lost a familiar security. At the last, however, he asked himself if he was to stay away for ever from the fear of this muddle about motives. After an interval neither longer nor shorter than usual he re-entered the church with a clear conviction that he should scarcely heed the presence or the absence of the lady of the concert. This indifference didn't prevent his instantly perceiving that for the only time since he had first seen her she was not on the spot. He had now no scruple about giving her time to arrive, but she didn't arrive, and when he went away still missing her he was quite profanely and consentingly sorry. If her absence made the tangle more intricate, that was only her fault. By the end of another year it was very intricate indeed; but by that time he didn't in the least care, and it was only his cultivated consciousness that had given him scruples. Three times in three months he had gone to church without finding her, and he felt that he had not needed these occasions to show him that his suspense had quite dropped. Yet it was, incongruously, not indifference, but a refinement of delicacy that had kept him from asking the sacristan, who would of course immediately have recognised his description of her, whether she had been seen at other hours. His delicacy had kept him from asking any question about her at any time, and it was exactly the same virtue that had left him so free to be decently civil to her at the concert.

This happy advantage now served him anew, enabling him when she finally met his eyes—it was after a fourth trial—to determine without hesitation to wait till she should retire. He joined her in the street as soon as she had done so, and asked her if he might accompany her a certain distance. With her placid permission he went as far as a house in the neighbourhood at which she had business: she let him know it was not where she lived. She lived, as she said, in a mere slum, with an old aunt, a person in connection with whom she spoke of the engrossment of humdrum duties and regular occupations. She was not, the mourning niece, in her first youth, and her vanished freshness had left something behind which, for Stransom, represented the proof that it had been tragically sacrificed. Whatever she gave him the assurance of she gave it without references. She might in fact have been a divorced duchess, and she might have been an old maid who taught the harp.

V

They fell at last into the way of walking together almost every time they met, though, for a long time, they never met anywhere save at church. He couldn't ask her to come and see him, and, as if she had not a proper place to receive him, she never invited him. As much as himself she knew the world of London, but from an undiscussed instinct of privacy they haunted the region not mapped on the social chart. On the return she always made him leave her at the same corner. She looked with him, as a pretext for a pause, at the depressed things in suburban shop-fronts; and there was never a word he had said to her that she had not beautifully understood. For long ages he never knew her name, any more than she had ever pronounced his own; but it was not their names that mattered, it was only their perfect practice and their common need.

These things made their whole relation so impersonal that they had not the rules or reasons people found in ordinary friendships. They didn't care for the things it was supposed necessary to care for in the intercourse of the world. They ended one day (they never knew which of them expressed it first) by throwing out the idea that they didn't care for each other. Over this idea they grew quite intimate; they rallied to it in a way that marked a fresh start in their confidence. If to feel deeply together about certain things wholly distinct from themselves didn't constitute a safety, where was safety to be looked for? Not lightly nor often, not without occasion nor without emotion, any more than in any other reference by serious people to a mystery of their faith; but when something had happened to warm, as it were, the air for it, they came as near as they could come to calling their Dead by name. They felt it was coming very near to utter their thought at all. The word "they" expressed enough; it limited the mention, it had a dignity of its own, and if, in their talk, you had heard our friends use it, you might have taken them for a pair of pagans of old alluding decently to the domesticated gods. They never knew—at least Stransom never knew—how they had learned to be sure about each other. If it had been with each a question of what the other was there for, the certitude had come in some fine way of its own. Any faith, after all, has the instinct of propagation, and it was as natural as it was beautiful that they should have taken pleasure on the spot in the imagination of a following. If the following was for each but a following of one, it had proved in the event to be sufficient. Her debt, however, of course, was much greater than his, because while she had only given him a worshipper he had given her a magnificent temple. Once she said she pitied him for the length of his list (she had counted his candles almost as often as himself) and this made him wonder what could have been the length of hers. He had wondered before at the coincidence of their losses, especially as from time to time a new candle was set up. On some occasion some accident led him to express this curiosity, and she answered as if she was surprised that he hadn't already understood. "Oh, for me, you know, the more there are the better   there could never be too many. I should like hundreds and hundreds—I should like thousands; I should like a perfect mountain of light."

Then of course, in a flash, he understood "Your Dead are only One?"

She hesitated as she had never hesitated. "Only One," she answered, colouring as if now he knew her innermost secret. It really made him feel that he knew less than before, so difficult was it for him to reconstitute a life in which a single experience had reduced all others to nought. His own life, round its central hollow, had been packed close enough. After this she appeared to have regretted her confession, though at the moment she spoke there had been pride in her very embarrassment. She declared to him that his own was the larger, the dearer possession—the portion one would have chosen if one had been able to choose; she assured him she could perfectly imagine some of the echoes with which his silences were peopled. He knew she couldn't: one's relation to what one had loved and hated had been a relation too distinct from the relations of others. But this didn't affect the fact that they were growing old together in their piety. She was a feature of that piety, but even at the ripe stage of acquaintance in which they occasionally arranged to meet at a concert or to go together to an exhibition she was not a feature of anything else. The most that happened was that his worship became paramount. Friend by friend dropped away till at last there were more emblems on his altar than houses left him to enter. She was more than any other the friend who remained, but she was unknown to all the rest. Once when she had discovered, as they called it, a new star, she used the expression that the chapel at last was full.

"Oh no," Stransom replied, "there is a great thing wanting for that! The chapel will never be full till a candle is set up before which all the others will pale. It will be the tallest candle of all."

Her mild wonder rested on him. "What candle do you mean?"

"I mean, dear lady, my own."

He had learned after a long time that she earned money by her pen, writing under a designation that she never told him in magazines that he never saw. She knew too well what he couldn't read and what she couldn't write, and she taught him to cultivate indifference with a success that did much for their good relations. Her invisible industry was a convenience to him; it helped his contented thought of her, the thought that rested in the dignity of her proud, obscure life, her little remunerated art and her little impenetrable home. Lost, with her obscure relative, in her dim suburban world, she came to the surface for him in distant places. She was really the priestess of his altar, and whenever he quitted England he committed it to her keeping. She proved to him afresh that women have more of the spirit of religion than men; he felt his fidelity pale and faint in comparison with hers. He often said to her that since he had so little time to live he rejoiced in her having so much; so glad was he to think she would guard the temple when he should have ceased. He had a great plan for that, which of course he told her too, a bequest of money to keep it up in undiminished state. Of the administration of this fund he would appoint her superintendent, and if the spirit should move her she might kindle a taper even for him.

"And who will kindle one even for me?" she gravely inquired.

VI

She was always in mourning, yet the day he came back from the longest absence he had yet made her appearance immediately told him she had lately had a bereavement. They met on this occasion as she was leaving the church, so that postponing his own entrance he instantly offered to turn round and walk away with her. She considered, then she said: "Go in now, but come and see me in an hour." He knew the small vista of her street, closed at the end and as dreary as an empty pocket, where the pairs of shabby little houses, semi-detached but indissolubly united, were like married couples on bad terms. Often, however, as he had gone to the beginning, he had never gone beyond. Her aunt was dead—that he immediately guessed, as well as that it made a difference; but when she had for the first time mentioned her number he found himself, on her leaving him, not a little agitated by this sudden liberality. She was not a person with whom, after all, one got on so very fast: it had taken him months and months to learn her name, years and years to learn her address. If she had looked, on this reunion, so much older to him, how in the world did he look to her? She had reached the period of life that he had long since reached, when, after separations, the dreadful clockface of the friend we meet announces the hour we have tried to forget. He couldn't have said what he expected as, at the end of his waiting, he turned the corner at which, for years, he had always paused; simply not to pause was a sufficient cause for emotion. It was an event, somehow; and in all their long acquaintance there had never been such a thing. The event grew larger when, five minutes later, in the faint elegance of her little drawing-room, she quavered out some greeting which showed the measure she took of it. He had a strange sense of having come for something in particular; strange because, literally, there was nothing particular between them, nothing save that they were at one on their great point, which had long ago become a magnificent matter of course. It was true that after she had said "You can always come now, you know," the thing he was there for seemed already to have happened. He asked her if it was the death of her aunt that made the difference; to which she replied: "She never knew I knew you. I wished her not to." The beautiful clearness of her candour—her faded beauty was like a summer twilight—disconnected the words from any image of deceit. They might have struck him as the record of a deep dissimulation; but she had always given him a sense of noble reasons. The vanished aunt was present, as he looked about him, in the small complacencies of the room, the beaded velvet and the fluted moreen; and though, as we know, he had the worship of the Dead, he found himself not definitely regretting this lady. If she was not in his long list, however, she was in her niece's short one, and Stransom presently observed to his friend that now, at least, in the place they haunted together, she would have another object of devotion.

"Yes, I shall have another. She was very kind to me. It's that that makes the difference."

He judged, wondering a good deal before he made any motion to leave her, that the difference would somehow be very great and would consist of still other things than her having let him come in. It rather chilled him, for they had been happy together as they were. He extracted from her at any rate an intimation that she should now have larger means, that her aunt's tiny fortune had come to her, so that there was henceforth only one to consume what had formerly been made to suffice for two. This was a joy to Stransom, because it had hitherto been equally impossible for him either to offer her presents or to find contentment in not doing so. It was too ugly to be at her side that way, abounding himself and yet not able to overflow—a demonstration that would have been a signally false note. Even her better situation too seemed only to draw out in a sense the loneliness of her future. It would merely help her to live more and more for their small ceremonial, at a time when he himself had begun wearily to feel that, having set it in motion, he might depart. When they had sat a while in the pale parlour she got up and said: "This isn't *my* room: let us go into mine." They had only to cross the narrow hall, as he found, to pass into quite another air. When she had closed the door of the second room, as she called it, he felt that he had at last real possession of her. The place had the flush of life—it was expressive; its dark red walls were articulate with memories and relics. These were simple things—photographs and water-colours, scraps of writing framed and ghosts of flowers embalmed; but only a moment was needed to show him they had a common meaning. It was here that she had lived and worked; and she had already told him she would make no change of scene. He saw that the objects about her mainly had reference to certain places and times; but after a minute he distinguished among them a small portrait of a gentleman. At a distance and without their glasses his eyes were only caught by it enough to feel a vague curiosity. Presently this impulse carried him nearer, and in another moment he was staring at the picture in stupefaction and with the sense that some sound had broken from him. He was further conscious that he showed his companion a white face when he turned round on her with the exclamation: "Acton Hague!"

She gave him back his astonishment. "Did you know him?"

"He was the friend of all my youth—my early manhood. And *you* knew him?"

She coloured at this, and for a moment her answer failed; her eyes took in everything in the place, and a strange irony reached her lips as she echoed: "Knew him?"

Then Stransom understood, while the room heaved like the cabin of a ship, that its whole contents cried out with him, that it was a museum in his honour, that all her later years had been addressed to him and that the shrine he himself had reared had been passionately converted to this use. It was all for Acton Hague that she had kneeled every day at his altar. What need had there been for a consecrated candle when he was present in the whole array? The revelation seemed to smite our friend in the face, and he dropped into a seat and sat silent. He had quickly become aware that she was shocked at the vision of his own shock, but as she sank on the sofa beside him and laid her hand on his arm he perceived almost as soon that she was unable to resent it as much as she would have liked.

VII

He learned in that instant two things: one of them was that even in so long a time she had gathered no knowledge of his great intimacy and his great quarrel; the other was that in spite of this ignorance, strangely enough, she supplied on the spot a reason for his confusion. "How extraordinary," he presently exclaimed, "that we should never have known!"

She gave a wan smile which seemed to Stransom stranger even than the fact itself. "I never, never spoke of him."

Stransom looked about the room again. "Why then, if your life had been so full of him?"

"Mayn't I put you that question as well? Hadn't your life also been full of him?"

"Any one's, every one's life was who had the wonderful experience of knowing him. I never spoke of him," Stransom added in a moment, "because he did me—years ago—an unforgettable wrong." She was silent, and with the full effect of his presence all about them it almost startled her visitor to hear no protest escape from her. She accepted his words; he turned his eyes to her again to see in what manner she accepted them. It was with rising tears and an extraordinary sweetness in the movement of putting out her hand to take his own. Nothing more wonderful had ever appeared to Stransom than, in that little chamber of remembrance and homage, to see her convey with such exquisite mildness that as from Acton Hague any injury was credible. The clock ticked in the stillness—Hague had probably given it to her—and while he let her hold his hand with a tenderness that was almost an assumption of responsibility for his old pain as well as his new, Stransom after a minute broke out: "Good God, how he must have used *you*!"

She dropped his hand at this, got up and, moving across the room, made straight a small picture to which, on examining it, he had given a slight push. Then turning round on him with her pale gaiety recovered: "I've forgiven him!" she declared.

"I know what you've done," said Stransom; "I know what you've done for years." For a moment they looked at each other across the room, with their long community of service in their eyes. This short passage made, to Stransom's sense, for the woman before him, an immense, an absolutely naked confession; which was presently, suddenly blushing red and changing her place again, what she appeared to become aware that he perceived in it. He got up. "How you must have loved him!" he cried.

"Women are not like men. They can love even where they've suffered."

"Women are wonderful," said Stransom. "But I assure you I've forgiven him too."

"If I had known of anything so strange I wouldn't have brought you here."

"So that we might have gone on in our ignorance to the last?"

"What do you call the last?" she asked, smiling still.

At this he could smile back at her. "You'll see—when it comes."

She reflected a moment. "This is better perhaps; but as we were—it was good."

"Did it never happen that he spoke of me?" Stransom inquired.

Considering more intently, she made no answer, and he quickly recognised that he would have been adequately answered by her asking how often he himself had spoken of their terrible friend. Suddenly a brighter light broke in her face, and an excited idea sprang to her lips in the question: "You *have* forgiven him?"

"How, if I hadn't, could I linger here?"

She winced, for an instant, at the deep but unintended irony of this; but even while she did so she panted quickly: "Then in the lights on your altar——?"

"There's never a light for Acton Hague!"

She stared, with a great visible fall. "But if he's one of your Dead?"

"He's one of the world's, if you like—he's one of yours. But he's not one of mine. Mine are only the Dead who died possessed of me. They're mine in death because they were mine in life."

"*He* was yours in life then, even if for a while he ceased to be. If you forgave him you went back to him. Those whom we've once loved——"

"Are those who can hurt us most," Stransom broke in.

"Ah, it's not true—you've *not* forgiven him!" she wailed with a passion that startled him.

He looked at her a moment. "What was it he did to you?"

"Everything!" Then abruptly she put out her hand in farewell. "Good-bye."

He turned as cold as he had turned that night he read of the death of Acton Hague. "You mean that we meet no more?"

"Not as we have met—not *there*!"

He stood aghast at this snap of their great bond, at the renouncement that rang out in the word she so passionately emphasised. "But what's changed—for you?"

She hesitated, in all the vividness of a trouble that, for the first time since he had known her, made her splendidly stern. "How can you understand now when you didn't understand before?"

"I didn't understand before only because I didn't know. Now that I know, I see what I've been living with for years," Stransom went on very gently.

She looked at him with a larger allowance, as if she appreciated his good-nature. "How can I, then, with this new knowledge of my own, ask you to continue to live with it?"

"I set up my altar, with its multiplied meanings," Stransom began; but she quickly interrupted him.

"You set up your altar, and when I wanted one most I found it magnificently ready. I used it, with the gratitude I've always shown you, for I knew from of old that it was dedicated to Death. I told you, long ago, that my Dead were not many. Yours were, but all you had done for them was none too much for *my* worship! You had placed a great light for Each—I gathered them together for One!"

"We had simply different intentions," Stransom replied. "That, as you say, I perfectly knew, and I don't see why your intention shouldn't still sustain you."

"That's because you're generous—you can imagine and think. But the spell is broken."

It seemed to poor Stransom, in spite of his resistance, that it really was, and the prospect stretched grey and void before him. All, however, that he could say was: "I hope you'll try before you give up."

"If I had known you had ever known him I should have taken for granted he had his candle," she presently rejoined. "What's changed, as you say, is that on making the discovery I find he never has had it. That makes *my* attitude—" she paused a moment, as if thinking how to express it, then said simply—"all wrong."

"Come once again," Stransom pleaded.

"Will you give him his candle?" she asked.

He hesitated, but only because it would sound ungracious; not because he had a doubt of his feeling. "I can't do that!" he declared at last.

"Then good bye." And she gave him her hand again.

He had got his dismissal; besides which, in the agitation of everything that had opened out to him, he felt the need to recover himself as he could only do in solitude. Yet he lingered—lingered to see if she had no compromise to express, no attenuation to propose. But he only met her great lamenting eyes, in which indeed he read that she was as sorry for him as for any one else. This made him say: "At least, at any rate, I may see you here."

"Oh, yes, come if you like. But I don't think it will do."

Stransom looked round the room once more; he felt in truth by no means sure it would do. He felt also stricken and more and more cold, and his chill was like an ague in which he had to make an effort not to shake. "I must try on my side, if you can't try on yours," he dolefully rejoined. She came out with him to the hall and into the doorway, and here he put to her the question that seemed to him the one he could least answer from his own wit. "Why have you never let me come before?"

"Because my aunt would have seen you, and I should have had to tell her how I came to know you."

"And what would have been the objection to that?"

"It would have entailed other explanations; there would at any rate have been that danger."

"Surely she knew you went every day to church," Stransom objected.

"She didn't know what I went for."

"Of me then she never even heard?"

"You'll think I was deceitful. But I didn't need to be!"

Stransom was now on the lower doorstep, and his hostess held the door half-closed behind him. Through what remained of the opening he saw her framed face. He made a supreme appeal. "What *did* he do to you?"

"It would have come out—*she* would have told you. That fear, at my heart—that was my reason!" And she closed the door, shutting him out.

VIII

He had ruthlessly abandoned her—that, of course, was what he had done. Stransom made it all out in solitude, at leisure, fitting the unmatched pieces gradually together and dealing one by one with a hundred obscure points. She had known Hague only after her present friend's relations with him had wholly terminated; obviously indeed a good while after; and it was natural enough that of his previous life she should have ascertained only what he had judged good to communicate. There were passages it was quite conceivable that even in moments of the tenderest expansion he should have withheld. Of many facts in the career of a man so in the eye of the world there was of course a common knowledge; but this lady lived apart from public affairs, and the only period perfectly clear to her would have been the period following the dawn of her own drama. A man, in her place, would have "looked up" the past—would even have consulted old newspapers. It remained singular indeed that in her long contact with the partner of her retrospect no accident had lighted a train; but there was no arguing about that; the accident had in fact come: it had simply been that security had prevailed. She had taken what Hague had given her, and her blankness in respect of his other connections was only a touch in the picture of that plasticity Stransom had supreme reason to know so great a master could have been trusted to produce.

This picture, for a while, was all that our friend saw: he caught his breath again and again as it came over him that the woman with whom he had had for years so fine a point of contact was a woman whom Acton Hague, of all men in the world, had more or less fashioned. Such as she sat there to-day, she was ineffaceably stamped with him. Beneficent, blameless as Stransom held her, he couldn't rid himself of the sense that he had been the victim of a fraud. She had imposed upon him hugely, though she had known it as little as he. All this later past came back to him as a time grotesquely mis-spent. Such at least were his first reflections; after a while he found himself more divided and only, as the end of it, more troubled. He imagined, recalled, reconstituted, figured out for himself the truth she had refused to give him; the effect of which was to make her seem to him only more saturated with her fate. He felt her spirit, in the strange business, to be finer than his own in the very degree in which she might have been, in which she certainly had been, more wronged. A woman, when she was wronged, was always more wronged than a man, and there were conditions when the least she could have got off with was more than the most he could have to endure. He was sure this rare creature wouldn't have got off with the least. He was awestruck at the thought of such a surrender—such a prostration. Moulded indeed she had been by powerful hands, to have converted her injury into an exaltation so sub-lime. The fellow had only had to die for everything that was ugly in him to be washed out in a torrent. It was vain to try to guess what had taken place, but nothing could be clearer than that she had ended by accusing herself. She absolved him at every point, she adored her very wounds. The passion by which he had profited had rushed back after its ebb, and now the tide of tenderness, arrested for ever at flood, was too deep even to fathom. Stransom sincerely considered that he had forgiven him; but how little he had achieved the miracle that she had achieved! His forgiveness was silence, but hers was mere unuttered sound. The light she had demanded for his altar would have broken his silence with a blare; whereas all the lights in the church were for her too great a hush.

She had been right about the difference—she had spoken the truth about the change: Stransom felt before long that he was perversely but definitely jealous. *His* tide had ebbed, not flowed; if he had "forgiven" Acton Hague, that forgiveness was a motive with a broken spring. The very fact of her appeal for a material sign, a sign that should make her dead lover equal there with the others, presented the concession to Stransom as too handsome for the case. He had never thought of himself as hard, but an exorbitant article might easily render him so. He moved round and round this one, but only in widening circles—the more he looked at it the less acceptable it appeared. At the same time he had no illusion about the effect of his refusal; he perfectly saw that it was the beginning of a separation. He left her alone for many days; but when at last he called upon her again this conviction acquired a depressing force. In the interval he had kept away from the church, and he needed no fresh assurance from her to know she had not entered it. The change was complete enough: it had broken up her life. Indeed it had broken up his, for all the fires of his shrine seemed to him suddenly to have been quenched. A great indifference fell upon him, the weight of which was in itself a pain; and he never knew what his devotion had been for him till, in that shock, it stopped like a dropped watch. Neither did he know with how large a confidence he had counted on the final service that had now failed: the mortal deception was that in this abandonment the whole future gave way.

These days of her absence proved to him of what she was capable; all the more that he never dreamed she was vindictive or even resentful. It was not in anger she had forsaken him; it was in absolute submission to hard reality, to crude destiny. This came home to him when he sat with her again in the room in which her late aunt's conversation lingered like the tone of a cracked piano. She tried to make him forget how much they were estranged; but in the very presence of what they had given up it was impossible not to be sorry for her. He had taken from her so much more than she had taken from him. He argued with her again, told her she could now have the altar to herself; but she only shook her head with pleading sadness, begging him not to waste his breath on the impossible, the extinct. Couldn't he see that in relation to her private need the rites he had established were practically an elaborate exclusion? She regretted nothing that had happened; it had all been right so long as she didn't know, and it was only that now she knew too much and that from the moment their eyes were open they would simply have to conform. It had doubtless been happiness enough for them to go on together so long. She was gentle, grateful, resigned; but this was only the form of a deep immutability. He saw that he should never more cross the threshold of the second room, and he felt how much this alone would make a stranger of him and give a conscious stiffness to his visits. He would have hated to plunge again into that well of reminders, but he enjoyed quite as little the vacant alternative.

After he had been with her three or four times it seemed to him that to have come at last into her house had had the horrid effect of diminishing their intimacy. He had known her better, had liked her in greater freedom, when they merely walked together or kneeled together. Now they only pretended; before they had been nobly sincere. They began to try their walks again, but it proved a lame imitation, for these things, from the first, beginning or ending, had been connected with their visits to the church. They had either strolled away as they came out or gone in to rest on the return. Besides, Stransom now grew weary; he couldn't walk as of old. The omission made everything false; it was a horrible mutilation of their lives. Our friend was frank and monotonous; he made no mystery of his remonstrance and no secret of his predicament. Her response, whatever it was, always came to the same thing—an implied invitation to him to judge, if he spoke of predicaments, of how much comfort she had in hers. For him indeed there was no comfort even in complaint, for every allusion to what had befallen them only made the author of their trouble more present. Acton Hague was between them, that was the essence of the matter; and he was never so much between them as when they were face to face. Stransom, even while he wanted to banish him, had the strangest

sense of desiring a satisfaction that could come only from having accepted him. Deeply disconcerted by what he knew, he
was still worse tormented by really not knowing. Perfectly
aware that it would have been horribly vulgar to abuse his old
friend or to tell his companion the story of their quarrel, it
yet vexed him that her depth of reserve should give him no
opening and should have the effect of a magnanimity greater
even than his own.

He challenged himself, denounced himself, asked himself if
he were in love with her that he should care so much what
adventures she had had. He had never for a moment admitted
that he was in love with her; therefore nothing could have
surprised him more than to discover that he was jealous. What
but jealousy could give a man that sore, contentious wish to
have the detail of what would make him suffer? Well enough
he knew indeed that he should never have it from the only
person who, to-day, could give it to him. She let him press
her with his sombre eyes, only smiling at him with an exquisite
mercy and breathing equally little the word that would expose
her secret and the word that would appear to deny his literal
right to bitterness. She told nothing, she judged nothing; she
accepted everything but the possibility of her return to the
old symbols. Stransom divined that for her too they had been
vividly individual, had stood for particular hours or particular
attributes—particular links in her chain. He made it clear to
himself, as he believed, that his difficulty lay in the fact that
the very nature of the plea for his faithless friend constituted
a prohibition; that it happened to have come from *her* was
precisely the vice that attached to it. To the voice of impersonal generosity he felt sure he would have listened; he
would have deferred to an advocate who, speaking from abstract justice, knowing of his omission without having
known Hague, should have had the imagination to say:
"Oh, remember only the best of him; pity him; provide for
him." To provide for him on the very ground of having discovered another of his turpitudes was not to pity him, but to
glorify him. The more Stransom thought the more he made
it out that this relation of Hague's, whatever it was, could
only have been a deception finely practised. Where had it
come into the life that all men saw? Why had he never heard

of it, if it had had the frankness of an attitude honourable? Stransom knew enough of his other ties, of his obligations and appearances, not to say enough of his general character, to be sure there had been some infamy. In one way or another the poor woman had been coldly sacrificed. That was why, at the last as well as the first, he must still leave him out.

IX

And yet this was no solution, especially after he had talked again to his friend of all it had been his plan that she should finally do for him. He had talked in the other days, and she had responded with a frankness qualified only by a courteous reluctance, a reluctance that touched him, to linger on the question of his death. She had then practically accepted the charge, suffered him to feel that he could depend upon her to be the eventual guardian of his shrine; and it was in the name of what had so passed between them that he appealed to her not to forsake him in his old age. She listened to him now with a sort of shining coldness and all her habitual forbearance to insist on her terms; her deprecation was even still tenderer, for it expressed the compassion of her own sense that he was abandoned. Her terms, however, remained the same, and scarcely the less audible for not being uttered; although he was sure that, secretly, even more than he, she felt bereft of the satisfaction his solemn trust was to have provided for her. They both missed the rich future, but she missed it most, because after all it was to have been entirely hers; and it was her acceptance of the loss that gave him the full measure of her preference for the thought of Acton Hague over any other thought whatever. He had humour enough to laugh rather grimly when he said to himself: "Why the deuce does she like him so much more than she likes me?"—the reasons being really so conceivable. But even his faculty of analysis left the irritation standing, and this irritation proved perhaps the greatest misfortune that had ever overtaken him. There had been nothing yet that made him so much want to give up. He had of course by this time well reached the age of renouncement; but it had not hitherto been vivid to him that it was time to give up everything.

Practically, at the end of six months, he had renounced the friendship that was once so charming and comforting. His privation had two faces, and the face it had turned to him on the occasion of his last attempt to cultivate that friendship was the one he could look at least. This was the privation he inflicted; the other was the privation he bore. The conditions she never phrased he used to murmur to himself in solitude: "One more, one more—only just one." Certainly he was going down; he often felt it when he caught himself, over his work, staring at vacancy and giving voice to that inanity. There was proof enough besides in his being so weak and so ill. His irritation took the form of melancholy, and his melancholy that of the conviction that his health had quite failed. His altar moreover had ceased to exist; his chapel, in his dreams, was a great dark cavern. All the lights had gone out—all his Dead had died again. He couldn't exactly see at first how it had been in the power of his late companion to extinguish them, since it was neither for her nor by her that they had been called into being. Then he understood that it was essentially in his own soul the revival had taken place, and that in the air of this soul they were now unable to breathe. The candles might mechanically burn, but each of them had lost its lustre. The church had become a void; it was his presence, her presence, their common presence, that had made the indispensable medium. If anything was wrong everything was—her silence spoiled the tune.

Then when three months were gone he felt so lonely that he went back; reflecting that as they had been his best society for years his Dead perhaps wouldn't let him forsake them without doing something more for him. They stood there, as he had left them, in their tall radiance, the bright cluster that had already made him, on occasions when he was willing to compare small things with great, liken them to a group of sea-lights on the edge of the ocean of life. It was a relief to him, after a while, as he sat there, to feel that they had still a virtue. He was more and more easily tired, and he always drove now; the action of his heart was weak and gave him none of the reassurance conferred by the action of his fancy. None the less he returned yet again, returned several times, and finally, during six months, haunted the place with a renewal of frequency and a strain of impatience. In winter the church was un-warmed, and exposure to cold was forbidden him, but the glow of his shrine was an influence in which he could almost bask. He sat and wondered to what he had reduced his absent associate and what she now did with the hours of her absence. There were other churches, there were other altars, there were other candles; in one way or another her piety would still operate; he couldn't absolutely have deprived her of her rites. So he argued, but without contentment; for he well enough knew there was no other such rare semblance of the mountain of light she had once mentioned to him as the satisfaction of her need. As this semblance again gradually grew great to him and his pious practice more regular, there was a sharper and sharper pang for him in the imagination of her darkness; for never so much as in these weeks had his rites been real, never had his gathered company seemed so to respond and even to invite. He lost himself in the large lustre, which was more and more what he had from the first wished it to be—as dazzling as the vision of heaven in the mind of a child. He wandered in the fields of light; he passed, among the tall tapers, from tier to tier, from fire to fire, from name to name, from the white intensity of one clear emblem, of one saved soul, to another. It was in the quiet sense of having saved his souls that his deep, strange instinct rejoiced. This was no dim theological rescue, no boon of a contingent world; they were saved better than faith or works could save them, saved for the warm world they had shrunk from dying to, for actuality, for continuity, for the certainty of human remembrance.

By this time he had survived all his friends; the last straight flame was three years old, there was no one to add to the list. Over and over he called his roll, and it appeared to him compact and complete. Where should he put in another, where, if there were no other objection, would it stand in its place in the rank? He reflected, with a want of sincerity of which he was quite conscious, that it would be difficult to determine that place. More and more, besides, face to face with his little legion, reading over endless histories, handling the empty shells and playing with the silence—more and more he could see that he had never introduced an alien. He had had his great compassions, his indulgences— there were cases in which they had been immense; but what had his devotion after all been if it hadn't been fundamentally a respect? He was, however, himself surprised at his stiffness; by the end of the winter the responsibility of it was what was uppermost in his thoughts. The refrain had grown old to them, the plea for just one more. There came a day when, for simple exhaustion, if symmetry should really demand just one more he was ready to take symmetry into account. Symmetry was harmony, and the idea of harmony began to haunt him; he said to himself that harmony was of course everything. He took, in fancy, his composition to pieces, redistributing it into other lines, making other juxtapositions and contrasts. He shifted this and that candle, he made the spaces different, he effaced the disfigurement of a possible gap. There were subtle and complex relations, a scheme of cross-reference, and moments in which he seemed to catch a glimpse of the void so sensible to the woman who wandered in exile or sat where he had seen her with the portrait of Acton Hague. Finally, in this way, he arrived at a conception of the total, the ideal, which left a clear opportunity for just another figure. "Just one more—to round it off; just one more, just one," continued to hum itself in his head. There was a strange confusion in the thought, for he felt the day to be near when he too should be one of the Others. What, in this case, would the Others matter to him, since they only mattered to the living? Even as one of the Dead, what would his altar matter to him, since his particular dream of keeping it up had melted away? What had harmony to do with the case if his lights were all to be quenched? What he had hoped for was an instituted thing. He might perpetuate it on some other pretext, but his special meaning would have dropped. This meaning was to have lasted with the life of the one other person who understood it.

In March he had an illness during which he spent a fortnight in bed, and when he revived a little he was told of two things that had happened. One was that a lady, whose name was not known to the servants (she left none) had been three times to ask about him; the other was that in his sleep, and on an occasion when his mind evidently wandered, he was heard to murmur again and again: "Just one more—just one." As soon as he found himself able to go out, and before the doctor in attendance had pronounced him so, he drove to see the lady who had come to ask about him. She was not at home; but this gave him the opportunity, before his strength should fail again, to take his way to the church. He entered the church alone; he had declined, in a happy manner he possessed of being able to decline effectively, the company of his servant or of a nurse. He knew now perfectly what these good people thought; they had discovered his clandestine connection, the magnet that had drawn him for so many years, and doubtless attached a significance of their own to the odd words they had repeated to him. The nameless lady was the clandestine connection—a fact nothing could have made clearer than his indecent haste to rejoin her. He sank on his knees before his altar, and his head fell over on his hands. His weakness, his life's weariness overtook him. It seemed to him he had come for the great surrender. At first he asked himself how he should get away; then, with the failing belief in the power, the very desire to move gradually left him. He had come, as he always came, to lose himself; the fields of light were still there to stray in; only this time, in straying, he would never come back. He had given himself to his Dead, and it was good: this time his Dead would keep him. He couldn't rise from his knees; he believed he should never rise again; all he could do was to lift his face and fix his eyes upon his lights. They looked unusually, strangely splendid, but the one that always drew him most had an unprecedented lustre. It was the central voice of the choir, the glowing heart of the brightness, and on this occasion it seemed to expand, to spread great wings of flame. The whole altar flared—it dazzled and blinded; but the source of the vast radiance burned clearer than the rest, it gathered itself into form, and the form was human beauty and human charity—it was the far-off face of Mary Antrim. She smiled at him from the glory of heaven— she brought the glory down with her to take him. He bowed his head in submission, and at the same moment another wave rolled over him. Was it the quickening of joy to pain? In the midst of his joy at any rate he felt his buried face grow hot as with some communicated knowledge that had the force of a reproach. It suddenly made him contrast that very rapture with the bliss he had refused to another. This breath of the passion immortal was all that other had asked; the descent of Mary Antrim opened his spirit with a great compunctious throb for the descent of Acton Hague. It was as if Stransom had read what her eyes said to him.

After a moment he looked round him in a despair which made him feel as if the source of life were ebbing. The church had been empty—he was alone; but he wanted to have something done, to make a last appeal. This idea gave him strength for an effort; he rose to his feet with a movement that made him turn, supporting himself by the back of a bench. Behind him was a prostrate figure, a figure he had seen before; a woman in deep mourning, bowed in grief or in prayer. He had seen her in other days—the first time he came into the church, and he slightly wavered there, looking at her again till she seemed to become aware he had noticed her. She raised her head and met his eyes: the partner of his long worship was there. She looked across at him an instant with a face wondering and scared; he saw that he had given her an alarm. Then quickly rising, she came straight to him with both hands out.

"Then you *could* come? God sent you!" he murmured with a happy smile.

"You're very ill—you shouldn't be here," she urged in anxious reply.

"God sent me too, I think. I was ill when I came, but the sight of you does wonders." He held her hands, and they steadied and quickened him. "I've something to tell you."

"Don't tell me!" she tenderly pleaded; "let me tell you. This afternoon, by a miracle, the sweetest of miracles, the sense of our difference left me. I was out—I was near, thinking, wandering alone, when, on the spot, something changed in my heart. It's my confession—there it is. To come back, to come back on the instant—the idea gave me wings. It was as if I suddenly saw something—as if it all became possible. I could come for what you yourself came for: that was enough. So here I am. It's not for my own—that's over. But I'm here for *them*." And breathless, infinitely relieved by her low, precipitate explanation, she looked with eyes that reflected all its splendour at the magnificence of their altar.

"They're here for you," Stransom said, "they're present to-night as they've never been. They speak for you—don't you see?—in a passion of light—they sing out like a choir of angels. Don't you hear what they say?—they offer the very thing you asked of me."

"Don't talk of it—don't think of it; forget it!" She spoke in hushed supplication, and while the apprehension deepened in her eyes she disengaged one of her hands and passed an arm round him, to support him better, to help him to sink into a seat.

He let himself go, resting on her; he dropped upon the bench, and she fell on her knees beside him with his arm on her shoulder. So he remained an instant, staring up at his shrine. "They say there's a gap in the array—they say it's not full, complete. Just one more," he went on, softly—"isn't that what you wanted? Yes, one more, one more."

"Ah, no more—no more!" she wailed, as if with a quick, new horror of it, under her breath.

"Yes, one more," he repeated, simply; "just one!" And with this his head dropped on her shoulder; she felt that in his weakness he had fainted. But alone with him in the dusky church a great dread was on her of what might still happen, for his face had the whiteness of death.

The Next Time

M RS. HIGHMORE'S errand this morning was odd enough to deserve commemoration: she came to ask me to write a notice of her great forthcoming work. Her great works have come forth so frequently without my assistance that I was sufficiently entitled on this occasion to open my eyes; but what really made me stare was the ground on which her request reposed, and what leads me to record the incident is the train of memory lighted by that explanation. Poor Ray Limbert, while we talked, seemed to sit there between us: she reminded me that my acquaintance with him had begun, eighteen years ago, with her having come in precisely as she came in this morning to bespeak my charity for him. If she didn't know then how little my charity was worth she is at least enlightened about it to-day, and this is just the circumstance that makes the drollery of her visit. As I hold up the torch to the dusky years—by which I mean as I cipher up with a pen that stumbles and stops the figured column of my reminiscences—I see that Limbert's public hour, or at least my small apprehension of it, is rounded by those two occasions. It was *finis*, with a little moralising flourish, that Mrs. Highmore seemed to trace to-day at the bottom of the page. "One of the most voluminous writers of the time," she has often repeated this sign; but never, I dare say, in spite of her professional command of appropriate emotion, with an equal sense of that mystery and that sadness of things which to people of imagination generally hover over the close of human histories. This romance at any rate is bracketed by her early and her late appeal; and when its melancholy protrusions had caught the declining light again from my half-hour's talk with her I took a private vow to recover while that light still lingers something of the delicate flush, to pick out with a brief patience the perplexing lesson.

It was wonderful to observe how for herself Mrs. Highmore had already done so: she wouldn't have hesitated to announce to me what was the matter with Ralph Limbert, or at all events to give me a glimpse of the high admonition she had read in his career. There could have been no better proof of the vividness of this parable, which we were really in our pleasant sympathy quite at one about, than that Mrs. Highmore, of all hardened sinners, should have been converted. This indeed was not news to me: she impressed upon me that for the last ten years she had wanted to do something artistic, something as to which she was prepared not to care a rap whether or no it should sell. She brought home to me further that it had been mainly seeing what her brother-in-law did and how he did it that had wedded her to this perversity. As *he* didn't sell dear soul, and as several persons, of whom I was one, thought highly of that, the fancy had taken her—taken her even quite early in her prolific course—of reaching, if only once, the same heroic eminence. She yearned to be, like Limbert, but of course only once, an exquisite failure. There was something a failure was, a failure in the market, that a success somehow wasn't. A success was as prosaic as a good dinner: there was nothing more to be said about it than that you had had it. Who but vulgar people, in such a case, made gloating remarks about the courses? It was often by such vulgar people that a success was attested. It made if you came to look at it nothing but money; that is it made so much that any other result showed small in comparison. A failure now could make—oh, with the aid of immense talent of course, for there were failures and failures—such a reputation! She did me the honour —she had often done it—to intimate that what she meant by reputation was seeing *me* toss a flower. If it took a failure to catch a failure I was by my own admission well qualified to place the laurel. It was because she had made so much money and Mr Highmore had taken such care of it that she could treat herself to an hour of pure glory. She perfectly remembered that as often as I had heard her heave that sigh I had been prompt with my declaration that a book sold might easily be as glorious as a book unsold. Of course she knew this, but she knew also that it was the age of trash triumphant and that she had never heard me speak of anything that had "done well" exactly as she had sometimes heard me speak of something that hadn't—with just two or three words of respect which, when I used them, seemed to convey more than they commonly stood for, seemed to hush up the discussion a little, as if for the very beauty of the secret.

I may declare in regard to these allusions that, whatever I then thought of myself as a holder of the scales I had never scrupled to laugh out at the humour of Mrs. Highmore's pursuit of quality at any price. It had never rescued her even for a day from the hard doom of popularity, and though I never gave her my word for it there was no reason at all why it should. The public *would* have her, as her husband used roguishly to remark; not indeed that, making her bargains, standing up to her publishers and even, in his higher flights, to her reviewers, he ever had a glimpse of her attempted conspiracy against her genius, or rather as I may say against mine. It was not that when she tried to be what she called subtle (for wasn't Limbert subtle, and wasn't I?) her fond consumers, bless them, didn't suspect the trick nor show what they thought of it: they straightway rose on the contrary to the morsel she had hoped to hold too high, and, making but a big, cheerful bite of it, wagged their great collective tail artlessly for more. It was not given to her not to please, nor granted even to her best refinements to affright. I have always respected the mystery of those humiliations, but I was fully aware this morning that they were practically the reason why she had come to me. Therefore when she said with the flush of a bold joke in her kind, coarse face, "What I feel is, you know, that *you* could settle me if you only would," I knew quite well what she meant. She meant that of old it had always appeared to be the fine blade, as some one had hyperbolically called it, of my particular opinion that snapped the silken thread by which Limbert's chance in the market was wont to hang. She meant that my favour was compromising, that my praise indeed was fatal. I had made myself a little specialty of seeing nothing in certain celebrities, of seeing overmuch in an occasional nobody, and of judging from a point of view that, say what I would for it (and I had a monstrous deal to say), remained perverse and obscure. Mine was in short the love that killed, for my subtlety, unlike Mrs. Highmore's, produced no tremor of the public tail. She had not forgotten how, toward the end, when his case was worst, Limbert would absolutely come to me with a funny, shy pathos in his eyes and say: "My dear fellow, I think I've done it this time, if you'll only keep quiet." If my keeping quiet in those days was to help him to appear to have hit the usual taste, for the want of which he was starving, so now my breaking out was to help Mrs. Highmore to appear to have hit the unusual.

The moral of all this was that I had frightened the public too much for our late friend, but that as she was not starving this was exactly what her grosser reputation required. And then, she good-naturedly and delicately intimated, there would always be, if further reasons were wanting, the price of my clever little article. I think she gave that hint with a flattering impression—spoiled child of the booksellers as she is—that the price of my clever little articles is high. Whatever it is, at any rate, she had evidently reflected that poor Limbert's anxiety for his own profit used to involve my sacrificing mine. Any inconvenience that my obliging her might entail would not in fine be pecuniary. Her appeal, her motive, her fantastic thirst for quality and her ingenious theory of my influence struck me all as excellent comedy, and when I consented contingently to oblige her she left me the sheets of her new novel. I could plead no inconvenience and have been looking them over; but I am frankly appalled at what she expects of me. What is she thinking of, poor dear, and what has put it into her head that "quality" has descended upon her? Why does she suppose that she has been "artistic?" She hasn't been anything whatever, I surmise, that she has not inveterately been. What does she imagine she has left out? What does she conceive she has put in? She has neither left out nor put in anything. I shall have to write her an embarrassed note. The book doesn't exist, and there's nothing in life to say about it. How can there be anything but the same old faithful rush for it?

I

This rush had already begun when, early in the seventies, in the interest of her prospective brother-in-law, she approached me on the singular ground of the unencouraged sentiment I had entertained for her sister. Pretty pink Maud had cast me out, but I appear to have passed in the flurried little circle for a magnanimous youth. Pretty pink Maud, so lovely then, before her troubles, that dusky Jane was gratefully conscious of all she made up for, Maud Stannace, very literary too, very languishing and extremely bullied by her mother, had yielded, invidiously as it might have struck me, to Ray Limbert's suit, which Mrs. Stannace was not the woman to stomach. Mrs. Stannace was seldom the woman to do anything: she had been shocked at the way her children, with the grubby taint of their father's blood (he had published pale Remains or flat Conversations of *his* father) breathed the alien air of authorship. If not the daughter, nor even the niece, she was, if I am not mistaken, the second cousin of a hundred earls and a great stickler for relationship, so that she had other views for her brilliant child, especially after her quiet one (such had been her original discreet forecast of the producer of eighty volumes) became the second wife of an ex-army-surgeon, already the father of four children. Mrs. Stannace had too manifestly dreamed it would be given to pretty pink Maud to detach some one of the hundred, who wouldn't be missed, from the cluster. It was because she cared only for cousins that I unlearnt the way to her house, which she had once reminded me was one of the few paths of gentility I could hope to tread. Ralph Limbert, who belonged to nobody and had done nothing—nothing even at Cambridge—had only the uncanny spell he had cast upon her younger daughter to recommend him; but if her younger daughter had a spark of filial feeling she wouldn't commit the indecency of deserting for his sake a deeply dependent and intensely aggravated mother.

These things I learned from Jane Highmore, who, as if her books had been babies (they remained her only ones), had waited till after marriage to show what she could do and now bade fair to surround her satisfied spouse (he took, for some mysterious reason, a part of the credit) with a little family, in sets of triplets, which properly handled would be the support of his declining years. The young couple, neither of whom had a penny, were now virtually engaged: the thing was subject to Ralph's putting his hand on some regular employment. People more enamoured couldn't be conceived, and Mrs. Highmore, honest woman, who had moreover a professional sense for a love-story, was eager to take them under her wing. What was wanted was a decent opening for Limbert, which it had occurred to her I might assist her to find, though indeed I had not yet found any such matter for myself. But it was well known that I was too particular, whereas poor Ralph, with the easy manners of genius, was ready to accept almost anything to which a salary, even a small one, was attached. If he could only for instance get a place on a newspaper the rest of his maintenance would come freely enough. It was true that his two novels, one of which she had brought to leave with me, had passed unperceived and that to her, Mrs. Highmore personally, they didn't irresistibly appeal; but she could all the same assure me that I should have only to spend ten minutes with him (and our encounter must speedily take place) to receive an impression of latent power.

Our encounter took place soon after I had read the volumes Mrs. Highmore had left with me, in which I recognised an intention of a sort that I had then pretty well given up the hope of meeting. I daresay that without knowing it I had been looking out rather hungrily for an altar of sacrifice: however that may be I submitted when I came across Ralph Limbert to one of the rarest emotions of my literary life, the sense of an activity in which I could critically rest. The rest was deep and salutary, and it has not been disturbed to this hour. It has been a long, large surrender, the luxury of dropped discriminations. He couldn't trouble me, whatever he did, for I practically enjoyed him as much when he was worse as when he was better. It was a case, I suppose, of natural prearrangement, in which, I hasten to add, I keep excellent company. We are a numerous band, partakers of the same repose, who sit together in the shade of the tree, by the plash of the fountain, with the glare of the desert around us and no great vice that I know of but the habit perhaps of estimating people a little too much by what they think of a certain style. If it had been laid upon these few pages, none the less, to be the history of an enthusiasm, I should not have undertaken them: they are concerned with Ralph Limbert in relations to which I was a stranger or in which I participated only by sympathy. I used to talk about his work, but I seldom talk now: the brotherhood of the faith have become, like the Trappists, a silent order. If to the day of his death, after mortal disenchantments, the impression he first produced always evoked the word "ingenuous," those to whom his face was familiar can easily imagine what it must have been when it still had the light of youth. I had never seen a man of genius look so passive, a man of experience so off his guard. At the period I made his acquaintance this freshness was all unbrushed. His foot had begun to stumble, but he was full of big intentions and of sweet Maud Stannace. Black-haired and pale, deceptively languid, he had the eyes of a clever child and the voice of a bronze bell. He saw more even than I had done in the girl he was engaged to; as time went on I became conscious that we had both, properly enough, seen rather more than there was. Our odd situation, that of the three of us, became perfectly possible from the moment I observed that he had more patience with her than I should have had. I was happy at not having to supply this quantity, and she, on her side, found pleasure in being able to be impertinent to me without incurring the reproach of a bad wife.

Limbert's novels appeared to have brought him no money: they had only brought him, so far as I could then make out, tributes that took up his time. These indeed brought him from several quarters some other things, and on my part at the end of three months *The Blackport Beacon*. I don't to-day remember how I obtained for him the London correspondence of the great northern organ, unless it was through somebody's having obtained it for myself. I seem to recall that I got rid of it in Limbert's interest, persuaded the editor that he was much the better man. The better man was naturally the man who had pledged himself to support a charming wife. We were neither of us good, as the event proved, but he had a finer sort of badness. *The Blackport Beacon* had two London correspondents—one a supposed haunter of political circles, the other a votary of questions sketchily classified as literary. They were both expected to be lively, and what was held out to each was that it was honourably open to him to be livelier than the other. I recollect the political correspondent of that period and how the problem offered to Ray Limbert was to try to be livelier than Pat Moyle. He had not yet seemed to me so candid as when he undertook this exploit, which brought matters to a head with Mrs. Stannace, inasmuch as her opposition to the marriage now logically fell to the ground. It's all tears and laughter as I look back upon that admirable time, in which nothing was so romantic as our intense vision of the real. No fool's paradise ever rustled such a cradle-song. It was anything but Bohemia—it was the very temple of Mrs. Grundy. We knew we were too critical, and that made us sublimely indulgent; we believed we did our duty or wanted to, and that made us free to dream. But we dreamed over the multiplication-table; we were nothing if not practical. Oh, the long smokes and sudden ideas, the knowing hints and banished scruples! The great thing was for Limbert to bring out his next book, which was just what his delightful engagement with the *Beacon* would give him leisure and liberty to do. The kind of work, all human and elastic and suggestive, was capital experience: in picking up things for his bi-weekly letter he would pick up life as well, he would pick up literature. The new publications, the new pictures, the new people—there would be nothing too novel for us and nobody too sacred. We introduced everything and everybody into Mrs. Stannace's drawing-room, of which I again became a familiar.

Mrs. Stannace, it was true, thought herself in strange company; she didn't particularly mind the new books, though some of them seemed queer enough, but to the new people she had decided objections. It was notorious however that poor Lady Robeck secretly wrote for one of the papers, and the thing had certainly, in its glance at the doings of the great world, a side that might be made attractive. But we were going to make every side attractive and we had everything to say about the sort of thing a paper like the *Beacon* would want. To give it what it would want and to give it nothing else was not doubtless an inspiring, but it was a perfectly respectable task, especially for a man with an appealing bride and a contentious mother-in-law. I thought Limbert's first letters as charming as the type allowed, though I won't deny that in spite of my sense of the importance of concessions I was just a trifle disconcerted at the way he had caught the tone. The tone was of course to be caught, but need it have been caught so in the act? The creature was even cleverer, as Maud Stannace said, than she had ventured to hope. Verily it was a good thing to have a dose of the wisdom of the serpent. If it had to be journalism—well, it *was* journalism. If he had to be "chatty"—well, he *was* chatty. Now and then he made a hit that—it was stupid of me—brought the blood to my face. I hated him to be so personal; but still, if it would make his fortune——! It wouldn't of course directly, but the book would, practically and in the sense to which our pure ideas of fortune were confined; and these things were all for the book. The daily balm meanwhile was in what one knew of the book—there were exquisite things to know; in the quiet monthly cheques from Blackport and in the deeper rose of Maud's little preparations, which were as dainty, on their tiny scale, as if she had been a humming-bird building a nest. When at the end of three months her betrothed had fairly settled down to his correspondence—in which Mrs. Highmore was the only person, so far as we could discover, disappointed, even she moreover being in this particular tortuous and possibly jealous; when the situation had assumed such a comfortable shape it was quite time to prepare. I published at that moment my first volume, mere faded ink to-day, a little collection of literary impressions, odds and ends of criticism contributed to a journal less remunerative but also less chatty than the *Beacon*, small ironies and ecstasies, great phrases and mistakes; and the very week it came out poor Limbert devoted half of one of his letters to it, with the happy sense this time of gratifying both himself and me as well as the Blackport breakfast-tables. I remember his saying it wasn't literature, the stuff, superficial stuff, he had to write about me; but what did that matter if it came back, as we knew, to the making for literature in the round-about way? I sold the thing, I remember, for ten pounds, and with the money I bought in Vigo Street a quaint piece of old silver for Maud Stannace, which I carried to her with my own hand as a wedding-gift. In her mother's small drawing-room, a faded bower of photography fenced in and bedimmed by folding screens out of which sallow persons of fashion with dashing signatures looked at you from retouched eyes and little windows of plush, I was left to wait long enough to feel in the air of the house a hushed vibration of disaster. When our young lady came in she was very pale and her eyes too had been retouched.

"Something horrid has happened," I immediately said; and having really all along but half believed in her mother's meagre permission I risked with an unguarded groan the introduction of Mrs. Stannace's name.

"Yes, she has made a dreadful scene; she insists on our putting it off again. We're very unhappy: poor Ray has been turned off." Her tears began to flow again.

I had such a good conscience that I stared. "Turned off what?"

"Why, his paper of course. The *Beacon* has given him what he calls the sack. They don't like his letters: they're not the style of thing they want."

My blankness could only deepen. "Then what style of thing *do* they want?"

"Something more chatty."

"More?" I cried, aghast.

"More gossipy, more personal. They want 'journalism.' They want tremendous trash."

"Why, that's just what his letters have *been*!" I broke out.

This was strong, and I caught myself up, but the girl offered me the pardon of a beautiful wan smile. "So Ray himself declares. He says he has stooped so low."

"Very well—he must stoop lower. He *must* keep the place."

"He can't!" poor Maud wailed. "He says he has tried all he knows, has been abject, has gone on all fours, and that if they don't like that— "

"He accepts his dismissal?" I interposed in dismay.

She gave a tragic shrug. "What other course is open to him? He wrote to them that such work as he has done is the very worst he can do for the money."

"Therefore," I inquired with a flash of hope, "they'll offer him more for worse?"

"No indeed," she answered, "they haven't even offered him to go on at a reduction. He isn't funny enough."

I reflected a moment. "But surely such a thing as his notice of my book— !"

"It was your wretched book that was the last straw! He should have treated it superficially."

"Well, if he didn't— -!" I began. Then I checked myself. "*Je vous porte malheur.*"

She didn't deny this; she only went on: "What on earth is he to do?"

"He's to do better than the monkeys! He's to write!"

"But what on earth are we to marry on?"

I considered once more. "You're to marry on *The Major Key*."

II

The Major Key was the new novel, and the great thing accordingly was to finish it; a consummation for which three months of the *Beacon* had in some degree prepared the way. The action of that journal was indeed a shock, but I didn't know then the worst, didn't know that in addition to being a shock it was also a symptom. It was the first hint of the difficulty to which poor Limbert was eventually to succumb. His state was the happier of a truth for his not immediately seeing all that it meant. Difficulty was the law of life, but one could thank heaven it was exceptionally present in that horrid quarter. There was the difficulty that inspired, the difficulty of *The Major Key* to wit, which it was after all base to sacrifice to the turning of somersaults for pennies. These convictions Ray Limbert beguiled his fresh wait by blandly entertaining: not indeed, I think, that the failure of his attempt to be chatty didn't leave him slightly humiliated. If it was bad enough to have grinned through a horse-collar it was very bad indeed to have grinned in vain. Well, he would try no more grinning or at least no more horse-collars. The only success worth one's powder was success in the line of one's idiosyncrasy. Consistency was in itself distinction, and what was talent but the art of being completely whatever it was that one happened to be? One's things were characteristic or they were nothing. I look back rather fondly on our having exchanged in those days these admirable remarks and many others; on our having been very happy too, in spite of postponements and obscurities, in spite also of such occasional hauntings as could spring from our lurid glimpse of the fact that even twaddle cunningly calculated was far above people's heads. It was easy to wave away spectres by the reflection that all one had to do was not to write for people; it was certainly not for people that Limbert wrote while he hammered at *The Major Key*. The taint of literature was fatal only in a certain kind of air, which was precisely the kind against which we had now closed our window. Mrs. Stannace rose from her crumpled cushions as soon as she had obtained an adjournment, and Maud looked pale and proud, quite victorious and superior, at her having obtained nothing more. Maud behaved well, I thought, to her mother, and well indeed for a girl who had mainly been taught to be flowerlike to every one. What she gave Ray Limbert her fine abundant needs made him then and ever pay for; but the gift was liberal, almost wonderful—an assertion I make even while remembering to how many clever women, early and late, his work has been dear. It was not only that the woman he was to marry was in love with him, but that (this was the strangeness) she had really seen almost better than any one what he could do. The greatest strangeness was that she didn't want him to do something different. This boundless belief was indeed the main way of her devotion; and as an act of faith it naturally asked for miracles. She was a rare wife for a poet if she was not perhaps the best who could have been picked out for a poor man.

Well, we were to have the miracles at all events and we were in a perfect state of mind to receive them. There were more of us every day, and we thought highly even of our friend's odd jobs and pot-boilers. The *Beacon* had had no successor, but he found some quiet corners and stray chances. Perpetually poking the fire and looking out of the window, he was certainly not a monster of facility, but he was, thanks perhaps to a certain method in that madness, a monster of certainty. It wasn't every one however who knew him for this: many editors printed him but once. He was getting a small reputation as a man it was well to have the first time; he created obscure apprehensions as to what might happen the second. He was good for making an impression, but no one seemed exactly to know what the impression was good for when made. The reason was simply that they had not seen yet *The Major Key*, that fiery-hearted rose as to which we watched in private the formation of petal after petal and flame after flame. Nothing mattered but this, for it had already elicited a splendid bid, much talked about in Mrs. Highmore's drawing-room, where at this point my reminiscences grow particularly thick. *Her* roses bloomed all the year and her sociability increased with her row of prizes. We had an idea that we "met every one" there—so we naturally thought when we met each other. Between our hostess and Ray Limbert flourished the happiest relation, the only cloud on which was that her husband eyed him rather askance. When he was called clever this personage wanted to know what he had to "show"; and it was certain that he showed nothing that could compare with Jane Highmore. Mr. Highmore took his stand on accomplished work and, turning up his coat-tails, warmed his rear with a good conscience at the neat bookcase in which the generations of triplets were chronologically arranged. The harmony between his companions rested on the fact that, as I have already hinted, each would have liked so much to be the other. Limbert couldn't but have a feeling about a woman who in addition to being the best creature and her sister's backer would have made, could she have condescended, such a success with the *Beacon*. On the other hand Mrs. Highmore used freely to say: "Do you know, he'll do exactly the thing that *I* want to do? I shall never do it myself, but he'll do it instead. Yes, he'll do *my* thing, and I shall hate him for it— the wretch." Hating him was her pleasant humour, for the wretch was personally to her taste.

She prevailed on her own publisher to promise to take *The Major Key* and to engage to pay a considerable sum down, as the phrase is, on the presumption of its attracting attention. This was good news for the evening's end at Mrs. Highmore's when there were only four or five left and cigarettes ran low; but there was better news to come, and I have never forgotten how, as it was I who had the good fortune to bring it, I kept it back on one of those occasions, for the sake of my effect, till only the right people remained. The right people were now more and more numerous, but this was a revelation addressed only to a choice residuum—a residuum including of course Limbert himself, with whom I haggled for another cigarette before I announced that as a consequence of an interview I had had with him that afternoon, and of a subtle argument I had brought to bear, Mrs. Highmore's pearl of publishers had agreed to put forth the new book as a serial. He was to "run" it in his magazine and he was to pay ever so much more for the privilege. I produced a fine gasp which presently found a more articulate relief, but poor Limbert's voice failed him once for all (he knew he was to walk away with me) and it was some one else who asked me in what my subtle argument had resided. I forget what florid description I then gave of it: to-day I have no reason not to confess that it had resided in the simple plea that the book was exquisite. I had said: "Come, my dear friend, be original; just risk it for that!" My dear friend seemed to rise to the chance, and I followed up my advantage, permitting him honestly no illusion as to the quality of the work. He clutched interrogatively at two or three attenuations, but I dashed them aside, leaving him face to face with the formidable truth. It was just a pure gem: was he the man not to flinch? His danger appeared to have acted upon him as the anaconda acts upon the rabbit; fascinated and paralysed, he had been engulfed in the long pink throat. When a week before, at my request, Limbert had let me possess for a day the complete manuscript, beautifully copied out by Maud Stannace, I had flushed with indignation at its having to be said of the author of such pages that he hadn't the common means to marry. I had taken the field in a great glow to repair this scandal, and it was therefore quite directly my fault if three months later, when *The Major Key* began to run, Mrs. Stannace was driven to the wall. She had made a condition of a fixed income; and at last a fixed income was achieved.

She had to recognise it, and after much prostration among the photographs she recognised it to the extent of accepting some of the convenience of it in the form of a project for a common household, to the expenses of which each party should proportionately contribute. Jane Highmore made a great point of her not being left alone, but Mrs. Stannace herself determined the proportion, which on Limbert's side at least and in spite of many other fluctuations was never altered. His income had been "fixed" with a vengeance: having painfully stooped to the comprehension of it Mrs. Stannace rested on this effort to the end and asked no further question on the subject. *The Major Key* in other words ran ever so long, and before it was half out Limbert and Maud had been married and the common household set up. These first months were probably the happiest in the family annals, with wedding-bells and budding laurels, the quiet, assured course of the book and the friendly, familiar note, round the corner, of

Mrs. Highmore's big guns. They gave Ralph time to block in another picture as well as to let me know after a while that he had the happy prospect of becoming a father. We had at times some dispute as to whether *The Major Key* was making an impression, but our contention could only be futile so long as we were not agreed as to what an impression consisted of. Several persons wrote to the author and several others asked to be introduced to him: wasn't that an impression? One of the lively "weeklies," snapping at the deadly "monthlies," said the whole thing was "grossly inartistic"—wasn't that? It was somewhere else proclaimed "a wonderfully subtle character-study"—wasn't that too? The strongest effect doubtless was produced on the publisher when, in its lemon-coloured volumes, like a little dish of three custards, the book was at last served cold: he never got his money back and so far as I know has never got it back to this day. *The Major Key* was rather a great performance than a great success. It converted readers into friends and friends into lovers; it placed the author, as the phrase is—placed him all too definitely; but it shrank to obscurity in the account of sales eventually rendered. It was in short an exquisite thing, but it was scarcely a thing to have published and certainly not a thing to have married on. I heard all about the matter, for my intervention had much exposed me. Mrs. Highmore said the second volume had given her ideas, and the ideas are probably to be found in some of her works, to the circulation of which they have even perhaps contributed. This was not absolutely yet the very thing she wanted to do, but it was on the way to it. So much, she informed me, she particularly perceived in the light of a critical study which I put forth in a little magazine; which the publisher in his advertisements quoted from profusely; and as to which there sprang up some absurd story that Limbert himself had written it. I remember that on my asking some one why such an idiotic thing had been said my interlocutor replied: "Oh, because, you know, it's just the way he *would* have written!" My spirit sank a little perhaps as I reflected that with such analogies in our manner there might prove to be some in our fate.

It was during the next four or five years that our eyes were open to what, unless something could be done, that fate, at least on Limbert's part, might be. The thing to be done was of course to write the book, the book that would make the difference, really justify the burden he had accepted and consummately express his power. For the works that followed upon *The Major Key* he had inevitably to accept conditions the reverse of brilliant, at a time too when the strain upon his resources had begun to show sharpness. With three babies in due course, an ailing wife and a complication still greater than these, it became highly important that a man should do only his best. Whatever Limbert did was his best; so at least each time I thought and so I unfailingly said somewhere, though it was not my saying it, heaven knows, that made the desired difference. Every one else indeed said it, and there was among multiplied worries always the comfort that his position was quite assured. The two books that followed *The Major Key* did more than anything else to assure it, and Jane Highmore was always crying out: "You stand alone, dear Ray; you stand absolutely alone!" Dear Ray used to tell me that he felt the truth of this in feebly-attempted discussions with his bookseller. His sister-in-law gave him good advice into the bargain; she was a repository of knowing hints, of esoteric learning. These things were doubtless not the less valuable to him for bearing wholly on the question of how a reputation might be with a little gumption, as Mrs. Highmore said, "worked." Save when she occasionally bore testimony to her desire to do, as Limbert did, something some day for her own very self, I never heard her speak of the literary motive as if it were distinguishable from the pecuniary. She cocked up his hat, she pricked up his prudence for him, reminding him that as one seemed to take one's self so the silly world was ready to take one. It was a fatal mistake to be too candid even with those who were all right—not to look and to talk prosperous, not at least to pretend that one had beautiful sales. To listen to her you would have thought the profession of letters a wonderful game of bluff. Wherever one's idea began it ended somehow in inspired paragraphs in the newspapers. "*I* pretend, I assure you, that you are going off like wildfire—I can at least do that for you!" she often declared, prevented as she was from doing much else by Mr. Highmore's insurmountable objection to *their* taking Mrs. Stannace.

I couldn't help regarding the presence of this latter lady in Limbert's life as the major complication: whatever he attempted it appeared given to him to achieve as best he could in the mere margin of the space in which she swung her petticoats. I may err in the belief that she practically lived on him, for though it was not in him to follow adequately Mrs. Highmore's counsel there were exasperated confessions he never made, scanty domestic curtains he rattled on their rings. I may exaggerate in the retrospect his apparent anxieties, for these after all were the years when his talent was freshest and when as a writer he most laid down his line. It wasn't of Mrs. Stannace nor even as time went on of Mrs. Limbert that we mainly talked when I got at longer intervals a smokier hour in the little grey den from which we could step out, as we used to say, to the lawn. The lawn was the back-garden, and Limbert's study was behind the dining-room, with folding doors not impervious to the clatter of the children's tea. We sometimes took refuge from it in the depths—a bush and a half deep—of the shrubbery, where was a bench that gave us a view while we gossiped of Mrs. Stannace's tiara-like head-dress nodding at an upper window. Within doors and without Limbert's life was overhung by an awful region that figured in his conversation, comprehensively and with unpremeditated art, as Upstairs. It was Upstairs that the thunder gathered, that Mrs. Stannace kept her accounts and her state, that Mrs. Limbert had her babies and her headaches, that the bells for ever jangled at the maids, that everything imperative in short took place—everything that he had somehow, pen in hand, to meet and dispose of in the little room on the garden-level. I don't think he liked to go Upstairs, but no special burst of confidence was needed to make me feel that a terrible deal of service went. It was the habit of the ladies of the Stannace family to be extremely waited on, and I've never been in a house where three maids and a nursery-governess gave such an impression of a retinue. "Oh, they're so deucedly, so hereditarily fine!"—I remember how that dropped from him in some worried hour. Well, it was because Maud was so universally fine that we had both been in love with her. It was not an air moreover for the plaintive note: no private inconvenience could long outweigh for him the great happiness of these years—the happiness that sat with us when we talked and that made it always amusing to talk, the sense of his being on the heels of success, coming closer and closer, touching it at last, knowing that he should touch it again and hold it fast and hold it high. Of course when we said success we didn't mean exactly what Mrs. Highmore for instance meant. He used to quote at me as a definition something from a nameless page of my own, some stray dictum to the effect that the man of his craft had achieved it when of a beautiful subject his expression was complete. Well, wasn't Limbert's in all conscience complete?

III

It was bang upon this completeness all the same that the turn arrived, the turn I can't say of his fortune—for what was that?—but of his confidence, of his spirits and, what was more to the point, of his system. The whole occasion on which the first symptom flared out is before me as I write. I had met them both at dinner: they were diners who had reached the penultimate stage—the stage which in theory is a rigid selection and in practice a wan submission. It was late in the season and stronger spirits than theirs were broken; the night was close and the air of the banquet such as to restrict conversation to the refusal of dishes and consumption to the sniffing of a flower. It struck me all the more that Mrs. Limbert was flying her flag. As vivid as a page of her husband's prose, she had one of those flickers of freshness that are the miracle of her sex and one of those expensive dresses that are the miracle of ours. She had also a neat brougham in which she had offered to rescue an old lady from the possibilities of a queer cab-horse; so that when she had rolled away with her charge I proposed a walk home with her husband, whom I had overtaken on the doorstep. Before I had gone far with him he told me he had news for me—he had accepted, of all people and of all things, an "editorial position." It had come to pass that very day, from one hour to another, without time for appeals or ponderations: Mr. Bousefield, the proprietor of a "high-class monthly," making, as they said, a sudden change, had

dropped on him heavily out of the blue. It was all right—
there was a salary and an idea, and both of them, as such
things went, rather high. We took our way slowly through the
vacant streets, and in the explanations and revelations that as
we lingered under lamp-posts I drew from him I found with
an apprehension that I tried to gulp down a foretaste of the
bitter end. He told me more than he had ever told me yet.
He couldn't balance accounts—that was the trouble: his expenses were too rising a tide. It was absolutely necessary that
he should at last make money, and now he must work only
for that. The need this last year had gathered the force of a
crusher: it had rolled over him and laid him on his back. He
had his scheme; this time he knew what he was about; on
some good occasion, with leisure to talk it over, he would tell
me the blessed whole. His editorship would help him, and for
the rest he must help himself. If he couldn't they would have
to do something fundamental—change their life altogether,
give up London, move into the country, take a house at thirty
pounds a year, send their children to the Board-school. I saw
that he was excited, and he admitted that he was: he had
waked out of a trance. He had been on the wrong tack; he
had piled mistake on mistake. It was the vision of his remedy
that now excited him: ineffably, grotesquely simple, it had yet
come to him only within a day or two. No, he wouldn't tell
me what it was; he would give me the night to guess, and if
I shouldn't guess it would be because I was as big an ass as
himself. However, a lone man might be an ass: he had room
in his life for his ears. Ray had a burden that demanded a
back: the back must therefore now be properly instituted. As
to the editorship, it was simply heaven-sent, being not at all
another case of *The Blackport Beacon* but a case of the very
opposite. The proprietor, the great Mr. Bousefield, had approached him precisely because his name, which was to be on
the cover, *didn't* represent the chatty. The whole thing was
to be—oh, on fiddling little lines of course—a protest against
the chatty. Bousefield wanted him to be himself; it was for
himself Bousefield had picked him out. Wasn't it beautiful and
brave of Bousefield? He wanted literature, he saw the great
reaction coming, the way the cat was going to jump. "Where
will you get literature?" I woefully asked; to which he replied

with a laugh that what he had to get was not literature but only what Bousefield would take for it.

In that single phrase without more ado I discovered his famous remedy. What was before him for the future was not to do his work but to do what somebody else would take for it. I had the question out with him on the next opportunity, and of all the lively discussions into which we had been destined to drift it lingers in my mind as the liveliest. This was not, I hasten to add, because I disputed his conclusions: it was an effect of the very force with which, when I had fathomed his wretched premises, I took them to my soul. It was very well to talk with Jane Highmore about his standing alone: the eminent relief of this position had brought him to the verge of ruin. Several persons admired his books—nothing was less contestable; but they appeared to have a mortal objection to acquiring them by subscription or by purchase: they begged or borrowed or stole, they delegated one of the party perhaps to commit the volumes to memory and repeat them, like the bards of old, to listening multitudes. Some ingenious theory was required at any rate to account for the inexorable limits of his circulation. It wasn't a thing for five people to live on; therefore either the objects circulated must change their nature or the organisms to be nourished must. The former change was perhaps the easier to consider first. Limbert considered it with extraordinary ingenuity from that time on, and the ingenuity, greater even than any I had yet had occasion to admire in him, made the whole next stage of his career rich in curiosity and suspense.

"I have been butting my skull against a wall," he had said in those hours of confidence; "and, to be as sublime a blockhead, if you'll allow me the word, you, my dear fellow, have kept sounding the charge. We've sat prating here of 'success,' heaven help us, like chanting monks in a cloister, hugging the sweet delusion that it lies somewhere in the work itself, in the expression, as you said, of one's subject or the intensification, as somebody else somewhere says, of one's note. One has been going on in short as if the only thing to do were to accept the law of one's talent and thinking that if certain consequences didn't follow it was only because one wasn't logical enough. My disaster has served me right—I mean for using

that ignoble word at all. It's a mere distributor's, a mere
hawker's word. What *is* 'success' anyhow? When a book's
right, it's right—shame to it surely if it isn't. When it sells it
sells—it brings money like potatoes or beer. If there's dishonour one way and inconvenience the other, it certainly is
comfortable, but it as certainly isn't glorious to have escaped
them. People of delicacy don't brag either about their probity
or about their luck. Success be hanged!—I want to sell. It's a
question of life and death. I must study the way. I've studied
too much the other way—I know the other way now, every
inch of it. I must cultivate the market—it's a science like another. I must go in for an infernal cunning. It will be very
amusing, I foresee that; I shall lead a dashing life and drive a
roaring trade. I haven't been obvious—I must *be* obvious. I
haven't been popular—I must *be* popular. It's another art—
or perhaps it isn't an art at all. It's something else; one must
find out *what* it is. Is it something awfully queer?—you
blush!—something barely decent? All the greater incentive to
curiosity! Curiosity's an immense motive; we shall have tremendous sport. They all do it; it's only a question of how. Of
course I've everything to unlearn; but what is life, as Jane
Highmore says, but a lesson? I must get all I can, all she can
give me, from Jane. She can't explain herself much; she's all
intuition; her processes are obscure; it's the spirit that swoops
down and catches her up. But I must study her reverently in
her works. Yes, you've defied me before, but now my loins
are girded: I declare I'll read one of them—I really will: I'll
put it through if I perish!"

I won't pretend that he made all these remarks at once; but
there wasn't one that he didn't make at one time or another,
for suggestion and occasion were plentiful enough, his life
being now given up altogether to his new necessity. It wasn't
a question of his having or not having, as they say, my intellectual sympathy: the brute force of the pressure left no room
for judgment; it made all emotion a mere recourse to the spy-
glass. I watched him as I should have watched a long race or
a long chase, irresistibly siding with him but much occupied
with the calculation of odds. I confess indeed that my heart,
for the endless stretch that he covered so fast, was often in
my throat. I saw him peg away over the sun-dappled plain, I

saw him double and wind and gain and lose; and all the while I secretly entertained a conviction. I wanted him to feed his many mouths, but at the bottom of all things was my sense that if he should succeed in doing so in this particular way I should think less well of him. Now I had an absolute terror of that. Meanwhile so far as I could I backed him up, I helped him: all the more that I had warned him immensely at first, smiled with a compassion it was very good of him not to have found exasperating over the complacency of his assumption that a man could escape from himself. Ray Limbert at all events would certainly never escape; but one could make believe for him, make believe very hard—an undertaking in which at first Mr. Bousefield was visibly a blessing. Limbert was delightful on the business of this being at last my chance too—my chance, so miraculously vouchsafed, to appear with a certain luxuriance. He didn't care how often he printed me, for wasn't it exactly in my direction. Mr. Bousefield held that the cat was going to jump? This was the least he could do for me. I might write on anything I liked—on anything at least but Mr. Limbert's second manner. He didn't wish attention strikingly called to his second manner; it was to operate insidiously; people were to be left to believe they had discovered it long ago. "Ralph Limbert? Why, when did we ever live without him?"—that's what he wanted them to say. Besides, they hated manners—let sleeping dogs lie. His understanding with Mr. Bousefield—on which he had had not at all to insist; it was the excellent man who insisted—was that he should run one of his beautiful stories in the magazine. As to the beauty of his story however Limbert was going to be less admirably straight than as to the beauty of everything else. That was another reason why I mustn't write about his new line: Mr. Bousefield was not to be too definitely warned that such a periodical was exposed to prostitution. By the time he should find it out for himself the public—*le gros public*—would have bitten, and then perhaps he would be conciliated and forgive. Everything else would be literary in short, and above all *I* would be; only Ralph Limbert wouldn't—he'd chuck up the whole thing sooner. He'd be vulgar, he'd be rudimentary, he'd be atrocious: he'd be elaborately what he hadn't been before.

I duly noticed that he had more trouble in making "every-thing else" literary than he had at first allowed for; but this was largely counteracted by the ease with which he was able to obtain that his mark should not be overshot. He had taken well to heart the old lesson of the *Beacon*; he remembered that he was after all there to keep his contributors down much rather than to keep them up. I thought at times that he kept them down a trifle too far, but he assured me that I needn't be nervous: he had his limit—his limit was inexorable. He would reserve pure vulgarity for his serial, over which he was sweating blood and water; elsewhere it should be qualified by the prime qualification, the mediocrity that attaches, that en-dears. Bousefield, he allowed, was proud, was difficult: noth-ing was really good enough for him but the middling good; but he himself was prepared for adverse comment, resolute for his noble course. Hadn't Limbert moreover in the event of a charge of laxity from headquarters the great strength of being able to point to my contributions? Therefore I must let myself go, I must abound in my peculiar sense, I must be a resource in case of accidents. Limbert's vision of accidents hovered mainly over the sudden awakening of Mr. Bousefield to the stuff that in the department of fiction his editor was palming off. He would then have to confess in all humility that this was not what the good old man wanted, but I should be all the more there as a salutary specimen. I would cross the scent with something showily impossible, splendidly un-popular—I must be sure to have something on hand. I always had plenty on hand—poor Limbert needn't have worried: the magazine was forearmed each month by my care with a retort to any possible accusation of trifling with Mr. Bousefield's standard. He had admitted to Limbert, after much consider-ation indeed, that he was prepared to be perfectly human; but he had added that he was not prepared for an abuse of this admission. The thing in the world I think I least felt myself was an abuse, even though (as I had never mentioned to my friendly editor) I too had my project for a bigger reverbera-tion. I daresay I trusted mine more than I trusted Limbert's; at all events the golden mean in which in the special case he saw his salvation as an editor was something I should be most sure of if I were to exhibit it myself. I exhibited it month after month in the form of a monstrous levity, only praying heaven that my editor might now not tell me, as he had so often told me, that my result was awfully good. I knew what that would signify—it would signify, sketchily speaking, disaster. What he did tell me heartily was that it was just what his game required: his new line had brought with it an earnest assumption—earnest save when we privately laughed about it—of the locutions proper to real bold enterprise. If I tried to keep him in the dark even as he kept Mr. Bousefield there was nothing to show that I was not tolerably successful: each case therefore presented a promising analogy for the other. He never noticed my descent, and it was accordingly possible that Mr. Bousefield would never notice his. But would nobody notice it at all?—that was a question that added a prospective zest to one's possession of a critical sense. So much depended upon it that I was rather relieved than otherwise not to know the answer too soon. I waited in fact a year—the year for which Limbert had cannily engaged on trial with Mr. Bousefield; the year as to which through the same sharpened shrewdness it had been conveyed in the agreement between them that Mr. Bousefield was not to intermeddle. It had been Limbert's general prayer that we would during this period let him quite alone. His terror of my direct rays was a droll, dreadful force that always operated: he explained it by the fact that I understood him too well, expressed too much of his intention, saved him too little from himself. The less he was saved the more he didn't sell: I literally interpreted, and that was simply fatal.

I held my breath accordingly; I did more—I closed my eyes, I guarded my treacherous ears. He induced several of us to do that (of such devotions we were capable) so that not even glancing at the thing from month to month, and having nothing but his shamed, anxious silence to go by, I participated only vaguely in the little hum that surrounded his act of sacrifice. It was blown about the town that the public would be surprised; it was hinted, it was printed that he was making a desperate bid. His new work was spoken of as "more calculated for general acceptance." These tidings produced in some quarters much reprobation, and nowhere more, I think, than on the part of certain persons who had never read a word of him, or assuredly had never spent a shilling on him, and who hung for hours over the other attractions of the newspaper that announced his abasement. So much asperity cheered me a little—seemed to signify that he might really be doing something. On the other hand I had a distinct alarm; some one sent me for some alien reason an American journal (containing frankly more than that source of affliction) in which was quoted a passage from our friend's last installment. The passage—I couldn't for my life help reading it—was simply superb. Ah, he *would* have to move to the country if that was the worst he could do! It gave me a pang to see how little after all he had improved since the days of his competition with Pat Moyle. There was nothing in the passage quoted in the American paper that Pat would for a moment have owned. During the last weeks, as the opportunity of reading the complete thing drew near, one's suspense was barely endurable, and I shall never forget the July evening on which I put it to rout. Coming home to dinner I found the two volumes on my table, and I sat up with them half the night, dazed, bewildered, rubbing my eyes, wondering at the monstrous joke. *Was* it a monstrous joke, his second manner—was *this* the new line, the desperate bid, the scheme for more general acceptance and the remedy for material failure? Had he made a fool of all his following, or had he most injuriously made a still bigger fool of himself? Obvious?—where the deuce was it obvious? Popular?—how on earth could it be popular? The thing was charming with all his charm and powerful with all his power: it was an unscrupulous, an unsparing, a shameless, merciless masterpiece. It was, no doubt, like the old letters to the *Beacon*, the worst he could do; but the perversity of the effort, even though heroic, had been frustrated by the purity of the gift. Under what illusion had he laboured, with what wavering, treacherous compass had he steered? His honour was inviolable, his measurements were all wrong. I was thrilled with the whole impression and with all that came crowding in its train. It was too grand a collapse—it was too hideous a triumph; I exulted almost with tears—I lamented with a strange delight. Indeed as the short night waned and, threshing about in my emotion, I fidgeted to my high-perched window for a glimpse of the summer dawn, I became at last aware that I was staring at it out of eyes that had compassionately and admiringly filled. The eastern sky, over the London housetops, had a wonderful tragic crimson. That was the colour of his magnificent mistake.

IV

If something less had depended on my impression I daresay I should have communicated it as soon as I had swallowed my breakfast; but the case was so embarrassing that I spent the first half of the day in reconsidering it, dipping into the book again, almost feverishly turning its leaves and trying to extract from them, for my friend's benefit, some symptom of reassurance, some ground for felicitation. This rash challenge had consequences merely dreadful; the wretched volumes, imperturbable and impeccable, with their shyer secrets and their second line of defence, were like a beautiful woman more denuded or a great symphony on a new hearing. There was something quite sinister in the way they stood up to me. I couldn't however be dumb—that was to give the wrong tinge to my disappointment; so that later in the afternoon, taking my courage in both hands, I approached with a vain tortuosity poor Limbert's door. A smart victoria waited before it in which from the bottom of the street I saw that a lady who had apparently just issued from the house was settling herself. I recognised Jane Highmore and instantly paused till she should drive down to me. She presently met me half-way and as soon as she saw me stopped her carriage in agitation. This was a relief—it postponed a moment the sight of that pale, fine face of our friend's fronting me for the right verdict. I gathered from the flushed eagerness with which Mrs. Highmore asked me if I had heard the news that a verdict of some sort had already been rendered.

"What news?—about the book?"

"About that horrid magazine. They're shockingly upset. He has lost his position—he has had a fearful flare-up with Mr. Bousefield."

I stood there blank, but not unaware in my blankness of how history repeats itself. There came to me across the years Maud's announcement of their ejection from the *Beacon*, and dimly, confusedly the same explanation was in the air. This time however I had been on my guard; I had had my suspicion. "He has made it too flippant?" I found breath after an instant to inquire.

Mrs. Highmore's vacuity exceeded my own. "Too 'flippant?' He has made it too oracular. Mr. Bousefield says he has killed it." Then perceiving my stupefaction: "Don't you know what has happened?" she pursued; "isn't it because in his trouble, poor love, he has sent for you that you've come? You've heard nothing at all? Then you had better know before you see them. Get in here with me—I'll take you a turn and tell you." We were close to the Park, the Regent's, and when with extreme alacrity I had placed myself beside her and the carriage had begun to enter it she went on: "It was what I feared, you know. It reeked with culture. He keyed it up too high."

I felt myself sinking in the general collapse. "What are you talking about?"

"Why, about that beastly magazine. They're all on the streets. I shall have to take mamma."

I pulled myself together. "What on earth then did Bousefield want? He said he wanted intellectual power."

"Yes, but Ray overdid it."

"Why, Bousefield said it was a thing he *couldn't* overdo."

"Well, Ray managed: he took Mr. Bousefield too literally. It appears the thing has been doing dreadfully, but the proprietor couldn't say anything, because he had covenanted to leave the editor quite free. He describes himself as having stood there in a fever and seen his ship go down. A day or two ago the year was up, so he could at last break out. Maud says he did break out quite fearfully; he came to the house and let poor Ray have it. Ray gave it to him back; he reminded him of his own idea of the way the cat was going to jump."

I gasped with dismay. "Has Bousefield abandoned that idea? Isn't the cat going to jump?"

Mrs. Highmore hesitated. "It appears that she doesn't seem in a hurry. Ray at any rate has jumped too far ahead of her. He should have temporised a little, Mr. Bousefield says; but I'm beginning to think, you know," said my companion, "that Ray *can't* temporise." Fresh from my emotions of the

previous twenty-four hours I was scarcely in a position to disagree with her. "He published too much pure thought."

"Pure thought?" I cried. "Why, it struck me so often—
certainly in a due proportion of cases—as pure drivel!"

"Oh, you're more keyed up than he! Mr. Bousefield says
that of course he wanted things that were suggestive and
clever, things that he could point to with pride. But he con-
tends that Ray didn't allow for human weakness. He gave
everything in too stiff doses."

Sensibly, I fear, to my neighbour I winced at her words; I
felt a prick that made me meditate. Then I said: "Is that, by
chance, the way he gave *me*?" Mrs. Highmore remained silent
so long that I had somehow the sense of a fresh pang; and
after a minute, turning in my seat, I laid my hand on her arm,
fixed my eyes upon her face and pursued pressingly: "Do you
suppose it to be to my 'Occasional Remarks' that Mr. Bousefield refers?"

At last she met my look. "Can you bear to hear it?"

"I think I can bear anything now."

"Well then, it was really what I wanted to give you an inkling of. It's largely over you that they've quarrelled. Mr.
Bousefield wants him to chuck you."

I grabbed her arm again. "And Limbert *won't*?"

"He seems to cling to you. Mr. Bousefield says no magazine
can afford you."

I gave a laugh that agitated the very coachman. "Why, my
dear lady, has he any idea of my price?"

"It isn't your price—he says you're dear at any price; you
do so much to sink the ship. Your 'Remarks' are called 'Occasional,' but nothing could be more deadly regular: you're
there month after month and you're never anywhere else. And
you supply no public want."

"I supply the most delicious irony."

"So Ray appears to have declared. Mr. Bousefield says that's
not in the least a public want. No one can make out what
you're talking about and no one would care if he could. I'm
only quoting *him*, mind."

"Quote, quote—if Limbert holds out. I think I must leave
you now, please: I must rush back to express to him what I
feel."

"I'll drive you to his door. That isn't all," said Mrs. High-more. And on the way, when the carriage had turned, she communicated the rest. "Mr. Bousefield really arrived with an ultimatum: it had the form of something or other by Minnie Meadows."

"Minnie Meadows?" I was stupefied.

"The new lady-humourist every one is talking about. It's the first of a series of screaming sketches for which poor Ray was to find a place."

"Is *that* Mr. Bousefield's idea of literature?"

"No, but he says it's the public's, and you've got to take *some* account of the public. *Aux grands maux les grands re-mèdes.* They had a tremendous lot of ground to make up, and no one would make it up like Minnie. She would be the best concession they could make to human weakness; she would strike at least this note of showing that it was not going to be quite all—well, all *you.* Now Ray draws the line at Minnie; he won't stoop to Minnie; he declines to touch, to look at Min-nie. When Mr. Bousefield—rather imperiously, I believe—made Minnie a *sine quâ non* of his retention of his post he said something rather violent, told him to go to some un-mentionable place and take Minnie with him. That of course put the fat on the fire. They had really a considerable scene."

"So had he with the *Beacon* man," I musingly replied. "Poor dear, he seems born for considerable scenes! It's on Minnie, then, that they've really split?" Mrs. Highmore ex-haled her despair in a sound which I took for an assent, and when we had rolled a little further I rather inconsequently and to her visible surprise broke out of my reverie. "It will never do in the world—he *must* stoop to Minnie!"

"It's too late—and what I've told you still isn't all. Mr. Bousefield raises another objection."

"What other, pray?"

"Can't you guess?"

I wondered. "No more of Ray's fiction?"

"Not a line. That's something else no magazine can stand. Now that his novel has run its course Mr. Bousefield is dis-tinctly disappointed."

I fairly bounded in my place. "Then it may do?"

Mrs. Highmore looked bewildered. "Why so, if he finds it too dull?"

"Dull? Ralph Limbert? He's as fine as a needle!"

"It comes to the same thing—he won't penetrate leather. Mr. Bousefield had counted on something that *would*, on something that would have a wider acceptance. Ray says he wants iron pegs." I collapsed again; my flicker of elation dropped to a throb of quieter comfort; and after a moment's silence I asked my neighbour if she had herself read the work our friend had just put forth. "No," she replied, "I gave him my word at the beginning, on his urgent request, that I wouldn't."

"Not even as a book?"

"He begged me never to look at it at all. He said he was trying a low experiment. Of course I knew what he meant and I entreated him to let me just for curiosity take a peep. But he was firm, he declared he couldn't bear the thought that a woman like me should see him in the depths."

"He's only, thank God, in the depths of distress," I replied. "His experiment's nothing worse than a failure."

"Then Bousefield *is* right—his circulation won't budge?"

"It won't move one, as they say in Fleet Street. The book has extraordinary beauty."

"Poor duck—after trying so hard!" Jane Highmore sighed with real tenderness. "What *will* then become of them?"

I was silent an instant. "You must take your mother."

She was silent too. "I must speak of it to Cecil!" she presently said. Cecil is Mr. Highmore, who then entertained, I knew, strong views on the inadjustability of circumstances in general to the idiosyncrasies of Mrs. Stannace. He held it supremely happy that in an important relation she should have met her match. Her match was Ray Limbert—not much of a writer but a practical man. "The dear things still think, you know," my companion continued, "that the book will be the beginning of their fortune. Their illusion, if you're right, will be rudely dispelled."

"That's what makes me dread to face them. I've just spent with his volumes an unforgettable night. His illusion has lasted because so many of us have been pledged till this moment to turn our faces the other way. We haven't known the truth and have therefore had nothing to say. Now that we do know it indeed we have practically quite as little. I hang back from the threshold. How can I follow up with a burst of enthusiasm such a catastrophe as Mr. Bousefield's visit?"

As I turned uneasily about my neighbour more comfortably snuggled. "Well, I'm glad then I haven't read him and have nothing unpleasant to say!" We had come back to Limbert's door, and I made the coachman stop short of it. "But he'll try again, with that determination of his: he'll build his hopes on the next time."

"On what else has he built them from the very first? It's never the present for him that bears the fruit; that's always postponed and for somebody else: there has always to be another try. I admit that his idea of a 'new line' has made him try harder than ever. It makes no difference," I brooded, still timorously lingering; "his achievement of his necessity, his hope of a market will continue to attach themselves to the future. But the next time will disappoint him as each last time has done—and then the next and the next and the next!"

I found myself seeing it all with a clearness almost inspired: it evidently cast a chill on Mrs. Highmore. "Then what on earth will become of him?" she plaintively asked.

"I don't think I particularly care what may become of *him*," I returned with a conscious, reckless increase of my exaltation; "I feel it almost enough to be concerned with what may become of one's enjoyment of him. I don't know in short what will become of his circulation; I am only quite at my ease as to what will become of his work. It will simply keep all its quality. He'll try again for the common with what he'll believe to be a still more infernal cunning, and again the common will fatally elude him, for his infernal cunning will have been only his genius in an ineffectual disguise." We sat drawn up by the pavement, facing poor Limbert's future as I saw it. It relieved me in a manner to know the worst, and I prophesied with an assurance which as I look back upon it strikes me as rather remarkable. *"Que voulez-vous?"* I went on; "you can't make a sow's ear of a silk purse! It's grievous indeed if you like—there are people who can't be vulgar for trying. *He* can't—it wouldn't come off, I promise you, even once. It takes more than trying—it comes by grace. It happens not to be given to Limbert to fall. He belongs to the heights—he breathes there, he lives there, and it's accordingly to the heights I must ascend," I said as I took leave of my conductress, "to carry him this wretched news from where *we* move!"

V

A few months were sufficient to show how right I had been about his circulation. It didn't move one, as I had said; it stopped short in the same place, fell off in a sheer descent, like some precipice gaped up at by tourists. The public in other words drew the line for him as sharply as he had drawn it for Minnie Meadows. Minnie has skipped with a flouncing caper over his line, however; whereas the mark traced by a lustier cudgel has been a barrier insurmountable to Limbert. Those next times I had spoken of to Jane Highmore, I see them simplified by retrocession. Again and again he made his desperate bid—again and again he tried to. His rupture with Mr. Bousefield caused him, I fear, in professional circles to be thought impracticable, and I am perfectly aware, to speak candidly, that no sordid advantage ever accrued to him from such public patronage of my performances as he had occasionally been in a position to offer. I reflect for my comfort that any injury I may have done him by untimely application of a faculty of analysis which could point to no converts gained by honourable exercise was at least equalled by the injury he did himself. More than once, as I have hinted, I held my tongue at his request, but my frequent plea that such favours weren't politic never found him, when in other connections there was an opportunity to give me a lift, anything but indifferent to the danger of the association. He let them have me in a word whenever he could; sometimes in periodicals in which he had credit, sometimes only at dinner. He talked about me when he couldn't get me in, but it was always part of the bargain that I shouldn't make him a topic. "How can I successfully serve you if you do?" he used to ask: he was more afraid than I thought he ought to have been of the charge of tit for tat. I didn't care, for I never could distinguish tat from tit; but as I have intimated I dropped into silence really more than anything else because there was a certain fascinated observation of his course which was quite testimony enough and to which in this huddled conclusion of it he practically reduced me.

I see it all foreshortened, his wonderful remainder—see it from the end backward, with the direction widening toward me as if on a level with the eye. The migration to the country promised him at first great things—smaller expenses, larger leisure, conditions eminently conducive on each occasion to the possible triumph of the next time. Mrs. Stannace, who altogether disapproved of it, gave as one of her reasons that her son-in-law, living mainly in a village on the edge of a goose-green, would be deprived of that contact with the great world which was indispensable to the painter of manners. She had the showiest arguments for keeping him in touch, as she called it, with good society; wishing to know with some force where, from the moment he ceased to represent it from ob-servation, the novelist could be said to be. In London fortu-nately a clever man was just a clever man; there were charming houses in which a person of Ray's undoubted ability, even though without the knack of making the best use of it, could always be sure of a quiet corner for watching decorously the social kaleidoscope. But the kaleidoscope of the goose-green, what in the world was that, and what such delusive thrift as drives about the land (with a fearful account for flys from the inn) to leave cards on the country magnates? This solicitude for Limbert's subject-matter was the specious colour with which, deeply determined not to affront mere tolerance in a cottage, Mrs. Stannace overlaid her indisposition to place her-self under the heel of Cecil Highmore. She knew that he ruled Upstairs as well as down, and she clung to the fable of the association of interests in the north of London. The High-mores had a better address—they lived now in Stanhope Gar-dens; but Cecil was fearfully artful—he wouldn't hear of an association of interests nor treat with his mother-in-law save as a visitor. She didn't like false positions; but on the other hand she didn't like the sacrifice of everything she was accus-tomed to. Her universe at all events was a universe full of card-leavings and charming houses, and it was fortunate that she couldn't Upstairs catch the sound of the doom to which, in his little grey den, describing to me his diplomacy, Limbert consigned alike the country magnates and the opportunities of London. Despoiled of every guarantee she went to Stanhope Gardens like a mere maidservant, with restrictions on her very luggage, while during the year that followed this upheaval Limbert, strolling with me on the goose-green, to which I often ran down, played extravagantly over the theme that with what he was now going in for it was a positive comfort not to have the social kaleidoscope. With a cold-blooded trick in view what had life or manners or the best society or flys from the inn to say to the question? It was as good a place as another to play his new game. He had found a quieter corner than any corner of the great world, and a damp old house at sixpence a year, which, beside leaving him all his margin to educate his children, would allow of the supreme luxury of his frankly presenting himself as a poor man. This was a convenience that *ces dames*, as he called them, had never yet fully permitted him.

It rankled in me at first to see his reward so meagre, his conquest so mean; but the simplification effected had a charm that I finally felt: it was a forcing-house for the three or four other fine miscarriages to which his scheme was evidently condemned. I limited him to three or four, having had my sharp impression, in spite of the perpetual broad joke of the thing, that a spring had really snapped in him on the occasion of that deeply disconcerting sequel to the episode of his editorship. He never lost his sense of the grotesque want, in the difference made, of adequate relation to the effort that had been the intensest of his life. He had from that moment a charge of shot in him, and it slowly worked its way to a vital part. As he met his embarrassments each year with his punctual false remedy I wondered periodically where he found the energy to return to the attack. He did it every time with a rage more blanched, but it was clear to me that the tension must finally snap the cord. We got again and again the irrepressible work of art, but what did *he* get, poor man, who wanted something so different? There were likewise odder questions than this in the matter, phenomena more curious and mysteries more puzzling, which often for sympathy if not for illumination I intimately discussed with Mrs. Limbert. She had her burdens, dear lady: after the removal from London and a considerable interval she twice again became a mother. Mrs. Stannace too, in a more restricted sense, exhibited afresh, in relation to the home she had abandoned, the same exemplary character. In her poverty of guarantees at Stanhope Gardens there had been least of all, it appeared, a proviso that she shouldn't resentfully revert again from Goneril to Regan. She came down to the goose-green like Lear himself, with fewer knights, or at least baronets, and the joint household was at last patched up. It fell to pieces and was put together on various occasions before Ray Limbert died. He was ridden to the end by the superstition that he had broken up Mrs. Stannace's original home on pretences that had proved hollow and that if he hadn't given Maud what she might have had he could at least give her back her mother. I was always sure that a sense of the compensations he owed was half the motive of the dogged pride with which he tried to wake up the libraries. I believed Mrs. Stannace still had money, though she pretended that, called upon at every turn to retrieve deficits, she had long since poured it into the general fund. This conviction haunted me; I suspected her of secret hoards, and I said to myself that she couldn't be so infamous as not some day on her deathbed to leave everything to her less opulent daughter. My compassion for the Limberts led me to hover perhaps indiscreetly round that closing scene, to dream of some happy time when such an accession of means would make up a little for their present penury.

This however was crude comfort, as in the first place I had nothing definite to go by and in the second I held it for more and more indicated that Ray wouldn't outlive her. I never ventured to sound him as to what in this particular he hoped or feared, for after the crisis marked by his leaving London I had new scruples about suffering him to be reminded of where he fell short. The poor man was in truth humiliated, and there were things as to which that kept us both silent. In proportion as he tried more fiercely for the market the old plaintive arithmetic, fertile in jokes, dropped from our conversation. We joked immensely still about the process, but our treatment of the results became sparing and superficial. He talked as much as ever, with monstrous arts and borrowed hints, of the traps he kept setting, but we all agreed to take

merely for granted that the animal was caught. This propriety
had really dawned upon me the day that after Mr. Bousefield's
visit Mrs. Highmore put me down at his door. Mr. Bousefield
in that juncture had been served up to me anew, but after we
had disposed of him we came to the book, which I was
obliged to confess I had already rushed through. It was from
this moment—the moment at which my terrible impression
of it had blinked out at his anxious query—that the image of
his scared face was to abide with me. I couldn't attenuate
then—the cat was out of the bag; but later, each of the next
times, I did, I acknowledge, attenuate. We all did religiously,
so far as was possible; we cast ingenious ambiguities over the
strong places, the beauties that betrayed him most, and found
ourselves in the queer position of admirers banded to mislead
a confiding artist. If we stifled our cheers however and dissimulated our joy our fond hypocrisy accomplished little, for Limbert's finger was on a pulse that told a plainer story. It was a
satisfaction to have secured a greater freedom with his wife,
who at last, much to her honour, entered into the conspiracy
and whose sense of responsibility was flattered by the frequency of our united appeal to her for some answer to the
marvellous riddle. We had all turned it over till we were tired
of it, threshing out the question why the note he strained
every chord to pitch for common ears should invariably insist
on addressing itself to the angels. Being, as it were, ourselves
the angels we had only a limited quarrel in each case with the
event; but its inconsequent character, given the forces set in
motion, was peculiarly baffling. It was like an interminable
sum that wouldn't come straight; nobody had the time to
handle so many figures. Limbert gathered, to make his pudding, dry bones and dead husks; how then was one to formulate the law that made the dish prove a feast? What was
the cerebral treachery that defied his own vigilance? There was
some obscure interference of taste, some obsession of the exquisite. All one could say was that genius was a fatal disturber
or that the unhappy man had no effectual *flair*. When he went
abroad to gather garlic he came home with heliotrope.

I hasten to add that if Mrs. Limbert was not directly illuminating she was yet rich in anecdote and example, having
found a refuge from mystification exactly where the rest of us

had found it, in a more devoted embrace and the sense of a finer glory. Her disappointments and eventually her privations had been many, her discipline severe; but she had ended by accepting the long grind of life and was now quite willing to take her turn at the mill. She was essentially one of us—she always understood. Touching and admirable at the last, when through the unmistakable change in Limbert's health her troubles were thickest, was the spectacle of the particular pride that she wouldn't have exchanged for prosperity. She had said to me once—only once, in a gloomy hour in London days when things were not going at all—that one really had to think him a very great man because if one didn't one would be rather ashamed of him. She had distinctly felt it at first—and in a very tender place—that almost every one passed him on the road; but I believe that in these final years she would almost have been ashamed of him if he had suddenly gone into editions. It is certain indeed that her complacency was not subjected to that shock. She would have liked the money immensely, but she would have missed something she had taught herself to regard as rather rare. There is another remark I remember her making, a remark to the effect that of course if she could have chosen she would have liked him to be Shakespeare or Scott, but that failing this she was very glad he wasn't—well, she named the two gentlemen, but I won't. I daresay she sometimes laughed out to escape an alternative. She contributed passionately to the capture of the second manner, foraging for him further afield than he could conveniently go, gleaning in the barest stubble, picking up shreds to build the nest and in particular in the study of the great secret of how, as we always said, they all did it laying waste the circulating libraries. If Limbert had a weakness he rather broke down in his reading. It was fortunately not till after the appearance of *The Hidden Heart* that he broke down in everything else. He had had rheumatic fever in the spring, when the book was but half finished, and this ordeal in addition to interrupting his work had enfeebled his powers of resistance and greatly reduced his vitality. He recovered from the fever and was able to take up the book again, but the organ of life was pronounced ominously weak and it was enjoined upon him with some sharpness that he should lend himself to no worries. It might have struck me as on the cards that his worries would now be surmountable, for when he began to mend he expressed to me a conviction almost contagious that he had never yet made so adroit a bid as in the idea of *The Hidden Heart*. It is grimly droll to reflect that this superb little composition, the shortest of his novels but perhaps the loveliest, was planned from the first as an "adventure-story" on approved lines. It was the way they all did the adventure-story that he tried most dauntlessly to emulate. I wonder how many readers ever divined to which of their bookshelves *The Hidden Heart* was so exclusively addressed. High medical advice early in the summer had been quite viciously clear as to the inconvenience that might ensue to him should he neglect to spend the winter in Egypt. He was not a man to neglect anything; but Egypt seemed to us all then as unattainable as a second edition. He finished *The Hidden Heart* with the energy of apprehension and desire, for if the book should happen to do what "books of that class," as the publisher said, sometimes did he might well have a fund to draw on. As soon as I read the deep and delicate thing I knew, as I had known in each case before, exactly how well it would do. Poor Limbert in this long business always figured to me an undiscourageable parent to whom only girls kept being born. A bouncing boy, a son and heir was devoutly prayed for and almanacks and old wives consulted; but the spell was inveterate, incurable, and *The Hidden Heart* proved, so to speak, but another female child. When the winter arrived accordingly Egypt was out of the question. Jane Highmore, to my knowledge, wanted to lend him money, and there were even greater devotees who did their best to induce him to lean on them. There was so marked a "movement" among his friends that a very considerable sum would have been at his disposal; but his stiffness was invincible: it had its root, I think, in his sense, on his own side, of sacrifices already made. He had sacrificed honour and pride, and he had sacrificed them precisely to the question of money. He would evidently, should he be able to go on, have to continue to sacrifice them, but it must be all in the way to which he had now, as he considered, hardened himself. He had spent years in plotting for favour, and since on favour he must live it could only be as a bargain and a price.

He got through the early part of the season better than we feared, and I went down in great elation to spend Christmas on the goose-green. He told me late on Christmas eve, after our simple domestic revels had sunk to rest and we sat together by the fire, that he had been visited the night before in wakeful hours by the finest fancy for a really good thing that he had ever felt descend in the darkness. "It's just the vision of a situation that contains, upon my honour, everything," he said, "and I wonder that I've never thought of it before." He didn't describe it further, contrary to his common practice, and I only knew later, by Mrs. Limbert, that he had begun *Derogation* and that he was completely full of his subject. It was a subject however that he was not to live to treat. The work went on for a couple of months in happy mystery, without revelations even to his wife. He had not invited her to help him to get up his case—she had not taken the field with him as on his previous campaigns. We only knew he was at it again but that less even than ever had been said about the impression to be made on the market. I saw him in February and thought him sufficiently at ease. The great thing was that he was immensely interested and was pleased with the omens. I got a strange, stirring sense that he had not consulted the usual ones and indeed that he had floated away into a grand indifference, into a reckless consciousness of art. The voice of the market had suddenly grown faint and far: he had come back at the last, as people so often do, to one of the moods, the sincerities of his prime. Was he really with a blurred sense of the urgent doing something now only for himself? We wondered and waited—we felt that he was a little confused. What had happened, I was afterwards satisfied, was that he had quite forgotten whether he generally sold or not. He had merely waked up one morning again in the country of the blue and had stayed there with a good conscience and a great idea. He stayed till death knocked at the gate, for the pen dropped from his hand only at the moment when from sudden failure of the heart his eyes, as he sank back in his chair, closed for ever. *Derogation* is a splendid fragment; it evidently would have been one of his high successes. I am not prepared to say it would have waked up the libraries.

Glasses

Y ES INDEED, I say to myself, pen in hand, I can keep hold of the thread and let it lead me back to the first impression. The little story is all there, I can touch it from point to point; for the thread, as I call it, is a row of coloured beads on a string. None of the beads are missing—at least I think they're not: that's exactly what I shall amuse myself with finding out.

I had been all summer working hard in town and then had gone down to Folkestone for a blow. Art was long, I felt, and my holiday short; my mother was settled at Folkestone, and I paid her a visit when I could. I remember how on this occasion, after weeks, in my stuffy studio, with my nose on my palette, I sniffed up the clean salt air and cooled my eyes with the purple sea. The place was full of lodgings, and the lodgings were at that season full of people, people who had nothing to do but to stare at one another on the great flat down. There were thousands of little chairs and almost as many little Jews; and there was music in an open rotunda, over which the little Jews wagged their big noses. We all strolled to and fro and took pennyworths of rest; the long, level cliff top, edged in places with its iron rail, might have been the deck of a huge crowded ship. There were old folks in Bath chairs, and there was one dear chair, creeping to its last full stop, by the side of which I always walked. There was in fine weather the coast of France to look at, and there were the usual things to say about it; there was also in every state of the atmosphere our friend Mrs Meldrum, a subject of remark not less inveterate. The widow of an officer in the Engineers, she had settled, like many members of the martial miscellany, well within sight of the hereditary enemy, who however had left her leisure to form in spite of the difference of their years a close alliance with my mother. She was the heartiest, the keenest, the ugliest of women, the least apologetic, the least morbid in her misfortune. She carried it high aloft, with loud sounds and free gestures, made it flutter in the breeze as if it had been the flag of her country. It consisted mainly of a big red

525

face, indescribably out of drawing, from which she glared at you through gold-rimmed aids to vision, optic circles of such diameter and so frequently displaced that some one had vividly spoken of her as flattening her nose against the glass of her spectacles. She was extraordinarily near-sighted, and whatever they did to other objects they magnified immensely the kind eyes behind them. Blessed conveniences they were, in their hideous, honest strength—they showed the good lady everything in the world but her own queerness. This element was enhanced by wild braveries of dress, reckless charges of colour and stubborn resistances of cut, wondrous encounters in which the art of the toilet seemed to lay down its life. She had the tread of a grenadier and the voice of an angel.

In the course of a walk with her the day after my arrival I found myself grabbing her arm with sudden and undue familiarity. I had been struck by the beauty of a face that approached us and I was still more affected when I saw the face, at the sight of my companion, open like a window thrown wide. A smile fluttered out of it as brightly as a drapery dropped from a sill—a drapery shaken there in the sun by a young lady flanked with two young men, a wonderful young lady who, as we drew nearer, rushed up to Mrs. Meldrum with arms flourished for an embrace. My immediate impression of her had been that she was dressed in mourning, but during the few moments she stood talking with our friend I made more discoveries. The figure from the neck down was meagre, the stature insignificant, but the desire to please towered high, as well as the air of infallibly knowing how and of never, never missing it. This was a little person whom I would have made a high bid for a good chance to paint. The head, the features, the colour, the whole facial oval and radiance had a wonderful purity; the deep grey eyes—the most agreeable, I thought, that I had ever seen—brushed with a kind of wing-like grace every object they encountered. Their possessor was just back from Boulogne, where she had spent a week with dear Mrs. Floyd-Taylor: this accounted for the effusiveness of her reunion with dear Mrs. Meldrum. Her black garments were of the freshest and daintiest; she suggested a pink-and-white wreath at a showy funeral. She confounded us for three minutes with her presence; she was a beauty of the great conscious, public, responsible order. The young men, her companions, gazed at her and grinned: I could see there were very few moments of the day at which young men, these or others, would not be so occupied. The people who approached took leave of their manners; every one seemed to linger and gape. When she brought her face close to Mrs. Meldrum's—and she appeared to be always bringing it close to somebody's—it was a marvel that objects so dissimilar should express the same general identity, the unmistakable character of the English gentlewoman. Mrs. Meldrum sustained the comparison with her usual courage, but I wondered why she didn't introduce me: I should have had no objection to the bringing of such a face close to mine. However, when the young lady moved on with her escort she herself bequeathed me a sense that some such *rapprochement* might still occur. Was this by reason of the general frequency of encounters at Folkestone, or by reason of a subtle acknowledgment that she contrived to make of the rights, on the part of others, that such beauty as hers created? I was in a position to answer that question after Mrs. Meldrum had answered a few of mine.

II

Flora Saunt, the only daughter of an old soldier, had lost both her parents, her mother within a few months. Mrs. Meldrum had known them, disapproved of them, considerably avoided them: she had watched the girl, off and on, from her early childhood. Flora, just twenty, was extraordinarily alone in the world—so alone that she had no natural chaperon, no one to stay with but a mercenary stranger, Mrs. Hammond Synge, the sister-in-law of one of the young men I had just seen. She had lots of friends, but none of them nice: she kept picking up impossible people. The Floyd-Taylors, with whom she had been at Boulogne, were simply horrid. The Hammond Synges were perhaps not so vulgar, but they had no conscience in their dealings with her.

"She knows what I think of them," said Mrs. Meldrum, "and indeed she knows what I think of most things."

"She shares that privilege with most of your friends!" I replied laughing.

"No doubt; but possibly to some of my friends it makes a little difference. That girl doesn't care a button. She knows best of all what I think of Flora Saunt."

"And what may your opinion be?"

"Why, that she's not worth talking about—an idiot too abysmal."

"Doesn't she care for that?"

"Just enough, as you saw, to hug me till I cry out. She's too pleased with herself for anything else to matter."

"Surely, my dear friend," I rejoined, "she has a good deal to be pleased with!"

"So every one tells her, and so you would have told her if I had given you a chance. However, that doesn't signify either, for her vanity is beyond all making or mending. She believes in herself, and she's welcome, after all, poor dear, having only herself to look to. I've seldom met a young woman more completely at liberty to be silly. She has a clear course—she'll make a showy finish."

"Well," I replied, "as she probably will reduce many persons to the same degraded state, her partaking of it won't stand out so much."

"If you mean that the world's full of twaddlers I quite agree with you!" cried Mrs. Meldrum, trumpeting her laugh half across the Channel.

I had after this to consider a little what she would call my mother's son, but I didn't let it prevent me from insisting on her making me acquainted with Flora Saunt; indeed I took the bull by the horns, urging that she had drawn the portrait of a nature which common charity now demanded that she should put into relation with a character really fine. Such a frail creature was just an object of pity. This contention on my part had at first of course been jocular; but strange to say it was quite the ground I found myself taking with regard to our young lady after I had begun to know her. I couldn't have said what I felt about her except that she was undefended; from the first of my sitting with her there after dinner, under the stars—that was a week at Folkestone of balmy nights and muffled tides and crowded chairs—I became aware both that protection was wholly absent from her life and that she was wholly indifferent to its absence. The odd thing was

that she was not appealing: she was abjectly, divinely conceited, absurdly, fantastically happy. Her beauty was as yet all
the world to her, a world she had plenty to do to live in. Mrs.
Meldrum told me more about her, and there was nothing
that, as the centre of a group of giggling, nudging spectators,
she was not ready to tell about herself. She held her little court
in the crowd, upon the grass, playing her light over Jews and
Gentiles, completely at ease in all promiscuities. It was an effect of these things that from the very first, with every one
listening, I could mention that my main business with her
would be just to have a go at her head and to arrange in that
view for an early sitting. It would have been as impossible, I
think, to be impertinent to her as it would have been to throw
a stone at a plate-glass window; so any talk that went forward
on the basis of her loveliness was the most natural thing in
the world and immediately became the most general and sociable. It was when I saw all this that I judged how, though
it was the last thing she asked for, what one would ever most
have at her service was a curious compassion. That sentiment
was coloured by the vision of the dire exposure of a being
whom vanity had put so off her guard. Hers was the only
vanity I have ever known that made its possessor superlatively
soft. Mrs. Meldrum's further information contributed moreover to these indulgences—her account of the girl's neglected
childhood and queer continental relegations, with straying,
squabbling, Monte-Carlo-haunting parents; the more invidious picture, above all, of her pecuniary arrangement, still in
force, with the Hammond Synges, who really, though they
never took her out—practically she went out alone—had their
hands half the time in her pocket. She had to pay for every
thing, down to her share of the wine-bills and the horses'
fodder, down to Bertie Hammond Synge's fare in the
"Underground" when he went to the City for her. She had
been left with just money enough to turn her head; and it
hadn't even been put in trust, nothing prudent or proper had
been done with it. She could spend her capital, and at the rate
she was going, expensive, extravagant and with a swarm of
parasites to help, it certainly wouldn't last very long.

"Couldn't *you* perhaps take her, independent, unencum-
bered as you are?" I asked of Mrs. Meldrum. "You're prob-

ably, with one exception, the sanest person she knows, and you at least wouldn't scandalously fleece her."

"How do you know what I wouldn't do?" my humorous friend demanded. "Of course I've thought how I can help her—it has kept me awake at night. But I can't help her at all; she'll take nothing from me. You know what she does—she hugs me and runs away. She has an instinct about me, she feels that I've one about her. And then she dislikes me for another reason that I'm not quite clear about, but that I'm well aware of and that I shall find out some day. So far as her settling with me goes it would be impossible moreover here: she wants naturally enough a much wider field. She must live in London—her game is there. So she takes the line of adoring me, of saying she can never forget that I was devoted to her mother—which I wouldn't for the world have been—and of giving me a wide berth. I think she positively dislikes to look at me. It's all right; there's no obligation; though people in general can't take their eyes off me."

"I see that at this moment," I replied. "But what does it matter where or how, for the present, she lives? She'll marry infallibly, marry early, and everything then will change."

"Whom will she marry?" my companion gloomily asked.

"Any one she likes. She's so abnormally pretty she can do anything. She'll fascinate some nabob or some prince."

"She'll fascinate him first and bore him afterwards. Moreover she's not so pretty as you make her out; she has a scrappy little figure."

"No doubt; but one doesn't in the least notice it."

"Not now," said Mrs. Meldrum, "but one will when she's older."

"When she's older she'll be a princess, so it won't matter."

"She has other drawbacks," my companion went on. "Those wonderful eyes are good for nothing but to roll about like sugar-balls—which they greatly resemble—in a child's mouth. She can't use them."

"Use them? Why, she does nothing else."

"To make fools of young men, but not to read or write, not to do any sort of work. She never opens a book, and her maid writes her notes. You'll say that those who live in glass houses shouldn't throw stones. Of course I know that if I didn't wear my goggles I shouldn't be good for much."

"Do you mean that Miss Saunt ought to sport such things?" I exclaimed with more horror than I meant to show.

"I don't prescribe for her; I don't know that they're what she requires."

"What's the matter with her eyes?" I asked after a moment.

"I don't exactly know; but I heard from her mother years ago that even as a child they had had for a while to put her into spectacles and that, though she hated them and had been in a fury of disgust, she would always have to be extremely careful. I'm sure I hope she is!"

I echoed the hope, but I remember well the impression this made upon me—my immediate pang of resentment, a disgust almost equal to Flora's own. I felt as if a great rare sapphire had split in my hand.

III

This conversation occurred the night before I went back to town. I settled on the morrow to take a late train, so that I had still my morning to spend at Folkestone, where during the greater part of it I was out with my mother. Every one in the place was as usual out with some one else, and even had I been free to go and take leave of her I should have been sure that Flora Saunt would not be at home. Just where she was I presently discovered: she was at the far end of the cliff, the point at which it overhangs the pretty view of Sandgate and Hythe. Her back however was turned to this attraction; it rested with the aid of her elbows, thrust slightly behind her so that her scanty little shoulders were raised toward her ears, on the high rail that inclosed the down. Two gentlemen stood before her whose faces we couldn't see but who even as observed from the rear were visibly absorbed in the charming figure-piece submitted to them. I was freshly struck with the fact that this meagre and defective little person, with the cock of her hat and the flutter of her crape, with her eternal idleness, her eternal happiness, her absence of moods and mysteries and the pretty presentation of her feet, which especially now in the supported slope of her posture occupied with their imperceptibility so much of the foreground—I was reminded anew, I say, how our young lady dazzled by some art that the enumeration of her merits didn't explain and that the mention of her lapses didn't affect. Where she was amiss nothing counted, and where she was right everything did. I say she was wanting in mystery, but that after all was her secret. This happened to be my first chance of introducing her to my mother, who had not much left in life but the quiet look from under the hood of her chair at the things which, when she should have quitted those she loved, she could still trust to make the world good for them. I wondered an instant how much she might be moved to trust Flora Saunt, and then while the chair stood still and she waited I went over and asked the girl to come and speak to her. In this way I saw that if one of Flora's attendants was the inevitable young Hammond Synge, master of ceremonies of her regular court, always offering the use of a telescope and accepting that of a cigar, the other was a personage I had not yet encountered, a small pale youth in showy knickerbockers, whose eyebrows and nose and the glued points of whose little moustache were extraordinarily uplifted and sustained. I remember taking him at first for a foreigner and for something of a pretender: I scarcely know why, unless because of the motive I felt in the stare he fixed on me when I asked Miss Saunt to come away. He struck me a little as a young man practising the social art of impertinence; but it didn't matter, for Flora came away with alacrity, bringing all her prettiness and pleasure and gliding over the grass in that rustle of delicate mourning which made the endless variety of her garments, as a painter could take heed, strike one always as the same obscure elegance. She seated herself on the floor of my mother's chair, a little too much on her right instep as I afterwards gathered, caressing her stiff hand, smiling up into her cold face, commending and approving her without a reserve and without a doubt. She told her immediately, as if it were something for her to hold on by, that she was soon to sit to me for a "likeness," and these words gave me a chance to inquire if it would be the fate of the picture, should I finish it, to be presented to the young man in the knickerbockers. Her lips, at this, parted in a stare;

her eyes darkened to the purple of one of the shadow-patches on the sea. She showed for the passing instant the face of some splendid tragic mask, and I remembered for the inconsequence of it what Mrs. Meldrum had said about her sight. I had derived from this lady a worrying impulse to catechise her, but that didn't seem exactly kind; so I substituted another question, inquired who the pretty young man in knicker-bockers might happen to be.

"Oh, a gentleman I met at Boulogne. He has come over to see me." After a moment she added: "He's Lord Iffield."

I had never heard of Lord Iffield, but her mention of his having been at Boulogne helped me to give him a niche. Mrs. Meldrum had incidentally thrown a certain light on the manners of Mrs. Floyd-Taylor, Flora's recent hostess in that charming town, a lady who, it appeared, had a special vocation for helping rich young men to find a use for their leisure. She had always one or other in hand and she had apparently on this occasion pointed her lesson at the rare creature on the opposite coast. I had a vague idea that Boulogne was not a resort of the aristocracy, at the same time there might very well have been a strong attraction there even for one of the darlings of fortune. I could perfectly understand in any case that such a darling should be drawn to Folkestone by Flora Saunt. But it was not in truth of these things I was thinking; what was uppermost in my mind was a matter which, though it had no sort of keeping, insisted just then on coming out.

"Is it true, Miss Saunt," I suddenly demanded, "that you're so unfortunate as to have had some warning about your beautiful eyes?"

I was startled by the effect of my words; the girl threw back her head, changing colour from brow to chin. "True? Who in the world says so?" I repented of my question in a flash; the way she met it made it seem cruel, and I saw that my mother looked at me in some surprise. I took care, in answer to Flora's challenge, not to incriminate Mrs. Meldrum. I answered that the rumour had reached me only in the vaguest form and that if I had been moved to put it to the test my very real interest in her must be held responsible. Her blush died away, but a pair of still prettier tears glistened in its track. "If you ever hear such a thing said again you can say it's a

horrid lie!'' I had brought on a commotion deeper than any
I was prepared for; but it was explained in some degree by
the next words she uttered: "I'm happy to say there's nothing
the matter with any part of my body; not the least little
thing!'' She spoke with her habitual complacency, with triumphant assurance; she smiled again, and I could see that she
was already sorry she had shown herself too disconcerted. She
turned it off with a laugh. "I've good eyes, good teeth, a good
digestion and a good temper. I'm sound of wind and limb!''
Nothing could have been more characteristic than her blush
and her tears, nothing less acceptable to her than to be
thought not perfect in every particular. She couldn't submit
to the imputation of a flaw. I expressed my delight in what
she told me, assuring her I should always do battle for her;
and as if to rejoin her companions she got up from her place
on my mother's toes. The young men presented their backs
to us; they were leaning on the rail of the cliff. Our incident
had produced a certain awkwardness, and while I was thinking
of what next to say she exclaimed irrelevantly: "Don't you
know? He'll be Lord Considine.'' At that moment the youth
marked for this high destiny turned round, and she went on,
to my mother: "I'll introduce him to you—he's awfully nice.''
She beckoned and invited him with her parasol; the movement
struck me as taking everything for granted. I had heard of
Lord Considine and if I had not been able to place Lord
Iffield it was because I didn't know the name of his eldest
son. The young man took no notice of Miss Saunt's appeal;
he only stared a moment and then on her repeating it quietly
turned his back. She was an odd creature: she didn't blush at
this; she only said to my mother apologetically, but with the
frankest, sweetest amusement: "You don't mind, do you? He's
a monster of shyness!'' It was as if she were sorry for every
one—for Lord Iffield, the victim of a complaint so painful,
and for my mother, the object of a trifling incivility. "I'm sure
I don't want him!'' said my mother; but Flora added some
remark about the rebuke she would give him for slighting us.
She would clearly never explain anything by any failure of her
own power. There rolled over me while she took leave of us
and floated back to her friends a wave of tenderness superstitious and silly. I seemed somehow to see her go forth to her

fate; and yet what should fill out this orb of a high destiny if not such beauty and such joy? I had a dim idea that Lord Considine was a great proprietor, and though there mingled with it a faint impression that I shouldn't like his son the result of the two images was a whimsical prayer that the girl mightn't miss her possible fortune.

IV

One day in the course of the following June there was ushered into my studio a gentleman whom I had not yet seen but with whom I had been very briefly in correspondence. A letter from him had expressed to me some days before his regret on learning that my "splendid portrait" of Miss Flora Louisa Saunt, whose full name figured by her own wish in the catalogue of the exhibition of the Academy, had found a purchaser before the close of the private view. He took the liberty of inquiring whether I might have at his service some other memorial of the same lovely head, some preliminary sketch, some study for the picture. I had replied that I had indeed painted Miss Saunt more than once and that if he were interested in my work I should be happy to show him what I had done. Mr. Geoffrey Dawling, the person thus introduced to me, stumbled into my room with awkward movements and equivocal sounds—a long, lean, confused, confusing young man, with a bad complexion and large, protrusive teeth. He bore in its most indelible pressure the postmark, as it were, of Oxford, and as soon as he opened his mouth I perceived, in addition to a remarkable revelation of gums, that the text of the queer communication matched the registered envelope. He was full of refinements and angles, of dreary and distinguished knowledge. Of his unconscious drollery his dress freely partook; it seemed, from the gold ring into which his red necktie was passed to the square toe-caps of his boots, to conform with a high sense of modernness to the fashion before the last. There were moments when his overdone urbanity, all suggestive stammers and interrogative quavers, made him scarcely intelligible; but I felt him to be a gentleman and I liked the honesty of his errand and the expression of his good green eyes.

As a worshipper at the shrine of beauty however he needed

explaining, especially when I found he had no acquaintance with my brilliant model; had on the mere evidence of my picture taken, as he said, a tremendous fancy to her face. I ought doubtless to have been humiliated by the simplicity of his judgment of it, a judgment for which the rendering was lost in the subject, quite leaving out the element of art. He was like the innocent reader for whom the story is "really true" and the author a negligible quantity. He had come to me only because he wanted to purchase, and I remember being so amused at his attitude, which I had never seen equally marked in a person of education, that I asked him why, for the sort of enjoyment he desired, it wouldn't be more to the point to deal directly with the lady. He stared and blushed at this: it was plain the idea frightened him. He was an extraordinary case—personally so modest that I could see it had never occurred to him. He had fallen in love with a painted sign and seemed content just to dream of what it stood for. He was the young prince in the legend or the comedy who loses his heart to the miniature of the outland princess. Until I knew him better this puzzled me much—the link was so missing between his sensibility and his type. He was of course bewildered by my sketches, which implied in the beholder some sense of intention and quality; but for one of them, a comparative failure, he ended by conceiving a preference so arbitrary and so lively that, taking no second look at the others, he expressed the wish to possess it and fell into the extremity of confusion over the question of the price. I simplified that problem, and he went off without having asked me a direct question about Miss Saunt, yet with his acquisition under his arm. His delicacy was such that he evidently considered his rights to be limited; he had acquired none at all in regard to the original of the picture. There were others—for I was curious about him—that I wanted him to feel I conceded: I should have been glad of his carrying away a sense of ground acquired for coming back. To ensure this I had probably only to invite him, and I perfectly recall the impulse that made me forbear. It operated suddenly from within while he hung about the door and in spite of the diffident appeal that blinked in his gentle grin. If he was smitten with Flora's ghost what mightn't be the direct force of the luminary that could cast such a shadow? This source of radiance, flooding my poor place, might very well happen to be present the next time he should turn up. The idea was sharp within me that there were complications it was no mission of mine to bring about. If they were to occur they might occur by a logic of their own.

Let me say at once that they did occur and that I perhaps after all had something to do with it. If Mr. Dawling had departed without a fresh appointment he was to reappear six months later under protection no less adequate than that of our young lady herself. I had seen her repeatedly for months: she had grown to regard my studio as the tabernacle of her face. This prodigy was frankly there the sole object of interest; in other places there were occasionally other objects. The freedom of her manners continued to be stupefying; there was nothing so extraordinary save the absence in connection with it of any catastrophe. She was kept innocent by her egotism, but she was helped also, though she had now put off her mourning, by the attitude of the lone orphan who had to be a law unto herself. It was as a lone orphan that she came and went, as a lone orphan that she was the centre of a crush. The neglect of the Hammond Synges gave relief to this character, and she paid them handsomely to be, as every one said, shocking. Lord Iffield had gone to India to shoot tigers, but he returned in time for the private view: it was he who had snapped up, as Flora called it, the gem of the exhibition. My hope for the girl's future had slipped ignominiously off his back, but after his purchase of the portrait I tried to cultivate a new faith. The girl's own faith was wonderful. It couldn't however be contagious: too great was the limit of her sense of what painters call values. Her colours were laid on like blankets on a cold night. How indeed could a person speak the truth who was always posturing and bragging? She was after all vulgar enough, and by the time I had mastered her profile and could almost with my eyes shut do it in a single line I was decidedly tired of her perfection. There grew to be something silly in its eternal smoothness. One moved with her moreover among phenomena mismated and unrelated; nothing in her talk ever matched with anything out of it. Lord Iffield was dying of love for her, but his family was leading him a life. His mother, horrid woman, had told some one that she would rather he should be swallowed by a tiger than marry a girl not absolutely one of themselves. He had given his young friend unmistakable signs, but he was lying low, gaining time: it was in his father's power to be, both in personal and in pecuniary ways, excessively nasty to him. His father wouldn't last for ever—quite the contrary; and he knew how thoroughly, in spite of her youth, her beauty and the swarm of her admirers, some of them positively threatening in their passion, he could trust her to hold out. There were richer, cleverer men, there were greater personages too, but she liked her "little viscount" just as he was, and liked to think that, bullied and persecuted, he had her there so luxuriously to rest upon. She came back to me with tale upon tale, and it all might be or mightn't. I never met my pretty model in the world—she moved, it appeared, in exalted circles—and could only admire, in her wealth of illustration, the grandeur of her life and the freedom of her hand.

I had on the first opportunity spoken to her of Geoffrey Dawling, and she had listened to my story so far as she had the art of such patience, asking me indeed more questions about him than I could answer; then she had capped my anecdote with others much more striking, revelations of effects produced in the most extraordinary quarters: on people who had followed her into railway-carriages; guards and porters even who had literally stuck there; others who had spoken to her in shops and hung about her house-door; cabmen, upon her honour, in London, who, to gaze their fill at her, had found excuses to thrust their petrifaction through the very glasses of four-wheelers. She lost herself in these reminiscences, the moral of which was that poor Mr. Dawling was only one of a million. When therefore the next autumn she flourished into my studio with her odd companion at her heels her first care was to make clear to me that if he was now in servitude it wasn't because she had run after him. Dawling hilariously explained that when one wished very much to get anything one usually ended by doing so—a proposition which led me wholly to dissent and our young lady to asseverate that she hadn't in the least wished to get Mr. Dawling. She mightn't have wished to get him, but she wished to show him, and I seemed to read that if she could treat him as a trophy her affairs were rather at the ebb. True there always hung from her belt a promiscuous fringe of scalps. Much at any rate would have come and gone since our separation in July. She had spent four months abroad, where, on Swiss and Italian lakes, in German cities, in Paris, many accidents might have happened.

V

I had been again with my mother, but except Mrs. Meldrum and the gleam of France had not found at Folkestone my old resources and pastimes. Mrs. Meldrum, much edified by my report of the performances, as she called them, in my studio, had told me that to her knowledge Flora would soon be on the straw: she had cut from her capital such fine fat slices that there was almost nothing more left to swallow. Perched on her breezy cliff the good lady dazzled me as usual by her universal light: she knew so much more about everything and everybody than I could ever squeeze out of my colour tubes. She knew that Flora was acting on system and absolutely declined to be interfered with: her precious reasoning was that her money would last as long as she should need it, that a magnificent marriage would crown her charms before she should be really pinched. She had a sum put by for a liberal outfit; meanwhile the proper use of the rest was to decorate her for the approaches to the altar, keep her afloat in the society in which she would most naturally meet her match. Lord Iffield had been seen with her at Lucerne, at Cadenabbia, but it was Mrs. Meldrum's conviction that nothing was to be expected of him but the most futile flirtation. The girl had a certain hold of him, but with a great deal of swagger he hadn't the spirit of a sheep: he was in fear of his father and would never commit himself in Lord Considine's lifetime. The most Flora might achieve would be that he wouldn't marry some one else. Geoffrey Dawling, to Mrs. Meldrum's knowledge (I had told her of the young man's visit) had attached himself on the way back from Italy to the Hammond Synge group. My informant was in a position to be definite about this dangler; she knew about his people: she had heard of him before.

Hadn't he been, at Oxford, a friend of one of her nephews? Hadn't he spent the Christmas holidays precisely three years before at her brother-in-law's in Yorkshire, taking that occasion to get himself refused with derision by wilful Betty, the second daughter of the house? Her sister, who liked the floundering youth, had written to her to complain of Betty, and that the young man should now turn up as an appendage of Flora's was one of those oft-cited proofs that the world is small and that there are not enough people to go round. His father had been something or other in the Treasury; his grandfather, on the mother's side, had been something or other in the Church. He had come into the paternal estate, two or three thousand a year in Hampshire; but he had let the place advantageously and was generous to four ugly sisters who lived at Bournemouth and adored him. The family was hideous all round, but the salt of the earth. He was supposed to be unspeakably clever; he was fond of London, fond of books, of intellectual society and of the idea of a political career. That such a man should be at the same time fond of Flora Saunt attested, as the phrase in the first volume of Gibbon has it, the variety of his inclinations. I was soon to learn that he was fonder of her than of all the other things together. Betty, one of five and with views above her station, was at any rate felt at home to have dished herself by her perversity. Of course no one had looked at her since and no one would ever look at her again. It would be eminently desirable that Flora should learn the lesson of Betty's fate.

I was not struck, I confess, with all this in my mind, by any symptoms on our young lady's part of that sort of meditation. The only moral she saw in anything was that of her incomparable countenance, which Mr. Dawling, smitten even like the railway porters and the cabmen by the doom-dealing gods, had followed from London to Venice and from Venice back to London again. I afterwards learned that her version of this episode was profusely inexact: his personal acquaintance with her had been determined by an accident remarkable enough, I admit, in connection with what had gone before—a coincidence at all events superficially striking. At Munich, returning from a tour in the Tyrol with two of his sisters, he had found himself at the *table d'hôte* of his inn opposite to the full presentment of that face of which the mere clumsy copy had made him dream and desire. He had been tossed by it to a height so vertiginous as to involve a retreat from the table; but the next day he had dropped with a resounding thud at the very feet of his apparition. On the following, with an equal incoherence, a sacrifice even of his bewildered sisters, whom he left behind, he made an heroic effort to escape by flight from a fate of which he already felt the cold breath. That fate, in London, very little later, drove him straight before it—drove him one Sunday afternoon, in the rain, to the door of the Hammond Synges. He marched in other words close up to the cannon that was to blow him to pieces. But three weeks, when he reappeared to me, had elapsed since then, yet (to vary my metaphor) the burden he was to carry for the rest of his days was firmly lashed to his back. I don't mean by this that Flora had been persuaded to contract her scope; I mean that he had been treated to the unconditional snub which, as the event was to show, couldn't have been bettered as a means of securing him. She hadn't calculated, but she had said "Never!" and that word had made a bed big enough for his long-legged patience. He became from this moment to my mind the interesting figure in the piece.

Now that he had acted without my aid I was free to show him this, and having on his own side something to show me he repeatedly knocked at my door. What he brought with him on these occasions was a simplicity so huge that, as I turn my ear to the past, I seem even now to hear it bumping up and down my stairs. That was really what I saw of him in the light of his behaviour. He had fallen in love as he might have broken his leg, and the fracture was of a sort that would make him permanently lame. It was the whole man who limped and lurched, with nothing of him left in the same position as before. The tremendous cleverness, the literary society, the political ambition, the Bournemouth sisters all seemed to flop with his every movement a little nearer to the floor. I hadn't had an Oxford training and I had never encountered the great man at whose feet poor Dawling had most submissively sat and who had addressed him his most destructive sniffs; but I remember asking myself if such privileges had been an indispensable preparation to the career on which my friend

appeared now to have embarked. I remember too making up
my mind about the cleverness, which had its uses and I suppose in impenetrable shades even its critics, but from which
the friction of mere personal intercourse was not the sort of
process to extract a revealing spark. He accepted without a
question both his fever and his chill, and the only thing he
showed any subtlety about was this convenience of my friendship. He doubtless told me his simple story, but the matter
comes back to me in a kind of sense of *my* being rather the
mouthpiece, of my having had to thresh it out for him. He
took it from me without a groan, and I gave it to him, as we
used to say, pretty hot; he took it again and again, spending
his odd half-hours with me as if for the very purpose of learning how idiotically he was in love. He told me I made him
see things: to begin with, hadn't I first made him see Flora
Saunt? I wanted him to give her up and luminously informed
him why; on which he never protested nor contradicted, never
was even so alembicated as to declare just for the sake of the
drama that he wouldn't. He simply and undramatically didn't,
and when at the end of three months I asked him what was
the use of talking with such a fellow his nearest approach to
a justification was to say that what made him want to help her
was just the deficiencies I dwelt on. I could only reply without
pointing the moral: "Oh, if you're as sorry for her as that!"
I too was nearly as sorry for her as that, but it only led me to
be sorrier still for other victims of this compassion. With
Dawling as with me the compassion was at first in excess of
any visible motive; so that when eventually the motive was
supplied each could to a certain extent compliment the other
on the fineness of his foresight.

After he had begun to haunt my studio Miss Saunt quite
gave it up, and I finally learned that she accused me of con-
spiring with him to put pressure on her to marry him. She
didn't know I would take it that way; else she wouldn't have
brought him to see me. It was in her view a part of the conspiracy; that to show him a kindness I asked him at last to sit
to me. I dare say moreover she was disgusted to hear that I
had ended by attempting almost as many sketches of his
beauty as I had attempted of hers. What was the value of
tributes to beauty by a hand that luxuriated in ugliness? My

relation to poor Dawling's want of modelling was simple
enough. I was really digging in that sandy desert for the
buried treasure of his soul.

VI

It befell at this period, just before Christmas, that on my having gone under pressure of the season into a great shop to
buy a toy or two, my eye, fleeing from superfluity, lighted at
a distance on the bright concretion of Flora Saunt, an exhibit-
ability that held its own even against the most plausible pink-
ness of the most developed dolls. A huge quarter of the place,
the biggest bazaar "on earth," was peopled with these and
other effigies and fantasies, as well as with purchasers and ven-
dors, haggard alike in the blaze of the gas with hesitations. I
was just about to appeal to Flora to avert that stage of my
errand when I saw that she was accompanied by a gentleman
whose identity, though more than a year had elapsed, came
back to me from the Folkestone cliff. It had been associated
in that scene with showy knickerbockers; at present it overflowed more splendidly into a fur-trimmed overcoat. Lord Iffield's presence made me waver an instant before crossing over;
and during that instant Flora, blank and undistinguishing, as
if she too were after all weary of alternatives, looked straight
across at me. I was on the point of raising my hat to her when
I observed that her face gave no sign. I was exactly in the line
of her vision, but she either didn't see me or didn't recognise
me, or else had a reason to pretend she didn't. Was her reason
that I had displeased her and that she wished to punish me?
I had always thought it one of her merits that she wasn't
vindictive. She at any rate simply looked away; and at this
moment one of the shop-girls, who had apparently gone off
in search of it, bustled up to her with a small mechanical toy.
It so happened that I followed closely what then took place,
afterwards recognising that I had been led to do so, led even
through the crowd to press nearer for the purpose, by an impression of which in the act I was not fully conscious.

Flora, with the toy in her hand, looked round at her companion; then seeing his attention had been solicited in another
quarter she moved away with the shop-girl, who had evidently

offered to conduct her into the presence of more objects of the same sort. When she reached the indicated spot I was in a position still to observe her. She had asked some question about the working of the toy, and the girl, taking it herself, began to explain the little secret. Flora bent her head over it, but she clearly didn't understand. I saw her, in a manner that quickened my curiosity, give a glance back at the place from which she had come. Lord Iffield was talking with another young person: she satisfied herself of this by the aid of a question addressed to her own attendant. She then drew closer to the table near which she stood and, turning her back to me, bent her head lower over the collection of toys and more particularly over the small object the girl had attempted to explain. She took it back and, after a moment, with her face well averted, made an odd motion of her arms and a significant little duck of her head. These slight signs, singular as it may appear, produced in my bosom an agitation so great that I failed to notice Lord Iffield's whereabouts. He had rejoined her; he was close upon her before I knew it or before she knew it herself. I felt at that instant the strangest of all impulses: if it could have operated more rapidly it would have caused me to dash between them in some such manner as to give Flora a warning. In fact as it was I think I could have done this in time had I not been checked by a curiosity stronger still than my impulse. There were three seconds during which I saw the young man and yet let him come on. Didn't I make the quick calculation that if he didn't catch what Flora was doing I too might perhaps not catch it? She at any rate herself took the alarm. On perceiving her companion's nearness she made, still averted, another duck of her head and a shuffle of her hands so precipitate that a little tin steamboat she had been holding escaped from them and rattled down to the floor with a sharpness that I hear at this hour. Lord Iffield had already seized her arm; with a violent jerk he brought her round toward him. Then it was that there met my eyes a quite distressing sight: this exquisite creature, blushing, glaring, exposed, with a pair of big black-rimmed eye-glasses, defacing her by their position, crookedly astride of her beautiful nose. She made a grab at them with her free hand while I turned confusedly away.

VII

I don't remember how soon it was I spoke to Geoffrey Dawling; his sittings were irregular, but it was certainly the very next time he gave me one.

"Has any rumour ever reached you of Miss Saunt's having anything the matter with her eyes?" He stared with a candour that was a sufficient answer to my question, backing it up with a shocked and mystified "Never!" Then I asked him if he had observed in her any symptom, however disguised, of embarrassed sight: on which, after a moment's thought, he exclaimed "Disguised?" as if my use of that word had vaguely awakened a train. "She's not a bit myopic," he said; "she doesn't blink or contract her lids." I fully recognised this and I mentioned that she altogether denied the impeachment; owing it to him moreover to explain the ground of my inquiry, I gave him a sketch of the incident that had taken place before me at the shop. He knew all about Lord Iffield: that nobleman had figured freely in our conversation as his preferred, his injurious rival. Poor Dawling's contention was that if there had been a definite engagement between his lordship and the young lady, the sort of thing that was announced in *The Morning Post*, renunciation and retirement would be comparatively easy to him; but that having waited in vain for any such assurance he was entitled to act as if the door were not really closed or were at any rate not cruelly locked. He was naturally much struck with my anecdote and still more with my interpretation of it.

"There *is* something, there *is* something—possibly something very grave, certainly something that requires she should make use of artificial aids. She won't admit it publicly, because with her idolatry of her beauty, the feeling she is all made up of, she sees in such aids nothing but the humiliation and the disfigurement. She has used them in secret, but that is evidently not enough, for the affection she suffers from, apparently some definite ailment, has lately grown much worse. She looked straight at me in the shop, which was violently lighted, without seeing it was I. At the same distance, at Folkestone, where as you know I first met her, where I heard this mystery hinted at and where she indignantly denied the thing, she appeared easily enough to recognise people. At present she couldn't really make out anything the shop-girl showed her. She has successfully concealed from the man I saw her with that she resorts in private to a pince-nez and that she does so not only under the strictest orders from an oculist, but because literally the poor thing can't accomplish without such help half the business of life. Iffield however has suspected something, and his suspicions, whether expressed or kept to himself, have put him on the watch. I happened to have a glimpse of the movement at which he pounced on her and caught her in the act."

I had thought it all out; my idea explained many things, and Dawling turned pale as he listened to me.

"Was he rough with her?" he anxiously asked.

"How can I tell what passed between them? I fled from the place."

My companion stared at me a moment. "Do you mean to say her eyesight's going?"

"Heaven forbid! In that case how could she take life as she does?"

"How *does* she take life? That's the question!" He sat there bewilderedly brooding; the tears had come into his eyes; they reminded me of those I had seen in Flora's the day I risked my inquiry. The question he had asked was one that to my own satisfaction I was ready to answer, but I hesitated to let him hear as yet all that my reflections had suggested. I was indeed privately astonished at their ingenuity. For the present I only rejoined that it struck me she was playing a particular game; at which he went on as if he hadn't heard me, suddenly haunted with a fear, lost in the dark possibility I had opened up: "Do you mean there's a danger of anything very bad?"

"My dear fellow, you must ask her oculist."

"Who in the world *is* her oculist?"

"I haven't a conception. But we mustn't get too excited. My impression would be that she has only to observe a few ordinary rules, to exercise a little common sense."

Dawling jumped at this. "I see—to stick to the pince-nez."

"To follow to the letter her oculist's prescription, whatever it is and at whatever cost to her prettiness. It's not a thing to be trifled with."

"Upon my honour it *shan't* be trifled with!" he roundly declared; and he adjusted himself to his position again as if we had quite settled the business. After a considerable interval, while I botched away, he suddenly said: "Did they make a great difference?"

"A great difference?"

"Those things she had put on."

"Oh, the glasses—in her beauty? She looked queer of course, but it was partly because one was unaccustomed. There are women who look charming in nippers. What, at any rate, if she does look queer? She must be mad not to accept that alternative."

"She *is* mad," said Geoffrey Dawling.

"Mad to refuse you, I grant. Besides," I went on, "the pince-nez, which was a large and peculiar one, was all awry: she had half pulled it off, but it continued to stick, and she was crimson, she was angry."

"It must have been horrible!" my companion murmured.

"It *was* horrible. But it's still more horrible to defy all warnings; it's still more horrible to be landed in——" Without saying in what I disgustedly shrugged my shoulders.

After a glance at me Dawling jerked round. "Then you do believe that she may be?"

I hesitated. "The thing would be to make *her* believe it. She only needs a good scare."

"But if that fellow is shocked at the precautions she does take?"

"Oh, who knows?" I rejoined with small sincerity. "I don't suppose Iffield is absolutely a brute."

"I would take her with leather blinders, like a shying mare!" cried Geoffrey Dawling.

I had an impression that Iffield wouldn't, but I didn't communicate it, for I wanted to pacify my friend, whom I had discomposed too much for the purposes of my sitting. I recollect that I did some good work that morning, but it also comes back to me that before we separated he had practically revealed to me that my anecdote, connecting itself in his mind with a series of observations at the time unconscious and unregistered, had covered with light the subject of our colloquy. He had had a formless perception of some secret that drove

Miss Saunt to subterfuges, and the more he thought of it the more he guessed this secret to be the practice of making believe she saw when she didn't and of cleverly keeping people from finding out how little she saw. When one patched things together it was astonishing what ground they covered. Just as he was going away he asked me from what source, at Folkestone, the horrid tale had proceeded. When I had given him, as I saw no reason not to do, the name of Mrs. Meldrum he exclaimed: "Oh, I know all about her; she's a friend of some friends of mine!" At this I remembered wilful Betty and said to myself that I knew some one who would probably prove more wilful still.

VIII

A few days later I again heard Dawling on my stairs, and even before he passed my threshold I knew he had something to tell me.

"I've been down to Folkestone—it was necessary I should see her!" I forget whether he had come straight from the station; he was at any rate out of breath with his news, which it took me however a minute to interpret.

"You mean that you've been with Mrs. Meldrum?"

"Yes; to ask her what she knows and how she comes to know it. It worked upon me awfully—I mean what you told me." He made a visible effort to seem quieter than he was, and it showed me sufficiently that he had not been reassured. I laid, to comfort him and smiling at a venture, a friendly hand on his arm, and he dropped into my eyes, fixing them an instant, a strange, distended look which might have expressed the cold clearness of all that was to come. "I *know*—now!" he said with an emphasis he rarely used.

"What then did Mrs. Meldrum tell you?"

"Only one thing that signified, for she has no real knowledge. But that one thing was everything."

"What is it then?"

"Why, that she can't bear the sight of her." His pronouns required some arranging, but after I had successfully dealt with them I replied that I knew perfectly Miss Saunt had a trick of turning her back on the good lady of Folkestone. But what did that prove? "Have you never guessed? I guessed as soon as she spoke!" Dawling towered over me in dismal triumph. It was the first time in our acquaintance that, intellectually speaking, this had occurred; but even so remarkable an incident still left me sufficiently at sea to cause him to continue: "Why, the effect of those spectacles!"

I seemed to catch the tail of his idea. "Mrs. Meldrum's?"

"They're so awfully ugly and they increase so the dear woman's ugliness." This remark began to flash a light, and when he quickly added "She sees herself, she sees her own fate!" my response was so immediate that I had almost taken the words out of his mouth. While I tried to fix this sudden image of Flora's face glazed in and cross-barred even as Mrs. Meldrum's was glazed and barred, he went on to assert that only the horror of that image, looming out at herself, could be the reason of her avoiding such a monitress. The fact he had encountered made everything hideously vivid and more vivid than anything else that just such another pair of goggles was what would have been prescribed to Flora.

"I see—I see," I presently rejoined. "What would become of Lord Iffield if she were suddenly to come out in them? What indeed would become of every one, what would become of everything?" This was an inquiry that Dawling was evidently unprepared to meet, and I completed it by saying at last: "My dear fellow, for that matter, what would become of *you*?"

Once more he turned on me his good green eyes. "Oh, I shouldn't mind!"

The tone of his words somehow made his ugly face beautiful, and I felt that there dated from this moment in my heart a confirmed affection for him. None the less, at the same time, perversely and rudely, I became aware of a certain drollery in our discussion of such alternatives. It made me laugh out and say to him while I laughed: "You'd take her even with those things of Mrs. Meldrum's?"

He remained mournfully grave; I could see that he was surprised at my rude mirth. But he summoned back a vision of the lady at Folkestone and conscientiously replied: "Even with those things of Mrs. Meldrum's." I begged him not to think my laughter in bad taste: it was only a practical recognition of the fact that we had built a monstrous castle in the air. Didn't he see on what flimsy ground the structure rested? The evidence was preposterously small. He believed the worst, but we were utterly ignorant.

"I shall find out the truth," he promptly replied.

"How can you? If you question her you'll simply drive her to perjure herself. Wherein after all does it concern you to know the truth? It's the girl's own affair."

"Then why did you tell me your story?"

I was a trifle embarrassed. "To warn you off," I returned smiling. He took no more notice of these words than presently to remark that Lord Iffield had no serious intentions. "Very possibly," I said. "But you mustn't speak as if Lord Iffield and you were her only alternatives."

Dawling thought a moment. "Wouldn't the people she has consulted give some information? She must have been to people. How else can she have been condemned?"

"Condemned to what? Condemned to perpetual nippers? Of course she has consulted some of the big specialists, but she has done it, you may be sure, in the most clandestine manner; and even if it were supposable that they would tell you anything—which I altogether doubt—you would have great difficulty in finding out which men they are. Therefore leave it alone; never show her what you suspect."

I even, before he quitted me, asked him to promise me this. "All right, I promise," he said gloomily enough. He was a lover who could tacitly grant the proposition that there was no limit to the deceit his loved one was ready to practise: it made so remarkably little difference. I could see that from this moment he would be filled with a passionate pity ever so little qualified by a sense of the girl's fatuity and folly. She was always accessible to him—that I knew; for if she had told him he was an idiot to dream she could dream of him, she would have resented the imputation of having failed to make it clear that she would always be glad to regard him as a friend. What were most of her friends—what were all of them—but repudiated idiots? I was perfectly aware that in her conversations and confidences I myself for instance had a niche in the gallery. As regards poor Dawling I knew how often he still called

on the Hammond Synges. It was not there but under the wing
of the Floyd-Taylors that her intimacy with Lord Iffield most
flourished. At all events when a week after the visit I have just
summarised Flora's name was one morning brought up to me
I jumped at the conclusion that Dawling had been with her
and even I fear briefly entertained the thought that he had
broken his word.

IX

She left me, after she had been introduced, in no suspense
about her present motive; she was on the contrary in a visible
fever to enlighten me; but I promptly learned that for the
alarm with which she pitiably panted our young man was not
accountable. She had but one thought in the world, and that
thought was for Lord Iffield. I had the strangest, saddest scene
with her, and if it did me no other good it at least made me
at last completely understand why insidiously, from the first,
she had struck me as a creature of tragedy. In showing me the
whole of her folly it lifted the curtain of her misery. I don't
know how much she meant to tell me when she came—I think
she had had plans of elaborate misrepresentation; at any rate
she found it at the end of ten minutes the simplest way to
break down and sob, to be wretched and true. When she had
once begun to let herself go the movement took her off her
feet: the relief of it was like the cessation of a cramp. She
shared in a word her long secret; she shifted her sharp pain.
She brought, I confess, tears to my own eyes, tears of helpless
tenderness for her helpless poverty. Her visit however was not
quite so memorable in itself as in some of its consequences,
the most immediate of which was that I went that afternoon
to see Geoffrey Dawling, who had in those days rooms in
Welbeck Street, where I presented myself at an hour late
enough to warrant the supposition that he might have come
in. He had not come in, but he was expected, and I was invited to enter and wait for him: a lady, I was informed, was
already in his sitting-room. I hesitated, a little at a loss: it had
wildly coursed through my brain that the lady was perhaps
Flora Saunt. But when I asked if she were young and remark-

ably pretty I received so significant a "No, sir!" that I risked
an advance and after a minute in this manner found myself,
to my astonishment, face to face with Mrs. Meldrum.

"Oh, you dear thing," she exclaimed, "I'm delighted to
see you: you spare me another compromising *démarche*! But
for this I should have called on you also. Know the worst at
once: if you see me here it's at least deliberate—it's planned,
plotted, shameless. I came up on purpose to see him; upon
my word, I'm in love with him. Why, if you valued my peace
of mind, did you let him, the other day at Folkestone, dawn
upon my delighted eyes? I took there in half an hour the most
extraordinary fancy to him. With a perfect sense of everything
that can be urged against him, I find him none the less the
very pearl of men. However, I haven't come up to declare my
passion—I've come to bring him news that will interest him
much more. Above all I've come to urge upon him to be
careful."

"About Flora Saunt?"

"About what he says and does: he must be as still as a
mouse! She's at last really engaged."

"But it's a tremendous secret?" I was moved to merriment.

"Precisely: she telegraphed me this noon, and spent another
shilling to tell me that not a creature in the world is yet to
know it."

"She had better have spent it to tell you that she had just
passed an hour with the creature you see before you."

"She has just passed an hour with every one in the place!"
Mrs. Meldrum cried. "They've vital reasons, she wired, for
it's not coming out for a month. Then it will be formally
announced, but meanwhile her happiness is delirious. I daresay Mr. Dawling already knows, and he may, as it's nearly
seven o'clock, have jumped off London Bridge; but an effect
of the talk I had with him the other day was to make me, on
receipt of my telegram, feel it to be my duty to warn him in
person against taking action, as it were, on the horrid certitude which I could see he carried away with him. I had added
somehow to that certitude. He told me what you had told
him you had seen in your shop."

Mrs. Meldrum, I perceived, had come to Welbeck Street on
an errand identical with my own—a circumstance indicating

her rare sagacity, inasmuch as her ground for undertaking it was a very different thing from what Flora's wonderful visit had made of mine. I remarked to her that what I had seen in the shop was sufficiently striking, but that I had seen a great deal more that morning in my studio. "In short," I said, "I've seen everything."

She was mystified. "Everything?"

"The poor creature is under the darkest of clouds. Oh, she came to triumph, but she remained to talk something approaching to sense! She put herself completely in my hands—she does me the honour to intimate that of all her friends I'm the most disinterested. After she had announced to me that Lord Iffield was bound hands and feet and that for the present I was absolutely the only person in the secret, she arrived at her real business. She had had a suspicion of me ever since the day, at Folkestone, I asked her for the truth about her eyes. The truth is what you and I both guessed. She has no end of a danger hanging over her."

"But from what cause? I, who by God's mercy have kept mine, know everything that can be known about eyes," said Mrs. Meldrum.

"She might have kept hers if she had profited by God's mercy, if she had done in time, done years ago, what was imperatively ordered her; if she hadn't in fine been cursed with the loveliness that was to make her behaviour a thing of fable. She may keep them still if she'll sacrifice—and after all so little—that purely superficial charm. She must do as you've done; she must wear, dear lady, what you wear!"

What my companion wore glittered for the moment like a melon-frame in August. "Heaven forgive her—now I understand!" She turned pale.

But I wasn't afraid of the effect on her good nature of her thus seeing, through her great goggles, why it had always been that Flora held her at such a distance. "I can't tell you," I said, "from what special affection, what state of the eye, her danger proceeds: that's the one thing she succeeded this morning in keeping from me. She knows it herself perfectly; she has had the best advice in Europe. 'It's a thing that's awful, simply awful'—that was the only account she would give me. Year before last, while she was at Boulogne, she went

for three days with Mrs. Floyd-Taylor to Paris. She there surreptitiously consulted the greatest man—even Mrs. Floyd-
Taylor doesn't know. Last autumn, in Germany, she did the
same. 'First put on certain special spectacles with a straight
bar in the middle: then we'll talk'—that's practically what they
say. What *she* says is that she'll put on anything in nature when
she's married, but that she must get married first. She has
always meant to do everything as soon as she's married. Then
and then only she'll be safe. How will any one ever look at
her if she makes herself a fright? How could she ever have got
engaged if she had made herself a fright from the first? It's no
use to insist that with her beauty she can never *be* a fright.
She said to me this morning, poor girl, the most characteristic,
the most harrowing things. 'My face is all I have—and *such* a
face! I knew from the first I could do anything with it. But I
needed it all—I need it still, every exquisite inch of it. It isn't
as if I had a figure or anything else. Oh, if God had only given
me a figure too, I don't say! Yes, with a figure, a really good
one, like Fanny Floyd-Taylor's, who's hideous, I'd have risked
plain glasses. *Que voulez-vous?* No one is perfect.' She says she
still has money left, but I don't believe a word of it. She has
been speculating on her impunity, on the idea that her danger
would hold off: she has literally been running a race with it.
Her theory has been, as you from the first so clearly saw, that
she'd get in ahead. She swears to me that though the 'bar' is
too cruel she wears when she's alone what she has been ordered to wear. But when the deuce is she alone? It's herself
of course that she has swindled worst: she has put herself off,
so insanely that even her vanity but half accounts for it, with
little inadequate concessions, little false measures and preposterous evasions and childish hopes. Her great terror is now
that Iffield, who already has suspicions, who has found out
her pince-nez but whom she has beguiled with some unblush-
ing hocus-pocus, may discover the dreadful facts; and the essence of what she wanted this morning was in that interest to
square me, to get me to deny indignantly and authoritatively
(for isn't she my 'favourite sitter?') that she has anything whatever the matter with any part of her. She sobbed, she 'went
on,' she entreated; after we got talking her extraordinary
nerve left her and she showed me what she has been

through—showed me also all her terror of the harm I could do her. 'Wait till I'm married! wait till I'm married!' She took hold of me, she almost sank on her knees. It seems to me highly immoral, one's participation in her fraud; but there's no doubt that she *must* be married: I don't know what I don't see behind it! Therefore," I wound up, "Dawling must keep his hands off."

Mrs. Meldrum had held her breath; she exhaled a long moan. "Well, that's exactly what I came here to tell him."

"Then here he is." Our unconscious host had just opened the door. Immensely startled at finding us he turned a frightened look from one to the other, as if to guess what disaster we were there to announce or avert.

Mrs. Meldrum, on the spot, was all gaiety. "I've come to return your sweet visit. Ah," she laughed, "I mean to keep up the acquaintance!"

"Do—do," he murmured mechanically and absently, continuing to look at us. Then abruptly he broke out: "He's going to marry her."

I was surprised. "You already know?"

He had had in his hand an evening newspaper; he tossed it down on the table. "It's in that."

"Published—already?" I was still more surprised.

"Oh, Flora can't keep a secret!" Mrs. Meldrum humorously declared. She went up to poor Dawling and laid a motherly hand upon him. "It's all right—it's just as it ought to be: don't think about her ever any more." Then as he met this adjuration with a dismal stare in which the thought of her was as abnormally vivid as the colour of the pupil, the excellent woman put up her funny face and tenderly kissed him on the cheek.

X

I have spoken of these reminiscences as of a row of coloured beads, and I confess that as I continue to straighten out my chaplet I am rather proud of the comparison. The beads are all there, as I said—they slip along the string in their small, smooth roundness. Geoffrey Dawling accepted like a gentleman the event his evening paper had proclaimed; in view of

which I snatched a moment to murmur him a hint to offer
Mrs. Meldrum his hand. He returned me a heavy head-shake,
and I judged that marriage would henceforth strike him very
much as the traffic of the street may strike some poor incurable at the window of an hospital. Circumstances arising at
this time promptly led to my making an absence from England, and circumstances already existing offered him a solid
basis for similar action. He had after all the usual resource of
a Briton—he could take to his boats. He started on a journey
round the globe, and I was left with nothing but my inference
as to what might have happened. Later observation however
only confirmed my belief that if at any time during the couple
of months that followed Flora Saunt's brilliant engagement he
had made up, as they say, to the good lady of Folkestone, that
good lady would not have pushed him over the cliff. Strange
as she was to behold I knew of cases in which she had been
obliged to administer that shove. I went to New York to paint
a couple of portraits; but I found, once on the spot, that I
had counted without Chicago, where I was invited to blot out
this harsh discrimination by the production of no less than
ten. I spent a year in America and should probably have spent
a second had I not been summoned back to England by
alarming news from my mother. Her strength had failed, and
as soon as I reached London I hurried down to Folkestone,
arriving just at the moment to offer a welcome to some slight
symptom of a rally. She had been much worse, but she was
now a little better; and though I found nothing but satisfaction in having come to her I saw after a few hours that my
London studio, where arrears of work had already met me,
would be my place to await whatever might next occur. Before
returning to town however I had every reason to sally forth
in search of Mrs. Meldrum, from whom, in so many months,
I had not had a line, and my view of whom, with the adjacent
objects, as I had left them, had been intercepted by a luxuriant
foreground.

Before I had gained her house I met her, as I supposed,
coming toward me across the down, greeting me from afar
with the familiar twinkle of her great vitreous badge; and as
it was late in the autumn and the esplanade was a blank I was
free to acknowledge this signal by cutting a caper on the grass.

My enthusiasm dropped indeed the next moment, for it had taken me but a few seconds to perceive that the person thus assaulted had by no means the figure of my military friend. I felt a shock much greater than any I should have thought possible as on this person's drawing near I identified her as poor little Flora Saunt. At what moment Flora had recognised me belonged to an order of mysteries over which, it quickly came home to me, one would never linger again: I could intensely reflect that once we were face to face it chiefly mattered that I should succeed in looking still more intensely unastonished. All I saw at first was the big gold bar crossing each of her lenses, over which something convex and grotesque, like the eyes of a large insect, something that now represented her whole personality, seemed, as out of the orifice of a prison, to strain forward and press. The face had shrunk away: it looked smaller, appeared even to look plain; it was at all events, so far as the effect on a spectator was concerned, wholly sacrificed to this huge apparatus of sight. There was no smile in it, and she made no motion to take my offered hand.

"I had no idea you were down here!" I exclaimed, and I wondered whether she didn't know me at all or knew me only by my voice.

"You thought I was Mrs. Meldrum," she very quietly remarked.

It was the quietness itself that made me feel the necessity of an answer almost violently gay. "Oh yes," I laughed, "you have a tremendous deal in common with Mrs. Meldrum! I've just returned to England after a long absence and I'm on my way to see her. Won't you come with me?" It struck me that her old reason for keeping clear of our friend was well disposed of now.

"I've just left her; I'm staying with her." She stood solemnly fixing me with her goggles. "Would you like to paint me *now*?" she asked. She seemed to speak, with intense gravity, from behind a mask or a cage.

There was nothing to do but to treat the question with the same exuberance. "It would be a fascinating little artistic problem!" That something was wrong it was not difficult to perceive; but a good deal more than met the eye might be presumed to be wrong if Flora was under Mrs. Meldrum's roof. I had not for a year had much time to think of her, but my imagination had had sufficient warrant for lodging her in more gilded halls. One of the last things I had heard before leaving England was that in commemoration of the new relationship she had gone to stay with Lady Considine. This had made me take everything else for granted, and the noisy American world had deafened my ears to possible contradictions. Her spectacles were at present a direct contradiction; they seemed a negation not only of new relationships but of every old one as well. I remember nevertheless that when after a moment she walked beside me on the grass I found myself nervously hoping she wouldn't as yet at any rate tell me anything very dreadful; so that to stave off this danger I harried her with questions about Mrs. Meldrum and, without waiting for replies, became profuse on the subject of my own doings. My companion was completely silent, and I felt both as if she were watching my nervousness with a sort of sinister irony and as if I were talking to some different, strange person. Flora plain and obscure and soundless was no Flora at all. At Mrs. Meldrum's door she turned off with the observation that as there was certainly a great deal I should have to say to our friend she had better not go in with me. I looked at her again—I had been keeping my eyes away from her—but only to meet her magnified stare. I greatly desired in truth to see Mrs. Meldrum alone, but there was something so pitiful in the girl's predicament that I hesitated to fall in with this idea of dropping her. Yet one couldn't express a compassion without seeming to take too much wretchedness for granted. I reflected that I must really figure to her as a fool, which was an entertainment I had never expected to give her. It rolled over me there for the first time—it has come back to me since—that there is, strangely, in very deep misfortune a dignity finer even than in the most inveterate habit of being all right. I couldn't have to her the manner of treating it as a mere detail that I was face to face with a part of what, at our last meeting, we had had such a scene about; but while I was trying to think of some manner that I *could* have she said quite colourlessly, yet somehow as if she might never see me again: "Good-bye. I'm going to take my walk."

"All alone?"

She looked round the great bleak cliff-top. "With whom should I go? Besides, I like to be alone—for the present."

This gave me the glimmer of a vision that she regarded her disfigurement as temporary, and the confidence came to me that she would never, for her happiness, cease to be a creature of illusions. It enabled me to exclaim, smiling brightly and feeling indeed idiotic: "Oh, I shall see you again! But I hope you'll have a very pleasant walk."

"All my walks are very pleasant, thank you—they do me such a lot of good." She was as quiet as a mouse, and her words seemed to me stupendous in their wisdom. "I take several a day," she continued. She might have been an ancient woman responding with humility at the church door to the patronage of the parson. "The more I take the better I feel. I'm ordered by the doctors to keep all the while in the air and go in for plenty of exercise. It keeps up my general health, you know, and if that goes on improving as it has lately done everything will soon be all right. All that was the matter with me before—and always; it was too reckless!—was that I neglected my general health. It acts directly on the state of the particular organ. So I'm going three miles."

I grinned at her from the doorstep while Mrs. Meldrum's maid stood there to admit me. "Oh, I'm so glad," I said, looking at her as she paced away with the pretty flutter she had kept and remembering the day when, while she rejoined Lord Iffield, I had indulged in the same observation. Her air of assurance was on this occasion not less than it had been on that; but I recalled that she had then struck me as marching off to her doom. Was she really now marching away from it?

XI

As soon as I saw Mrs. Meldrum I broke out to her. "Is there anything in it? *Is* her general health——?"

Mrs. Meldrum interrupted me with her great amused blare. "You've already seen her and she has told you her wondrous tale? What's 'in it' is what has been in everything she has ever done—the most comical, tragical belief in herself. She thinks she's doing a 'cure.' "

"And what does her husband think?"

"Her husband? What husband?"

"Hasn't she then married Lord Iffield?"

"Vous-en-êtes là?" cried my hostess. "He behaved like a regular beast."

"How should I know? You never wrote to me."

Mrs. Meldrum hesitated, covering me with what poor Flora called the particular organ. "No, I didn't write to you; and I abstained on purpose. If I didn't I thought you mightn't, over there, hear what had happened. If you should hear I was afraid you would stir up Mr. Dawling."

"Stir him up?"

"Urge him to fly to the rescue; write out to him that there was another chance for him."

"I wouldn't have done it," I said.

"Well," Mrs. Meldrum replied, "it was not my business to give you an opportunity."

"In short you were afraid of it."

Again she hesitated and though it may have been only my fancy I thought she considerably reddened. At all events she laughed out. Then "I was afraid of it!" she very honestly answered.

"But doesn't he know? Has he given no sign?"

"Every sign in life—he came straight back to her. He did everything to get her to listen to him; but she hasn't the smallest idea of it."

"Has he seen her as she is now?" I presently and just a trifle awkwardly inquired.

"Indeed he has, and borne it like a hero. He told me all about it."

"How much you've all been through!" I ventured to ejaculate. "Then what has become of him?"

"He's at home in Hampshire. He has got back his old place and I believe by this time his old sisters. It's not half a bad little place."

"Yet its attractions say nothing to Flora?"

"Oh, Flora's by no means on her back!" my interlocutress laughed.

"She's not on her back because she's on yours. Have you got her for the rest of your life?"

Once more my hostess genially glared at me. "Did she tell you how much the Hammond Synges have kindly left her to live on? Not quite eighty pounds a year."

"That's a good deal, but it won't pay the oculist. What was it that at last induced her to submit to him?"

"Her general collapse after that brute of an Iffield's rupture. She cried her eyes out—she passed through a horror of black darkness. Then came a gleam of light, and the light appears to have broadened. She went into goggles as repentant Magdalens go into the Catholic Church."

"Yet you don't think she'll be saved?"

"*She* thinks she will—that's all I can tell you. There's no doubt that when once she brought herself to accept her real remedy, as she calls it, she began to enjoy a relief that she had never known. That feeling, very new and in spite of what she pays for it most refreshing, has given her something to hold on by, begotten in her foolish little mind a belief that, as she says, she's on the mend and that in the course of time, if she leads a tremendously healthy life, she'll be able to take off her muzzle and become as dangerous again as ever. It keeps her going."

"And what keeps *you*? You're good until the parties begin again."

"Oh, she doesn't object to me now!" smiled Mrs. Meldrum. "I'm going to take her abroad; we shall be a pretty pair." I was struck with this energy and after a moment I inquired the reason of it. "It's to divert her mind," my friend replied, reddening again, I thought, a little. "We shall go next week: I've only waited, to start, to see how your mother would be." I expressed to her hereupon my sense of her extraordinary merit and also that of the inconceivability of Flora's fancying herself still in a situation not to jump at the chance of marrying a man like Dawling. "She says he's too ugly; she says he's too dreary; she says in fact he's 'nobody,' " Mrs. Meldrum pursued. "She says above all that he's not 'her own sort.' She doesn't deny that he's good, but she insists on the fact that he's grotesque. He's quite the last person she would ever dream of." I was almost disposed on hearing this to protest that if the girl had so little proper feeling her noble suitor had perhaps served her right; but after a while my curiosity as to just how her noble suitor *had* served her got the better of that emotion, and I asked a question or two which led my companion again to apply to him the invidious epithet I have already quoted. What had happened was simply that Flora had at the eleventh hour broken down in the attempt to put him off with an uncandid account of her infirmity and that his lordship's interest in her had not been proof against the discovery of the way she had practised on him. Her dissimulation, he was obliged to perceive, had been infernally deep. The future in short assumed a new complexion for him when looked at through the grim glasses of a bride who, as he had said to some one, couldn't really, when you came to find out, see her hand before her face. He had conducted himself like any other jockeyed customer—he had returned the animal as unsound. He had backed out in his own way, giving the business, by some sharp shuffle, such a turn as to make the rupture ostensibly Flora's, but he had none the less remorselessly and basely backed out. He had cared for her lovely face, cared for it in the amused and haunted way it had been her poor little delusive gift to make men care; and her lovely face, damn it, with the monstrous gear she had begun to rig upon it, was just what had let him in. He had in the judgment of his family done everything that could be expected of him; he had made—Mrs. Meldrum had herself seen the letter—a "handsome" offer of pecuniary compensation. Oh, if Flora, with her incredible buoyancy, was in a manner on her feet again now, it was not that she had not for weeks and weeks been prone in the dust. Strange were the humiliations, the prostrations it was given to some natures to survive. That Flora had survived was perhaps after all a sort of sign that she was reserved for some final mercy. "But she has been in the abysses at any rate," said Mrs. Meldrum, "and I really don't think I can tell you what pulled her through."

"I think I can tell *you*," I said. "What in the world but Mrs. Meldrum?"

At the end of an hour Flora had not come in, and I was obliged to announce that I should have but time to reach the station, where, in charge of my mother's servant, I was to find my luggage. Mrs. Meldrum put before me the question of waiting till a later train, so as not to lose our young lady; but

I confess I gave this alternative a consideration less profound than I pretended. Somehow I didn't care if I did lose our young lady. Now that I knew the worst that had befallen her it struck me still less as possible to meet her on the ground of condolence; and with the melancholy aspect she wore to me what other ground was left? I lost her, but I caught my train. In truth she was so changed that one hated to see it; and now that she was in charitable hands one didn't feel compelled to make great efforts. I had studied her face for a particular beauty; I had lived with that beauty and reproduced it; but I knew what belonged to my trade well enough to be sure it was gone for ever.

XII

I was soon called back to Folkestone; but Mrs. Meldrum and her young friend had already left England, finding to that end every convenience on the spot and not having had to come up to town. My thoughts however were so painfully engaged there that I should in any case have had little attention for them: the event occurred that was to bring my series of visits to a close. When this high tide had ebbed I returned to America and to my interrupted work, which had opened out on such a scale that, with a deep plunge into a great chance, I was three good years in rising again to the surface. There are nymphs and naiads moreover in the American depths: they may have had something to do with the duration of my dive. I mention them to account for a grave misdemeanor—the fact that after the first year I rudely neglected Mrs. Meldrum. She had written to me from Florence after my mother's death and had mentioned in a postscript that in our young lady's calculations the lowest numbers were now Italian counts. This was a good omen, and if in subsequent letters there was no news of a sequel I was content to accept small things and to believe that grave tidings, should there be any, would come to me in due course. The gravity of what might happen to a featherweight became indeed with time and distance less appreciable, and I was not without an impression that Mrs. Meldrum, whose sense of proportion was not the least of her merits, had no idea of boring the world with the ups and downs of her pensioner. The poor girl grew dusky and dim, a small fitful memory, a regret tempered by the comfortable consciousness of how kind Mrs. Meldrum would always be to her. I was professionally more preoccupied than I had ever been, and I had swarms of pretty faces in my eyes and a chorus of high voices in my ears. Geoffrey Dawling had on his return to England written me two or three letters: his last information had been that he was going into the figures of rural illiteracy. I was delighted to receive it and had no doubt that if he should go into figures they would, as they are said to be able to prove anything, prove at least that my advice was sound and that he had wasted time enough. This quickened on my part another hope, a hope suggested by some round-about rumour—I forget how it reached me—that he was engaged to a girl down in Hampshire. He turned out not to be, but I felt sure that if only he went into figures deep enough he would become, among the girls down in Hampshire or elsewhere, one of those numerous prizes of battle whose defences are practically not on the scale of their provocations. I nursed in short the thought that it was probably open to him to become one of the types as to which, as the years go on, frivolous and superficial spectators lose themselves in the wonder that they ever succeeded in winning even the least winsome mates. He never alluded to Flora Saunt; and there was in his silence about her, quite as in Mrs. Meldrum's, an element of instinctive tact, a brief implication that if you didn't happen to have been in love with her she was not an inevitable topic.

Within a week after my return to London I went to the opera, of which I had always been much of a devotee. I arrived too late for the first act of "Lohengrin," but the second was just beginning, and I gave myself up to it with no more than a glance at the house. When it was over I treated myself, with my glass, from my place in the stalls, to a general survey of the boxes, making doubtless on their contents the reflections, pointed by comparison, that are most familiar to the wanderer restored to London. There was a certain proportion of pretty women, but I suddenly became aware that one of these was far prettier than the others. This lady, alone in one of the smaller receptacles of the grand tier and already the aim of

fifty tentative glasses, which she sustained with admirable serenity—this single exquisite figure, placed in the quarter furthest removed from my stall, was a person, I immediately felt,
to cause one's curiosity to linger. Dressed in white, with diamonds in her hair and pearls on her neck, she had a pale
radiance of beauty which even at that distance made her a
distinguished presence and, with the air that easily attaches to
lonely loveliness in public places, an agreeable mystery. A mystery however she remained to me only for a minute after I
had levelled my glass at her: I feel to this moment the startled
thrill, the shock almost of joy with which I suddenly encountered in her vague brightness a rich revival of Flora Saunt. I
say a revival because, to put it crudely, I had on that last occasion left poor Flora for dead. At present perfectly alive again,
she was altered only, as it were, by resurrection. A little older,
a little quieter, a little finer and a good deal fairer, she was
simply transfigured by recovery. Sustained by the reflection
that even recovery wouldn't enable her to distinguish me in
the crowd, I was free to look at her well. Then it was it came
home to me that my vision of her in her great goggles had
been cruelly final. As her beauty was all there was of her, that
machinery had extinguished her, and so far as I had thought
of her in the interval I had thought of her as buried in the
tomb her stern specialist had built. With the sense that she
had escaped from it came a lively wish to return to her; and
if I didn't straightway leave my place and rush round the theatre and up to her box it was because I was fixed to the spot
some moments longer by the simple inability to cease looking
at her.

She had been from the first of my seeing her practically
motionless, leaning back in her chair with a kind of thoughtful
grace and with her eyes vaguely directed, as it seemed to me,
to one of the boxes on my side of the house and consequently
over my head and out of my sight. The only movement she
made for some time was to finger with an ungloved hand and
as if with the habit of fondness the row of pearls on her neck,
which my glass showed me to be large and splendid. Her diamonds and pearls, in her solitude, mystified me, making me,
as she had had no such brave jewels in the days of the Hammond Synges, wonder what undreamt-of improvement had

taken place in her fortunes. The ghost of a question hovered there a moment: could anything so prodigious have happened as that on her tested and proved amendment Lord Iffield had taken her back? This could not have occurred without my hearing of it; and moreover if she had become a person of such fashion where was the little court one would naturally see at her elbow? Her isolation was puzzling, though it could easily suggest that she was but momentarily alone. If she had come with Mrs. Meldrum that lady would have taken advantage of the interval to pay a visit to some other box—doubtless the box at which Flora had just been looking. Mrs. Meldrum didn't account for the jewels, but the refreshment of Flora's beauty accounted for anything. She presently moved her eyes over the house, and I felt them brush me again like the wings of a dove. I don't know what quick pleasure flickered into the hope that she would at last see me. She did see me: she suddenly bent forward to take up the little double-barrelled ivory glass that rested on the edge of the box and, to all appearance, fix me with it. I smiled from my place straight up at the searching lenses, and after an instant she dropped them and smiled as straight back at me. Oh, her smile: it was her old smile, her young smile, her peculiar smile made perfect! I instantly left my stall and hurried off for a nearer view of it; quite flushed, I remember, as I went, with the annoyance of having happened to think of the idiotic way I had tried to paint her. Poor Iffield with his sample of that error, and still poorer Dawling in particular with *his*! I hadn't touched her, I was professionally humiliated, and as the attendant in the lobby opened her box for me I felt that the very first thing I should have to say to her would be that she must absolutely sit to me again.

XIII

She gave me the smile once more as over her shoulder, from her chair, she turned her face to me. "Here you are again!" she exclaimed with her disgloved hand put up a little backward for me to take. I dropped into a chair just behind her and, having taken it and noted that one of the curtains of the box would make the demonstration sufficiently private, bent my lips over it and impressed them on its finger-tips. It was given me however, to my astonishment, to feel next that all the privacy in the world couldn't have sufficed to mitigate the start with which she greeted this free application of my moustache: the blood had jumped to her face, she quickly recovered her hand and jerked at me, twisting herself round, a vacant, challenging stare. During the next few instants several extraordinary things happened, the first of which was that now I was close to them the eyes of loveliness I had come up to look into didn't show at all the conscious light I had just been pleased to see them flash across the house: they showed on the contrary, to my confusion, a strange, sweet blankness, an expression I failed to give a meaning to until, without delay, I felt on my arm, directed to it as if instantly to efface the effect of her start, the grasp of the hand she had impulsively snatched from me. It was the irrepressible question in this grasp that stopped on my lips all sound of salutation. She had mistaken my entrance for that of another person, a pair of lips without a moustache. She was feeling me to see who I was! With the perception of this and of her not seeing me I sat gaping at her and at the wild word that didn't come, the right word to express or to disguise my stupefaction. What *was* the right word to commemorate one's sudden discovery, at the very moment too at which one had been most encouraged to count on better things, that one's dear old friend had gone blind? Before the answer to this question dropped upon me—and the moving moments, though few, seemed many—I heard, with the sound of voices, the click of the attendant's key on the other side of the door. Poor Flora heard also, and with the hearing, still with her hand on my arm, she brightened again as I had a minute since seen her brighten across the house: she had the sense of the return of the person she had taken me for—the person with the right pair of lips, as to whom I was for that matter much more in the dark than she. I gasped, but my word had come: if she had lost her sight it was in this very loss that she had found again her beauty. I managed to speak while we were still alone, before her companion had appeared. "You're lovelier at this day than you have ever been in your life!" At the sound of my voice and that of the opening of the door her excitement broke into

audible joy. She sprang up, recognising me, always holding
me, and gleefully cried to a gentleman who was arrested in
the doorway by the sight of me: "He has come back, he has
come back, and you should have heard what he says of me!"
The gentleman was Geoffrey Dawling, and I thought it best
to let him hear on the spot. "How beautiful she is, my dear
man—but how extraordinarily beautiful! More beautiful at
this hour than ever, ever before!"

It gave them almost equal pleasure and made Dawling blush
up to his eyes; while this in turn produced, in spite of deepened astonishment, a blessed snap of the strain that I had been
under for some moments. I wanted to embrace them both,
and while the opening bars of another scene rose from the
orchestra I almost did embrace Dawling, whose first emotion
on beholding me had visibly and ever so oddly been a consciousness of guilt. I had caught him somehow in the act,
though that was as yet all I knew; but by the time we had
sunk noiselessly into our chairs again (for the music was supreme, Wagner passed first) my demonstration ought pretty
well to have given him the limit of the criticism he had to
fear. I myself indeed, while the opera blazed, was only too
afraid he might divine in our silent closeness the very moral
of my optimism, which was simply the comfort I had gathered
from seeing that if our companion's beauty lived again her
vanity partook of its life. I had hit on the right note—that
was what eased me off: it drew all pain for the next half-hour
from the sense of the deep darkness in which the stricken
woman sat there. If the music, in that darkness, happily soared
and swelled for her, it beat its wings in unison with those of
a gratified passion. A great deal came and went between us
without profaning the occasion, so that I could feel at the end
of twenty minutes as if I knew almost everything he might in
kindness have to tell me; knew even why Flora, while I stared
at her from the stalls, had misled me by the use of ivory and
crystal and by appearing to recognise me and smile. She
leaned back in her chair in luxurious ease: I had from the first
become aware that the way she fingered her pearls was a sharp
image of the wedded state. Nothing of old had seemed wanting to her assurance; but I hadn't then dreamed of the art
with which she would wear that assurance as a married

woman. She had taken him when everything had failed; he had taken her when she herself had done so. His embarrassed eyes confessed it all, confessed the deep peace he found in it. They only didn't tell me why he had not written to me, nor clear up as yet a minor obscurity. Flora after a while again lifted the glass from the ledge of the box and elegantly swept the house with it. Then, by the mere instinct of her grace, a motion but half conscious, she inclined her head into the void with the sketch of a salute, producing, I could see, a perfect imitation of a response to some homage. Dawling and I looked at each other again: the tears came into his eyes. She was playing at perfection still, and her misfortune only simplified the process.

I recognised that this was as near as I should ever come, certainly as I should come that night, to pressing on her misfortune. Neither of us would name it more than we were doing then, and Flora would never name it at all. Little by little I perceived that what had occurred was, strange as it might appear, the best thing for her happiness. The question was now only of her beauty and her being seen and marvelled at: with Dawling to do for her everything in life her activity was limited to that. Such an activity was all within her scope: it asked nothing of her that she couldn't splendidly give. As from time to time in our delicate communion she turned her face to me with the parody of a look I lost none of the signs of its strange new glory. The expression of the eyes was a bit of pastel put in by a master's thumb; the whole head, stamped with a sort of showy suffering, had gained a fineness from what she had passed through. Yes, Flora was settled for life— nothing could hurt her further. I foresaw the particular praise she would mostly incur—she would be incomparably "interesting." She would charm with her pathos more even than she had charmed with her pleasure. For herself above all she was fixed for ever, rescued from all change and ransomed from all doubt. Her old certainties, her old vanities were justified and sanctified, and in the darkness that had closed upon her one object remained clear. That object, as unfading as a mosaic mask, was fortunately the loveliest she could possibly look upon. The greatest blessing of all was of course that Dawling thought so. Her future was ruled with the straightest line, and so for that matter was his. There were two facts to which before I left my friends I gave time to sink into my spirit. One of them was that he had changed by some process as effective as Flora's change; had been simplified somehow into service as she had been simplified into success. He was such a picture of inspired intervention as I had never yet encountered: he would exist henceforth for the sole purpose of rendering unnecessary, or rather impossible, any reference even on her own part to his wife's infirmity. Oh yes, how little desire he would ever give *me* to refer to it! He principally after a while made me feel—and this was my second lesson—that, good-natured as he was, my being there to see it all oppressed him; so that by the time the act ended I recognised that I too had filled out my hour. Dawling remembered things; I think he caught in my very face the irony of old judgments: they made him thresh about in his chair. I said to Flora as I took leave of her that I would come to see her; but I may mention that I never went. I'll go to-morrow if I hear she wants me; but what in the world can she ever want? As I quitted them I laid my hand on Dawling's arm and drew him for a moment into the lobby.

"Why did you never write to me of your marriage?"

He smiled uncomfortably, showing his long yellow teeth and something more. "I don't know—the whole thing gave me such a tremendous lot to do."

This was the first dishonest speech I had heard him make: he really hadn't written to me because he had an idea I would think him a still bigger fool than before. I didn't insist, but I tried there, in the lobby, so far as a pressure of his hand could serve me, to give him a notion of what I thought him. "I can't at any rate make out," I said, "why I didn't hear from Mrs. Meldrum."

"She didn't write to you?"

"Never a word. What has become of her?"

"I think she's at Folkestone," Dawling returned; "but I'm sorry to say that practically she has ceased to see us."

"You haven't quarrelled with her?"

"How *could* we? Think of all we owe her. At the time of our marriage, and for months before, she did everything for us: I don't know how we should have managed without her. But since then she has never been near us and has given us rather markedly little encouragement to try and keep up our relations with her."

I was struck with this though of course I admit I am struck with all sorts of things. "Well," I said after a moment, "even if I could imagine a reason for that attitude it wouldn't explain why she shouldn't have taken account of *my* natural interest."

"Just so." Dawling's face was a windowless wall. He could contribute nothing to the mystery, and, quitting him, I carried it away. It was not till I went down to see Mrs. Meldrum that it was really dispelled. She didn't want to hear of them or to talk of them, not a bit, and it was just in the same spirit that she hadn't wanted to write of them. She had done everything in the world for them, but now, thank heaven, the hard business was over. After I had taken this in, which I was quick to do, we quite avoided the subject. She simply couldn't bear it.

The Figure in the Carpet

I HAD DONE a few things and earned a few pence—I had perhaps even had time to begin to think I was finer than was perceived by the patronising; but when I take the little measure of my course (a fidgety habit, for it's none of the longest yet) I count my real start from the evening George Corvick, breathless and worried, came in to ask me a service. He had done more things than I, and earned more pence, though there were chances for cleverness I thought he sometimes missed. I could only however that evening declare to him that he never missed one for kindness. There was almost rapture in hearing it proposed to me to prepare for *The Middle*, the organ of our lucubrations, so called from the position in the week of its day of appearance, an article for which he had made himself responsible and of which, tied up with a stout string, he laid on my table the subject. I pounced upon my opportunity—that is on the first volume of it—and paid scant attention to my friend's explanation of his appeal. What explanation could be more to the point than my obvious fitness for the task? I had written on Hugh Vereker, but never a word in *The Middle*, where my dealings were mainly with the ladies and the minor poets. This was his new novel, an advance copy, and whatever much or little it should do for his reputation I was clear on the spot as to what it should do for mine. Moreover if I always read him as soon as I could get hold of him I had a particular reason for wishing to read him now: I had accepted an invitation to Bridges for the following Sunday, and it had been mentioned in Lady Jane's note that Mr. Vereker was to be there. I was young enough to have an emotion about meeting a man of his renown and innocent enough to believe the occasion would demand the display of an acquaintance with his "last."

Corvick, who had promised a review of it, had not even had time to read it; he had gone to pieces in consequence of news requiring—as on precipitate reflection he judged—that he should catch the night-mail to Paris. He had had a telegram from Gwendolen Erme in answer to his letter offering to fly to her aid. I knew already about Gwendolen Erme; I had never seen her, but I had my ideas, which were mainly to the effect that Corvick would marry her if her mother would only die. That lady seemed now in a fair way to oblige him; after some dreadful mistake about some climate or some waters she had suddenly collapsed on the return from abroad. Her daughter, unsupported and alarmed, desiring to make a rush for home but hesitating at the risk, had accepted our friend's assistance, and it was my secret belief that at the sight of him Mrs. Erme would pull round. His own belief was scarcely to be called secret; it discernibly at any rate differed from mine. He had showed me Gwendolen's photograph with the remark that she wasn't pretty but was awfully interesting; she had published at the age of nineteen a novel in three volumes, "Deep Down," about which, in *The Middle*, he had been really splendid. He appreciated my present eagerness and undertook that the periodical in question should do no less; then at the last, with his hand on the door, he said to me: "Of course you'll be all right, you know." Seeing I was a trifle vague he added: "I mean you won't be silly."

"Silly—about Vereker! Why, what do I ever find him but awfully clever?"

"Well, what's that but silly? What on earth does 'awfully clever' mean? For God's sake try to get *at* him. Don't let him suffer by our arrangement. Speak of him, you know, if you can, as *I* should have spoken of him."

I wondered an instant. "You mean as far and away the biggest of the lot—that sort of thing?"

Corvick almost groaned. "Oh, you know, I don't put them back to back that way; it's the infancy of art! But he gives me a pleasure so rare; the sense of"—he mused a little—"something or other."

I wondered again. "The sense, pray, of what?"

"My dear man, that's just what I want *you* to say!"

Even before Corvick had banged the door I had begun, book in hand, to prepare myself to say it. I sat up with Vereker half the night; Corvick couldn't have done more than that. He was awfully clever—I stuck to that, but he wasn't a bit the biggest of the lot. I didn't allude to the lot, however; I flattered myself that I emerged on this occasion from the infancy of art. "It's all right," they declared vividly at the office; and when the number appeared I felt there was a basis on which I could meet the great man. It gave me confidence for a day or two, and then that confidence dropped. I had fancied him reading it with relish, but if Corvick was not satisfied how could Vereker himself be? I reflected indeed that the heat of the admirer was sometimes grosser even than the appetite of the scribe. Corvick at all events wrote me from Paris a little ill-humouredly. Mrs. Erme was pulling round, and I hadn't at all said what Vereker gave him the sense of.

II

The effect of my visit to Bridges was to turn me out for more profundity. Hugh Vereker, as I saw him there, was of a contact so void of angles that I blushed for the poverty of imagination involved in my small precautions. If he was in spirits it was not because he had read my review; in fact on the Sunday morning I felt sure he hadn't read it, though *The Middle* had been out three days and bloomed, I assured myself, in the stiff garden of periodicals which gave one of the ormolu tables the air of a stand at a station. The impression he made on me personally was such that I wished him to read it, and I corrected to this end with a surreptitious hand what might be wanting in the careless conspicuity of the sheet. I am afraid I even watched the result of my manœuvre, but up to luncheon I watched in vain.

When afterwards, in the course of our gregarious walk, I found myself for half an hour, not perhaps without another manœuvre, at the great man's side, the result of his affability was a still livelier desire that he should not remain in ignorance of the peculiar justice I had done him. It was not that he seemed to thirst for justice; on the contrary I had not yet caught in his talk the faintest grunt of a grudge—a note for which my young experience had already given me an ear. Of late he had had more recognition, and it was pleasant, as we used to say in *The Middle*, to see that it drew him out. He wasn't of course popular, but I judged one of the sources of his good humour to be precisely that his success was independent of that. He had none the less become in a manner the fashion; the critics at least had put on a spurt and caught up with him. We had found out at last how clever he was, and he had had to make the best of the loss of his mystery. I was strongly tempted, as I walked beside him, to let him know how much of that unveiling was my act; and there was a moment when I probably should have done so had not one of the ladies of our party, snatching a place at his other elbow, just then appealed to him in a spirit comparatively selfish. It was very discouraging: I almost felt the liberty had been taken with myself.

I had had on my tongue's end, for my own part, a phrase or two about the right word at the right time; but later on I was glad not to have spoken, for when on our return we clustered at tea I perceived Lady Jane, who had not been out with us, brandishing *The Middle* with her longest arm. She had taken it up at her leisure; she was delighted with what she had found, and I saw that, as a mistake in a man may often be a felicity in a woman, she would practically do for me what I hadn't been able to do for myself. "Some sweet little truths that needed to be spoken," I heard her declare, thrusting the paper at rather a bewildered couple by the fireplace. She grabbed it away from them again on the reappearance of Hugh Vereker, who after our walk had been upstairs to change something. "I know you don't in general look at this kind of thing, but it's an occasion really for doing so. You *haven't* seen it? Then you must. The man has actually got *at* you, at what *I* always feel, you know." Lady Jane threw into her eyes a look evidently intended to give an idea of what she always felt; but she added that she couldn't have expressed it. The man in the paper expressed it in a striking manner. "Just see there, and there, where I've dashed it, how he brings it out." She had literally marked for him the brightest patches of my prose, and if I was a little amused Vereker himself may well have been. He showed how much he was when before us all Lady Jane wanted to read something aloud. I liked at any rate the way he defeated her purpose by jerking the paper affectionately out of her clutch. He would take it upstairs with him, would look at it on going to dress. He did this half an hour later—I saw it in his hand when he repaired to his room. That was the moment at which, thinking to give her pleasure,

I mentioned to Lady Jane that I was the author of the review. I did give her pleasure, I judged, but perhaps not quite so much as I had expected. If the author was "only me" the thing didn't seem quite so remarkable. Hadn't I had the effect rather of diminishing the lustre of the article than of adding to my own? Her ladyship was subject to the most extraordinary drops. It didn't matter; the only effect I cared about was the one it would have on Vereker up there by his bedroom fire.

At dinner I watched for the signs of this impression, tried to fancy there was some happier light in his eyes; but to my disappointment Lady Jane gave me no chance to make sure. I had hoped she would call triumphantly down the table, publicly demand if she hadn't been right. The party was large—there were people from outside as well, but I had never seen a table long enough to deprive Lady Jane of a triumph. I was just reflecting in truth that this interminable board would deprive *me* of one when the guest next me, dear woman—she was Miss Poyle, the vicar's sister, a robust, unmodulated person—had the happy inspiration and the unusual courage to address herself across it to Vereker, who was opposite, but not directly, so that when he replied they were both leaning forward. She inquired, artless body, what he thought of Lady Jane's "panegyric," which she had read—not connecting it however with her right-hand neighbour; and while I strained my ear for his reply I heard him, to my stupefaction, call back gaily, with his mouth full of bread: "Oh, it's all right—it's the usual twaddle!"

I had caught Vereker's glance as he spoke, but Miss Poyle's surprise was a fortunate cover for my own. "You mean he doesn't do you justice?" said the excellent woman.

Vereker laughed out, and I was happy to be able to do the same. "It's a charming article," he tossed us.

Miss Poyle thrust her chin half across the cloth. "Oh you're so deep!" she drove home.

"As deep as the ocean! All I pretend is, the author doesn't see——"

A dish was at this point passed over his shoulder, and we had to wait while he helped himself.

"Doesn't see what?" my neighbour continued.

"Doesn't see anything."

"Dear me—how very stupid!"

"Not a bit," Vereker laughed again. "Nobody does."

The lady on his further side appealed to him, and Miss Poyle sank back to me. "Nobody sees anything!" she cheerfully announced; to which I replied that I had often thought so too, but had somehow taken the thought for a proof on my own part of a tremendous eye. I didn't tell her the article was mine; and I observed that Lady Jane, occupied at the end of the table, had not caught Vereker's words.

I rather avoided him after dinner, for I confess he struck me as cruelly conceited, and the revelation was a pain. "The usual twaddle"—my acute little study! That one's admiration should have had a reserve or two could gall him to that point? I had thought him placid, and he was placid enough; such a surface was the hard, polished glass that encased the bauble of his vanity. I was really ruffled, and the only comfort was that if nobody saw anything George Corvick was quite as much out of it as I. This comfort however was not sufficient, after the ladies had dispersed, to carry me in the proper manner—I mean in a spotted jacket and humming an air—into the smoking-room. I took my way in some dejection to bed; but in the passage I encountered Mr. Vereker, who had been up once more to change, coming out of his room. *He* was humming an air and had on a spotted jacket, and as soon as he saw me his gaiety gave a start.

"My dear young man," he exclaimed, "I'm so glad to lay hands on you! I'm afraid I most unwittingly wounded you by those words of mine at dinner to Miss Poyle. I learned but half an hour ago from Lady Jane that you wrote the little notice in *The Middle*."

I protested that no bones were broken; but he moved with me to my own door, his hand on my shoulder, kindly feeling for a fracture; and on hearing that I had come up to bed he asked leave to cross my threshold and just tell me in three words what his qualification of my remarks had represented. It was plain he really feared I was hurt, and the sense of his solicitude suddenly made all the difference to me. My cheap review fluttered off into space, and the best things I had said in it became flat enough beside the brilliancy of his being there. I can see him there still, on my rug, in the firelight and his spotted jacket, his fine, clear face all bright with the desire to be tender to my youth. I don't know what he had at first meant to say, but I think the sight of my relief touched him, excited him, brought up words to his lips from far within. It was so these words presently conveyed to me something that, as I afterwards knew, he had never uttered to any one. I have always done justice to the generous impulse that made him speak; it was simply compunction for a snub unconsciously administered to a man of letters in a position inferior to his own, a man of letters moreover in the very act of praising him. To make the thing right he talked to me exactly as an equal and on the ground of what we both loved best. The hour, the place, the unexpectedness deepened the impression: he couldn't have done anything more exquisitely successful.

III

"I don't quite know how to explain it to you," he said, "but it was the very fact that your notice of my book had a spice of intelligence, it was just your exceptional sharpness that produced the feeling—a very old story with me, I beg you to believe—under the momentary influence of which I used in speaking to that good lady the words you so naturally resent. I don't read the things in the newspapers unless they're thrust upon me as that one was—it's always one's best friend that does it! But I used to read them sometimes—ten years ago. I daresay they were in general rather stupider then; at any rate it always seemed to me that they missed my little point with a perfection exactly as admirable when they patted me on the back as when they kicked me in the shins. Whenever since I've happened to have a glimpse of them they were still blazing away—still missing it, I mean, deliciously. *You* miss it, my dear fellow, with inimitable assurance; the fact of your being awfully clever and your article's being awfully nice doesn't make a hair's breadth of difference. It's quite with you rising young men," Vereker laughed, "that I feel most what a failure I am!"

I listened with intense interest; it grew intenser as he talked. "*You* a failure—heavens! What then may your 'little point' happen to be?"

"Have I got to *tell* you, after all these years and labours?" There was something in the friendly reproach of this—jocosely exaggerated—that made me, as an ardent young seeker for truth, blush to the roots of my hair. I'm as much in the dark as ever, though I've grown used in a sense to my obtuseness; at that moment, however, Vereker's happy accent made me appear to myself, and probably to him, a rare donkey. I was on the point of exclaiming "Ah, yes, don't tell me: for my honour, for that of the craft, don't!" when he went on in a manner that showed he had read my thought and had his own idea of the probability of our some day redeeming ourselves. "By my little point I mean—what shall I call it?—the particular thing I've written my books most *for*. Isn't there for every writer a particular thing of that sort, the thing that most makes him apply himself, the thing without the effort to achieve which he wouldn't write at all, the very passion of his passion, the part of the business in which, for him, the flame of art burns most intensely? Well, it's *that*!"

I considered a moment. I was fascinated—easily, you'll say; but I wasn't going after all to be put off my guard. "Your description's certainly beautiful, but it doesn't make what you describe very distinct."

"I promise you it would be distinct if it should dawn on you at all." I saw that the charm of our topic overflowed for my companion into an emotion as lively as my own. "At any rate," he went on, "I can speak for myself: there's an idea in my work without which I wouldn't have given a straw for the whole job. It's the finest, fullest intention of the lot, and the application of it has been, I think, a triumph of patience, of ingenuity. I ought to leave that to somebody else to say; but that nobody does say it is precisely what we're talking about. It stretches, this little trick of mine, from book to book, and everything else, comparatively, plays over the surface of it. The order, the form, the texture of my books will perhaps some day constitute for the initiated a complete representation of it. So it's naturally the thing for the critic to look for. It strikes me," my visitor added, smiling, "even as the thing for the critic to find."

This seemed a responsibility indeed. "You call it a little trick?"

"That's only my little modesty. It's really an exquisite scheme."

"And you hold that you've carried the scheme out?"

"The way I've carried it out is the thing in life I think a bit well of myself for."

I was silent a moment. "Don't you think you ought—just a trifle—to assist the critic?"

"Assist him? What else have I done with every stroke of my pen? I've shouted my intention in his great blank face!" At this, laughing out again, Vereker laid his hand on my shoulder to show that the allusion was not to my personal appearance.

"But you talk about the initiated. There must therefore, you see, be initiation."

"What else in heaven's name is criticism supposed to be?" I'm afraid I coloured at this too; but I took refuge in repeating that his account of his silver lining was poor in something or other that a plain man knows things by. "That's only because you've never had a glimpse of it," he replied. "If you had had one the element in question would soon have become practically all you'd see. To me it's exactly as palpable as the marble of this chimney. Besides, the critic just *isn't* a plain man: if he were, pray, what would he be doing in his neighbour's garden? You're anything but a plain man yourself, and the very *raison d'être* of you all is that you're little demons of subtlety. If my great affair's a secret, that's only because it's a secret in spite of itself—the amazing event has made it one. I not only never took the smallest precaution to do so, but never dreamed of any such accident. If I had I shouldn't in advance have had the heart to go on. As it was I only became aware little by little, and meanwhile I had done my work."

"And now you quite like it?" I risked.

"My work?"

"Your secret. It's the same thing."

"Your guessing that," Vereker replied, "is a proof that you're as clever as I say!" I was encouraged by this to remark that he would clearly be pained to part with it, and he confessed that it was indeed with him now the great amusement of life. "I live almost to see if it will ever be detected." He looked at me for a jesting challenge; something at the back of his eyes seemed to peep out. "But I needn't worry—it won't!"

"You fire me as I've never been fired," I returned; "you make me determined to do or die." Then I asked: "Is it a kind of esoteric message?"

His countenance fell at this—he put out his hand as if to bid me good-night. "Ah, my dear fellow, it can't be described in cheap journalese!"

I knew of course he would be awfully fastidious, but our talk had made me feel how much his nerves were exposed. I was unsatisfied—I kept hold of his hand. "I won't make use of the expression then," I said, "in the article in which I shall eventually announce my discovery, though I daresay I shall have hard work to do without it. But meanwhile, just to hasten that difficult birth, can't you give a fellow a clue?" I felt much more at my ease.

"My whole lucid effort gives him the clue—every page and line and letter. The thing's as concrete there as a bird in a cage, a bait on a hook, a piece of cheese in a mouse-trap. It's stuck into every volume as your foot is stuck into your shoe. It governs every line, it chooses every word, it dots every i, it places every comma."

I scratched my head. "Is it something in the style or something in the thought? An element of form or an element of feeling?"

He indulgently shook my hand again, and I felt my questions to be crude and my distinctions pitiful. "Good-night, my dear boy—don't bother about it. After all, you do like a fellow."

"And a little intelligence might spoil it?" I still detained him.

He hesitated. "Well, you've got a heart in your body. Is that an element of form or an element of feeling? What I contend that nobody has ever mentioned in my work is the organ of life."

"I see—it's some idea about life, some sort of philosophy. Unless it be," I added with the eagerness of a thought perhaps still happier, "some kind of game you're up to with your style, something you're after in the language. Perhaps it's a preference for the letter P!" I ventured profanely to break out. "Papa, potatoes, prunes—that sort of thing?" He was suitably indulgent: he only said I hadn't got the right letter. But his amusement was over; I could see he was bored. There was nevertheless something else I had absolutely to learn. "Should you be able, pen in hand, to state it clearly yourself—to name it, phrase it, formulate it?"

"Oh," he almost passionately sighed, "if I were only, pen in hand, one of *you* chaps!"

"That would be a great chance for you of course. But why should you despise us chaps for not doing what you can't do yourself?"

"Can't do?" He opened his eyes. "Haven't I done it in twenty volumes? I do it in my way," he continued. "You don't do it in yours."

"Ours is so devilish difficult," I weakly observed.

"So is mine. We each choose our own. There's no compulsion. You won't come down and smoke?"

"No. I want to think this thing out."

"You'll tell me then in the morning that you've laid me bare?"

"I'll see what I can do; I'll sleep on it. But just one word more," I added. We had left the room—I walked again with him a few steps along the passage. "This extraordinary 'general intention,' as you call it—for that's the most vivid description I can induce you to make of it—is then generally a sort of buried treasure?"

His face lighted. "Yes, call it that, though it's perhaps not for me to do so."

"Nonsense!" I laughed. "You know you're hugely proud of it."

"Well, I didn't propose to tell you so; but it *is* the joy of my soul!"

"You mean it's a beauty so rare, so great?"

He hesitated a moment. "The loveliest thing in the world!" We had stopped, and on these words he left me; but at the end of the corridor, while I looked after him rather yearningly, he turned and caught sight of my puzzled face. It made him earnestly, indeed I thought quite anxiously, shake his head and wave his finger. "Give it up—give it up!"

This wasn't a challenge—it was fatherly advice. If I had had one of his books at hand I would have repeated my recent act of faith—I would have spent half the night with him. At three o'clock in the morning, not sleeping, remembering moreover how indispensable he was to Lady Jane, I stole down to the library with a candle. There wasn't, so far as I could discover, a line of his writing in the house.

IV

Returning to town I feverishly collected them all; I picked out each in its order and held it up to the light. This gave me a maddening month, in the course of which several things took place. One of these, the last, I may as well immediately mention, was that I acted on Vereker's advice: I renounced my ridiculous attempt. I could really make nothing of the business; it proved a dead loss. After all, before, as he had himself observed, I liked him; and what now occurred was simply that my new intelligence and vain preoccupation damaged my liking. I not only failed to find his general intention—I found myself missing the subordinate intentions I had formerly found. His books didn't even remain the charming things they had been for me; the exasperation of my search put me out of conceit of them. Instead of being a pleasure the more they became a resource the less; for from the moment I was unable to follow up the author's hint I of course felt it a point of honour not to make use professionally of my knowledge of them. I *had* no knowledge—nobody had any. It was humiliating, but I could bear it—they only annoyed me now. At last they even bored me, and I accounted for my confusion—perversely, I confess—by the idea that Vereker had made a fool of me. The buried treasure was a bad joke, the general intention a monstrous *pose*.

The great incident of the time however was that I told George Corvick all about the matter and that my information had an immense effect upon him. He had at last come back, but so, unfortunately, had Mrs. Erme, and there was as yet, I could see, no question of his nuptials. He was immensely stirred up by the anecdote I had brought from Bridges; it fell in so completely with the sense he had had from the first that there was more in Vereker than met the eye. When I remarked that the eye seemed what the printed page had been expressly invented to meet he immediately accused me of being spiteful because I had been foiled. Our commerce had always that pleasant latitude. The thing Vereker had mentioned to me was exactly the thing he, Corvick, had wanted me to speak of in my review. On my suggesting at last that with the assistance I had now given him he would doubtless be prepared to speak of it himself he admitted freely that before doing this there was more he must understand. What he would have said, had he reviewed the new book, was that there was evidently in the writer's inmost art something to *be* understood. I hadn't so much as hinted at that: no wonder the writer hadn't been flattered! I asked Corvick what he really considered he meant by his own supersubtlety, and, unmistakably kindled, he replied: "It isn't for the vulgar—it isn't for the vulgar!" He had hold of the tail of something; he would pull hard, pull it right out. He pumped me dry on Vereker's strange confidence and, pronouncing me the luckiest of mortals, mentioned half a dozen questions he wished to goodness I had had the gumption to put. Yet on the other hand he didn't want to be told too much—it would spoil the fun of seeing what would come. The failure of my fun was at the moment of our meeting not complete, but I saw it ahead, and Corvick saw that I saw it. I, on my side, saw likewise that one of the first things he would do would be to rush off with my story to Gwendolen.

On the very day after my talk with him I was surprised by the receipt of a note from Hugh Vereker, to whom our encounter at Bridges had been recalled, as he mentioned, by his falling, in a magazine, on some article to which my signature was appended. "I read it with great pleasure," he wrote, "and remembered under its influence our lively conversation by your bedroom fire. The consequence of this has been that I begin to measure the temerity of my having saddled you with a knowledge that you may find something of a burden. Now that the fit's over I can't imagine how I came to be moved so much beyond my wont. I had never before related, no matter in what expansion, the history of my little secret, and I shall never speak of the business again. I was accidentally so much more explicit with you than it had ever entered into my game to be, that I find this game—I mean the pleasure of playing it—suffers considerably. In short, if you can understand it, I've spoiled a part of my fun. I really don't want to give anybody what I believe you clever young men call the tip. That's of course a selfish solicitude, and I name it to you for what it may be worth to you. If you're disposed to humour me don't repeat my revelation. Think me demented—it's your right; but don't tell anybody why."

The sequel to this communication was that as early on the morrow as I dared I drove straight to Mr. Vereker's door. He occupied in those years one of the honest old houses in Kensington-square. He received me immediately, and as soon as I came in I saw I had not lost my power to minister to his mirth. He laughed out at the sight of my face, which doubtless expressed my perturbation. I had been indiscreet—my compunction was great. "I *have* told somebody," I panted, "and I'm sure that person will by this time have told somebody else! It's a woman, into the bargain."

"The person you've told?"

"No, the other person. I'm quite sure he must have told her."

"For all the good it will do her—or do *me*! A woman will never find out."

"No, but she'll talk all over the place: she'll do just what you don't want."

Vereker thought a moment, but he was not so disconcerted as I had feared: he felt that if the harm was done it only served him right. "It doesn't matter—don't worry."

"I'll do my best, I promise you, that your talk with me shall go no further."

"Very good; do what you can."

"In the meantime," I pursued, "George Corvick's possession of the tip may, on his part, really lead to something."

"That will be a brave day."

I told him about Corvick's cleverness, his admiration, the intensity of his interest in my anecdote; and without making too much of the divergence of our respective estimates mentioned that my friend was already of opinion that he saw much further into a certain affair than most people. He was quite as fired as I had been at Bridges. He was moreover in love with the young lady: perhaps the two together would puzzle something out.

Vereker seemed struck with this. "Do you mean they're to be married?"

"I daresay that's what it will come to."

"That may help them," he conceded, "but we must give them time!"

I spoke of my own renewed assault and confessed my difficulties; whereupon he repeated his former advice: "Give it up, give it up!" He evidently didn't think me intellectually equipped for the adventure. I stayed half an hour, and he was most good-natured, but I couldn't help pronouncing him a man of shifting moods. He had been free with me in a mood, he had repented in a mood, and now in a mood he had turned indifferent. This general levity helped me to believe that, so far as the subject of the tip went, there wasn't much in it. I contrived however to make him answer a few more questions about it, though he did so with visible impatience. For himself, beyond doubt, the thing we were all so blank about was vividly there. It was something, I guessed, in the primal plan, something like a complex figure in a Persian carpet. He highly approved of this image when I used it, and he used another himself. "It's the very string," he said, "that my pearls are strung on!" The reason of his note to me had been that he really didn't want to give us a grain of succour—our destiny was a thing too perfect in its way to touch. He had formed the habit of depending upon it, and if the spell was to break it must break by some force of its own. He comes back to me from that last occasion—for I was never to speak to him again—as a man with some safe secret for enjoyment. I wondered as I walked away where he had got *his* tip.

V

When I spoke to George Corvick of the caution I had received he made me feel that any doubt of his delicacy would be almost an insult. He had instantly told Gwendolen, but Gwendolen's ardent response was in itself a pledge of discretion. The question would now absorb them, and they would enjoy their fun too much to wish to share it with the crowd. They appeared to have caught instinctively Vereker's peculiar notion of fun. Their intellectual pride, however, was not such as to make them indifferent to any further light I might throw on the affair they had in hand. They were indeed of the "artistic temperament," and I was freshly struck with my colleague's power to excite himself over a question of art. He called it letters, he called it life—it was all one thing. In what he said I now seemed to understand that he spoke equally for Gwendolen, to whom, as soon as Mrs. Erme was sufficiently better to allow her a little leisure, he made a point of introducing me. I remember our calling together one Sunday in August at a huddled house in Chelsea, and my renewed envy of Corvick's possession of a friend who had some light to mingle with his own. He could say things to her that I could never say to him. She had indeed no sense of humour and, with her pretty way of holding her head on one side, was one of those persons whom you want, as the phrase is, to shake, but who have learnt Hungarian by themselves. She conversed perhaps in Hungarian with Corvick; she had remarkably little English for his friend. Corvick afterwards told me that I had chilled her by my apparent indisposition to oblige her with the detail of what Vereker had said to me. I admitted that I felt I had given thought enough to this exposure: hadn't I even made up my mind that it was hollow, wouldn't stand the test? The importance they attached to it was irritating—it rather envenomed my dissent.

That statement looks unamiable, and what probably happened was that I felt humiliated at seeing other persons derive a daily joy from an experiment which had brought me only chagrin. I was out in the cold while, by the evening fire, under the lamp, they followed the chase for which I myself had sounded the horn. They did as I had done, only more deliberately and sociably—they went over their author from the beginning. There was no hurry, Corvick said—the future was before them and the fascination could only grow; they would take him page by page, as they would take one of the classics, inhale him in slow draughts and let him sink deep in. I doubt whether they would have got so wound up if they had not been in love: poor Vereker's secret gave them endless occasion to put their young heads together. None the less it represented the kind of problem for which Corvick had a special aptitude, drew out the particular pointed patience of which, had he lived, he would have given more striking and, it is to be hoped, more fruitful examples. He at least was, in Vereker's words, a little demon of subtlety. We had begun by disputing, but I soon saw that without my stirring a finger his infatuation would have its bad hours. He would bound off on false scents as I had done—he would clap his hands over new lights and see them blown out by the wind of the turned page. He was like nothing, I told him, but the maniacs who embrace some bedlamitical theory of the cryptic character of Shakespeare. To this he replied that if we had had Shakespeare's own word for his being cryptic he would immediately have accepted it. The case there was altogether different—we had nothing but the word of Mr. Snooks. I rejoined that I was stupefied to see him attach such importance even to the word of Mr. Vereker. He inquired thereupon whether I treated Mr. Vereker's word as a lie. I wasn't perhaps prepared, in my unhappy rebound, to go as far as that, but I insisted that till the contrary was proved I should view it as too fond an imagination. I didn't, I confess, say—I didn't at that time quite know—all I felt. Deep down, as Miss Erme would have said, I was uneasy, I was expectant. At the core of my personal confusion—for my curiosity lived in its ashes—was the sharpness of a sense that Corvick would at last probably come out somewhere. He made, in defence of his credulity, a great point of the fact that from of old, in his study of this genius, he had caught whiffs and hints of he didn't know what, faint wandering notes of a hidden music. That was just the rarity, that was the charm: it fitted so perfectly into what I reported.

If I returned on several occasions to the little house in Chelsea I daresay it was as much for news of Vereker as for news of Miss Erme's mamma. The hours spent there by Corvick were present to my fancy as those of a chessplayer bent with a silent scowl, all the lamplit winter, over his board and his moves. As my imagination filled it out the picture held me fast. On the other side of the table was a ghostlier form, the faint figure of an antagonist good-humouredly but a little wearily secure—an antagonist who leaned back in his chair with his hands in his pockets and a smile on his fine clear face. Close to Corvick, behind him, was a girl who had begun to strike me as pale and wasted and even, on more familiar view, as rather handsome, and who rested on his shoulder and hung upon his moves. He would take up a chessman and hold it poised a while over one of the little squares, and then he would put it back in its place with a long sigh of disappointment. The young lady, at this, would slightly but uneasily shift her position and look across, very hard, very long, very strangely, at their dim participant. I had asked them at an early stage of the business if it mightn't contribute to their success to have some closer communication with him. The special circumstances would surely be held to have given me a right to introduce them. Corvick immediately replied that he had no wish to approach the altar before he had prepared the sacrifice. He quite agreed with our friend both as to the sport and as to the honour—he would bring down the animal with his own rifle. When I asked him if Miss Erme were as keen a shot he said after an hesitation: "No; I'm ashamed to say she wants to set a trap. She'd give anything to see him; she says she requires another tip. She's really quite morbid about it. But she must play fair—she *shan't* see him!" he emphatically added. I had a suspicion that they had even quarrelled a little on the subject—a suspicion not corrected by the way he more than once exclaimed to me: "She's quite incredibly literary, you know   quite fantastically!" I remember his saying of her that she felt in italics and thought in capitals. "Oh, when I've run him to earth," he also said, "then, you know, I shall knock at his door. Rather—I beg you to believe. I'll have it from his own lips: 'Right you are, my boy; you've done it this time!' He shall crown me victor—with the critical laurel."

Meanwhile he really avoided the chances London life might have given him of meeting the distinguished novelist; a danger however that disappeared with Vereker's leaving England for an indefinite absence, as the newspapers announced—going to the south for motives connected with the health of his wife, which had long kept her in retirement. A year—more than a year—had elapsed since the incident at Bridges, but I had not encountered him again. I think at bottom I was rather ashamed—I hated to remind him that though I had irremediably missed his point a reputation for acuteness was rapidly overtaking me. This scruple led me a dance; kept me out of Lady Jane's house, made me even decline, when in spite of my bad manners she was a second time so good as to make me a sign, an invitation to her beautiful seat. I once saw her with Vereker at a concert and was sure I was seen by them, but I slipped out without being caught. I felt, as on that occasion I splashed along in the rain, that I couldn't have done anything else; and yet I remember saying to myself that it was hard, was even cruel. Not only had I lost the books, but I had lost the man himself: they and their author had been alike spoiled for me. I knew too which was the loss I most regretted. I had liked the man still better than I had liked the books.

VI

Six months after Vereker had left England George Corvick, who made his living by his pen, contracted for a piece of work which imposed on him an absence of some length and a journey of some difficulty, and his undertaking of which was much of a surprise to me. His brother-in-law had become editor of a great provincial paper, and the great provincial paper, in a fine flight of fancy, had conceived the idea of sending a "special commissioner" to India. Special commissioners had begun, in the "metropolitan press," to be the fashion, and the journal in question felt that it had passed too long for a mere country cousin. Corvick had no hand, I knew, for the big brush of the correspondent, but that was his brother-in-law's affair, and the fact that a particular task was not in his line was apt to be with himself exactly a reason for accepting it. He was prepared to out-Herod the metropolitan press; he took solemn precautions against priggishness, he exquisitely outraged taste. Nobody ever knew it—the taste was all his own. In addition to his expenses he was to be conveniently paid, and I found myself able to help him, for the usual fat book, to a plausible arrangement with the usual fat publisher. I naturally inferred that his obvious desire to make a little money was not unconnected with the prospect of a union with Gwendolen Erme. I was aware that her mother's opposition was largely addressed to his want of means and of lucrative abilities, but it so happened that, on my saying the last time I saw him something that bore on the question of his separation from our young lady, he exclaimed with an emphasis that startled me: "Ah, I'm not a bit engaged to her, you know!"

"Not overtly," I answered, "because her mother doesn't like you. But I've always taken for granted a private understanding."

"Well, there *was* one. But there isn't now." That was all he said, except something about Mrs. Erme's having got on her feet again in the most extraordinary way—a remark from which I gathered he wished me to think he meant that private understandings were of little use when the doctor didn't share them. What I took the liberty of really thinking was that the girl might in some way have estranged him. Well, if he had taken the turn of jealousy for instance it could scarcely be jealousy of me. In that case (besides the absurdity of it) he wouldn't have gone away to leave us together. For some time before his departure we had indulged in no allusion to the buried treasure, and from his silence, of which mine was the consequence, I had drawn a sharp conclusion. His courage had dropped, his ardour had gone the way of mine—this inference at least he left me to enjoy. More than that he couldn't do; he couldn't face the triumph with which I might have greeted an explicit admission. He needn't have been afraid, poor dear, for I had by this time lost all need to triumph. In fact I considered that I showed magnanimity in not reproaching him with his collapse, for the sense of his having thrown up the game made me feel more than ever how much I at last depended on him. If Corvick had broken down I should never know; no one would be of any use if *he* wasn't. It wasn't a bit true that I had ceased to care for knowledge; little by little my curiosity had not only begun to ache again, but had become the familiar torment of my consciousness. There are doubtless people to whom torments of such an order appear hardly more natural than the contortions of disease; but I don't know after all why I should in this connection so much as mention them. For the few persons, at any rate, abnormal or not, with whom my anecdote is concerned, literature was a game of skill, and skill meant courage, and courage meant honour, and honour meant passion, meant life. The stake on the table was of a different substance, and our roulette was the revolving mind, but we sat round the green board as intently as the grim gamblers at Monte Carlo. Gwendolen Erme, for that matter, with her white face and her fixed eyes, was of the very type of the lean ladies one had met in the temples of chance. I recognised in Corvick's absence that she made this analogy vivid. It was extravagant, I admit, the way she lived for the art of the pen. Her passion visibly preyed upon her, and in her presence I felt almost tepid. I got hold of "Deep Down" again: it was a desert in which she had lost herself, but in which too she had dug a wonderful hole in the sand—a cavity out of which Corvick had still more remarkably pulled her.

Early in March I had a telegram from her, in consequence of which I repaired immediately to Chelsea, where the first thing she said to me was: "He has got it, he has got it!"

She was moved, as I could see, to such depths that she must mean the great thing. "Vereker's idea?"

"His general intention. George has cabled from Bombay."

She had the missive open there; it was emphatic, but it was brief. "Eureka. Immense." That was all—he had saved the money of the signature. I shared her emotion, but I was disappointed. "He doesn't say what it is."

"How could he—in a telegram? He'll write it."

"But how does he know?"

"Know it's the real thing? Oh, I'm sure when you see it you do know. *Vera incessu patuit dea!*"

"It's you, Miss Erme, who are a dear for bringing me such news!"—I went all lengths in my high spirits. "But fancy finding our goddess in the temple of Vishnu! How strange of George to have been able to go into the thing again in the midst of such different and such powerful solicitations!"

"He hasn't gone into it, I know; it's the thing itself, let severely alone for six months, that has simply sprung out at him like a tigress out of the jungle. He didn't take a book with him—on purpose; indeed he wouldn't have needed to— he knows every page, as I do, by heart. They all worked in him together, and some day somewhere, when he wasn't thinking, they fell, in all their superb intricacy, into the one right combination. The figure in the carpet came out. That's the way he knew it would come and the real reason—you didn't in the least understand, but I suppose I may tell you now—why he went and why I consented to his going. We knew the change would do it, the difference of thought, of scene, would give the needed touch, the magic shake. We had perfectly, we had admirably calculated. The elements were all in his mind, and in the *secousse* of a new and intense experience they just struck light." She positively struck light herself—she was literally, facially luminous. I stammered something about unconscious cerebration, and she continued: "He'll come right home—this will bring him."

"To see Vereker, you mean?"

"To see Vereker—and to see *me*. Think what he'll have to tell me!"

I hesitated. "About India?"

"About fiddlesticks! About Vereker—about the figure in the carpet."

"But, as you say, we shall surely have that in a letter."

She thought like one inspired, and I remembered how Corvick had told me long before that her face was interesting. "Perhaps it won't go in a letter if it's 'immense.' "

"Perhaps not if it's immense bosh. If he has got something that won't go in a letter he hasn't got *the* thing. Vereker's own statement to me was exactly that the 'figure' *would* go in a letter."

"Well, I cabled to George an hour ago—two words," said Gwendolen.

"Is it indiscreet of me to inquire what they were?"

She hung fire, but at last she brought them out. " 'Angel, write.' "

"Good!" I exclaimed. "I'll make it sure—I'll send him the same."

VII

My words however were not absolutely the same—I put something instead of "angel"; and in the sequel my epithet seemed the more apt, for when eventually we heard from Corvick it was merely, it was thoroughly to be tantalised. He was magnificent in his triumph, he described his discovery as stupendous; but his ecstasy only obscured it—there were to be no particulars till he should have submitted his conception to the supreme authority. He had thrown up his commission, he had thrown up his book, he had thrown up everything but the instant need to hurry to Rapallo, on the Genoese shore, where Vereker was making a stay. I wrote him a letter which was to await him at Aden—I besought him to relieve my suspense. That he found my letter was indicated by a telegram which, reaching me after weary days and without my having received an answer to my laconic dispatch at Bombay, was evidently intended as a reply to both communications. Those few words were in familiar French, the French of the day, which Corvick often made use of to show he wasn't a prig. It had for some persons the opposite effect, but his message may fairly be paraphrased. "Have patience; I want to see, as it breaks on you, the face you'll make!" *"Tellement envie de voir ta tête!"*—that was what I had to sit down with. I can certainly not be said to have sat down, for I seem to remember myself at this time as rushing constantly between the little house in Chelsea and my own. Our impatience, Gwendolen's and mine, was equal, but I kept hoping her light would be greater. We all spent during this episode, for people of our means, a great deal of money in telegrams, and I counted on the receipt of news from Rapallo immediately after the junction of the discoverer with the discovered. The interval seemed an age, but late one day I heard a hansom rattle up to my door with the crash engendered by a hint of liberality. I lived with my heart in my mouth and I bounded to the window—a movement which gave me a view of a young lady erect on the footboard of the vehicle and eagerly looking up at my house. At sight of me she flourished a paper with a movement that brought me straight down, the movement with which, in melodramas, handkerchiefs and reprieves are flourished at the foot of the scaffold.

"Just seen Vereker—not a note wrong. Pressed me to bosom—keeps me a month." So much I read on her paper while the cabby dropped a grin from his perch. In my excitement I paid him profusely and in hers she suffered it; then as he drove away we started to walk about and talk. We had talked, heaven knows, enough before, but this was a wondrous lift. We pictured the whole scene at Rapallo, where he would have written, mentioning my name, for permission to call; that is *I* pictured it, having more material than my companion, whom I felt hang on my lips as we stopped on purpose before shop-windows we didn't look into. About one thing we were clear: if he was staying on for fuller communication we should at least have a letter from him that would help us through the dregs of delay. We understood his staying on, and yet each of us saw, I think, that the other hated it. The letter we were clear about arrived; it was for Gwendolen, and I called upon her in time to save her the trouble of bringing it to me. She didn't read it out, as was natural enough; but she repeated to me what it chiefly embodied. This consisted of the remarkable statement that he would tell her when they were married exactly what she wanted to know.

"Only when we're married—not before," she explained. "It's tantamount to saying—isn't it?—that I must marry him straight off!" She smiled at me while I flushed with disappointment, a vision of fresh delay that made me at first unconscious of my surprise. It seemed more than a hint that on me as well he would impose some tiresome condition. Suddenly, while she reported several more things from his letter, I remembered what he had told me before going away. He found Mr. Vereker deliriously interesting and his own possession of the secret a kind of intoxication. The buried treasure was all gold and gems. Now that it was there it seemed to grow and grow before him; it was in all time, in all tongues, one of the most wonderful flowers of art. Nothing, above all, when once one was face to face with it, had been more consummately done. When once it came out it came out, was there with a splendour that made you ashamed; and there had not been, save in the bottomless vulgarity of the age, with every one tasteless and tainted, every sense stopped, the smallest reason why it should have been overlooked. It was immense, but it was simple—it was simple, but it was immense, and the final knowledge of it was an experience quite apart. He intimated that the charm of such an experience, the desire to drain it, in its freshness, to the last drop, was what kept him there close to the source. Gwendolen, frankly radiant as she tossed me these fragments, showed the elation of a prospect more assured than my own. That brought me back to the question of her marriage, prompted me to ask her if what she meant by what she had just surprised me with was that she was under an engagement.

"Of course I am!" she answered. "Didn't you know it?" She appeared astonished; but I was still more so, for Corvick had told me the exact contrary. I didn't mention this, however; I only reminded her that I had not been to that degree in her confidence, or even in Corvick's, and that moreover I was not in ignorance of her mother's interdict. At bottom I was troubled by the disparity of the two assertions; but after a moment I felt that Corvick's was the one I least doubted. This simply reduced me to asking myself if the girl had on the spot improvised an engagement—vamped up an old one or dashed off a new—in order to arrive at the satisfaction she desired. I reflected that she had resources of which I was destitute; but she made her case slightly more intelligible by rejoining presently: "What the state of things has been is that we felt of course bound to do nothing in mamma's lifetime."

"But now you think you'll just dispense with your mother's consent?"

"Ah, it may not come to that!" I wondered what it might come to, and she went on: "Poor dear, she may swallow the dose. In fact, you know," she added with a laugh, "she really *must*!"—a proposition of which, on behalf of every one concerned, I fully acknowledged the force.

VIII

Nothing more annoying had ever happened to me than to become aware before Corvick's arrival in England that I should not be there to put him through. I found myself abruptly called to Germany by the alarming illness of my younger brother, who, against my advice, had gone to Munich to study, at the feet indeed of a great master, the art of portraiture in oils. The near relative who made him an allowance had threatened to withdraw it if he should, under specious pretexts, turn for superior truth to Paris—Paris being somehow, for a Cheltenham aunt, the school of evil, the abyss. I deplored this prejudice at the time, and the deep injury of it was now visible—first in the fact that it had not saved the poor boy, who was clever, frail and foolish, from congestion of the lungs, and second in the greater remoteness from London to which the event condemned me. I am afraid that what was uppermost in my mind during several anxious weeks was the sense that if we had only been in Paris I might have run over to see Corvick. This was actually out of the question from every point of view: my brother, whose recovery gave us both plenty to do, was ill for three months, during which I never left him and at the end of which we had to face the absolute prohibition of a return to England. The consideration of climate imposed itself, and he was in no state to meet it alone. I took him to Meran and there spent the summer with him, trying to show him by example how to get back to work and nursing a rage of another sort that I tried not to show him.

The whole business proved the first of a series of phenomena so strangely combined that, taken together (which was how I had to take them) they form as good an illustration as I can recall of the manner in which, for the good of his soul doubtless, fate sometimes deals with a man's avidity. These incidents certainly had larger bearings than the comparatively meagre consequence we are here concerned with—though I feel that consequence also to be a thing to speak of with some respect. It's mainly in such a light, I confess, at any rate, that at this hour the ugly fruit of my exile is present to me. Even at first indeed the spirit in which my avidity, as I have called it, made me regard this term owed no element of ease to the fact that before coming back from Rapallo George Corvick addressed me in a way I didn't like. His letter had none of the sedative action that I must to day profess myself sure he had wished to give it, and the march of occurrences was not so ordered as to make up for what it lacked. He had begun on the spot, for one of the quarterlies, a great last word on Vereker's writings, and this exhaustive study, the only one that would have counted, have existed, was to turn on the new light, to utter—oh, so quietly!—the unimagined truth. It was in other words to trace the figure in the carpet through every convolution, to reproduce it in every tint. The result, said Corvick, was to be the greatest literary portrait ever painted, and what he asked of me was just to be so good as not to trouble him with questions till he should hang up his masterpiece before me. He did me the honour to declare that, putting aside the great sitter himself, all aloft in his indifference, I was individually the connoisseur he was most working for. I was therefore to be a good boy and not try to peep under the curtain before the show was ready: I should enjoy it all the more if I sat very still.

I did my best to sit very still, but I couldn't help giving a jump on seeing in *The Times*, after I had been a week or two in Munich and before, as I knew, Corvick had reached London, the announcement of the sudden death of poor Mrs. Erme. I instantly wrote to Gwendolen for particulars, and she replied that her mother had succumbed to long-threatened failure of the heart. She didn't say, but I took the liberty of reading into her words, that from the point of view of her marriage and also of her eagerness, which was quite a match for mine, this was a solution more prompt than could have been expected and more radical than waiting for the old lady to swallow the dose. I candidly admit indeed that at the time—for I heard from her repeatedly—I read some singular things into Gwendolen's words and some still more extraordinary ones into her silences. Pen in hand, this way, I live the time over, and it brings back the oddest sense of my having been for months and in spite of myself a kind of coerced spectator. All my life had taken refuge in my eyes, which the procession of events appeared to have committed itself to keep astare. There were days when I thought of writing to Hugh Vereker and simply throwing myself on his charity. But I felt more deeply that I hadn't fallen quite so low, besides which, quite properly, he would send me about my business. Mrs. Erme's death brought Corvick straight home, and within the month he was united "very quietly"—as quietly I suppose as he meant in his article to bring out his *trouvaille*—to the young lady he had loved and quitted. I use this last term, I may parenthetically say, because I subsequently grew sure that at the time he went to India, at the time of his great news from Bombay, there was no engagement whatever. There was none at the moment she affirmed the opposite. On the other hand he certainly became engaged the day he returned. The happy pair went down to Torquay for their honeymoon, and there, in a reckless hour, it occurred to poor Corvick to take his young bride out for a drive. He had no command of that business: this had been brought home to me of old in a little tour we had once made together in a dogcart. In a dogcart he perched his companion for a rattle over Devonshire hills, on one of the likeliest of which he brought his horse, who, it was true, had bolted, down with such violence that the occupants of the cart were hurled forward and that he fell horribly on his head. He was killed on the spot; Gwendolen escaped unhurt.

I pass rapidly over the question of this unmitigated tragedy, of what the loss of my best friend meant for me, and I complete my little history of my patience and my pain by the frank statement of my having, in a postscript to my very first letter to her after the receipt of the hideous news, asked Mrs. Corvick whether her husband had not at least finished the great article on Vereker. Her answer was as prompt as my inquiry: the article, which had been barely begun, was a mere heartbreaking scrap. She explained that Corvick had just settled down to it when he was interrupted by her mother's death; then, on his return, he had been kept from work by the engrossments into which that calamity plunged them. The opening pages were all that existed; they were striking, they were promising, but they didn't unveil the idol. That great intellectual feat was obviously to have formed his climax. She said nothing more, nothing to enlighten me as to the state of her own knowledge—the knowledge for the acquisition of which I had conceived her doing prodigious things. This was above all what I wanted to know: had *she* seen the idol unveiled? Had there been a private ceremony for a palpitating audience of one? For what else but that ceremony had the previous ceremony been enacted? I didn't like as yet to press her, though when I thought of what had passed between us on the subject in Corvick's absence her reticence surprised me. It was therefore not till much later, from Meran, that I risked another appeal, risked it in some trepidation, for she continued to tell me nothing. "Did you hear in those few days of your blighted bliss," I wrote, "what we desired so to hear?" I said, "we" as a little hint; and she showed me she could take a little hint. "I heard everything," she replied, "and I mean to keep it to myself!"

IX

It was impossible not to be moved with the strongest sympathy for her, and on my return to England I showed her every kindness in my power. Her mother's death had made her means sufficient, and she had gone to live in a more convenient quarter. But her loss had been great and her visitation cruel; it never would have occurred to me moreover to suppose she could come to regard the enjoyment of a technical tip, of a piece of literary experience, as a counterpoise to her grief. Strange to say, none the less, I couldn't help fancying after I had seen her a few times that I caught a glimpse of some such oddity. I hasten to add that there had been other things I couldn't help fancying; and as I never felt I was really clear about these, so, as to the point I here touch on, I give her memory the benefit of every doubt. Stricken and solitary, highly accomplished and now, in her deep mourning, her maturer grace and her uncomplaining sorrow incontestably handsome, she presented herself as leading a life of singular dignity and beauty. I had at first found a way to believe that I should soon get the better of the reserve formulated the week after the catastrophe in her reply to an appeal as to which I was not unconscious that it might strike her as mistimed. Certainly that reserve was something of a shock to me—certainly it puzzled me the more I thought of it, though I tried to explain it, with moments of success, by the supposition of exalted sentiments, of superstitious scruples, of a refinement of loyalty. Certainly it added at the same time hugely to the price of Vereker's secret, precious as that mystery already appeared. I may as well confess abjectly that Mrs. Corvick's unexpected attitude was the final tap on the nail that was to fix, as they say, my luckless idea, convert it into the obsession of which I am for ever conscious.

But this only helped me the more to be artful, to be adroit, to allow time to elapse before renewing my suit. There were plenty of speculations for the interval, and one of them was deeply absorbing. Corvick had kept his information from his young friend till after the removal of the last barriers to their intimacy; then he had let the cat out of the bag. Was it Gwendolen's idea, taking a hint from him, to liberate this animal

only on the basis of the renewal of such a relation? Was the
figure in the carpet traceable or describable only for husbands
and wives—for lovers supremely united? It came back to me
in a mystifying manner that in Kensington Square, when I told
him that Corvick would have told the girl he loved, some
word had dropped from Vereker that gave colour to this possibility. There might be little in it, but there was enough to
make me wonder if I should have to marry Mrs. Corvick to
get what I wanted. Was I prepared to offer her this price for
the blessing of her knowledge? Ah! that way madness lay—so
I said to myself at least in bewildered hours. I could see meanwhile the torch she refused to pass on flame away in her chamber of memory—pour through her eyes a light that made a
glow in her lonely house. At the end of six months I was fully
sure of what this warm presence made up to her for. We had
talked again and again of the man who had brought us together, of his talent, his character, his personal charm, his certain career, his dreadful doom, and even of his clear purpose
in that great study which was to have been a supreme literary
portrait, a kind of critical Vandyke or Velasquez. She had conveyed to me in abundance that she was tongue-tied by her
perversity, by her piety, that she would never break the silence
it had not been given to the "right person," as she said, to
break. The hour however finally arrived. One evening when I
had been sitting with her longer than usual I laid my hand
firmly on her arm.

"Now, at last, what *is* it?"

She had been expecting me; she was ready. She gave a long,
slow, soundless headshake, merciful only in being inarticulate.
This mercy didn't prevent its hurling at me the largest, finest,
coldest "Never!" I had yet, in the course of a life that had
known denials, had to take full in the face. I took it and was
aware that with the hard blow the tears had come into my
eyes. So for a while we sat and looked at each other; after
which I slowly rose. I was wondering if some day she would
accept me; but this was not what I brought out. I said as I
smoothed down my hat: "I know what to think then; it's
nothing!"

A remote, disdainful pity for me shone out of her dim smile;
then she exclaimed in a voice that I hear at this moment: "It's

my *life*!" As I stood at the door she added: "You've insulted him!"

"Do you mean Vereker?"

"I mean—the Dead!"

I recognised when I reached the street the justice of her charge. Yes, it was her life—I recognised that too; but her life none the less made room with the lapse of time for another interest. A year and a half after Corvick's death she published in a single volume her second novel, "Overmastered," which I pounced on in the hope of finding in it some tell-tale echo or some peeping face. All I found was a much better book than her younger performance, showing I thought the better company she had kept. As a tissue tolerably intricate it was a carpet with a figure of its own; but the figure was not the figure I was looking for. On sending a review of it to *The Middle* I was surprised to learn from the office that a notice was already in type. When the paper came out I had no hesitation in attributing this article, which I thought rather vulgarly overdone, to Drayton Deane, who in the old days had been something of a friend of Corvick's, yet had only within a few weeks made the acquaintance of his widow. I had had an early copy of the book, but Deane had evidently had an earlier. He lacked all the same the light hand with which Corvick had gilded the gingerbread—he laid on the tinsel in splotches.

X

Six months later appeared "The Right of Way," the last chance, though we didn't know it, that we were to have to redeem ourselves. Written wholly during Vereker's absence, the book had been heralded, in a hundred paragraphs, by the usual ineptitudes. I carried it, as early a copy as any, I this time flattered myself, straightway to Mrs. Corvick. This was the only use I had for it; I left the inevitable tribute of *The Middle* to some more ingenious mind and some less irritated temper. "But I already have it," Gwendolen said. "Drayton Deane was so good as to bring it to me yesterday, and I've just finished it."

"Yesterday? How did he get it so soon?"

"He gets everything soon. He's to review it in *The Middle*."

"He—Drayton Deane—review Vereker?" I couldn't believe my ears.

"Why not? One fine ignorance is as good as another."

I winced, but I presently said: "You ought to review him yourself!"

"I don't 'review,' " she laughed. "I'm reviewed!"

Just then the door was thrown open. "Ah yes, here's your reviewer!" Drayton Deane was there with his long legs and his tall forehead: he had come to see what she thought of "The Right of Way," and to bring news which was singularly relevant. The evening papers were just out with a telegram on the author of that work, who, in Rome, had been ill for some days with an attack of malarial fever. It had at first not been thought grave, but had taken in consequence of complications a turn that might give rise to anxiety. Anxiety had indeed at the latest hour begun to be felt.

I was struck in the presence of these tidings with the fundamental detachment that Mrs. Corvick's public regret quite failed to conceal: it gave me the measure of her consummate independence. That independence rested on her knowledge, the knowledge which nothing now could destroy and which nothing could make different. The figure in the carpet might take on another twist or two, but the sentence had virtually been written. The writer might go down to his grave: she was the person in the world to whom—as if she had been his favoured heir—his continued existence was least of a need. This reminded me how I had observed at a particular moment—after Corvick's death—the drop of her desire to see him face to face. She had got what she wanted without that. I had been sure that if she hadn't got it she wouldn't have been restrained from the endeavour to sound him personally by those superior reflections, more conceivable on a man's part than on a woman's, which in my case had served as a deterrent. It wasn't however, I hasten to add, that my case, in spite of this invidious comparison, wasn't ambiguous enough. At the thought that Vereker was perhaps at that moment dying there rolled over me a wave of anguish—a poignant sense of how inconsistently I still depended on him. A delicacy that it was my one compensation to suffer to rule me had left the Alps and the Apennines between us, but the vision of the waning opportunity made me feel as if I might in my despair at last have gone to him. Of course I would really have done nothing of the sort. I remained five minutes, while my companions talked of the new book, and when Drayton Deane appealed to me for my opinion of it I replied, getting up, that I detested Hugh Vereker—simply couldn't read him. I went away with the moral certainty that as the door closed behind me Deane would remark that I was awfully superficial. His hostess wouldn't contradict him.

I continue to trace with a briefer touch our intensely odd concatenation. Three weeks after this came Vereker's death, and before the year was out the death of his wife. That poor lady I had never seen, but I had had a futile theory that, should she survive him long enough to be decorously accessible, I might approach her with the feeble flicker of my petition. Did she know and if she knew would she speak? It was much to be presumed that for more reasons than one she would have nothing to say; but when she passed out of all reach I felt that renouncement was indeed my appointed lot. I was shut up in my obsession for ever—my gaolers had gone off with the key. I find myself quite as vague as a captive in a dungeon about the time that further elapsed before Mrs. Corvick became the wife of Drayton Deane. I had foreseen, through my bars, this end of the business, though there was no indecent haste and our friendship had rather fallen off. They were both so "awfully intellectual" that it struck people as a suitable match, but I knew better than any one the wealth of understanding the bride would contribute to the partnership. Never, for a marriage in literary circles—so the newspapers described the alliance—had a bride been so handsomely dowered. I began with due promptness to look for the fruit of their union—that fruit, I mean, of which the premonitory symptoms would be peculiarly visible in the husband. Taking for granted the splendour of the lady's nuptial gift, I expected to see him make a show commensurate with his increase of means. I knew what his means had been—his article on "The Right of Way" had distinctly given one the figure. As he was now exactly in the position in which still more exactly I was not I watched from month to month, in the likely periodicals, for the heavy mes-

sage poor Corvick had been unable to deliver and the responsibility of which would have fallen on his successor. The widow
and wife would have broken by the rekindled hearth the silence
that only a widow and wife might break, and Deane would be
as aflame with the knowledge as Corvick in his own hour, as
Gwendolen in hers had been. Well, he was aflame doubtless,
but the fire was apparently not to become a public blaze. I
scanned the periodicals in vain: Drayton Deane filled them with
exuberant pages, but he withheld the page I most feverishly
sought. He wrote on a thousand subjects, but never on the
subject of Vereker. His special line was to tell truths that other
people either "funked," as he said, or overlooked, but he
never told the only truth that seemed to me in these days to
signify. I met the couple in those literary circles referred to in
the papers: I have sufficiently intimated that it was only in
such circles we were all constructed to revolve. Gwendolen was
more than ever committed to them by the publication of her
third novel, and I myself definitely classed by holding the opinion that this work was inferior to its immediate predecessor.
Was it worse because she had been keeping worse company?
If her secret was, as she had told me, her life—a fact discernible in her increasing bloom, an air of conscious privilege that,
cleverly corrected by pretty charities, gave distinction to her
appearance—it had yet not a direct influence on her work.
That only made—everything only made—one yearn the more
for it, rounded it off with a mystery finer and subtler.

XI

It was therefore from her husband I could never remove my
eyes: I hovered about him in a manner that might have made
him uneasy. I went even so far as to engage him in conversation. *Didn't* he know, hadn't he come into it as a matter of
course?—that question hummed in my brain. Of course he
knew; otherwise he wouldn't return my stare so queerly. His
wife had told him what I wanted, and he was amiably amused
at my impotence. He didn't laugh—he was not a laugher: his
system was to present to my irritation, so that I should crudely
expose myself, a conversational blank as vast as his big bare
brow. It always happened that I turned away with a settled

conviction from these unpeopled expanses, which seemed to complete each other geographically and to symbolise together Drayton Deane's want of voice, want of form. He simply hadn't the art to use what he knew; he literally was incompetent to take up the duty where Corvick had left it. I went still further—it was the only glimpse of happiness I had. I made up my mind that the duty didn't appeal to him. He wasn't interested, he didn't care. Yes, it quite comforted me to believe him too stupid to have joy of the thing I lacked. He was as stupid after as before, and that deepened for me the golden glory in which the mystery was wrapped. I had of course however to recollect that his wife might have imposed her conditions and exactions. I had above all to recollect that with Vereker's death the major incentive dropped. He was still there to be honoured by what might be done—he was no longer there to give it his sanction. Who, alas, but he had the authority?

Two children were born to the pair, but the second cost the mother her life. After this calamity I seemed to see another ghost of a chance. I jumped at it in thought, but I waited a certain time for manners, and at last my opportunity arrived in a remunerative way. His wife had been dead a year when I met Drayton Deane in the smoking-room of a small club of which we both were members, but where for months—perhaps because I rarely entered it—I had not seen him. The room was empty and the occasion propitious. I deliberately offered him, to have done with the matter for ever, that advantage for which I felt he had long been looking.

"As an older acquaintance of your late wife's than even you were," I began, "you must let me say to you something I have on my mind. I shall be glad to make any terms with you that you see fit to name for the information she had from George Corvick—the information, you know, that he, poor fellow, in one of the happiest hours of his life, had straight from Hugh Vereker."

He looked at me like a dim phrenological bust. "The information——?"

"Vereker's secret, my dear man—the general intention of his books: the string the pearls were strung on, the buried treasure, the figure in the carpet."

He began to flush—the numbers on his bumps to come out. "Vereker's books had a general intention?"

I stared in my turn. "You don't mean to say you don't know it?" I thought for a moment he was playing with me. "Mrs. Deane knew it; she had it, as I say, straight from Corvick, who had, after infinite search and to Vereker's own delight, found the very mouth of the cave. Where *is* the mouth? He told after their marriage—and told alone—the person who, when the circumstances were reproduced, must have told you. Have I been wrong in taking for granted that she admitted you, as one of the highest privileges of the relation in which you stood to her, to the knowledge of which she was after Corvick's death the sole depositary? All *I* know is that that knowledge is infinitely precious, and what I want you to understand is that if you will in your turn admit *me* to it you will do me a kindness for which I shall be everlastingly grateful."

He had turned at last very red; I daresay he had begun by thinking I had lost my wits. Little by little he followed me; on my own side I stared with a livelier surprise. "I don't know what you're talking about," he said.

He wasn't acting—it was the absurd truth. "She *didn't* tell you——?"

"Nothing about Hugh Vereker."

I was stupefied; the room went round. It had been too good even for that! "Upon your honour?"

"Upon my honour. What the devil's the matter with you?" he demanded.

"I'm astounded—I'm disappointed. I wanted to get it out of you."

"It isn't *in* me!" he awkwardly laughed. "And even if it were——"

"If it were you'd let me have it—oh yes, in common humanity. But I believe you. I see—I see!" I went on, conscious, with the full turn of the wheel, of my great delusion, my false view of the poor man's attitude. What I saw, though I couldn't say it, was that his wife hadn't thought him worth enlightening. This struck me as strange for a woman who had thought him worth marrying. At last I explained it by the reflection that she couldn't possibly have married him for his understanding. She had married him for something else. He was to some extent enlightened now, but he was even more astonished, more disconcerted: he took a moment to compare my story with his quickened memories. The result of his meditation was his presently saying with a good deal of rather feeble form:

"This is the first I hear of what you allude to. I think you must be mistaken as to Mrs. Drayton Deane's having had any unmentioned, and still less any unmentionable, knowledge about Hugh Vereker. She would certainly have wished it—if it bore on his literary character—to be used."

"It *was* used. She used it herself. She told me with her own lips that she 'lived' on it."

I had no sooner spoken than I repented of my words; he grew so pale that I felt as if I had struck him. "Ah, 'lived'——!" he murmured, turning short away from me.

My compunction was real; I laid my hand on his shoulder. "I beg you to forgive me—I've made a mistake. You *don't* know what I thought you knew. You could, if I had been right, have rendered me a service; and I had my reasons for assuming that you would be in a position to meet me."

"Your reasons?" he asked. "What were your reasons?"

I looked at him well; I hesitated; I considered. "Come and sit down with me here, and I'll tell you." I drew him to a sofa, I lighted another cigarette and, beginning with the anecdote of Vereker's one descent from the clouds, I gave him an account of the extraordinary chain of accidents that had in spite of it kept me till that hour in the dark. I told him in a word just what I've written out here. He listened with deepening attention, and I became aware, to my surprise, by his ejaculations, by his questions, that he would have been after all not unworthy to have been trusted by his wife. So abrupt an experience of her want of trust had an agitating effect on him, but I saw that immediate shock throb away little by little and then gather again into waves of wonder and curiosity— waves that promised, I could perfectly judge, to break in the end with the fury of my own highest tides. I may say that to-day as victims of unappeased desire there isn't a pin to choose between us. The poor man's state is almost my consolation; there are indeed moments when I feel it to be almost my revenge.

The Way It Came

I FIND, as you prophesied, much that's interesting, but little that helps the delicate question—the possibility of publication. Her diaries are less systematic than I hoped; she only had a blessed habit of noting and narrating. She summarised, she saved; she appears seldom indeed to have let a good story pass without catching it on the wing. I allude of course not so much to things she heard as to things she saw and felt. She writes sometimes of herself, sometimes of others, sometimes of the combination. It's under this last rubric that she's usually most vivid. But it's not, you will understand, when she's most vivid that she's always most publishable. To tell the truth she's fearfully indiscreet, or has at least all the material for making *me* so. Take as an instance the fragment I send you, after dividing it for your convenience into several small chapters. It is the contents of a thin blank-book which I have had copied out and which has the merit of being nearly enough a rounded thing, an intelligible whole. These pages evidently date from years ago. I've read with the liveliest wonder the statement they so circumstantially make and done my best to swallow the prodigy they leave to be inferred. These things would be striking, wouldn't they? to any reader; but can you imagine for a moment my placing such a document before the world, even though, as if she herself had desired the world should have the benefit of it, she has given her friends neither name nor initials? Have you any sort of clue to their identity? I leave her the floor.

I

I know perfectly of course that I brought it upon myself; but that doesn't make it any better. I was the first to speak of her to him—he had never even heard her mentioned. Even if I had happened not to speak some one else would have made up for it: I tried afterwards to find comfort in that reflection. But the comfort of reflections is thin: the only comfort that counts in life is not to have been a fool. That's a beatitude I shall doubtless never enjoy. "Why, you ought to meet her and talk it over," is what I immediately said. "Birds of a feather flock together." I told him who she was and that they were birds of a feather because if he had had in youth a strange adventure she had had about the same time just such another. It was well known to her friends—an incident she was constantly called on to describe. She was charming, clever, pretty, unhappy; but it was none the less the thing to which she had originally owed her reputation.

Being at the age of eighteen somewhere abroad with an aunt she had had a vision of one of her parents at the moment of death. The parent was in England, hundreds of miles away and so far as she knew neither dying nor dead. It was by day, in the museum of some great foreign town. She had passed alone, in advance of her companions, into a small room containing some famous work of art and occupied at that moment by two other persons. One of these was an old custodian; the second, before observing him, she took for a stranger, a tourist. She was merely conscious that he was bareheaded and seated on a bench. The instant her eyes rested on him however she beheld to her amazement her father, who, as if he had long waited for her, looked at her in singular distress, with an impatience that was akin to reproach. She rushed to him with a bewildered cry, "Papa, what *is* it?" but this was followed by an exhibition of still livelier feeling when on her movement he simply vanished, leaving the custodian and her relations, who were at her heels, to gather round her in dismay. These persons, the official, the aunt, the cousins were therefore in a manner witnesses of the fact—the fact at least of the impression made on her; and there was the further testimony of a doctor who was attending one of the party and to whom it was immediately afterwards communicated. He gave her a remedy for hysterics but said to the aunt privately: "Wait and see if something doesn't happen at home." Something *had* happened—the poor father, suddenly and violently seized, had died that morning. The aunt, the mother's sister, received before the day was out a telegram announcing the event and requesting her to prepare her niece for it. Her niece was already prepared, and the girl's sense of this visitation remained of course indelible. We had all as her friends had it conveyed to us and had conveyed it creepily to each other. Twelve years had elapsed and as a woman who had made an unhappy marriage and lived apart from her husband she had become interesting from other sources; but since the name she now bore was a name frequently borne, and since moreover her judicial separation, as things were going, could hardly count as a distinction, it was usual to qualify her as "the one, you know, who saw her father's ghost."

As for him, dear man, he had seen his mother's. I had never heard of that till this occasion on which our closer, our pleasanter acquaintance led him, through some turn of the subject of our talk, to mention it and to inspire me in so doing with the impulse to let him know that he had a rival in the field—a person with whom he could compare notes. Later on his story became for him, perhaps because of my unduly repeating it, likewise a convenient worldly label; but it had not a year before been the ground on which he was introduced to me. He had other merits, just as she, poor thing! had others. I can honestly say that I was quite aware of them from the first—I discovered them sooner than he discovered mine. I remember how it struck me even at the time that his sense of mine was quickened by my having been able to match, though not in deed straight from my own experience, his curious anecdote. It dated, this anecdote, as hers did, from some dozen years before—a year in which, at Oxford, he had for some reason of his own been staying on into the "Long." He had been in the August afternoon on the river. Coming back into his room while it was still distinct daylight he found his mother standing there as if her eyes had been fixed on the door. He had had a letter from her that morning out of Wales, where she was staying with her father. At the sight of him she smiled with extraordinary radiance and extended her arms to him, and then as he sprang forward and joyfully opened his own she vanished from the place. He wrote to her that night, telling her what had happened; the letter had been carefully preserved. The next morning he heard of her death. He was through this chance of our talk extremely struck with the little prodigy I was able to produce for him. He had never encountered another case. Certainly they ought to meet, my friend and he; certainly they would have something in com-

mon. I would arrange this, wouldn't I?—if *she* didn't mind;
for himself he didn't mind in the least. I had promised to
speak to her of the matter as soon as possible, and within the
week I was able to do so. She "minded" as little as he; she
was perfectly willing to see him. And yet no meeting was to
occur—as meetings are commonly understood.

II

That's just half my tale—the extraordinary way it was hindered. This was the fault of a series of accidents; but the accidents continued for years and became, for me and for others,
a subject of hilarity with either party. They were droll enough
at first; then they grew rather a bore. The odd thing was that
both parties were amenable: it wasn't a case of their being
indifferent, much less of their being indisposed. It was one of
the caprices of chance, aided I suppose by some opposition of
their interests and habits. His were centred in his office, his
eternal inspectorship, which left him small leisure, constantly
calling him away and making him break engagements. He
liked society, but he found it everywhere and took it at a run.
I never knew at a given moment where he was, and there were
times when for months together I never saw him. She was on
her side practically suburban: she lived at Richmond and never
went "out." She was a woman of distinction, but not of fashion, and felt, as people said, her situation. Decidedly proud
and rather whimsical she lived her life as she had planned it.
There were things one could do with her, but one couldn't
make her come to one's parties. One went indeed a little more
than seemed quite convenient to hers, which consisted of her
cousin, a cup of tea and the view. The tea was good; but the
view was familiar, though perhaps not, like the cousin—a disagreeable old maid who had been of the group at the museum
and with whom she now lived—offensively so. This connection with an inferior relative, which had partly an economical
motive—she proclaimed her companion a marvellous manager—was one of the little perversities we had to forgive her.
Another was her estimate of the proprieties created by her
rupture with her husband. That was extreme—many persons
called it even morbid. She made no advances; she cultivated

scruples; she suspected, or I should perhaps rather say she remembered slights: she was one of the few women I have known whom that particular predicament had rendered modest rather than bold. Dear thing! she had some delicacy. Especially marked were the limits she had set to possible attentions from men: it was always her thought that her husband was waiting to pounce on her. She discouraged if she didn't forbid the visits of male persons not senile: she said she could never be too careful.

When I first mentioned to her that I had a friend whom fate had distinguished in the same weird way as herself I put her quite a liberty to say "Oh, bring him out to see me!" I should probably have been able to bring him, and a situation perfectly innocent or at any rate comparatively simple would have been created. But she uttered no such word; she only said: "I must meet him certainly; yes, I shall look out for him!" That caused the first delay, and meanwhile various things happened. One of them was that as time went on she made, charming as she was, more and more friends, and that it regularly befell that these friends were sufficiently also friends of his to bring him up in conversation. It was odd that without belonging, as it were, to the same world or, according to the horrid term, the same set, my baffled pair should have happened in so many cases to fall in with the same people and make them join in the funny chorus. She had friends who didn't know each other but who inevitably and punctually recommended *him*. She had also the sort of originality, the intrinsic interest that led her to be kept by each of us as a kind of private resource, cultivated jealously, more or less in secret, as a person whom one didn't meet in society, whom it was not for every one—whom it was not for the vulgar—to approach, and with whom therefore acquaintance was particularly difficult and particularly precious We saw her separately, with appointments and conditions, and found it made on the whole for harmony not to tell each other. Somebody had always had a note from her still later than somebody else. There was some silly woman who for a long time, among the unprivileged, owed to three simple visits to Richmond a reputation for being intimate with "lots of awfully clever out-of-the-way people."

Every one has had friends it has seemed a happy thought to bring together, and every one remembers that his happiest thoughts have not been his greatest successes; but I doubt if there was ever a case in which the failure was in such direct proportion to the quantity of influence set in motion. It is really perhaps here the quantity of influence that was most remarkable. My lady and gentleman each declared to me and others that it was like the subject of a roaring farce. The reason first given had with time dropped out of sight and fifty better ones flourished on top of it. They were so awfully alike: they had the same ideas and tricks and tastes, the same prejudices and superstitions and heresies; they said the same things and sometimes did them; they liked and disliked the same persons and places, the same books, authors and styles; any one could see a certain identity even in their looks and their features. It established much of a propriety that they were in common parlance equally "nice" and almost equally handsome. But the great sameness, for wonder and chatter, was their rare per-versity in regard to being photographed. They were the only persons ever heard of who had never been "taken" and who had a passionate objection to it. They just *wouldn't* be, for anything any one could say. I had loudly complained of this; him in particular I had so vainly desired to be able to show on my drawing-room chimney-piece in a Bond Street frame. It was at any rate the very liveliest of all the reasons why they ought to know each other—all the lively reasons reduced to naught by the strange law that had made them bang so many doors in each other's face, made them the buckets in the well, the two ends of the see-saw, the two parties in the state, so that when one was up the other was down, when one was out the other was in; neither by any possibility entering a house till the other had left it, or leaving it, all unawares, till the other was at hand. They only arrived when they had been given up, which was precisely also when they departed. They were in a word alternate and incompatible; they missed each other with an inveteracy that could be explained only by its being preconcerted. It was however so far from preconcerted that it had ended—literally after several years—by disappoint-ing and annoying them. I don't think their curiosity was lively till it had been proved utterly vain. A great deal was of course done to help them, but it merely laid wires for them to trip. To give examples I should have to have taken notes; but I happen to remember that neither had ever been able to dine on the right occasion. The right occasion for each was the occasion that would be wrong for the other. On the wrong one they were most punctual, and there were never any but wrong ones. The very elements conspired and the constitution of man reinforced them. A cold, a headache, a bereavement, a storm, a fog, an earthquake, a cataclysm infallibly intervened. The whole business was beyond a joke.

Yet as a joke it had still to be taken, though one couldn't help feeling that the joke had made the situation serious, had produced on the part of each a consciousness, an awkwardness, a positive dread of the last accident of all, the only one with any freshness left, the accident that would bring them face to face. The final effect of its predecessors had been to kindle this instinct. They were quite ashamed—perhaps even a little of each other. So much preparation, so much frustration: what indeed could be good enough for it all to lead up to? A mere meeting would be mere flatness. Did I see them at the end of years, they often asked, just stupidly confronted? If they were bored by the joke they might be worse bored by something else. They made exactly the same reflections, and each in some manner was sure to hear of the other's. I really think it was this peculiar diffidence that finally controlled the situation. I mean that if they had failed for the first year or two because they couldn't help it they kept up the habit because they had—what shall I call it?—grown nervous. It really took some lurking volition to account for anything so absurd.

III

When to crown our long acquaintance I accepted his renewed offer of marriage it was humorously said, I know, that I had made the gift of his photograph a condition. This was so far true that I had refused to give him mine without it. At any rate I had him at last, in his high distinction, on the chimney-piece, where the day she called to congratulate me she came nearer than she had ever done to seeing him. He had set her in being taken an example which I invited her to follow; he had sacrificed his perversity—wouldn't she sacrifice hers? She too must give me something on my engagement—wouldn't she give me the companion-piece? She laughed and shook her head; she had headshakes whose impulse seemed to come from as far away as the breeze that stirs a flower. The companion-piece to the portrait of my future husband was the portrait of his future wife. She had taken her stand—she could depart from it as little as she could explain it. It was a prejudice, an *entêtement*, a vow—she would live and die unphotographed. Now too she was alone in that state: this was what she liked; it made her so much more original. She rejoiced in the fall of her late associate and looked a long time at his picture, about which she made no memorable remark, though she even turned it over to see the back. About our engagement she was charming—full of cordiality and sympathy. "You've known him even longer than I've *not*," she said, "and that seems a very long time." She understood how we had jogged together over hill and dale and how inevitable it was that we should now rest together. I'm definite about all this because what followed is so strange that it's a kind of relief to me to mark the point up to which our relations were as natural as ever. It was I myself who in a sudden madness altered and destroyed them. I see now that she gave me no pretext and that I only found one in the way she looked at the fine face in the Bond Street frame. How then would I have had her look at it? What I had wanted from the first was to make her care for him. Well, that was what I still wanted— up to the moment of her having promised me that he would on this occasion really aid me to break the silly spell that had kept them asunder. I had arranged with him to do his part if she would as triumphantly do hers. I was on a different footing now—I was on a footing to answer for him. I would positively engage that at five on the following Saturday he would be on that spot. He was out of town on pressing business; but pledged to keep his promise to the letter he would return on purpose and in abundant time. "Are you perfectly sure?" I remember she asked, looking grave and considering: I thought she had turned a little pale. She was tired, she was indisposed: it was a pity he was to see her after all at so poor a moment. If he only *could* have seen her five years before!

However, I replied that this time I was sure and that success therefore depended simply on herself. At five o'clock on the Saturday she would find him in a particular chair I pointed out, the one in which he usually sat and in which—though this I didn't mention—he had been sitting when, the week before, he put the question of our future to me in the way that had brought me round. She looked at it in silence, just as she had looked at the photograph, while I repeated for the twentieth time that it was too preposterous it shouldn't somehow be feasible to introduce to one's dearest friend one's second self. "*Am* I your dearest friend?" she asked with a smile that for a moment brought back her beauty. I replied by pressing her to my bosom; after which she said: "Well, I'll come. I'm extraordinarily afraid, but you may count on me."

When she had left me I began to wonder what she was afraid of, for she had spoken as if she fully meant it. The next day, late in the afternoon, I had three lines from her: she had found on getting home the announcement of her husband's death. She had not seen him for seven years, but she wished me to know it in this way before I should hear of it in another. It made however in her life, strange and sad to say, so little difference that she would scrupulously keep her appointment. I rejoiced for her—I supposed it would make at least the difference of her having more money; but even in this diversion, far from forgetting that she had said she was afraid, I seemed to catch sight of a reason for her being so. Her fear as the evening went on became contagious, and the contagion took in my breast the form of a sudden panic. It wasn't jealousy—it was the dread of jealousy. I called myself a fool for not having been quiet till we were man and wife. After that I should somehow feel secure. It was only a question of waiting another month—a trifle surely for people who had waited so long. It had been plain enough she was nervous, and now that she was free she naturally wouldn't be less so. What was her nervousness therefore but a presentiment? She had been hitherto the victim of interference, but it was quite possible she would henceforth be the source of it. The victim in that case would be my simple self. What had the interference been but the finger of providence pointing out a danger? The danger was of course for poor *me*. It had been kept at bay by

THE WAY IT CAME

a series of accidents unexampled in their frequency; but the reign of accident was now visibly at an end. I had an intimate conviction that both parties would keep the tryst. It was more and more impressed upon me that they were approaching, converging. We had talked about breaking the spell; well, it would be effectually broken—unless indeed it should merely take another form and overdo their encounters as it had overdone their escapes. This was something I couldn't sit still for thinking of; it kept me awake—at midnight I was full of unrest. At last I felt there was only one way of laying the ghost. If the reign of accident was over I must just take up the succession. I sat down and wrote a hurried note which would meet him on his return and which as the servants had gone to bed I sallied forth bare-headed into the empty, gusty street to drop into the nearest pillar-box. It was to tell him that I shouldn't be able to be at home in the afternoon as I had hoped and that he must postpone his visit till dinner-time. This was an implication that he would find me alone.

IV

When accordingly at five she presented herself I naturally felt false and base. My act had been a momentary madness, but I had at least to be consistent. She remained an hour; he of course never came; and I could only persist in my perfidy. I had thought it best to let her come; singular as this now seems to me I thought it diminished my guilt. Yet as she sat there so visibly white and weary, stricken with a sense of everything her husband's death had opened up, I felt an almost intolerable pang of pity and remorse. If I didn't tell her on the spot what I had done it was because I was too ashamed. I feigned astonishment—I feigned it to the end; I protested that if ever I had had confidence I had had it that day. I blush as I tell my story—I take it as my penance. There was nothing indignant I didn't say about him; I invented suppositions, attenuations; I admitted in stupefaction, as the hands of the clock travelled, that their luck hadn't turned. She smiled at this vision of their "luck," but she looked anxious—she looked unusual: the only thing that kept me up was the fact that, oddly enough, she wore mourning—no great depths of crape, but simple and scrupulous black. She had in her bonnet three small black feathers. She carried a little muff of astrachan. This put me by the aid of some acute reflection a little in the right. She had written to me that the sudden event made no difference for her, but apparently it made as much difference as that. If she was inclined to the usual forms why didn't she observe that of not going the first day or two out to tea? There was some one she wanted so much to see that she couldn't wait till her husband was buried. Such a betrayal of eagerness made me hard and cruel enough to practise my odious deceit, though at the same time, as the hour waxed and waned, I suspected in her something deeper still than disappointment and somewhat less successfully concealed. I mean a strange underlying relief, the soft, low emission of the breath that comes when a danger is past. What happened as she spent her barren hour with me was that at last she gave him up. She let him go for ever. She made the most graceful joke of it that I've ever seen made of anything; but it was for all that a great date in her life. She spoke with her mild gaiety of all the other vain times, the long game of hide-and-seek, the unprecedented queerness of such a relation. For it *was*, or had been, a relation, wasn't it, hadn't it? That was just the absurd part of it. When she got up to go I said to her that it was more a relation than ever, but that I hadn't the face after what had occurred to propose to her for the present another opportunity. It was plain that the only valid opportunity would be my accomplished marriage. Of course she would be at my wedding? It was even to be hoped that *he* would.

"If *I* am, he won't be!" she declared with a laugh. I admitted there might be something in that. The thing was therefore to get us safely married first. "That won't help us. Nothing will help us!" she said as she kissed me farewell. "I shall never, never see him!" It was with those words she left me.

I could bear her disappointment as I've called it; but when a couple of hours later I received him at dinner I found that I couldn't bear his. The way my manœuvre might have affected him had not been particularly present to me; but the result of it was the first word of reproach that had ever yet dropped from him. I say "reproach" because that expression is scarcely too strong for the terms in which he conveyed to me his surprise that under the extraordinary circumstances I should not have found some means not to deprive him of such an occasion. I might really have managed either not to be obliged to go out or to let their meeting take place all the same. They would probably have got on in my drawing-room without me. At this I quite broke down—I confessed my iniquity and the miserable reason of it. I had not put her off and I had not gone out; she had been there and after waiting for him an hour had departed in the belief that he had been absent by his own fault.

"She must think me a precious brute!" he exclaimed. "Did she say of me—what she had a right to say?"

"I assure you she said nothing that showed the least feeling. She looked at your photograph, she even turned round the back of it, on which your address happens to be inscribed. Yet it provoked her to no demonstration. She doesn't care so much as all that."

"Then why are you afraid of her?"

"It was not of her I was afraid. It was of you."

"Did you think I would fall in love with her? You never alluded to such a possibility before," he went on as I remained silent. "Admirable person as you pronounced her, that wasn't the light in which you showed her to me."

"Do you mean that if it *had* been you would have managed by this time to catch a glimpse of her? I didn't fear things then," I added. "I hadn't the same reason."

He kissed me at this, and when I remembered that she had done so an hour or two before I felt for an instant as if he were taking from my lips the very pressure of hers. In spite of kisses the incident had shed a certain chill, and I suffered horribly from the sense that he had seen me guilty of a fraud. He had seen it only through my frank avowal, but I was as unhappy as if I had a stain to efface. I couldn't get over the manner of his looking at me when I spoke of her apparent indifference to his not having come. For the first time since I had known him he seemed to have expressed a doubt of my word. Before we parted I told him that I would undeceive her, start the first thing in the morning for Richmond and there let her know that he had been blameless. At this he kissed me again. I would expiate my sin, I said; I would humble myself in the dust; I would confess and ask to be forgiven. At this he kissed me once more.

V

In the train the next day this struck me as a good deal for him to have consented to; but my purpose was firm enough to carry me on. I mounted the long hill to where the view begins, and then I knocked at her door. I was a trifle mystified by the fact that her blinds were still drawn, reflecting that if in the stress of my compunction I had come early I had certainly yet allowed people time to get up.

"At home, mum? She has left home for ever."

I was extraordinarily startled by this announcement of the elderly parlour-maid. "She has gone away?"

"She's dead, mum, please." Then as I gasped at the horrible word: "She died last night."

The loud cry that escaped me sounded even in my own ears like some harsh violation of the hour. I felt for the moment as if I had killed her; I turned faint and saw through a vagueness the woman hold out her arms to me. Of what next happened I have no recollection, nor of anything but my friend's poor stupid cousin, in a darkened room, after an interval that I suppose very brief, sobbing at me in a smothered accusatory way. I can't say how long it took me to understand, to believe and then to press back with an immense effort that pang of responsibility which, superstitiously, insanely, had been at first almost all I was conscious of. The doctor, after the fact, had been superlatively wise and clear: he was satisfied of a long-latent weakness of the heart, determined probably years before by the agitations and terrors to which her marriage had introduced her. She had had in those days cruel scenes with her husband, she had been in fear of her life. All emotion, everything in the nature of anxiety and suspense had been after that to be strongly deprecated, as in her marked cultivation of a quiet life she was evidently well aware; but who could say that any one, especially a "real lady," could be successfully protected from every little rub? She had had one a day or two before in the news of her husband's death; for there were shocks of all kinds, not only those of grief and surprise. For that matter she had never dreamed of so near a release: it had looked uncommonly as if he would live as long as herself. Then in the evening, in town, she had manifestly had another: something must have happened there which it would be indispensable to clear up. She had come back very late—it was past eleven o'clock, and on being met in the hall by her cousin, who was extremely anxious, had said that she was tired and must rest a moment before mounting the stairs. They had passed together into the dining-room, her companion proposing a glass of wine and bustling to the sideboard to pour it out. This took but a moment, and when my informant turned round our poor friend had not had time to seat herself. Suddenly, with a little moan that was barely audible, she dropped upon the sofa. She was dead. What unknown "little rub" had dealt her the blow? What shock, in the name of wonder, *had* she had in town? I mentioned immediately the only one I could imagine—her having failed to meet at my house, to which by invitation for the purpose she had come at five o'clock, the gentleman I was to be married to, who had been accidentally kept away and with whom she had no acquaintance whatever. This obviously counted for little; but something else might easily have occurred: nothing in the London streets was more possible than an accident, especially an accident in those desperate cabs. What had she done, where had she gone on leaving my house? I had taken for granted she had gone straight home. We both presently remembered that in her excursions to town she sometimes, for convenience, for refreshment, spent an hour or two at the "Gentlewomen," the quiet little ladies' club, and I promised that it should be my first care to make at that establishment thorough inquiry. Then we entered the dim and dreadful chamber where she lay locked up in death and where, asking after a little to be left alone with her, I remained for half an hour. Death had made her, had kept her beautiful; but I felt above all, as I knelt at her bed, that it had made her, had kept her silent. It had turned the key on something I was concerned to know.

On my return from Richmond and after another duty had been performed I drove to his chambers. It was the first time, but I had often wanted to see them. On the staircase, which,

as the house contained twenty sets of rooms, was unrestrictedly public, I met his servant, who went back with me and
ushered me in. At the sound of my entrance he appeared in
the doorway of a further room, and the instant we were alone
I produced my news: "She's dead!"

"Dead?"

He was tremendously struck, and I observed that he had
no need to ask whom, in this abruptness, I meant.

"She died last evening—just after leaving me."

He stared with the strangest expression, his eyes searching
mine as if they were looking for a trap. "Last evening—after
leaving you?" He repeated my words in stupefaction. Then
he brought out so that it was in stupefaction I heard: "Impossible! I saw her."

"You 'saw' her?"

"On that spot—where you stand."

This called back to me after an instant, as if to help me to
take it in, the great wonder of the warning of his youth. "In
the hour of death—I understand: as you so beautifully saw
your mother."

"Ah! *not* as I saw my mother—not that way, not that way!"
He was deeply moved by my news—far more moved, I perceived, than he would have been the day before: it gave me a
vivid sense that, as I had then said to myself, there was indeed
a relation between them and that he had actually been face to
face with her. Such an idea, by its reassertion of his extraordinary privilege, would have suddenly presented him as painfully abnormal had he not so vehemently insisted on the
difference. "I saw her living—I saw her to speak to her—I
saw her as I see you now!"

It is remarkable that for a moment, though only for a
moment, I found relief in the more personal, as it were, but
also the more natural of the two odd facts. The next, as I
embraced this image of her having come to him on leaving
me and of just what it accounted for in the disposal of her
time, I demanded with a shade of harshness of which I was
aware—

"What on earth did she come for?"

He had now had a minute to think—to recover himself and
judge of effects, so that if it was still with excited eyes he spoke

he showed a conscious redness and made an inconsequent attempt to smile away the gravity of his words.

"She came just to see me. She came—after what had passed at your house—so that we *should*, after all, at last meet. The impulse seemed to me exquisite, and that was the way I took it."

I looked round the room where she had been—where she had been and I never had been.

"And was the way you took it the way she expressed it?"

"She only expressed it by being here and by letting me look at her. That was enough!" he exclaimed with a singular laugh.

I wondered more and more. "You mean she didn't speak to you?"

"She said nothing. She only looked at me as I looked at her."

"And you didn't speak either?"

He gave me again his painful smile. "I thought of *you*. The situation was every way delicate. I used the finest tact. But she saw she had pleased me." He even repeated his dissonant laugh.

"She evidently pleased you!" Then I thought a moment. "How long did she stay?"

"How can I say? It seemed twenty minutes, but it was probably a good deal less."

"Twenty minutes of silence!" I began to have my definite view and now in fact quite to clutch at it. "Do you know you're telling me a story positively monstrous?"

He had been standing with his back to the fire; at this, with a pleading look, he came to me. "I beseech you, dearest, to take it kindly."

I could take it kindly, and I signified as much; but I couldn't somehow, as he rather awkwardly opened his arms, let him draw me to him. So there fell between us for an appreciable time the discomfort of a great silence.

VI

He broke it presently by saying: "There's absolutely no doubt of her death?"

"Unfortunately none. I've just risen from my knees by the bed where they've laid her out."

He fixed his eyes hard on the floor; then he raised them to mine. "How does she look?"

"She looks—at peace."

He turned away again, while I watched him; but after a moment he began: "At what hour, then——?"

"It must have been near midnight. She dropped as she reached her house—from an affection of the heart which she knew herself and her physician knew her to have, but of which, patiently, bravely she had never spoken to me."

He listened intently and for a minute he was unable to speak. At last he broke out with an accent of which the almost boyish confidence, the really sublime simplicity rings in my ears as I write: "Wasn't she *wonderful*!" Even at the time I was able to do it justice enough to remark in reply that I had always told him so; but the next minute, as if after speaking he had caught a glimpse of what he might have made me feel, he went on quickly: "You see that if she didn't get home till midnight——"

I instantly took him up. "There was plenty of time for you to have seen her? How so," I inquired, "when you didn't leave my house till late? I don't remember the very moment— I was preoccupied. But you know that though you said you had lots to do you sat for some time after dinner. She, on her side, was all the evening at the 'Gentlewomen.' I've just come from there—I've ascertained. She had tea there; she remained a long, long time."

"What was she doing all the long, long time?"

I saw that he was eager to challenge at every step my account of the matter; and the more he showed this the more I found myself disposed to insist on that account, to prefer with apparent perversity an explanation which only deepened the marvel and the mystery, but which, of the two prodigies it had to choose from, my reviving jealousy found easiest to accept. He stood there pleading with a candour that now seems to me beautiful for the privilege of having in spite of supreme defeat known the living woman; while I, with a passion I wonder at to-day, though it still smoulders in a manner in its ashes, could only reply that, through a strange gift shared by her with his mother and on her own side likewise hereditary, the miracle of his youth had been renewed for him, the miracle of hers for her. She had been to him—yes, and by an impulse as charming as he liked; but oh! she had not been in the body. It was a simple question of evidence. I had had, I assured him, a definite statement of what she had done— most of the time—at the little club. The place was almost empty, but the servants had noticed her. She had sat motion-less in a deep chair by the drawing-room fire; she had leaned back her head, she had closed her eyes, she had seemed softly to sleep.

"I see. But till what o'clock?"

"There," I was obliged to answer, "the servants fail me a little. The portress in particular is unfortunately a fool, though even she too is supposed to be a Gentlewoman. She was ev-idently at that period of the evening, without a substitute and against regulations, absent for some little time from the cage in which it's her business to watch the comings and goings. She's muddled, she palpably prevaricates; so I can't positively, from her observation, give you an hour. But it was remarked toward half-past ten that our poor friend was no longer in the club."

"She came straight here; and from here she went straight to the train."

"She couldn't have run it so close," I declared. "That was a thing she particularly never did."

"There was no need of running it close, my dear—she had plenty of time. Your memory is at fault about my having left you late: I left you, as it happens, unusually early. I'm sorry my stay with you seemed long; for I was back here by ten."

"To put yourself into your slippers," I rejoined, "and fall asleep in your chair. You slept till morning—you saw her in a dream!" He looked at me in silence and with sombre eyes— eyes that showed me he had some irritation to repress. Pres-ently I went on: "You had a visit, at an extraordinary hour, from a lady—*soit*: nothing in the world is more probable. But there are ladies and ladies. How in the name of goodness, if she was unannounced and dumb and you had into the bargain never seen the least portrait of her—how could you identify the person we're talking of?"

"Haven't I to absolute satiety heard her described? I'll de-scribe her for you in every particular."

"Don't!" I exclaimed with a promptness that made him laugh once more. I coloured at this, but I continued: "Did your servant introduce her?"

"He wasn't here—he's always away when he's wanted. One of the features of this big house is that from the street-door the different floors are accessible practically without challenge. My servant makes love to a young person employed in the rooms above these, and he had a long bout of it last evening. When he's out on that job he leaves my outer door, on the staircase, so much ajar as to enable him to slip back without a sound. The door then only requires a push. She pushed it—that simply took a little courage."

"A little? It took tons! And it took all sorts of impossible calculations."

"Well, she had them—she made them. Mind you, I don't deny for a moment," he added, "that it was very, very wonderful!"

Something in his tone prevented me for a while from trusting myself to speak. At last I said: "How did she come to know where you live?"

"By remembering the address on the little label the shop-people happily left sticking to the frame I had had made for my photograph."

"And how was she dressed?"

"In mourning, my own dear. No great depths of crape, but simple and scrupulous black. She had in her bonnet three small black feathers. She carried a little muff of astrachan. She has near the left eye," he continued, "a tiny vertical scar——"

I stopped him short. "The mark of a caress from her husband." Then I added: "How close you must have been to her!" He made no answer to this, and I thought he blushed, observing which I broke straight off. "Well, good-bye."

"You won't stay a little?" He came to me again tenderly, and this time I suffered him. "Her visit had its beauty," he murmured as he held me, "but yours has a greater one."

I let him kiss me, but I remembered, as I had remembered the day before, that the last kiss she had given, as I supposed, in this world had been for the lips he touched.

"I'm life, you see," I answered. "What you saw last night was death."

"It was life—it was life!"

He spoke with a kind of soft stubbornness, and I disengaged myself. We stood looking at each other hard.

"You describe the scene—so far as you describe it at all—in terms that are incomprehensible. She was in the room before you knew it?"

"I looked up from my letter-writing—at that table under the lamp I had been wholly absorbed in it—and she stood before me."

"Then what did you do?"

"I sprang up with an ejaculation, and she, with a smile, laid her finger, ever so warningly, yet with a sort of delicate dignity, to her lips. I knew it meant silence, but the strange thing was that it seemed immediately to explain and to justify her. We at any rate stood for a time that, as I've told you, I can't calculate, face to face. It was just as you and I stand now."

"Simply staring?"

He impatiently protested. "Ah! *we're* not staring!"

"Yes, but we're talking."

"Well, *we* were—after a fashion." He lost himself in the memory of it. "It was as friendly as this." I had on my tongue's point to ask if that were saying much for it, but I remarked instead that what they had evidently done was to gaze in mutual admiration. Then I inquired whether his recognition of her had been immediate. "Not quite," he replied, "for of course I didn't expect her; but it came to me long before she went who she was—who she could only be."

I thought a little. "And how did she at last go?"

"Just as she arrived. The door was open behind her, and she passed out."

"Was she rapid—slow?"

"Rather quick. But looking behind her," he added, with a smile. "I let her go, for I perfectly understood that I was to take it as she wished."

I was conscious of exhaling a long, vague sigh. "Well, you must take it now as *I* wish—you must let *me* go."

At this he drew near me again, detaining and persuading me, declaring with all due gallantry that I was a very different matter. I would have given anything to have been able to ask him if he had touched her, but the words refused to form themselves: I knew well enough how horrid and vulgar they would sound. I said something else—I forget exactly what; it was feebly tortuous and intended to make him tell me without my putting the question. But he didn't tell me; he only repeated, as if from a glimpse of the propriety of soothing and consoling me, the sense of his declaration of some minutes before—the assurance that she was indeed exquisite, as I had always insisted, but that I was his "real" friend and his very own for ever. This led me to reassert, in the spirit of my previous rejoinder, that I had at least the merit of being alive; which in turn drew from him again the flash of contradiction I dreaded. "Oh, *she* was alive! she was, she was!"

"She was dead! she was dead!" I asseverated with an energy, a determination that it should *be* so, which comes back to me now almost as grotesque. But the sound of the word as it rang out filled me suddenly with horror, and all the natural emotion the meaning of it might have evoked in other conditions gathered and broke in a flood. It rolled over me that here was a great affection quenched and how much I had loved and trusted her. I had a vision at the same time of the lonely beauty of her end. "She's gone—she's lost to us for ever!" I burst into sobs.

"That's exactly what I feel," he exclaimed, speaking with extreme kindness and pressing me to him for comfort. "She's gone; she's lost to us for ever: so what does it matter now?" He bent over me, and when his face had touched mine I scarcely knew if it were wet with my tears or with his own.

VII

It was my theory, my conviction, it became, as I may say, my attitude, that they had still never "met;" and it was just on this ground that I said to myself it would be generous to ask him to stand with me beside her grave. He did so, very modestly and tenderly, and I assumed, though he himself clearly cared nothing for the danger, that the solemnity of the occasion, largely made up of persons who had known them both and had a sense of the long joke, would sufficiently deprive his presence of all light association. On the question of what had happened the evening of her death little more passed between us; I had been overtaken by a horror of the element of evidence. It seemed gross and prying on either hypothesis. He on his side had none to produce, none at least but a statement of his house-porter—on his own admission a most casual and intermittent personage—that between the hours of ten o'clock and midnight no less than three ladies in deep black had flitted in and out of the place. This proved far too much; we had neither of us any use for three. He knew that I considered I had accounted for every fragment of her time, and we dropped the matter as settled; we abstained from further discussion. What *I* knew however was that he abstained to please me rather than because he yielded to my reasons. He didn't yield—he was only indulgent; he clung to his interpretation because he liked it better. He liked it better, I held, because it had more to say to his vanity. That, in a similar position, would not have been its effect on me, though I had doubtless quite as much; but these are things of individual humour, as to which no person can judge for another. I should have supposed it more gratifying to be the subject of one of those inexplicable occurrences that are chronicled in thrilling books and disputed about at learned meetings; I could conceive, on the part of a being just engulfed in the infinite and still vibrating with human emotion, of nothing more fine and pure, more high and august than such an impulse of reparation, of admonition or even of curiosity. *That* was beautiful, if one would, and I should in his place have thought more of myself for being so distinguished. It was public that he had already, that he had long been distinguished, and what was this in itself but almost a proof? Each of the strange visitations contributed to establish the other. He had a different feeling; but he had also, I hasten to add, an unmistakable desire not to make a stand or, as they say, a fuss about it. I might believe what I liked—the more so that the whole thing was in a manner a mystery of my producing. It was an event of my history, a puzzle of my consciousness, not of his; therefore he would take about it any tone that struck me as convenient. We had both at all events other business on hand; we were pressed with preparations for our marriage.

Mine were assuredly urgent, but I found as the days went on that to believe what I "liked" was to believe what I was more and more intimately convinced of. I found also that I didn't like it so much as that came to, or that the pleasure at all events was far from being the cause of my conviction. My obsession, as I may really call it and as I began to perceive, refused to be elbowed away, as I had hoped, by my sense of paramount duties. If I had a great deal to do I had still more to think about, and the moment came when my occupations were gravely menaced by my thoughts. I see it all now, I feel it, I live it over. It's terribly void of joy, it's full indeed to overflowing of bitterness; and yet I must do myself justice— I couldn't possibly be other than I was. The same strange impressions, had I to meet them again, would produce the same deep anguish, the same sharp doubts, the same still sharper certainties. Oh, it's all easier to remember than to write, but even if I could retrace the business hour by hour, could find terms for the inexpressible, the ugliness and the pain would quickly stay my hand. Let me then note very simply and briefly that a week before our wedding-day, three weeks after her death, I became fully aware that I had something very serious to look in the face and that if I was to make this effort I must make it on the spot and before another hour should elapse. My unextinguished jealousy—that was the Medusa-mask. It hadn't died with her death, it had lividly survived, and it was fed by suspicions unspeakable. They *would* be unspeakable to-day, that is, if I hadn't felt the sharp need of uttering them at the time. This need took possession of me—to save me, as it appeared, from my fate. When once it had done so I saw—in the urgency of the case, the diminishing hours and shrinking interval—only one issue, that of absolute promptness and frankness. I could at least not do him the wrong of delaying another day; I could at least treat my difficulty as too fine for a subterfuge. Therefore very quietly, but none the less abruptly and hideously, I put it before him on a certain evening that we must reconsider our situation and recognise that it had completely altered.

He stared bravely. "How has it altered?"

"Another person has come between us."

He hesitated a moment. "I won't pretend not to know whom you mean." He smiled in pity for my aberration, but he meant to be kind. "A woman dead and buried!"

"She's buried, but she's not dead. She's dead for the world—she's dead for me. But she's not dead for *you*."

"You hark back to the different construction we put on her appearance that evening?"

"No," I answered, "I hark back to nothing. I've no need of it. I've more than enough with what's before me."

"And pray, darling, what is that?"

"You're completely changed."

"By that absurdity?" he laughed.

"Not so much by that one as by other absurdities that have followed it."

"And what may they have been?"

We had faced each other fairly, with eyes that didn't flinch; but his had a dim, strange light, and my certitude triumphed in his perceptible paleness. "Do you really pretend," I asked, "not to know what they are?"

"My dear child," he replied, "you describe them too sketchily!"

I considered a moment. "One may well be embarrassed to finish the picture! But from that point of view—and from the beginning—what was ever more embarrassing than your idiosyncrasy?"

He was extremely vague. "My idiosyncrasy?"

"Your notorious, your peculiar power."

He gave a great shrug of impatience, a groan of overdone disdain. "Oh, my peculiar power!"

"Your accessibility to forms of life," I coldly went on, "your command of impressions, appearances, contacts closed—for our gain or our loss—to the rest of us. That was originally a part of the deep interest with which you inspired me—one of the reasons I was amused, I was indeed positively proud to know you. It was a magnificent distinction; it's a magnificent distinction still. But of course I had no prevision then of the way it would operate now; and even had that been the case I should have had none of the extraordinary way in which its action would affect me."

"To what in the name of goodness," he pleadingly inquired, "are you fantastically alluding?" Then as I remained silent, gathering a tone for my charge, "How in the world *does* it operate?" he went on; "and how in the world are you affected?"

"She missed you for five years," I said, "but she never misses you now. You're making it up!"

"Making it up?" He had begun to turn from white to red.

"You see her—you see her: you see her every night!" He gave a loud sound of derision, but it was not a genuine one. "She comes to you as she came that evening," I declared; "having tried it she found she liked it!" I was able, with God's help, to speak without blind passion or vulgar violence; but those were the exact words—and far from "sketchy" they then appeared to me—that I uttered. He had turned away in his laughter, clapping his hands at my folly, but in an instant he faced me again with a change of expression that struck me. "Do you dare to deny," I asked, "that you habitually see her?"

He had taken the line of indulgence, of meeting me halfway and kindly humouring me. At all events to my astonishment he suddenly said: "Well, my dear, what if I do?"

"It's your natural right; it belongs to your constitution and to your wonderful if not perhaps quite enviable fortune. But you will easily understand that it separates us. I unconditionally release you."

"Release me?"

"You must choose between me and her."

He looked at me hard. "I see." Then he walked away a little, as if grasping what I had said and thinking how he had best treat it. At last he turned upon me afresh. "How on earth do you know such an awfully private thing?"

"You mean because you've tried so hard to hide it? It is awfully private, and you may believe I shall never betray you. You've done your best, you've acted your part, you've behaved, poor dear! loyally and admirably. Therefore I've watched you in silence, playing my part too; I've noted every drop in your voice, every absence in your eyes, every effort in your indifferent hand: I've waited till I was utterly sure and miserably unhappy. How *can* you hide it when you're abjectly in love with her, when you're sick almost to death with the joy of what she gives you?" I checked his quick protest with a quicker gesture. "You love her as you've *never* loved, and, passion for passion, she gives it straight back! She rules you, she holds you, she has you all! A woman, in such a case as mine, divines and feels and sees; she's not an idiot who has to be credibly informed. You come to me mechanically, compunctiously, with the dregs of your tenderness and the remnant of your life. I can renounce you, but I can't share you; the best of you is hers; I know what it is and I freely give you up to her for ever!"

He made a gallant fight, but it couldn't be patched up; he repeated his denial, he retracted his admission, he ridiculed my charge, of which I freely granted him moreover the indefensible extravagance. I didn't pretend for a moment that we were talking of common things; I didn't pretend for a moment that he and she were common people. Pray, if they *had* been, how should I ever have cared for them? They had enjoyed a rare extension of being and they had caught me up in their flight; only I couldn't breathe in such an air and I promptly asked to be set down. Everything in the facts was monstrous, and most of all my lucid perception of them; the only thing allied to nature and truth was my having to act on that perception. I felt after I had spoken in this sense that my assurance was complete; nothing had been wanting to it but the sight of my effect on him. He disguised indeed the effect in a cloud of chaff, a diversion that gained him time and covered his retreat. He challenged my sincerity, my sanity, almost my humanity, and that of course widened our breach and confirmed our rupture. He did everything in short but convince me either that I was wrong or that he was unhappy: we separated and I left him to his inconceivable communion.

He never married, any more than I've done. When six years later, in solitude and silence, I heard of his death I hailed it as a direct contribution to my theory. It was sudden, it was never properly accounted for, it was surrounded by circumstances in which—for oh, I took them to pieces!—I distinctly read an intention, the mark of his own hidden hand. It was the result of a long necessity, of an unquenchable desire. To say exactly what I mean, it was a response to an irresistible call.

The Turn of the Screw

THE STORY had held us, round the fire, sufficiently breathless, but except the obvious remark that it was gruesome, as, on Christmas eve in an old house, a strange tale should essentially be, I remember no comment uttered till somebody happened to say that it was the only case he had met in which such a visitation had fallen on a child. The case, I may mention, was that of an apparition in just such an old house as had gathered us for the occasion—an appearance, of a dreadful kind, to a little boy sleeping in the room with his mother and waking her up in the terror of it; waking her not to dissipate his dread and soothe him to sleep again, but to encounter also, herself, before she had succeeded in doing so, the same sight that had shaken him. It was this observation that drew from Douglas—not immediately, but later in the evening—a reply that had the interesting consequence to which I call attention. Someone else told a story not particularly effective, which I saw he was not following. This I took for a sign that he had himself something to produce and that we should only have to wait. We waited in fact till two nights later; but that same evening, before we scattered, he brought out what was in his mind.

"I quite agree—in regard to Griffin's ghost, or whatever it was—that its appearing first to the little boy, at so tender an age, adds a particular touch. But it's not the first occurrence of its charming kind that I know to have involved a child. If the child gives the effect another turn of the screw, what do you say to *two* children——?"

"We say, of course," somebody exclaimed, "that they give two turns! Also that we want to hear about them."

I can see Douglas there before the fire, to which he had got up to present his back, looking down at his interlocutor with his hands in his pockets. "Nobody but me, till now, has ever heard. It's quite too horrible." This, naturally, was declared by several voices to give the thing the utmost price, and our friend, with quiet art, prepared his triumph by turning his eyes over the rest of us and going on: "It's beyond everything. Nothing at all that I know touches it."

"For sheer terror?" I remember asking.

He seemed to say it was not so simple as that; to be really at a loss how to qualify it. He passed his hand over his eyes, made a little wincing grimace. "For dreadful—dreadfulness!"

"Oh, how delicious!" cried one of the women.

He took no notice of her; he looked at me, but as if, instead of me, he saw what he spoke of. "For general uncanny ugliness and horror and pain."

"Well then," I said, "just sit right down and begin."

He turned round to the fire, gave a kick to a log, watched it an instant. Then as he faced us again: "I can't begin. I shall have to send to town." There was a unanimous groan at this, and much reproach; after which, in his preoccupied way, he explained. "The story's written. It's in a locked drawer—it has not been out for years. I could write to my man and enclose the key; he could send down the packet as he finds it." It was to me in particular that he appeared to propound this—appeared almost to appeal for aid not to hesitate. He had broken a thickness of ice, the formation of many a winter; had had his reasons for a long silence. The others resented postponement, but it was just his scruples that charmed me. I adjured him to write by the first post and to agree with us for an early hearing; then I asked him if the experience in question had been his own. To this his answer was prompt. "Oh, thank God, no!"

"And is the record yours? You took the thing down?"

"Nothing but the impression. I took that *here*"—he tapped his heart. "I've never lost it."

"Then your manuscript——?"

"Is in old, faded ink, and in the most beautiful hand." He hung fire again. "A woman's. She has been dead these twenty years. She sent me the pages in question before she died." They were all listening now, and of course there was somebody to be arch, or at any rate to draw the inference. But if he put the inference by without a smile it was also without irritation. "She was a most charming person, but she was ten years older than I. She was my sister's governess," he quietly said. "She was the most agreeable woman I've ever known in her position; she would have been worthy of any whatever. It was long ago, and this episode was long before. I was at Trinity, and I found her at home on my coming down the second summer. I was much there that year—it was a beautiful one; and we had, in her off-hours, some strolls and talks in the garden—talks in which she struck me as awfully clever and nice. Oh yes; don't grin: I liked her extremely and am glad to this day to think she liked me too. If she hadn't she wouldn't have told me. She had never told anyone. It wasn't simply that she said so, but that I knew she hadn't. I was sure; I could see. You'll easily judge why when you hear."

"Because the thing had been such a scare?"

He continued to fix me. "You'll easily judge," he repeated: "*you* will."

I fixed him too. "I see. She was in love."

He laughed for the first time. "You *are* acute. Yes, she was in love. That is, she had been. That came out—she couldn't tell her story without its coming out. I saw it, and she saw I saw it, but neither of us spoke of it. I remember the time and the place—the corner of the lawn, the shade of the great beeches and the long, hot summer afternoon. It wasn't a scene for a shudder; but oh——!" He quitted the fire and dropped back into his chair.

"You'll receive the packet Thursday morning?" I inquired.

"Probably not till the second post."

"Well then; after dinner——"

"You'll all meet me here?" He looked us round again. "Isn't anybody going?" It was almost the tone of hope.

"Everybody will stay!"

"*I* will—and *I* will!" cried the ladies whose departure had been fixed. Mrs. Griffin, however, expressed the need for a little more light. "Who was it she was in love with?"

"The story will tell," I took upon myself to reply.

"Oh, I can't wait for the story!"

"The story *won't* tell," said Douglas; "not in any literal, vulgar way."

"More's the pity, then. That's the only way I ever understand."

"Won't *you* tell, Douglas?" somebody else inquired.

He sprang to his feet again. "Yes—to-morrow. Now I must go to bed. Good-night." And quickly catching up a candle-stick, he left us slightly bewildered. From our end of the great brown hall we heard his step on the stair; whereupon Mrs. Griffin spoke. "Well, if I don't know who she was in love with, I know who *he* was."

"She was ten years older," said her husband.

"*Raison de plus*—at that age! But it's rather nice, his long reticence."

"Forty years!" Griffin put in.

"With this outbreak at last."

"The outbreak," I returned, "will make a tremendous oc-casion of Thursday night;" and everyone so agreed with me that, in the light of it, we lost all attention for everything else. The last story, however incomplete and like the mere opening of a serial, had been told; we handshook and "candlestuck," as somebody said, and went to bed.

I knew the next day that a letter containing the key had, by the first post, gone off to his London apartments; but in spite of—or perhaps just on account of—the eventual diffusion of this knowledge we quite let him alone till after dinner, till such an hour of the evening, in fact, as might best accord with the kind of emotion on which our hopes were fixed. Then he became as communicative as we could desire and indeed gave us his best reason for being so. We had it from him again before the fire in the hall, as we had had our mild wonders of the previous night. It appeared that the narrative he had promised to read us really required for a proper intelligence a few words of prologue. Let me say here distinctly, to have done with it, that this narrative, from an exact transcript of my own made much later, is what I shall presently give. Poor Douglas, before his death—when it was in sight—committed to me the manuscript that reached him on the third of these days and that, on the same spot, with immense effect, he be-gan to read to our hushed little circle on the night of the fourth. The departing ladies who had said they would stay didn't, of course, thank heaven, stay: they departed, in con-sequence of arrangements made, in a rage of curiosity, as they professed, produced by the touches with which he had already worked us up. But that only made his little final auditory more compact and select, kept it, round the hearth, subject to a common thrill.

The first of these touches conveyed that the written statement took up the tale at a point after it had, in a manner, begun. The fact to be in possession of was therefore that his old friend, the youngest of several daughters of a poor country parson, had, at the age of twenty, on taking service for the first time in the schoolroom, come up to London, in trepidation, to answer in person an advertisement that had already placed her in brief correspondence with the advertiser. This person proved, on her presenting herself, for judgment, at a house in Harley Street, that impressed her as vast and imposing this prospective patron proved a gentleman, a bachelor in the prime of life, such a figure as had never risen, save in a dream or an old novel, before a fluttered, anxious girl out of a Hampshire vicarage. One could easily fix his type; it never, happily, dies out. He was handsome and bold and pleasant, off-hand and gay and kind. He struck her, inevitably, as gallant and splendid, but what took her most of all and gave her the courage she afterwards showed was that he put the whole thing to her as a kind of favour, an obligation he should gratefully incur. She conceived him as rich, but as fearfully extravagant—saw him all in a glow of high fashion, of good looks, of expensive habits, of charming ways with women. He had for his own town residence a big house filled with the spoils of travel and the trophies of the chase; but it was to his country home, an old family place in Essex, that he wished her immediately to proceed.

He had been left, by the death of their parents in India, guardian to a small nephew and a small niece, children of a younger, a military brother, whom he had lost two years before. These children were, by the strangest of chances for a man in his position,—a lone man without the right sort of experience or a grain of patience, very heavily on his hands. It had all been a great worry and, on his own part doubtless, a series of blunders, but he immensely pitied the poor chicks and had done all he could; had in particular sent them down to his other house, the proper place for them being of course the country, and kept them there, from the first, with the best people he could find to look after them, parting even with his

own servants to wait on them and going down himself, whenever he might, to see how they were doing. The awkward
thing was that they had practically no other relations and that
his own affairs took up all his time. He had put them in possession of Bly, which was healthy and secure, and had placed
at the head of their little establishment—but below stairs
only—an excellent woman, Mrs. Grose, whom he was sure his
visitor would like and who had formerly been maid to his
mother. She was now housekeeper and was also acting for the
time as superintendent to the little girl, of whom, without
children of her own, she was, by good luck, extremely fond.
There were plenty of people to help, but of course the young
lady who should go down as governess would be in supreme
authority. She would also have, in holidays, to look after the
small boy, who had been for a term at school—young as he
was to be sent, but what else could be done?—and who, as
the holidays were about to begin, would be back from one
day to the other. There had been for the two children at first
a young lady whom they had had the misfortune to lose. She
had done for them quite beautifully—she was a most respectable person—till her death, the great awkwardness of which
had, precisely, left no alternative but the school for little Miles.
Mrs. Grose, since then, in the way of manners and things, had
done as she could for Flora; and there were, further, a cook,
a housemaid, a dairywoman, an old pony, an old groom, and
an old gardener, all likewise thoroughly respectable.

So far had Douglas presented his picture when someone
put a question. "And what did the former governess die of?—
of so much respectability?"

Our friend's answer was prompt. "That will come out. I
don't anticipate."

"Excuse me—I thought that was just what you *are* doing."

"In her successor's place," I suggested, "I should have
wished to learn if the office brought with it——"

"Necessary danger to life?" Douglas completed my
thought. "She did wish to learn, and she did learn. You shall
hear tomorrow what she learnt. Meanwhile, of course, the
prospect struck her as slightly grim. She was young, untried,
nervous: it was a vision of serious duties and little company,

of really great loneliness. She hesitated—took a couple of days to consult and consider. But the salary offered much exceeded her modest measure, and on a second interview she faced the music, she engaged." And Douglas, with this, made a pause that, for the benefit of the company, moved me to throw in—

"The moral of which was of course the seduction exercised by the splendid young man. She succumbed to it."

He got up and, as he had done the night before, went to the fire, gave a stir to a log with his foot, then stood a moment with his back to us. "She saw him only twice."

"Yes, but that's just the beauty of her passion."

A little to my surprise, on this, Douglas turned round to me. "It *was* the beauty of it. There were others," he went on, "who hadn't succumbed. He told her frankly all his difficulty—that for several applicants the conditions had been prohibitive. They were, somehow, simply afraid. It sounded dull—it sounded strange; and all the more so because of his main condition."

"Which was——?"

"That she should never trouble him—but never, never: neither appeal nor complain nor write about anything; only meet all questions herself, receive all moneys from his solicitor, take the whole thing over and let him alone. She promised to do this, and she mentioned to me that when, for a moment, disburdened, delighted, he held her hand, thanking her for the sacrifice, she already felt rewarded."

"But was that all her reward?" one of the ladies asked.

"She never saw him again."

"Oh!" said the lady; which, as our friend immediately left us again, was the only other word of importance contributed to the subject till, the next night, by the corner of the hearth, in the best chair, he opened the faded red cover of a thin old-fashioned gilt-edged album. The whole thing took indeed more nights than one, but on the first occasion the same lady put another question. "What is your title?"

"I haven't one."

"Oh, *I* have!" I said. But Douglas, without heeding me, had begun to read with a fine clearness that was like a rendering to the ear of the beauty of his author's hand.

I

I remember the whole beginning as a succession of flights and drops, a little see-saw of the right throbs and the wrong. After rising, in town, to meet his appeal, I had at all events a couple of very bad days—found myself doubtful again, felt indeed sure I had made a mistake. In this state of mind I spent the long hours of bumping, swinging coach that carried me to the stopping-place at which I was to be met by a vehicle from the house. This convenience, I was told, had been ordered, and I found, toward the close of the June afternoon, a commodious fly in waiting for me. Driving at that hour, on a lovely day, through a country to which the summer sweetness seemed to offer me a friendly welcome, my fortitude mounted afresh and, as we turned into the avenue, encountered a reprieve that was probably but a proof of the point to which it had sunk. I suppose I had expected, or had dreaded, something so melancholy that what greeted me was a good surprise. I remember as a most pleasant impression the broad, clear front, its open windows and fresh curtains and the pair of maids looking out; I remember the lawn and the bright flowers and the crunch of my wheels on the gravel and the clustered tree-tops over which the rooks circled and cawed in the golden sky. The scene had a greatness that made it a different affair from my own scant home, and there immediately appeared at the door, with a little girl in her hand, a civil person who dropped me as decent a curtsey as if I had been the mistress or a distinguished visitor. I had received in Harley Street a narrower notion of the place, and that, as I recalled it, made me think the proprietor still more of a gentleman, suggested that what I was to enjoy might be something beyond his promise.

I had no drop again till the next day, for I was carried triumphantly through the following hours by my introduction to the younger of my pupils. The little girl who accompanied Mrs. Grose appeared to me on the spot a creature so charming as to make it a great fortune to have to do with her. She was the most beautiful child I had ever seen, and I afterwards wondered that my employer had not told me more of her. I slept little that night—I was too much excited; and this aston-

ished me too, I recollect, remained with me, adding to my
sense of the liberality with which I was treated. The large,
impressive room, one of the best in the house, the great state
bed, as I almost felt it, the full, figured draperies, the long
glasses in which, for the first time, I could see myself from
head to foot, all struck me—like the extraordinary charm of
my small charge—as so many things thrown in. It was thrown
in as well, from the first moment, that I should get on with
Mrs. Grose in a relation over which, on my way, in the coach,
I fear I had rather brooded. The only thing indeed that in
this early outlook might have made me shrink again was the
clear circumstance of her being so glad to see me. I perceived
within half an hour that she was so glad—stout, simple, plain,
clean, wholesome woman—as to be positively on her guard
against showing it too much. I wondered even then a little
why she should wish not to show it, and that, with reflection,
with suspicion, might of course have made me uneasy.

But it was a comfort that there could be no uneasiness in
a connection with anything so beatific as the radiant image of
my little girl, the vision of whose angelic beauty had probably
more than anything else to do with the restlessness that, before morning, made me several times rise and wander about
my room to take in the whole picture and prospect; to watch,
from my open window, the faint summer dawn, to look at
such portions of the rest of the house as I could catch, and
to listen, while, in the fading dusk, the first birds began to
twitter, for the possible recurrence of a sound or two, less
natural and not without, but within, that I had fancied I
heard. There had been a moment when I believed I recog
nised, faint and far, the cry of a child; there had been another
when I found myself just consciously starting as at the passage,
before my door, of a light footstep. But these fancies were not
marked enough not to be thrown off, and it is only in the
light, or the gloom, I should rather say, of other and subsequent matters that they now come back to me. To watch,
teach, "form" little Flora would too evidently be the making
of a happy and useful life. It had been agreed between us
downstairs that after this first occasion I should have her as a
matter of course at night, her small white bed being already
arranged, to that end, in my room. What I had undertaken

was the whole care of her, and she had remained, just this last time, with Mrs. Grose only as an effect of our consideration for my inevitable strangeness and her natural timidity. In spite of this timidity—which the child herself, in the oddest way in the world, had been perfectly frank and brave about, allowing it, without a sign of uncomfortable consciousness, with the deep, sweet serenity indeed of one of Raphael's holy infants, to be discussed, to be imputed to her and to determine us— I felt quite sure she would presently like me. It was part of what I already liked Mrs. Grose herself for, the pleasure I could see her feel in my admiration and wonder as I sat at supper with four tall candles and with my pupil, in a high chair and a bib, brightly facing me, between them, over bread and milk. There were naturally things that in Flora's presence could pass between us only as prodigious and gratified looks, obscure and roundabout allusions.

"And the little boy—does he look like her? Is he too so very remarkable?"

One wouldn't flatter a child. "Oh, Miss, *most* remarkable. If you think well of this one!"—and she stood there with a plate in her hand, beaming at our companion, who looked from one of us to the other with placid heavenly eyes that contained nothing to check us.

"Yes; if I do——?"

"You *will* be carried away by the little gentleman!"

"Well, that, I think, is what I came for—to be carried away. I'm afraid, however," I remember feeling the impulse to add, "I'm rather easily carried away. I was carried away in London!"

I can still see Mrs. Grose's broad face as she took this in. "In Harley Street?"

"In Harley Street."

"Well, Miss, you're not the first—and you won't be the last."

"Oh, I've no pretension," I could laugh, "to being the only one. My other pupil, at any rate, as I understand, comes back tomorrow?"

"Not tomorrow—Friday, Miss. He arrives, as you did, by the coach, under care of the guard, and is to be met by the same carriage."

I forthwith expressed that the proper as well as the pleasant and friendly thing would be therefore that on the arrival of the public conveyance I should be in waiting for him with his little sister; an idea in which Mrs. Grose concurred so heartily that I somehow took her manner as a kind of comforting pledge—never falsified, thank heaven!—that we should on every question be quite at one. Oh, she was glad I was there!

What I felt the next day was, I suppose, nothing that could be fairly called a reaction from the cheer of my arrival; it was probably at the most only a slight oppression produced by a fuller measure of the scale, as I walked round them, gazed up at them, took them in, of my new circumstances. They had, as it were, an extent and mass for which I had not been prepared and in the presence of which I found myself, freshly, a little scared as well as a little proud. Lessons, in this agitation, certainly suffered some delay; I reflected that my first duty was, by the gentlest arts I could contrive, to win the child into the sense of knowing me. I spent the day with her out of doors; I arranged with her, to her great satisfaction, that it should be she, she only, who might show me the place. She showed it step by step and room by room and secret by secret, with droll, delightful, childish talk about it and with the result, in half an hour, of our becoming immense friends. Young as she was, I was struck, throughout our little tour, with her confidence and courage with the way, in empty chambers and dull corridors, on crooked staircases that made me pause and even on the summit of an old machicolated square tower that made me dizzy, her morning music, her disposition to tell me so many more things than she asked, rang out and led me on. I have not seen Bly since the day I left it, and I dare say that to my older and more informed eyes it would now appear sufficiently contracted. But as my little conductress, with her hair of gold and her frock of blue, danced before me round corners and pattered down passages, I had the view of a castle of romance inhabited by a rosy sprite, such a place as would somehow, for diversion of the young idea, take all colour out of storybooks and fairy-tales. Wasn't it just a storybook over which I had fallen a-doze and a-dream? No; it was a big, ugly, antique, but convenient house, embodying a few features of a building still older, half replaced and half utilised, in which I had the fancy of our being almost as lost as a handful of passengers in a great drifting ship. Well, I was, strangely, at the helm!

II

This came home to me when, two days later, I drove over with Flora to meet, as Mrs. Grose said, the little gentleman; and all the more for an incident that, presenting itself the second evening, had deeply disconcerted me. The first day had been, on the whole, as I have expressed, reassuring; but I was to see it wind up in keen apprehension. The postbag, that evening,—it came late,—contained a letter for me, which, however, in the hand of my employer, I found to be composed but of a few words enclosing another, addressed to himself, with a seal still unbroken. "This, I recognise, is from the head-master, and the head-master's an awful bore. Read him, please; deal with him; but mind you don't report. Not a word. I'm off!" I broke the seal with a great effort—so great a one that I was a long time coming to it; took the unopened missive at last up to my room and only attacked it just before going to bed. I had better have let it wait till morning, for it gave me a second sleepless night. With no counsel to take, the next day, I was full of distress; and it finally got so the better of me that I determined to open myself at least to Mrs. Grose.

"What does it mean? The child's dismissed his school."

She gave me a look that I remarked at the moment; then, visibly, with a quick blankness, seemed to try to take it back. "But aren't they all——?"

"Sent home—yes. But only for the holidays. Miles may never go back at all."

Consciously, under my attention, she reddened. "They won't take him?"

"They absolutely decline."

At this she raised her eyes, which she had turned from me; I saw them fill with good tears. "What has he done?"

I hesitated; then I judged best simply to hand her my letter—which, however, had the effect of making her, without taking it, simply put her hands behind her. She shook her head sadly. "Such things are not for me, Miss."

My counsellor couldn't read! I winced at my mistake, which I attenuated as I could, and opened my letter again to repeat it to her; then, faltering in the act and folding it up once more, I put it back in my pocket. "Is he really *bad*?"

The tears were still in her eyes. "Do the gentlemen say so?"

"They go into no particulars. They simply express their regret that it should be impossible to keep him. That can have only one meaning." Mrs. Grose listened with dumb emotion; she forbore to ask me what this meaning might be; so that, presently, to put the thing with some coherence and with the mere aid of her presence to my own mind, I went on: "That he's an injury to the others."

At this, with one of the quick turns of simple folk, she suddenly flamed up. "Master Miles! *him* an injury?"

There was such a flood of good faith in it that, though I had not yet seen the child, my very fears made me jump to the absurdity of the idea. I found myself, to meet my friend the better, offering it, on the spot, sarcastically. "To his poor little innocent mates!"

"It's too dreadful," cried Mrs. Grose, "to say such cruel things! Why, he's scarce ten years old."

"Yes, yes; it would be incredible."

She was evidently grateful for such a profession. "See him, Miss, first. *Then* believe it!" I felt forthwith a new impatience to see him; it was the beginning of a curiosity that, for all the next hours, was to deepen almost to pain. Mrs. Grose was aware, I could judge, of what she had produced in me, and she followed it up with assurance. "You might as well believe it of the little lady. Bless her," she added the next moment—"*look* at her!"

I turned and saw that Flora, whom, ten minutes before, I had established in the schoolroom with a sheet of white paper, a pencil, and a copy of nice "round O's," now presented herself to view at the open door. She expressed in her little way an extraordinary detachment from disagreeable duties, looking to me, however, with a great childish light that seemed to offer it as a mere result of the affection she had conceived for my person, which had rendered necessary that she should follow me. I needed nothing more than this to feel the full force of Mrs. Grose's comparison, and, catching my pupil in my arms, covered her with kisses in which there was a sob of atonement.

None the less, the rest of the day, I watched for further occasion to approach my colleague, especially as, toward evening, I began to fancy she rather sought to avoid me. I overtook her, I remember, on the staircase; we went down together, and at the bottom I detained her, holding her there with a hand on her arm. "I take what you said to me at noon as a declaration that *you've* never known him to be bad."

She threw back her head; she had clearly, by this time, and very honestly, adopted an attitude. "Oh, never known him— I don't pretend *that*!"

I was upset again. "Then you *have* known him——?"

"Yes indeed, Miss, thank God!"

On reflection I accepted this. "You mean that a boy who never is——?"

"Is no boy for *me*!"

I held her tighter. "You like them with the spirit to be naughty?" Then, keeping pace with her answer, "So do I!" I eagerly brought out. "But not to the degree to contaminate——"

"To contaminate?"—my big word left her at a loss. I explained it. "To corrupt."

She stared, taking my meaning in; but it produced in her an odd laugh. "Are you afraid he'll corrupt *you*?" She put the question with such a fine bold humour that, with a laugh, a little silly doubtless, to match her own, I gave way for the time to the apprehension of ridicule.

But the next day, as the hour for my drive approached, I cropped up in another place. "What was the lady who was here before?"

"The last governess? She was also young and pretty—almost as young and almost as pretty, Miss, even as you."

"Ah, then, I hope her youth and her beauty helped her!" I recollect throwing off. "He seems to like us young and pretty!"

"Oh, he *did*," Mrs. Grose assented: "it was the way he liked everyone!" She had no sooner spoken indeed than she caught herself up. "I mean that's *his* way—the master's."

I was struck. "But of whom did you speak first?"

She looked blank, but she coloured. "Why, of *him*."

"Of the master?"

"Of who else?"

There was so obviously no one else that the next moment I had lost my impression of her having accidentally said more than she meant; and I merely asked what I wanted to know. "Did *she* see anything in the boy——?"

"That wasn't right? She never told me."

I had a scruple, but I overcame it. "Was she careful—particular?"

Mrs. Grose appeared to try to be conscientious. "About some things—yes."

"But not about all?"

Again she considered. "Well, Miss—she's gone. I won't tell tales."

"I quite understand your feeling," I hastened to reply; but I thought it, after an instant, not opposed to this concession to pursue: "Did she die here?"

"No— she went off."

I don't know what there was in this brevity of Mrs. Grose's that struck me as ambiguous. "Went off to die?" Mrs. Grose looked straight out of the window, but I felt that, hypothetically, I had a right to know what young persons engaged for Bly were expected to do. "She was taken ill, you mean, and went home?"

"She was not taken ill, so far as appeared, in this house. She left it, at the end of the year, to go home, as she said, for a short holiday, to which the time she had put in had certainly given her a right. We had then a young woman—a nursemaid who had stayed on and who was a good girl and clever; and *she* took the children altogether for the interval. But our young lady never came back, and at the very moment I was expecting her I heard from the master that she was dead."

I turned this over. "But of what?"

"He never told me! But please, Miss," said Mrs. Grose, "I must get to my work."

III

Her thus turning her back on me was fortunately not, for my just preoccupations, a snub that could check the growth of our mutual esteem. We met, after I had brought home little

Miles, more intimately than ever on the ground of my stupefaction, my general emotion: so monstrous was I then ready
to pronounce it that such a child as had now been revealed
to me should be under an interdict. I was a little late on the
scene, and I felt, as he stood wistfully looking out for me
before the door of the inn at which the coach had put him
down, that I had seen him, on the instant, without and within,
in the great glow of freshness, the same positive fragrance of
purity, in which I had, from the first moment, seen his little
sister. He was incredibly beautiful, and Mrs. Grose had put
her finger on it: everything but a sort of passion of tenderness
for him was swept away by his presence. What I then and there
took him to my heart for was something divine that I have
never found to the same degree in any child—his indescribable
little air of knowing nothing in the world but love. It would
have been impossible to carry a bad name with a greater sweetness of innocence, and by the time I had got back to Bly with
him I remained merely bewildered—so far, that is, as I was not
outraged—by the sense of the horrible letter locked up in my
room, in a drawer. As soon as I could compass a private word
with Mrs. Grose I declared to her that it was grotesque.

She promptly understood me. "You mean the cruel
charge——?"

"It doesn't live an instant. My dear woman, *look* at him!"

She smiled at my pretension to have discovered his charm.
"I assure you, Miss, I do nothing else! What will you say,
then?" she immediately added.

"In answer to the letter?" I had made up my mind.
"Nothing."

"And to his uncle?"

I was incisive. "Nothing."

"And to the boy himself?"

I was wonderful. "Nothing."

She gave with her apron a great wipe to her mouth. "Then
I'll stand by you. We'll see it out."

"We'll see it out!" I ardently echoed, giving her my hand
to make it a vow.

She held me there a moment, then whisked up her apron
again with her detached hand. "Would you mind, Miss, if I
used the freedom——"

"To kiss me? No!" I took the good creature in my arms and, after we had embraced like sisters, felt still more fortified and indignant.

This, at all events, was for the time: a time so full that, as I recall the way it went, it reminds me of all the art I now need to make it a little distinct. What I look back at with amazement is the situation I accepted. I had undertaken, with my companion, to see it out, and I was under a charm, apparently, that could smooth away the extent and the far and difficult connections of such an effort. I was lifted aloft on a great wave of infatuation and pity. I found it simple, in my ignorance, my confusion, and perhaps my conceit, to assume that I could deal with a boy whose education for the world was all on the point of beginning. I am unable even to remember at this day what proposal I framed for the end of his holidays and the resumption of his studies. Lessons with me, indeed, that charming summer, we all had a theory that he was to have; but I now feel that, for weeks, the lessons must have been rather my own. I learnt something—at first certainly—that had not been one of the teachings of my small, smothered life; learnt to be amused, and even amusing, and not to think for the morrow. It was the first time, in a manner, that I had known space and air and freedom, all the music of summer and all the mystery of nature. And then there was consideration—and consideration was sweet. Oh, it was a trap—not designed, but deep—to my imagination, to my delicacy, perhaps to my vanity; to whatever, in me, was most excitable. The best way to picture it all is to say that I was off my guard. They gave me so little trouble—they were of a gentleness so extraordinary. I used to speculate—but even this with a dim disconnectedness—as to how the rough future (for all futures are rough!) would handle them and might bruise them. They had the bloom of health and happiness; and yet, as if I had been in charge of a pair of little grandees, of princes of the blood, for whom everything, to be right, would have to be enclosed and protected, the only form that, in my fancy, the after-years could take for them was that of a romantic, a really royal extension of the garden and the park. It may be, of course, above all, that what suddenly broke into this gives the previous time a charm of stillness—that hush in which

something gathers or crouches. The change was actually like
the spring of a beast.

In the first weeks the days were long; they often, at their
finest, gave me what I used to call my own hour, the hour
when, for my pupils, tea-time and bed-time having come and
gone, I had, before my final retirement, a small interval alone.
Much as I liked my companions, this hour was the thing in
the day I liked most; and I liked it best of all when, as the
light faded—or rather, I should say, the day lingered and the
last calls of the last birds sounded, in a flushed sky, from the
old trees—I could take a turn into the grounds and enjoy,
almost with a sense of property that amused and flattered me,
the beauty and dignity of the place. It was a pleasure at these
moments to feel myself tranquil and justified; doubtless, perhaps, also to reflect that by my discretion, my quiet good
sense and general high propriety, I was giving pleasure—if he
ever thought of it!—to the person to whose pressure I had
responded. What I was doing was what he had earnestly
hoped and directly asked of me, and that I *could*, after all, do
it proved even a greater joy than I had expected. I dare say I
fancied myself, in short, a remarkable young woman and took
comfort in the faith that this would more publicly appear.
Well, I needed to be remarkable to offer a front to the remarkable things that presently gave their first sign.

It was plump, one afternoon, in the middle of my very
hour: the children were tucked away and I had come out for
my stroll. One of the thoughts that, as I don't in the least
shrink now from noting, used to be with me in these wan-
derings was that it would be as charming as a charming story
suddenly to meet someone. Someone would appear there at
the turn of a path and would stand before me and smile and
approve. I didn't ask more than that—I only asked that he
should *know*; and the only way to be sure he knew would be
to see it, and the kind light of it, in his handsome face. That
was exactly present to me—by which I mean the face was—
when, on the first of these occasions, at the end of a long June
day, I stopped short on emerging from one of the plantations
and coming into view of the house. What arrested me on the
spot—and with a shock much greater than any vision had allowed for—was the sense that my imagination had, in a flash,

turned real. He did stand there!—but high up, beyond the lawn and at the very top of the tower to which, on that first morning, little Flora had conducted me. This tower was one of a pair—square, incongruous, crenelated structures—that were distinguished, for some reason, though I could see little difference, as the new and the old. They flanked opposite ends of the house and were probably architectural absurdities, redeemed in a measure indeed by not being wholly disengaged nor of a height too pretentious, dating, in their gingerbread antiquity, from a romantic revival that was already a respectable past. I admired them, had fancies about them, for we could all profit in a degree, especially when they loomed through the dusk, by the grandeur of their actual battlements; yet it was not at such an elevation that the figure I had so often invoked seemed most in place.

It produced in me, this figure, in the clear twilight, I remember, two distinct gasps of emotion, which were, sharply, the shock of my first and that of my second surprise. My second was a violent perception of the mistake of my first: the man who met my eyes was not the person I had precipitately supposed. There came to me thus a bewilderment of vision of which, after these years, there is no living view that I can hope to give. An unknown man in a lonely place is a permitted object of fear to a young woman privately bred; and the figure that faced me was—a few more seconds assured me—as little anyone else I knew as it was the image that had been in my mind. I had not seen it in Harley Street—I had not seen it anywhere. The place, moreover, in the strangest way in the world, had, on the instant, and by the very fact of its appearance, become a solitude. To me at least, making my statement here with a deliberation with which I have never made it, the whole feeling of the moment returns. It was as if, while I took in—what I did take in—all the rest of the scene had been stricken with death. I can hear again, as I write, the intense hush in which the sounds of evening dropped. The rooks stopped cawing in the golden sky and the friendly hour lost, for the minute, all its voice. But there was no other change in nature, unless indeed it were a change that I saw with a stranger sharpness. The gold was still in the sky, the clearness in the air, and the man who looked at me over the battlements was as definite as a picture in a frame. That's how I thought, with extraordinary quickness, of each person that he might have been and that he was not. We were confronted across our distance quite long enough for me to ask myself with intensity who then he was and to feel, as an effect of my inability to say, a wonder that in a few instants more became intense.

The great question, or one of these, is, afterwards, I know, with regard to certain matters, the question of how long they have lasted. Well, this matter of mine, think what you will of it, lasted while I caught at a dozen possibilities, none of which made a difference for the better, that I could see, in there having been in the house—and for how long, above all?—a person of whom I was in ignorance. It lasted while I just bridled a little with the sense that my office demanded that there should be no such ignorance and no such person. It lasted while this visitant, at all events,—and there was a touch of the strange freedom, as I remember, in the sign of familiarity of his wearing no hat,—seemed to fix me, from his position, with just the question, just the scrutiny through the fading light, that his own presence provoked. We were too far apart to call to each other, but there was a moment at which, at shorter range, some challenge between us, breaking the hush, would have been the right result of our straight mutual stare. He was in one of the angles, the one away from the house, very erect, as it struck me, and with both hands on the ledge. So I saw him as I see the letters I form on this page; then, exactly, after a minute, as if to add to the spectacle, he slowly changed his place—passed, looking at me hard all the while, to the opposite corner of the platform. Yes, I had the sharpest sense that during this transit he never took his eyes from me, and I can see at this moment the way his hand, as he went, passed from one of the crenelations to the next. He stopped at the other corner, but less long, and even as he turned away still markedly fixed me. He turned away; that was all I knew.

IV

It was not that I didn't wait, on this occasion, for more, for I was rooted as deeply as I was shaken. Was there a "secret"

at Bly—a mystery of Udolpho or an insane, an unmentionable
relative kept in unsuspected confinement? I can't say how long
I turned it over, or how long, in a confusion of curiosity and
dread, I remained where I had had my collision; I only recall
that when I re-entered the house darkness had quite closed
in. Agitation, in the interval, certainly had held me and driven
me, for I must, in circling about the place, have walked three
miles; but I was to be, later on, so much more overwhelmed
that this mere dawn of alarm was a comparatively human chill.
The most singular part of it in fact—singular as the rest had
been—was the part I became, in the hall, aware of in meeting
Mrs. Grose. This picture comes back to me in the general
train—the impression, as I received it on my return, of the
wide white panelled space, bright in the lamplight and with
its portraits and red carpet, and of the good surprised look of
my friend, which immediately told me she had missed me. It
came to me straightway, under her contact, that, with plain
heartiness, mere relieved anxiety at my appearance, she knew
nothing whatever that could bear upon the incident I had
there ready for her. I had not suspected in advance that her
comfortable face would pull me up, and I somehow measured
the importance of what I had seen by my thus finding myself
hesitate to mention it. Scarce anything in the whole history
seems to me so odd as this fact that my real beginning of fear
was one, as I may say, with the instinct of sparing my companion. On the spot, accordingly, in the pleasant hall and with
her eyes on me, I, for a reason that I couldn't then have
phrased, achieved an inward revolution—offered a vague pretext for my lateness and, with the plea of the beauty of the
night and of the heavy dew and wet feet, went as soon as
possible to my room.

Here it was another affair; here, for many days after, it was
a queer affair enough. There were hours, from day to day,—
or at least there were moments, snatched even from clear
duties,—when I had to shut myself up to think. It was not so
much yet that I was more nervous than I could bear to be as
that I was remarkably afraid of becoming so; for the truth I
had now to turn over was, simply and clearly, the truth that
I could arrive at no account whatever of the visitor with whom
I had been so inexplicably and yet, as it seemed to me, so

intimately concerned. It took little time to see that I could sound without forms of inquiry and without exciting remark any domestic complication. The shock I had suffered must have sharpened all my senses; I felt sure, at the end of three days and as the result of mere closer attention, that I had not been practised upon by the servants nor made the object of any "game." Of whatever it was that I knew nothing was known around me. There was but one sane inference: someone had taken a liberty rather gross. That was what, repeatedly, I dipped into my room and locked the door to say to myself. We had been, collectively, subject to an intrusion; some unscrupulous traveller, curious in old houses, had made his way in unobserved, enjoyed the prospect from the best point of view, and then stolen out as he came. If he had given me such a bold hard stare, that was but a part of his indiscretion. The good thing, after all, was that we should surely see no more of him.

This was not so good a thing, I admit, as not to leave me to judge that what, essentially, made nothing else much signify was simply my charming work. My charming work was just my life with Miles and Flora, and through nothing could I so like it as through feeling that I could throw myself into it in trouble. The attraction of my small charges was a constant joy, leading me to wonder afresh at the vanity of my original fears, the distaste I had begun by entertaining for the probable grey prose of my office. There was to be no grey prose, it appeared, and no long grind; so how could work not be charming that presented itself as daily beauty? It was all the romance of the nursery and the poetry of the schoolroom. I don't mean by this, of course, that we studied only fiction and verse; I mean I can express no otherwise the sort of interest my companions inspired. How can I describe that except by saying that instead of growing used to them—and it's a marvel for a governess: I call the sisterhood to witness!—I made constant fresh discoveries. There was one direction, assuredly, in which these discoveries stopped: deep obscurity continued to cover the region of the boy's conduct at school. It had been promptly given me, I have noted, to face that mystery without a pang. Perhaps even it would be nearer the truth to say that—without a word—he himself had cleared it up. He had made the whole charge absurd. My conclusion bloomed there with the real rose-flush of his innocence: he was only too fine and fair for the little horrid, unclean school-world, and he had paid a price for it. I reflected acutely that the sense of such differences, such superiorities of quality, always, on the part of the majority—which could include even stupid, sordid headmasters—turns infallibly to the vindictive.

Both the children had a gentleness (it was their only fault, and it never made Miles a muff) that kept them—how shall I express it?—almost impersonal and certainly quite unpunishable. They were like the cherubs of the anecdote, who had—morally, at any rate—nothing to whack! I remember feeling with Miles in especial as if he had had, as it were, no history. We expect of a small child a scant one, but there was in this beautiful little boy something extraordinarily sensitive, yet extraordinarily happy, that, more than in any creature of his age I have seen, struck me as beginning anew each day. He had never for a second suffered. I took this as a direct disproof of his having really been chastised. If he had been wicked he would have "caught" it, and I should have caught it by the rebound—I should have found the trace. I found nothing at all, and he was therefore an angel. He never spoke of his school, never mentioned a comrade or a master; and I, for my part, was quite too much disgusted to allude to them. Of course I was under the spell, and the wonderful part is that, even at the time, I perfectly knew I was. But I gave myself up to it; it was an antidote to any pain, and I had more pains than one. I was in receipt in these days of disturbing letters from home, where things were not going well. But with my children, what things in the world mattered? That was the question I used to put to my scrappy retirements. I was dazzled by their loveliness.

There was a Sunday—to get on—when it rained with such force and for so many hours that there could be no procession to church; in consequence of which, as the day declined, I had arranged with Mrs. Grose that, should the evening show improvement, we would attend together the late service. The rain happily stopped, and I prepared for our walk, which, through the park and by the good road to the village, would be a matter of twenty minutes. Coming downstairs to meet

my colleague in the hall, I remembered a pair of gloves that
had required three stitches and that had received them—with
a publicity perhaps not edifying—while I sat with the children
at their tea, served on Sundays, by exception, in that cold,
clean temple of mahogany and brass, the "grown-up" dining-
room. The gloves had been dropped there, and I turned in
to recover them. The day was grey enough, but the afternoon
light still lingered, and it enabled me, on crossing the threshold, not only to recognise, on a chair near the wide window,
then closed, the articles I wanted, but to become aware of a
person on the other side of the window and looking straight
in. One step into the room had sufficed; my vision was instantaneous; it was all there. The person looking straight in
was the person who had already appeared to me. He appeared
thus again with I won't say greater distinctness, for that was
impossible, but with a nearness that represented a forward
stride in our intercourse and made me, as I met him, catch
my breath and turn cold. He was the same—he was the same,
and seen, this time, as he had been seen before, from the waist
up, the window, though the dining-room was on the ground-
floor, not going down to the terrace on which he stood. His
face was close to the glass, yet the effect of this better view
was, strangely, only to show me how intense the former had
been. He remained but a few seconds—long enough to convince me he also saw and recognised; but it was as if I had
been looking at him for years and had known him always.
Something, however, happened this time that had not happened before; his stare into my face, through the glass and
across the room, was as deep and hard as then, but it quitted
me for a moment during which I could still watch it, see it
fix successively several other things. On the spot there came
to me the added shock of a certitude that it was not for me
he had come there. He had come for someone else.

The flash of this knowledge—for it was knowledge in the
midst of dread—produced in me the most extraordinary effect, started, as I stood there, a sudden vibration of duty and
courage. I say courage because I was beyond all doubt already
far gone. I bounded straight out of the door again, reached
that of the house, got, in an instant, upon the drive, and,
passing along the terrace as fast as I could rush, turned a

corner and came full in sight. But it was in sight of nothing now—my visitor had vanished. I stopped, I almost dropped, with the real relief of this; but I took in the whole scene—I gave him time to reappear. I call it time, but how long was it? I can't speak to the purpose today of the duration of these things. That kind of measure must have left me: they couldn't have lasted as they actually appeared to me to last. The terrace and the whole place, the lawn and the garden beyond it, all I could see of the park, were empty with a great emptiness. There were shrubberies and big trees, but I remember the clear assurance I felt that none of them concealed him. He was there or was not there: not there if I didn't see him. I got hold of this; then, instinctively, instead of returning as I had come, went to the window. It was confusedly present to me that I ought to place myself where he had stood. I did so; I applied my face to the pane and looked, as he had looked, into the room. As if, at this moment, to show me exactly what his range had been, Mrs. Grose, as I had done for himself just before, came in from the hall. With this I had the full image of a repetition of what had already occurred. She saw me as I had seen my own visitant, she pulled up short as I had done; I gave her something of the shock that I had received. She turned white, and this made me ask myself if I had blanched as much. She stared, in short, and retreated on just *my* lines, and I knew she had then passed out and come round to me and that I should presently meet her. I remained where I was, and while I waited I thought of more things than one. But there's only one I take space to mention. I wondered why *she* should be scared.

V

Oh, she let me know as soon as, round the corner of the house, she loomed again into view. "What in the name of goodness is the matter——?" She was now flushed and out of breath.

I said nothing till she came quite near. "With me?" I must have made a wonderful face. "Do I show it?"

"You're as white as a sheet. You look awful."

I considered; I could meet on this, without scruple, any innocence. My need to respect the bloom of Mrs. Grose's had dropped, without a rustle, from my shoulders, and if I wavered for the instant it was not with what I kept back. I put out my hand to her and she took it; I held her hard a little, liking to feel her close to me. There was a kind of support in the shy heave of her surprise. "You came for me for church, of course, but I can't go."

"Has anything happened?"

"Yes. You must know now. Did I look very queer?"

"Through this window? Dreadful!"

"Well," I said, "I've been frightened." Mrs. Grose's eyes expressed plainly that *she* had no wish to be, yet also that she knew too well her place not to be ready to share with me any marked inconvenience. Oh, it was quite settled that she *must* share! "Just what you saw from the dining-room a minute ago was the effect of that. What *I* saw—just before—was much worse."

Her hand tightened. "What was it?"

"An extraordinary man. Looking in."

"What extraordinary man?"

"I haven't the least idea."

Mrs. Grose gazed round us in vain. "Then where is he gone?"

"I know still less."

"Have you seen him before?"

"Yes—once. On the old tower."

She could only look at me harder. "Do you mean he's a stranger?"

"Oh, very much!"

"Yet you didn't tell me?"

"No—for reasons. But now that you've guessed——"

Mrs. Grose's round eyes encountered this charge. "Ah, I haven't guessed!" she said very simply. "How can I if *you* don't imagine?"

"I don't in the very least."

"You've seen him nowhere but on the tower?"

"And on this spot just now."

Mrs. Grose looked round again. "What was he doing on the tower?"

"Only standing there and looking down at me."

She thought a minute. "Was he a gentleman?"

I found I had no need to think. "No." She gazed in deeper wonder. "No."

"Then nobody about the place? Nobody from the village?"

"Nobody—nobody. I didn't tell you, but I made sure."

She breathed a vague relief: this was, oddly, so much to the good. It only went indeed a little way. "But if he isn't a gentleman——"

"What *is* he? He's a horror."

"A horror?"

"He's—God help me if I know *what* he is!"

Mrs. Grose looked round once more; she fixed her eyes on the duskier distance, then, pulling herself together, turned to me with abrupt inconsequence. "It's time we should be at church."

"Oh, I'm not fit for church!"

"Won't it do you good?"

"It won't do *them*——!" I nodded at the house.

"The children?"

"I can't leave them now."

"You're afraid——?"

I spoke boldly. "I'm afraid of *him*."

Mrs. Grose's large face showed me, at this, for the first time, the far-away faint glimmer of a consciousness more acute: I somehow made out in it the delayed dawn of an idea I myself had not given her and that was as yet quite obscure to me. It comes back to me that I thought instantly of this as something I could get from her; and I felt it to be connected with the desire she presently showed to know more. "When was it—on the tower?"

"About the middle of the month. At this same hour."

"Almost at dark," said Mrs. Grose.

"Oh no, not nearly. I saw him as I see you."

"Then how did he get in?"

"And how did he get out?" I laughed. "I had no opportunity to ask him! This evening, you see," I pursued, "he has not been able to get in."

"He only peeps?"

"I hope it will be confined to that!" She had now let go my hand; she turned away a little. I waited an instant; then I brought out: "Go to church. Good-bye. I must watch."

Slowly she faced me again. "Do you fear for them?"

We met in another long look. "Don't *you*?" Instead of answering she came nearer to the window and, for a minute, applied her face to the glass. "You see how he could see," I meanwhile went on.

She didn't move. "How long was he here?"

"Till I came out. I came to meet him."

Mrs. Grose at last turned round, and there was still more in her face. "*I* couldn't have come out."

"Neither could I!" I laughed again. "But I did come. I have my duty."

"So have I mine," she replied; after which she added: "What is he like?"

"I've been dying to tell you. But he's like nobody."

"Nobody?" she echoed.

"He has no hat." Then seeing in her face that she already, in this, with a deeper dismay, found a touch of picture, I quickly added stroke to stroke. "He has red hair, very red, close-curling, and a pale face, long in shape, with straight, good features and little, rather queer whiskers that are as red as his hair. His eyebrows are, somehow, darker; they look particularly arched and as if they might move a good deal. His eyes are sharp, strange—awfully; but I only know clearly that they're rather small and very fixed. His mouth's wide, and his lips are thin, and except for his little whiskers he's quite clean-shaven. He gives me a sort of sense of looking like an actor."

"An actor!" It was impossible to resemble one less, at least, than Mrs. Grose at that moment.

"I've never seen one, but so I suppose them. He's tall, active, erect," I continued, "but never—no, never!—a gentleman."

My companion's face had blanched as I went on; her round eyes started and her mild mouth gaped. "A gentleman?" she gasped, confounded, stupefied: "a gentleman *he*?"

"You know him then?"

She visibly tried to hold herself. "But he *is* handsome?"

I saw the way to help her. "Remarkably!"

"And dressed——?"

"In somebody's clothes. They're smart, but they're not his own."

She broke into a breathless affirmative groan. "They're the master's!"

I caught it up. "You *do* know him?"

She faltered but a second. "Quint!" she cried.

"Quint?"

"Peter Quint—his own man, his valet, when he was here!"

"When the master was?"

Gaping still, but meeting me, she pieced it all together. "He never wore his hat, but he did wear—well, there were waistcoats missed! They were both here—last year. Then the master went, and Quint was alone."

I followed, but halting a little. "Alone?"

"Alone with *us*." Then, as from a deeper depth, "In charge," she added.

"And what became of him?"

She hung fire so long that I was still more mystified. "He went too," she brought out at last.

"Went where?"

Her expression, at this, became extraordinary. "God knows where! He died."

"Died?" I almost shrieked.

She seemed fairly to square herself, plant herself more firmly to utter the wonder of it. "Yes. Mr. Quint is dead."

VI

It took of course more than that particular passage to place us together in presence of what we had now to live with as we could—my dreadful liability to impressions of the order so vividly exemplified, and my companion's knowledge, henceforth,—a knowledge half consternation and half compassion,—of that liability. There had been, this evening, after the revelation that left me, for an hour, so prostrate—there had been, for either of us, no attendance on any service but a little service of tears and vows, of prayers and promises, a climax to the series of mutual challenges and pledges that had straightway ensued on our retreating together to the schoolroom and shutting ourselves up there to have everything out. The result of our having everything out was simply to reduce our situation to the last rigour of its elements. She herself had seen nothing, not the shadow of a shadow, and nobody in the house but the governess was in the governess's plight; yet she accepted without directly impugning my sanity the truth as I gave it to her, and ended by showing me, on this ground, an awe-stricken tenderness, an expression of the sense of my more than questionable privilege, of which the very breath has remained with me as that of the sweetest of human charities.

What was settled between us, accordingly, that night, was that we thought we might bear things together; and I was not even sure that, in spite of her exemption, it was she who had the best of the burden. I knew at this hour, I think, as well as I knew later what I was capable of meeting to shelter my pupils; but it took me some time to be wholly sure of what my honest ally was prepared for to keep terms with so compromising a contract. I was queer company enough—quite as queer as the company I received; but as I trace over what we went through I see how much common ground we must have found in the one idea that, by good fortune, *could* steady us. It was the idea, the second movement, that led me straight out, as I may say, of the inner chamber of my dread. I could take the air in the court, at least, and there Mrs. Grose could join me. Perfectly can I recall now the particular way strength came to me before we separated for the night. We had gone over and over every feature of what I had seen.

"He was looking for someone else, you say—someone who was not you?"

"He was looking for little Miles." A portentous clearness now possessed me. "*That's* whom he was looking for."

"But how do you know?"

"I know, I know, I know!" My exaltation grew. "And *you* know, my dear!"

She didn't deny this, but I required, I felt, not even so much telling as that. She resumed in a moment, at any rate: "What if *he* should see him?"

"Little Miles? That's what he wants!"

She looked immensely scared again. "The child?"

"Heaven forbid! The man. He wants to appear to *them*." That he might was an awful conception, and yet, somehow, I could keep it at bay; which, moreover, as we lingered there, was what I succeeded in practically proving. I had an absolute certainty that I should see again what I had already seen, but something within me said that by offering myself bravely as the sole subject of such experience, by accepting, by inviting, by surmounting it all, I should serve as an expiatory victim and guard the tranquillity of my companions. The children, in especial, I should thus fence about and absolutely save. I recall one of the last things I said that night to Mrs. Grose.

"It does strike me that my pupils have never mentioned——"

She looked at me hard as I musingly pulled up. "His having been here and the time they were with him?"

"The time they were with him, and his name, his presence, his history, in any way."

"Oh, the little lady doesn't remember. She never heard or knew."

"The circumstances of his death?" I thought with some intensity. "Perhaps not. But Miles would remember—Miles would know."

"Ah, don't try him!" broke from Mrs. Grose.

I returned her the look she had given me. "Don't be afraid." I continued to think. "It *is* rather odd."

"That he has never spoken of him?"

"Never by the least allusion. And you tell me they were 'great friends'?"

"Oh, it wasn't *him*!" Mrs. Grose with emphasis declared. "It was Quint's own fancy. To play with him, I mean—to spoil him." She paused a moment; then she added: "Quint was much too free."

This gave me, straight from my vision of his face—*such a face!*—a sudden sickness of disgust. "Too free with *my* boy?"

"Too free with everyone!"

I forbore, for the moment, to analyse this description further than by the reflection that a part of it applied to several of the members of the household, of the half-dozen maids and men who were still of our small colony. But there was everything, for our apprehension, in the lucky fact that no discomfortable legend, no perturbation of scullions, had ever, within anyone's memory, attached to the kind old place. It had neither bad name nor ill fame, and Mrs. Grose, most apparently, only desired to cling to me and to quake in silence. I even put her, the very last thing of all, to the test. It was when, at midnight, she had her hand on the schoolroom door to take leave. "I have it from you then—for it's of great importance—that he was definitely and admittedly bad?"

"Oh, not admittedly. *I* knew it—but the master didn't."

"And you never told him?"

"Well, he didn't like tale-baring—he hated complaints. He was terribly short with anything of that kind, and if people were all right to *him*——"

"He wouldn't be bothered with more?" This squared well enough with my impression of him: he was not a trouble-loving gentleman, nor so very particular perhaps about some of the company *he* kept. All the same, I pressed my interlocutress. "I promise you *I* would have told!"

She felt my discrimination. "I dare say I was wrong. But, really, I was afraid."

"Afraid of what?"

"Of things that man could do. Quint was so clever—he was so deep."

I took this in still more than, probably, I showed. "You weren't afraid of anything else? Not of his effect——?"

"His effect?" she repeated with a face of anguish and waiting while I faltered.

"On innocent little precious lives. They were in your charge."

"No, they were not in mine!" she roundly and distressfully returned. "The master believed in him and placed him here because he was supposed not to be well and the country air so good for him. So he had everything to say. Yes"—she let me have it—"even about *them*."

"Them—that creature?" I had to smother a kind of howl. "And you could bear it!"

"No. I couldn't—and I can't now!" And the poor woman burst into tears.

A rigid control, from the next day, was, as I have said, to follow them; yet how often and how passionately, for a week, we came back together to the subject! Much as we had discussed it that Sunday night, I was, in the immediate later hours in especial—for it may be imagined whether I slept—

still haunted with the shadow of something she had not told me. I myself had kept back nothing, but there was a word Mrs. Grose had kept back. I was sure, moreover, by morning, that this was not from a failure of frankness, but because on every side there were fears. It seems to me indeed, in retrospect, that by the time the morrow's sun was high I had restlessly read into the facts before us almost all the meaning they were to receive from subsequent and more cruel occurrences. What they gave me above all was just the sinister figure of the living man—the dead one would keep awhile!—and of the months he had continuously passed at Bly, which, added up, made a formidable stretch. The limit of this evil time had arrived only when, on the dawn of a winter's morning, Peter Quint was found, by a labourer going to early work, stone dead on the road from the village: a catastrophe explained— superficially at least—by a visible wound to his head; such a wound as might have been produced—and as, on the final evidence, *had* been—by a fatal slip, in the dark and after leaving the public house, on the steepish icy slope, a wrong path altogether, at the bottom of which he lay. The icy slope, the turn mistaken at night and in liquor, accounted for much— practically, in the end and after the inquest and boundless chatter, for everything; but there had been matters in his life— strange passages and perils, secret disorders, vices more than suspected—that would have accounted for a good deal more.

I scarce know how to put my story into words that shall be a credible picture of my state of mind; but I was in these days literally able to find a joy in the extraordinary flight of heroism the occasion demanded of me. I now saw that I had been asked for a service admirable and difficult, and there would be a greatness in letting it be seen—oh, in the right quarter!— that I could succeed where many another girl might have failed. It was an immense help to me—I confess I rather applaud myself as I look back!—that I saw my service so strongly and so simply. I was there to protect and defend the little creatures in the world the most bereaved and the most loveable, the appeal of whose helplessness had suddenly become only too explicit, a deep, constant ache of one's own committed heart. We were cut off, really, together; we were united in our danger. They had nothing but me, and I—well, I had *them*. It was in short a magnificent chance. This chance presented itself to me in an image richly material. I was a screen—I was to stand before them. The more I saw, the less they would. I began to watch them in a stifled suspense, a disguised excitement that might well, had it continued too long, have turned to something like madness. What saved me, as I now see, was that it turned to something else altogether. It didn't last as suspense—it was superseded by horrible proofs. Proofs, I say, yes—from the moment I really took hold.

This moment dated from an afternoon hour that I happened to spend in the grounds with the younger of my pupils alone. We had left Miles indoors, on the red cushion of a deep window-seat; he had wished to finish a book, and I had been glad to encourage a purpose so laudable in a young man whose only defect was an occasional excess of the restless. His sister, on the contrary, had been alert to come out, and I strolled with her half an hour, seeking the shade, for the sun was still high and the day exceptionally warm. I was aware afresh, with her, as we went, of how, like her brother, she contrived—it was the charming thing in both children—to let me alone without appearing to drop me and to accompany me without appearing to surround. They were never importunate and yet never listless. My attention to them all really went to seeing them amuse themselves immensely without me: this was a spectacle they seemed actively to prepare and that engaged me as an active admirer. I walked in a world of their invention—they had no occasion whatever to draw upon mine; so that my time was taken only with being, for them, some remarkable person or thing that the game of the moment required and that was merely, thanks to my superior, my exalted stamp, a happy and highly distinguished sinecure. I forget what I was on the present occasion; I only remember that I was something very important and very quiet and that Flora was playing very hard. We were on the edge of the lake, and, as we had lately begun geography, the lake was the Sea of Azof.

Suddenly, in these circumstances, I became aware that, on the other side of the Sea of Azof, we had an interested spectator. The way this knowledge gathered in me was the strangest thing in the world—the strangest, that is, except the very much stranger in which it quickly merged itself. I had sat down with a piece of work—for I was something or other that could sit—on the old stone bench which overlooked the pond; and in this position I began to take in with certitude, and yet without direct vision, the presence, at a distance, of a third person. The old trees, the thick shrubbery, made a great and pleasant shade, but it was all suffused with the brightness of the hot, still hour. There was no ambiguity in anything; none whatever, at least, in the conviction I from one moment to another found myself forming as to what I should see straight before me and across the lake as a consequence of raising my eyes. They were attached at this juncture to the stitching in which I was engaged, and I can feel once more the spasm of my effort not to move them till I should so have steadied myself as to be able to make up my mind what to do. There was an alien object in view—a figure whose right of presence I instantly, passionately questioned. I recollect counting over perfectly the possibilities, reminding myself that nothing was more natural, for instance, than the appearance of one of the men about the place, or even of a messenger, a postman or a tradesman's boy, from the village. That reminder had as little effect on my practical certitude as I was conscious—still even without looking—of its having upon the character and attitude of our visitor. Nothing was more natural than that these things should be the other things that they absolutely were not.

Of the positive identity of the apparition I would assure myself as soon as the small clock of my courage should have ticked out the right second; meanwhile, with an effort that was already sharp enough, I transferred my eyes straight to little Flora, who, at the moment, was about ten yards away. My heart had stood still for an instant with the wonder and terror of the question whether she too would see; and I held my breath while I waited for what a cry from her, what some sudden innocent sign either of interest or of alarm, would tell me. I waited, but nothing came; then, in the first place—and there is something more dire in this, I feel, than in anything I have to relate—I was determined by a sense that, within a minute, all sounds from her had previously dropped; and, in the second, by the circumstance that, also within the minute, she had, in her play, turned her back to the water. This was her attitude when I at last looked at her—looked with the confirmed conviction that we were still, together, under direct personal notice. She had picked up a small flat piece of wood, which happened to have in it a little hole that had evidently suggested to her the idea of sticking in another fragment that might figure as a mast and make the thing a boat. This second morsel, as I watched her, she was very markedly and intently attempting to tighten in its place. My apprehension of what she was doing sustained me so that after some seconds I felt I was ready for more. Then I again shifted my eyes—I faced what I had to face.

VII

I got hold of Mrs. Grose as soon after this as I could; and I can give no intelligible account of how I fought out the interval. Yet I still hear myself cry as I fairly threw myself into her arms: "They *know*—it's too monstrous: they know, they know!"

"And what on earth——?" I felt her incredulity as she held me.

"Why, all that *we* know—and heaven knows what else besides!" Then, as she released me, I made it out to her, made it out perhaps only now with full coherency even to myself. "Two hours ago, in the garden"—I could scarce articulate—"Flora *saw*!"

Mrs. Grose took it as she might have taken a blow in the stomach. "She has told you?" she panted.

"Not a word—that's the horror. She kept it to herself! The child of eight, *that* child!" Unutterable still, for me, was the stupefaction of it.

Mrs. Grose, of course, could only gape the wider. "Then how do you know?"

"I was there—I saw with my eyes: saw that she was perfectly aware."

"Do you mean aware of *him*?"

"No—of *her*." I was conscious as I spoke that I looked prodigious things, for I got the slow reflection of them in my companion's face. "Another person—this time; but a figure of quite as unmistakeable horror and evil: a woman in black, pale and dreadful—with such an air also, and such a face!—on the other side of the lake. I was there with the child—quiet for the hour; and in the midst of it she came."

"Came how—from where?"

"From where they come from! She just appeared and stood there—but not so near."

"And without coming nearer?"

"Oh, for the effect and the feeling, she might have been as close as you!"

My friend, with an odd impulse, fell back a step. "Was she someone you've never seen?"

"Yes. But someone the child has. Someone *you* have." Then, to show how I had thought it all out: "My predecessor—the one who died."

"Miss Jessel?"

"Miss Jessel. You don't believe me?" I pressed.

She turned right and left in her distress. "How can you be sure?"

This drew from me, in the state of my nerves, a flash of impatience. "Then ask Flora—*she's* sure!" But I had no sooner spoken than I caught myself up. "No, for God's sake, *don't!* She'll say she isn't—she'll lie!"

Mrs. Grose was not too bewildered instinctively to protest. "Ah, how *can* you?"

"Because I'm clear. Flora doesn't want me to know."

"It's only then to spare you."

"No, no—there are depths, depths! The more I go over it, the more I see in it, and the more I see in it the more I fear. I don't know what I *don't* see—what I *don't* fear!"

Mrs. Grose tried to keep up with me. "You mean you're afraid of seeing her again?"

"Oh, no; that's nothing—now!" Then I explained. "It's of *not* seeing her."

But my companion only looked wan. "I don't understand you."

"Why, it's that the child may keep it up—and that the child assuredly *will*—without my knowing it."

At the image of this possibility Mrs. Grose for a moment collapsed, yet presently to pull herself together again, as if from the positive force of the sense of what, should we yield an inch, there would really be to give way to. "Dear, dear— we must keep our heads! And after all, if she doesn't mind it——!" She even tried a grim joke. "Perhaps she likes it!"

"Likes *such* things—a scrap of an infant!"

"Isn't it just a proof of her blessed innocence?" my friend bravely inquired.

She brought me, for the instant, almost round. "Oh, we must clutch at *that*—we must cling to it! If it isn't a proof of what you say, it's a proof of—God knows what! For the woman's a horror of horrors."

"Mrs. Grose, at this, fixed her eyes a minute on the ground; then at last raising them, "Tell me how you know," she said.

"Then you admit it's what she was?" I cried.

"Tell me how you know," my friend simply repeated.

"Know? By seeing her! By the way she looked."

"At you, do you mean—so wickedly?"

"Dear me, no—I could have borne that. She gave me never a glance. She only fixed the child."

Mrs. Grose tried to see it. "Fixed her?"

"Ah, with such awful eyes!"

She stared at mine as if they might really have resembled them. "Do you mean of dislike?"

"God help us, no. Of something much worse."

"Worse than dislike?"—this left her indeed at a loss.

"With a determination—indescribable. With a kind of fury of intention."

I made her turn pale. "Intention?"

"To get hold of her." Mrs. Grose—her eyes just lingering on mine—gave a shudder and walked to the window; and while she stood there looking out I completed my statement. "*That's* what Flora knows."

After a little she turned round. "The person was in black, you say?"

"In mourning—rather poor, almost shabby. But—yes— with extraordinary beauty." I now recognised to what I had at last, stroke by stroke, brought the victim of my confidence, for she quite visibly weighed this. "Oh, handsome—very, very," I insisted; "wonderfully handsome. But infamous."

She slowly came back to me. "Miss Jessel—*was* infamous." She once more took my hand in both her own, holding it as tight as if to fortify me against the increase of alarm I might draw from this disclosure. "They were both infamous," she finally said.

So, for a little, we faced it once more together; and I found absolutely a degree of help in seeing it now so straight. "I appreciate," I said, "the great decency of your not having hitherto spoken; but the time has certainly come to give me the whole thing." She appeared to assent to this, but still only in silence; seeing which I went on: "I must have it now. Of what did she die? Come, there was something between them."

"There was everything."

"In spite of the difference——?"

"Oh, of their rank, their condition"—she brought it woefully out. "*She* was a lady."

I turned it over; I again saw. "Yes—she was a lady."

"And he so dreadfully below," said Mrs. Grose.

I felt that I doubtless needn't press too hard, in such company, on the place of a servant in the scale; but there was nothing to prevent an acceptance of my companion's own measure of my predecessor's abasement. There was a way to deal with that, and I dealt; the more readily for my full vision—on the evidence—of our employer's late clever, goodlooking "own" man; impudent, assured, spoiled, depraved. "The fellow was a hound."

Mrs. Grose considered as if it were perhaps a little a case for a sense of shades. "I've never seen one like him. He did what he wished."

"With *her*?"

"With them all."

It was as if now in my friend's own eyes Miss Jessel had again appeared. I seemed at any rate, for an instant, to see their evocation of her as distinctly as I had seen her by the pond; and I brought out with decision: "It must have been also what *she* wished!"

Mrs. Grose's face signified that it had been indeed, but she said at the same time: "Poor woman—she paid for it!"

"Then you do know what she died of?" I asked.

"No—I know nothing. I wanted not to know; I was glad enough I didn't; and I thanked heaven she was well out of this!"

"Yet you had, then, your idea——"

"Of her real reason for leaving? Oh, yes—as to that. She couldn't have stayed. Fancy it here—for a governess! And afterwards I imagined—and I still imagine. And what I imagine is dreadful."

"Not so dreadful as what *I* do," I replied; on which I must have shown her—as I was indeed but too conscious—a front of miserable defeat. It brought out again all her compassion for me, and at the renewed touch of her kindness my power to resist broke down. I burst, as I had, the other time, made her burst, into tears; she took me to her motherly breast, and my lamentation overflowed. "I don't do it!" I sobbed in despair; "I don't save or shield them! It's far worse than I dreamed—they're lost!"

VIII

What I had said to Mrs. Grose was true enough: there were in the matter I had put before her depths and possibilities that I lacked resolution to sound; so that when we met once more in the wonder of it we were of a common mind about the duty of resistance to extravagant fancies. We were to keep our heads if we should keep nothing else—difficult indeed as that might be in the face of what, in our prodigious experience, was least to be questioned. Late that night, while the house slept, we had another talk in my room, when she went all the way with me as to its being beyond doubt that I had seen exactly what I had seen. To hold her perfectly in the pinch of that, I found I had only to ask her how, if I had "made it up," I came to be able to give, of each of the persons appearing to me, a picture disclosing, to the last detail, their special marks—a portrait on the exhibition of which she had instantly recognised and named them. She wished, of course,—small blame to her!—to sink the whole subject; and I was quick to assure her that my own interest in it had now violently taken the form of a search for the way to escape from it. I encountered her on the ground of a probability that with recurrence—for recurrence we took for granted—I should get used to my danger, distinctly professing that my personal exposure had suddenly become the least of my discomforts. It was my new suspicion that was intolerable; and yet even to this complication the later hours of the day had brought a little ease.

On leaving her, after my first outbreak, I had of course returned to my pupils, associating the right remedy for my dismay with that sense of their charm which I had already found to be a thing I could positively cultivate and which had never failed me yet. I had simply, in other words, plunged afresh into Flora's special society and there become aware—it was almost a luxury!—that she could put her little conscious hand straight upon the spot that ached. She had looked at me in sweet speculation and then had accused me to my face of having "cried." I had supposed I had brushed away the ugly signs: but I could literally—for the time, at all events—rejoice, under this fathomless charity, that they had not entirely disappeared. To gaze into the depths of blue of the child's eyes and pronounce their loveliness a trick of premature cunning was to be guilty of a cynicism in preference to which I naturally preferred to abjure my judgment and, so far as might be, my agitation. I couldn't abjure for merely wanting to, but I could repeat to Mrs. Grose—as I did there, over and over, in the small hours—that with their voices in the air, their pressure on one's heart and their fragrant faces against one's cheek, everything fell to the ground but their incapacity and their beauty. It was a pity that, somehow, to settle this once for all, I had equally to re-enumerate the signs of subtlety that, in the afternoon, by the lake, had made a miracle of my show of self-possession. It was a pity to be obliged to re-investigate the certitude of the moment itself and repeat how it had come to me as a revelation that the inconceivable communion I then surprised was a matter, for either party, of habit. It was a pity that I should have had to quaver out again the reasons for my not having, in my delusion, so much as questioned that the little girl saw our visitant even as I actually saw Mrs. Grose herself, and that she wanted, by just so much as she did thus see, to make me suppose she didn't, and at the same time, without showing anything, arrive at a guess as to whether I myself did! It was a pity that I needed once more to describe the portentous little activity by which she sought to divert my attention—the perceptible increase of movement, the greater intensity of play, the singing, the gabbling of nonsense, and the invitation to romp.

Yet if I had not indulged, to prove there was nothing in it, in this review, I should have missed the two or three dim elements of comfort that still remained to me. I should not for instance have been able to asseverate to my friend that I was certain—which was so much to the good—that *I* at least had not betrayed myself. I should not have been prompted, by stress of need, by desperation of mind,—I scarce know what to call it,—to invoke such further aid to intelligence as might spring from pushing my colleague fairly to the wall. She had told me, bit by bit, under pressure, a great deal; but a small shifty spot on the wrong side of it all still sometimes brushed my brow like the wing of a bat; and I remember how on this occasion—for the sleeping house and the concentration alike of our danger and our watch seemed to help—I felt the importance of giving the last jerk to the curtain. "I don't believe anything so horrible," I recollect saying; "no, let us put it definitely, my dear, that I don't. But if I did, you know, there's a thing I should require now, just without sparing you the least bit more—oh, not a scrap, come!—to get out of you. What was it you had in mind when, in our distress, before Miles came back, over the letter from his school, you said, under my insistence, that you didn't pretend for him that he had not literally *ever* been 'bad'? He has *not* literally 'ever,' in these weeks that I myself have lived with him and so closely watched him; he has been an imperturbable little prodigy of delightful, loveable goodness. Therefore you might perfectly have made the claim for him if you had not, as it happened, seen an exception to take. What was your exception, and to what passage in your personal observation of him did you refer?"

It was a dreadfully austere inquiry, but levity was not our note, and, at any rate, before the grey dawn admonished us to separate I had got my answer. What my friend had had in mind proved to be immensely to the purpose. It was neither more nor less than the circumstance that for a period of several months Quint and the boy had been perpetually together. It was in fact the very appropriate truth that she had ventured to criticise the propriety, to hint at the incongruity, of so close an alliance, and even to go so far on the subject as a frank overture to Miss Jessel. Miss Jessel had, with a most strange manner, requested her to mind her business, and the good woman had, on this, directly approached little Miles. What she had said to him, since I pressed, was that *she* liked to see young gentlemen not forget their station.

I pressed again, of course, at this. "You reminded him that Quint was only a base menial?"

"As you might say! And it was his answer, for one thing, that was bad."

"And for another thing?" I waited. "He repeated your words to Quint?"

"No, not that. It's just what he *wouldn't*!" she could still impress upon me. "I was sure, at any rate," she added, "that he didn't. But he denied certain occasions."

"What occasions?"

"When they had been about together quite as if Quint were his tutor—and a very grand one—and Miss Jessel only for the little lady. When he had gone off with the fellow, I mean, and spent hours with him."

"He then prevaricated about it—he said he hadn't?" Her assent was clear enough to cause me to add in a moment: "I see. He lied."

"Oh!" Mrs. Grose mumbled. This was a suggestion that it didn't matter; which indeed she backed up by a further remark. "You see, after all, Miss Jessel didn't mind. She didn't forbid him."

I considered. "Did he put that to you as a justification?"

At this she dropped again. "No, he never spoke of it."

"Never mentioned her in connection with Quint?"

She saw, visibly flushing, where I was coming out. "Well, he didn't show anything. He denied," she repeated; "he denied."

Lord, how I pressed her now! "So that you could see he knew what was between the two wretches?"

"I don't know—I don't know!" the poor woman groaned.

"You do know, you dear thing," I replied; "only you haven't my dreadful boldness of mind, and you keep back, out of timidity and modesty and delicacy, even the impression that, in the past, when you had, without my aid, to flounder about in silence, most of all made you miserable. But I shall get it out of you yet! There was something in the boy that suggested to you," I continued, "that he covered and concealed their relation."

"Oh, he couldn't prevent——"

"Your learning the truth? I dare say! But, heavens," I fell, with vehemence, a-thinking, "what it shows that they must, to that extent, have succeeded in making of him!"

"Ah, nothing that's not nice *now*!" Mrs. Grose lugubriously pleaded.

"I don't wonder you looked queer," I persisted, "when I mentioned to you the letter from his school!"

"I doubt if I looked as queer as you!" she retorted with homely force. "And if he was so bad then as that comes to, how is he such an angel now?"

"Yes, indeed—and if he was a fiend at school! How, how, how? Well," I said in my torment, "you must put it to me again, but I shall not be able to tell you for some days. Only, put it to me again!" I cried in a way that made my friend stare. "There are directions in which I must not for the present let myself go." Meanwhile I returned to her first example—the one to which she had just previously referred—of the boy's happy capacity for an occasional slip. "If Quint—on your remonstrance at the time you speak of—was a base menial, one of the things Miles said to you, I find myself guessing, was that you were another." Again her admission was so adequate that I continued: "And you forgave him that?"

"Wouldn't *you*?"

"Oh, yes!" And we exchanged there, in the stillness, a sound of the oddest amusement. Then I went on: "At all events, while he was with the man——"

"Miss Flora was with the woman. It suited them all!"

It suited me too, I felt, only too well; by which I mean that it suited exactly the particularly deadly view I was in the very act of forbidding myself to entertain. But I so far succeeded in checking the expression of this view that I will throw, just here, no further light on it than may be offered by the mention of my final observation to Mrs. Grose. "His having lied and been impudent are, I confess, less engaging specimens than I had hoped to have from you of the outbreak in him of the little natural man. Still," I mused, "they must do, for they make me feel more than ever that I must watch."

It made me blush, the next minute, to see in my friend's face how much more unreservedly she had forgiven him than her anecdote struck me as presenting to my own tenderness an occasion for doing. This came out when, at the schoolroom door, she quitted me. "Surely you don't accuse *him*——"

"Of carrying on an intercourse that he conceals from me? Ah, remember that, until further evidence, I now accuse nobody." Then, before shutting her out to go, by another passage, to her own place, "I must just wait," I wound up.

IX

I waited and waited, and the days, as they elapsed, took something from my consternation. A very few of them, in fact, passing, in constant sight of my pupils, without a fresh incident, sufficed to give to grievous fancies and even to odious memories a kind of brush of the sponge. I have spoken of the surrender to their extraordinary childish grace as a thing I could actively cultivate, and it may be imagined if I neglected now to address myself to this source for whatever it would yield. Stranger than I can express, certainly, was the effort to struggle against my new lights; it would doubtless have been, however, a greater tension still had it not been so frequently successful. I used to wonder how my little charges could help guessing that I thought strange things about them, and the circumstance that these things only made them more interesting was not by itself a direct aid to keeping them in the dark. I trembled lest they should see that they *were* so immensely more interesting. Putting things at the worst, at all events, as in meditation I so often did, any clouding of their innocence could only be—blameless and foredoomed as they were—a reason the more for taking risks. There were mo-

ments when, by an irresistible impulse, I found myself catching them up and pressing them to my heart. As soon as I had
done so I used to say to myself: "What will they think of that?
Doesn't it betray too much?" It would have been easy to get
into a sad, wild tangle about how much I might betray; but
the real account, I feel, of the hours of peace that I could still
enjoy was that the immediate charm of my companions was
a beguilement still effective even under the shadow of the
possibility that it was studied. For if it occurred to me that I
might occasionally excite suspicion by the little outbreaks of
my sharper passion for them, so too I remember wondering
if I mightn't see a queerness in the traceable increase of their
own demonstrations.

They were at this period extravagantly and preternaturally
fond of me; which, after all, I could reflect, was no more than
a graceful response in children perpetually bowed over and
hugged. The homage of which they were so lavish succeeded,
in truth, for my nerves, quite as well as if I never appeared to
myself, as I may say, literally to catch them at a purpose in it.
They had never, I think, wanted to do so many things for
their poor protectress; I mean—though they got their lessons
better and better, which was naturally what would please her
most—in the way of diverting, entertaining, surprising her;
reading her passages, telling her stories, acting her charades,
pouncing out at her, in disguises, as animals and historical
characters, and above all astonishing her by the "pieces" they
had secretly got by heart and could interminably recite. I
should never get to the bottom—were I to let myself go even
now—of the prodigious private commentary, all under still
more private correction, with which, in these days, I over-
scored their full hours. They had shown me from the first a
facility for everything, a general faculty which, taking a fresh
start, achieved remarkable flights. They got their little tasks as
if they loved them, and indulged, from the mere exuberance
of the gift, in the most unimposed little miracles of memory.
They not only popped out at me as tigers and as Romans, but
as Shakespeareans, astronomers, and navigators. This was so
singularly the case that it had presumably much to do with
the fact as to which, at the present day, I am at a loss for a
different explanation: I allude to my unnatural composure on

the subject of another school for Miles. What I remember is that I was content not, for the time, to open the question, and that contentment must have sprung from the sense of his perpetually striking show of cleverness. He was too clever for a bad governess, for a parson's daughter, to spoil; and the strangest if not the brightest thread in the pensive embroidery I just spoke of was the impression I might have got, if I had dared to work it out, that he was under some influence operating in his small intellectual life as a tremendous incitement.

If it was easy to reflect, however, that such a boy could postpone school, it was at least as marked that for such a boy to have been "kicked out" by a school-master was a mystification without end. Let me add that in their company now—and I was careful almost never to be out of it—I could follow no scent very far. We lived in a cloud of music and love and success and private theatricals. The musical sense in each of the children was of the quickest, but the elder in especial had a marvellous knack of catching and repeating. The schoolroom piano broke into all gruesome fancies; and when that failed there were confabulations in corners, with a sequel of one of them going out in the highest spirits in order to "come in" as something new. I had had brothers myself, and it was no revelation to me that little girls could be slavish idolaters of little boys. What surpassed everything was that there was a little boy in the world who could have for the inferior age, sex, and intelligence so fine a consideration. They were extraordinarily at once, and to say that they never either quarrelled or complained is to make the note of praise coarse for their quality of sweetness. Sometimes, indeed, when I dropped into coarseness, I perhaps came across traces of little understandings between them by which one of them should keep me occupied while the other slipped away. There is a *naïf* side, I suppose, in all diplomacy; but if my pupils practised upon me, it was surely with the minimum of grossness. It was all in the other quarter that, after a lull, the grossness broke out.

I find that I really hang back; but I must take my plunge. In going on with the record of what was hideous at Bly, I not only challenge the most liberal faith—for which I little care; but—and this is another matter—I renew what I myself suffered, I again push my way through it to the end. There came suddenly an hour after which, as I look back, the affair seems to me to have been all pure suffering; but I have at least reached the heart of it, and the straightest road out is doubtless to advance. One evening—with nothing to lead up or to prepare it—I felt the cold touch of the impression that had breathed on me the night of my arrival and which, much lighter then, as I have mentioned, I should probably have made little of in memory had my subsequent sojourn been less agitated. I had not gone to bed; I sat reading by a couple of candles. There was a roomful of old books at Bly—last-century fiction, some of it, which, to the extent of a distinctly deprecated renown, but never to so much as that of a stray specimen, had reached the sequestered home and appealed to the unavowed curiosity of my youth. I remember that the book I had in my hand was Fielding's *Amelia*; also that I was wholly awake. I recall further both a general conviction that it was horribly late and a particular objection to looking at my watch. I figure, finally, that the white curtain draping, in the fashion of those days, the head of Flora's little bed, shrouded, as I had assured myself long before, the perfection of childish rest. I recollect in short that, though I was deeply interested in my author, I found myself, at the turn of a page and with his spell all scattered, looking straight up from him and hard at the door of my room. There was a moment during which I listened, reminded of the faint sense I had had, the first night, of there being something undefineably astir in the house, and noted the soft breath of the open casement just move the half-drawn blind. Then, with all the marks of a deliberation that must have seemed magnificent had there been anyone to admire it, I laid down my book, rose to my feet, and, taking a candle, went straight out of the room and, from the passage, on which my light made little impression, noiselessly closed and locked the door.

I can say now neither what determined nor what guided me, but I went straight along the lobby, holding my candle high, till I came within sight of the tall window that presided over the great turn of the staircase. At this point I precipitately found myself aware of three things. They were practically simultaneous, yet they had flashes of succession. My candle,

under a bold flourish, went out, and I perceived, by the uncovered window, that the yielding dusk of earliest morning
rendered it unnecessary. Without it, the next instant, I saw
that there was someone on the stair. I speak of sequences, but
I required no lapse of seconds to stiffen myself for a third
encounter with Quint. The apparition had reached the landing half-way up and was therefore on the spot nearest the
window, where at sight of me, it stopped short and fixed me
exactly as it had fixed me from the tower and from the garden.
He knew me as well as I knew him; and so, in the cold, faint
twilight, with a glimmer in the high glass and another on the
polish of the oak stair below, we faced each other in our common intensity. He was absolutely, on this occasion, a living,
detestable, dangerous presence. But that was not the wonder
of wonders; I reserve this distinction for quite another circumstance: the circumstance that dread had unmistakeably quitted
me and that there was nothing in me there that didn't meet
and measure him.

I had plenty of anguish after that extraordinary moment,
but I had, thank God, no terror. And he knew I had not—I
found myself at the end of an instant magnificently aware of
this. I felt, in a fierce rigour of confidence, that if I stood my
ground a minute I should cease—for the time, at least—to
have him to reckon with; and during the minute, accordingly,
the thing was as human and hideous as a real interview: hideous just because it *was* human, as human as to have met
alone, in the small hours, in a sleeping house, some enemy,
some adventurer, some criminal. It was the dead silence of
our long gaze at such close quarters that gave the whole horror, huge as it was, its only note of the unnatural. If I had
met a murderer in such a place and at such an hour, we still
at least would have spoken. Something would have passed, in
life, between us; if nothing had passed one of us would have
moved. The moment was so prolonged that it would have
taken but little more to make me doubt if even *I* were in life.
I can't express what followed it save by saying that the silence
itself—which was indeed in a manner an attestation of my
strength—became the element into which I saw the figure
disappear; in which I definitely saw it turn as I might have
seen the low wretch to which it had once belonged turn on

receipt of an order, and pass, with my eyes on the villainous back that no hunch could have more disfigured, straight down the staircase and into the darkness in which the next bend was lost.

X

I remained awhile at the top of the stair, but with the effect presently of understanding that when my visitor had gone, he had gone: then I returned to my room. The foremost thing I saw there by the light of the candle I had left burning was that Flora's little bed was empty; and on this I caught my breath with all the terror that, five minutes before, I had been able to resist. I dashed at the place in which I had left her lying and over which (for the small silk counterpane and the sheets were disarranged) the white curtains had been deceivingly pulled forward; then my step, to my unutterable relief, produced an answering sound: I perceived an agitation of the window-blind, and the child, ducking down, emerged rosily from the other side of it. She stood there in so much of her candour and so little of her nightgown, with her pink bare feet and the golden glow of her curls. She looked intensely grave, and I had never had such a sense of losing an advantage acquired (the thrill of which had just been so prodigious) as on my consciousness that she addressed me with a reproach. "You naughty: where *have* you been?"—instead of challenging her own irregularity I found myself arraigned and explaining. She herself explained, for that matter, with the loveliest, eagerest simplicity. She had known suddenly, as she lay there, that I was out of the room, and had jumped up to see what had become of me. I had dropped, with the joy of her reappearance, back into my chair—feeling then, and then only, a little faint; and she had pattered straight over to me, thrown herself upon my knee, given herself to be held with the flame of the candle full in the wonderful little face that was still flushed with sleep. I remember closing my eyes an instant, yieldingly, consciously, as before the excess of something beautiful that shone out of the blue of her own. "You were looking for me out of the window?" I said. "You thought I might be walking in the grounds?"

"Well, you know, I thought someone was"—she never blanched as she smiled out that at me.

Oh, how I looked at her now! "And did you see anyone?"

"Ah, *no!*" she returned, almost with the full privilege of childish inconsequence, resentfully, though with a long sweetness in her little drawl of the negative.

At that moment, in the state of my nerves, I absolutely believed she lied; and if I once more closed my eyes it was before the dazzle of the three or four possible ways in which I might take this up. One of these, for a moment, tempted me with such singular intensity that, to withstand it, I must have gripped my little girl with a spasm that, wonderfully, she submitted to without a cry or a sign of fright. Why not break out at her on the spot and have it all over?—give it to her straight in her lovely little lighted face? "You see, you see, you *know* that you do and that you already quite suspect I believe it; therefore why not frankly confess it to me, so that we may at least live with it together and learn perhaps, in the strangeness of our fate, where we are and what it means?" This solicitation dropped, alas, as it came: if I could immediately have succumbed to it I might have spared myself——well you'll see what. Instead of succumbing I sprang again to my feet, looked at her bed, and took a helpless middle way. "Why did you pull the curtain over the place to make me think you were still there?"

Flora luminously considered; after which, with her little divine smile: "Because I don't like to frighten you!"

"But if I had, by your idea, gone out——?"

She absolutely declined to be puzzled; she turned her eyes to the flame of the candle as if the question were as irrelevant, or at any rate as impersonal, as Mrs. Marcel or nine-times-nine. "Oh, but you know," she quite adequately answered, "that you might come back, you dear, and that you *have!*" And after a little, when she had got into bed, I had, for a long time, by almost sitting on her to hold her hand, to prove that I recognised the pertinence of my return.

You may imagine the general complexion, from that moment, of my nights. I repeatedly sat up till I didn't know when; I selected moments when my room-mate unmistakeably slept, and, stealing out, took noiseless turns in the passage and even pushed as far as to where I had last met Quint. But I never met him there again; and I may as well say at once that I on no other occasion saw him in the house. I just missed, on the staircase, on the other hand, a different adventure. Looking down it from the top I once recognised the presence of a woman seated on one of the lower steps with her back presented to me, her body half bowed and her head, in an attitude of woe, in her hands. I had been there but an instant, however, when she vanished without looking round at me. I knew, none the less, exactly what dreadful face she had to show; and I wondered whether, if instead of being above I had been below, I should have had, for going up, the same nerve I had lately shown Quint. Well, there continued to be plenty of chance for nerve. On the eleventh night after my latest encounter with that gentleman—they were all numbered now—I had an alarm that perilously skirted it and that indeed, from the particular quality of its unexpectedness, proved quite my sharpest shock. It was precisely the first night during this series that, weary with watching, I had felt that I might again without laxity lay myself down at my old hour. I slept immediately and, as I afterwards knew, till about one o'clock; but when I woke it was to sit straight up, as completely roused as if a hand had shook me. I had left a light burning, but it was now out, and I felt an instant certainty that Flora had extinguished it. This brought me to my feet and straight, in the darkness, to her bed, which I found she had left. A glance at the window enlightened me further, and the striking of a match completed the picture.

The child had again got up—this time blowing out the taper, and had again, for some purpose of observation or response, squeezed in behind the blind and was peering out into the night. That she now saw—as she had not, I had satisfied myself, the previous time—was proved to me by the fact that she was disturbed neither by my re-illumination nor by the haste I made to get into slippers and into a wrap. Hidden, protected, absorbed, she evidently rested on the sill—the casement opened forward—and gave herself up. There was a great still moon to help her, and this fact had counted in my quick decision. She was face to face with the apparition we had met at the lake, and could now communicate with it as she had not then been able to do. What I, on my side, had to care for was, without disturbing her, to reach, from the corridor, some other window in the same quarter. I got to the door without her hearing me; I got out of it, closed it and listened, from the other side, for some sound from her. While I stood in the passage I had my eyes on her brother's door, which was but ten steps off and which, indescribably, produced in me a renewal of the strange impulse that I lately spoke of as my temptation. What if I should go straight in and march to *his* window?—what if, by risking to his boyish bewilderment a revelation of my motive, I should throw across the rest of the mystery the long halter of my boldness?

This thought held me sufficiently to make me cross to his threshold and pause again. I preternaturally listened; I figured to myself what might portentously be; I wondered if his bed were also empty and he too were secretly at watch. It was a deep, soundless minute, at the end of which my impulse failed. He was quiet; he might be innocent; the risk was hideous; I turned away. There was a figure in the grounds—a figure prowling for a sight, the visitor with whom Flora was engaged; but it was not the visitor most concerned with my boy. I hesitated afresh, but on other grounds and only a few seconds; then I had made my choice. There were empty rooms at Bly, and it was only a question of choosing the right one. The right one suddenly presented itself to me as the lower one—though high above the gardens—in the solid corner of the house that I have spoken of as the old tower. This was a large, square chamber, arranged with some state as a bedroom, the extravagant size of which made it so inconvenient that it had not for years, though kept by Mrs. Grose in exemplary order, been occupied. I had often admired it and I knew my way about in it; I had only, after just faltering at the first chill gloom of its disuse, to pass across it and unbolt as quietly as I could one of the shutters. Achieving this transit, I uncovered the glass without a sound and, applying my face to the pane, was able, the darkness without being much less than within, to see that I commanded the right direction. Then I saw something more. The moon made the night extraordinarily penetrable and showed me on the lawn a person, diminished by distance, who stood there motionless and as if fascinated, looking up to where I had appeared—looking, that is, not so much straight at me as at something that was apparently above me. There was clearly another person above me—there was a person on the tower; but the presence on the lawn was not in the least what I had conceived and had confidently hurried to meet. The presence on the lawn—I felt sick as I made it out—was poor little Miles himself.

XI

It was not till late next day that I spoke to Mrs. Grose; the rigour with which I kept my pupils in sight making it often difficult to meet her privately, and the more as we each felt the importance of not provoking—on the part of the servants quite as much as on that of the children—any suspicion of a secret flurry or of a discussion of mysteries. I drew a great security in this particular from her mere smooth aspect. There was nothing in her fresh face to pass on to others my horrible confidences. She believed me, I was sure, absolutely: if she hadn't I don't know what would have become of me, for I couldn't have borne the business alone. But she was a magnificent monument to the blessing of a want of imagination, and if she could see in our little charges nothing but their beauty and amiability, their happiness and cleverness, she had no direct communication with the sources of my trouble. If they had been at all visibly blighted or battered, she would doubtless have grown, on tracing it back, haggard enough to match them; as matters stood, however, I could feel her, when she surveyed them, with her large white arms folded and the habit of serenity in all her look, thank the Lord's mercy that if they were ruined the pieces would still serve. Flights of fancy gave place, in her mind, to a steady fireside glow, and I had already begun to perceive how, with the development of the conviction that—as time went on without a public accident— our young things could, after all, look out for themselves, she addressed her greatest solicitude to the sad case presented by their instructress. That, for myself, was a sound simplification: I could engage that, to the world, my face should tell no tales, but it would have been, in the conditions, an immense added strain to find myself anxious about hers.

At the hour I now speak of she had joined me, under pressure, on the terrace, where, with the lapse of the season, the afternoon sun was now agreeable; and we sat there together while, before us, at a distance, but within call if we wished, the children strolled to and fro in one of their most manageable moods. They moved slowly, in unison, below us, over the lawn, the boy, as they went, reading aloud from a storybook and passing his arm round his sister to keep her quite in touch. Mrs. Grose watched them with positive placidity; then I caught the suppressed intellectual creak with which she conscientiously turned to take from me a view of the back of the tapestry. I had made her a receptacle of lurid things, but there was an odd recognition of my superiority—my accomplishments and my function—in her patience under my pain. She offered her mind to my disclosures as, had I wished to mix a witch's broth and proposed it with assurance, she would have held out a large clean saucepan. This had become thoroughly her attitude by the time that, in my recital of the events of the night, I reached the point of what Miles had said to me when, after seeing him, at such a monstrous hour, almost on the very spot where he happened now to be, I had gone down to bring him in; choosing then, at the window, with a concentrated need of not alarming the house, rather that method than a signal more resonant. I had left her meanwhile in little doubt of my small hope of representing with success even to her actual sympathy my sense of the real splendour of the little inspiration with which, after I had got him into the house, the boy met my final articulate challenge. As soon as I appeared in the moonlight on the terrace, he had come to me as straight as possible; on which I had taken his hand without a word and led him, through the dark spaces, up the staircase where Quint had so hungrily hovered for him, along the lobby where I had listened and trembled, and so to his forsaken room.

Not a sound, on the way, had passed between us, and I had wondered—oh, *how* I had wondered!—if he were groping about in his little mind for something plausible and not too grotesque. It would tax his invention, certainly, and I felt, this time, over his real embarrassment, a curious thrill of triumph. It was a sharp trap for the inscrutable! He couldn't play any longer at innocence; so how the deuce would he get out of it? There beat in me indeed, with the passionate throb of this question, an equal dumb appeal as to how the deuce *I* should. I was confronted at last, as never yet, with all the risk attached even now to sounding my own horrid note. I remember in fact that as we pushed into his little chamber, where the bed had not been slept in at all and the window, uncovered to the moonlight, made the place so clear that there was no need of striking a match—I remember how I suddenly dropped, sank upon the edge of the bed from the force of the idea that he must know how he really, as they say, "had" me. He could do what he liked, with all his cleverness to help him, so long as I should continue to defer to the old tradition of the criminality of those caretakers of the young who minister to superstitions and fears. He "had" me indeed, and in a cleft stick; for who would ever absolve me, who would consent that I should go unhung, if, by the faintest tremor of an overture, I were the first to introduce into our perfect intercourse an element so dire? No, no: it was useless to attempt to convey to Mrs. Grose, just as it is scarcely less so to attempt to suggest here, how, in our short, stiff brush in the dark, he fairly shook me with admiration. I was of course thoroughly kind and merciful; never, never yet had I placed on his little shoulders hands of such tenderness as those with which, while I rested against the bed, I held him there well under fire. I had no alternative but, in form at least, to put it to him.

"You must tell me now—and all the truth. What did you go out for? What were you doing there?"

I can still see his wonderful smile, the whites of his beautiful eyes, and the uncovering of his little teeth shine to me in the dusk. "If I tell you why, will you understand?" My heart, at this, leaped into my mouth. *Would* he tell me why? I found no sound on my lips to press it, and I was aware of replying only with a vague, repeated, grimacing nod. He was gentleness itself, and while I wagged my head at him he stood there more than ever a little fairy prince. It was his brightness indeed that gave me a respite. Would it be so great if he were really going to tell me? "Well," he said at last, "just exactly in order that you should do this."

"Do what?"

"Think me—for a change—*bad!*" I shall never forget the sweetness and gaiety with which he brought out the word, nor how, on top of it, he bent forward and kissed me. It was practically the end of everything. I met his kiss and I had to make, while I folded him for a minute in my arms, the most stupendous effort not to cry. He had given exactly the account of himself that permitted least of my going behind it, and it was only with the effect of confirming my acceptance of it that, as I presently glanced about the room, I could say—

"Then you didn't undress at all?"

He fairly glittered in the gloom. "Not at all. I sat up and read."

"And when did you go down?"

"At midnight. When I'm bad I *am* bad!"

"I see, I see—it's charming. But how could you be sure I would know it?"

"Oh, I arranged that with Flora." His answers rang out with a readiness! "She was to get up and look out."

"Which is what she did do." It was I who fell into the trap!

"So she disturbed you, and, to see what she was looking at, you also looked—you saw."

"While you," I concurred, "caught your death in the night air!"

He literally bloomed so from this exploit that he could afford radiantly to assent. "How otherwise should I have been bad enough?" he asked. Then, after another embrace, the incident and our interview closed on my recognition of all the reserves of goodness that, for his joke, he had been able to draw upon.

XII

The particular impression I had received proved in the morning light, I repeat, not quite successfully presentable to Mrs. Grose, though I reinforced it with the mention of still another remark that he had made before we separated. "It all lies in half-a-dozen words," I said to her, "words that really settle the matter. 'Think, you know, what I *might* do!' He threw that off to show me how good he is. He knows down to the ground what he 'might' do. That's what he gave them a taste of at school."

"Lord, you do change!" cried my friend.

"I don't change—I simply make it out. The four, depend upon it, perpetually meet. If on either of these last nights you had been with either child, you would clearly have understood. The more I've watched and waited the more I've felt that if there were nothing else to make it sure it would be made so by the systematic silence of each. *Never*, by a slip of the tongue, have they so much as alluded to either of their old friends, any more than Miles has alluded to his expulsion. Oh yes, we may sit here and look at them, and they may show off to us there to their fill; but even while they pretend to be lost in their fairy-tale they're steeped in their vision of the dead restored. He's not reading to her," I declared; "they're talking of *them*—they're talking horrors! I go on, I know, as if I were crazy; and it's a wonder I'm not. What I've seen would have made *you* so; but it has only made me more lucid, made me get hold of still other things."

My lucidity must have seemed awful, but the charming creatures who were victims of it, passing and repassing in their interlocked sweetness, gave my colleague something to hold on by; and I felt how tight she held as, without stirring in the breath of my passion, she covered them still with her eyes. "Of what other things have you got hold?"

"Why, of the very things that have delighted, fascinated, and yet, at bottom, as I now so strangely see, mystified and troubled me. Their more than earthly beauty, their absolutely unnatural goodness. It's a game," I went on; "it's a policy and a fraud!"

"On the part of little darlings——?"

"As yet mere lovely babies? Yes, mad as that seems!" The very act of bringing it out really helped me to trace it—follow it all up and piece it all together. "They haven't been good—they've only been absent. It has been easy to live with them, because they're simply leading a life of their own. They're not mine—they're not ours. They're his and they're hers!"

"Quint's and that woman's?"

"Quint's and that woman's. They want to get to them."

Oh, how, at this, poor Mrs. Grose appeared to study them! "But for what?"

"For the love of all the evil that, in those dreadful days, the pair put into them. And to ply them with that evil still, to keep up the work of demons, is what brings the others back."

"Laws!" said my friend under her breath. The exclamation was homely, but it revealed a real acceptance of my further proof of what, in the bad time—for there had been a worse even than this!—must have occurred. There could have been no such justification for me as the plain assent of her experience to whatever depth of depravity I found credible in our brace of scoundrels. It was in obvious submission of memory that she brought out after a moment: "They *were* rascals! But what can they now do?" she pursued.

"Do?" I echoed so loud that Miles and Flora, as they passed at their distance, paused an instant in their walk and looked at us. "Don't they do enough?" I demanded in a lower tone, while the children, having smiled and nodded and kissed hands to us, resumed their exhibition. We were held by it a minute; then I answered: "They can destroy them!" At this my companion did turn, but the inquiry she launched was a silent one, the effect of which was to make me more explicit. "They don't know, as yet, quite how—but they're trying hard. They're seen only across, as it were, and beyond—in strange places and on high places, the top of towers, the roof of houses, the outside of windows, the further edge of pools; but there's a deep design, on either side, to shorten the distance and overcome the obstacle; and the success of the tempters is only a question of time. They've only to keep to their suggestions of danger."

"For the children to come?"

"And perish in the attempt!" Mrs. Grose slowly got up, and I scrupulously added: "Unless, of course, we can prevent!"

Standing there before me while I kept my seat, she visibly turned things over. "Their uncle must do the preventing. He must take them away."

"And who's to make him?"

She had been scanning the distance, but she now dropped on me a foolish face. "You, Miss."

"By writing to him that his house is poisoned and his little nephew and niece mad?"

"But if they *are*, Miss?"

"And if I am myself, you mean? That's charming news to be sent him by a governess whose prime undertaking was to give him no worry."

Mrs. Grose considered, following the children again. "Yes, he do hate worry. That was the great reason——"

"Why those fiends took him in so long? No doubt, though his indifference must have been awful. As I'm not a fiend, at any rate, I shouldn't take him in."

My companion, after an instant and for all answer, sat down again and grasped my arm. "Make him at any rate come to you."

I stared. "To *me*?" I had a sudden fear of what she might do. " 'Him'?"

"He ought to *be* here—he ought to help."

I quickly rose, and I think I must have shown her a queerer face than ever yet. "You see me asking him for a visit?" No, with her eyes on my face she evidently couldn't. Instead of it even—as a woman reads another—she could see what I myself saw: his derision, his amusement, his contempt for the breakdown of my resignation at being left alone and for the fine machinery I had set in motion to attract his attention to my slighted charms. She didn't know—no one knew—how proud I had been to serve him and to stick to our terms; yet she none the less took the measure, I think, of the warning I now gave her. "If you should so lose your head as to appeal to him for me——"

She was really frightened. "Yes, Miss?"

"I would leave, on the spot, both him and you."

XIII

It was all very well to join them, but speaking to them proved quite as much as ever an effort beyond my strength—offered, in close quarters, difficulties as insurmountable as before. This situation continued a month, and with new aggravations and particular notes, the note above all, sharper and sharper, of the small ironic consciousness on the part of my pupils. It was not, I am as sure today as I was sure then, my mere infernal imagination: it was absolutely traceable that they were aware

of my predicament and that this strange relation made, in a
manner, for a long time, the air in which we moved. I don't
mean that they had their tongues in their cheeks or did anything vulgar, for that was not one of their dangers: I do mean,
on the other hand, that the element of the unnamed and un-
touched became, between us, greater than any other, and that
so much avoidance could not have been so successfully effected without a great deal of tacit arrangement. It was as if,
at moments, we were perpetually coming into sight of subjects
before which we must stop short, turning suddenly out of
alleys that we perceived to be blind, closing with a little bang
that made us look at each other—for, like all bangs, it was
something louder than we had intended—the doors we had
indiscreetly opened. All roads lead to Rome, and there were
times when it might have struck us that almost every branch
of study or subject of conversation skirted forbidden ground.
Forbidden ground was the question of the return of the dead
in general and of whatever, in especial, might survive, in memory, of the friends little children had lost. There were days
when I could have sworn that one of them had, with a small
invisible nudge, said to the other: "She thinks she'll do it this
time—but she *won't*!" To "do it" would have been to indulge
for instance—and for once in a way—in some direct reference
to the lady who had prepared them for my discipline. They
had a delightful endless appetite for passages in my own his
tory, to which I had again and again treated them; they were
in possession of everything that had ever happened to me, had
had, with every circumstance the story of my smallest adventures and of those of my brothers and sisters and of the cat
and the dog at home, as well as many particulars of the eccentric nature of my father, of the furniture and arrangement
of our house, and of the conversation of the old women of
our village. There were things enough, taking one with another, to chatter about, if one went very fast and knew by
instinct when to go round. They pulled with an art of their
own the strings of my invention and my memory; and nothing
else perhaps, when I thought of such occasions afterwards,
gave me so the suspicion of being watched from under cover.
It was in any case over *my* life, *my* past, and *my* friends alone
that we could take anything like our ease—a state of affairs

that led them sometimes without the least pertinence to break out into sociable reminders. I was invited—with no visible connection—to repeat afresh Goody Gosling's celebrated *mot* or to confirm the details already supplied as to the cleverness of the vicarage pony.

It was partly at such junctures as these and partly at quite different ones that, with the turn my matters had now taken, my predicament, as I have called it, grew most sensible. The fact that the days passed for me without another encounter ought, it would have appeared, to have done something toward soothing my nerves. Since the light brush, that second night on the upper landing, of the presence of a woman at the foot of the stair, I had seen nothing, whether in or out of the house, that one had better not have seen. There was many a corner round which I expected to come upon Quint, and many a situation that, in a merely sinister way, would have favoured the appearance of Miss Jessel. The summer had turned, the summer had gone; the autumn had dropped upon Bly and had blown out half our lights. The place, with its grey sky and withered garlands, its bared spaces and scattered dead leaves, was like a theatre after the performance—all strewn with crumpled playbills. There were exactly states of the air, conditions of sound and of stillness, unspeakable impressions of the *kind* of ministering moment, that brought back to me, long enough to catch it, the feeling of the medium in which, that June evening out-of-doors, I had had my first sight of Quint, and in which, too, at those other instants, I had, after seeing him through the window, looked for him in vain in the circle of shrubbery. I recognised the signs, the portents—I recognised the moment, the spot. But they remained unaccompanied and empty, and I continued unmolested; if unmolested one could call a young woman whose sensibility had, in the most extraordinary fashion, not declined but deepened. I had said in my talk with Mrs. Grose on that horrid scene of Flora's by the lake—and had perplexed her by so saying—that it would from that moment distress me much more to lose my power than to keep it. I had then expressed what was vividly in my mind: the truth that, whether the children really saw or not—since, that is, it was not yet definitely proved— I greatly preferred, as a safeguard, the fulness of my own exposure. I was ready to know the very worst that was to be known. What I had then had an ugly glimpse of was that my eyes might be sealed just while theirs were most opened. Well, my eyes *were* sealed, it appeared, at present—a consummation for which it seemed blasphemous not to thank God. There was, alas, a difficulty about that: I would have thanked him with all my soul had I not had in a proportionate measure this conviction of the secret of my pupils.

How can I retrace today the strange steps of my obsession? There were times of our being together when I would have been ready to swear that, literally, in my presence, but with my direct sense of it closed, they had visitors who were known and were welcome. Then it was that, had I not been deterred by the very chance that such an injury might prove greater than the injury to be averted, my exultation would have broken out. "They're here, they're here, you little wretches," I would have cried, "and you can't deny it now!" The little wretches denied it with all the added volume of their sociability and their tenderness, in just the crystal depths of which—like the flash of a fish in a stream —the mockery of their advantage peeped up. The shock, in truth, had sunk into me still deeper than I knew on the night when, looking out to see either Quint or Miss Jessel under the stars, I had beheld the boy over whose rest I watched and who had immediately brought in with him—had straightway, there, turned it on me— the lovely upward look with which, from the battlements above me, the hideous apparition of Quint had played. If it was a question of a scare, my discovery on this occasion had scared me more than any other, and it was in the condition of nerves produced by it that I made my actual inductions. They harassed me so that sometimes, at odd moments, I shut myself up audibly to rehearse—it was at once a fantastic relief and a renewed despair—the manner in which I might come to the point. I approached it from one side and the other while, in my room, I flung myself about, but I always broke down in the monstrous utterance of names. As they died away on my lips, I said to myself that I should indeed help them to represent something infamous if, by pronouncing them, I should violate as rare a little case of instinctive delicacy as any schoolroom, probably, had ever known. When I said to myself: "*They* have the manners to be silent, and you, trusted as you are, the baseness to speak!" I felt myself crimson and I covered my face with my hands. After these secret scenes I chattered more than ever, going on volubly enough till one of our prodigious, palpable hushes occurred—I can call them nothing else—the strange, dizzy lift or swim (I try for terms!) into a stillness, a pause of all life, that had nothing to do with the more or less noise that at the moment we might be engaged in making and that I could hear through any deepened exhilaration or quickened recitation or louder strum of the piano. Then it was that the others, the outsiders, were there. Though they were not angels, they "passed," as the French say, causing me, while they stayed, to tremble with the fear of their addressing to their younger victims some yet more infernal message or more vivid image than they had thought good enough for myself.

What it was most impossible to get rid of was the cruel idea that, whatever I had seen, Miles and Flora saw *more*—things terrible and unguessable and that sprang from dreadful passages of intercourse in the past. Such things naturally left on the surface, for the time, a chill which we vociferously denied that we felt; and we had, all three, with repetition, got into such splendid training that we went, each time, almost automatically, to mark the close of the incident, through the very same movements. It was striking of the children, at all events, to kiss me inveterately with a kind of wild irrelevance and never to fail—one or the other—of the precious question that had helped us through many a peril. "When do you think he *will* come? Don't you think we *ought* to write?"—there was nothing like that inquiry, we found by experience, for carrying off an awkwardness. "He" of course was their uncle in Harley Street; and we lived in much profusion of theory that he might at any moment arrive to mingle in our circle. It was impossible to have given less encouragement than he had done to such a doctrine, but if we had not had the doctrine to fall back upon we should have deprived each other of some of our finest exhibitions. He never wrote to them—that may have been selfish, but it was a part of the flattery of his trust of me; for the way in which a man pays his highest tribute to a woman is apt to be but by the more festal celebration of

one of the sacred laws of his comfort; and I held that I carried
out the spirit of the pledge given not to appeal to him when
I let my charges understand that their own letters were but
charming literary exercises. They were too beautiful to be
posted; I kept them myself; I have them all to this hour. This
was a rule indeed which only added to the satiric effect of my
being plied with the supposition that he might at any moment
be among us. It was exactly as if my charges knew how almost
more awkward than anything else that might be for me. There
appears to me, moreover, as I look back, no note in all this
more extraordinary than the mere fact that, in spite of my
tension and of their triumph, I never lost patience with them.
Adorable they must in truth have been, I now reflect, that I
didn't in these days hate them! Would exasperation, however,
if relief had longer been postponed, finally have betrayed me?
It little matters, for relief arrived. I call it relief, though it was
only the relief that a snap brings to a strain or the burst of a
thunderstorm to a day of suffocation. It was at least change,
and it came with a rush.

XIV

Walking to church a certain Sunday morning, I had little Miles
at my side and his sister, in advance of us and at Mrs. Grose's,
well in sight. It was a crisp, clear day, the first of its order for
some time, the night had brought a touch of frost, and the
autumn air, bright and sharp, made the church-bells almost
gay. It was an odd accident of thought that I should have
happened at such a moment to be particularly and very gratefully struck with the obedience of my little charges. Why did
they never resent my inexorable, my perpetual society? Something or other had brought nearer home to me that I had all
but pinned the boy to my shawl and that, in the way our
companions were marshalled before me, I might have appeared to provide against some danger of rebellion. I was like
a gaoler with an eye to possible surprises and escapes. But all
this belonged—I mean their magnificent little surrender—just
to the special array of the facts that were most abysmal.
Turned out for Sunday by his uncle's tailor, who had had a
free hand and a notion of pretty waistcoats and of his grand

little air, Miles's whole title to independence, the rights of his sex and situation, were so stamped upon him that if he had suddenly struck for freedom I should have had nothing to say. I was by the strangest of chances wondering how I should meet him when the revolution unmistakeably occurred. I call it a revolution because I now see how, with the word he spoke, the curtain rose on the last act of my dreadful drama and the catastrophe was precipitated. "Look here, my dear, you know," he charmingly said, "when in the world, please, am I going back to school?"

Transcribed here the speech sounds harmless enough, particularly as uttered in the sweet, high, casual pipe with which, at all interlocutors, but above all at his eternal governess, he threw off intonations as if he were tossing roses. There was something in them that always made one "catch," and I caught, at any rate, now so effectually that I stopped as short as if one of the trees of the park had fallen across the road. There was something new, on the spot, between us, and he was perfectly aware that I recognised it, though, to enable me to do so, he had no need to look a whit less candid and charming than usual. I could feel in him how he already, from my at first finding nothing to reply, perceived the advantage he had gained. I was so slow to find anything that he had plenty of time, after a minute, to continue with his suggestive but inconclusive smile: "You know, my dear, that for a fellow to be with a lady *always*——!" His "my dear" was constantly on his lips for me, and nothing could have expressed more the exact shade of the sentiment with which I desired to inspire my pupils than its fond familiarity. It was so respectfully easy.

But, oh, how I felt that at present I must pick my own phrases! I remember that, to gain time, I tried to laugh, and I seemed to see in the beautiful face with which he watched me how ugly and queer I looked. "And always with the same lady?" I returned.

He neither blenched nor winked. The whole thing was virtually out between us. "Ah, of course, she's a jolly, 'perfect' lady; but, after all, I'm a fellow, don't you see? that's—well, getting on."

I lingered there with him an instant ever so kindly. "Yes, you're getting on." Oh, but I felt helpless!

I have kept to this day the heartbreaking little idea of how he seemed to know that and to play with it. "And you can't say I've not been awfully good, can you?"

I laid my hand on his shoulder, for, though I felt how much better it would have been to walk on, I was not yet quite able. "No, I can't say that, Miles."

"Except just that one night, you know——!"

"That one night?" I couldn't look as straight as he.

"Why, when I went down—went out of the house."

"Oh, yes. But I forget what you did it for."

"You forget?"—he spoke with the sweet extravagance of childish reproach. "Why, it was to show you I could!"

"Oh, yes, you could."

"And I can again."

I felt that I might, perhaps, after all, succeed in keeping my wits about me. "Certainly. But you won't."

"No, not *that* again. It was nothing."

"It was nothing," I said. "But we must go on."

He resumed our walk with me, passing his hand into my arm. "Then when *am* I going back?"

I wore, in turning it over, my most responsible air. "Were you very happy at school?"

He just considered. "Oh, I'm happy enough anywhere!"

"Well, then," I quavered, "if you're just as happy here——!"

"Ah, but that isn't everything! Of course *you* know a lot——"

"But you hint that you know almost as much?" I risked as he paused.

"Not half I want to!" Miles honestly professed. "But it isn't so much that."

"What is it, then?"

"Well—I want to see more life."

"I see; I see." We had arrived within sight of the church and of various persons, including several of the household of Bly, on their way to it and clustered about the door to see us go in. I quickened our step; I wanted to get there before the question between us opened up much further; I reflected hungrily that, for more than an hour, he would have to be silent; and I thought with envy of the comparative dusk of the pew and of the almost spiritual help of the hassock on which I might bend my knees. I seemed literally to be running a race with some confusion to which he was about to reduce me, but I felt that he had got in first when, before we had even entered the churchyard, he threw out—

"I want my own sort!"

It literally made me bound forward. "There are not many of your own sort, Miles!" I laughed. "Unless perhaps dear little Flora!"

"You really compare me to a baby girl?"

This found me singularly weak. "Don't you, then, *love* our sweet Flora?"

"If I didn't—and you too; if I didn't——!" he repeated as if retreating for a jump, yet leaving his thought so unfinished that, after we had come into the gate, another stop, which he imposed on me by the pressure of his arm, had become inevitable. Mrs. Grose and Flora had passed into the church, the other worshippers had followed, and we were, for the minute, alone among the old, thick graves. We had paused, on the path from the gate, by a low oblong, table-like tomb.

"Yes, if you didn't——?"

He looked, while I waited, about at the graves. "Well, you know what!" But he didn't move, and he presently produced something that made me drop straight down on the stone slab, as if suddenly to rest. "Does my uncle think what *you* think?"

I markedly rested. "How do you know what I think?"

"Ah, well, of course I don't; for it strikes me you never tell me. But I mean does *he* know?"

"Know what, Miles?"

"Why, the way I'm going on."

I perceived quickly enough that I could make, to this inquiry, no answer that would not involve something of a sacrifice of my employer. Yet it appeared to me that we were all, at Bly, sufficiently sacrificed to make that venial. "I don't think your uncle much cares."

Miles, on this, stood looking at me. "Then don't you think he can be made to?"

"In what way?"

"Why, by his coming down."

"But who'll get him to come down?"

"*I* will!" the boy said with extraordinary brightness and emphasis. He gave me another look charged with that expression and then marched off alone into church.

XV

The business was practically settled from the moment I never followed him. It was a pitiful surrender to agitation, but my being aware of this had somehow no power to restore me. I only sat there on my tomb and read into what my little friend had said to me the fulness of its meaning; by the time I had grasped the whole of which I had also embraced, for absence, the pretext that I was ashamed to offer my pupils and the rest of the congregation such an example of delay. What I said to myself above all was that Miles had got something out of me and that the proof of it, for him, would be just this awkward collapse. He had got out of me that there was something I was much afraid of and that he should probably be able to make use of my fear to gain, for his own purpose, more freedom. My fear was of having to deal with the intolerable question of the grounds of his dismissal from school, for that was really but the question of the horrors gathered behind. That his uncle should arrive to treat with me of these things was a solution that, strictly speaking, I ought now to have desired to bring on; but I could so little face the ugliness and the pain of it that I simply procrastinated and lived from hand to mouth. The boy, to my deep discomposure, was immensely in the right, was in a position to say to me: "Either you clear up with my guardian the mystery of this interruption of my studies, or you cease to expect me to lead with you a life that's so unnatural for a boy." What was so unnatural for the particular boy I was concerned with was this sudden revelation of a consciousness and a plan.

That was what really overcame me, what prevented my going in. I walked round the church, hesitating, hovering; I reflected that I had already, with him, hurt myself beyond repair. Therefore I could patch up nothing, and it was too extreme an effort to squeeze beside him into the pew: he would be so much more sure than ever to pass his arm into mine and make me sit there for an hour in close, silent contact with his commentary on our talk. For the first minute since his arrival I wanted to get away from him. As I paused beneath the high east window and listened to the sounds of worship, I was taken with an impulse that might master me, I felt, completely should I give it the least encouragement. I might easily put an end to my predicament by getting away altogether. Here was my chance; there was no one to stop me; I could give the whole thing up—turn my back and retreat. It was only a question of hurrying again, for a few preparations, to the house which the attendance at church of so many of the servants would practically have left unoccupied. No one, in short, could blame me if I should just drive desperately off. What was it to get away if I got away only till dinner? That would be in a couple of hours, at the end of which—I had the acute prevision—my little pupils would play at innocent wonder about my non-appearance in their train.

"What *did* you do, you naughty, bad thing? Why in the world, to worry us so—and take our thoughts off too, don't you know?—did you desert us at the very door?" I couldn't meet such questions nor, as they asked them, their false little lovely eyes; yet it was all so exactly what I should have to meet that, as the prospect grew sharp to me, I at last let myself go.

I got, so far as the immediate moment was concerned, away; I came straight out of the churchyard and, thinking hard, retracted my steps through the park. It seemed to me that by the time I reached the house I had made up my mind I would fly. The Sunday stillness both of the approaches and of the interior, in which I met no one, fairly excited me with a sense of opportunity. Were I to get off quickly, this way, I should get off without a scene, without a word. My quickness would have to be remarkable, however, and the question of a conveyance was the great one to settle. Tormented, in the hall, with difficulties and obstacles, I remember sinking down at the foot of the staircase—suddenly collapsing there on the lowest step and then, with a revulsion, recalling that it was exactly where more than a month before, in the darkness of night and just so bowed with evil things, I had seen the spectre of the most horrible of women. At this I was able to straighten myself; I went the rest of the way up; I made, in my bewilderment, for the schoolroom, where there were objects belonging to me that I should have to take. But I opened the door to find again, in a flash, my eyes unsealed. In the presence of what I saw I reeled straight back upon my resistance.

Seated at my own table in clear noonday light I saw a person whom, without my previous experience, I should have taken at the first blush for some housemaid who might have stayed at home to look after the place and who, availing herself of rare relief from observation and of the schoolroom table and my pens, ink, and paper, had applied herself to the considerable effort of a letter to her sweetheart. There was an effort in the way that, while her arms rested on the table, her hands with evident weariness supported her head; but at the moment I took this in I had already become aware that, in spite of my entrance, her attitude strangely persisted. Then it was—with the very act of its announcing itself—that her identity flared up in a change of posture. She rose, not as if she had heard me, but with an indescribable grand melancholy of indifference and detachment, and, within a dozen feet of me, stood there as my vile predecessor. Dishonoured and tragic, she was all before me; but even as I fixed and, for memory, secured it, the awful image passed away. Dark as midnight in her black dress, her haggard beauty and her unutterable woe, she had looked at me long enough to appear to say that her right to sit at my table was as good as mine to sit at hers. While these instants lasted indeed I had the extraordinary chill of a feeling that it was I who was the intruder. It was as a wild protest against it that, actually addressing her—"You terrible, miserable woman!"—I heard myself break into a sound that, by the open door, rang through the long passage and the empty house. She looked at me as if she heard me, but I had recovered myself and cleared the air. There was nothing in the room the next minute but the sunshine and a sense that I must stay.

XVI

I had so perfectly expected that the return of my pupils would be marked by a demonstration that I was freshly upset at having to take into account that they were dumb about my absence. Instead of gaily denouncing and caressing me, they made no allusion to my having failed them, and I was left, for the time, on perceiving that she too said nothing, to study Mrs. Grose's odd face. I did this to such purpose that I made sure they had in some way bribed her to silence; a silence that, however, I would engage to break down on the first private opportunity. This opportunity came before tea: I secured five minutes with her in the housekeeper's room, where, in the twilight, amid a smell of lately-baked bread, but with the place all swept and garnished, I found her sitting in pained placidity before the fire. So I see her still, so I see her best: facing the flame from her straight chair in the dusky, shining room, a large clean image of the "put away"—of drawers closed and locked and rest without a remedy.

"Oh, yes, they asked me to say nothing; and to please them—so long as they were there—of course I promised. But what had happened to you?"

"I only went with you for the walk," I said. "I had then to come back to meet a friend."

She showed her surprise. "A friend—*you*?"

"Oh, yes, I have a couple!" I laughed. "But did the children give you a reason?"

"For not alluding to your leaving us? Yes; they said you would like it better. Do you like it better?"

My face had made her rueful. "No, I like it worse!" But after an instant I added: "Did they say why I should like it better?"

"No; Master Miles only said, 'We must do nothing but what she likes!' "

"I wish indeed he would! And what did Flora say?"

"Miss Flora was too sweet. She said, 'Oh, of course, of course!'—and I said the same."

I thought a moment. "You were too sweet too—I can hear you all. But none the less, between Miles and me, it's now all out."

"All out?" My companion stared. "But what, Miss?"

"Everything. It doesn't matter. I've made up my mind. I came home, my dear," I went on, "for a talk with Miss Jessel."

I had by this time formed the habit of having Mrs. Grose literally well in hand in advance of my sounding that note; so that even now, as she bravely blinked under the signal of my word, I could keep her comparatively firm. "A talk! Do you mean she spoke?"

"It came to that. I found her, on my return, in the school-room."

"And what did she say?" I can hear the good woman still, and the candour of her stupefaction.

"That she suffers the torments——!"

It was this, of a truth, that made her, as she filled out my picture, gape. "Do you mean," she faltered, "—of the lost?"

"Of the lost. Of the damned. And that's why, to share them——" I faltered myself with the horror of it.

But my companion, with less imagination, kept me up. "To share them——?"

"She wants Flora." Mrs. Grose might, as I gave it to her, fairly have fallen away from me had I not been prepared. I still held her there, to show I was. "As I've told you, however, it doesn't matter."

"Because you've made up your mind? But to what?"

"To everything."

"And what do you call 'everything'?"

"Why, sending for their uncle."

"Oh, Miss, in pity do," my friend broke out.

"Ah, but I will, I *will!* I see it's the only way. What's 'out,' as I told you, with Miles is that if he thinks I'm afraid to— and has ideas of what he gains by that—he shall see he's mistaken. Yes, yes; his uncle shall have it here from me on the spot (and before the boy himself if necessary) that if I'm to be reproached with having done nothing again about more school——"

"Yes, Miss——" my companion pressed me.

"Well, there's that awful reason."

There were now clearly so many of these for my poor colleague that she was excusable for being vague. "But —a— which?"

"Why, the letter from his old place."

"You'll show it to the master?"

"I ought to have done so on the instant."

"Oh, no!" said Mrs. Grose with decision.

"I'll put it before him," I went on inexorably, "that I can't undertake to work the question on behalf of a child who has been expelled——"

"For we've never in the least known what!" Mrs. Grose declared.

"For wickedness. For what else—when he's so clever and beautiful and perfect? Is he stupid? Is he untidy? Is he infirm? Is he ill-natured? He's exquisite—so it can be only *that*; and that would open up the whole thing. After all," I said, "it's their uncle's fault. If he left here such people——!"

"He didn't really in the least know them. The fault's mine." She had turned quite pale.

"Well, you shan't suffer," I answered.

"The children shan't!" she emphatically returned.

I was silent awhile; we looked at each other. "Then what am I to tell him?"

"You needn't tell him anything. *I'll* tell him."

I measured this. "Do you mean you'll write——?" Remembering she couldn't, I caught myself up. "How do you communicate?"

"I tell the bailiff. *He* writes."

"And should you like him to write our story?"

My question had a sarcastic force that I had not fully intended, and it made her, after a moment, inconsequently break down. The tears were again in her eyes. "Ah, Miss, *you* write!"

"Well—tonight," I at last answered; and on this we separated.

XVII

I went so far, in the evening, as to make a beginning. The weather had changed back, a great wind was abroad, and beneath the lamp, in my room, with Flora at peace beside me, I sat for a long time before a blank sheet of paper and listened to the lash of the rain and the batter of the gusts. Finally I went out, taking a candle; I crossed the passage and listened a minute at Miles's door. What, under my endless obsession, I had been impelled to listen for was some betrayal of his not being at rest, and I presently caught one, but not in the form

I had expected. His voice tinkled out. "I say, you there—come in." It was a gaiety in the gloom!

I went in with my light and found him, in bed, very wide awake, but very much at his ease. "Well, what are *you* up to?" he asked with a grace of sociability in which it occurred to me that Mrs. Grose, had she been present, might have looked in vain for proof that anything was "out."

I stood over him with my candle. "How did you know I was there?"

"Why, of course I heard you. Did you fancy you made no noise? You're like a troop of cavalry!" he beautifully laughed.

"Then you weren't asleep?"

"Not much! I lie awake and think."

I had put my candle, designedly, a short way off, and then, as he held out his friendly old hand to me, had sat down on the edge of his bed. "What is it," I asked, "that you think of?"

"What in the world, my dear, but *you*?"

"Ah, the pride I take in your appreciation doesn't insist on that! I had so far rather you slept."

"Well, I think also, you know, of this queer business of ours."

I marked the coolness of his firm little hand. "Of what queer business, Miles?"

"Why, the way you bring me up. And all the rest!"

I fairly held my breath a minute, and even from my glimmering taper there was light enough to show how he smiled up at me from his pillow. "What do you mean by all the rest?"

"Oh, you know, you know!"

I could say nothing for a minute, though I felt, as I held his hand and our eyes continued to meet, that my silence had all the air of admitting his charge and that nothing in the whole world of reality was perhaps at that moment so fabulous as our actual relation. "Certainly you shall go back to school," I said, "if it be that that troubles you. But not to the old place—we must find another, a better. How could I know it did trouble you, this question, when you never told me so, never spoke of it at all?" His clear, listening face, framed in its smooth whiteness, made him for the minute as appealing as some wistful patient in a children's hospital; and I would have given, as the resemblance came to me, all I possessed on earth really to be the nurse or the sister of charity who might have helped to cure him. Well, even as it was, I perhaps might help! "Do you know you've never said a word to me about your school—I mean the old one; never mentioned it in any way?"

He seemed to wonder; he smiled with the same loveliness. But he clearly gained time; he waited, he called for guidance. "Haven't I?" It wasn't for *me* to help him—it was for the thing I had met!

Something in his tone and the expression of his face, as I got this from him, set my heart aching with such a pang as it had never yet known; so unutterably touching was it to see his little brain puzzled and his little resources taxed to play, under the spell laid on him, a part of innocence and consistency. "No, never—from the hour you came back. You've never mentioned to me one of your masters, one of your comrades, nor the least little thing that ever happened to you at school. Never, little Miles—no, never—have you given me an inkling of anything that *may* have happened there. Therefore you can fancy how much I'm in the dark. Until you came out, that way, this morning, you had, since the first hour I saw you, scarce even made a reference to anything in your previous life. You seemed so perfectly to accept the present." It was extraordinary how my absolute conviction of his secret precocity (or whatever I might call the poison of an influence that I dared but half to phrase) made him, in spite of the faint breath of his inward trouble, appear as accessible as an older person—imposed him almost as an intellectual equal. "I thought you wanted to go on as you are."

It struck me that at this he just faintly coloured. He gave, at any rate, like a convalescent slightly fatigued, a languid shake of his head. "I don't—I don't. I want to get away."

"You're tired of Bly?"

"Oh, no, I like Bly."

"Well, then——?"

"Oh, *you* know what a boy wants!"

I felt that I didn't know so well as Miles, and I took temporary refuge. "You want to go to your uncle?"

Again, at this, with his sweet ironic face, he made a movement on the pillow. "Ah, you can't get off with that!"

I was silent a little, and it was I, now, I think, who changed colour. "My dear, I don't want to get off!"

"You can't, even if you do. You can't, you can't!"—he lay beautifully staring. "My uncle must come down, and you must completely settle things."

"If we do," I returned with some spirit, "you may be sure it will be to take you quite away."

"Well, don't you understand that that's exactly what I'm working for? You'll have to tell him—about the way you've let it all drop; you'll have to tell him a tremendous lot!"

The exultation with which he uttered this helped me somehow, for the instant, to meet him rather more. "And how much will *you*, Miles, have to tell him? There are things he'll ask you!"

He turned it over. "Very likely. But what things?"

"The things you've never told me. To make up his mind what to do with you. He can't send you back——"

"Oh, I don't want to go back!" he broke in. "I want a new field."

He said it with admirable serenity, with positive unimpeachable gaiety; and doubtless it was that very note that most evoked for me the poignancy, the unnatural childish tragedy, of his probable reappearance at the end of three months with all this bravado and still more dishonour. It overwhelmed me now that I should never be able to bear that, and it made me let myself go. I threw myself upon him and in the tenderness of my pity I embraced him. "Dear little Miles, dear little Miles——!"

My face was close to his, and he let me kiss him, simply taking it with indulgent good-humour. "Well, old lady?"

"Is there nothing—nothing at all that you want to tell me?"

He turned off a little, facing round toward the wall and holding up his hand to look at as one had seen sick children look. "I've told you—I told you this morning."

Oh, I was sorry for him! "That you just want me not to worry you?"

He looked round at me now, as if in recognition of my understanding him; then ever so gently, "To let me alone," he replied.

There was even a singular little dignity in it, something that made me release him, yet, when I had slowly risen, linger beside him. God knows I never wished to harass him, but I felt that merely, at this, to turn my back on him was to abandon or, to put it more truly, to lose him. "I've just begun a letter to your uncle," I said.

"Well, then, finish it!"

I waited a minute. "What happened before?"

He gazed up at me again. "Before what?"

"Before you came back. And before you went away."

For some time he was silent, but he continued to meet my eyes. "What happened?"

It made me, the sound of the words, in which it seemed to me that I caught for the very first time a small faint quaver of consenting consciousness—it made me drop on my knees beside the bed and seize once more the chance of possessing him. "Dear little Miles, dear little Miles, if you *knew* how I want to help you! It's only that, it's nothing but that, and I'd rather die than give you a pain or do you a wrong—I'd rather die than hurt a hair of you. Dear little Miles"—oh, I brought it out now even if I *should* go too far—"I just want you to help me to save you!" But I knew in a moment after this that I had gone too far. The answer to my appeal was instantaneous, but it came in the form of an extraordinary blast and chill, a gust of frozen air and a shake of the room as great as if, in the wild wind, the casement had crashed in. The boy gave a loud, high shriek, which, lost in the rest of the shock of sound, might have seemed, indistinctly, though I was so close to him, a note either of jubilation or of terror. I jumped to my feet again and was conscious of darkness. So for a moment we remained, while I stared about me and saw that the drawn curtains were unstirred and the window tight. "Why, the candle's out!" I then cried.

"It was I who blew it, dear!" said Miles.

XVIII

The next day, after lessons, Mrs. Grose found a moment to say to me quietly: "Have you written, Miss?"

"Yes—I've written." But I didn't add—for the hour—that

my letter, sealed and directed, was still in my pocket. There would be time enough to send it before the messenger should go to the village. Meanwhile there had been, on the part of my pupils, no more brilliant, more exemplary morning. It was exactly as if they had both had at heart to gloss over any recent little friction. They performed the dizziest feats of arithmetic, soaring quite out of *my* feeble range, and perpetrated, in higher spirits than ever, geographical and historical jokes. It was conspicuous of course in Miles in particular that he appeared to wish to show how easily he could let me down. This child, to my memory, really lives in a setting of beauty and misery that no words can translate; there was a distinction all his own in every impulse he revealed; never was a small natural creature, to the uninitiated eye all frankness and freedom, a more ingenious, a more extraordinary little gentleman. I had perpetually to guard against the wonder of contemplation into which my initiated view betrayed me; to check the irrelevant gaze and discouraged sigh in which I constantly both attacked and renounced the enigma of what such a little gentleman could have done that deserved a penalty. Say that, by the dark prodigy I knew, the imagination of all evil *had* been opened up to him: all the justice within me ached for the proof that it could ever have flowered into an act.

He had never, at any rate, been such a little gentleman as when, after our early dinner on this dreadful day, he came round to me and asked if I shouldn't like him, for half an hour, to play to me. David playing to Saul could never have shown a finer sense of the occasion. It was literally a charming exhibition of tact, of magnanimity, and quite tantamount to his saying outright: "The true knights we love to read about never push an advantage too far. I know what you mean now: you mean that—to be let alone yourself and not followed up—you'll cease to worry and spy upon me, won't keep me so close to you, will let me go and come. Well, I 'come,' you see—but I don't go! There'll be plenty of time for that. I do really delight in your society, and I only want to show you that I contended for a principle." It may be imagined whether I resisted this appeal or failed to accompany him again, hand in hand, to the schoolroom. He sat down at the old piano and played as he had never played, and if there are those who think he had better have been kicking a football I can only say that I wholly agree with them. For at the end of a time that under his influence I had quite ceased to measure I started up with a strange sense of having literally slept at my post. It was after luncheon, and by the schoolroom fire, and yet I hadn't really, in the least, slept: I had only done something much worse—I had forgotten. Where, all this time, was Flora? When I put the question to Miles he played on a minute before answering, and then could only say: "Why, my dear, how do *I* know?"—breaking moreover into a happy laugh which, immediately after, as if it were a vocal accompaniment, he prolonged into incoherent, extravagant song.

I went straight to my room, but his sister was not there; then, before going downstairs, I looked into several others. As she was nowhere about she would surely be with Mrs. Grose, whom, in the comfort of that theory, I accordingly proceeded in quest of. I found her where I had found her the evening before, but she met my quick challenge with blank, scared ignorance. She had only supposed that, after the repast, I had carried off both the children; as to which she was quite in her right, for it was the very first time I had allowed the little girl out of my sight without some special provision. Of course now indeed she might be with the maids, so that the immediate thing was to look for her without an air of alarm. This we promptly arranged between us; but when, ten minutes later and in pursuance of our arrangement, we met in the hall, it was only to report on either side that after guarded inquiries we had altogether failed to trace her. For a minute there, apart from observation, we exchanged mute alarms, and I could feel with what high interest my friend returned me all those I had from the first given her.

"She'll be above," she presently said—"in one of the rooms you haven't searched."

"No; she's at a distance." I had made up my mind. "She has gone out."

Mrs. Grose stared. "Without a hat?"

I naturally also looked volumes. "Isn't that woman always without one?"

"She's with *her*?"

"She's with *her*!" I declared. "We must find them."

My hand was on my friend's arm, but she failed for the moment, confronted with such an account of the matter, to respond to my pressure. She communed, on the contrary, on the spot, with her uneasiness. "And where's Master Miles?"

"Oh, *he's* with Quint. They're in the schoolroom."

"Lord, Miss!" My view, I was myself aware—and therefore I suppose my tone—had never yet reached so calm an assurance.

"The trick's played," I went on; "they've successfully worked their plan. He found the most divine little way to keep me quiet while she went off."

" 'Divine'?" Mrs. Grose bewilderedly echoed.

"Infernal, then!" I almost cheerfully rejoined. "He has provided for himself as well. But come!"

She had helplessly gloomed at the upper regions. "You leave him——?"

"So long with Quint? Yes—I don't mind that now."

She always ended, at these moments, by getting possession of my hand, and in this manner she could at present still stay me. But after gasping an instant at my sudden resignation, "Because of your letter?" she eagerly brought out.

I quickly, by way of answer, felt for my letter, drew it forth, held it up, and then, freeing myself, went and laid it on the great hall-table. "Luke will take it," I said as I came back. I reached the house-door and opened it; I was already on the steps.

My companion still demurred: the storm of the night and the early morning had dropped, but the afternoon was damp and grey. I came down to the drive while she stood in the doorway. "You go with nothing on?"

"What do I care when the child has nothing? I can't wait to dress," I cried, "and if you must do so, I leave you. Try meanwhile, yourself, upstairs."

"With *them*?" Oh, on this, the poor woman promptly joined me!

XIX

We went straight to the lake, as it was called at Bly, and I dare say rightly called, though I reflect that it may in fact have been a sheet of water less remarkable than it appeared to my untravelled eyes. My acquaintance with sheets of water was small, and the pool of Bly, at all events on the few occasions of my consenting, under the protection of my pupils, to affront its surface in the old flat-bottomed boat moored there for our use, had impressed me both with its extent and its agitation. The usual place of embarkation was half a mile from the house, but I had an intimate conviction that, wherever Flora might be, she was not near home. She had not given me the slip for any small adventure, and, since the day of the very great one that I had shared with her by the pond, I had been aware, in our walks, of the quarter to which she most inclined. This was why I had now given to Mrs. Grose's steps so marked a direction—a direction that made her, when she perceived it, oppose a resistance that showed me she was freshly mystified. "You're going to the water, Miss?—you think she's *in*——?"

"She may be, though the depth is, I believe, nowhere very great. But what I judge most likely is that she's on the spot from which, the other day, we saw together what I told you."

"When she pretended not to see——?"

"With that astounding self-possession! I've always been sure she wanted to go back alone. And now her brother has managed it for her."

Mrs. Grose still stood where she had stopped. "You suppose they really *talk* of them?"

I could meet this with a confidence! "They say things that, if we heard them, would simply appal us."

"And if she *is* there——?"

"Yes?"

"Then Miss Jessel is?"

"Beyond a doubt. You shall see."

"Oh, thank you!" my friend cried, planted so firm that, taking it in, I went straight on without her. By the time I reached the pool, however, she was close behind me, and I knew that, whatever, to her apprehension, might befall me, the exposure of my society struck her as her least danger. She exhaled a moan of relief as we at last came in sight of the greater part of the water without a sight of the child. There was no trace of Flora on that nearer side of the bank where my observation of her had been most startling, and none on the opposite edge, where, save for a margin of some twenty yards, a thick copse came down to the water. The pond, oblong in shape, had a width so scant compared to its length that, with its ends out of view, it might have been taken for a scant river. We looked at the empty expanse, and then I felt the suggestion of my friend's eyes. I knew what she meant and I replied with a negative headshake.

"No, no; wait! She has taken the boat."

My companion stared at the vacant mooring-place and then again across the lake. "Then where is it?"

"Our not seeing it is the strongest of proofs. She has used it to go over, and then has managed to hide it."

"All alone—that child?"

"She's not alone, and at such times she's not a child: she's an old, old woman." I scanned all the visible shore while Mrs. Grose took again, into the queer element I offered her, one of her plunges of submission; then I pointed out that the boat might perfectly be in a small refuge formed by one of the recesses of the pool, an indentation masked, for the hither side, by a projection of the bank and by a clump of trees growing close to the water.

"But if the boat's there, where on earth's *she*?" my colleague anxiously asked.

"That's exactly what we must learn." And I started to walk further.

"By going all the way round?"

"Certainly, far as it is. It will take us but ten minutes, but it's far enough to have made the child prefer not to walk. She went straight over."

"Laws!" cried my friend again; the chain of my logic was ever too much for her. It dragged her at my heels even now, and when we had got half-way round—a devious, tiresome process, on ground much broken and by a path choked with overgrowth—I paused to give her breath. I sustained her with a grateful arm, assuring her that she might hugely help me; and this started us afresh, so that in the course of but few minutes more we reached a point from which we found the boat to be where I had supposed it. It had been intentionally left as much as possible out of sight and was tied to one of the stakes of a fence that came, just there, down to the brink and that had been an assistance to disembarking. I recognised, as I looked at the pair of short, thick oars, quite safely drawn up, the prodigious character of the feat for a little girl; but I had lived, by this time, too long among wonders and had panted to too many livelier measures. There was a gate in the fence, through which we passed, and that brought us, after a trifling interval, more into the open. Then, "There she is!" we both exclaimed at once.

Flora, a short way off, stood before us on the grass and smiled as if her performance was now complete. The next thing she did, however, was to stoop straight down and pluck—quite as if it were all she was there for—a big, ugly spray of withered fern. I instantly became sure she had just come out of the copse. She waited for us, not herself taking a step, and I was conscious of the rare solemnity with which we presently approached her. She smiled and smiled, and we met; but it was all done in a silence by this time flagrantly ominous. Mrs. Grose was the first to break the spell: she threw herself on her knees and, drawing the child to her breast, clasped in a long embrace the little tender, yielding body. While this dumb convulsion lasted I could only watch it— which I did the more intently when I saw Flora's face peep at me over our companion's shoulder. It was serious now—the flicker had left it; but it strengthened the pang with which I at that moment envied Mrs. Grose the simplicity of *her* relation. Still, all this while, nothing more passed between us save that Flora had let her foolish fern again drop to the ground. What she and I had virtually said to each other was that pretexts were useless now. When Mrs. Grose finally got up she kept the child's hand, so that the two were still before me; and the singular reticence of our communion was even more marked in the frank look she launched me. "I'll be hanged," it said, "if *I'll* speak!"

It was Flora who, gazing all over me in candid wonder, was the first. She was struck with our bareheaded aspect. "Why, where are your things?"

"Where yours are, my dear!" I promptly returned.

She had already got back her gaiety, and appeared to take this as an answer quite sufficient. "And where's Miles?" she went on.

There was something in the small valour of it that quite finished me: these three words from her were, in a flash like the glitter of a drawn blade, the jostle of the cup that my hand, for weeks and weeks, had held high and full to the brim and that now, even before speaking, I felt overflow in a deluge. "I'll tell you if you'll tell *me*——" I heard myself say, then heard the tremor in which it broke.

"Well, what?"

Mrs. Grose's suspense blazed at me, but it was too late now, and I brought the thing out handsomely. "Where, my pet, is Miss Jessel?"

XX

Just as in the churchyard with Miles, the whole thing was upon us. Much as I had made of the fact that this name had never once, between us, been sounded, the quick, smitten glare with which the child's face now received it fairly likened my breach of the silence to the smash of a pane of glass. It added to the interposing cry, as if to stay the blow, that Mrs. Grose, at the same instant, uttered over my violence—the shriek of a creature scared, or rather wounded, which, in turn, within a few seconds, was completed by a gasp of my own. I seized my colleague's arm. "She's there, she's there!"

Miss Jessel stood before us on the opposite bank exactly as she had stood the other time, and I remember, strangely, as the first feeling now produced in me, my thrill of joy at having brought on a proof. She was there, and I was justified; she was there, and I was neither cruel nor mad. She was there for poor scared Mrs. Grose, but she was there most for Flora; and no moment of my monstrous time was perhaps so extraordinary as that in which I consciously threw out to her—with the sense that, pale and ravenous demon as she was, she would catch and understand it—an inarticulate message of gratitude. She rose erect on the spot my friend and I had lately quitted, and there was not, in all the long reach of her desire, an inch of her evil that fell short. This first vividness of vision and emotion were things of a few seconds, during which Mrs. Grose's dazed blink across to where I pointed struck me as a sovereign sign that she too at last saw, just as it carried my own eyes precipitately to the child. The revelation then of the manner in which Flora was affected startled me, in truth, far more than it would have done to find her also merely agitated, for direct dismay was of course not what I had expected. Prepared and on her guard as our pursuit had actually made her, she would repress every betrayal; and I was therefore shaken, on the spot, by my first glimpse of the particular one for which I had not allowed. To see her, without a convulsion of her small pink face, not even feign to glance in the direction of the prodigy I announced, but only, instead of that, turn at *me* an expression of hard, still gravity, an expression absolutely new and unprecedented and that appeared to read and accuse and judge me—this was a stroke that somehow converted the little girl herself into the very presence that could make me quail. I quailed even though my certitude that she thoroughly saw was never greater than at that instant, and in the immediate need to defend myself I called it passionately to witness. "She's there, you little unhappy thing—there, there, *there*, and you see her as well as you see me!" I had said shortly before to Mrs. Grose that she was not at these times a child, but an old, old woman, and that description of her could not have been more strikingly confirmed than in the way in which, for all answer to this, she simply showed me, without a concession, an admission, of her eyes, a countenance of deeper and deeper, of indeed suddenly quite fixed, reprobation. I was by this time—if I can put the whole thing at all together— more appalled at what I may properly call her manner than at anything else, though it was simultaneously with this that I became aware of having Mrs. Grose also, and very formidably, to reckon with. My elder companion, the next moment, at any rate, blotted out everything but her own flushed face and her loud, shocked protest, a burst of high disapproval. "What a dreadful turn, to be sure, Miss! Where on earth do you see anything?"

I could only grasp her more quickly yet, for even while she spoke the hideous plain presence stood undimmed and undaunted. It had already lasted a minute, and it lasted while I continued, seizing my colleague, quite thrusting her at it and presenting her to it, to insist with my pointing hand. "You don't see her exactly as *we* see?—you mean to say you don't now—*now*? She's as big as a blazing fire! Only look, dearest woman, *look*——!" She looked, even as I did, and gave me, with her deep groan of negation, repulsion, compassion—the mixture with her pity of her relief at her exemption—a sense, touching to me even then, that she would have backed me up if she could. I might well have needed that, for with this hard blow of the proof that her eyes were hopelessly sealed I felt my own situation horribly crumble, I felt—I saw—my livid predecessor press, from her position, on my defeat, and I was conscious, more than all, of what I should have from this instant to deal with in the astounding little attitude of Flora. Into this attitude Mrs. Grose immediately and violently entered, breaking, even while there pierced through my sense of ruin a prodigious private triumph, into breathless reassurance.

"She isn't there, little lady, and nobody's there—and you never see nothing, my sweet! How can poor Miss Jessel—when poor Miss Jessel's dead and buried? *We* know, don't we, love?"—and she appealed, blundering in, to the child. "It's all a mere mistake and a worry and a joke—and we'll go home as fast as we can!"

Our companion, on this, had responded with a strange, quick primness of propriety, and they were again, with Mrs. Grose on her feet, united, as it were, in pained opposition to me. Flora continued to fix me with her small mask of reprobation, and even at that minute I prayed God to forgive me for seeming to see that, as she stood there holding tight to our friend's dress, her incomparable childish beauty had suddenly failed, had quite vanished. I've said it already—she was literally, she was hideously, hard; she had turned common and almost ugly. "I don't know what you mean. I see nobody. I see nothing. I never *have*. I think you're cruel. I don't like you!" Then, after this deliverance, which might have been that of a vulgarly pert little girl in the street, she hugged Mrs. Grose more closely and buried in her skirts the dreadful little face. In this position she produced an almost furious wail. "Take me away, take me away—oh, take me away from *her*!"

"From *me*?" I panted.

"From you—from you!" she cried.

Even Mrs. Grose looked across at me dismayed, while I had nothing to do but communicate again with the figure that, on the opposite bank, without a movement, as rigidly still as if catching, beyond the interval, our voices, was as vividly there for my disaster as it was not there for my service. The wretched child had spoken exactly as if she had got from some outside source each of her stabbing little words, and I could therefore, in the full despair of all I had to accept, but sadly shake my head at her. "If I had ever doubted, all my doubt would at present have gone. I've been living with the miserable truth, and now it has only too much closed round me. Of course I've lost you: I've interfered, and you've seen— under *her* dictation"—with which I faced, over the pool again, our infernal witness—"the easy and perfect way to meet it. I've done my best, but I've lost you. Good-bye." For Mrs. Grose I had an imperative, an almost frantic "Go, go!" before which, in infinite distress, but mutely possessed of the little girl and clearly convinced, in spite of her blindness, that something awful had occurred and some collapse engulfed us, she retreated, by the way we had come, as fast as she could move.

Of what first happened when I was left alone I had no subsequent memory. I only knew that at the end of, I suppose, a quarter of an hour, an odorous dampness and roughness, chilling and piercing my trouble, had made me understand that I must have thrown myself, on my face, on the ground and given way to a wildness of grief. I must have lain there long and cried and sobbed, for when I raised my head the day was almost done. I got up and looked a moment, through the twilight, at the grey pool and its blank, haunted edge, and then I took, back to the house, my dreary and difficult course. When I reached the gate in the fence the boat, to my surprise, was gone, so that I had a fresh reflection to make on Flora's extraordinary command of the situation. She passed that night, by the most tacit, and I should add, were not the word so grotesque a false note, the happiest of arrangements, with Mrs. Grose. I saw neither of them on my return, but, on the other hand, as by an ambiguous compensation, I saw a great deal of Miles. I saw—I can use no other phrase—so much of him that it was as if it were more than it had ever been. No evening I had passed at Bly had the portentous quality of this one; in spite of which—and in spite also of the deeper depths of consternation that had opened beneath my feet—there was literally, in the ebbing actual, an extraordinarily sweet sadness. On reaching the house I had never so much as looked for the boy; I had simply gone straight to my room to change what I was wearing and to take in, at a glance, much material testimony to Flora's rupture. Her little belongings had all been removed. When later, by the schoolroom fire, I was served with tea by the usual maid, I indulged, on the article of my other pupil, in no inquiry whatever. He had his freedom now—he might have it to the end! Well, he did have it; and it consisted—in part at least—of his coming in at about eight o'clock and sitting down with me in silence. On the removal of the tea-things I had blown out the candles and drawn my chair closer: I was conscious of a mortal coldness and felt as if I should never again be warm. So, when he appeared, I was sitting in the glow with my thoughts. He paused a moment by the door as if to look at me; then—as if to share them—came to the other side of the hearth and sank into a chair. We sat there in absolute stillness; yet he wanted, I felt, to be with me.

XXI

Before a new day, in my room, had fully broken, my eyes opened to Mrs. Grose, who had come to my bedside with worse news. Flora was so markedly feverish that an illness was perhaps at hand; she had passed a night of extreme unrest, a night agitated above all by fears that had for their subject not in the least her former, but wholly her present, governess. It was not against the possible re-entrance of Miss Jessel on the scene that she protested—it was conspicuously and passionately against mine. I was promptly on my feet of course, and with an immense deal to ask; the more that my friend had discernibly now girded her loins to meet me once more. This I felt as soon as I had put to her the question of her sense of the child's sincerity as against my own. "She persists in denying to you that she saw, or has ever seen, anything?"

My visitor's trouble, truly, was great. "Ah, Miss, it isn't a matter on which I can push her! Yet it isn't either, I must say, as if I much needed to. It has made her, every inch of her, quite old."

"Oh, I see her perfectly from here. She resents, for all the world like some high little personage, the imputation on her truthfulness and, as it were, her respectability. 'Miss Jessel indeed—*she*!' Ah, she's 'respectable,' the chit! The impression she gave me there yesterday was, I assure you, the very strangest of all; it was quite beyond any of the others. I *did* put my foot in it! She'll never speak to me again."

Hideous and obscure as it all was, it held Mrs. Grose briefly silent; then she granted my point with a frankness which, I made sure, had more behind it. "I think indeed, Miss, she never will. She do have a grand manner about it!"

"And that manner"—I summed it up—"is practically what's the matter with her now!"

Oh, that manner, I could see in my visitor's face, and not a little else besides! "She asks me every three minutes if I think you're coming in."

"I see—I see." I too, on my side, had so much more than worked it out. "Has she said to you since yesterday—except to repudiate her familiarity with anything so dreadful—a single other word about Miss Jessel?"

"Not one, Miss. And of course you know," my friend added, "I took it from her, by the lake, that, just then and there at least, there *was* nobody."

"Rather! And, naturally, you take it from her still."

"I don't contradict her. What else can I do?"

"Nothing in the world! You've the cleverest little person to deal with. They've made them—their two friends, I mean—still cleverer even than nature did; for it was wondrous material to play on! Flora has now her grievance, and she'll work it to the end."

"Yes, Miss; but to *what* end?"

"Why, that of dealing with me to her uncle. She'll make me out to him the lowest creature——!"

I winced at the fair show of the scene in Mrs. Grose's face; she looked for a minute as if she sharply saw them together. "And him who thinks so well of you!"

"He has an odd way—it comes over me now," I laughed, "—of proving it! But that doesn't matter. What Flora wants, of course, is to get rid of me."

My companion bravely concurred. "Never again to so much as look at you."

"So that what you've come to me now for," I asked, "is to speed me on my way?" Before she had time to reply, however, I had her in check. "I've a better idea—the result of my reflections. My going *would* seem the right thing, and on Sunday I was terribly near it. Yet that won't do. It's *you* who must go. You must take Flora."

My visitor, at this, did speculate. "But where in the world——?"

"Away from here. Away from *them*. Away, even most of all, now, from me. Straight to her uncle."

"Only to tell on you——?"

"No, not 'only'! To leave me, in addition, with my remedy."

She was still vague. "And what *is* your remedy?"

"Your loyalty, to begin with. And then Miles's."

She looked at me hard. "Do you think he——?"

"Won't if he has the chance, turn on me? Yes, I venture still to think it. At all events, I want to try. Get off with his sister as soon as possible and leave me with him alone." I was amazed, myself, at the spirit I had still in reserve, and therefore perhaps a trifle the more disconcerted at the way in which, in spite of this fine example of it, she hesitated. "There's one thing, of course," I went on: "they mustn't, before she goes, see each for three seconds." Then it came over me that, in spite of Flora's presumable sequestration from the instant of her return from the pool, it might already be too late. "Do you mean, " I anxiously asked, "that they *have* met?"

At this she quite flushed. "Ah, Miss, I'm not such a fool as that! If I've been obliged to leave her three or four times, it has been each time with one of the maids, and at present, though she's alone, she's locked in safe. And yet—and yet!" There were too many things.

"And yet what?"

"Well, are you so sure of the little gentleman?"

"I'm not sure of anything but *you*. But I have, since last evening, a new hope. I think he wants to give me an opening.

I do believe that—poor little exquisite wretch!—he wants to speak. Last evening, in the firelight and the silence, he sat with me for two hours as if it were just coming."

Mrs. Grose looked hard, through the window, at the grey, gathering day. "And did it come?"

"No, though I waited and waited, I confess it didn't, and it was without a breach of the silence or so much as a faint allusion to his sister's condition and absence that we at last kissed for good-night. All the same," I continued, "I can't, if her uncle sees her, consent to his seeing her brother without my having given the boy—and most of all because things have got so bad—a little more time."

My friend appeared on this ground more reluctant than I could quite understand. "What do you mean by more time?"

"Well, a day or two—really to bring it out. He'll then be on *my* side—of which you see the importance. If nothing comes, I shall only fail, and you will, at the worst, have helped me by doing, on your arrival in town, whatever you may have found possible." So I put it before her, but she continued for a little so inscrutably embarrassed that I came again to her aid. "Unless, indeed," I wound up, "you really want *not* to go."

I could see it, in her face, at last clear itself; she put out her hand to me as a pledge. "I'll go—I'll go. I'll go this morning."

I wanted to be very just. "If you *should* wish still to wait, I would engage she shouldn't see me."

"No, no: it's the place itself. She must leave it." She held me a moment with heavy eyes, then brought out the rest. "Your idea's the right one. I myself, Miss——"

"Well?"

"I can't stay."

The look she gave me with it made me jump at possibilities. "You mean that, since yesterday, you *have* seen——?"

She shook her head with dignity. "I've *heard*——!"

"Heard?"

"From that child—horrors! There!" she sighed with tragic relief. "On my honour, Miss, she says things——!" But at this evocation she broke down; she dropped, with a sudden sob, upon my sofa and, as I had seen her do before, gave way to all the grief of it.

It was quite in another matter that I, for my part, let myself go. "Oh, thank God!"

She sprang up again at this, drying her eyes with a groan. " 'Thank God'?"

"It so justifies me!"

"It does that, Miss!"

I couldn't have desired more emphasis, but I just hesitated. "She's so horrible?"

I saw my colleague scarce knew how to put it. "Really shocking."

"And about me?"

"About you, Miss—since you must have it. It's beyond everything, for a young lady; and I can't think wherever she must have picked up——"

"The appalling language she applied to me? I can, then!" I broke in with a laugh that was doubtless significant enough.

It only, in truth, left my friend still more grave. "Well, perhaps I ought to also—since I've heard some of it before! Yet I can't bear it," the poor woman went on while, with the same movement, she glanced, on my dressing-table, at the face of my watch. "But I must go back."

I kept her, however. "Ah, if you can't bear it——!"

"How can I stop with her, you mean? Why, just *for* that: to get her away. Far from this," she pursued, "far from *them*——"

"She may be different? she may be free?" I seized her almost with joy. "Then, in spite of yesterday, you *believe*——"

"In such doings?" Her simple description of them required, in the light of her expression, to be carried no further, and she gave me the whole thing as she had never done. "I believe."

Yes, it was a joy, and we were still shoulder to shoulder: if I might continue sure of that I should care but little what else happened. My support in the presence of disaster would be the same as it had been in my early need of confidence, and if my friend would answer for my honesty, I would answer for all the rest. On the point of taking leave of her, none the less, I was to some extent embarrassed. "There's one thing of course—it occurs to me—to remember. My letter, giving the alarm, will have reached town before you."

I now perceived still more how she had been beating about the bush and how weary at last it had made her. "Your letter won't have got there. Your letter never went."

"What then became of it?"

"Goodness knows! Master Miles——"

"Do you mean *he* took it?" I gasped.

She hung fire, but she overcame her reluctance. "I mean that I saw yesterday, when I came back with Miss Flora, that it wasn't where you had put it. Later in the evening I had the chance to question Luke, and he declared that he had neither noticed nor touched it." We could only exchange, on this, one of our deeper mutual soundings, and it was Mrs. Grose who first brought up the plumb with an almost elate "You see!"

"Yes, I see that if Miles took it instead he probably will have read it and destroyed it."

"And don't you see anything else?"

I faced her a moment with a sad smile. "It strikes me that by this time your eyes are open even wider than mine."

They proved to be so indeed, but she could still blush, almost, to show it. "I make out now what he must have done at school." And she gave, in her simple sharpness, an almost droll disillusioned nod. "He stole!"

I turned it over—I tried to be more judicial. "Well—perhaps."

She looked as if she found me unexpectedly calm. "He stole *letters*!"

She couldn't know my reasons for a calmness after all pretty shallow; so I showed them off as I might. "I hope then it was to more purpose than in this case! The note, at any rate, that I put on the table yesterday," I pursued, "will have given him so scant an advantage—for it contained only the bare demand for an interview—that he is already much ashamed of having gone so far for so little, and that what he had on his mind last evening was precisely the need of confession." I seemed to myself, for the instant, to have mastered it, to see it all. "Leave us, leave us"—I was already, at the door, hurrying her off. "I'll get it out of him. He'll meet me—he'll confess. If he confesses, he's saved. And if he's saved——"

"Then *you* are?" The dear woman kissed me on this, and I took her farewell. "I'll save you without him!" she cried as she went.

XXII

Yet it was when she had got off—and I missed her on the spot—that the great pinch really came. If I had counted on what it would give me to find myself alone with Miles, I speedily perceived, at least, that it would give me a measure. No hour of my stay in fact was so assailed with apprehensions as that of my coming down to learn that the carriage containing Mrs. Grose and my younger pupil had already rolled out of the gates. Now I *was*, I said to myself, face to face with the elements, and for much of the rest of the day, while I fought my weakness, I could consider that I had been supremely rash. It was a tighter place still than I had yet turned round in; all the more that, for the first time, I could see in the aspect of others a confused reflection of the crisis. What had happened naturally caused them all to stare; there was too little of the explained, throw out whatever we might, in the suddenness of my colleague's act. The maids and the men looked blank; the effect of which on my nerves was an aggravation until I saw the necessity of making it a positive aid. It was precisely, in short, by just clutching the helm that I avoided total wreck; and I dare say that, to bear up at all, I became, that morning, very grand and very dry. I welcomed the consciousness that I was charged with much to do, and I caused it to be known as well that, left thus to myself, I was quite remarkably firm. I wandered with that manner, for the next hour or two, all over the place and looked, I have no doubt, as if I were ready for any onset. So, for the benefit of whom it might concern, I paraded with a sick heart.

The person it appeared least to concern proved to be, till dinner, little Miles himself. My perambulations had given me, meanwhile, no glimpse of him, but they had tended to make more public the change taking place in our relation as a consequence of his having at the piano, the day before, kept me, in Flora's interest, so beguiled and befooled. The stamp of publicity had of course been fully given by her confinement and departure, and the change itself was now ushered in by our non-observance of the regular custom of the schoolroom. He had already disappeared when, on my way down, I pushed open his door, and I learned below that he had breakfasted—in the presence of a couple of the maids—with Mrs. Grose and his sister. He had then gone out, as he said, for a stroll; than which nothing, I reflected, could better have expressed his frank view of the abrupt transformation of my office. What he would now permit this office to consist of was yet to be settled: there was a queer relief, at all events—I mean for myself in especial—in the renouncement of one pretension. If so much had sprung to the surface, I scarce put it too strongly in saying that what had perhaps sprung highest was the absurdity of our prolonging the fiction that I had anything more to teach him. It sufficiently stuck out that, by tacit little tricks in which even more than myself he carried out the care for my dignity, I had had to appeal to him to let me off straining to meet him on the ground of his true capacity. He had at any rate his freedom now; I was never to touch it again; as I had amply shown, moreover, when, on his joining me in the schoolroom the previous night, I had uttered, on the subject of the interval just concluded, neither challenge nor hint. I had too much, from this moment, my other ideas. Yet when he at last arrived the difficulty of applying them, the accumulations of my problem, were brought straight home to me by the beautiful little presence on which what had occurred had as yet, for the eye, dropped neither stain nor shadow.

To mark, for the house, the high state I cultivated I decreed that my meals with the boy should be served, as we called it, downstairs; so that I had been awaiting him in the ponderous pomp of the room outside of the window of which I had had from Mrs. Grose, that first scared Sunday, my flash of something it would scarce have done to call light. Here at present I felt afresh—for I had felt it again and again—how my equilibrium depended on the success of my rigid will, the will to shut my eyes as tight as possible to the truth that what I had to deal with was, revoltingly, against nature. I could only get on at all by taking "nature" into my confidence and my account, by treating my monstrous ordeal as a push in a direction unusual, of course, and unpleasant, but demanding, after all, for a fair front, only another turn of the screw of ordinary human virtue. No attempt, none the less, could well require more tact than just this attempt to supply, one's self, *all* the nature. How could I put even a little of that article into a suppression of reference to what had occurred? How, on the other hand, could I make a reference without a new plunge into the hideous obscure? Well, a sort of answer, after a time, had come to me, and it was so far confirmed as that I was met, incontestably, by the quickened vision of what was rare in my little companion. It was indeed as if he had found even now—as he had so often found at lessons—still some other delicate way to ease me off. Wasn't there light in the fact which, as we shared our solitude, broke out with a specious glitter it had never yet quite worn?—the fact that (opportunity aiding, precious opportunity which had now come) it would be preposterous, with a child so endowed, to forgo the help one might wrest from absolute intelligence? What had his intelligence been given him for but to save him? Mightn't one, to reach his mind, risk the stretch of an angular arm over his character? It was as if, when we were face to face in the dining-room, he had literally shown me the way. The roast mutton was on the table, and I had dispensed with attendance. Miles, before he sat down, stood a moment with his hands in his pockets and looked at the joint, on which he seemed on the point of passing some humorous judgment. But what he presently produced was: "I say, my dear, is she really very awfully ill?"

"Little Flora? Not so bad but that she'll presently be better. London will set her up. Bly had ceased to agree with her. Come here and take your mutton."

He alertly obeyed me, carried the plate carefully to his seat, and, when he was established, went on. "Did Bly disagree with her so terribly suddenly?"

"Not so suddenly as you might think. One had seen it coming on."

"Then why didn't you get her off before?"

"Before what?"

"Before she became too ill to travel."

I found myself prompt. "She's *not* too ill to travel: she only might have become so if she had stayed. This was just the

moment to seize. The journey will dissipate the influence"—
oh, I was grand!—"and carry it off."

"I see, I see"—Miles, for that matter, was grand too. He
settled to his repast with the charming little "table manner"
that, from the day of his arrival, had relieved me of all grossness of admonition. Whatever he had been driven from school
for, it was not for ugly feeding. He was irreproachable, as
always, today; but he was unmistakeably more conscious. He
was discernibly trying to take for granted more things than
he found, without assistance, quite easy; and he dropped into
peaceful silence while he felt his situation. Our meal was of
the briefest—mine a vain pretence, and I had the things immediately removed. While this was done Miles stood again
with his hands in his little pockets and his back to me—stood
and looked out of the wide window through which, that other
day, I had seen what pulled me up. We continued silent while
the maid was with us—as silent, it whimsically occurred to
me, as some young couple who, on their wedding-journey, at
the inn, feel shy in the presence of the waiter. He turned
round only when the waiter had left us. "Well—so we're
alone!"

XXIII

"Oh, more or less." I fancy my smile was pale. "Not absolutely. We shouldn't like that!" I went on.

"No—I suppose we shouldn't. Of course we have the
others."

"We have the others—we have indeed the others," I concurred.

"Yet even though we have them," he returned, still with
his hands in his pockets and planted there in front of me,
"they don't much count, do they?"

I made the best of it, but I felt wan. "It depends on what
you call 'much'!"

"Yes"—with all accommodation—"everything depends!"
On this, however, he faced to the window again and presently
reached it with his vague, restless, cogitating step. He remained there awhile, with his forehead against the glass, in
contemplation of the stupid shrubs I knew and the dull things

of November. I had always my hypocrisy of "work," behind
which, now, I gained the sofa. Steadying myself with it there
as I had repeatedly done at those moments of torment that I
have described as the moments of my knowing the children
to be given to something from which I was barred, I sufficiently obeyed my habit of being prepared for the worst. But
an extraordinary impression dropped on me as I extracted a
meaning from the boy's embarrassed back—none other than
the impression that I was not barred now. This inference grew
in a few minutes to sharp intensity and seemed bound up with
the direct perception that it was positively *he* who was. The
frames and squares of the great window were a kind of image,
for him, of a kind of failure. I felt that I saw him, at any rate,
shut in or shut out. He was admirable, but not comfortable:
I took it in with a throb of hope. Wasn't he looking, through
the haunted pane, for something he couldn't see?—and wasn't
it the first time in the whole business that he had known such
a lapse? The first, the very first: I found it a splendid portent.
It made him anxious, though he watched himself; he had been
anxious all day and, even while in his usual sweet little manner
he sat at table, had needed all his small strange genius to give
it a gloss. When he at last turned round to meet me, it was
almost as if this genius had succumbed. "Well, I think I'm
glad Bly agrees with *me*!"

"You would certainly seem to have seen, these twenty four
hours, a good deal more of it than for some time before. I
hope," I went on bravely, "that you've been enjoying yourself."

"Oh, yes, I've been ever so far; all round about—miles and
miles away. I've never been so free."

He had really a manner of his own, and I could only try to
keep up with him. "Well, do you like it?"

He stood there smiling; then at last he put into two
words—"Do *you*?"—more discrimination than I had ever
heard two words contain. Before I had time to deal with that,
however, he continued as if with the sense that this was an
impertinence to be softened. "Nothing could be more charm
ing than the way you take it, for of course if we're alone
together now it's you that are alone most. But I hope," he
threw in, "you don't particularly mind!"

"Having to do with you?" I asked. "My dear child, how can I help minding? Though I've renounced all claim to your company,—you're so beyond me,—I at least greatly enjoy it. What else should I stay on for?"

He looked at me more directly, and the expression of his face, graver now, struck me as the most beautiful I had ever found in it. "You stay on just for *that*?"

"Certainly. I stay on as your friend and from the tremendous interest I take in you till something can be done for you that may be more worth your while. That needn't surprise you." My voice trembled so that I felt it impossible to suppress the shake. "Don't you remember how I told you, when I came and sat on your bed the night of the storm, that there was nothing in the world I wouldn't do for you?"

"Yes, yes!" He, on his side, more and more visibly nervous, had a tone to master; but he was so much more successful than I that, laughing out through his gravity, he could pretend we were pleasantly jesting. "Only that, I think, was to get me to do something for *you*!"

"It was partly to get you to do something," I conceded. "But, you know, you didn't do it."

"Oh, yes," he said with the brightest superficial eagerness, "you wanted me to tell you something."

"That's it. Out, straight out. What you have on your mind, you know."

"Ah, then, is *that* what you've stayed over for?"

He spoke with a gaiety through which I could still catch the finest little quiver of resentful passion; but I can't begin to express the effect upon me of an implication of surrender even so faint. It was as if what I had yearned for had come at last only to astonish me. "Well, yes—I may as well make a clean breast of it. It was precisely for that."

He waited so long that I supposed it for the purpose of repudiating the assumption on which my action had been founded; but what he finally said was: "Do you mean now— here?"

"There couldn't be a better place or time." He looked round him uneasily, and I had the rare—oh, the queer!—impression of the very first symptom I had seen in him of the approach of immediate fear. It was as if he were suddenly afraid of me—which struck me indeed as perhaps the best thing to make him. Yet in the very pang of the effort I felt it vain to try sternness, and I heard myself the next instant so gentle as to be almost grotesque. "You want so to go out again?"

"Awfully!" He smiled at me heroically, and the touching little bravery of it was enhanced by his actually flushing with pain. He had picked up his hat, which he had brought in, and stood twirling it in a way that gave me, even as I was just nearly reaching port, a perverse horror of what I was doing. To do it in *any* way was an act of violence, for what did it consist of but the obtrusion of the idea of grossness and guilt on a small helpless creature who had been for me a revelation of the possibilities of beautiful intercourse? Wasn't it base to create for a being so exquisite a mere alien awkwardness? I suppose I now read into our situation a clearness it couldn't have had at the time, for I seem to see our poor eyes already lighted with some spark of a prevision of the anguish that was to come. So we circled about, with terrors and scruples, like fighters not daring to close. But it was for each other we feared! That kept us a little longer suspended and unbruised. "I'll tell you everything," Miles said—"I mean I'll tell you anything you like. You'll stay on with me, and we shall both be all right and I *will* tell you—I *will*. But not now."

"Why not now?"

My insistence turned him from me and kept him once more at his window in a silence during which, between us, you might have heard a pin drop. Then he was before me again with the air of a person for whom, outside, someone who had frankly to be reckoned with was waiting. "I have to see Luke."

I had not yet reduced him to quite so vulgar a lie, and I felt proportionately ashamed. But, horrible as it was, his lies made up my truth. I achieved thoughtfully a few loops of my knitting. "Well, then, go to Luke, and I'll wait for what you promise. Only, in return for that, satisfy, before you leave me, one very much smaller request."

He looked as if he felt he had succeeded enough to be able still a little to bargain. "Very much smaller——?"

"Yes, a mere fraction of the whole. Tell me"—oh, my work preoccupied me, and I was off-hand!—"if, yesterday afternoon, from the table in the hall, you took, you know, my letter."

XXIV

My sense of how he received this suffered for a minute from something that I can describe only as a fierce split of my attention—a stroke that at first, as I sprang straight up, reduced me to the mere blind movement of getting hold of him, drawing him close, and, while I just fell for support against the nearest piece of furniture, instinctively keeping him with his back to the window. The appearance was full upon us that I had already had to deal with here: Peter Quint had come into view like a sentinel before a prison. The next thing I saw was that, from outside, he had reached the window, and then I knew that, close to the glass and glaring in through it, he offered once more to the room his white face of damnation. It represents but grossly what took place within me at the sight to say that on the second my decision was made; yet I believe that no woman so overwhelmed ever in so short a time recovered her grasp of the *act*. It came to me in the very horror of the immediate presence that the act would be, seeing and facing what I saw and faced, to keep the boy himself unaware. The inspiration—I can call it by no other name— was that I felt how voluntarily, how transcendently, I *might*. It was like fighting with a demon for a human soul, and when I had fairly so appraised it I saw how the human soul—held out, in the tremor of my hands, at arm's length—had a perfect dew of sweat on a lovely childish forehead. The face that was close to mine was as white as the face against the glass, and out of it presently came a sound, not low nor weak, but as if from much further away, that I drank like a waft of fragrance.

"Yes—I took it."

At this, with a moan of joy, I enfolded, I drew him close; and while I held him to my breast, where I could feel in the sudden fever of his little body the tremendous pulse of his little heart, I kept my eyes on the thing at the window and saw it move and shift its posture. I have likened it to a sentinel, but its slow wheel, for a moment, was rather the prowl of a baffled beast. My present quickened courage, however, was

such that, not too much to let it through, I had to shade, as
it were, my flame. Meanwhile the glare of the face was again
at the window, the scoundrel fixed as if to watch and wait. It
was the very confidence that I might now defy him, as well
as the positive certitude, by this time, of the child's unconsciousness, that made me go on. "What did you take it for?"

"To see what you said about me."

"You opened the letter?"

"I opened it."

My eyes were now, as I held him off a little again, on Miles's
own face, in which the collapse of mockery showed me how
complete was the ravage of uneasiness. What was prodigious
was that at last, by my success, his sense was sealed and his
communication stopped: he knew that he was in presence, but
knew not of what, and knew still less that I also was and that
I did know. And what did this strain of trouble matter when
my eyes went back to the window only to see that the air was
clear again and—by my personal triumph—the influence
quenched? There was nothing there. I felt that the cause was
mine and that I should surely get *all*. "And you found nothing!"—I let my elation out.

He gave the most mournful, thoughtful little headshake.
"Nothing."

"Nothing, nothing!" I almost shouted in my joy.

"Nothing, nothing," he sadly repeated.

I kissed his forehead; it was drenched. "So what have you
done with it?"

"I've burnt it."

"Burnt it?" It was now or never. "Is that what you did at
school?"

Oh, what this brought up! "At school?"

"Did you take letters?—or other things?"

"Other things?" He appeared now to be thinking of something far off and that reached him only through the pressure
of his anxiety. Yet it did reach him. "Did I *steal*?"

I felt myself redden to the roots of my hair as well as wonder if it were more strange to put to a gentleman such a question or to see him take it with allowances that gave the very
distance of his fall in the world. "Was it for that you mightn't
go back?"

The only thing he felt was rather a dreary little surprise. "Did you know I mightn't go back?"

"I know everything."

He gave me at this the longest and strangest look. "Everything?"

"Everything. Therefore *did* you——?" But I couldn't say it again.

Miles could, very simply. "No. I didn't steal."

My face must have shown him I believed him utterly; yet my hands—but it was for pure tenderness—shook him as if to ask him why, if it was all for nothing, he had condemned me to months of torment. "What then did you do?"

He looked in vague pain all round the top of the room and drew his breath, two or three times over, as if with difficulty. He might have been standing at the bottom of the sea and raising his eyes to some faint green twilight. "Well—I said things."

"Only that?"

"They thought it was enough!"

"To turn you out for?"

Never, truly, had a person "turned out" shown so little to explain it as this little person! He appeared to weigh my question, but in a manner quite detached and almost helpless. "Well, I suppose I oughtn't."

"But to whom did you say them?"

He evidently tried to remember, but it dropped—he had lost it. "I don't know!"

He almost smiled at me in the desolation of his surrender, which was indeed practically, by this time, so complete that I ought to have left it there. But I was infatuated—I was blind with victory, though even then the very effect that was to have brought him so much nearer was already that of added separation. "Was it to everyone?" I asked.

"No; it was only to——" But he gave a sick little head-shake. "I don't remember their names."

"Were they then so many?"

"No—only a few. Those I liked."

Those he liked? I seemed to float not into clearness, but into a darker obscure, and within a minute there had come to me out of my very pity the appalling alarm of his being per-

haps innocent. It was for the instant confounding and bottomless, for if he *were* innocent, what then on earth was *I*?
Paralysed, while it lasted, by the mere brush of the question,
I let him go a little, so that, with a deep-drawn sigh, he turned
away from me again; which, as he faced toward the clear window, I suffered, feeling that I had nothing now there to keep
him from. "And did they repeat what you said?" I went on
after a moment.

He was soon at some distance from me, still breathing hard
and again with the air, though now without anger for it, of
being confined against his will. Once more, as he had done
before, he looked up at the dim day as if, of what had hitherto
sustained him, nothing was left but an unspeakable anxiety.
"Oh, yes," he nevertheless replied—"they must have repeated
them. To those *they* liked," he added.

There was, somehow, less of it than I had expected; but I
turned it over. "And these things came round——?"

"To the masters? Oh, yes!" he answered very simply. "But
I didn't know they'd tell."

"The masters? They didn't—they've never told. That's why
I ask you."

He turned to me again his little beautiful fevered face. "Yes,
it was too bad."

"Too bad?"

"What I suppose I sometimes said. To write home."

I can't name the exquisite pathos of the contradiction given
to such a speech by such a speaker; I only know that the next
instant I heard myself throw off with homely force: "Stuff and
nonsense!" But the next after that I must have sounded stern
enough. "What *were* these things?"

My sternness was all for his judge, his executioner; yet it
made him avert himself again, and that movement made *me*,
with a single bound and an irrepressible cry, spring straight
upon him. For there again, against the glass, as if to blight his
confession and stay his answer, was the hideous author of our
woe—the white face of damnation. I felt a sick swim at the
drop of my victory and all the return of my battle, so that the
wildness of my veritable leap only served as a great betrayal.
I saw him, from the midst of my act, meet it with a divination,
and on the perception that even now he only guessed, and

that the window was still to his own eyes free, I let the impulse flame up to convert the climax of his dismay into the very proof of his liberation. "No more, no more, no more!" I shrieked, as I tried to press him against me, to my visitant.

"Is she *here*?" Miles panted as he caught with his sealed eyes the direction of my words. Then as his strange "she" staggered me and, with a gasp, I echoed it, "Miss Jessel, Miss Jessel!" he with a sudden fury gave me back.

I seized, stupefied, his supposition—some sequel to what we had done to Flora, but this made me only want to show him that it was better still than that. "It's not Miss Jessel! But it's at the window—straight before us. It's *there*—the coward horror, there for the last time!"

At this, after a second in which his head made the movement of a baffled dog's on a scent and then gave a frantic little shake for air and light, he was at me in a white rage, bewildered, glaring vainly over the place and missing wholly, though it now, to my sense, filled the room like the taste of poison, the wide, overwhelming presence. "It's *he*?"

I was so determined to have all my proof that I flashed into ice to challenge him. "Whom do you mean by 'he'?"

"Peter Quint—you devil!" His face gave again, round the room, its convulsed supplication. "*Where*?"

They are in my ears still, his supreme surrender of the name and his tribute to my devotion. "What does he matter now, my own?—what will he *ever* matter? *I* have you," I launched at the beast, "but he has lost you for ever!" Then, for the demonstration of my work, "There, *there*!" I said to Miles.

But he had already jerked straight round, stared, glared again, and seen but the quiet day. With the stroke of the loss I was so proud of he uttered the cry of a creature hurled over an abyss, and the grasp with which I recovered him might have been that of catching him in his fall. I caught him, yes, I held him—it may be imagined with what a passion; but at the end of a minute I began to feel what it truly was that I held. We were alone with the quiet day, and his little heart, dispossessed, had stopped.

Covering End

A T THE FOOT of the staircase he waited and listened, thinking he had heard her call to him from the gallery, high aloft but out of view, to which he had allowed her independent access and whence indeed, on her first going up, the sound of her appreciation had reached him in rapid movements, evident rushes and dashes, and in droll, charming cries that echoed through the place. He had afterwards, expectant and restless, been, for another look, to the house-door, and then had fidgetted back into the hall, where her voice again caught him. It was many a day since such a voice had sounded in those empty chambers, and never perhaps, in all the years, for poor Chivers, had any voice at all launched a note so friendly and so free.

"Oh no, mum, there ain't no one whatever come yet. It's quite all right, mum— you can please yourself!" If he left her to range, all his pensive little economy seemed to say, wasn't it just his poor pickings? He quitted the stairs, but stopped again, with his hand to his ear, as he heard her once more appeal to him. "Lots of lovely——? Lovely *what*, mum? Little ups and downs?" he quavered aloft. "Oh, as you say, mum: as many as in a poor man's life!" She was clearly disposed, as she roamed in delight from point to point, to continue to talk, and, with his better ear and his scooped hand, he continued to listen hard. " 'Dear little crooked steps'? Yes, mum; please mind 'em, mum: they be cruel in the dark corners!" She appeared to take another of her light scampers, the sign of a fresh discovery and a fresh response; at which he felt his heart warm with the success of a trust of her that might after all have been rash. Once more her voice reached him and once more he gossiped back. "Coming up too? Not if you'll kindly indulge, me, mum—I must be where I can watch the bell. It takes watching as well as hearing!"—he dropped, as he resumed his round, to a murmur of great patience. This was taken up the next moment by the husky plaint of the signal itself, which seemed to confess equally to short wind and creaking joints. It moved, however, distinguishably, and its

motion made him start much more as if he had been guilty
of sleeping at his post than as if he had waited half the day.
"Mercy, if I *didn't* watch——!" He shuffled across the wide
stone-paved hall and, losing himself beneath the great arch of
the short passage to the entrance-front, hastened to admit his
new visitor. He gives us thereby the use of his momentary
absence for a look at the place he has left.

This is the central hall, high and square, brown and grey,
flagged beneath and timbered above, of an old English country-house; an apartment in which a single survey is a perception of long and lucky continuities. It would have been
difficult to find elsewhere anything at once so old and so actual, anything that had plainly come so far, far down without,
at any moment of the endless journey, losing its way. To stand
there and look round was to wonder a good deal—yet without
arriving at an answer—whether it had been most neglected or
most cherished; there was such resignation in its long survival
and yet such bravery in its high polish. If it had never been
spoiled, this was partly, no doubt, because it had been, for a
century, given up; but what it had been given up to was, after
all, homely and familiar use. It had in it at the present moment
indeed much of the chill of fallen fortunes; but there was no
concession in its humility and no hypocrisy in its welcome. It
was magnificent and shabby, and the eyes of the dozen dark
old portraits seemed, in their eternal attention, to count the
cracks in the pavement, the rents in the seats of the chairs and
the missing tones in the Flemish tapestry. Above the tapestry,
which, in its turn, was above the high oak wainscot, most of
these stiff images—on the side on which it principally
reigned—were placed; and they held up their heads to assure
all comers that a tone or two was all that *was* missing, and
that they had never waked up in winter dawns to any glimmer
of bereavement, in the long night, of any relic or any feature.
Such as it was, the company was all there; every inch of old
oak, every yard of old arras, every object of ornament or of
use to which these surfaces formed so rare a background. If
the watchers on the walls had ever found a gap in their own
rank the ancient roof, of a certainty, would have been shaken
by their collective gasp. As a matter of fact it was rich and
firm—it had almost the dignity of the vault of a church. On

this Saturday afternoon in August, a hot, still day, such of the casements as freely worked in the discoloured glass of the windows stood open in one quarter to a terrace that overlooked a park and in another to a wonderful old empty court that communicated with a wonderful old empty garden. The staircase, wide and straight, mounted, full in sight, to a landing that was halfway up; and on the right, as you faced this staircase, a door opened out of the brown panelling into a glimpse of a little morning-room where, in a slanted, gilded light, there was brownness too, mixed with notes of old yellow. On the left, toward court and garden, another door stood open to the warm air. Still as you faced the staircase you had at your right, between that monument and the morning-room, the arch through which Chivers had disappeared.

His reappearance interrupts and yet in a manner, after all, quickens our intense impression; Chivers on the spot, and in this severe but spacious setting, was so perfect an image of immemorial domesticity. It would have been impossible perhaps, however, either to tell his age or to name his use: he was of the age of all the history that lurked in all the corners and of any use whatever you might be so good as still to find for him. Considerably shrunken and completely silvered, he had perpetual agreement in the droop of his kind white head and perpetual inquiry in the jerk of the idle old hands now almost covered by the sleeves of the black dress-coat which, twenty years before, must have been by a century or two the newest thing in the house and into which his years appeared to have declined very much as a shrunken family moves into a part of its habitation. This attire was completed by a white necktie that, in honour of the day, he himself had this morning done up. The humility he betrayed and the oddity he concealed were alike brought out by his juxtaposition with the gentleman he had admitted.

To admit Mr. Prodmore was anywhere and at any time, as you would immediately have recognised, an immense admission. He was a personage of great presence and weight, with a large smooth face in which a small sharp meaning was planted like a single pin in the tight red toilet-cushion of a guest-chamber. He wore a blue frock-coat and a stiff white waistcoat and a high white hat that he kept on his head with a kind of protesting cock, while in his buttonhole nestled a bold prize plant on which he occasionally lowered a proprietary eye that seemed to remind it of its being born to a public career. Mr. Prodmore's appearance had evidently been thought out, but it might have struck you that the old portraits took it in with a sterner stare, with a fixedness indeed in which a visitor more sensitive would have read a consciousness of his remaining, in their presence, so jauntily, so vulgarly covered. He had never a glance for them, and it would have been easy after a minute to see that this was an old story between them. Their manner, as it were, sensibly increased the coolness. This coolness became a high rigour as Mr. Prodmore encountered, from the very threshold, a disappointment.

"No one here?" he indignantly demanded.

"I'm sorry to say no one has come, sir," Chivers replied; "but I've had a telegram from Captain Yule."

Mr. Prodmore's apprehension flared out. "Not to say he ain't coming?"

"He was to take the 2.20 from Paddington: he certainly *should* be here!" The old man spoke as if his non-arrival were the most unaccountable thing in the world, especially for a poor person ever respectful of the mystery of causes.

"He should have been here this hour or more. And so should my fly-away daughter!"

Chivers surrounded this description of Miss Prodmore with the deep discretion of silence, and then, after a moment, evidently reflected that silence, in a world bestrewn with traps to irreverence, might be as rash as speech. "Were they coming—a—together, sir?"

He had scarcely mended the matter, for his visitor gave an inconsequent stare. "Together?—for what do you take Miss Prodmore?" This young lady's parent glared about him again as if to alight on something else that was out of place; but the good intentions expressed in the attitude of every object might presently have been presumed to soothe his irritation. It had at any rate the effect of bridging, for poor Chivers, some of his gaps. "It *is* in a sense true that their 'coming together,' as you call it, is exactly what I've made my plans for to-day: my calculation was that we should all punctually converge on this spot. Attended by her trusty maid, Miss Prodmore, who happens to be on a week's visit to her grandmother at Bellborough, was to take the 1.40 from that place. I was to drive over—ten miles—from the most convenient of my seats. Captain Yule"—the speaker wound up his statement as with the mention of the last touch in a masterpiece of his own sketching—"was finally to shake off for a few hours the peculiar occupations that engage him."

The old man listened with his head askance to favour his good ear, but his visible attention all on a sad spot in one of the half-dozen worn rugs. "They *must* be peculiar, sir, when a gentleman comes into a property like this and goes three months without so much as a nat'ral curiosity——! I don't speak of anything but what *is* nat'ral, sir; but there have *been* people here——"

"There have repeatedly been people here!" Mr. Prodmore complacently interrupted.

"As you say, sir—to be shown over. With the master himself never shown!" Chivers dismally commented.

"He *shall* be, so that nobody can miss him!" Mr. Prodmore, for his own reassurance as well, hastened to retort.

His companion risked a tiny explanation. "It will be a mercy indeed to look on him; but I meant that he has not been taken round."

"That's what I meant too. *I'll* take him—round and round: it's exactly what I've come for!" Mr. Prodmore rang out; and his eyes made the lower circuit again, looking as pleased as such a pair of eyes could look with nobody as yet quite good enough either to terrify or to tickle. "He can't fail to be affected, though he *has* been up to his neck in such a different class of thing."

Chivers clearly wondered a while what class of thing it could be. Then he expressed a timid hope. "In nothing, I dare say, but what's right, sir——?"

"In everything," Mr. Prodmore distinctly informed him, "that's wrong! But here he is!" that gentleman added with elation as the doorbell again sounded. Chivers, under the double agitation of the appeal and the disclosure, proceeded to

the front as fast as circumstances allowed; while Mr. Prodmore, left alone, would have been observed—had not his solitude been so bleak—to recover a degree of cheerfulness.
Cheerfulness in solitude at Covering End was certainly not
irresistible, but particular feelings and reasons had pitched, for
their campaign, the starched, if now somewhat ruffled, tent
of his large white waistcoat. If they had issued audibly from
that pavilion they would have represented to us his consciousness of the reinforcement he might bring up for attack should
Captain Yule really resist the house. The sound he next heard
from the front caused him none the less, for that matter, to
articulate a certain drop. "Only Cora?—Well," he added in a
tone somewhat at variance with his "only," "he sha'n't, at any
rate, resist *her*!" This announcement would have quickened a
spectator's interest in the young lady whom Chivers now introduced and followed, a young lady who straightway found
herself the subject of traditionary discipline. "I've waited.
What do you mean?"

Cora Prodmore, who had a great deal of colour in her
cheeks and a great deal more—a bold variety of kinds—in the
extremely high pitch of her new, smart clothes, meant, on the
whole, it was easy to see, very little, and met this challenge
with still less show of support either from the sources I have
mentioned or from any others. A dull, fresh, honest, over-
dressed damsel of two-and-twenty, she was too much out of
breath, too much flurried and frightened, to do more than
stammer: "Waited, papa? Oh, I'm sorry!"

Her regret appeared to strike her father still more as an
impertinence than as a vanity. "Would you then, if I had not
had patience for you, have wished not to find me? Why the
dickens are you so late?"

Agitated, embarrassed, the girl was at a loss. "I'll tell you,
papa!" But she followed up her pledge with an air of vacuity and then, dropping into the nearest seat, simply closed
her eyes to her danger. If she desired relief she had caught
at the one way to get it. "I feel rather faint. Could I have
some tea?"

Mr. Prodmore considered both the idea and his daughter's substantial form. "Well, as I shall expect you to put forth
all your powers—yes!" He turned to Chivers. "Some tea."

The old man's eyes had attached themselves to Miss Prodmore's symptoms with more solicitude than those of her parent. "I did think it might be required!" Then as he gained the door of the morning-room: "I'll lay it out here."

The young lady, on his withdrawal, recovered herself sufficiently to rise again. "It was my train, papa—so very awfully behind. I walked up, you know, also, from the station—there's such a lovely footpath across the park."

"You've been roaming the country then alone?" Mr. Prodmore inquired.

The girl protested with instant eagerness against any such picture. "Oh, dear no, not *alone*!" She spoke, absurdly, as if she had had a train of attendants; but it was an instant before she could complete the assurance. "There were ever so many people about."

"Nothing is more possible than that there should be *too* many!" said her father, speaking as for his personal convenience, but presenting that as enough. "But where, among them all," he demanded, "is your trusty maid?"

Cora's reply made up in promptitude what it lacked in felicity. "I didn't bring her." She looked at the old portraits as if to appeal to them to help her to remember why. Apparently indeed they gave a sign, for she presently went on: "She was so extremely unwell."

Mr. Prodmore met this with reprobation. "Wasn't she to understand from the first that we don't permit——"

"Anything of that sort?"—the girl recalled it at least as a familiar law. "Oh yes, papa—I *thought* she did."

"But she doesn't?"—Mr. Prodmore pressed the point. Poor Cora, at a loss again, appeared to wonder if the point had better be a failure of brain or of propriety, but her companion continued to press. "What on earth's the matter with her?"

She again communed with their silent witnesses. "I really don't quite know, but I think that at Granny's she eats too much."

"I'll soon put an end to *that*!" Mr. Prodmore returned with decision. "You expect then to pursue your adventures quite into the night—to return to Bellborough as you came?"

The girl had by this time begun a little to find her feet. "Exactly as I came, papa dear—under the protection of a new friend I've just made, a lady whom I met in the train and who is also going back by the 6.19. She was, like myself, on her way to this place, and I expected to find her here."

Mr. Prodmore chilled on the spot any such expectations. "What does she want at this place?"

Cora was clearly stronger for her new friend than for herself. "She wants to see it."

Mr. Prodmore reflected on this complication. "To-day?" It was practically presumptuous. "To-day won't do."

"So I suggested," the girl declared. "But do you know what she said?"

"How should I know," he coldly demanded, "what a nobody says?"

But on this, as if with the returning taste of a new strength, his daughter could categorically meet him. "She's not a nobody. She's an American."

Mr. Prodmore, for a moment, was struck: he embraced the place, instinctively, in a flash of calculation. "An American?"

"Yes, and she's wild——"

He knew all about that. "Americans mostly *are*!"

"I mean," said Cora, "to see this place. 'Wild' was what she herself called it—and I think she also said she was 'mad.'"

"She gave"—Mr. Prodmore reviewed the affair—"a fine account of herself! But she won't do."

The effect of her new acquaintance on his companion had been such that she could, after an instant, react against this sentence. "Well, when I told her that this particular day perhaps wouldn't, she said it would just *have* to."

"Have to do?" Mr. Prodmore showed again, through a chink, his speculative eye. "For *what* then, with such grand airs?"

"Why, I suppose, for what Americans want."

He measured the quantity. "They want everything."

"Then I wonder," said Cora, "that she hasn't arrived."

"When she does arrive," he answered, "I'll tackle her; and I shall thank you, in future, not to take up, in trains, with indelicate women of whom you know nothing."

"Oh, I did know something," his daughter pleaded; "for I saw her yesterday at Bellborough."

Mr. Prodmore contested even this freedom. "And what was she doing at Bellborough?"

"Staying at the Blue Dragon, to see the old abbey. She says she just loves old abbeys. It seems to be the same feeling," the girl went on, "that brought her over, to-day, to see this old house."

"She 'just loves' old houses? Then why the deuce didn't she accompany you properly, since she *is* so pushing, to the door?"

"Because she went off in a fly," Cora explained, "to see, first, the old hospital. She just loves old hospitals. She asked me if this isn't a show-house. I told her"—the girl was anxious to disclaim responsibility—"that I hadn't the least idea."

"It *is*!" Mr. Prodmore cried almost with ferocity. "I wonder, on such a speech, what she thought of *you*!"

Miss Prodmore meditated with distinct humbleness. "I know. She told me."

He had looked her up and down. "That you're really a hopeless frump?"

Cora, oddly enough, seemed almost to court this description. "That I'm not, as she rather funnily called it, a show-girl."

"Think of your having to be reminded—by the very strangers you pick up," Mr. Prodmore groaned, "of what my daughter should pre-eminently be! Your friend, all the same," he bethought himself, "is evidently loud."

"Well, when she comes," the girl again so far agreed as to reply, "you'll certainly hear her. But don't judge her, papa, till you do. She's tremendously clever," she risked—"there seems to be nothing she doesn't know."

"And there seems to be nothing you do! You're *not* tremendously clever," Mr. Prodmore pursued; "so you'll permit me to demand of you a slight effort of intelligence." Then, as for the benefit of the listening walls themselves, he struck the high note. "I'm expecting Captain Yule."

Cora's consciousness blinked. "The owner of this property?"

Her father's tone showed his reserves. "That's what it depends on you to make him!"

"On me?" the girl gasped.

"He came into it three months ago by the death of his great-uncle, who had lived to ninety-three, but who, having quarrelled mortally with his father, had always refused to receive either sire or son."

Our young lady bent her eyes on this page of family history, then raised them but dimly lighted. "But now, at least, doesn't he live here?"

"So little," her companion replied, "that he comes here today for the very first time. I've some business to discuss with him that can best be discussed on this spot; and it's a vital part of that business that you too should take pains to make him welcome."

Miss Prodmore failed to ignite. "In his own house?"

"That it's *not* his own house is just the point I seek to make! The way I look at it is that it's *my* house. The way I look at it even, my dear"—in his demonstration of his ways of looking Mr. Prodmore literally expanded—"is that it's *our* house. The whole thing is mortgaged, as it stands, for every penny of its value; and I'm in the pleasant position—do you follow me?" he trumpeted.

Cora jumped. "Of holding the mortgages?"

He caught her with a smile of approval and indeed of surprise. "You keep up with me better than I hoped. I hold every scrap of paper, and it's a precious collection."

She smothered, perceptibly, a vague female sigh, glancing over the place more attentively than she had yet done. "Do you mean that you can come down on him?"

"I don't need to 'come,' my dear—I *am* 'down.' *This* is down!"—and the iron point of Mr. Prodmore's stick fairly struck, as he rapped it, a spark from the cold pavement. "I came many weeks ago—commercially speaking—and haven't since budged from the place."

The girl moved a little about the hall, then turned with a spasm of courage. "Are you going to be very hard?"

If she read the eyes with which he met her she found in them, in spite of a certain accompanying show of pleasantry, her answer. "Hard with *you*?"

"No—that doesn't matter. Hard with the Captain."

Mr. Prodmore thought an instant. " 'Hard' is a stupid, shuffling term. What do you mean by it?"

"Well, I don't understand business," Cora said; "but I think I understand *you*, papa, enough to gather that you've got, as usual, a striking advantage."

"As usual, I *have* scored; but my advantage won't be striking perhaps till I have sent the blow home. What I appeal to you, as a father, at present to do"—he continued broadly to demonstrate—"is to nerve my arm. I look to you to see me through."

"Through what, then?"

"Through this most important transaction. Through the speculation of which you've been the barely-dissimulated subject. I've brought you here to receive an impression, and I've brought you, even more, to make one."

The girl turned honestly flat. "But on whom?"

"On me, to begin with—by not being a fool. And then, Miss, on *him*."

Erect, but as if paralysed, she had the air of facing the worst. "On Captain Yule?"

"By bringing him to the point."

"But, father," she asked in evident anguish—"to *what* point?"

"The point where a gentleman *has* to."

Miss Prodmore faltered. "Go down on his knees?"

Her father considered. "No—they don't do that now."

"What *do* they do?"

Mr. Prodmore carried his eyes with a certain sustained majesty to a remote point. "He will know himself."

"Oh no indeed, he won't," the girl cried; "they don't *ever*!"

"Then the sooner they learn—whoever teaches 'em!—the better: the better I mean in particular," Mr. Prodmore added with an intention discernibly vicious, "for the master of this house. I'll guarantee that he shall understand that," he concluded, "for I shall do my part."

She looked at him as if his part were really to be hated. "But how on earth, sir, can I ever do mine? To begin with, you know, I've never even seen him."

Mr. Prodmore took out his watch; then, having consulted it, put it back with a gesture that seemed to dispose at the same time and in the same manner of the objection. "You'll

see him *now*—from one moment to the other. He's remarkably handsome, remarkably young, remarkably ambitious and
remarkably clever. He has one of the best and oldest names
in this part of the country—a name that, far and wide here,
one could do so much with that I'm simply indignant to see
him do so little. I propose, my dear, to do with it all he hasn't,
and I further propose, to that end, first to get hold of it. It's
you, Miss Prodmore, who shall take it out of the fire."

"The fire?"—he had terrible figures.

"Out of the mud, if you prefer. You must pick it up, do
you see? My plan is, in short," Mr. Prodmore pursued, "that
when we've brushed it off and rubbed it down a bit, blown
away the dust and touched up the rust, my daughter shall
gracefully bear it."

She could only oppose, now, a stiff, thick transparency that
yielded a view of the course in her own veins, after all, however, mingled with a feebler fluid, of the passionate blood of
the Prodmores. "And pray is it also Captain Yule's plan?"

Her father's face warned her off the ground of irony, but
he replied without violence. "His plans have not yet quite
matured. But nothing is more natural," he added with an
ominous smile, "than that they shall do so on the sunny south
wall of Miss Prodmore's best manner."

Miss Prodmore's spirit was visibly rising, and a note that
might have meant warning for warning sounded in the laugh
produced by this sally. "You speak of them, papa, as if they
were sour little plums! You exaggerate, I think, the warmth
of Miss Prodmore's nature. It has always been thought remarkably cold."

"Then you'll be so good, my dear, as to confound—it
mightn't be amiss even a little to scandalize—that opinion.
I've spent twenty years in giving you what your poor mother
used to call advantages, and they've cost me hundreds and
hundreds of pounds. It's now time that, both as a parent and
as a man of business, I should get my money back. I couldn't
help your temper," Mr. Prodmore conceded, "nor your taste,
nor even your unfortunate resemblance to the estimable, but
far from ornamental woman who brought you forth; but I
paid out a small fortune that you should have, damn you,
don't you know? a good manner. You never show it to me,

certainly; but do you mean to tell me that, at this time of day—for other persons—you *haven't* got one?"

This pulled our young lady perceptibly up; there was a directness in the argument that was like the ache of old pinches. "If you mean by 'other persons' persons who are particularly civil—well, Captain Yule may not see his way to be one of them. He may not *think*—don't you see?—that I've a good manner."

"Do your duty, miss, and never mind what he thinks!" Her father's conception of her duty momentarily sharpened. "Don't look at him like a sick turkey, and he'll be sure to think right."

The colour that sprang into Cora's face at this rude comparison was such, unfortunately, as perhaps a little to justify it. Yet she retained, in spite of her emotion, some remnant of presence of mind. "I remember your saying once, some time ago, that that was just what he would be sure *not* to do: I mean when he began to go in for his dreadful ideas——"

Mr. Prodmore took her boldly up. "About the 'radical programme,' the 'social revolution,' the spoliation of everyone and the destruction of everything? Why, you stupid thing, I've worked round to a complete agreement with him. The taking from those who have by those who haven't——"

"Well?" said the girl, with some impatience, as he sought the right way of expressing his notion.

"What is it but to receive, from consenting hands, the principal treasure of the rich? If I'm rich my daughter is my largest property, and I freely make her over. I shall, in other words, forgive my young friend his low opinions if he renounces them for *you*."

Cora, at this, started as with a glimpse of delight. "He won't renounce them! He *sha'n't*!"

Her father appeared still to enjoy the ingenious way he had put it, so that he had good humour to spare. "If you suggest that you're in political sympathy with him, you mean then that you'll take him as he *is*?"

"I won't take him at all!" she protested with her head very high; but she had no sooner uttered the words than the sound of the approach of wheels caused her dignity to drop. "A fly?—it must be *he*!" She turned right and left, for a retreat or an escape, but her father had already caught her by the wrist. "Surely," she pitifully panted, "you don't want me to bounce on him *thus?*"

Mr. Prodmore, as he held her, estimated the effect. "Your frock won't do—with what it cost me?"

"It's not my frock, papa—it's his thinking I've come here for him to see me!"

He let her go and, as she moved away, had another look for the social value of the view of her stout back. It appeared to determine him, for, with a touch of mercy, he passed his word. "He doesn't think it, and he sha'n't know it."

The girl had made for the door of the morning-room, before reaching which she flirted breathlessly round. "But he knows you want me to hook him!"

Mr. Prodmore was already in the parliamentary attitude the occasion had suggested to him for the reception of his visitor. "The way to 'hook' him will be not to be hopelessly vulgar. He doesn't know that you know anything." The house-bell clinked, and he waved his companion away. "Await us there with tea, and mind you toe the mark!"

Chivers, at this moment, summoned by the bell, reappeared in the morning-room doorway, and Cora's dismay brushed him as he sidled past her and off into the passage to the front. Then, from the threshold of her refuge, she launched a last appeal. "Don't *kill* me, father: give me time!" With which she dashed into the room, closing the door with a bang.

II

Mr. Prodmore, in Chivers's absence, remained staring as if at a sudden image of something rather fine. His child had left with him the sense of a quick irradiation, and he failed to see why, at the worst, such lightnings as she was thus able to dart shouldn't strike somewhere. If he had spoken to her of her best manner perhaps *that* was her best manner. He heard steps and voices, however, and immediately invited to his aid his own, which was simply magnificent. Chivers, returning, announced solemnly "Captain Yule!" and ushered in a tall young man in a darkish tweed suit and a red necktie, attached in a sailor's knot, who, as he entered, removed a soft brown hat. Mr. Prodmore, at this, immediately saluted him by un-covering. "Delighted at last to see you here!"

It was the young man who first, in his comparative sim-plicity, put out a hand. "If I've not come before, Mr. Prod-more, it was—very frankly speaking—from the dread of seeing *you*!" His speech contradicted, to some extent, his gesture, but Clement Yule's was an aspect in which contra-dictions were rather remarkably at home. Erect and slender, but as strong as he was straight, he was set up, as the phrase is, like a soldier, and yet finished, in certain details—matters of expression and suggestion only indeed—like a man in whom sensibility had been recklessly cultivated. He was hard and fine, just as he was sharp and gentle, just as he was frank and shy, just as he was serious and young, just as he looked, though you could never have imitated it, distinctly "kept up" and yet considerably reduced. His features were thoroughly regular, but his complete shaving might have been designed to show that they were, after all, not absurd. The face Mr. Prodmore offered him fairly glowed, on this new showing, with instant pride of possession, and there was that in Captain Yule's whole air which justified such a senti-ment without consciously rewarding it.

"Ah, surely," said the elder man, "my presence is not with-out a motive!"

"It's just the motive," Captain Yule returned, "that makes me wince at it! Certainly I've no illusions," he added, "about the ground of our meeting. Your thorough knowledge of what you're about has placed me at your mercy—you hold me in the hollow of your hand."

It was vivid in every inch that Mr. Prodmore's was a nature to expand in the warmth, or even in the chill, of any tribute to his financial subtlety. "Well, I won't, on my side, deny that when, in general, I go in deep I don't go in for nothing. I make it pay double!" he smiled.

"You make it pay so well—'double' surely doesn't do you justice!—that, if I've understood you, you can do quite as you like with this preposterous place. Haven't you brought me down exactly that I may *see* you do it?"

"I've certainly brought you down that you may open your eyes!" This, apparently, however, was not what Mr. Prodmore himself had arrived to do with his own. These fine points of expression literally contracted with intensity. "Of course, you know, you can always clear the property. You can pay off the mortgages."

Captain Yule, by this time, had, as he had not done at first, looked up and down, round about and well over the scene, taking in, though at a mere glance, it might have seemed, more particularly, the row, high up, of strenuous ancestors. But Mr. Prodmore's last words rang none the less on his ear, and he met them with mild amusement. "Pay off——? What can I pay off with?"

"You can always raise money."

"What can I raise it on?"

Mr. Prodmore looked massively gay. "On your great political future."

"Oh, I've not taken—for the short run at least—the lucrative line," the young man said, "and I know what you think of *that*."

Mr. Prodmore's blandness confessed, by its instant increase, to this impeachment. There was always the glory of intimacy in Yule's knowing what he thought. "I hold that you keep, in public, very dangerous company; but I also hold that you're extravagant mainly because you've nothing at stake. A man has the right opinions," he developed with pleasant confidence, "as soon as he has something to lose by having the wrong. Haven't I already hinted to you how to set your political house in order? You drop into the lower regions because you keep the best rooms empty. You're a firebrand, in other words my dear Captain, simply because you're a bachelor. That's one of the early complaints we all pass through, but it's soon over, and the treatment for it quite simple. I have your remedy."

The young man's eyes, wandering again about the house, might have been those of an auditor of the fiddling before the rise of the curtain. "A remedy worse than the disease?"

"There's nothing worse, that I've ever heard of," Mr. Prodmore sharply replied, "than your particular fix. Least of all a heap of gold——"

"A heap of gold?" His visitor idly settled, as if the curtain were going up.

Mr. Prodmore raised it bravely. "In the lap of a fine fresh lass! Give pledges to fortune, as somebody says—*then* we'll talk. You want money—that's what you want. Well, marry it!"

Clement Yule, for a little, never stirred, save that his eyes yet again strayed vaguely. At last they stopped with a smile. "Of course I could do that in a moment!"

"It's even just my own danger from you," his companion returned. "I perfectly recognise that *any* woman would now jump——"

"I don't like jumping women," Captain Yule threw in; "but that perhaps is a detail. It's more to the point that I've yet to see the woman whom, by an advance of my own——"

"You'd care to keep in the really attractive position——?"

"Which can never, of course, be anything"—Yule took his friend up again—"but that of waiting quietly."

"Never, never anything!" Mr. Prodmore, most assentingly, banished all other thought. "But I haven't asked you, you know, to make an advance."

"You've only asked me to receive one?"

Mr. Prodmore waited a little. "Well, I've asked you—I asked you a month ago—to think it all over."

"I *have* thought it all over," Clement Yule said; "and the strange sequel seems to be that my eyes have got accustomed to my darkness. I seem to make out, in the gloom of my meditations, that, at the worst, I can let the whole thing slide."

"The property?"—Mr. Prodmore jerked back as if it were about to start.

"Isn't it the property," his visitor inquired, "that positively throws me up? If I can afford neither to live on it nor to disencumber it, I can at least let it save its own bacon and pay its own debts. I can say to you simply: 'Take it, my dear sir, and the devil take *you*'!"

Mr. Prodmore gave a quick, strained smile. "You wouldn't be so shockingly rude!"

"Why not—if I'm a firebrand and a keeper of low company and a general nuisance? Sacrifice for sacrifice, that might very well be the least!"

This was put with such emphasis that Mr. Prodmore was for a moment arrested. He could stop very short, however, and yet talk as still going. "How do you know, if you haven't compared them? It's just to make the comparison—in all the proper circumstances—that you're here at this hour." He took, with a large, though vague, exhibitory gesture, a few turns about. "Now that you stretch yourself—for an hour's relaxation and rocked, as it were, by my friendly hand—in the ancient cradle of your race, can you seriously entertain the idea of parting with such a venerable family relic?"

It was evident that, as he decorously embraced the scene, the young man, in spite of this dissuasive tone, *was* entertaining ideas. It might have appeared at the moment to a spectator in whom fancy was at all alert that the place, becoming in a manner conscious of the question, felt itself on its honour, and that its honour could make no compromise. It met Clement Yule with no grimace of invitation, with no attenuation of its rich old sadness. It was as if the two hard spirits, the grim *genius loci* and the quick modern conscience, stood an instant confronted. "The cradle of my race bears, for me, Mr. Prodmore, a striking resemblance to its tomb." The sigh that dropped from him, however, was not quite void of tenderness. It might, for that matter, have been a long, sad creak, portending collapse, of some immemorial support of the Yules. "Heavens, how melancholy——!"

Mr. Prodmore, somewhat ambiguously, took up the sound. "Melancholy?"—he just balanced. That well might be, even a little *should* be—yet agreement might depreciate.

"Musty, mouldy;" then with a poke of his stick at a gap in the stuff with which an old chair was covered, "mangy!" Captain Yule responded. "Is this the character throughout?"

Mr. Prodmore fixed a minute the tell-tale tatter. "You must judge for yourself—you must go over the house." He hesitated again; then his indecision vanished—the right line was clear. "It does look a bit run down, but I'll tell you what I'll do. I'll do it up for you—neatly: I'll throw *that* in!"

His young friend turned on him an eye that, though markedly enlivened by his offer, was somehow only the more inscrutable. "Will you put in the electric light?"

Mr. Prodmore's own twinkle—at this touch of a spring he had not expected to work—was, on the other hand, temporarily veiled. "Well, if you'll meet me half way! We're dealing here"—he backed up his gravity—"with fancy-values. Don't you feel," he appealed, "as you take it all in, a kind of a something-or-other down your back?"

Clement Yule gazed a while at one of the pompous quarterings in the faded old glass that, in tones as of late autumn, crowned with armorial figures the top of the great hall-window; then with abruptness he turned away. "Perhaps I *don't* take it all in; but what I do feel is—since you mention it—a sort of stiffening of the spine! The whole thing is too queer—too cold—too cruel."

"Cruel?"—Mr. Prodmore's demur was virtuous.

"Like the face of some stuck-up distant relation who won't speak first. I see in the stare of the old dragon, I taste in his very breath, all the helpless mortality he has tucked away!"

"Lord, sir—you *have* fancies!" Mr. Prodmore was almost scandalised.

But the young man's fancies only multiplied as he moved, not at all critical, but altogether nervous, from object to object. "I don't know what's the matter—but there *is* more here than meets the eye." He tried as for his amusement or his relief to figure it out. "I miss the old presences. I feel the old absences. I hear the old voices. I see the old ghosts."

This last was a profession that offered some common ground. "The old ghosts, Captain Yule," his companion promptly replied, "are worth so much a dozen, and with no reduction, I must remind you—with the price indeed rather raised—for the quantity taken!" Feeling then apparently that he had cleared the air a little by this sally, Mr. Prodmore proceeded to pat his interlocutor on a back that he by no means wished to cause to be put to the wall. "Look about you, at any rate, a little more." He crossed with his toes well out the line that divides encouragement from patronage. "Do make yourself at home."

"Thank you very much, Mr. Prodmore. May I light a cigarette?" his visitor asked.

"In your own house, Captain?"

"That's just the question: it seems so much less my own house than before I had come into it!" The Captain offered Mr. Prodmore a cigarette which that gentleman, also taking a light from him, accepted; then he lit his own and began to smoke. "As I understand you," he went on, "you *lump* your two conditions? I mean I must accept both or neither?"

Mr. Prodmore threw back his shoulders with a high recognition of the long stride represented by this question. "You *will* accept both, for, by doing so, you'll clear the property at a stroke. The way I put it is—see?—that if you'll stand for Gossage you'll get returned for Gossage."

"And if I get returned for Gossage I shall marry your daughter. Accordingly," the young man pursued, "if I marry your daughter——"

"I'll burn up, before your eyes," said this young lady's proprietor, "every scratch of your pen. It will be a bonfire of signatures. There won't be a penny to pay—there'll only be a position to take. You'll take it with peculiar grace."

"Peculiar, Mr. Prodmore—very!"

The young man had assented more than he desired, but he was not deterred by it from completing the picture. "You'll settle down here in comfort and honour."

Clement Yule took several steps; the effect of his host was the reverse of soothing; yet the latter watched his irritation as if it were the working of a charm. "Are you very sure of the 'honour' if I turn my political coat?"

"You'll only be turning it back again to the way it was always worn. Gossage will receive you with open arms and press you to a heaving Tory bosom. That bosom"—Mr. Prodmore followed himself up—"has never heaved but to sound Conservative principles. The cradle, as I've called it—or at least the rich, warm coverlet—of your race, Gossage was the political property, so to speak, of generations of your family. Stand therefore in the good old interest and you'll stand like a lion."

"I'm afraid you mean," Captain Yule laughed, "that I must first roar like one."

"Oh, *I'll* do the roaring!"—and Mr. Prodmore shook his mane. "Leave that to me."

"Then why the deuce don't you stand yourself?"

Mr. Prodmore knew so familiarly why! "Because I'm not a remarkably handsome young man with the grand old home and the right old name. Because I'm a different sort of matter altogether. But if I haven't these advantages," he went on, "you'll do justice to my natural desire that my daughter at least shall have them."

Clement Yule watched himself smoke a minute. "Doing justice to natural desires is just what, of late, I've tried to make a study of. But I confess I don't quite grasp the deep attraction you appear to discover in so large a surrender of your interests."

"My surrenders are my own affair," Mr. Prodmore rang out, "and as for my interests, as I never, on principle, give anything for nothing, I dare say I may be trusted to know them when I see them. You come high—I don't for a moment deny it; but when I look at you, in this pleasant, intimate way, my dear boy—if you'll allow me so to describe things—I recognise one of those cases, unmistakeable when really met, in which one must put down one's money. There's not an article in the whole shop, if you don't mind the comparison, that strikes me as better value. I intend you shall be, Captain," Mr. Prodmore wound up in a frank, bold burst, "the true comfort of my life!"

The young man was as hushed for a little as if an organ-tone were still in the air. "May I inquire," he at last returned, "if Miss Prodmore's ideas of comfort are as well defined—and in her case, I may add, as touchingly modest—as her father's? Is she a responsible party of this ingenious arrangement?"

Mr. Prodmore rendered homage—his appreciation was marked—to the elevated character of his young friend's scruple. "Miss Prodmore, Captain Yule, may be perhaps best described as a large smooth sheet of blank, though gilt-edged, paper. No image of any tie but the true and perfect filial has yet, I can answer for it, formed itself on the considerable expanse. But for that image to be projected——"

"I've only, in person, to appear?" Yule asked with an embarrassment that he tried to laugh off.

"And, naturally, in person," Mr. Prodmore intelligently assented, "do yourself, as well as the young lady, justice. Do you remember what you said when I first, in London, laid the matter before you?"

Clement Yule did remember, but his amusement increased. "I think I said it struck me I should first take a look at—what do you call it?—the *corpus delicti*."

"You should first see for yourself what you had really come into? I was not only eager for that," said Mr. Prodmore, "but I'm willing to go further: I'm quite ready to hear you say that you think you should also first see the young lady."

Captain Yule continued to laugh. "There *is* something in that then, since you mention it!"

"I think you'll find that there's everything." Mr. Prodmore again looked at his watch. "Which will you take first?"

"First?"

"The young lady or the house?"

His companion, at this, unmistakeably started. "Do you mean your daughter's *here*?"

Mr. Prodmore glowed with consciousness. "In the morning-room."

"Waiting for me?"

The tone showed a consternation that Mr. Prodmore's was alert to soothe. "Ah, as long, you know, as you like!"

Yule's alarm, however, was not assuaged: it appeared to grow as he stared, much discomposed, yet sharply thinking, at the door to which his friend had pointed. "Oh, longer than *this*, please!" Then as he turned away: "Do you mean she knows——?"

"That she's here on view?" Mr. Prodmore hung fire a moment, but was equal to the occasion. "She knows nothing whatever. She's as unconscious as the rose on its stem!"

His companion was visibly relieved. "That's right—let her remain so! I'll first take the house," said Clement Yule.

"Shall I go round *with* you?" Mr. Prodmore asked.

The young man's reflection was brief. "Thank you. I'd rather, on the whole, go round alone."

The old servant who had admitted the gentlemen came back at this crisis from the morning-room, looking from under a bent brow and with much limpid earnestness from one of them to the other. The one he first addressed had evidently, though quite unaware of it, inspired him with a sympathy from which he now took a hint. "There's tea on, sir!" he persuasively jerked as he passed the younger man.

The elder answered. "Then I'll join my daughter." He gained the morning-room door, whence he repeated with an appropriate gesture—that of offering proudly, with light, firm fingers, a flower of his own celebrated raising—his happy formula of Miss Prodmore's state. "The rose on its stem!" Scattering petals, diffusing fragrance, he thus passed out.

Chivers, meanwhile, had rather pointlessly settled once more in its place some small object that had not strayed; to whom Clement Yule, absently watching him, abruptly broke out. "I say, my friend, what colour is the rose?"

The old man looked up with a dimness that presently glimmered. "The rose, sir?" He turned to the open door and the shining day. "Rather a brilliant——"

"A brilliant——?" Yule was interested.

"Kind of old-fashioned red." Chivers smiled with the pride of being thus able to testify, but the next instant his smile went out. "It's the only one left—on the old west wall."

His visitor's mirth, at this, quickly enough revived. "My dear fellow, I'm not alluding to the sole ornament of the garden, but to the young lady at present in the morning-room. Do you happen to have noticed if she's pretty?"

Chivers stood queerly rueful. "Laws, sir—it's a matter I mostly notice; but isn't it, at the same time, sir, a matter—like—of taste?"

"Pre-eminently. That's just why I appeal with such confidence to yours."

The old man acknowledged with a flush of real embarrassment a responsibility he had so little invited. "Well, sir—mine was always a sort of fancy for something more merry-like."

"She isn't merry-like then, poor Miss Prodmore?" Captain Yule's attention, however, dropped before the answer came, and he turned off the subject with an "Ah, if you come to that, neither am I! But it doesn't signify," he went on. "What are *you*?" he more sociably demanded.

Chivers clearly had to think a bit. "Well, sir, I'm not quite *that*. Whatever has there been to make me, sir?" he asked in dim extenuation.

"How in the world do *I* know? I mean to whom do you belong?"

Chivers seemed to scan impartially the whole field. "If you could just only *tell* me, sir! I quite seem to waste away—for some one to take an order of."

Clement Yule, by this time, had become aware he was amusing. "Who pays your wages?"

"No one at all, sir," said the old man very simply.

His friend, fumbling an instant in a waistcoat pocket, produced something that his hand, in obedience to a little peremptory gesture and by a trick of which he had unlearned, through scant custom, the neatness, though the propriety was instinctive, placed itself in a shy practical relation to. "Then there's a sovereign. And I haven't many!" the young man, turning away resignedly, threw after it.

Chivers, for an instant, intensely studied him. "Ah, then, shouldn't it stay in the family?"

Clement Yule wheeled round, first struck, then, at the sight of the figure made by his companion in this offer, visibly touched. "I think it does, old boy."

Chivers kept his eyes on him now. "I've served your house, sir."

"How long?"

"All my life."

So, for a time, they faced each other, and something in Chivers made Yule at last speak. "Then I won't give *you* up!"

"Indeed, sir, I hope you won't give up anything."

The Captain took up his hat. "It remains to be seen." He looked over the place again; his eyes wandered to the open door. "Is that the garden?"

"It *was*!"—and the old man's sigh was like the creak of the wheel of time. "Shall I show you how it used to be?"

"It's just as it *is*, alas, that I happen to require it!" Captain Yule reached the door and stood looking beyond. "Don't come," he then said; "I want to think." With which he walked out.

Chivers, left alone, appeared to wonder at it, and his wonder, like that of most old people, lay near his lips. "What does he want, poor dear, to think about?" This speculation, however, was immediately checked by a high, clear voice that preceded the appearance on the stairs, before she had reached the middlemost landing, of the wonderful figure of a lady, a lady who, with the almost trumpeted cheer of her peremptory but friendly call—"Housekeeper, Butler, old Family Servant!"—fairly waked the sleeping echoes. Chivers gazed up at her in quick remembrance, half dismayed, half dazzled, of a duty neglected. She appeared now; she shone at him out of the upper dusk; reaching the middle, she had begun to descend, with beautiful laughter and rustling garments; and though she was alone she gave him the sense of coming in a crowd and with music. "Oh, I should have told him of *her*!"

III

She was indeed an apparition, a presence requiring announcement and explanation just in the degree in which it seemed to show itself in a relation quite of its own to all social preliminaries. It evidently either assumed them to be already over or wished to forestall them altogether; what was clear at any rate was that it allowed them scant existence. She was young, tall, radiant, lovely, and dressed in a manner determined at once, obviously, by the fact and by the humour of her journey—it might have proclaimed her so a pilgrim or so set her up as a priestess. Most journeys, for this lady, at all events, were clearly a brush of Paris. "Did you think I had got snapped down in an old box like that poor girl—what's her name? the one who was poking round too—in the celebrated poem? You dear, delightful man, why didn't you tell me?"

"Tell you, mum——?"

"Well, that you're so perfectly—perfect! You're ever so much better than anyone has ever said. Why, in the name of common sense, has nobody ever said *anything*? You're everything in the world you ought to be, and not the shade of a shade of anything you oughtn't!"

It was a higher character to be turned out with than poor Chivers had ever dreamed. "Well, mum, I try!" he gaped.

"Oh no, you don't—that's just your charm! *I* try," cried his friend, "but you do nothing: here you simply *are* you can't help it!"

He stood overwhelmed. "Me, mum?"

She took him in at the eyes—she could take everything at once. "Yes, you too, you positive old picture! I've seen the old masters—but you're the old master!"

"The master—I?" He fairly fell back.

" 'The good and faithful servant'—Rembrandt van Rhyn: with three stars. *That's* what you are!" Nothing would have been more droll to a spectator than her manner of meeting his humbleness, or more charming indeed than the practical sweetness of her want of imagination of it. "The house is a vision of beauty, and you're simply worthy of the house. I can't say more for you!"

"I find it a bit of a strain, mum," Chivers candidly replied, "to keep up—fairly to call it—with what you *do* say."

"That's just what everyone finds it!"—she broke into the happiest laugh. "Yet I haven't come here to suffer in silence, you know—to suffer, I mean, from envy and despair." She was in constant movement, from side to side, observing, comparing, returning, taking notes while she gossiped and gossiping, too, for remembrance. The intention of remembrance even had in it, however, some prevision of failure or some alloy of irritation. "You're so fatally right and so deadly complete, all the same, that I can really scarcely bear it: with every fascinating feature that I had already heard of and thought I was prepared for, and ever so many others that, strange to say, I hadn't and wasn't, and that you just spring right *at* me like a series of things going off. What do you call it," she asked—"a royal salute, a hundred guns?"

Her enthusiasm had a bewildering form, but it had by this time warmed the air, and the old man rubbed his hands as over a fire to which the bellows had been applied. "I saw as soon as you arrived, mum, that you were looking for more things than ever *I* heard tell of!"

"Oh, I had got you by heart," she returned, "from books and drawings and photos; I had you in my pocket when I came: so, you see, as soon as you were so good as to give me my head and let me loose, I knew my way about. It's all here, every inch of it," she competently continued, "and now at last I can do what I want!"

A light of consternation, at this, just glimmered in Chivers's face. "And pray, mum, what might that be?"

"Why, take you right back with me—to Missoura Top."

This answer seemed to fix his bewilderment, but he was there for the general convenience. "Do I understand you, mum, that you require to take *me*?"

Her particular convenience, on the spot, embraced him, so new and delightful a sense had he suddenly read into her words. "Do you mean to say you'd come—as the old Family Servant? Then *do*, you nice real thing: it's just what I'm dying for—an old Family Servant! You're somebody's else, yes—but everything, over here, is somebody's else, and I want, too, a first-rate second-hand one, all ready made, as you are, but not too much done up. You're the best I've seen yet, and I wish I could have you packed—put up in paper and bran—as I shall have my old pot there." She whisked about, remembering, recovering, eager: "Don't let me *forget* my precious pot!" Excited, with quick transitions, she quite sociably appealed to her companion, who shuffled sympathetically to where, out of harm, the object had been placed on a table. "Don't you just love old crockery? That's awfully sweet old Chelsea."

He took up the piece with tenderness, though, in his general agitation, not perhaps with all the caution with which, for daily service, he handled ancient frailities. He at any rate turned on this fresh subject an interested, puzzled eye. "Where is it I've known this very bit—though not to say, as *you* do, by name?" Suddenly it came to him. "In the pew-opener's front parlour!"

"No," his interlocutress cried, "in the pew-opener's best bedroom: on the old chest of drawers, you know—with those ducks of brass handles. I've got the handles too—I mean the whole thing; and the brass fender and fire irons, and the chair her grandmother died in. Not in the fly," she added—"it was such a bore that they have to be sent."

Chivers, with the pot still in his hands, fairly rocked in the high wind of so much confidence and such great transactions. He had nothing for these, however, but approval. "You did right to take this out, mum, when the fly went to the stables. Them flymen do be cruel rash with anything that's delicate." Of the delicacy of the vessel it now rested with him to deposit safely again he was by this time so appreciatively aware that in returning with it to its safe niche he stumbled into some obscure trap literally laid for him by his nervousness. It was the matter of a few seconds, of a false movement, a knock of the elbow, a gasp, a shriek, a complete little crash. There was the pot on the pavement, in several pieces, and the clumsy cup-bearer blue with fear. "Mercy *on* us, mum—I've brought shame on my old grey hairs!"

The little shriek of his companion had smothered itself in the utterance, and the next minute, with the ruin between them, they were contrastedly face to face. The charming woman, who had already found more voices in the air than anyone had found before, could, in the happy play of this power, find a poetry in her accident. "Oh, but the way you *take* it!" she laughed—"you're too quaint to live!" She looked at him as if he alone had suffered—as if his suffering indeed positively added to his charm. "The way you said that now—it's just the very 'type'! That's all I want of you now—to *be* the very type. It's what you are, you poor dear thing—for you *can't* help it; and it's what everything and everyone else is, over here; so that you had just better all make up your minds to it and not try to shirk it. There was a type in the train with me—the 'awfully nice girl' of all the English novels, the 'simple maiden in her flower' of—who is it?—your great poet. *She* couldn't help it either—in fact I wouldn't have *let* her!" With this, while Chivers picked up his fragments, his lady had a happy recall. His face, as he stood there with the shapeless elements of his humiliation fairly rattling again in his hands, was a reflection of her extraordinary manner of enlarging the subject, or rather, more beneficently perhaps, the space that contained it. "By the way, the girl was coming right here. Has she come?"

Chivers crept solemnly away, as if to bury his dead, which he consigned, with dumb rites, to a situation of honourable publicity; then, as he came back, he replied without elation: "Miss Prodmore is here, mum. She's having her tea."

This, for his friend, was a confirmatory touch to be fitted with eagerness into the picture. "Yes, that's exactly it—they're always having their tea!"

"With Mr. Prodmore—in the morning-room," the old man supplemented. "Captain Yule's in the garden."

"Captain Yule?"

"The new master. He's also just arrived."

The wonderful lady gave an immediate "Oh!" to the effect of which her silence for another moment seemed to add. "She didn't tell me about *him*."

"Well, mum," said Chivers, "it do be a strange thing to tell. He had never—like, mum—so much as seen the place."

"Before to-day—his very own?" This too, for the visitor, was an impression among impressions, and, like most of her others, it ended after an instant as a laugh. "Well, I hope he likes it!"

"I haven't seen many, mum," Chivers boldly declared, "that like it as much as *you*."

She made with her handsome head a motion that appeared to signify still deeper things than he had caught. Her beautiful wandering eyes played high and low, like the flight of an imprisoned swallow, then, as she sank upon a seat, dropped at last as if the creature were bruised with its limits. "I should like it still better if it were *my* very own!"

"Well, mum," Chivers sighed, "if it wasn't against my duty I could wish indeed it were! But the Captain, mum," he conscientiously added, "is the lawful heir."

It was a wonder what she found in whatever he said; he touched with every word the spring of her friendly joy. "That's another of your lovely old things—I adore your lawful heirs!" She appeared to have, about everything that came up, a general lucid vision that almost glorified the particular case. "He has come to take possession?"

Chivers accepted, for the credit of the house, this sustaining suggestion. "He's a-taking of it now."

This evoked, for his companion, an instantaneous show. "What does he do and how does he do it? Can't I *see*?" She was all impatience, but she dropped to disappointment as her guide looked blank. "There's no grand fuss —?"

"I scarce think him, mum," Chivers with propriety hastened to respond, "the gentleman to make any about anything."

She had to resign herself, but she smiled as she thought. "Well, perhaps I like them better when they don't!" She had clearly a great range of taste, and it all came out in the wistfulness with which, before the notice apparently served on her, she prepared to make way. "I also"—she lingered and sighed—"have taken possession!"

Poor Chivers really rose to her. "It was you, mum," he smiled, "took it first!"

She sadly shook her head. "Ah, but for a poor little hour! *He's* for life."

The old man gave up, after a little, with equal depression, the pretence of dealing with such realities. "For mine, mum, I do at least hope."

She made again the circuit of the great place, picking up without interest the jacket she had on her previous entrance laid down. "I shall think of you, you know, here together." She vaguely looked about her as for anything else to take; then abruptly, with her eyes again on Chivers: "Do you suppose he'll be kind to you?"

His hand, in his trousers-pocket, seemed to turn the matter over. "He has already been, mum."

"Then be sure to be so to *him*!" she replied with some emphasis. The house-bell sounded as she spoke, giving her quickly another thought. "Is that his bell?"

Chivers was hardly less struck. "I must see whose!"—and hurrying, on this, to the front, he presently again vanished.

His companion, left alone, stood a minute with an air in which happy possession was oddly and charmingly mingled with desperate surrender; so much as to have left you in doubt if the next of her lively motions were curiosity or disgust. Impressed, in her divided state, with a small framed plaque of enamel, she impulsively detached it from the wall and examined it with hungry tenderness. Her hovering thought was so vivid that you might almost have traced it in sound. "Why, bless me if it isn't Limoges! I wish awfully I were a *bad* woman: then, I do devoutly hope, I'd just quietly take it!" It testified to the force of this temptation that on hearing a sound behind her she started like a guilty thing; recovering herself, however, and—just, of course, not to appear at fault—keeping the object familiarly in her hand as she jumped to a recognition of the gentleman who, coming in from the garden, had stopped in the open doorway. She gathered indeed from his being there a positive advantage, the full confidence of which was already in her charming tone. "Oh, Captain Yule, I'm delighted to meet you! It's such a comfort to ask you if I *may*!"

His surprise kept him an instant dumb, but the effort not too closely to betray it appeared in his persuasive inflection. "If you 'may,' madam——?"

"Why, just *be* here, don't you know? and poke round!"
She presented such a course as almost vulgarly natural.
"Don't tell me I can't now, because I already *have*: I've
been upstairs and downstairs and in my lady's chamber—I
won't answer for it even perhaps that I've not been in my
lord's! I got round your lovely servant—if you don't look
out I'll grab him. If you don't look out, you know, I'll grab
everything." She gave fair notice and went on with amazing
serenity; she gathered positive gaiety from his frank stupefaction. "That's what I came over for—just to lay your
country waste. Your house is a wild old dream; and besides"—she dropped, oddly and quaintly, into real responsible judgment—"you've got some quite good things. Oh
yes, you *have*—several: don't coyly pretend you haven't!"
Her familiarity took these flying leaps, and she alighted, as
her victim must have phrased it to himself, without turning
a hair. "Don't you *know* you have? Just look at that!" She
thrust her enamel before him, but he took it and held it so
blankly, with an attention so absorbed in the mere woman,
that at the sight of his manner her zeal for his interest and
her pity for his detachment again flashed out. "Don't you
know *anything*? Why, it's Limoges!"

Clement Yule simply broke into a laugh—though his laugh
indeed was comprehensive. "It seems absurd, but I'm not in
the least acquainted with my house. I've never happened to
see it."

She seized his arm. "Then do let me show it to you!"

"I shall be delighted." His laughter had redoubled in a way
that spoke of his previous tension; yet his tone, as he saw
Chivers return breathless from the front, showed that he had
responded sincerely enough to desire a clear field. "Who in
the world's there?"

The old man was full of it. "A party!"

"A party?"

Chivers confessed to the worst. "Over from Gossage—to
see the house."

The worst, however, clearly was quite good enough for
their companion, who embraced the incident with sudden enthusiasm. "Oh, let *me* show it!" But before either of the men
could reply she had, addressing herself to Chivers, one of

those droll drops that betrayed the quickness of her wit and the freedom of her fancy. "Dear me, I forgot—*you* get the tips! But, you dear old creature," she went on, "I'll get them too, and I'll simply make them over to you." She again pressed Yule—pressed him into this service. "Perhaps they'll be bigger—for me!"

He continued to be highly amused. "I should think they'd be enormous—for you! But I *should* like," he added with more concentration—"I should like extremely, you know, to go over with you alone."

She was held a moment. "Just you and me?"

"Just you and me—as you kindly proposed."

She stood reminded; but, throwing it off, she had her first inconsequence. "That must be for after——!"

"Ah, but not too late." He looked at his watch. "I go back to-night."

"Laws, sir!" Chivers irrepressibly groaned.

"You want to keep him?" the stranger asked. Captain Yule turned away at the question, but her look went after him, and she found herself, somehow, instantly answered. "Then I'll help you," she said to Chivers; "and the oftener we go over the better."

Something further, on this, quite immaterial, but quite adequate, passed, while the young man's back was turned, between the two others; in consequence of which Chivers again appealed to his master. "Shall I show them straight in, sir?"

His master, still detached, replied without looking at him. "By all means—if there's money in it!" This was jocose, but there would have been, for an observer, an increase of hope in the old man's departing step. The lady had exerted an influence.

She continued, for that matter, with a start of genial remembrance, to exert one in his absence. "Oh, and I promised to show it to Miss Prodmore!" Her conscience, with a kind smile for the young person she named, put the question to Clement Yule. "Won't you call her?"

The coldness of his quick response made it practically none. " 'Call' her? Dear lady, I don't *know* her!"

"You must, then—she's wonderful." The face with which he met this drew from the dear lady a sharper look; but, for the aid of her good-nature, Cora Prodmore, at the moment she spoke, presented herself in the doorway of the morning-room. "See? She's charming!" The girl, with a glare of recognition, dashed across the open as if under heavy fire; but heavy fire, alas—the extremity of exposure—was promptly embodied in her friend's public embrace. "Miss Prodmore," said this terrible friend, "let me present Captain Yule." Never had so great a gulf been bridged in so free a span. "Captain Yule, Miss Prodmore. Miss Prodmore, Captain Yule."

There was stiffness, the cold mask of terror, in such notice as either party took of this demonstration, the convenience of which was not enhanced for the divided pair by the perception that Mr. Prodmore had now followed his daughter. Cora threw herself confusedly into it indeed, as with a vain rebound into the open. "Papa, let me 'present' you to Mrs. Gracedew. Mrs. Gracedew, Mr. Prodmore. Mr. Prodmore, Mrs. Gracedew."

Mrs. Gracedew, with a free salute and a distinct repetition, took in Mr. Prodmore as she had taken everything else. "Mr. Prodmore"—oh, she pronounced him, spared him nothing of himself. "So happy to meet your daughter's father. Your daughter's so perfect a specimen."

Mr. Prodmore, for the first moment, had simply looked large and at sea, then, like a practical man and without more question, had quickly seized the long perch held out to him in this statement. "So perfect a specimen, yes!"—he seemed to pass it on to his young friend.

Mrs. Gracedew, if she observed his emphasis, drew from it no deterrence; she only continued to cover Cora with a gaze that kept her well in the middle. "So fresh, so quaint, so droll!"

It was apparently a result of what had passed in the morning-room that Mr. Prodmore had grasped afresh the need for effective action, which he clearly felt he did something to meet in clutching precipitately the helping hand popped so suddenly out of space, yet so beautifully gloved and so pressingly and gracefully brandished. "So fresh, so quaint, so droll!"— he again gave Captain Yule the advantage of the stranger's impression.

To what further appreciation this might have prompted the lady herself was not, however, just then manifest; for the return of Chivers had been almost simultaneous with the advance of the Prodmores, and it had taken place with forms that made it something of a circumstance. There was positive pomp in the way he preceded several persons of both sexes, not tourists at large, but simple sightseers of the half-holiday order, plain provincial folk already, on the spot, rather awestruck. The old man, with suppressed pulls and prayers, had drawn them up in a broken line, and the habit of more peopled years, the dull drone of the dead lesson, sounded out in his prompt beginning. The party stood close, in this manner, on one side of the apartment, while the master of the house and his little circle were grouped on the other. But as Chivers, guiding his squad, reached the centre of the space, Mrs. Gracedew, markedly moved, quite unreservedly engaged, came slowly forward to meet him. "This, ladies and gentlemen," he mechanically quavered, "is perhaps the most important feature—the grand old feudal, baronial 'all. Being, from all accounts, the most ancient portion of the edifice, it was erected in the very earliest ages." He paused a moment, to mark his effect, then gave a little cough which had become, obviously, in these great reaches of time, an essential part of the trick. "Some do say," he dispassionately remarked, "in the course of the fifteenth century."

Mrs. Gracedew, who had visibly thrown herself into the working of the charm, following him with vivid sympathy and hanging on his lips, took the liberty, at this, of quite affectionately pouncing on him. "*I* say in the fourteenth, my dear—you're robbing us of a hundred years!"

Her victim yielded without a struggle. "I do seem, in them dark old centuries, sometimes to trip a little." Yet the interruption of his ancient order distinctly discomposed him, all the more that his audience, gaping with a sense of the importance of the fine point, moved in its mass a little nearer. Thus put upon his honour, he endeavoured to address the group with a dignity undiminished. "The Gothic roof is much admired, but the west gallery is a modern addition."

His discriminations had the note of culture, but his candour, all too promptly, struck Mrs. Gracedew as excessive. "What in the name of Methuselah do you call 'modern'? It was here at the visit of James the First, in 1611, and is supposed to have served, in the charming detail of its ornament, as a model for several that were constructed in his reign. The great fireplace," she handsomely conceded, "*is* Jacobean."

She had taken him up with such wondrous benignant authority—as if, for her life, if they *were* to have it, she couldn't help taking care that they had it out; she had interposed with an assurance that so converted her—as by the wave of a great wand, the motion of one of her own free arms—from mere passive alien to domesticated dragon, that poor Chivers could only assent with grateful obeisances. She so plunged into the old book that he had quite lost his place. The two gentlemen and the young lady, moreover, were held there by the magic of her manner. His own, as he turned again to his cluster of sightseers, took refuge in its last refinement. "The tapestry on the left Italian—the elegant wood-work Flemish."

Mrs. Gracedew was upon him again. "Excuse me if I just deprecate a misconception. The elegant wood-work Italian— the tapestry on the left Flemish." Suddenly she put it to him before them all, pleading as familiarly and gaily as she had done when alone with him and looking now at the others, all round, gentry and poor folk alike, for sympathy and support. She had an idea that made her dance. "Do you really mind if *I* just do it? Oh, I know how: I can do quite beautifully the housekeeper last week at Castle Gaunt." She fraternised with the company as if it were a game they must play with her, though this first stage sufficiently hushed them "How do you do? Ain't it thrilling?" Then with a laugh as free as if, for a disguise, she had thrown her handkerchief over her head or made an apron of her tucked-up skirt, she passed to the grand manner. "Keep well together, please —we're not doing puss-in-the-corner. I've my duty to all parties—I can't be partial to one!"

The contingent from Gossage had, after all, like most contingents, its spokesman— a very erect little personage in a very new suit and a very green necktie, with a very long face and upstanding hair. It was on an evident sense of having been practically selected for encouragement that he, in turn, made choice of a question which drew all eyes. "How many parties, now, can you manage?"

Mrs. Gracedew was superbly definite. "Two. The party up and the party down." Chivers gasped at the way she dealt with this liberty, and his impression was conspicuously deepened as she pointed to one of the escutcheons in the high hall-window. "Observe in the centre compartment the family arms." She did take his breath away, for before he knew it she had crossed with the lightest but surest of gestures to the black old portrait, on the opposite wall, of a long-limbed gentleman in white trunk-hose. "And observe the family legs!" Her method was wholly her own, irregular and broad; she flew, familiarly, from the pavement to the roof and then dropped from the roof to the pavement as if the whole air of the place were an element in which she floated. "Observe the suit of armour worn at Tewkesbury—observe the tattered banner carried at Blenheim." They bobbed their heads wherever she pointed, but it would have come home to any spectator that they saw her alone. This was the case quite as much with the opposite trio—the case especially with Clement Yule, who indeed made no pretence of keeping up with her signs. It was the signs themselves he looked at—not at the subjects indicated. But he never took his eyes from her, and it was as if, at last, she had been peculiarly affected by a glimpse of his attention. All her own, for a moment, frankly went back to him and was immediately determined by it. "Observe, above all, that you're in one of the most interesting old houses, of its type, in England; for which the ages have been tender and the generations wise: letting it change so slowly that there's always more left than taken—living their lives in it, but letting it shape their lives!"

Though this pretty speech had been unmistakeably addressed to the younger of the temporary occupants of Covering End, it was the elder who, on the spot, took it up. "A most striking and appropriate tribute to a real historical monument!" Mr. Prodmore had a natural ease that could deal handsomely with compliments, and he manifestly, moreover, like a clever man, saw even more in such an explosion of them than fully met the ear. "You do, madam, bring the whole thing out!"

The visitor who had already with such impunity ventured had, on this, a loud renewal of boldness, but for the benefit of a near neighbour. "Doesn't she indeed, Jane, bring it out?"

Mrs. Gracedew, with a friendly laugh, caught the words in their passage. "But who in the world wants to keep it *in*? It isn't a secret—it isn't a strange cat or a political party!" The housekeeper, as she talked, had already dropped from her; her sense of the place was too fresh for control, though instead of half an hour it might have taken six months to become so fond. She soared again, at random, to the noble spring of the roof. "Just look at those lovely lines!" They all looked, all but Clement Yule, and several of the larger company, subdued, overwhelmed, nudged each other with strange sounds. Wherever she turned Mrs. Gracedew appeared to find a pretext for breaking out. "Just look at the tone of that glass, and the gilding of that leather, and the cutting of that oak, and the dear old flags of the very floor." It came back, came back easily, her impulse to appeal to the lawful heir, and she seemed, with her smile of universal intelligence, just to demand the charity of another moment for it. "To look, in this place, is to love!"

A voice from the party she had in hand took it up with an artless guffaw that resounded more than had doubtless been meant and that, at any rate, was evidently the accompaniment of some private pinch applied to one of the ladies. "I *say*—to love!"

It was one of the ladies who very properly replied. "It depends on who you look at!"

Mr. Prodmore, in the geniality of the hour, made his profit of the simple joke. "Do you hear *that*, Captain? You must look at the right person!"

Mrs. Gracedew certainly had not been looking at the wrong one. "I don't think Captain Yule cares. He doesn't do justice——!"

Though her face was still gay, she had faltered, which seemed to strike the young man even more than if she had gone on. "To what, madam?"

Well, on the chance, she let him have it. "To the value of your house."

He took it beautifully. "I like to hear *you* express it!"

"I *can't* express it!" She once more looked all round, and so much more gravely than she had yet done that she might have appeared in trouble. She tried but, with a sigh, broke down. "It's too inexpressible!"

This was a view of the case to which Mr. Prodmore, for his own reasons, was not prepared to assent. Expression and formulation were what he naturally most desired, and he had just encountered a fountain of these things that he couldn't prematurely suffer to fail him. "Do what you can for it, madam. It would bring it quite home."

Thus excited, she gave with sudden sombre clearness another try. "Well—the value's a fancy value!"

Mr. Prodmore, receiving it as more than he could have hoped, turned triumphant to his young friend. "Exactly what I told you!"

Mrs. Gracedew explained indeed as if Mr. Prodmore's triumph was not perhaps exactly what she had argued for. Still, the truth was too great. "When a thing's unique, it's unique!"

That was every bit Mr. Prodmore required. "It's unique!"

This met, moreover, the perception of the gentleman in the green necktie. "It's unique!" They all, in fact, demonstratively—almost vociferously now—caught the point.

Mrs. Gracedew, finding herself so sustained, and still with her eyes on the lawful heir's, put it yet more strongly. "It's worth anything you like."

What was this but precisely what Mr. Prodmore had always striven to prove? "Anything you like!" he richly reverberated.

The pleasant discussion and the general interest seemed to bring them all together. "Twenty thousand now?" one of the gentlemen from Gossage archly inquired—a very young gentleman with an almost coaxing voice, who blushed immensely as soon as he had spoken.

He blushed still more at the way Mrs. Gracedew faced him. "I wouldn't *look* at twenty thousand!"

Mr. Prodmore, on the other hand, was proportionately uplifted. "She wouldn't look at twenty thousand!" he announced with intensity to the Captain.

The visitor who had been the first to speak gave a shrewder guess. "Thirty then, as it stands?"

Mrs. Gracedew looked more and more responsible; she communed afresh with the place; but she too evidently had her conscience. "It would be giving it away!"

Mr. Prodmore, at this, could scarcely contain himself. "It would be giving it away!"

The second speaker had meanwhile conceived the design of showing that, though still crimson, he was not ashamed. "You'd hold out for forty——?"

Mrs. Gracedew required a minute to answer—a very marked minute during which the whole place, pale old portraits and lurking old echoes and all, might have made you feel how much depended on her; to the degree that the consciousness in her face became finally a reason for her not turning it to Gossage. "Fifty thousand, Captain Yule, is what I think I should propose."

If the place had seemed to listen it might have been the place that, in admiring accents from the gentleman with the green tie, took up the prodigious figure. "Fifty thousand pound!"

It was echoed in a high note from the lady he had previously addressed. "Fifty thousand!"

Yet it was Mr. Prodmore who caught it up loudest and appeared to make it go furthest. "Fifty thousand—fifty thousand!" Mrs. Gracedew had put him in such spirits that he found on the spot, indicating to her his young friend, both the proper humour and the proper rigour for any question of what anyone might "propose." "He'll never part with the dear old home!"

Mrs. Gracedew could match at least the confidence. "Then I'll go over it again while I have the chance." Her own humour enjoined that she should drop into the housekeeper, in the perfect tone of which character she addressed herself once more to the party. "We now pass to the grand staircase." She gathered her band with a brave gesture, but before she had fairly impelled them to the ascent she heard herself rather sharply challenged by Captain Yule, who, during the previous scene, had uttered no sound, yet had remained as attentive as he was impenetrable. "Please let them pass without you!"

She was taken by surprise. "And stay here with *you*?"

"If you'll be so good. I want to speak to you." Turning then to Chivers and frowning on the party, he delivered himself for the first time as a person in a position. "For God's sake, remove them!"

The old man, at this blast of impatience, instantly fluttered forward. "We now pass to the grand staircase."

They all passed, Chivers covering their scattered ascent as a shepherd scales a hillside with his flock; but it became evident during the manœuvre that Cora Prodmore was quite out of tune. She had been standing beyond and rather behind Captain Yule; but she now moved quickly round and reached her new friend's right. "Mrs. Gracedew, may *I* speak to you?"

Her father, before the reply could come, had taken up the place. "*After* Captain Yule, my dear." He was in a state of positively polished lucidity. "You must make the most—don't you see?—of the opportunity of the others!"

He waved her to the staircase as one who knew what he was about, but, while the young man, turning his back, moved consciously and nervously away, the girl renewed her effort to provoke Mrs. Gracedew to detain her. It happened, to her sorrow, that this lady appeared for the moment, to the detriment of any free attention, to be absorbed in Captain Yule's manner; so that Cora could scarce disengage her without some air of invidious reference to it. Recognising as much, she could only for two seconds, but with great yearning, parry her own antagonist. "She'll *help* me, I think, papa!"

"That's exactly what strikes me, love!" he cheerfully replied. "But *I'll* help you too!" He gave her, towards the stairs, a push proportioned both to his authority and to her weight; and while she reluctantly climbed in the wake of the visitors he laid on Mrs. Gracedew's arm, with a portentous glance at Captain Yule, a hand of commanding significance. "Just pile it on!"

Her attention came back—she seemed to see. "He doesn't like it?"

"Not half enough. Bring him round."

Her eyes rested again on their companion, who had fidgetted further away and who now, with his hands in his pockets and unaware of this private passage, stood again in the open doorway and gazed into the grey court. Something in the sight determined her. "I'll bring him round."

But at this moment Cora, pausing half-way up, sent down another entreaty. "Mrs. Gracedew, will you see *me?*"

The charming woman looked at her watch. "In ten minutes," she smiled back.

Mr. Prodmore, bland and assured, looked at his own. "You could put him through in five—but I'll allow you twenty. There!" he decisively cried to his daughter, whom he quickly rejoined and hustled on her course. Mrs. Gracedew kissed after her a hand of vague comfort.

IV

The silence that reigned between the pair might have been registered as embarrassing had it lasted a trifle longer. Yule had continued to turn his back, but he faced about, though he was distinctly grave, in time to avert an awkwardness. "How do you come to know so much about my house?"

She was as distinctly not grave. "How do *you* come to know so little?"

"It's not my fault," he said very gently. "A particular combination of misfortunes has forbidden me, till this hour, to come within a mile of it."

These words evidently struck her as so exactly the right ones to proceed from the lawful heir that such a felicity of misery could only quicken her interest. He was plainly as good in his way as the old butler—the particular combination of misfortunes corresponded to the life-long service. Her interest, none the less, in its turn, could only quicken her pity, and all her emotions, we have already seen, found prompt enough expression. What could any expression do indeed now but mark the romantic reality? "Why, you poor thing!"—she came toward him on the weary road. "Now that you've got here I hope at least you'll stay." Their intercourse must pitch itself—so far as she was concerned—in some key that would make up for things. "Do make yourself comfortable. Don't mind me."

Yule looked a shade less serious. "That's exactly what I wanted to say to *you*!"

She was struck with the way it came in. "Well, if you *had* been haughty I shouldn't have been quite crushed, should I?"

The young man's gravity, at this, completely yielded. "I'm never haughty—oh no!"

She seemed even more amused. "Fortunately then, as *I'm* never crushed. I don't think," she added, "that I'm really as crushable as you."

The smile with which he received this failed to conceal completely that it was something of a home-thrust. "Aren't we really *all* crushable—by the right thing?"

She considered a little. "Don't you mean rather by the wrong?"

He had got, clearly, a trifle more accustomed to her being extraordinary. "Are you sure we always know them apart?"

She weighed the responsibility. "I always do. Don't you?"

"Not quite every time!"

"Oh," she replied, "I don't think, thank goodness, we have positively 'every time' to distinguish."

"Yet we must always act," he objected.

She turned this over; then with her wonderful living look, "I'm glad to hear it," she exclaimed, "because, I fear, I always *do*! You'll certainly think," she added with more gravity, "that I've taken a line to-day!"

"Do you mean that of mistress of the house? Yes—you do seem in possession!"

"*You* don't!" she honestly answered; after which, as to attenuate a little the rigour of the charge: "You don't comfortably look it, I mean. You don't look"—she was very serious—"as I want you to."

It was when she was most serious that she was funniest. "How do you 'want' me to look?"

She endeavoured, while he watched her, to make up her mind, but seemed only, after an instant, to recognise a difficulty. "When you look at *me*, you're all right!" she sighed. It was an obstacle to her lesson, and she cast her eyes about. "Look at that chimney-piece."

"Well—?" he inquired as his eyes came back from it.

"You mean to say it isn't lovely?"

He returned to it without passion—gave a vivid sign of mere disability. "I'm sure I don't know. I don't mean to say anything. I'm a rank outsider."

It had an instant effect on her—she almost pounced upon him. "Then you must let me put you up!"

"Up to what?"

"Up to everything!"—his levity added to her earnestness. "You were smoking when you came in," she said as she glanced about. "Where's your cigarette?"

The young man appreciatively produced another. "I thought perhaps I mightn't—here."

"You may everywhere."

He bent his head to the information. "Everywhere."

She laughed at his docility, yet could only wish to presume upon it. "It's a rule of the house!"

He took in the place with greater pleasure. "What delightful rules!"

"How could such a house have any others?"—she was already launched again in her brave relation to it. "I *may* go up just once more—mayn't I—to the long gallery?"

How could he tell? "The long gallery?"

With an added glow she remembered. "I forgot you've never seen it. Why, it's the leading thing about you!" She was full, on the spot, of the pride of showing it. "Come right up!"

Clement Yule, half seated on a table from which his long left leg nervously swung, only looked at her and smiled and smoked. "There's a party up."

She remembered afresh. "So *we* must be the party down? Well, you must give me a chance. That long gallery's the principal thing I came over for."

She was strangest of all when she explained. "Where in heaven's name did you come over from?"

"Missoura Top, where I'm building—just in this style. I came for plans and ideas," Mrs. Gracedew serenely pursued. "I felt I must look right *at* you."

"But what did you know about us?"

She kept it a moment as if it were too good to give him all at once. "Everything!"

He seemed indeed almost afraid to touch it. "At 'Missoura Top'?"

"Why not? It's a growing place—forty thousand the last census." She hesitated; then as if her warrant should be slightly more personal: "My husband left it to me."

The young man presently changed his posture. "You're a widow?"

Nothing was wanting to the simplicity of her quiet assent. "A very lone woman." Her face, for a moment, had the vision of a long distance. "My loneliness is great enough to want something big to hold it—and my taste good enough to want something beautiful. You see, I had your picture."

Yule's innocence made a movement. "Mine?"

Her smile reassured him; she nodded toward the main entrance. "A watercolour I chanced on in Boston."

"In Boston?"

She stared. "Haven't you heard of Boston either?"

"Yes—but what has Boston heard of *me*?"

"It wasn't 'you,' unfortunately—it was your divine south front. The drawing struck me so that I got you up—in the books."

He appeared, however, rather comically, but half to make it out, or to gather at any rate that there was even more of it than he feared. "Are we in the books?"

"Did you never discover it?" Before his blankness, the dim apprehension in his fine amused and troubled face of how much there was of it, her frank, gay concern for him sprang again to the front. "Where in heaven's name, Captain Yule, have *you* come over from?"

He looked at her very kindly, but as if scarce expecting her to follow. "The East End of London."

She had followed perfectly, he saw the next instant, but she had by no means equally accepted. "What were you doing there?"

He could only put it, though a little over-consciously, very simply. "Working, you see. When I left the army—it was much too slow, unless one was personally a whirlwind of war—I began to make out that, for a fighting man——"

"There's always," she took him up, "somebody or other to go for?"

He considered her, while he smoked, with more confidence; as if she might after all understand. "The enemy, yes—everywhere in force. I went for *him*: misery and ignorance and vice—injustice and privilege and wrong. Such as you see me——"

"You're a rabid reformer?"—she understood beautifully. "I wish we had you at Missoura Top!"

He literally, for a moment, in the light of her beauty and familiarity, appeared to measure his possible use there; then, looking round him again, announced with a sigh that, predicament for predicament, his own would do. "I fear my work is nearer home. I hope," he continued, "since you're so good as to seem to care, to perform a part of that work in the next House of Commons. My electors have wanted me——"

"And you've wanted *them*," she lucidly put in, "and that has been why you couldn't come down."

"Yes, for all this last time. And before that, from my childhood up, there was another reason." He took a few steps away and brought it out as rather a shabby one. "A family feud."

She proved to be quite delighted with it. "Oh, I'm so glad—I *hoped* I'd strike a 'feud'! That rounds it off, and spices it up, and, for the heartbreak with which I take leave of you, just neatly completes the fracture!" Her reference to her going seemed suddenly, on this, to bring her back to a sense of proportion and propriety, and she glanced about once more for some wrap or reticule. This, in turn, however, was another recall. "Must I really wait—to go up?"

He had watched her movement, had changed colour, had shifted his place, had tossed away, plainly unwitting, a cigarette but half smoked; and now he stood in her path to the staircase as if, still unsatisfied, he abruptly sought a way to turn the tables. "Only till you tell me this: if you absolutely meant, a while ago, that this old thing is so precious."

She met his doubt with amazement and his density with compassion. "Do you literally need I should *say* it? Can you stand here and not feel it?" If he had the misfortune of bandaged eyes she could at least rejoice in her own vision, which grew intenser with her having to speak for it. She spoke as with a new rush of her impression. "It's a place to love——"

Yet to say the whole thing was not easy.

"To love——?" he impatiently insisted.

"Well, as you'd love a person!" If that was saying the whole thing, saying the whole thing could only be to go. A sound from the "party up" came down at that moment, and she took it so clearly as a call that, for a sign of separation, she passed straight to the stairs. "Goodbye!"

The young man let her reach the foot, but then, though the greatest width of the hall now divided them, spoke, anxiously and nervously, as if the point she had just made brought them still more together. "I think I 'feel' it, you know; but it's simply you—your presence, as I may say, and the remarkable way you put it—that make me. I'm afraid that in your absence——" He struck a match to smoke again.

It gave her time apparently to make out something to pause for. "In my absence?"

He lit his cigarette. "I may come back——"

"Come back?" she took him almost sharply up. "I should like to see you *not*!"

He smoked a moment. "I mean to my old idea——"

She had quite turned round on him now. "Your old idea——?"

He faced her over the width still between them. "Well—that one *could* give it up."

Her stare, at this, fairly filled the space. "Give up Covering? How in the world—or why?"

"Because I can't afford to keep it."

It brought her straight back, but only half-way: she pulled up short as at a flash. "Can't you let it?"

Again he smoked before answering. "Let it to *you*?"

She gave a laugh, and her laugh brought her nearer. "I'd take it in a minute!"

Clement Yule remained grave. "I shouldn't have the face to charge you a rent that would make it worth one's while, and I think even you, dear lady"—his voice just trembled as he risked that address—"wouldn't have the face to offer me one." He paused, but something in his aspect and manner checked in her now any impulse to read his meaning too soon. "My lovely inheritance is Dead Sea fruit. It's mortgaged for all it's worth and I haven't the means to pay the interest. If by a miracle I could scrape the money together it would leave me without a penny to live on." He puffed his cigarette profusely. "So if I find the old home at last—I lose it by the same luck!"

Mrs. Gracedew had hung upon his words, and she seemed still to wait, in visible horror, for something that would improve on them. But when she had to take them for his last, "I never heard of anything so awful!" she broke out. "Do you mean to say you can't arrange——?"

"Oh yes," he promptly replied, "an arrangement—if that be the name to give it—has been definitely proposed to me."

"What's the matter then?"—she had dropped into relief. "For heaven's sake, you poor thing, definitely accept it!"

He laughed, though with little joy, at her sweet simplifications. "I've made up my mind in the last quarter of an hour that I can't. It's such a peculiar case."

Mrs. Gracedew frankly wondered; her bias was clearly sceptical. "*How* peculiar——?"

He found the measure difficult to give. "Well—more peculiar than most cases."

Still she was not satisfied. "More peculiar than mine?"

"Than yours?"—Clement Yule knew nothing about that.

Something, at this, in his tone, his face—it might have been his "British" density—seemed to pull her up. "I forgot—you don't know mine. No matter. What *is* yours?"

He took a few steps in thought. "Well, the fact that I'm asked to change."

"To change what?"

He wondered how he could put it; then at last, on his own side, simplified. "My attitude."

"Is that all?"—she was relieved again. "Well, you're not a statue."

"No, I'm not a statue; but on the other hand, don't you see? I'm not a windmill." There was good humour, none the less, in his rigour. "The mortgages I speak of have all found their way, like gregarious silly sheep, into the hands of one person—a devouring wolf, a very rich, a very sharp man of money. He holds me in this manner at his mercy. He consents to make things comfortable for me, but he requires that, in return, I shall do something for him that—don't you know?—rather sticks in my crop."

It appeared on this light showing to stick for a moment even in Mrs. Gracedew's. "Do you mean something wrong?"

He had not a moment's hesitation. "Exceedingly so!"

She turned it over as if pricing a Greek Aldus. "Anything immoral?"

"Yes—I may literally call it immoral."

She courted however, frankly enough, the strict truth. "Too bad to tell?"

He indulged in another pensive fidget, then left her to judge. "He wants me to give up——" Yet again he faltered.

"To give up what?" What could it be, she appeared to ask, that was barely nameable?

He quite blushed to her indeed as he came to the point. "My fundamental views."

She was disappointed—she had waited for more "Nothing but *them?*"

He met her with astonishment. "Surely they're quite enough, when one has unfortunately"—he rather ruefully smiled—"so very many!"

She laughed aloud; this was frankly so odd a plea. "Well, *I've* a neat collection too, but I'd 'swap,' as they say in the West, the whole set——!" She looked about the hall for something of equivalent price; after which she pointed, as it caught her eye, to the great cave of the fireplace. "I'd take *that* set!"

The young man scarcely followed. "The fire-irons?"

"For the whole fundamental lot!" She gazed with real yearning at the antique group. "*They're* three hundred years old. Do you mean to tell me your wretched 'views'——?"

"Have anything like that age? No, thank God," Clement Yule laughed, "my views—wretched as you please!—are quite in their prime! They're a hungry little family that has got to be fed. They keep me awake at night."

"Then you must make up your sleep!" Her impatience grew with her interest. "Listen to *me!*"

"That would scarce be the way!" he returned. But he added more sincerely: "You must surely see a fellow can't chuck his politics."

" 'Chuck' them——?"

"Well—sacrifice them."

"I'd sacrifice mine," she cried, "for that old fire-back with your arms!" He glanced at the object in question, but with such a want of intelligence that she visibly resented it. "See how it has stood!"

"See how *I've* stood!" he answered with spirit. "I've glowed with a hotter fire than anything in any chimney, and the warmth and light I diffuse have attracted no little atten- tion. How can I consent to reduce them to the state of that desolate hearth?"

His companion, freshly struck with the fine details of the desolation, had walked over to the chimney-corner, where, lost in her deeper impression, she lingered and observed. At last she turned away with her impatience controlled. "It's magnificent!"

"The fire-back?"

"Everything—everywhere. I don't understand your haggling."

He hesitated. "That's because you're ignorant." Then seeing in the light of her eye that he had applied to her the word in the language she least liked, he hastened to attenuate. "I mean of what's behind my reserves."

She was silent in a way that made their talk more of a discussion than if she had spoken. "What *is* behind them?" she presently asked.

"Why, my whole political history. Everything I've said, everything I've done. My scorching addresses and letters, reproduced in all the papers. I needn't go into details, but I'm a pure, passionate, pledged Radical."

Mrs. Gracedew looked him full in the face. "Well, what if you *are*?"

He broke into mirth at her tone. "Simply this—that I can't therefore, from one day to the other, pop up at Gossage in the purple pomp of the opposite camp. There's a want of transition. It may be timid of me—it may be abject. But I can't."

If she was not yet prepared to contest she was still less prepared to surrender it, and she confined herself for the instant to smoothing down with her foot the corner of an old rug. "Have you thought very much about it?"

He was vague. "About what?"

"About what Mr. Prodmore wants you to do."

He flushed up. "Oh then, you know it's *he*?"

"I'm not," she said, still gravely enough, "of an intelligence absolutely infantile."

"You're the cleverest Tory I've ever met!" he laughed. "I didn't mean to mention my friend's name, but since *you've* done so——!" He gave up with a shrug his scruple.

Oh, she had already cleared the ground of it! "It's he who's the devouring wolf? It's he who holds your mortgages?"

The very lucidity of her interest just checked his assent. "He holds plenty of others, and he treats me very handsomely."

She showed of a sudden an inconsequent face. "Do you call *that* handsome—such a condition?"

He shed surprise. "Why, I thought it was just the condition you could meet."

She measured her inconsistency, but was not abashed. "We're not talking of what *I* can meet." Yet she found also a relief in dropping the point. "Why doesn't he stand himself?"

"Well, like other devouring wolves, he's not personally adored."

"Not even," she asked, "when he offers such liberal terms?"

Clement Yule had to explain. "I dare say he doesn't offer them to everyone."

"Only to you?"—at this she quite sprang. "You *are* personally adored; you will be still more if you stand; and that, you poor lamb, is why he wants you!"

The young man, obviously pleased to find her after all more at one with him, accepted gracefully enough the burden her sympathy imposed. "I'm the bearer of my name, I'm the representative of my family; and to my family and my name— since you've led me to it—this countryside has been for generations indulgently attached."

She listened to him with a sentiment in her face that showed how now, at last, she felt herself deal with the lawful heir. She seemed to perceive it with a kind of passion. "You do of course what you will with the countryside!"

"Yes"—he went with her—"if we do it as genuine Yules. I'm obliged of course to grant you that your genuine Yule's a Tory of Tories. It's Mr. Prodmore's belief that I should carry Gossage in that character, but in that character only. They won't look at me in any other."

It might have taxed a spectator to say in what character Mrs. Gracedew, on this, for a little, considered him. "Don't be too sure of people's not looking at you!"

He blushed again, but he laughed. "We must leave out my personal beauty."

"We can't!" she replied with decision. "Don't we take in Mr. Prodmore's?"

Captain Yule was not prepared. "You call him beautiful?"

"Hideous." She settled it; then pursued her investigation. "What's the extraordinary interest that he attaches——?"

"To the return of a Tory?" Here the young man *was* prepared. "Oh, his desire is born of his fear—his terror on behalf of Property, which he sees, somehow, with an intensely Personal, with a quite colossal 'P.' He has a great deal of that article, and very little of anything else."

Mrs. Gracedew, accepting provisionally his demonstration, had one of her friendly recalls. "Do you call that nice daughter 'very little'?"

The young man looked quite at a loss. "Is she very big? I really didn't notice her— and moreover she's just a part of the Property. He thinks things are going too far."

She sat straight down on a stiff chair; on which, with high distinctness: "Well, they *are*!"

He stood before her in the discomposure of her again thus appearing to fail him. "Aren't you then a lover of justice?"

"A passionate one!" She sat there as upright as if she held the scales. "Where's the justice of your losing this house?" Generous as well as strenuous, all her fairness thrown out by her dark old high-backed seat, she put it to him as from the judicial bench. "To keep Covering, you must carry Gossage!"

The odd face he made at it might have betrayed a man dazzled. "As a renegade?"

"As a genuine Yule. What business have you to be anything else?" She had already arranged it all. "You must close with Mr. Prodmore—you must stand in the Tory interest." She hung fire a moment; then as she got up: "If you will, I'll conduct your canvas!"

He stared at the distracting picture. "That puts the temptation high!"

But she brushed the mere picture away. "Ah, don't look at me as if *I* were the temptation! Look at this sweet old human home, and feel all its gathered memories. Do you want to know what they do to me?" She took the survey herself again, as if to be really sure. "They speak to me for Mr. Prodmore."

He followed with a systematic docility the direction of her eyes, but as if with the result only of its again coming home to him that there was no accounting for what things might do. "Well, there are others than these, you know," he good-naturedly pleaded—"things for which I've spoken, repeatedly and loudly, to others than you." The very manner of his speaking on such occasions appeared, for that matter, now to come back to him. "One's 'human home' is all very well, but the rest of one's humanity is better!" She gave, at this, a droll soft wail; she turned impatiently away. "I see you're disgusted with me, and I'm sorry; but one must take one's self as circumstances and experience have made one, and it's not my fault, don't you know? if they've made me a very modern man. I see something else in the world than the beauty of old show-houses and the glory of old show-families. There are thousands of people in England who can show no houses at all, and I don't feel it utterly shameful to share their poor fate!"

She had moved away with impatience, and it was the advantage of this for her that the back she turned prevented him from seeing how intently she listened. She seemed to continue to listen even after he had stopped; but if that gave him a sense of success he might have been checked by the way she at last turned round with a sad and beautiful headshake. "We share the poor fate of humanity whatever we do, and we do something to help and console when we've something precious to show. What on earth is more precious than what the ages have slowly wrought? They've trusted us, in such a case, to keep it—to do something, in our turn, for *them*." She shone out at him as if her contention had the evidence of the noonday sun, and yet in her generosity she superabounded and explained. "It's such a virtue, in anything, to have lasted; it's such an honour, for anything, to have been spared. To all strugglers from the wreck of time hold out a pitying hand!"

Yule, on this argument—of a strain which even a good experience of debate could scarce have prepared him to meet—had not a congruous rejoinder absolutely pat, and his hesitation unfortunately gave him time to see how soon his companion made out that what had touched him most in it was her particular air in presenting it. She would manifestly have preferred he should have been floored by her mere moral reach; yet he was aware that his own made no great show as he took refuge in general pleasantry. "What a plea for looking backward, dear lady, to come from Missoura Top!"

"We're making a Past at Missoura Top as fast as ever we can, and I should like to see you lay your hand on an hour of the one we've made! It's a tight fit, as yet, I grant," she said, "and that's just why I like, in yours, to find room, don't you see? to turn round. You're *in* it, over here, and you can't get out; so just make the best of that and treat the thing as part of the fun!"

"The whole of the fun, to me," the young man replied, "is in hearing you defend it! It's like your defending hereditary gout or chronic rheumatism and sore throat—the things I feel aching in every old bone of these walls and groaning in every old draught that, I'm sure, has for centuries blown through them."

Mrs. Gracedew looked as if no woman could be shaken who was so prepared to be just all round. "If there be aches—there may be—you're here to soothe them, and if there be draughts—there *must* be!—you're here to stop them up. And do you know what *I'm* here for? If I've come so far and so straight I've almost wondered myself. I've felt with a kind of passion—but now I see *why* I've felt." She moved about the hall with the excitement of this perception and, separated from him at last by a distance across which he followed her discovery with a visible suspense, she brought out the news. "I'm here for an act of salvation—I'm here to avert a sacrifice!"

So they stood a little, with more, for the minute, passing between them than either really could say. She might have flung down a glove that he decided on the whole, passing his hand over his head as the seat of some confusion, not to pick up. Again, but flushed as well as smiling, he sought the easiest cover. "You're here, I think, madam, to be a memory for all my future!"

Well, she was willing, she showed as she came nearer, to take it, at the worst, for that. "You'll be one for mine, if I can see you by that hearth. Why do you make such a fuss about changing your politics? If you'd come to Missoura Top you'd change them quick enough!" Then, as she saw further and struck harder, her eyes grew deep, her face even seemed to pale, and she paused, splendid and serious, with the force of her plea. "What do politics amount to, compared with religions? Parties and programmes come and go, but a duty like this abides. There's nothing you can break with"—she pressed him closer, ringing out—"that would be like breaking *here*. The very words are violent and ugly—as much a sacrilege as if you had been trusted with the key of the temple. This *is* the temple—don't profane it! Keep up the old altar kindly—you can't set up a new one as good. You *must* have beauty in your life, don't you see?—that's the only way to make sure of it for the lives of others. Keep leaving it to *them*, to all the poor others," she went on with her bright irony, "and heaven only knows what will become of it! Does it take one of *us* to feel that?—to preach you the truth? Then it's good, Captain Yule, we come right over—just to see, you know, what you may happen to be about. We know," she went on while her sense of proportion seemed to play into her sense of humour, "what we haven't got, worse luck; so that if you've happily got it you've got it also for *us*. You've got it in trust, you see, and oh! we have an eye on you. You've had it so for me, all these dear days that I've been drinking it in, that, to be grateful, I've wanted regularly to *do* something." With which, as if in the rich confidence of having convinced him, she came so near as almost to touch him. "Tell me now I shall have done it—I shall have kept you at your post!"

If he moved, on this, immediately further, it was with the oddest air of seeking rather to study her remarks at his ease than to express an independence of them. He kept, to this end, his face averted—he was so completely now in intelligent possession of her own. The sacrifice in question carried him even to the door of the court, where he once more stood so long engaged that the persistent presentation of his back might at last have suggested either a confession or a request.

Mrs. Gracedew, meanwhile, a little spent with her sincerity, seated herself again in the great chair, and if she sought, visibly enough, to read a meaning into his movement, she had as little triumph for one possible view of it as she had resentment for the other. The possibility that he yielded left her after all as vague in respect to a next step as the possibility that he merely wished to get rid of her. The moments elapsed without her abdicating; and indeed when he finally turned round his expression was an equal check to any power to feel she might have won. "You have," he queerly smiled at her, "a standpoint quite your own and a style of eloquence that the few scraps of parliamentary training I've picked up don't seem at all to fit me to deal with. Of course I don't pretend, you know, that I don't *care* for Covering."

That, at all events, she could be glad to hear, if only perhaps for the tone in it that was so almost comically ingenuous. But her relief was reasonable and her exultation temperate. "You haven't even seen it yet." She risked, however, a laugh. "Aren't you a bit afraid?"

He took a minute to reply, then replied—as if to make it up—with a grand collapse. "Yes; awfully. But if I am," he hastened in decency to add, "it isn't only Covering that makes me."

This left his friend apparently at a loss. "What else is it?"

"Everything. But it doesn't in the least matter," he loosely pursued. "You may be quite correct. When we talk of the house your voice comes to me somehow as the wind in its old chimneys."

Her amusement distinctly revived. "I hope you don't mean I roar!"

He blushed again, there was no doubt he was confused. "No—nor yet perhaps that you whistle! I don't believe the wind does either, here. It only whispers," he sought gracefully to explain; "and it sighs——"

"And I hope," she broke in, "that it sometimes laughs!"

The sound she gave only made him, as he looked at her, more serious. "Whatever it does, it's all right."

"All right?"   they were sufficiently together again for her to lay her hand straight on his arm. "Then you promise?"

"Promise what?"

He had turned as pale as if she hurt him, and she took her hand away. "To meet Mr. Prodmore."

"Oh dear no; not yet!"—he quite recovered himself. "I must wait—I must think."

She looked disappointed, and there was a momentary silence. "When have you to answer him?"

"Oh, he gives me time!" Clement Yule spoke very much as he might have said "Oh, in two minutes!"

"*I* wouldn't give you time," Mrs. Gracedew cried with force—"I'd give you a shaking! For God's sake, at any rate"— and she really tried to push him off—"go upstairs!"

"And literally *find* the dreadful man?" This was so little his personal idea that, distinctly dodging her pressure, he had already reached the safe quarter.

But it befell that at the same moment she saw Cora reappear on the upper landing—a circumstance that promised her a still better conclusion. "He's coming down!"

Cora, in spite of this announcement, came down boldly enough without him and made directly for Mrs. Gracedew, to whom her eyes had attached themselves with an undeviating glare. Her plain purpose of treating this lady as an isolated presence allowed their companion perfect freedom to consider her arrival with sharp alarm. His disconcerted stare seemed for a moment to balance; it wandered, gave a wild glance at the open door, then searched the ascent of the staircase, in which, apparently, it now found a coercion. "I'll go up!" he gasped; and he took three steps at a time.

V

The girl threw herself, in her flushed eagerness, straight upon the wonderful lady. "I've come back to you—I want to speak to you!" The need had been a rapid growth, but it was clearly immense. "May I confide in you?"

Her instant overflow left Mrs. Gracedew both astonished and amused. "You too?" she laughed. "Why, it *is* good we come over!"

"It is indeed!" Cora gratefully echoed. "You were so very kind to me and seemed to think me so curious."

The mirth of her friend redoubled. "Well, I loved you for it, and it was nothing moreover to what you thought *me*!"

Miss Prodmore found, for this, no denial—she only presented her frank high colour. "I loved *you*. But I'm the worst!" she generously added. "And I'm solitary."

"Ah, so am I!" Mrs. Gracedew declared with gaiety, but with emphasis. "A *very* queer thing always *is* solitary! But, since we have that link, by all means confide."

"Well, I was met here by tremendous news." Cora produced it with a purple glow. "He wants me to marry him!"

Mrs. Gracedew looked amiably receptive, but as if she failed as yet to follow. "'He' wants you?"

"Papa, of course. He has settled it!"

Mrs. Gracedew was still vague. "Settled what?"

"Why, the whole question. That I must take him."

Mrs. Gracedew seemed to frown at her own scattered wits. "But, my dear, take *whom*?"

The girl looked surprised at this lapse of her powers. "Why, Captain Yule, who just went up."

"Oh!" said Mrs. Gracedew with a full stare. "Oh!" she repeated looking straight away.

"I thought you would know," Cora gently explained.

Her friend's eyes, with a kinder light now, came back to her. "I didn't know." Mrs. Gracedew looked, in truth, as if that had been sufficiently odd, and seemed also to wonder at two or three things more. It all, however, broke quickly into a question. "Has Captain Yule asked you?"

"No, but he *will*"—Cora was clear as a bell. "He'll do it to keep the house. It's mortgaged to papa, and Captain Yule buys it back."

Her friend had an illumination that was rapid for the way it spread. "By marrying you?" she quavered.

Cora, under further parental instruction, had plainly mastered the subject. "By giving me his name and his position. They're awfully great, and they're the price, don't you see?" she modestly mentioned. "*My* price. Papa's price. Papa wants them."

Mrs. Gracedew had caught hold; yet there were places where her grasp was weak, and she had, strikingly, begun again to reflect. "But his name and his position, great as they may be, are his dreadful politics!"

Cora threw herself with energy into this advance. "You *know* about his dreadful politics? He's to change them," she recited, "to get *me*. And if he gets me——"

"He keeps the house?"—Mrs. Gracedew snatched it up.

Cora continued to show her schooling. "I go *with* it—he's to have us both. But only," she admonishingly added, "if he changes. The question is—*will* he change?"

Mrs. Gracedew appeared profoundly to entertain it. "I see. *Will* he change?"

Cora's consideration of it went even further. "*Has* he changed?"

It went—and the effect was odd—a little too far for her companion, in whom, just discernibly, it had touched the spring of impatience. "My dear child, how in the world should *I* know?"

But Cora knew exactly how anyone would know. "He hasn't seemed to care enough for the house. *Does* he care?"

Mrs. Gracedew moved away, passed over to the fireplace and stood a moment looking at the old armorial fire-back she had praised to its master—yet not, it must be added, as if she particularly saw it. Then as she faced about: "You had better ask him!"

They stood thus confronted, with the fine old interval between them, and the girl's air was for a moment that of considering such a course. "If he does care," she said at last, "he'll propose."

Mrs. Gracedew, from where she stood in relation to the stairs, saw at this point the subject of their colloquy restored to view: Captain Yule was just upon them—he had turned the upper landing. The sight of him forced from her in a flash an ejaculation that she tried, however, to keep private—"He does care!" She passed swiftly, before he reached them, back to the girl and, in a quick whisper, but with full conviction, let her have it: "He'll propose!"

Her movement had made her friend aware, and the young man, hurrying down, was now in the hall. Cora, at his hurry, looked dismay—"Then I fly!" With which, casting about for a direction, she reached the door to the court.

Captain Yule, however, at this result of his return, expressed instant regret. "I drive Miss Prodmore away!"

Mrs. Gracedew, more quickly still, eased off the situation. "It's all right!" She had embraced both parties with a smile, but it was most liberal now for Cora. "Do you mind, one moment?"—it conveyed, unmistakeably, a full intelligence and a fine explanation. "I've something to say to Captain Yule."

Cora stood in the doorway, robust against the garden-light, and looking from one to the other. "Yes—but I've also something more to say to *you*."

"Do you mean now?" the young man asked.

It was the first time he had spoken to her, and her hesitation might have signified a maidenly flutter. "No—but before she goes."

Mrs. Gracedew took it amiably up. "Come back, then; I'm not going." And there was both dismissal and encouragement in the way that, as on the occasion of the girl's former retreat, she blew her a familiar kiss. Cora, still with her face to them, waited just enough to show that she took it without a response; then, with a quick turn, dashed out, while Mrs. Gracedew looked at their visitor in vague surprise. "What's the matter with her?"

She had turned away as soon as she spoke, moving as far from him as she had moved a few moments before from Cora. The silence that, as he watched her, followed her question would have been seen by a spectator to be a hard one for either to break. "I don't know what's the matter with her," he said at last. "I'm afraid I only know what's the matter with *me*. It will doubtless give you pleasure to learn," he added, "that I've closed with Mr. Prodmore."

It was a speech that, strangely enough, seemed but half to dissipate the hush. Mrs. Gracedew reached the great chimney again, again she stood there with her face averted; and when she finally replied it was in other words than he might have supposed himself naturally to inspire. "I thought you said he gave you time."

"Yes; but you produced just now so deep an effect on me that I thought best not to take any." He appeared to listen to a sound from above, and, for a moment, under this impulse, his eyes travelled about almost as if he were alone. Then he completed, with deliberation, his statement. "I came upon him right there, and I burnt my ships."

Mrs. Gracedew continued not to meet his face. "You do what he requires?"

The young man was markedly, consciously caught. "I do what he requires. I felt the tremendous force of all you said to me."

She turned round on him now, as if perhaps with a slight sharpness, the face of responsibility—even, it might be, of reproach. "So did I—or I shouldn't have said it!"

It was doubtless this element of justification in her tone that drew from him a laugh a tiny trifle dry. "You're perhaps not aware that you wield an influence of which it's not too much to say——"

But he paused at the important point so long that she took him up. "To say what?"

"Well, that it's practically irresistible!"

It sounded a little as if it had not been what he first meant; but it made her, none the less, still graver and just faintly ironical. "You've given me the most flattering proof of my influence that I've ever enjoyed in my life!"

He fixed her very hard, now distinctly so mystified that he could only wonder what different recall of her previous attitude she would have looked for. "This was inevitable, dear madam, from the moment you had converted me—and in about three minutes too!—into the absolute echo of your raptures."

Nothing was, indeed, more extraordinary than her air of having suddenly forgotten them. "My 'raptures'?"

He was amazed. "Why, about my home."

He might look her through and through, but she had no eyes for himself, though she had now quitted the fireplace and finally recognised this allusion. "Oh yes—your home!" From where had she come back to it? "It's a nice tattered, battered old thing." This account of it was the more shrunken that her observation, even as she spoke, freshly went the rounds. "It has defects of course"—with this renewed attention they appeared suddenly to strike her. They had popped out, conspicuous, and for a little it might have been a matter of conscience. However, her conscience dropped. "But it's no use mentioning them now!"

They had half an hour earlier been vividly present to himself, but to see her thus oddly pulled up by them was to forget on the spot the ground he had taken. "I'm particularly sorry," he returned with some spirit, "that you didn't mention them before!"

At this imputation of inconsequence, of a levity not, after all, without its excuse, Mrs. Gracedew was reduced, in keeping her resentment down, to an effort not quite successfully disguised. It was in a tone, nevertheless, all the more mild in intention that she reminded him of where he had equally failed. "If you had really gone over the house, as I almost went on my knees to you to do, you might have discovered some of them yourself!"

"How can you say that," the young man asked with heat, "when I was precisely in the very act of it? It was just *because* I was that the first person I met above was Mr. Prodmore; on which, feeling that I must come to it sooner or later, I simply gave in to him on the spot—yielded him, to have it well over, the whole of his point."

She listened to this account of the matter as she might have gazed, from afar, at some queer object that was scarce distinguishable. It left her a moment in the deepest thought, but she presently recovered her tone. "Let me then congratulate you on at last knowing what you want!"

But there were, after all, he instantly showed, no such great reasons for that. "I only know it so far as *you* know it! I struck while the iron was hot—or at any rate while the hammer was."

"Of course I recognise"—she adopted his image with her restored gaiety—"that it can rarely have been exposed to such a fire. I blazed up, and I know that when I burn——"

She had pulled up with the foolish sense of this. "When you burn?"

"Well, I do it as Chicago does."

He also could laugh out now. "Isn't that usually down to the ground?"

Meeting his laugh, she threw up her light arms. "As high as the sky!" Then she came back, as with a scruple, to the real question. "I suppose you've still formalities to go through."

"With Mr. Prodmore?" Well, he would suppose it too if she liked. "Oh, endless, tiresome ones, no doubt!"

This sketch of them made her wonder. "You mean they'll take so very, very long?"

He seemed after all to know perfectly what he meant. "Every hour, every month, that I can possibly make them last!"

She was with him here, however, but to a certain point. "You mustn't drag them out *too* much—must you? Won't he think in that case you may want to retract?"

Yule apparently tried to focus Mr. Prodmore under this delusion, and with a success that had a quick, odd result. "I shouldn't be so terribly upset by his mistake, you know, even if he did!"

His manner, with its slight bravado, left her proportionately shocked. "Oh, it would never do to give him any colour whatever for supposing you to have any doubt that, as one may say, you've pledged your honour."

He devoted to this proposition more thought than its simplicity would have seemed to demand; but after a minute, at all events, his intelligence triumphed. "Of course not—not when I *haven't* any doubt!"

Though his intelligence had triumphed, she still wished to show she was there to support it. "How can you *possibly* have any—any more than you can possibly have that one's honour is everything in life?" And her charming eyes expressed to him her need to feel that he was quite at one with her on *that* point.

He could give her every assurance. "Oh yes—everything in life!"

It did her much good, brought back the rest of her brightness. "Wasn't it just of the question of the honour of things that we talked a while ago—and of the difficulty of sometimes keeping our sense of it clear? There's no more to be said therefore," she went on with the faintest soft sigh about it, "except that I leave you to your ancient glory as I leave you to your strict duty." She had these things there before her; they might have been a well-spread board from which she turned away fasting. "I hope you'll do justice to dear old Covering in spite of its weak points, and I hope above all you'll not be incommoded——"

As she hesitated here he was too intent. "Incommoded——?"

She saw it better than she could express it. "Well, by such a rage——!"

He challenged this description with a strange gleam. "You suppose it will be a rage?"

She laughed out at his look. "Are you afraid of the love that kills?"

He grew singularly grave. "*Will* it kill——?"

"Great passions *have*!"—she was highly amused.

But he could only stare. "Is it a great passion?"

"Surely—when so many feel it!"

He was fairly bewildered. "But how many— ?"

She reckoned them up. "Let's see. If you count them all——"

"'All'?" Clement Yule gasped.

She looked at him, in turn, slightly mystified. "I see. You knock off some. About half?"

It was too obscure—he broke down. "Whom on earth are you talking about?"

"Why, the electors ——"

"Of Gossage?"—he leaped at it. "Oh!"

"I got the whole thing up—there are six thousand. It's such a fine figure!" said Mrs. Gracedew.

He had sharply passed from her, to cover his mistake, and it carried him half round the hall. Then, as if aware that this pause itself compromised him, he came back confusedly and with her last words in his ear. "*Has* she a fine figure?"

But her own thoughts were off. "'She'?"

He blushed and recovered himself. "Aren't we talking——"

"Of Gossage? Oh yes—she has every charm! Good bye," said Mrs. Gracedew.

He pulled, at this, the longest face, but was kept dumb a moment by the very decision with which she again began to gather herself. It held him helpless, and there was finally real despair in his retarded protest. "You don't mean to say you're going?"

"You don't mean to say you're surprised at it? Haven't I done," she luminously asked, "what I told you I had been so mystically moved to come for?" She recalled to him by her renewed supreme survey the limited character of this errand, which she then in a brisk familiar word expressed to the house itself. "You dear old thing—you're saved!"

Clement Yule might, on the other hand, by his simultaneous action, have given himself out for lost. "For God's sake," he cried as he circled earnestly round her, "don't go till I can come back to thank you!" He pulled out his watch. "I promised to return immediately to Prodmore."

This completely settled his visitor. "Then don't let me, for a moment more, keep you away from him. You must have such lots"—it went almost without saying—"to talk comfortably over."

The young man's embrace of that was, in his restless movement, to roam to the end of the hall furthest from the stairs. But here his assent was entire. "I certainly feel, you know, that I must see him again." He rambled even to the open door and looked with incoherence into the court. "Yes, decidedly, I *must*!"

"Is he out there?" Mrs. Gracedew lightly asked.

He turned short round. "No—I left him in the long gallery."

"You *saw* that then?"—she flashed back into eagerness. "Isn't it lovely?"

Clement Yule rather wondered. "I didn't notice it. How *could* I?"

His face was so woeful that she broke into a laugh. "How *couldn't* you? Notice it now, then. Go up to him!"

He crossed at last to the staircase, but at the foot he stopped again. "Will you wait for me?"

He had such an air of proposing a bargain, of making the wait a condition, that she had to look it well in the face. The result of her doing so, however, was apparently a strong sense that she could give him no pledge. Her silence, after a moment, expressed that; but, for a further emphasis, moving away, she sank suddenly into the chair she had already occupied and in which, serious again and very upright, she continued to withhold her promise. "Go up to him!" she simply repeated. He obeyed, with an abrupt turn, mounting briskly enough several steps, but pausing midway and looking back at her as if he were after all irresolute. He was in fact so much so that, at the sight of her still in her chair and alone by his cold hearth, he descended a few steps again and seemed, with too much decidedly on his mind, on the point of breaking out. She had sat a minute in such thought, figuring him clearly as gone, that at the sound of his return she sprang up with a protest. This checked him afresh, and he remained where he had paused, still on the ascent and exchanging with her a look to which neither party was inspired, oddly enough, to contribute a word. It struck him, without words, at all events, as enough, and he now took his upward course at such a pace that he presently disappeared. She listened a while to his retreating tread; then her own, on the old flags of the hall, became rapid, though, it may perhaps be added, directed to no visible end. It conveyed her, in the great space, from point to point, but she now for the first time moved there without attention and without joy, her course determined by a series of such inward throbs as might have been the suppressed beats of a speech. A real observer, had such a monster been present, would have followed this tacit evolution from sign to sign and from shade to shade. "Why didn't he tell me *all?*—But it was none of my business!—What does he mean to do?—What should he do but what he *has* done?—And what *can* he do, when he's so deeply committed, when he's practically engaged, when he's just the same as married—and buried? —The thing for *me* to 'do' is just to pull up short and bundle out: to remove from the scene they encumber the numerous fragments—well, of what?"

Her thought was plainly arrested by the sight of Cora Prodmore, who, returning from the garden, reappeared first in the court and then in the open doorway. Mrs. Gracedew's was a thought, however, that, even when desperate, was never quite vanquished, and it found a presentable public solution in the pieces of the vase smashed by Chivers and just then, on the table where he had laid them, catching her eye. "Of my old Chelsea pot!" Her gay, sad headshake as she took one of them up pronounced for Cora's benefit its funeral oration. She laid the morsel thoughtfully down, while her visitor seemed with simple dismay to read the story.

VI

"Has he been *breaking*——?" the girl asked in horror.

Mrs. Gracedew laughingly tapped her heart. "Yes, we've had a scene! He went up again to your father."

Cora was disconcerted. "Papa's not there. He just came down to me by the other way."

"Then he can join you here," said Mrs. Gracedew with instant resignation. "I'm going."

"Just when I've come back to you—at the risk," Cora made bold to throw off, "of again interrupting, though I really hoped he had gone, your conversation with Captain Yule?"

But Mrs. Gracedew let the ball quite drop. "I've nothing to say to Captain Yule."

Cora picked it up for another toss. "You had a good deal to say a few minutes ago!"

"Well, I've said it, and it's over. I've nothing more to say at all," Mrs. Gracedew insisted. But her announcement of departure left her on this occasion, as each of its predecessors had done, with a last, with indeed a fresh solicitude. "What has become of my delightful 'party'?"

"They've been dismissed, through the grounds, by the other door. But they mentioned," the girl pursued, "the probable arrival of a fresh lot."

Mrs. Gracedew showed on this such a revival of interest as fairly amounted to yearning. "Why, what times you have! *You*," she nevertheless promptly decreed, "must take the fresh lot—since the house is now practically yours!"

Poor Cora looked blank. "Mine?"

Her companion matched her stare. "Why, if you're going to marry Captain Yule."

Cora coloured, in a flash, to the eyes. "I'm *not* going to marry Captain Yule!"

Her friend as quickly paled again. "Why on earth then did you tell me only ten minutes ago that you were?"

Cora could only look bewildered at the charge. "I told you nothing of the sort. I only told you"—she was almost indignantly positive—"that he had been ordered me!"

It sent Mrs. Gracedew off; she moved away to indulge an emotion that presently put on the form of extravagant mirth.

"Like a dose of medicine or a course of baths?"

The girl's gravity and lucidity sustained themselves. "As a remedy for the single life." Oh, she had mastered the matter now! "But I won't take him!"

"Ah then, why didn't you let me know?" Mrs. Gracedew panted.

"I was on the very point of it when he came in and interrupted us." Cora clearly felt she might be wicked, but was at least not stupid. "It's just to let you know that I'm here now."

Ah, the difference it made! This difference, for Mrs. Gracedew, suddenly shimmered in all the place, and her companion's fixed eyes caught in her face the reflection of it. "Excuse me—I misunderstood. I somehow took for granted——!" She stopped, a trifle awkwardly—suddenly tender, for Cora, as to the way she had inevitably seen it.

"You took for granted I'd jump at him? Well, now you can take for granted I won't!"

Mrs. Gracedew, fairly admiring her, put it sympathetically. "You prefer the single life?"

"No—but I don't prefer *him*!" Cora was crystal-bright.

Her light indeed, for her friend, was at first almost blinding; it took Mrs. Gracedew a moment to distinguish—which she then did, however, with immense eagerness. "You prefer someone else?" Cora's promptitude dropped at this, and, starting to hear it, as you might well have seen, for the first time publicly phrased, she abruptly moved away. A minute's sense of her scruple was enough for Mrs. Gracedew: this was proved by the tone of soft remonstrance and high benevolence with which that lady went on. She had looked very hard, first, at one of the old warriors hung on the old wall, and almost spoke as if he represented their host. "He seems remarkably clever."

Cora, at something in the sound, quite jumped about. "Then why don't you marry him yourself?"

Mrs. Gracedew gave a sort of happy sigh. "Well, I've got fifty reasons! I rather think one of them must be that he hasn't happened to ask me."

It was a speech, however, that her visitor could easily better. "I haven't got fifty reasons, but I *have* got one."

Mrs. Gracedew smiled as if it were indeed a stroke of wit. "You mean your case is one of those in which safety is *not* in numbers?" And then on Cora's visibly not understanding: "It *is* when reasons are bad that one needs so many!"

The proposition was too general for the girl to embrace, but the simplicity of her answer was far from spoiling it. "My reason is awfully good."

Mrs. Gracedew did it complete justice. "I see. An older friend."

Cora listened as at a warning sound; yet she had by this time practically let herself go, and it took but Mrs. Gracedew's extended encouraging hand, which she quickly seized, to bring the whole thing out. "I've been trying this hour, in my terrible need of advice, to tell you about him!" It came in a small clear torrent, a soft tumble-out of sincerity. "After we parted—you and I—at the station, he suddenly turned up there, and I took a little quiet walk with him which gave you time to get here before me and of which my father is in a state of ignorance that I don't know whether to regard as desirable or dreadful."

Mrs. Gracedew, attentive and wise, might have been, for her face, the old family solicitor. "You want me then to *inform* your father?" It was a wonderful intonation.

Poor Cora, for that matter too, might suddenly have become under this touch the prodigal with a list of debts. She seemed an instant to look out of a blurred office window-pane at a grey London sky; then she broke away. "I really don't know *what* I want. I think," she honestly admitted, "I just want kindness."

Mrs. Gracedew's expression might have hinted—but not for too long—that Bedford Row was an odd place to apply for it: she appeared for an instant to make the revolving office-chair creak. "What do you mean by kindness?"

Cora was a model client—she perfectly knew. "I mean help."

Mrs. Gracedew closed an inkstand with a clap and locked a couple of drawers. "What do you mean by help?"

The client's inevitable answer seemed to perch on the girl's lips: "A thousand pounds." But it came out in another, in a much more charming form. "I mean that I love him."

The family solicitor got up: it was a high figure. "And does he love *you?*"

Cora hesitated. "Ask *him*."

Mrs. Gracedew weighed the necessity. "Where is he?"

"Waiting." And the girl's glance, removed from her companion and wandering aloft and through space, gave the scale of his patience.

Her adviser, however, required the detail. "But *where*?"

Cora briefly demurred again. "In that funny old grotto."

Mrs. Gracedew thought. "Funny?"

"Half way from the park gate. It's very *nice*!" Cora more eagerly added.

Mrs. Gracedew continued to reflect. "Oh, I know it!" She spoke as if she had known it most of her life.

Her tone encouraged her client. "Then will you see him?"

"No." This time it was almost dry.

"No?"

"No. If you want help——" Mrs. Gracedew, still musing, explained.

"Yes?"

"Well—you want a great deal."

"Oh, so much!"—Cora but too woefully took it in. "I want," she quavered, "all there is!"

"Well—you shall have it."

"All there is?"—she convulsively held her to it.

Mrs. Gracedew had finally mastered it. "I'll see your father."

"You dear, delicious lady!" Her young friend had again encompassed her; but, passive and preoccupied, she showed some of the chill of apprehension. It was indeed as if to meet this that Cora went earnestly on: "He's intensely sympathetic!"

"Your father?" Mrs. Gracedew had her reserves.

"Oh no—the other person. I so believe in him!" Cora cried.

Mrs. Gracedew looked at her a moment. "Then so do I—and I like him for believing in *you*."

"Oh, he does that," the girl hurried on, "far more than Captain Yule—I could see just with one glance that *he* doesn't at all. Papa has of course seen the young man I mean, but we've been so sure papa would hate it that we've had to be awfully careful. He's the son of the richest man at Bellborough, he's Granny's godson, and he'll inherit his father's business, which is simply immense. Oh, from the point of view of the things he's *in*"—and Cora found herself sharp on this—"he's quite as good as papa himself. He has been away for three days, and if he met me at the station, where, on his way back, he has to change, it was by the merest chance in the world. I wouldn't love him," she brilliantly wound up, "if he wasn't nice."

"A man's always nice if you *will* love him!" Mrs. Gracedew laughed.

Her young friend more than met it. "He's nicer still if he 'will' love *you*!"

But Mrs. Gracedew kept her head. "Nicer of course than if he won't! But are you sure this gentleman *does* love you?"

"As sure as that the other one doesn't."

"Ah, but the other one doesn't know you."

"Yes, thank goodness—and never shall!"

Mrs. Gracedew watched her a little, but on the girl's meeting her eyes turned away with a quick laugh. "You mean of course till it's too late!"

"Altogether!" Cora spoke as with quite the measure of the time.

Mrs. Gracedew, revolving a moment in silence, appeared to accept her showing. "Then what's the matter?" she impatiently asked.

"The matter?"

"Your father's objection to the gentleman in the grotto."

Cora now for the first time faltered. "His name."

This for a moment pulled up her friend, in whom, however, relief seemed to contend with alarm. "Only his name?"

"Yes, but——" Cora's eyes rolled.

Her companion invitingly laughed. "But it's enough?"

Her roll confessingly fixed itself. "*Not* enough—that's just the trouble!"

Mrs. Gracedew looked kindly curious. "What then *is* it?"

Cora faced the music. "Pegg."

Mrs. Gracedew stared. "Nothing else?"

"Nothing to speak of." The girl was quite candid now. "Hall."

"Nothing before——?"

"Not a letter."

"Hall Pegg?" Mrs. Gracedew had winced, but she quickly recovered herself, and, for a further articulation, appeared, from delicacy, to form the sound only with her mind. The sound she formed with her lips was, after an instant, simply "Oh!"

It was to the combination of the spoken and the unspoken that Cora desperately replied. "It sounds like a hat-rack!"

" 'Hall Pegg? Hall Pegg'?" Mrs. Gracedew now made it, like a questionable coin, ring upon the counter. But it lay there as lead and without, for a moment, her taking it up again. "How many has your father?" she inquired instead.

"How many names?" Miss Prodmore seemed dimly to see that there was no hope in that. "He somehow makes out five."

"Oh, that's *too* many!" Mrs. Gracedew jeeringly declared.

"Papa unfortunately doesn't think so, when Captain Yule, I believe, has six."

"Six?" Mrs. Gracedew, alert, looked as if that might be different.

"Papa, in the morning-room, told me them all."

Mrs. Gracedew visibly considered, then for a moment dropped Mr. Pegg. "And what are they?"

"Oh, all sorts. 'Marmaduke Clement——'." Cora tried to recall.

Mrs. Gracedew, however, had already checked her. "I see— 'Marmaduke Clement' will do." She appeared for a minute intent, but, as with an energetic stoop, she picked up Mr. Pegg. "But so will yours," she said, with decision.

"Mine?—you mean *his*!"

"The same thing—what you'll *be*."

"Mrs. Hall Pegg!"—Cora tried it, with resolution, loudly.

It fell a little flat in the noble space, but Mrs. Gracedew's manner quickly covered it. "It won't make you a bit less charming."

Cora wondered—she hoped. "Only for papa."

And what was *he*? Mrs. Gracedew by this time seemed assentingly to ask. "Never for *me*!" she soothingly declared.

Cora took this in with deep thanks that gripped and patted her companion's hand. "You accept it more than gracefully. But if you could only make *him*——!"

Mrs. Gracedew was all concentration. " 'Him'? Mr. Pegg?"

"No—he naturally *has* to accept it. But papa."

She looked harder still at this greater feat, then seemed to see light. "Well, it will be difficult—but I will."

Doubt paled before it. "Oh, you heavenly thing!"

Mrs. Gracedew after an instant, sustained by this appreciation, went a step further. "And I'll make him *say* he does!"

Cora closed her eyes with the dream of it. "Oh, if I could only hear him!"

Her benefactress had at last run it to earth. "It will be enough if *I* do."

Cora quickly considered; then, with prompt accommodation, gave the comfortable measure of her faith. "Yes—I think it will." She was quite ready to retire. "I'll give you time."

"Thank you," said Mrs. Gracedew; "but before you give me time give me something better."

This pulled the girl up a little, as if in parting with her secret she had parted with her all. "Something better?"

"If I help you, you know," Mrs. Gracedew explained, "you must help me."

"But how?"

"By a clear assurance." The charming woman's fine face now gave the real example of clearness. "That if Captain Yule should propose to you, you would unconditionally refuse him."

Cora flushed with the surprise of its being only that. "With my dying breath!"

Mrs. Gracedew scanned her robust vitality. "Will you make it even a promise?"

The girl looked about her in solid certainty. "Do you want me to sign——?"

Mrs. Gracedew was quick. "No, don't sign!"

Yet Cora was so ready to oblige. "Then what shall I do?"

Mrs. Gracedew turned away, but after a few vague steps faced her again. "Kiss me."

Cora flew to her arms, and the compact had scarce been sealed before the younger of the parties was already at the passage to the front. "We meet of course at the station."

Mrs. Gracedew thought. "If all goes well. But where shall you be meanwhile?"

Her confederate had no need to think. "Can't you guess?"

The bang of the house-door, the next minute, so helped the answer to the riddle as fairly to force it, when she found herself alone, from her lips. "At that funny old grotto? Well," she sighed, "I *like* funny old grottos!" She found herself alone, however, only for a minute; Mr. Prodmore's formidable presence had darkened the door from the court.

VII

"My daughter's not here?" he demanded from the threshold.

"Your daughter's not here." She had rapidly got under arms. "But it's a convenience to me, Mr. Prodmore, that *you* are, for I've something very particular to ask you."

Her interlocutor crossed straight to the morning-room. "I shall be delighted to answer your question, but I must first put my hand on Miss Prodmore." This hand the next instant stayed itself on the latch, and he appealed to the amiable visitor. "Unless indeed she's occupied in there with Captain Yule?"

The amiable visitor met the appeal. "I don't think she's occupied—anywhere—with Captain Yule."

Mr. Prodmore came straight away from the door. "Then where the deuce *is* Captain Yule?"

The amiable visitor turned a trifle less direct. "His absence, for which I'm responsible, is just what renders the inquiry I speak of to you possible." She had already assumed a most inquiring air, yet it was soon clear that she needed every advantage her manner could give her. "What will you take——? what will you take——?"

It had the sound, as she faltered, of a general question, and Mr. Prodmore raised his eyebrows. "Take? Nothing, thank you—I've just had a cup of tea." Then suddenly, as if on the broad hint: "Won't *you* have one?"

"Yes, with pleasure—but not yet." She looked about her again; she was now at close quarters and, concentrated, anxious, pressed her hand a moment to her brow.

This struck her companion. "Don't you think you'd be better for it immediately?"

"Why, it's only when you're kept in the dark that your daughter's kept in the light!" She argued it with a candour that might have served for brilliancy. "It's at her own earnest request that I plead to you for her liberty of choice. She's an honest girl—perhaps even a peculiar girl; and she's not a baby. You overdo, I think, the nursing. She has a perfect right to her preference."

Poor Mr. Prodmore couldn't help taking it from her, and, this being the case, he still took it in the most convenient way. "And pray haven't I a perfect right to mine?" he asked from his chair.

She fairly seemed to serve it up to him—to put down the dish with a flourish. "Not at her expense. You expect her to give up too much."

"And what has she," he appealed, "expected *me* to give up? What but the desire of my heart and the dream of my life? Captain Yule announced to me but a few minutes since his intention to offer her his hand."

She faced him on it as over the table. "Well, if he does, I think he'll simply find——"

"Find what?" They looked at each other hard.

"Why, that she won't have it."

Oh, Mr. Prodmore now sprang up. "She *will!*"

"She won't!" Mrs. Gracedew more distinctly repeated.

"She *shall!*" returned her adversary, making for the staircase with the evident sense of where reinforcement might be most required.

Mrs. Gracedew, however, with a spring, was well before him. "She sha'n't!" She spoke with positive passion and practically so barred the way that he stood arrested and bewildered and they faced each other, for a flash, like enemies. But it all went out, on her part, in a flash too—in a sudden wonderful smile. "Now tell me how much!"

Mr. Prodmore continued to glare—the sweat was on his brow. But while he slowly wiped it with a pocket-handkerchief of splendid scarlet silk he remained so silent that he would have had for a spectator the effect of meeting in a manner her question. More formally to answer it he had at last to turn away. "How can I tell you anything so preposterous?"

She was all ready to inform him. "Simply by computing the total amount to which, for your benefit, this unhappy estate is burdened." He listened with his back presented, but that appeared to strike her, as she fixed this expanse, as an encouragement to proceed. "If I've troubled you by showing you that your speculation is built on the sand, let me atone for it by my eagerness to take off your hands an investment from which you derive so little profit."

He at last gave her his attention, but quite as if there were nothing in it. "And pray what profit will *you* derive——?"

"Ah, that's my own secret!" She would show him as well no glimpse of it—her laugh but rattled the box. "I want this house!"

"So do I, damn me!" he roundly returned; "and that's why I've practically paid for it!" He stuffed away his pocket handkerchief.

There was nevertheless something in her that could hold him, and it came out, after an instant, quietly and reasonably enough. "I'll practically pay for it, Mr. Prodmore—if you'll only tell me your figure."

"My figure?"

"Your figure."

Mr. Prodmore waited—then removed his eyes from her face. He appeared to have waited on purpose to let her hope of a soft answer fall from a greater height. "My figure would be quite my own!"

"Then it will match, in that respect," Mrs. Gracedew laughed, "this overture, which is quite *my* own! As soon as you've let me know it I cable to Missoura Top to have the money sent right out to you."

Mr. Prodmore surveyed in a superior manner this artless picture of a stroke of business. "You imagine that having the money sent right out to me will make you owner of this place?"

She herself, with her head on one side, studied her sketch and seemed to twirl her pencil. "No—not quite. But I'll settle the rest with Captain Yule."

Her companion looked, over his white waistcoat, at his large tense shoes, the patent-leather shine of which so flashed propriety back at him that he became, the next moment, doubly erect on it. "Captain Yule has nothing to sell."

She received the remark with surprise. "Then what have you been trying to buy?"

She had touched in himself even a sharper spring. "Do you mean to say," he cried, "you want to buy *that*?" She stared at his queer emphasis, which was intensified by a queer grimace; then she turned from him with a change of colour and an ejaculation that led to nothing more, after a few seconds, than a somewhat conscious silence—a silence of which Mr. Prodmore made use to follow up his unanswered question with another. "Is your proposal that I should transfer my investment to you for the mere net amount of it your conception of a fair bargain?"

This second inquiry, however, she could, as she slowly came round, substantially meet. "Pray then what is yours?"

"Mine would be, not that I should simply get my money back, but that I should get the effective value of the house."

Mrs. Gracedew considered it. "But isn't the effective value of the house just what your money expresses?"

The lid of his hard left eye, the harder of the two, just dipped with the effect of a wink. "No, madam. It's just what *yours* does. It's moreover just what your lips have already expressed so distinctly!"

She clearly did her best to follow him. "To those people—when I showed the place off?"

Mr. Prodmore laughed. "You seemed to be *taking* bids then!"

She was candid, but earnest. "Taking them?"

"Oh, like an auctioneer! You ran it up high!" And Mr. Prodmore laughed again.

She turned a little pale, but it added to her brightness. "I certainly did, if saying it was charming——"

"Charming?" Mr. Prodmore broke in. "You said it was magnificent. You said it was unique. That was your very word. You said it was the *perfect* specimen of its class in England." He was more than accusatory, he was really crushing. "Oh, you got in deep!"

It was indeed an indictment, and her smile was perhaps now rather set. "Possibly. But taunting me with my absurd high spirits and the dreadful liberties I took doesn't in the least tell me how deep *you're* in!"

"For you, Mrs. Gracedew?" He took a few steps, looking at his shoes again and as if to give her time to plead—since he wished to be quite fair—that it was *not* for her. "I'm in to the tune of fifty thousand."

She was silent, on this announcement, so long that he once more faced her; but if what he showed her in doing so at last made her speak, it also took the life from her tone. "That's a great deal of money, Mr. Prodmore."

The tone didn't matter, but only the truth it expressed, which he so thoroughly liked to hear. "So I've often had occasion to say to myself!"

"If it's a large sum for you then," said Mrs. Gracedew, "it's a still larger one for me." She sank into a chair with a vague melancholy; such a mass loomed huge, and she sat down before it as a solitary herald, resigning himself with a sigh to wait, might have leaned against a tree before a besieged city. "We women,"—she wished to conciliate—"have more modest ideas."

But Mr. Prodmore would scarce condescend to parley. "Is it as a 'modest idea' that you describe your extraordinary intrusion——?"

His question scarce reached her; she was so lost for the moment in the sense of innocent community with her sex. "I mean I think we measure things often rather more exactly."

There would have been no doubt of Mr. Prodmore's very different community as he rudely replied: "Then you measured *this* thing exactly half an hour ago!"

It was a long way to go back, but Mrs. Gracedew, in her seat, musingly made the journey, from which she then suddenly returned with a harmless, indeed quite a happy, memento. "Was I *very* grotesque?"

He demurred. "Grotesque?"

"I mean—did I go on about it?"

Mr. Prodmore would have no general descriptions; he was specific, he was vivid. "You banged the desk. You raved. You shrieked."

This was a note she appeared indulgently, almost tenderly, to recognise. "We *do* shriek at Missoura Top!"

"I don't know what you do at Missoura Top, but I know what you did at Covering End!"

She warmed at last to his tone. "So do *I* then! I surprised you. You weren't at all prepared——"

He took her briskly up. "No—and I'm not prepared yet!"

Mrs. Gracedew could quite see it. "Yes, you're too astonished."

"My astonishment's my own affair," he retorted—"not less so than my memory!"

"Oh, I yield to your memory," said the charming woman, "and I confess my extravagance. But quite, you know, *as* extravagance."

"I don't at all know,"—Mr. Prodmore shook it off—"nor what you *call* extravagance."

"Why, banging the desk. Raving. Shrieking. I overdid it," she exclaimed; "I wanted to please you!"

She had too happy a beauty, as she sat in her high-backed chair, to have been condemned to say that to any man without a certain effect. The effect on Mr. Prodmore was striking. "So you said," he sternly inquired, "what you didn't believe?"

She flushed with the avowal. "Yes—for you."

He looked at her hard. "For *me?*"

Under his eye—for her flush continued—she slowly got up. "And for those good people."

"Oh!"—he sounded most sarcastic. "Should you like me to call them back?"

"No." She was still gay enough, but very decided. "I took them in."

"And now you want to take *me?*"

"Oh, Mr. Prodmore!" she almost pitifully, but not quite adequately, moaned.

He appeared to feel he had gone a little far. "Well, if we're not what you say——"

"Yes?"—she looked up askance at the stroke.

"Why the devil do you want us?" The question rang out and was truly for the poor lady, as the quick suffusion of her eyes showed, a challenge it would take more time than he left her properly to pick up. He left her in fact no time at all before he went on: "Why the devil did you say you'd offer fifty?"

She looked quite wan and seemed to wonder. "*Did* I say that?" She could only let his challenge lie. "It was a figure of speech!"

"Then that's the kind of figure we're talking about!" Mr. Prodmore's sharpness would have struck an auditor as the more effective that, on the heels of this thrust, seeing the ancient butler reappear, he dropped the victim of it as comparatively unimportant and directed his fierceness instantly to Chivers, who mildly gaped at him from the threshold of the court. "Have you seen Miss Prodmore? If you haven't, find her!"

Mrs. Gracedew addressed their visitor in a very different tone, though with the full authority of her benevolence. "You won't, my dear man." To Mr. Prodmore also she continued bland. "I happen to know she has gone for a walk."

"A walk—alone?" Mr. Prodmore gasped.

"No—not alone." Mrs. Gracedew looked at Chivers with a vague smile of appeal for help, but he could only give her, from under his bent old brow, the blank decency of his wonder. It seemed to make her feel afresh that she was, after all, alone—so that in her loneliness, which had also its fine sad charm, she risked another brush with their formidable friend. "Cora has gone with Mr. Pegg."

"Pegg has *been* here?"

It was like a splash in a full basin, but she launched the whole craft. "He walked with her from the station."

"When she arrived?" Mr. Prodmore rose like outraged Neptune. "That's why she was so late?"

Mrs. Gracedew assented. "Why I got here first. I get everywhere first!" she bravely laughed.

Mr. Prodmore looked round him in purple dismay—it was so clearly a question for him where *he* should get, and what! "In which direction did they go?" he imperiously asked.

His rudeness was too evident to be more than lightly recognised. "I think I must let you ascertain for yourself!"

All he could do then was to shout it to Chivers. "Call my carriage, you ass!" After which, as the old man melted into the vestibule, he dashed about blindly for his hat, pounced upon it and seemed, furious but helpless, on the point of hurling it at his contradictress as a gage of battle. "So you abetted and protected this wicked, low intrigue?"

She had something in her face now that was indifferent to any violence. "You're too disappointed to see your real interest: oughtn't I therefore in common charity to point it out to you?"

He faced her question so far as to treat it as one. "What do *you* know of my disappointment?"

There was something in his very harshness that even helped her, for it added at this moment to her sense of making out in his narrowed glare a couple of tears of rage. "I know everything."

"What do you know of my real interest?" he went on as if he had not heard her.

"I know enough for my purpose—which is to offer you a handsome condition. I think it's not I who have protected the happy understanding that you call by so ugly a name; it's the happy understanding that has put me"—she gained confidence—"well, in a position. Do drive after them, if you like—but catch up with them only to forgive them. If you'll do that, I'll pay your price."

The particular air with which, a minute after Mrs. Gracedew had spoken these words, Mr. Prodmore achieved a transfer of his attention to the inside of his hat—this special shade of majesty would have taxed the descriptive resources of the most accomplished reporter. It is none the less certain that he appeared for some time absorbed in that receptacle—appeared at last to breathe into it hard. "What do you call my price?"

"Why the sum you just mentioned—fifty thousand!" Mrs. Gracedew feverishly quavered.

He looked at her as if stupefied. "*That's* not my price—and it never for a moment was!" If derision can be dry, Mr. Prodmore's was of the driest. "Besides," he rang out, "my price is up!"

She caught it with a long wail. "Up?"

Oh, he let her have it now! "Seventy thousand."

She turned away overwhelmed, but still with voice for her despair. "Oh, deary me!"

Mr. Prodmore was already at the door, from which he launched his ultimatum. "It's to take or to leave!"

She would have had to leave it, perhaps, had not something happened at this moment to nerve her for the effort of staying him with a quick motion. Captain Yule had come into sight on the staircase and, after just faltering at what he himself saw, had marched resolutely enough down. She watched him arrive—watched him with an attention that visibly and responsively excited his own; after which she passed nearer to their companion. "Seventy thousand then!"—it gleamed between them, in her muffled hiss, as if she had planted a dagger.

Mr. Prodmore, to do him justice, took his wound in front. "Seventy thousand—done!" And, without another look at Yule, he was presently heard to bang the outer door after him for a sign.

VIII

The young man, meanwhile, had approached in surprise. "He's gone? I've been looking for him!"

Mrs. Gracedew was out of breath; there was a disturbed whiteness of bosom in her which needed time to subside and which she might have appeared to retreat before him on purpose to veil. "I don't think, you know, that you need him—now."

Clement Yule was mystified. "Now?"

She recovered herself enough to explain—made an effort at least to be plausible. "I mean that—if you don't mind—you must deal with *me*. I've arranged with Mr. Prodmore to take it over."

Oh, he gave her no help! "Take what over?"

She looked all about as if not quite thinking what it could be called; at last, however, she offered with a smile a sort of substitute for a name. "Why, your debt."

But he was only the more bewildered. "*Can* you—without arranging with *me*?"

She turned it round, but as if merely to oblige him. "That's precisely what I want to do." Then, more brightly, as she thought further: "That is, I mean, I want you to arrange with *me*. Surely you will," she said encouragingly.

His own processes, in spite of a marked earnestness, were much less rapid. "But if I arrange with anybody——"

"Yes?" She cheerfully waited.

"How do I perform my engagement?"

"The one to Mr. Prodmore?"

He looked surprised at her speaking as if he had half-a-dozen. "Yes—that's the worst."

"Certainly—the worst!" And she gave a happy laugh that made him stare.

He broke into quite a different one. "You speak as if its being the worst made it the best!"

"It does—for me. You don't," said Mrs. Gracedew, "perform any engagement."

He required a moment to take it in; then something extraordinary leaped into his face. "He lets me off?"

Ah, she could ring out now! "He lets you off."

It lifted him high, but only to drop him with an audible thud. "Oh, I see—I lose my house!"

"Dear no—*that* doesn't follow!" She spoke as if the absurdity he indicated were the last conceivable, but there was a certain want of sharpness of edge in her expression of the alternative. "You arrange with *me* to keep it."

There was quite a corresponding want, clearly, in the image presented to the Captain—of which, for a moment, he seemed with difficulty to follow the contour. "How do I arrange?"

"Well, we must think," said Mrs. Gracedew; "we must wait." She spoke as if this were a detail for which she had not yet had much attention; only bringing out, however, the next instant in an encouraging cry and as if it were by itself almost a solution: "We must find some way!" She might have been talking to a reasonable child.

But even reasonable children ask too many questions. "Yes—and what way *can* we find?" Clement Yule, glancing about him, was so struck with the absence of ways that he appeared to remember with something of regret how different it had been before. "With Prodmore it was simple enough. You see I could marry his daughter."

Mrs. Gracedew was silent just long enough for her soft ironic smile to fill the cup of the pause. "*Could* you?"

It was as if he had tasted in the words the wine at the brim; for he gave, under the effect of them, a sudden headshake and an awkward laugh. "Well, never perhaps *that* exactly—when it came to the point. But I had to, you see——" It was difficult to say just what.

She took advantage of it, looking hard, but not seeing at all. "You had to——?"

"Well," he repeated ruefully, "think a lot about it. You didn't suspect that?"

Oh, if he came to suspicions she could only break off! "Don't ask me too many questions."

He looked an instant as if he wondered why. "But isn't this just the moment for them?" He fronted her, with a quickness he tried to dissimulate, from the other side. "What *did* you suppose?"

She looked everywhere but into his face. "Why, I supposed you were in distress."

He was very grave. "About his terms?"

"About his terms of course!" she laughed. "Not about his religious opinions."

His gratitude was too great for gaiety. "You really, in your beautiful sympathy, *guessed* my fix?"

But she declined to be too solemn. "Dear Captain Yule, it all quite stuck out of you!"

"You mean I floundered like a drowning man——?"

Well, she consented to have meant that. "Till I plunged in!" He appeared there, for a few seconds, to see her again take the jump and to listen again to the splash; then, with an odd, sharp impulse, he turned his back. "You saved me."

She wouldn't deny it— on the contrary. "What a pity, now, *I* haven't a daughter!"

On this he slowly came round again. "What should I do with her?"

"You'd treat her, I hope, better than you've treated Miss Prodmore."

The young man positively coloured. "But I haven't been bad——?"

The sight of this effect of her small joke produced on Mrs. Gracedew's part an emotion less controllable than any she had yet felt. "Oh, you delightful goose!" she irrepressibly dropped.

She made his blush deepen, but the aggravation was a relief. "Of course—I'm all right, and there's only one pity in the matter. I've nothing—nothing whatever, not a scrap of service nor a thing you'd care for—to offer you in compensation."

She looked at him ever so kindly. "I'm not, as they say, 'on the make.'" Never had he been put right with a lighter hand. "I didn't do it for payment."

"Then what did you do it for?"

For something, it might have seemed, as her eyes dropped and strayed, that had got brushed into a crevice of the old pavement. "Because I hated Mr. Prodmore."

He conscientiously demurred. "So much as all that?"

"Oh, well," she replied impatiently, "of course you also know how much I like the house. My hates and my likes," she subtly explained, "can never live together. I get one of them out. The one this time was that man."

He showed a candour of interest. "Yes—you got him out. Yes—I saw him go." And his inner vision appeared to attend for some moments Mr. Prodmore's departure. "But how did you do it?"

"Oh, I don't know. Women——!" Mrs. Gracedew but vaguely sketched it.

A touch or two, however, for that subject, could of course almost always suffice. "Precisely—women. May I smoke again?" Clement Yule abruptly asked.

"Certainly. But I managed Mr. Prodmore," she laughed as he re-lighted, "without cigarettes."

Her companion puffed. "*I* couldn't manage him."

"So I saw!"

"*I* couldn't get him out."

"So *he* saw!"

Captain Yule, for a little, lost himself in his smoke. "Where is he gone?"

"I haven't the least idea. But I meet him again," she hastened to add—"very soon."

"And when do you meet *me*?"

"Why, whenever you'll come to see me." For the twentieth time she gathered herself as if the words she had just spoken were quite her last hand. "At present, you see, I *have* a train to catch."

Absorbed in the trivial act that engaged him, he gave her no help. "A train?"

"Surely. I didn't walk."

"No; but even trains——!" His eyes clung to her now. "You fly?"

"I try to. Good-bye."

He had got between her and the door of departure quite as, on her attempt to quit him half an hour before, he had anticipated her approach to the stairs; and in this position he took no notice of her farewell. "I said just now that I had nothing to offer you. But of course I've the house itself."

"The house?" She stared. "Why, I've *got* it!"

"Got it?"

"All in my head, I mean. That's all I want " She had not yet, save to Mr. Prodmore, made quite so light of it.

This had its action in his markedly longer face. "Why, I thought you loved it so!"

Ah, she was perfectly consistent. "I love it far too much to deprive *you* of it."

Yet Clement Yule could in a fashion meet her. "Oh, it wouldn't be depriving——!"

She altogether protested. "Not to turn you out—— ?"

"Dear lady, I've never been *in*!"

Oh, she was none the less downright. "You're in *now*—I've put you, and you must stay." He looked round so woefully, however, that she presently attenuated. "I don't mean *all* the while, but long enough——!"

"Long enough for what?"

"For me to feel you're here."

"And how long will that take?"

"Well, you think me very fast—but sometimes I'm slow. I told you just now, at any rate," she went on, "that I had arranged you should lose nothing. Is the very next thing I do, then, to make you lose everything?"

"It isn't a question of what I lose," the young man anxiously cried; "it's a question of what I *do*! What *have* I done to find it all so plain?" Fate was really—fate reversed, improved and unnatural—too much for him, and his heated young face showed honest stupefaction. "I haven't lifted a finger. It's you who have done all."

"Yes, but if you're just where you were before, how in the world are you saved?" She put it to him with still superior lucidity.

"By my life's being my own again—to do what I want."

"What you 'want' "—Mrs. Gracedew's handsome uplifted head had it all there, every inch of it—"is to keep your house."

"Ah, but only," he perfectly assented, "if, as you said, you find a way!"

"I *have* found a way—and there the way is: for *me* just simply not to touch the place. What you 'want,' " she argued more closely, "is what made you give in to Prodmore. What you 'want' is these walls and these acres. What you 'want' is to take the way I first showed you."

Her companion's eyes, quitting for the purpose her face, looked to the quarter marked by her last words as at an horizon now remote. "Why, the way you first showed me was to marry Cora!"

She had to admit it, but as little as possible. "Practically —yes."

"Well, it's just 'practically' that I can't!"

"I didn't know that then," said Mrs. Gracedew. "You didn't tell me."

He passed, with an approach to a grimace, his hand over the back of his head. "I felt a delicacy!"

"I didn't even know *that*." She spoke it almost sadly.

"It didn't strike you that I might?"

She thought a moment. "No." She thought again. "No. But don't quarrel with me about it *now*!"

"Quarrel with you?" he looked amazement.

She laughed, but she had changed colour. "Cora, at any rate, felt no delicacy. Cora told me."

Clement Yule fairly gaped. "Then she did know——?"

"She knew all; and if her father said she didn't he simply told you what was not." She frankly gave him this, but the next minute, as if she had startled him more than she meant, she jumped to reassurance. "It was quite right of her. She would have refused you."

The young man stared. "Oh!" He was quick, however, to show—by an amusement perhaps a trifle overdone—that he felt no personal wound. "Do you call that quite right?"

Mrs. Gracedew looked at it again. "For *her*—yes; and for Prodmore."

"Oh, for Prodmore"—his laugh grew more grim—"with all my heart!"

This then—her kind eyes seemed to drop it upon him—was all she meant. "To stay at your post—*that* was the way I showed you."

He had come round to it now, as mechanically, in intenser thought, he smoothed down the thick hair he had rubbed up; but his face soon enough gave out, in wonder and pain, that his freedom was somehow only a new predicament. "How can I take any way at all, dear lady——?"

"If I only stick here in your path?" She had taken him straight up, and with spirit; and the same spirit bore her to the end "I won't stick a moment more! Haven't I been trying this age to leave you?"

Clement Yule, for all answer, caught her sharply, in her passage, by the arm. "You surrender your rights?" He was for an instant almost terrible.

She quite turned pale with it. "Weren't you ready to surrender *yours*?"

"I hadn't any, so it was deuced easy. I hadn't paid for them."

Oh that, she let him see— even though with his continued grasp he might hurt her—had nothing in it! "Your ancestors had paid: it's the same thing." Erect there in the brightness of her triumph and the force of her logic, she must yet, to anticipate his return, take a stride—like a sudden dip into a gully and the scramble up on the other bank —that put her dignity to the test. "You're just, in a manner, my tenant."

"But how can I treat that as such a mere detail? I'm your tenant on what terms?"

"Oh, *any* terms—choose them for yourself!" She made an attempt to free her arm—gave it a small vain shake. Then, as if to bribe him to let her go: "You can write me about them."

He appeared to consider it. "To Missoura Top?"

She fully assented. "I go right back." As if it had put him off his guard she broke away. "Farewell!"

She broke away, but he broke faster, and once more, nearer the door, he had barred her escape. "Just one little moment, please. If you won't tell me your own terms, you must at least tell me Prodmore's."

Ah, the fiend—she could never squeeze past *that*! All she could do, for the instant, was to reverberate foolishly "Prodmore's?"

But there was nothing foolish, at last, about *him*. "How you did it—how you managed him." His feet were firm while he waited, though he had to wait some time. "You bought him out?"

She made less of it than, clearly, he had ever heard made of a stroke of business; it might have been a case of his owing her ninepence. "I bought him out."

He wanted at least the exact sum."For how much?" Her silence seemed to say that she had made no note of it, but his pressure only increased. "I really must know."

She continued to try to treat it as if she had merely paid for his cab—she put even what she could of that suggestion into a tender, helpless, obstinate headshake. "You shall never know!"

The only thing his own manner met was the obstinacy. "I'll get it from *him*!"

She repeated her headshake, but with a world of sadness added. "Get it if you can!"

He looked into her eyes now as if it was the sadness that struck him most. "He won't say, because he *did* you?"

They showed each other, on this, the least separated faces yet. "He'll never, never say."

The confidence in it was so tender that it sounded almost like pity, and the young man took it up with all the flush of the sense that pity could be but for *him*. This sense broke full in her face. "The scoundrel!"

"Not a bit!" she returned, with equal passion—"I was only too clever for him!" The thought of it was again an exaltation in which she pushed her friend aside. "So let me go!"

The push was like a jar that made the vessel overflow, and he was before her now as if he stretched across the hall. "With the heroic view of your power and the barren beauty of your sacrifice? You pour out money, you move a mountain, and to let you 'go,' to close the door fast behind you, is all I can figure out to do for you?" His emotion trembled out of him with the stammer of a new language, but it was as if in a minute or two he had thrown over all consciousness. "You're the most generous—you're the noblest of women! The wonderful chance that brought you here——!"

His own arm was grasped now—she knew better than he about the wonderful chance. "It brought *you* at the same happy hour! I've done what I liked," she went on very simply; "and the only way to thank me is to believe it."

"You've done it for a proud, poor man"—his answer was quite as direct. "He has nothing—in the light of such a magic as yours—either to give or to hope; but you've made him, in a little miraculous hour, think of you——"

He stumbled with the rush of things, and if silence can, in its way, be active, there was a collapse too, for an instant, on her closed lips. These lips, however, she at last opened. "How have I made him think of me?"

"As he has thought of no other woman!" He had personal possession of her now, and it broke, as he pressed her, as he pleaded, the helpless fall of his eloquence. "Mrs. Gracedew—don't leave me." He jerked his head passionately at the whole place and the yellow afternoon. "If you made me care——"

"It was surely that you had made *me* first!" She laughed, and her laugh disengaged her, so that before he could reply she had again put space between them.

He accepted the space now—he appeared so sure of his point. "Then let me go on caring. When I asked you a while back for some possible adjustment to my new source of credit, you simply put off the question—told me I must trust to time for it. Well," said Clement Yule, "I've trusted to time so effectually that ten little minutes have made me find it. I've found it because I've so quickly found *you*. May I, Mrs. Gracedew, keep *all* that I've found? I offer you in return the only thing I have to give—I offer you my hand and my life."

She held him off, across the hall, for a time almost out of proportion to the previous wait he had just made so little of. Then at last also, when she answered, it might have passed for a plea for further postponement, even for a plea for mercy. "Ah, Captain Yule——!" But she turned suddenly off: the flower had been nipped in the bud by the re-entrance of Chivers, at whom his master veritably glowered.

"What the devil is it?"

The old man showed the shock, but he had his duty. "Another party."

Mrs. Gracedew, at this, wheeled round. "The 'party up'!" It brought back her voice—indeed, all her gaiety. And her gaiety was always determinant. "Show them in."

Clement Yule's face fell while Chivers proceeded to obey. "You'll *have* them?" he wailed across the hall.

"Ah, mayn't I be proud of my house?" she tossed back at him.

At this, radiant, he had rushed at her. "Then you accept——?"

Her raised hand checked him. "Hush!"

He fell back—the party was there. Chivers ushered it as he had ushered the other, making the most, this time, of more scanty material—four persons so spectacled, satchelled, shawled and handbooked that they testified on the spot to a particular foreign origin and presented themselves indeed very much as tourists who, at an hotel, casting up the promise of comfort or the portent of cost, take possession, while they wait for their keys, with expert looks and free sounds. Clement Yule, who had receded, effacing himself, to the quarter opposed to that of his companion, addressed to their visitors a covert but dismayed stare and then, edging round, in his agitation, to the rear, instinctively sought relief by escape through the open passage. One of the invaders meanwhile— a broad-faced gentleman with long hair tucked behind his ears and a ring on each forefinger—had lost no time in showing he knew where to begin. He began at the top—the proper place, and took in the dark pictures ranged above the tapestry. "Olt vamily bortraits?"—he appealed to Chivers and spoke very loud.

Chivers rose to the occasion and, gracefully pawing the air, began also at the beginning. "Dame Dorothy Yule—who lived to a hundred and one."

"A hundred and one—ach *so*!" broke, with a resigned absence of criticism, from each of the interested group; another member of which, however, indicated with a somewhat fatigued skip the central figure of the series, the personage with the long white legs that Mrs. Gracedew had invited the previous inquirers to remark. "Who's dis?" the present inquirer asked.

The question affected the lovely lady over by the fireplace as the trumpet of battle affects a generous steed. She flashed on the instant into the middle of the hall and into the friendliest and most familiar relation with everyone and with everything. "John Anthony Yule, sir—who passed away, poor duck, in his flower!"

They met her with low salutations, a sweep of ugly shawls and a brush of queer German hats: she had issued, to their glazed convergence, from the dusk of the Middle Ages and the shade of high pieces, and now stood there, beautiful and human and happy, in a light that, whatever it was for themselves, the very breadth of their attention, the expression of their serious faces, converted straightway for her into a new, and oh! into the right, one. To a detached observer of the whole it would have been promptly clear that she found herself striking these good people very much as the lawful heir had, half an hour before, struck another stranger—that she produced in them, in her setting of assured antiquity, quite the romantic vibration that she had responded to in the presence of that personage. They read her as she read *him*, and a bright and deepening cheer, reflected dimly in their thick thoroughness, went out from her as she accepted their reading. An impression was exchanged, for the minute, from side to side—their grave admiration of the finest feature of the curious house and the deep free radiance of her silent, grateful "Why not?" It made a passage of some intensity and some duration, of which the effect indeed, the next minute, was to cause the only lady of the party—a matron of rich Jewish type, with small nippers on a huge nose and a face out of proportion to her little Freischütz hat—to break the spell by an uneasy turn and a stray glance at one of the other pictures. "Who's *dat*?"

"That?" The picture chanced to be a portrait over the wide arch, and something happened, at the very moment, to arrest Mrs. Gracedew's eyes rather above than below. What took place, in a word, was that Clement Yule, already fidgetting in his impatience back from the front, just occupied the arch, completed her thought and filled her vision. "Oh, that's my future husband!" He caught the words, but answered them only by a long look at her as he moved, with a checked wildness of which she alone, of all the spectators, had a sense, straight across the hall again and to the other opening. He paused there as he had done before, then with a last dumb appeal to her dropped into the court and passed into the garden. Mrs. Gracedew, already so wonderful to their visitors, was, before she followed him, wonderful with a greater wonder to poor Chivers. "You dear old thing—I give it all back to you!"

In the Cage

IT HAD occurred to her early that in her position—that of a young person spending, in framed and wired confinement, the life of a guinea-pig or a magpie—she should know a great many persons without their recognising the acquaintance. That made it an emotion the more lively—though singularly rare and always, even then, with opportunity still very much smothered—to see any one come in whom she knew, as she called it, outside, and who could add something to the poor identity of her function. Her function was to sit there with two young men—the other telegraphist and the counter-clerk; to mind the "sounder," which was always going, to dole out stamps and postal-orders, weigh letters, answer stupid questions, give difficult change and, more than anything else, count words as numberless as the sands of the sea, the words of the telegrams thrust, from morning to night, through the gap left in the high lattice, across the encumbered shelf that her forearm ached with rubbing. This transparent screen fenced out or fenced in, according to the side of the narrow counter on which the human lot was cast, the duskiest corner of a shop pervaded not a little, in winter, by the poison of perpetual gas, and at all times by the presence of hams, cheese, dried fish, soap, varnish, paraffin, and other solids and fluids that she came to know perfectly by their smells without consenting to know them by their names.

The barrier that divided the little post-and-telegraph-office from the grocery was a frail structure of wood and wire; but the social, the professional separation was a gulf that fortune, by a stroke quite remarkable, had spared her the necessity of contributing at all publicly to bridge. When Mr. Cocker's young men stepped over from behind the other counter to change a five-pound note—and Mr. Cocker's situation, with the cream of the "Court Guide" and the dearest furnished apartments, Simpkin's, Ladle's, Thrupp's, just round the corner, was so select that his place was quite pervaded by the crisp rustle of these emblems—she pushed out the sovereigns as if the applicant were no more to her than one of the momentary appearances in the great procession; and this perhaps all the more from the very fact of the connection—only recognised outside indeed—to which she had lent herself with ridiculous inconsequence. She recognised the others the less because she had at last so unreservedly, so irredeemably, recognised Mr. Mudge. But she was a little ashamed, none the less, of having to admit to herself that Mr. Mudge's removal to a higher sphere—to a more commanding position, that is, though to a much lower neighbourhood—would have been described still better as a luxury than as the simplification that she contented herself with calling it. He had, at any rate, ceased to be all day long in her eyes, and this left something a little fresh for them to rest on of a Sunday. During the three months that he had remained at Cocker's after her consent to their engagement, she had often asked herself what it was that marriage would be able to add to a familiarity so final. Opposite there, behind the counter of which his superior stature, his whiter apron, his more clustering curls and more present, too present, h's had been for a couple of years the principal ornament, he had moved to and fro before her as on the small sanded floor of their contracted future. She was conscious now of the improvement of not having to take her present and her future at once. They were about as much as she could manage when taken separate.

She had, none the less, to give her mind steadily to what Mr. Mudge had again written her about, the idea of her applying for a transfer to an office quite similar—she couldn't yet hope for a place in a bigger—under the very roof where he was foreman, so that, dangled before her every minute of the day, he should see her, as he called it, "hourly," and in a part, the far N.W. district, where, with her mother, she would save, on their two rooms alone, nearly three shillings. It would be far from dazzling to exchange Mayfair for Chalk Farm, and it was something of a predicament that he so kept at her; still, it was nothing to the old predicaments, those of the early times of their great misery, her own, her mother's, and her elder sister's—the last of whom had succumbed to all but absolute want when, as conscious, incredulous ladies, suddenly bereaved, betrayed, overwhelmed, they had slipped faster and faster down the steep slope at the bottom of which she alone had rebounded. Her mother had never rebounded any more at the bottom than on the way; had only rumbled and grumbled down and down, making, in respect of caps and conversation, no effort whatever, and too often, alas! smelling of whisky.

II

It was always rather quiet at Cocker's while the contingent from Ladle's and Thrupp's and all the other great places were at luncheon, or, as the young men used vulgarly to say, while the animals were feeding. She had forty minutes in advance of this to go home for her own dinner; and when she came back, and one of the young men took his turn, there was often half an hour during which she could pull out a bit of work or a book—a book from the place where she borrowed novels, very greasy, in fine print and all about fine folks, at a ha'penny a day. This sacred pause was one of the numerous ways in which the establishment kept its finger on the pulse of fashion and fell into the rhythm of the larger life. It had something to do, one day, with the particular vividness marking the advent of a lady whose meals were apparently irregular, yet whom she was destined, she afterwards found, not to forget. The girl was *blasée*; nothing could belong more, as she perfectly knew, to the intense publicity of her profession; but she had a whimsical mind and wonderful nerves; she was subject, in short, to sudden flickers of antipathy and sympathy, red gleams in the grey, fitful awakings and followings, odd caprices of curiosity. She had a friend who had invented a new career for women—that of being in and out of people's houses to look after the flowers. Mrs. Jordan had a manner of her own of sounding this allusion; "the flowers," on her lips, were, in happy homes, as usual as the coals or the daily papers. She took charge of them, at any rate, in all the rooms, at so much a month, and people were quickly finding out what it was to make over this delicate duty to the widow of a clergyman. The widow, on her side, dilating on the initiations thus opened up to her, had been splendid to her young friend over the way she was made free of the greatest houses—the way, especially when she did the dinner-tables, set out so often for twenty, she felt that a single step more would socially, would absolutely, introduce her. On its being asked of her, then, if she circulated only in a sort of tropical solitude, with the upper servants for picturesque natives, and on her having to assent to this glance at her limitations, she had found a reply to the girl's invidious question. "You've no imagination, my dear!"—that was because the social door might at any moment open so wide.

Our young lady had not taken up the charge, had dealt with it good-humouredly, just because she knew so well what to think of it. It was at once one of her most cherished complaints and most secret supports that people didn't understand her, and it was accordingly a matter of indifference to her that Mrs. Jordan shouldn't; even though Mrs. Jordan, handed down from their early twilight of gentility and also the victim of reverses, was the only member of her circle in whom she recognised an equal. She was perfectly aware that her imaginative life was the life in which she spent most of her time; and she would have been ready, had it been at all worth while, to contend that, since her outward occupation didn't kill it, it must be strong indeed. Combinations of flowers and greenstuff, forsooth! What *she* could handle freely, she said to herself, was combinations of men and women. The only weakness in her faculty came from the positive abundance of her contact with the human herd; this was so constant, had the effect of becoming so cheap, that there were long stretches in which inspiration, divination and interest, quite dropped. The great thing was the flashes, the quick revivals, absolute accidents all, and neither to be counted on nor to be resisted. Some one had only sometimes to put in a penny for a stamp, and the whole thing was upon her. She was so absurdly constructed that these were literally the moments that made up—made up for the long stiffness of sitting there in the stocks, made up for the cunning hostility of Mr. Buckton and the importunate sympathy of the counter-clerk, made up for the daily, deadly, flourishy letter from Mr. Mudge, made up even for the most haunting of her worries, the rage at moments of not knowing how her mother did "get it."

She had surrendered herself moreover, of late, to a certain expansion of her consciousness; something that seemed perhaps vulgarly accounted for by the fact that, as the blast of the season roared louder and the waves of fashion tossed their spray further over the counter, there were more impressions to be gathered and really—for it came to that—more life to be led. Definite, at any rate, it was that by the time May was well started the kind of company she kept at Cocker's had begun to strike her as a reason—a reason she might almost put forward for a policy of procrastination. It sounded silly, of course, as yet, to plead such a motive, especially as the fascination of the place was, after all, a sort of torment. But she liked her torment; it was a torment she should miss at Chalk Farm. She was ingenious and uncandid, therefore, about leaving the breadth of London a little longer between herself and that austerity. If she had not quite the courage, in short, to say to Mr. Mudge that her actual chance for a play of mind was worth, any week, the three shillings he desired to help her to save, she yet saw something happen in the course of the month that, in her heart of hearts at least, answered the subtle question. This was connected precisely with the appearance of the memorable lady.

III

She pushed in three bescribbled forms which the girl's hand was quick to appropriate, Mr. Buckton having so frequent a perverse instinct for catching first any eye that promised the sort of entertainment with which she had her peculiar affinity. The amusements of captives are full of a desperate contrivance, and one of our young friend's ha'pennyworths had been the charming tale of *Picciola*. It was of course the law of the place that they were never to take no notice, as Mr. Buckton said, whom they served; but this also never prevented, certainly on the same gentleman's own part, what he was fond of describing as the underhand game. Both her companions, for that matter, made no secret of the number of favourites they had among the ladies; sweet familiarities in spite of which she had repeatedly caught each of them in stupidities and mistakes, confusions of identity and lapses of observation that never failed to remind her how the cleverness of men ended where the cleverness of women began. "Marguerite, Regent

Street. Try on at six. All Spanish lace. Pearls. The full length."
That was the first; it had no signature. "Lady Agnes Orme,
Hyde Park Place. Impossible to-night, dining Haddon. Opera
to-morrow, promised Fritz, but could do play Wednesday.
Will try Haddon for Savoy, and anything in the world you
like, if you can get Gussy. Sunday, Montenero. Sit Mason
Monday, Tuesday. Marguerite awful. Cissy." That was the second. The third, the girl noted when she took it, was on a
foreign form: "Everard, Hôtel Brighton, Paris. Only understand and believe. 22nd to 26th, and certainly 8th and 9th.
Perhaps others. Come. Mary."

Mary was very handsome, the handsomest woman, she felt
in a moment, she had ever seen—or perhaps it was only Cissy.
Perhaps it was both, for she had seen stranger things than
that—ladies wiring to different persons under different names.
She had seen all sorts of things and pieced together all sorts
of mysteries. There had once been one—not long before—
who, without winking, sent off five over five different signatures. Perhaps these represented five different friends who had
asked her—all women, just as perhaps now Mary and Cissy,
or one or other of them, were wiring by deputy. Sometimes
she put in too much—too much of her own sense; sometimes
she put in too little; and in either case this often came round
to her afterwards, for she had an extraordinary way of keeping
clues. When she noticed, she noticed; that was what it came
to. There were days and days, there were weeks sometimes,
of vacancy. This arose often from Mr. Buckton's devilish and
successful subterfuges for keeping her at the sounder whenever it looked as if anything might amuse; the sounder, which
it was equally his business to mind, being the innermost cell
of captivity, a cage within the cage, fenced off from the rest
by a frame of ground glass. The counter-clerk would have
played into her hands; but the counter-clerk was really reduced to idiocy by the effect of his passion for her. She flattered herself moreover, nobly, that with the unpleasant
conspicuity of this passion she would never have consented to
be obliged to him. The most she would ever do would be
always to shove off on him whenever she could the registra-
tion of letters, a job she happened particularly to loathe. After
the long stupors, at all events, there almost always suddenly

would come a sharp taste of something; it was in her mouth before she knew it; it was in her mouth now.

To Cissy, to Mary, whichever it was, she found her curiosity going out with a rush, a mute effusion that floated back to her, like a returning tide, the living colour and splendour of the beautiful head, the light of eyes that seemed to reflect such utterly other things than the mean things actually before them; and, above all, the high, curt consideration of a manner that, even at bad moments, was a magnificent habit and of the very essence of the innumerable things—her beauty, her birth, her father and mother, her cousins, and all her ancestors—that its possessor couldn't have got rid of if she had wished. How did our obscure little public servant know that, for the lady of the telegrams, this was a bad moment? How did she guess all sorts of impossible things, such as, almost on the very spot, the presence of drama, at a critical stage, and the nature of the tie with the gentleman at the Hôtel Brighton? More than ever before it floated to her through the bars of the cage that this at last was the high reality, the bristling truth that she had hitherto only patched up and eked out— one of the creatures, in fine, in whom all the conditions for happiness actually met, and who, in the air they made, bloomed with an unwitting insolence. What came home to the girl was the way the insolence was tempered by something that was equally a part of the distinguished life, the custom of a flowerlike bend to the less fortunate—a dropped fragrance, a mere quick breath, but which in fact pervaded and lingered. The apparition was very young, but certainly married, and our fatigued friend had a sufficient store of mythological comparison to recognise the port of Juno. Marguerite might be "awful," but she knew how to dress a goddess.

Pearls and Spanish lace—she herself, with assurance, could see them, and the "full length" too, and also red velvet bows, which, disposed on the lace in a particular manner (she could have placed them with the turn of a hand), were of course to adorn the front of a black brocade that would be like a dress in a picture. However, neither Marguerite, nor Lady Agnes, nor Haddon, nor Fritz, nor Gussy was what the wearer of this garment had really come in for. She had come in for Everard—and that was doubtless not *his* true name either. If our

young lady had never taken such jumps before, it was simply
that she had never before been so affected. She went all the
way. Mary and Cissy had been round together, in their single
superb person, to see him—he must live round the corner;
they had found that, in consequence of something they had
come, precisely, to make up for or to have another scene
about, he had gone off—gone off just on purpose to make
them feel it; on which they had come together to Cocker's as
to the nearest place; where they had put in the three forms
partly in order not to put in the one alone. The two others,
in a manner, covered it, muffled it, passed it off. Oh yes, she
went all the way, and this was a specimen of how she often
went. She would know the hand again any time. It was as
handsome and as everything else as the woman herself. The
woman herself had, on learning his flight, pushed past Everard's servant and into his room; she had written her missive
at his table and with his pen. All this, every inch of it, came
in the waft that she blew through and left behind her, the
influence that, as I have said, lingered. And among the things
the girl was sure of, happily, was that she should see her again.

IV

She saw her, in fact, and only ten days later; but this time she
was not alone, and that was exactly a part of the luck of it.
Being clever enough to know through what possibilities it
could range, our young lady had ever since had in her mind
a dozen conflicting theories about Everard's type; as to which,
the instant they came into the place, she felt the point settled
with a thump that seemed somehow addressed straight to her
heart. That organ literally beat faster at the approach of the
gentleman who was this time with Cissy, and who, as seen
from within the cage, became on the spot the happiest of the
happy circumstances with which her mind had invested the
friend of Fritz and Gussy. He was a very happy circumstance
indeed as, with his cigarette in his lips and his broken familiar
talk caught by his companion, he put down the half-dozen
telegrams which it would take them together some minutes
to despatch. And here it occurred, oddly enough, that if,
shortly before, the girl's interest in his companion had sharp-

ened her sense for the messages then transmitted, her immediate vision of himself had the effect, while she counted his
seventy words, of preventing intelligibility. *His* words were
mere numbers, they told her nothing whatever; and after he
had gone she was in possession of no name, of no address, of
no meaning, of nothing but a vague, sweet sound and an
immense impression. He had been there but five minutes, he
had smoked in her face, and, busy with his telegrams, with
the tapping pencil and the conscious danger, the odious betrayal that would come from a mistake, she had had no wandering glances nor roundabout arts to spare. Yet she had taken
him in; she knew everything; she had made up her mind.

He had come back from Paris; everything was re-arranged;
the pair were again shoulder to shoulder in their high encounter with life, their large and complicated game. The fine,
soundless pulse of this game was in the air for our young
woman while they remained in the shop. While they remained? They remained all day; their presence continued and
abode with her, was in everything she did till nightfall, in the
thousands of other words she counted, she transmitted, in all
the stamps she detached and the letters she weighed and the
change she gave, equally unconscious and unerring in each of
these particulars, and not, as the run on the little office thickened with the afternoon hours, looking up at a single ugly
face in the long sequence, nor really hearing the stupid questions that she patiently and perfectly answered. All patience
was possible now, and all questions stupid after his—all faces
ugly. She had been sure she should see the lady again; and
even now she should perhaps, she should probably, see her
often. But for him it was totally different; she should never,
never see him. She wanted it too much. There was a kind of
wanting that helped—she had arrived, with her rich experience, at that generalisation; and there was another kind that
was fatal. It was this time the fatal kind; it would prevent.

Well, she saw him the very next day, and on this second
occasion it was quite different; the sense of every syllable he
despatched was fiercely distinct; she indeed felt her progressive
pencil, dabbing as if with a quick caress the marks of his own,
put life into every stroke. He was there a long time—had not
brought his forms filled out, but worked them off in a nook

on the counter; and there were other people as well—a changing, pushing cluster, with every one to mind at once and
endless right change to make and information to produce.
But she kept hold of him throughout; she continued, for herself, in a relation with him as close as that in which, behind
the hated ground glass, Mr. Buckton luckily continued with
the sounder. This morning everything changed, but with a
kind of dreariness too; she had to swallow the rebuff to her
theory about fatal desires, which she did without confusion
and indeed with absolute levity; yet if it was now flagrant that
he did live close at hand—at Park Chambers—and belonged
supremely to the class that wired everything, even their expensive feelings (so that, as he never wrote, his correspondence cost him weekly pounds and pounds, and he might be
in and out five times a day), there was, all the same, involved
in the prospect, and by reason of its positive excess of light,
a perverse melancholy, almost a misery. This was rapidly to
give it a place in an order of feelings on which I shall presently
touch.

Meanwhile, for a month, he was very constant. Cissy, Mary,
never re-appeared with him; he was always either alone or
accompanied only by some gentleman who was lost in the
blaze of his glory. There was another sense, however—and
indeed there was more than one—in which she mostly found
herself counting in the splendid creature with whom she had
originally connected him. He addressed this correspondent
neither as Mary nor as Cissy; but the girl was sure of whom
it was, in Eaton Square, that he was perpetually wiring to—
and so irreproachably!—as Lady Bradeen. Lady Bradeen was
Cissy, Lady Bradeen was Mary, Lady Bradeen was the friend
of Fritz and of Gussy, the customer of Marguerite, and the
close ally, in short (as was ideally right, only the girl had not
yet found a descriptive term that was), of the most magnificent of men. Nothing could equal the frequency and variety
of his communications to her ladyship but their extraordinary,
their abysmal propriety. It was just the talk—so profuse sometimes that she wondered what was left for their real meetings—of the happiest people in the world. Their real meetings
must have been constant, for half of it was appointments and
allusions, all swimming in a sea of other allusions still, tangled

in a complexity of questions that gave a wondrous image of their life. If Lady Bradeen was Juno, it was all certainly Olympian. If the girl, missing the answers, her ladyship's own outpourings, sometimes wished that Cocker's had only been one of the bigger offices where telegrams arrived as well as departed, there were yet ways in which, on the whole, she pressed the romance closer by reason of the very quantity of imagination that it demanded. The days and hours of this new friend, as she came to account him, were at all events unrolled, and however much more she might have known she would still have wished to go beyond. In fact she did go beyond; she went quite far enough.

But she could none the less, even after a month, scarce have told if the gentlemen who came in with him recurred or changed; and this in spite of the fact that they too were always posting and wiring, smoking in her face and signing or not signing. The gentlemen who came in with him were nothing, at any rate, when he was there. They turned up alone at other times—then only perhaps with a dim richness of reference. He himself, absent as well as present, was all. He was very tall, very fair, and had, in spite of his thick pre-occupations, a good-humour that was exquisite, particularly as it so often had the effect of keeping him on. He could have reached over anybody, and anybody—no matter who—would have let him; but he was so extraordinarily kind that he quite pathetically waited, never waggling things at her out of his turn or saying "Here!" with horrid sharpness. He waited for pottering old ladies, for gaping slaveys, for the perpetual Buttonses from Thrupp's; and the thing in all this that she would have liked most unspeakably to put to the test was the possibility of her having for him a personal identity that might in a particular way appeal. There were moments when he actually struck her as on her side, arranging to help, to support, to spare her.

But such was the singular spirit of our young friend, that she could remind herself with a sort of rage that when people had awfully good manners—people of that class,—you couldn't tell. These manners were for everybody, and it might be drearily unavailing for any poor particular body to be over-worked and unusual. What he did take for granted was all sorts of facility; and his high pleasantness, his relighting of cigarettes while he waited, his unconscious bestowal of opportunities, of boons, of blessings, were all a part of his magnificent security, the instinct that told him there was nothing such an existence as his could ever lose by. He was, somehow, at once very bright and very grave, very young and immensely complete; and whatever he was at any moment, it was always as much as all the rest the mere bloom of his beatitude. He was sometimes Everard, as he had been at the Hôtel Brighton, and he was sometimes Captain Everard. He was sometimes Philip with his surname and sometimes Philip without it. In some directions he was merely Phil, in others he was merely Captain. There were relations in which he was none of these things, but a quite different person—"the Count." There were several friends for whom he was William. There were several for whom, in allusion perhaps to his complexion, he was "the Pink 'Un." Once, once only by good luck, he had, coinciding comically, quite miraculously, with another person also near to her, been "Mudge." Yes, whatever he was, it was a part of his happiness—whatever he was and probably whatever he wasn't. And his happiness was a part—it became so little by little—of something that, almost from the first of her being at Cocker's, had been deeply with the girl.

V

This was neither more nor less than the queer extension of her experience, the double life that, in the cage, she grew at last to lead. As the weeks went on there she lived more and more into the world of whiffs and glimpses, and found her divinations work faster and stretch further. It was a prodigious view as the pressure heightened, a panorama fed with facts and figures, flushed with a torrent of colour and accompanied with wondrous world-music. What it mainly came to at this period was a picture of how London could amuse itself; and that, with the running commentary of a witness so exclusively a witness, turned for the most part to a hardening of the heart. The nose of this observer was brushed by the bouquet, yet she could never really pluck even a daisy. What could still remain fresh in her daily grind was the immense disparity, the difference and contrast, from class to class, of every instant and every motion. There were times when all the wires in the country seemed to start from the little hole-and-corner where she plied for a livelihood, and where, in the shuffle of feet, the flutter of "forms," the straying of stamps and the ring of change over the counter, the people she had fallen into the habit of remembering and fitting together with others, and of having her theories and interpretations of, kept up before her their long procession and rotation. What twisted the knife in her vitals was the way the profligate rich scattered about them, in extravagant chatter over their extravagant pleasures and sins, an amount of money that would have held the stricken household of her frightened childhood, her poor pinched mother and tormented father and lost brother and starved sister, together for a lifetime. During her first weeks she had often gasped at the sums people were willing to pay for the stuff they transmitted—the "much love"s, the "awful" regrets, the compliments and wonderments and vain, vague gestures that cost the price of a new pair of boots. She had had a way then of glancing at the people's faces, but she had early learned that if you became a telegraphist you soon ceased to be astonished. Her eye for types amounted nevertheless to genius, and there were those she liked and those she hated, her feeling for the latter of which grew to a positive possession, an instinct of observation and detection. There were the brazen women, as she called them, of the higher and the lower fashion, whose squanderings and graspings, whose struggles and secrets and love-affairs and lies, she tracked and stored up against them, till she had at moments, in private, a triumphant, vicious feeling of mastery and power, a sense of having their silly, guilty secrets in her pocket, her small retentive brain, and thereby knowing so much more about them than they suspected or would care to think. There were those she would have liked to betray, to trip up, to bring down with words altered and fatal; and all through a personal hostility provoked by the lightest signs, by their accidents of tone and manner, by the particular kind of relation she always happened instantly to feel.

There were impulses of various kinds, alternately soft and severe, to which she was constitutionally accessible and which were determined by the smallest accidents. She was rigid, in

general, on the article of making the public itself affix its
stamps, and found a special enjoyment in dealing, to that end,
with some of the ladies who were too grand to touch them.
She had thus a play of refinement and subtlety greater, she
flattered herself, than any of which she could be made the
subject; and though most people were too stupid to be conscious of this, it brought her endless little consolations and
revenges. She recognised quite as much those of her sex
whom she would have liked to help, to warn, to rescue, to
see more of; and that alternative as well operated exactly
through the hazard of personal sympathy, her vision for silver
threads and moonbeams and her gift for keeping the clues
and finding her way in the tangle. The moonbeams and silver
threads presented at moments all the vision of what poor *she*
might have made of happiness. Blurred and blank as the whole
thing often inevitably, or mercifully, became, she could still,
through crevices and crannies, be stupefied, especially by
what, in spite of all seasoning, touched the sorest place in her
consciousness, the revelation of the golden shower flying
about without a gleam of gold for herself. It remained prodigious to the end, the money her fine friends were able to
spend to get still more, or even to complain to fine friends of
their own that they were in want. The pleasures they proposed
were equalled only by those they declined, and they made
their appointments often so expensively that she was left wondering at the nature of the delights to which the mere approaches were so paved with shillings. She quivered on
occasion into the perception of this and that one whom she
would, at all events, have just simply liked to *be*. Her conceit,
her baffled vanity were possibly monstrous; she certainly often
threw herself into a defiant conviction that she would have
done the whole thing much better. But her greatest comfort,
on the whole, was her comparative vision of the men; by
whom I mean the unmistakable gentlemen, for she had no
interest in the spurious or the shabby, and no mercy at all for
the poor. She could have found a sixpence, outside, for an
appearance of want; but her fancy, in some directions so alert,
had never a throb of response for any sign of the sordid. The
men she did follow, moreover, she followed mainly in one
relation, the relation as to which the cage convinced her, she

believed, more than anything else could have done, that it was quite the most diffused.

She found her ladies, in short, almost always in communication with her gentlemen, and her gentlemen with her ladies, and she read into the immensity of their intercourse stories and meanings without end. Incontestably she grew to think that the men cut the best figure; and in this particular, as in many others, she arrived at a philosophy of her own, all made up of her private notations and cynicisms. It was a striking part of the business, for example, that it was much more the women, on the whole, who were after the men than the men who were after the women: it was literally visible that the general attitude of the one sex was that of the object pursued and defensive, apologetic and attenuating, while the light of her own nature helped her more or less to conclude as to the attitude of the other. Perhaps she herself a little even fell into the custom of pursuit in occasionally deviating only for gentlemen from her high rigour about the stamps. She had early in the day made up her mind, in fine, that they had the best manners; and if there were none of them she noticed when Captain Everard was there, there were plenty she could place and trace and name at other times, plenty who, with their way of being "nice" to her, and of handling, as if their pockets were private tills, loose, mixed masses of silver and gold, were such pleasant appearances that she could envy them without dislike. *They* never had to give change—they only had to get it. They ranged through every suggestion, every shade of fortune, which evidently included indeed lots of bad luck as well as of good, declining even toward Mr. Mudge and his bland, firm thrift, and ascending, in wild signals and rocket-flights, almost to within hail of her highest standard. So, from month to month, she went on with them all, through a thousand ups and downs and a thousand pangs and indifferences. What virtually happened was that in the shuffling herd that passed before her by far the greater part only passed—a proportion but just appreciable stayed. Most of the elements swam straight away, lost themselves in the bottomless common, and by so doing really kept the page clear. On the clearness, therefore, what she did retain stood sharply out; she nipped and caught it, turned it over and interwove it.

VI

She met Mrs. Jordan whenever she could, and learned from her more and more how the great people, under her gentle shake, and after going through everything with the mere shops, were waking up to the gain of putting into the hands of a person of real refinement the question that the shop-people spoke of so vulgarly as that of the floral decorations. The regular dealers in these decorations were all very well; but there was a peculiar magic in the play of taste of a lady who had only to remember, through whatever intervening dusk, all her own little tables, little bowls and little jars and little other arrangements, and the wonderful thing she had made of the garden of the vicarage. This small domain, which her young friend had never seen, bloomed in Mrs. Jordan's discourse like a new Eden, and she converted the past into a bank of violets by the tone in which she said, "Of course you always knew my one passion!" She obviously met now, at any rate, a big contemporary need, measured what it was rapidly becoming for people to feel they could trust her without a tremor. It brought them a peace that—during the quarter of an hour before dinner in especial—was worth more to them than mere payment could express. Mere payment, none the less, was tolerably prompt; she engaged by the month, taking over the whole thing; and there was an evening on which, in respect to our heroine, she at last returned to the charge. "It's growing and growing, and I see that I must really divide the work. One wants an associate—of one's own kind, don't you know? You know the look they want it all to have?—of having come, not from a florist, but from one of themselves. Well, I'm sure *you* could give it—because you *are* one. Then we *should* win. Therefore just come in with me."

"And leave the P.O.?"

"Let the P.O. simply bring you your letters. It would bring you lots, you'd see: orders, after a bit, by the dozen." It was on this, in due course, that the great advantage again came up: "One seems to live again with one's own people." It had taken some little time (after their having parted company in the tempest of their troubles and then, in the glimmering dawn, finally sighted each other again) for each to admit that the other was, in her private circle, her only equal; but the admission came, when it did come, with an honest groan; and since equality *was* named, each found much personal profit in exaggerating the other's original grandeur. Mrs. Jordan was ten years the older, but her young friend was struck with the smaller difference this now made: it had counted otherwise at the time when, much more as a friend of her mother's, the bereaved lady, without a penny of provision, and with stop-gaps, like their own, all gone, had, across the sordid landing on which the opposite doors of the pair of scared miseries opened and to which they were bewilderedly bolted, bor-rowed coals and umbrellas that were repaid in potatoes and postage-stamps. It had been a questionable help, at that time, to ladies submerged, floundering, panting, swimming for their lives, that they *were* ladies; but such an advantage could come up again in proportion as others vanished, and it had grown very great by the time it was the only ghost of one they pos-sessed. They had literally watched it take to itself a portion of the substance of each that had departed; and it became pro-digious now, when they could talk of it together, when they could look back at it across a desert of accepted derogation, and when, above all, they could draw from each other a cre-dulity about it that they could draw from no one else. Noth-ing was really so marked as that they felt the need to cultivate this legend much more after having found their feet and stayed their stomachs in the ultimate obscure than they had done in the upper air of mere frequent shocks. The thing they could now oftenest say to each other was that they knew what they meant; and the sentiment with which, all round, they knew it was known had been a kind of promise to stick well together again

Mrs. Jordan was at present fairly dazzling on the subject of the way that, in the practice of her beautiful art, she more than peeped in—she penetrated. There was not a house of the great kind—and it was, of course, only a question of those, real homes of luxury—in which she was not, at the rate such people now had things, all over the place. The girl felt before the picture the cold breath of disinheritance as much as she had ever felt it in the cage; she knew, moreover, how much she betrayed this, for the experience of poverty had begun, in her life, too early, and her ignorance of the requirements of homes of luxury had grown, with other active knowledge, a depth of simplification. She had accordingly at first often found that in these colloquies she could only pretend she understood. Educated as she had rapidly been by her chances at Cocker's, there were still strange gaps in her learning—she could never, like Mrs. Jordan, have found her way about one of the "homes." Little by little, however, she had caught on, above all in the light of what Mrs. Jordan's redemption had materially made of that lady, giving her, though the years and the struggles had naturally not straightened a feature, an almost super-eminent air. There were women in and out of Cocker's who were quite nice and who yet didn't look well; whereas Mrs. Jordan looked well and yet, with her extraordinarily protrusive teeth, was by no means quite nice. It would seem, mystifyingly, that it might really come from all the greatness she could live with. It was fine to hear her talk so often of dinners of twenty and of her doing, as she said, exactly as she liked with them. She spoke as if, for that matter, she invited the company. "They simply *give* me the table—all the rest, all the other effects, come afterwards."

VII

"Then you *do* see them?" the girl again asked.

Mrs. Jordan hesitated, and indeed the point had been ambiguous before. "Do you mean the guests?"

Her young friend, cautious about an undue exposure of innocence, was not quite sure. "Well—the people who live there."

"Lady Ventnor? Mrs. Bubb? Lord Rye? Dear, yes. Why, they *like* one."

"But does one personally *know* them?" our young lady went on, since that was the way to speak. "I mean socially, don't you know?—as you know *me*."

"They're not so nice as you!" Mrs. Jordan charmingly cried. "But I *shall* see more and more of them."

Ah, this was the old story. "But how soon?"

"Why, almost any day. Of course," Mrs. Jordan honestly added, "they're nearly always out."

"Then why do they want flowers all over?"

"Oh, that doesn't make any difference." Mrs. Jordan was not philosophic; she was only evidently determined it shouldn't make any. "They're awfully interested in my ideas, and it's inevitable they should meet me over them."

Her interlocutress was sturdy enough. "What do you call your ideas?"

Mrs. Jordan's reply was fine. "If you were to see me some day with a thousand tulips, you'd soon discover."

"A thousand?"—the girl gaped at such a revelation of the scale of it; she felt, for the instant, fairly planted out. "Well, but if in fact they never do meet you?" she none the less pessimistically insisted.

"Never? They *often* do—and evidently quite on purpose. We have grand long talks."

There was something in our young lady that could still stay her from asking for a personal description of these apparitions; that showed too starved a state. But while she considered, she took in afresh the whole of the clergyman's widow. Mrs. Jordan couldn't help her teeth, and her sleeves were a distinct rise in the world. A thousand tulips at a shilling clearly took one further than a thousand words at a penny; and the betrothed of Mr. Mudge, in whom the sense of the race for life was always acute, found herself wondering, with a twinge of her easy jealousy, if it mightn't after all then, for *her* also, be better—better than where she was—to follow some such scent. Where she was was where Mr. Buckton's elbow could freely enter her right side and the counter-clerk's breathing—he had something the matter with his nose—pervade her left ear. It was something to fill an office under Government, and she knew but too well there were places commoner still than Cocker's; but it never required much of a chance to bring back to her the picture of servitude and promiscuity that she must present to the eye of comparative freedom. She was so boxed up with her young men, and anything like a margin so absent, that it needed more art than she should ever possess to pretend in the least to compass, with any one in the nature of an acquaintance— say with Mrs. Jordan herself, flying in, as it might happen, to wire sympathetically to Mrs. Bubb—an approach to a relation of elegant privacy. She remembered the day when Mrs. Jordan *had*, in fact, by the greatest chance, come in with fifty-three words for Lord Rye and a five-pound note to change. This had been the dramatic manner of their reunion—their mutual recognition was so great an event. The girl could at first only see her from the waist up, besides making but little of her long telegram to his lordship. It was a strange whirligig that had converted the clergyman's widow into such a specimen of the class that went beyond the sixpence.

Nothing of the occasion, all the more, had ever become dim; least of all the way that, as her recovered friend looked up from counting, Mrs. Jordan had just blown, in explanation, through her teeth and through the bars of the cage: "I *do* flowers, you know." Our young woman had always, with her little finger crooked out, a pretty movement for counting; and she had not forgotten the small secret advantage, a sharpness of triumph it might even have been called, that fell upon her at this moment and avenged her for the incoherence of the message, an unintelligible enumeration of numbers, colours, days, hours. The correspondence of people she didn't know was one thing; but the correspondence of people she did had an aspect of its own for her, even when she couldn't understand it. The speech in which Mrs. Jordan had defined a position and announced a profession was like a tinkle of bluebells; but, for herself, her one idea about flowers was that people had them at funerals, and her present sole gleam of light was that lords probably had them most. When she watched, a minute later, through the cage, the swing of her visitor's departing petticoats, she saw the sight from the waist down; and when the counter-clerk, after a mere male glance, remarked, with an intention unmistakably low, "Handsome woman!" she had for him the finest of her chills: "She's the widow of a bishop." She always felt, with the counter-clerk, that it was impossible sufficiently to put it on; for what she wished to express to him was the maximum of her contempt, and that element in her nature was confusedly stored. "A bishop" *was* putting it on, but the counter-clerk's approaches were vile. The night, after this, when, in the fulness of time, Mrs. Jordan mentioned the grand long talks, the girl at last brought out: "Should *I* see them?—I mean if I *were* to give up everything for you."

Mrs. Jordan at this became most arch. "I'd send you to all the bachelors!"

Our young lady could be reminded by such a remark that she usually struck her friend as pretty. "Do *they* have their flowers?"

"Oceans. And they're the most particular." Oh, it was a wonderful world. "You should see Lord Rye's."

"His flowers?"

"Yes, and his letters. He writes me pages on pages—with the most adorable little drawings and plans. You should see his diagrams!"

VIII

The girl had in course of time every opportunity to inspect these documents, and they a little disappointed her; but in the meanwhile there had been more talk, and it had led to her saying, as if her friend's guarantee of a life of elegance were not quite definite: "Well, I see every one at *my* place."

"Every one?"

"Lots of swells. They flock. They live, you know, all round, and the place is filled with all the smart people, all the fast people, those whose names are in the papers—mamma has still the *Morning Post*—and who come up for the season."

Mrs. Jordan took this in with complete intelligence. "Yes, and I dare say it's some of your people that *I* do."

Her companion assented, but discriminated. "I doubt if you 'do' them as much as I! Their affairs, their appointments and arrangements, their little games and secrets and vices— those things all pass before me."

This was a picture that could impose on a clergyman's widow a certain strain; it was in intention, moreover, something of a retort to the thousand tulips. "Their vices? Have they got vices?"

Our young critic even more remarkably stared; then with a touch of contempt in her amusement: "Haven't you found *that* out?" The homes of luxury, then, hadn't so much to give. "*I* find out everything," she continued.

Mrs. Jordan, at bottom a very meek person, was visibly struck. "I see. You do 'have' them."

"Oh, I don't care! Much good does it do me!"

Mrs. Jordan, after an instant, recovered her superiority. "No—it doesn't lead to much." Her own initiations so clearly did. Still—after all; and she was not jealous: "There must be a charm."

"In seeing them?" At this the girl suddenly let herself go. "I hate them; there's that charm!"

Mrs. Jordan gaped again. "The *real* 'smarts'?"

"Is that what you call Mrs. Bubb? Yes—it comes to me; I've had Mrs. Bubb. I don't think she has been in herself, but there are things her maid has brought. Well, my dear!"—and the young person from Cocker's, recalling these things and summing them up, seemed suddenly to have much to say. But she didn't say it; she checked it; she only brought out: "Her maid, who's horrid—*she* must have her!" Then she went on with indifference: "They're *too* real! They're selfish brutes."

Mrs. Jordan, turning it over, adopted at last the plan of treating it with a smile. She wished to be liberal. "Well, of course, they do lay it out."

"They bore me to death," her companion pursued with slightly more temperance.

But this was going too far. "Ah, that's because you've no sympathy!"

The girl gave an ironic laugh, only retorting that she wouldn't have any either if she had to count all day all the words in the dictionary; a contention Mrs. Jordan quite granted, the more that she shuddered at the notion of ever failing of the very gift to which she owed the vogue—the rage she might call it—that had caught her up. Without sympathy—or without imagination, for it came back again to that—how should she get, for big dinners, down the middle and toward the far corners at all? It wasn't the combinations, which were easily managed: the strain was over the ineffable simplicities, those that the bachelors above all, and Lord Rye perhaps most of any, threw off—just blew off, like cigarette-puffs—such sketches of. The betrothed of Mr. Mudge at all events accepted the explanation, which had the effect, as almost any turn of their talk was now apt to have, of bringing her round to the terrific question of that gentleman. She was tormented with the desire to get out of Mrs. Jordan, on this subject, what she was sure was at the back of Mrs. Jordan's head; and to get it out of her, queerly enough, if only to vent a certain irritation at it. She knew that what her friend would already have risked if she had not been timid and tortuous was: "Give him up—yes, give him up: you'll see that with your sure chances you'll be able to do much better."

Our young woman had a sense that if that view could only be put before her with a particular sniff for poor Mr. Mudge she should hate it as much as she morally ought. She was conscious of not, as yet, hating it quite so much as that. But she saw that Mrs. Jordan was conscious of something too, and that there was a sort of assurance she was waiting little by little to gather. The day came when the girl caught a glimpse of what was still wanting to make her friend feel strong; which was nothing less than the prospect of being able to announce the climax of sundry private dreams. The associate of the aristocracy had personal calculations—she pored over them in her lonely lodgings. If she did the flowers for the bachelors, in short, didn't she expect that to have consequences very different from the outlook, at Cocker's, that she had described as leading to nothing? There seemed in very truth something auspicious in the mixture of bachelors and flowers, though, when looked hard in the eye, Mrs. Jordan was not quite prepared to say she had expected a positive proposal from Lord Rye to pop out of it. Our young woman arrived at last, none the less, at a definite vision of what was in her mind. This was a vivid foreknowledge that the betrothed of Mr. Mudge would, unless conciliated in advance by a successful rescue, almost hate her on the day she should break a particular piece of news. How could that unfortunate otherwise endure to hear of what, under the protection of Lady Ventnor, was after all so possible?

IX

Meanwhile, since irritation sometimes relieved her, the betrothed of Mr. Mudge drew straight from that admirer an amount of it that was proportioned to her fidelity. She always walked with him on Sundays, usually in the Regent's Park, and quite often, once or twice a month, he took her, in the

Strand or thereabouts, to see a piece that was having a run. The productions he always preferred were the really good ones—Shakespeare, Thompson, or some funny American thing; which, as it also happened that she hated vulgar plays, gave him ground for what was almost the fondest of his approaches, the theory that their tastes were, blissfully, just the same. He was for ever reminding her of that, rejoicing over it, and being affectionate and wise about it. There were times when she wondered how in the world she could bear him, how she could bear any man so smugly unconscious of the immensity of her difference. It was just for this difference that, if she was to be liked at all, she wanted to be liked, and if that was not the source of Mr. Mudge's admiration, she asked herself, what on earth *could* be? She was not different only at one point, she was different all round; unless perhaps indeed in being practically human, which her mind just barely recognised that he also was. She would have made tremendous concessions in other quarters: there was no limit, for instance, to those she would have made to Captain Everard; but what I have named was the most she was prepared to do for Mr. Mudge. It was because *he* was different that, in the oddest way, she liked as well as deplored him; which was after all a proof that the disparity, should they frankly recognise it, wouldn't necessarily be fatal. She felt that, oleaginous—too oleaginous—as he was, he was somehow comparatively primitive: she had once, during the portion of his time at Cocker's that had overlapped her own, seen him collar a drunken soldier, a big, violent man, who, having come in with a mate to get a postal-order cashed, had made a grab at the money before his friend could reach it and had so produced, among the hams and cheeses and the lodgers from Thrupp's, reprisals instantly ensuing a scene of scandal and consternation. Mr. Buckton and the counter-clerk had crouched within the cage, but Mr. Mudge had, with a very quiet but very quick step round the counter, triumphantly interposed in the scrimmage, parted the combatants, and shaken the delinquent in his skin. She had been proud of him at that moment, and had felt that if their affair had not already been settled the neatness of his execution would have left her without resistance.

Their affair had been settled by other things: by the evident sincerity of his passion and by the sense that his high white apron resembled a front of many floors. It had gone a great way with her that he would build up a business to his chin, which he carried quite in the air. This could only be a question of time; he would have all Piccadilly in the pen behind his ear. That was a merit in itself for a girl who had known what she had known. There were hours at which she even found him good-looking, though, frankly, there could be no crown for her effort to imagine, on the part of the tailor or the barber, some such treatment of his appearance as would make him resemble even remotely a gentleman. His very beauty was the beauty of a grocer, and the finest future would offer it none too much room to expand. She had engaged herself, in short, to the perfection of a type, and perfection of anything was much for a person who, out of early troubles, had just escaped with her life. But it contributed hugely at present to carry on the two parallel lines of her contacts in the cage and her contacts out of it. After keeping quiet for some time about this opposition, she suddenly—one Sunday afternoon on a penny chair in the Regent's Park—broke, for him, capriciously, bewilderingly, into an intimation of what it came to. He naturally pressed more and more on the subject of her again placing herself where he could see her hourly, and for her to recognise that she had as yet given him no sane reason for delay she had no need to hear him say that he couldn't make out what she was up to. As if, with her absurd bad reasons, she knew it herself! Sometimes she thought it would be amusing to let him have them full in the face, for she felt she should die of him unless she once in a while stupefied him; and sometimes she thought it would be disgusting and perhaps even fatal. She liked him, however, to think her silly, for that gave her the margin which, at the best, she would always require; and the only difficulty about this was that he hadn't enough imagination to oblige her. It produced, none the less, something of the desired effect—to leave him simply wondering why, over the matter of their reunion, she didn't yield to his arguments. Then at last, simply as if by accident and out of mere boredom on a day that was rather flat, she pre-

posterously produced her own. "Well, wait a bit. Where I am
I still see things." And she talked to him even worse, if possible, than she had talked to Mrs. Jordan.

Little by little, to her own stupefaction, she caught that
he was trying to take it as she meant it, and that he was
neither astonished nor angry. Oh, the British tradesman—
this gave her an idea of his resources! Mr. Mudge would be
angry only with a person who, like the drunken soldier in
the shop, should have an unfavourable effect upon business.
He seemed positively to enter, for the time and without the
faintest flash of irony or ripple of laughter, into the whimsical grounds of her enjoyment of Cocker's custom, and instantly to be casting up whatever it might, as Mrs. Jordan
had said, lead to. What he had in mind was not, of course,
what Mrs. Jordan had had: it was obviously not a source of
speculation with him that his sweetheart might pick up a
husband. She could see perfectly that this was not, for a
moment, even what he supposed she herself dreamed of.
What she had done was simply to give his fancy another
push into the dim vast of trade. In that direction it was all
alert, and she had whisked before it the mild fragrance of a
"connection." That was the most he could see in any picture of her keeping in with the gentry; and when, getting
to the bottom of this, she quickly proceeded to show him
the kind of eye she turned on such people and to give him
a sketch of what that eye discovered, she reduced him to the
particular confusion in which he could still be amusing to her.

X

"They're the most awful wretches, I assure you—the lot all
about there."

"Then why do you want to stay among them?"

"My dear man, just because they *are*. It makes me hate
them so."

"Hate them? I thought you liked them."

"Don't be stupid. What I 'like' is just to loathe them. You
wouldn't believe what passes before my eyes."

"Then why have you never told me? You didn't mention
anything before I left."

"Oh, I hadn't got into it then. It's the sort of thing you don't believe at first; you have to look round you a bit and then you understand. You work into it more and more. Besides," the girl went on, "this is the time of the year when the worst lot come up. They're simply packed together in those smart streets. Talk of the numbers of the poor! What *I* can vouch for is the numbers of the rich! There are new ones every day, and they seem to get richer and richer. Oh, they do come up!" she cried, imitating, for her private recreation— she was sure it wouldn't reach Mr. Mudge—the low intonation of the counter-clerk.

"And where do they come from?" her companion candidly inquired.

She had to think a moment; then she found something. "From the 'spring meetings.' They bet tremendously."

"Well, they bet enough at Chalk Farm, if that's all."

"It *isn't* all. It isn't a millionth part!" she replied with some sharpness. "It's immense fun"—she would tantalise him. Then, as she had heard Mrs. Jordan say, and as the ladies at Cocker's even sometimes wired, "Its quite too dreadful!" She could fully feel how it was Mr. Mudge's propriety, which was extreme—he had a horror of coarseness and attended a Wesleyan chapel—that prevented his asking for details. But she gave him some of the more innocuous in spite of himself, especially putting before him how, at Simpkin's and Ladle's, they all made the money fly. That was indeed what he liked to hear: the connection was not direct, but one was somehow more in the right place where the money was flying than where it was simply and meagrely nesting. It enlivened the air, he had to acknowledge, much less at Chalk Farm than in the district in which his beloved so oddly enjoyed her footing. She gave him, she could see, a restless sense that these might be familiarities not to be sacrificed; germs, possibilities, faint foreshowings—heaven knew what—of the initiation it would prove profitable to have arrived at when, in the fulness of time, he should have his own shop in some such paradise. What really touched him—that was discernible—was that she could feed him with so much mere vividness of reminder, keep before him, as by the play of a fan, the very wind of the swift bank-notes and the charm of the existence of a class that

Providence had raised up to be the blessing of grocers. He liked to think that the class was there, that it was always there, and that she contributed in her slight but appreciable degree to keep it up to the mark. He couldn't have formulated his theory of the matter, but the exuberance of the aristocracy was the advantage of trade, and everything was knit together in a richness of pattern that it was good to follow with one's finger-tips. It was a comfort to him to be thus assured that there were no symptoms of a drop. What did the sounder, as she called it, nimbly worked, do but keep the ball going?

What it came to, therefore, for Mr. Mudge, was that all enjoyments were, in short, interrelated, and that the more people had the more they wanted to have. The more flirtations, as he might roughly express it, the more cheese and pickles. He had even in his own small way been dimly struck with the concatenation between the tender passion and cheap champagne. What he would have liked to say had he been able to work out his thought to the end was: "I see, I see. Lash them up then, lead them on, keep them going: some of it can't help, some time, coming *our* way." Yet he was troubled by the suspicion of subtleties on his companion's part that spoiled the straight view. He couldn't understand people's hating what they liked or liking what they hated; above all it hurt him somewhere—for he had his private delicacies—to see anything *but* money made out of his betters. To be curious at the expense of the gentry was vaguely wrong; the only thing that was distinctly right was to be prosperous. Wasn't it just because they were up there aloft that they were lucrative? He concluded, at any rate, by saying to his young friend: "If it's improper for you to remain at Cocker's, then that falls in exactly with the other reasons that I have put before you for your removal."

"Improper?"—her smile became a long, wide look at him. "My dear boy, there's no one like you!"

"I dare say," he laughed; "but that doesn't help the question."

"Well," she returned, "I can't give up my friends. I'm making even more than Mrs. Jordan."

Mr. Mudge considered. "How much is *she* making?"

"Oh, you dear donkey!"—and, regardless of all the Regent's Park, she patted his cheek. This was the sort of moment at which she was absolutely tempted to tell him that she liked to be near Park Chambers. There was a fascination in the idea of seeing if, on a mention of Captain Everard, he wouldn't do what she thought he might; wouldn't weigh against the obvious objection the still more obvious advantage. The advantage, of course, could only strike him at the best as rather fantastic; but it was always to the good to keep hold when you *had* hold, and such an attitude would also after all involve a high tribute to her fidelity. Of one thing she absolutely never doubted. Mr. Mudge believed in her with a belief——! She believed in herself too, for that matter: if there was a thing in the world no one could charge her with, it was being the kind of low barmaid person who rinsed tumblers and bandied slang. But she forbore as yet to speak; she had not spoken even to Mrs. Jordan; and the hush that on her lips surrounded the Captain's name maintained itself as a kind of symbol of the success that, up to this time, had attended something or other—she couldn't have said what—that she humoured herself with calling, without words, her relation with him.

XI

She would have admitted indeed that it consisted of little more than the fact that his absences, however frequent and however long, always ended with his turning up again. It was nobody's business in the world but her own if that fact continued to be enough for her. It was of course not enough just in itself; what it had taken on to make it so was the extraordinary possession of the elements of his life that memory and attention had at last given her. There came a day when this possession, on the girl's part, actually seemed to enjoy, between them, while their eyes met, a tacit recognition that was half a joke and half a deep solemnity. He bade her good morning always now; he often quite raised his hat to her. He passed a remark when there was time or room, and once she went so far as to say to him that she had not seen him for "ages." "Ages" was the word she consciously and carefully, though a trifle tremulously, used; "ages" was exactly what she meant.

To this he replied in terms doubtless less anxiously selected, but perhaps on that account not the less remarkable, "Oh yes, hasn't it been awfully wet?" That was a specimen of their give and take; it fed her fancy that no form of intercourse so transcendent and distilled had ever been established on earth. Everything, so far as they chose to consider it so, might mean almost anything. The want of margin in the cage, when he peeped through the bars, wholly ceased to be appreciable. It was a drawback only in superficial commerce. With Captain Everard she had simply the margin of the universe. It may be imagined, therefore, how their unuttered reference to all she knew about him could, in this immensity, play at its ease. Every time he handed in a telegram it was an addition to her knowledge: what did his constant smile mean to mark if it didn't mean to mark that? He never came into the place without saying to her in this manner: "Oh yes, you have me by this time so completely at your mercy that it doesn't in the least matter what I give you now. You've become a comfort, I assure you!"

She had only two torments; the greatest of which was that she couldn't, not even once or twice, touch with him on some individual fact. She would have given anything to have been able to allude to one of his friends by name, to one of his engagements by date, to one of his difficulties by the solution. She would have given almost as much for just the right chance—it would have to be tremendously right—to show him in some sharp, sweet way that she had perfectly penetrated the greatest of these last and now lived with it in a kind of heroism of sympathy. He was in love with a woman to whom, and to any view of whom, a lady-telegraphist, and especially one who passed a life among hams and cheeses, was as the sand on the floor; and what her dreams desired was the possibility of its somehow coming to him that her own interest in him could take a pure and noble account of such an infatuation and even of such an impropriety. As yet, however, she could only rub along with the hope that an accident, sooner or later, might give her a lift toward popping out with something that would surprise and perhaps even, some fine day, assist him. What could people mean, moreover—cheaply sarcastic people—by not feeling all that could be got out of the weather? *She* felt it all, and seemed literally to feel it most when she went quite wrong, speaking of the stuffy days as cold, of the cold ones as stuffy, and betraying how little she knew, in her cage, of whether it was foul or fair. It was, for that matter, always stuffy at Cocker's, and she finally settled down to the safe proposition that the outside element was "changeable." Anything seemed true that made him so radiantly assent.

This indeed is a small specimen of her cultivation of insidious ways of making things easy for him—ways to which of course she couldn't be at all sure that he did real justice. Real justice was not of this world: she had had too often to come back to that; yet, strangely, happiness was, and her traps had to be set for it in a manner to keep them unperceived by Mr. Buckton and the counter-clerk. The most she could hope for apart from the question, which constantly flickered up and died down, of the divine chance of his consciously liking her, would be that, without analysing it, he should arrive at a vague sense that Cocker's was—well, attractive; easier, smoother, sociably brighter, slightly more picturesque, in short more propitious in general to his little affairs, than any other establishment just thereabouts. She was quite aware that they couldn't be, in so huddled a hole, particularly quick; but she found her account in the slowness—she certainly could bear it if *he* could. The great pang was that, just thereabouts, post-offices were so awfully thick. She was always seeing him, in imagination, in other places and with other girls. But she would defy any other girl to follow him as she followed. And though they weren't, for so many reasons, quick at Cocker's, she could hurry for him when, through an intimation light as air, she gathered that he was pressed.

When hurry was, better still, impossible, it was because of the pleasantest thing of all, the particular element of their contact—she would have called it their friendship—that consisted of an almost humorous treatment of the look of some of his words. They would never perhaps have grown half so intimate if he had not, by the blessing of heaven, formed some of his letters with a queerness——! It was positive that the queerness could scarce have been greater if he had practised it for the very purpose of bringing their heads together over it as far as

was possible to heads on different sides of a cage. It had taken
her in reality but once or twice to master these tricks, but, at
the cost of striking him perhaps as stupid, she could still challenge them when circumstances favoured. The great circumstance that favoured was that she sometimes actually believed
he knew she only feigned perplexity. If he knew it, therefore,
he tolerated it; if he tolerated it he came back; and if he came
back he liked her. This was her seventh heaven; and she didn't
ask much of his liking—she only asked of it to reach the point
of his not going away because of her own. He had at times
to be away for weeks; he had to lead his life; he had to travel—
there were places to which he was constantly wiring for
"rooms": all this she granted him, forgave him; in fact, in the
long-run, literally blessed and thanked him for. If he had to
lead his life, that precisely fostered his leading it so much by
telegraph: therefore the benediction was to come in when he
could. That was all she asked—that he shouldn't wholly deprive her.

   Sometimes she almost felt that he couldn't have done so
even had he been minded, on account of the web of revelation
that was woven between them. She quite thrilled herself with
thinking what, with such a lot of material, a bad girl would
do. It would be a scene better than many in her ha'penny
novels, this going to him in the dusk of evening at Park
Chambers and letting him at last have it. "I know too much
about a certain person now not to put it to you—excuse my
being so lurid—that it's quite worth your while to buy me
off. Come, therefore; buy me!" There was a point indeed at
which such flights had to drop again—the point of an un-
readiness to name, when it came to that, the purchasing medium. It wouldn't, certainly, be anything so gross as money,
and the matter accordingly remained rather vague, all the
more that *she* was not a bad girl. It was not for any such reason
as might have aggravated a mere minx that she often hoped
he would again bring Cissy. The difficulty of this, however,
was constantly present to her, for the kind of communion to
which Cocker's so richly ministered rested on the fact that
Cissy and he were so often in different places. She knew by
this time all the places—Suchbury, Monkhouse, Whiteroy,
Finches,—and even how the parties, on these occasions, were

composed; but her subtlety found ways to make her knowledge fairly protect and promote their keeping, as she had
heard Mrs. Jordan say, in touch. So, when he actually sometimes smiled as if he really felt the awkwardness of giving her
again one of the same old addresses, all her being went out
in the desire—which her face must have expressed—that he
should recognise her forbearance to criticise as one of the
finest, tenderest sacrifices a woman had ever made for love.

XII

She was occasionally worried, all the same, by the impression
that these sacrifices, great as they were, were nothing to those
that his own passion had imposed; if indeed it was not rather
the passion of his confederate, which had caught him up and
was whirling him round like a great steam-wheel. He was at
any rate in the strong grip of a dizzy, splendid fate; the wild
wind of his life blew him straight before it. Didn't she catch
in his face, at times, even through his smile and his happy
habit, the gleam of that pale glare with which a bewildered
victim appeals, as he passes, to some pair of pitying eyes? He
perhaps didn't even himself know how scared he was, but *she*
knew. They were in danger, they were in danger, Captain Everard and Lady Bradeen: it beat every novel in the shop. She
thought of Mr. Mudge and his safe sentiment; she thought of
herself and blushed even more for her tepid response to it. It
was a comfort to her at such moments to feel that in another
relation—a relation supplying that affinity with her nature that
Mr. Mudge, deluded creature, would never supply—she
should have been no more tepid than her ladyship. Her deepest soundings were on two or three occasions of finding herself almost sure that, if she dared, her ladyship's lover would
have gathered relief from "speaking" to her. She literally fancied once or twice that, projected as he was toward his doom,
her own eyes struck him, while the air roared in his ears, as
the one pitying pair in the crowd. But how could he speak to
her while she sat sandwiched there between the counter-clerk
and the sounder?

She had long ago, in her comings and goings, made acquaintance with Park Chambers, and reflected, as she looked

up at their luxurious front, that *they*, of course, would supply
the ideal setting for the ideal speech. There was not a picture
in London that, before the season was over, was more
stamped upon her brain. She went round about to pass it, for
it was not on the short way; she passed on the opposite side
of the street and always looked up, though it had taken her a
long time to be sure of the particular set of windows. She had
made that out at last by an act of audacity that, at the time,
had almost stopped her heart-beats and that, in retrospect,
greatly quickened her blushes. One evening, late, she had lingered and watched—watched for some moment when the
porter, who was in uniform and often on the steps, had gone
in with a visitor. Then she followed boldly, on the calculation
that he would have taken the visitor up and that the hall
would be free. The hall *was* free, and the electric light played
over the gilded and lettered board that showed the names and
numbers of the occupants of the different floors. What she
wanted looked straight at her—Captain Everard was on the
third. It was as if, in the immense intimacy of this, they were,
for the instant and the first time, face to face outside the cage.
Alas! they were face to face but a second or two: she was
whirled out on the wings of a panic fear that he might just
then be entering or issuing. This fear was indeed, in her
shameless deflections, never very far from her, and was mixed
in the oddest way with depressions and disappointments. It
was dreadful, as she trembled by, to run the risk of looking
to him as if she basely hung about; and yet it was dreadful to
be obliged to pass only at such moments as put an encounter
out of the question.

At the horrible hour of her first coming to Cocker's he was
always—it was to be hoped—snug in bed; and at the hour of
her final departure he was of course—she had such things all
on her fingers'-ends—dressing for dinner. We may let it pass
that if she could not bring herself to hover till he was dressed,
this was simply because such a process for such a person could
only be terribly prolonged. When she went in the middle of
the day to her own dinner she had too little time to do anything but go straight, though it must be added that for a real
certainty she would joyously have omitted the repast. She had
made up her mind as to there being on the whole no decent

pretext to justify her flitting casually past at three o'clock in
the morning. That was the hour at which, if the ha'penny
novels were not all wrong, he probably came home for the
night. She was therefore reduced to merely picturing that miraculous meeting toward which a hundred impossibilities
would have to conspire. But if nothing was more impossible
than the fact, nothing was more intense than the vision. What
may not, we can only moralise, take place in the quickened,
muffled perception of a girl of a certain kind of soul? All our
young friend's native distinction, her refinement of personal
grain, of heredity, of pride, took refuge in this small throbbing
spot; for when she was most conscious of the abjection of her
vanity and the pitifulness of her little flutters and manœuvres,
then the consolation and the redemption were most sure to
shine before her in some just discernible sign. He did like her!

XIII

He never brought Cissy back, but Cissy came one day without
him, as fresh as before from the hands of Marguerite, or only,
at the season's end, a trifle less fresh. She was, however, distinctly less serene. She had brought nothing with her, and
looked about with some impatience for the forms and the
place to write. The latter convenience, at Cocker's, was obscure and barely adequate, and her clear voice had the light
note of disgust which her lover's never showed as she responded with a "There?" of surprise to the gesture made by
the counter-clerk in answer to her sharp inquiry. Our young
friend was busy with half a dozen people, but she had despatched them in her most business-like manner by the time
her ladyship flung through the bars the light of re-appearance.
Then the directness with which the girl managed to receive
this missive was the result of the concentration that had
caused her to make the stamps fly during the few minutes
occupied by the production of it. This concentration, in turn,
may be described as the effect of the apprehension of immi-
nent relief. It was nineteen days, counted and checked off,
since she had seen the object of her homage; and as, had he
been in London, she should, with his habits, have been sure
to see him often, she was now about to learn what other spot

his presence might just then happen to sanctify. For she thought of them, the other spots, as ecstatically conscious of it, expressively happy in it.

But, gracious, how handsome *was* her ladyship, and what an added price it gave him that the air of intimacy he threw out should have flowed originally from such a source! The girl looked straight through the cage at the eyes and lips that must so often have been so near his own—looked at them with a strange passion that, for an instant, had the result of filling out some of the gaps, supplying the missing answers, in his correspondence. Then, as she made out that the features she thus scanned and associated were totally unaware of it, that they glowed only with the colour of quite other and not at all guessable thoughts, this directly added to their splendour, gave the girl the sharpest impression she had yet received of the uplifted, the unattainable plains of heaven, and yet at the same time caused her to thrill with a sense of the high company she did somehow keep. She was with the absent through her ladyship and with her ladyship through the absent. The only pang—but it didn't matter—was the proof in the admirable face, in the sightless pre-occupation of its possessor, that the latter hadn't a notion of her. Her folly had gone to the point of half believing that the other party to the affair must sometimes mention in Eaton Square the extraordinary little person at the place from which he so often wired. Yet the perception of her visitor's blankness actually helped this extraordinary little person, the next instant, to take refuge in a reflection that could be as proud as it liked. "How little she knows, how little she knows!" the girl cried to herself; for what did that show after all but that Captain Everard's telegraphic confidant was Captain Everard's charming secret? Our young friend's perusal of her ladyship's telegram was literally prolonged by a momentary daze: what swam between her and the words, making her see them as through rippled, shallow, sunshot water, was the great, the perpetual flood of "How much *I* know—how much *I* know!" This produced a delay in her catching that, on the face, these words didn't give her what she wanted, though she was prompt enough with her remembrance that her grasp was, half the time, just of what was *not* on the face. "Miss Dolman, Parade Lodge, Parade Terrace, Dover. Let him instantly know right one, Hôtel de France, Ostend. Make it seven nine four nine six one. Wire me alternative Burfield's."

The girl slowly counted. Then he was at Ostend. This hooked on with so sharp a click that, not to feel she was as quickly letting it all slip from her, she had absolutely to hold it a minute longer and to do something to that end. Thus it was that she did on this occasion what she never did—threw off an "Answer paid?" that sounded officious, but that she partly made up for by deliberately affixing the stamps and by waiting till she had done so to give change. She had, for so much coolness, the strength that she considered she knew all about Miss Dolman.

"Yes—paid." She saw all sorts of things in this reply, even to a small, suppressed start of surprise at so correct an assumption; even to an attempt, the next minute, at a fresh air of detachment. "How much, with the answer?" The calculation was not abstruse, but our intense observer required a moment more to make it, and this gave her ladyship time for a second thought. "Oh, just wait!" The white, begemmed hand bared to write rose in sudden nervousness to the side of the wonderful face which, with eyes of anxiety for the paper on the counter, she brought closer to the bars of the cage. "I think I must alter a word!" On this she recovered her telegram and looked over it again; but she had a new, obvious trouble, and studied it without deciding and with much of the effect of making our young woman watch her.

This personage, meanwhile, at the sight of her expression, had decided on the spot. If she had always been sure they were in danger, her ladyship's expression was the best possible sign of it. There was a word wrong, but she had lost the right one, and much, clearly, depended on her finding it again. The girl, therefore, sufficiently estimating the affluence of customers and the distraction of Mr. Buckton and the counter-clerk, took the jump and gave it. "Isn't it Cooper's?"

It was as if she had bodily leaped—cleared the top of the cage and alighted on her interlocutress. "Cooper's?"—the stare was heightened by a blush. Yes, she had made Juno blush.

This was all the more reason for going on. "I mean instead of Burfield's."

Our young friend fairly pitied her; she had made her in an instant so helpless, and yet not a bit haughty nor outraged. She was only mystified and scared. "Oh, you know——?"

"Yes, I know!" Our young friend smiled, meeting the other's eyes, and, having made Juno blush, proceeded to patronise her. "*I'll* do it"—she put out a competent hand. Her ladyship only submitted, confused and bewildered, all presence of mind quite gone; and the next moment the telegram was in the cage again and its author out of the shop. Then quickly, boldly, under all the eyes that might have witnessed her tampering, the extraordinary little person at Cocker's made the proper change. People were really too giddy, and if they *were*, in a certain case, to be caught, it shouldn't be the fault of her own grand memory. Hadn't it been settled weeks before?—for Miss Dolman it was always to be "Cooper's."

XIV

But the summer "holidays" brought a marked difference; they were holidays for almost everyone but the animals in the cage. The August days were flat and dry, and, with so little to feed it, she was conscious of the ebb of her interest in the secrets of the refined. She was in a position to follow the refined to the extent of knowing—they had made so many of their arrangements with her aid—exactly where they were; yet she felt quite as if the panorama had ceased unrolling and the band stopped playing. A stray member of the latter occasionally turned up, but the communications that passed before her bore now largely on rooms at hotels, prices of furnished houses, hours of trains, dates of sailings and arrangements for being "met": she found them for the most part prosaic and coarse. The only thing was that they brought into her stuffy corner as straight a whiff of Alpine meadows and Scotch moors as she might hope ever to inhale; there were moreover, in especial, fat, hot, dull ladies who had out with her, to exasperation, the terms for seaside lodgings, which struck her as huge, and the matter of the number of beds required, which was not less portentous: this in reference to places of which the names—Eastbourne, Folkestone, Cromer, Scarborough, Whitby—tormented her with something of the sound of the plash of water that haunts the traveller in the desert. She had not been out of London for a dozen years, and the only thing to give a taste to the present dead weeks was the spice of a chronic resentment. The sparse customers, the people she did see, were the people who were "just off"—off on the decks of fluttered yachts, off to the uttermost point of rocky headlands where the very breeze was then playing for the want of which she said to herself that she sickened.

There was accordingly a sense in which, at such a period, the great differences of the human condition could press upon her more than ever; a circumstance drawing fresh force, in truth, from the very fact of the chance that at last, for a change, did squarely meet her—the chance to be "off," for a bit, almost as far as anybody. They took their turns in the cage as they took them both in the shop and at Chalk Farm, and she had known these two months that time was to be allowed in September—no less than eleven days—for her personal, private holiday. Much of her recent intercourse with Mr. Mudge had consisted of the hopes and fears, expressed mainly by himself, involved in the question of their getting the same dates— a question that, in proportion as the delight seemed assured, spread into a sea of speculation over the choice of where and how. All through July, on the Sunday evenings and at such other odd times as he could seize, he had flooded their talk with wild waves of calculation. It was practically settled that, with her mother, somewhere "on the south coast" (a phrase of which she liked the sound) they should put in their allowance together; but she already felt the prospect quite weary and worn with the way he went round and round on it. It had become his sole topic, the theme alike of his most solemn prudences and most placid jests, to which every opening led for return and revision and in which every little flower of a foretaste was pulled up as soon as planted. He had announced at the earliest day—characterising the whole business, from that moment, as their "plans," under which name he handled it as a syndicate handles a Chinese, or other, Loan—he had promptly declared that the question must be thoroughly studied, and he produced, on the whole subject, from day to day, an amount of information that excited her wonder and even, not a little, as she frankly let him know, her disdain. When she thought of the danger in which another pair of lovers rapturously lived, she inquired of him anew why he could leave nothing to chance. Then she got for answer that this profundity was just his pride, and he pitted Ramsgate against Bournemouth and even Boulogne against Jersey—for he had great ideas—with all the mastery of detail that was some day, professionally, to carry him far.

The longer the time since she had seen Captain Everard, the more she was booked, as she called it, to pass Park Chambers; and this was the sole amusement that, in the lingering August days and the long, sad twilights, it was left her to cultivate. She had long since learned to know it for a feeble one, though its feebleness was perhaps scarce the reason for her saying to herself each evening as her time for departure approached: "No, no—not to-night." She never failed of that silent remark, any more than she failed of feeling, in some deeper place than she had even yet fully sounded, that one's remarks were as weak as straws, and that, however one might indulge in them at eight o'clock, one's fate infallibly declared itself in absolute indifference to them at about eight-fifteen. Remarks were remarks, and very well for that; but fate was fate, and this young lady's was to pass Park Chambers every night in the working week. Out of the immensity of her knowledge of the life of the world there bloomed on these occasions a specific remembrance that it was regarded in that region, in August and September, as rather pleasant just to be caught for something or other in passing through town. Somebody was always passing and somebody might catch somebody else. It was in full cognisance of this subtle law that she adhered to the most ridiculous circuit she could have made to get home. One warm, dull, featureless Friday, when an accident had made her start from Cocker's a little later than usual, she became aware that something of which the infinite possibilities had for so long peopled her dreams was at last prodigiously upon her, though the perfection in which the conditions happened to present it was almost rich enough to be but the positive creation of a dream. She saw, straight before her, like a vista painted in a picture, the empty street and the lamps that burned pale in the dusk not yet established. It was into the convenience of this quiet twilight that a gentleman on the doorstep of the Chambers gazed with a vagueness that our young lady's little figure violently trembled, in the approach, with the measure of its power to dissipate. Everything indeed grew in a flash terrific and distinct; her old uncertainties fell away from her, and, since she was so familiar with fate, she felt as if the very nail that fixed it were driven in by the hard look with which, for a moment, Captain Everard awaited her.

The vestibule was open behind him and the porter as absent as on the day she had peeped in; he had just come out—was in town, in a tweed suit and a pot hat, but between two journeys—duly bored over his evening and at a loss what to do with it. Then it was that she was glad she had never met him in that way before: she reaped with such ecstasy the benefit of his not being able to think she passed often. She jumped in two seconds to the determination that he should even suppose it to be the first time and the queerest chance: this was while she still wondered if he would identify or notice her. His original attention had not, she instinctively knew, been for the young woman at Cocker's; it had only been for any young woman who might advance with an air of not upholding ugliness. Ah, but then, and just as she had reached the door, came his second observation, a long, light reach with which, visibly and quite amusedly, he recalled and placed her. They were on different sides, but the street, narrow and still, had only made more of a stage for the small momentary drama. It was not over, besides it was far from over, even on his sending across the way, with the pleasantest laugh she had ever heard, a little lift of his hat and an "Oh, good evening!" It was still less over on their meeting, the next minute, though rather indirectly and awkwardly, in the middle of the road—a situation to which three or four steps of her own had unmistakably contributed,—and then passing not again to the side on which she had arrived, but back toward the portal of Park Chambers.

"I didn't know you at first. Are you taking a walk?"

"Oh, I don't take walks at night! I'm going home after my work."

"Oh!"

That was practically what they had meanwhile smiled out, and his exclamation, to which, for a minute, he appeared to have nothing to add, left them face to face and in just such an attitude as, for his part, he might have worn had he been wondering if he could properly ask her to come in. During this interval, in fact, she really felt his question to be just "*How* properly——?" It was simply a question of the degree of properness.

XV

She never knew afterwards quite what she had done to settle it, and at the time she only knew that they presently moved, with vagueness, but with continuity, away from the picture of the lighted vestibule and the quiet stairs and well up the street together. This also must have been in the absence of a definite permission, of anything vulgarly articulate, for that matter, on the part of either; and it was to be, later on, a thing of remembrance and reflection for her that the limit of what, just here, for a longish minute, passed between them was his taking in her thoroughly successful deprecation, though conveyed without pride or sound or touch, of the idea that she might be, out of the cage, the very shopgirl at large that she hugged the theory she was not. Yes, it was strange, she afterwards thought, that so much could have come and gone and yet not troubled the air either with impertinence or with resentment, with any of the horrid notes of that kind of acquaintance. He had taken no liberty, as she would have called it; and, through not having to betray the sense of one, she herself had, still more charmingly, taken none. Yet on the spot, nevertheless, she could speculate as to what it meant that, if his relation with Lady Bradeen continued to be what her mind had built it up to, he should feel free to proceed in any private direction. This was one of the questions he was to leave her to deal with—the question whether people of his sort still asked girls up to their rooms when they were so awfully in love with other women. Could people of his sort do that without what people of *her* sort would call being "false to their love"? She had already a vision of how the true answer was that people of her sort didn't, in such cases, matter— didn't count as infidelity, counted only as something else:

she might have been curious, since it came to that, to see exactly what.

Strolling together slowly in their summer twilight and their empty corner of Mayfair, they found themselves emerge at last opposite to one of the smaller gates of the Park; upon which, without any particular word about it—they were talking so of other things—they crossed the street and went in and sat down on a bench. She had gathered by this time one magnificent hope about him—the hope that he would say nothing vulgar. She knew what she meant by that; she meant something quite apart from any matter of his being "false." Their bench was not far within; it was near the Park Lane paling and the patchy lamplight and the rumbling cabs and 'buses. A strange emotion had come to her, and she felt indeed excitement within excitement; above all a conscious joy in testing him with chances he didn't take. She had an intense desire he should know the type she really was without her doing anything so low as tell him, and he had surely begun to know it from the moment he didn't seize the opportunities into which a common man would promptly have blundered. These were on the mere surface, and *their* relation was behind and below them. She had questioned so little on the way what they were doing, that as soon as they were seated she took straight hold of it. Her hours, her confinement, the many conditions of service in the post-office, had—with a glance at his own postal resources and alternatives—formed, up to this stage, the subject of their talk. "Well, here we are, and it may be right enough; but this isn't the least, you know, where I was going."

"You were going home?"

"Yes, and I was already rather late. I was going to my supper."

"You haven't had it?"

"No, indeed!"

"Then you haven't eaten——?"

He looked, of a sudden, so extravagantly concerned that she laughed out. "All day? Yes, we do feed once. But that was long ago. So I must presently say good-bye."

"Oh, deary *me*!" he exclaimed, with an intonation so droll and yet a touch so light and a distress so marked—a confession of helplessness for such a case, in short, so unre-lieved—that she felt sure, on the spot, she had made the great difference plain. He looked at her with the kindest eyes and still without saying what she had known he wouldn't. She had known he wouldn't say, "Then sup with *me*!" but the proof of it made her feel as if she had feasted.

"I'm not a bit hungry," she went on.

"Ah, you *must* be, awfully!" he made answer, but settling himself on the bench as if, after all, that needn't interfere with his spending his evening. "I've always quite wanted the chance to thank you for the trouble you so often take for me."

"Yes, I know," she replied; uttering the words with a sense of the situation far deeper than any pretence of not fitting his allusion. She immediately saw that he was surprised and even a little puzzled at her frank assent; but, for herself, the trouble she had taken could only, in these fleeting minutes—they would probably never come back—be all there like a little hoard of gold in her lap. Certainly he might look at it, handle it, take up the pieces. Yet if he understood anything he must understand all. "I consider you've already immensely thanked me." The horror was back upon her of having seemed to hang about for some reward. "It's awfully odd that you should have been there just the one time——!"

"The one time you've passed my place?"

"Yes; you can fancy I haven't many minutes to waste. There was a place to-night I had to stop at."

"I see, I see"—he knew already so much about her work. "It must be an awful grind—for a lady."

"It is; but I don't think I groan over it any more than my companions—and you've seen *they're* not ladies!" She mildly jested, but with an intention. "One gets used to things, and there are employments I should have hated much more." She had the finest conception of the beauty of not, at least, boring him. To whine, to count up her wrongs, was what a barmaid or a shopgirl would do, and it was quite enough to sit there like one of these.

"If you had had another employment," he remarked after a moment, "we might never have become acquainted."

"It's highly probable—and certainly not in the same way." Then, still with her heap of gold in her lap and something of the pride of it in her manner of holding her head, she continued not to move—she only smiled at him. The evening had thickened now; the scattered lamps were red; the Park, all before them, was full of obscure and ambiguous life; there were other couples on other benches, whom it was impossible not to see, yet at whom it was impossible to look. "But I've walked so much out of my way with you only just to show you that—that"—with this she paused; it was not, after all, so easy to express—"that anything you may have thought is perfectly true."

"Oh, I've thought a tremendous lot!" her companion laughed. "Do you mind my smoking?"

"Why should I? You always smoke *there*."

"At your place? Oh yes, but here it's different."

"No," she said, as he lighted a cigarette, "that's just what it isn't. It's quite the same."

"Well, then, that's because 'there' it's so wonderful!"

"Then you're conscious of how wonderful it is?" she returned.

He jerked his handsome head in literal protest at a doubt. "Why, that's exactly what I mean by my gratitude for all your trouble. It has been just as if you took a particular interest." She only looked at him in answer to this, in such sudden, immediate embarrassment, as she was quite aware, that, while she remained silent, he showed he was at a loss to interpret her expression. "You *have*—haven't you?—taken a particular interest?"

"Oh, a particular interest!" she quavered out, feeling the whole thing—her immediate embarrassment—get terribly the better of her, and wishing, with a sudden scare, all the more to keep her emotion down. She maintained her fixed smile a moment and turned her eyes over the peopled darkness, unconfused now, because there was something much more confusing. This, with a fatal great rush, was simply the fact that they were thus together. They were near, near, and all that she had imagined of that had only become more true, more dreadful and overwhelming. She stared straight away in silence till she felt that she looked like an idiot; then, to say something, to say nothing, she attempted a sound which ended in a flood of tears.

Her tears helped her really to dissimulate, for she had instantly, in so public a situation, to recover herself. They had
come and gone in half a minute, and she immediately explained them. "It's only because I'm tired. It's that—it's
that!" Then she added a trifle incoherently: "I shall never see
you again."

"Ah, but why not?" The mere tone in which her companion asked this satisfied her once for all as to the amount of
imagination for which she could count on him. It was naturally not large: it had exhausted itself in having arrived at what
he had already touched upon—the sense of an intention in
her poor zeal at Cocker's. But any deficiency of this kind was
no fault in him: *he* wasn't obliged to have an inferior cleverness—to have second-rate resources and virtues. It had been
as if he almost really believed she had simply cried for fatigue,
and he had accordingly put in some kind, confused plea—
"You ought really to take something: won't you have something or other *somewhere*?"—to which she had made no response but a headshake of a sharpness that settled it. "Why
shan't we all the more keep meeting?"

"I mean meeting this way—only this way. At my place
there—*that* I've nothing to do with, and I hope of course
you'll turn up, with your correspondence, when it suits you.
Whether I stay or not, I mean; for I shall probably not stay."

"You're going somewhere else?"—he put it with positive
anxiety.

"Yes; ever so far away—to the other end of London. There
are all sorts of reasons I can't tell you; and it's practically
settled. It's better for me, much; and I've only kept on at
Cocker's for you."

"For me?"

Making out in the dusk that he fairly blushed, she now
measured how far he had been from knowing too much. Too
much, she called it at present; and that was easy, since it
proved so abundantly enough for her that he should simply
be where he was. "As we shall never talk this way but to-
night—never, never again!—here it all is; I'll say it; I don't
care what you think; it doesn't matter; I only want to help

you. Besides, you're kind—you're kind. I've been thinking, then, of leaving for ever so long. But you've come so often—at times,—and you've had so much to do, and it has been so pleasant and interesting, that I've remained, I've kept putting off any change. More than once, when I had nearly decided, you've turned up again and I've thought, 'Oh no!' That's the simple fact!" She had by this time got her confusion down so completely that she could laugh. "This is what I meant when I said to you just now that I 'knew.' I've known perfectly that you knew I took trouble for you; and that knowledge has been for me, and I seemed to see it was for you, as if there were something—I don't know what to call it!—between us. I mean something unusual and good—something not a bit horrid or vulgar."

She had by this time, she could see, produced a great effect upon him; but she would have spoken the truth to herself if she had at the same moment declared that she didn't in the least care: all the more that the effect must be one of extreme perplexity. What, in it all, was visibly clear for him, none the less, was that he was tremendously glad he had met her. She held him, and he was astonished at the force of it; he was intent, immensely considerate. His elbow was on the back of the seat, and his head, with the pot-hat pushed quite back, in a boyish way, so that she really saw almost for the first time his forehead and hair, rested on the hand into which he had crumpled his gloves. "Yes," he assented, "it's not a bit horrid or vulgar."

She just hung fire a moment; then she brought out the whole truth. "I'd do anything for you. I'd do anything for you." Never in her life had she known anything so high and fine as this, just letting him have it and bravely and magnificently leaving it. Didn't the place, the associations and circumstances, perfectly make it sound what it was not? and wasn't that exactly the beauty?

So she bravely and magnificently left it, and little by little she felt him take it up, take it down, as if they had been on a satin sofa in a boudoir. She had never seen a boudoir, but there had been lots of boudoirs in the telegrams. What she had said, at all events, sank into him, so that after a minute he simply made a movement that had the result of placing his

hand on her own—presently indeed that of her feeling herself
firmly enough grasped. There was no pressure she need return, there was none she need decline; she just sat admirably
still, satisfied, for the time, with the surprise and bewilderment
of the impression she made on him. His agitation was even
greater, on the whole, than she had at first allowed for. "I say,
you know, you mustn't think of leaving!" he at last broke out.

"Of leaving Cocker's, you mean?"

"Yes, you must stay on there, whatever happens, and help
a fellow."

She was silent a little, partly because it was so strange and
exquisite to feel him watch her as if it really mattered to him
and he were almost in suspense. "Then you *have* quite recognised what I've tried to do?" she asked.

"Why, wasn't that exactly what I dashed over from my door
just now to thank you for?"

"Yes; so you said."

"And don't you believe it?"

She looked down a moment at his hand, which continued
to cover her own; whereupon he presently drew it back, rather
restlessly folding his arms. Without answering his question she
went on: "Have you ever spoken of me?"

"Spoken of you?"

"Of my being there—of my knowing, and that sort of
thing."

"Oh, never to a human creature!" he eagerly declared.

She had a small drop at this, which was expressed in another
pause; after which she returned to what he had just asked her.
"Oh yes, I quite believe you like it—my always being there
and our taking things up so familiarly and successfully: if not
exactly where we left them," she laughed, "almost always, at
least, in an interesting place!" He was about to say something
in reply to this, but her friendly gaiety was quicker. "You want
a great many things in life, a great many comforts and helps
and luxuries—you want everything as pleasant as possible.
Therefore, so far as it's in the power of any particular person
to contribute to all that——" She had turned her face to him
smiling, just thinking.

"Oh, see here!" But he was highly amused. "Well, what
then?" he inquired, as if to humour her.

"Why, the particular person must never fail. We must manage it for you somehow."

He threw back his head, laughing out; he was really exhilarated. "Oh yes, somehow!"

"Well, I think we each do—don't we?—in one little way and another and according to our limited lights. I'm pleased, at any rate, for myself, that you are; for I assure you I've done my best."

"You do better than any one!" He had struck a match for another cigarette, and the flame lighted an instant his responsive, finished face, magnifying into a pleasant grimace the kindness with which he paid her this tribute. "You're awfully clever, you know; cleverer, cleverer, cleverer——!" He had appeared on the point of making some tremendous statement; then suddenly, puffing his cigarette and shifting almost with violence on his seat, let it altogether fall.

XVII

In spite of this drop, if not just by reason of it, she felt as if Lady Bradeen, all but named out, had popped straight up; and she practically betrayed her consciousness by waiting a little before she rejoined: "Cleverer than who?"

"Well, if I wasn't afraid you'd think I swagger, I should say—than anybody! If you leave your place there, where shall you go?" he more gravely demanded.

"Oh, too far for you ever to find me!"

"I'd find you anywhere."

The tone of this was so still more serious that she had but her one acknowledgment. "I'd do anything for you—I'd do anything for you," she repeated. She had already, she felt, said it all; so what did anything more, anything less, matter? That was the very reason indeed why she could, with a lighter note, ease him generously of any awkwardness produced by solemnity, either his own or hers. "Of course it must be nice for you to be able to think there are people all about who feel in such a way."

In immediate appreciation of this, however, he only smoked without looking at her. "But you don't want to give up your present work?" he at last inquired. "I mean you *will* stay in the post-office?"

"Oh yes; I think I've a genius for that."

"Rather! No one can touch you." With this he turned more to her again. "But you can get, with a move, greater advantages?"

"I can get, in the suburbs, cheaper lodgings. I live with my mother. We need some space; and there's a particular place that has other inducements."

He just hesitated. "Where is it?"

"Oh, quite out of *your* way. You'd never have time."

"But I tell you I'd go anywhere. Don't you believe it?"

"Yes, for once or twice. But you'd soon see it wouldn't do for you."

He smoked and considered; seemed to stretch himself a little and, with his legs out, surrender himself comfortably. "Well, well, well—I believe everything you say. I take it from you—anything you like—in the most extraordinary way." It struck her certainly—and almost without bitterness—that the way in which she was already, as if she had been an old friend, arranging for him and preparing the only magnificence she could muster, was quite the most extraordinary. "Don't, *don't* go!" he presently went on. "I shall miss you too horribly!"

"So that you just put it to me as a definite request?"—oh, how she tried to divest this of all sound of the hardness of bargaining! That ought to have been easy enough, for what was she arranging to get? Before he could answer she had continued: "To be perfectly fair, I should tell you I recognise at Cocker's certain strong attractions. All you people come. I like all the horrors."

"The horrors?"

"Those you all—you know the set I mean, *your* set—show me with as good a conscience as if I had no more feeling than a letter-box."

He looked quite excited at the way she put it. "Oh, they don't know!"

"Don't know I'm not stupid? No, how should they?"

"Yes, how should they?" said the Captain sympathetically. "But isn't 'horrors' rather strong?"

"What you *do* is rather strong!" the girl promptly returned.

"What *I* do?"

"Your extravagance, your selfishness, your immorality, your crimes," she pursued, without heeding his expression.

"I *say!*"—her companion showed the queerest stare.

"I like them, as I tell you—I revel in them. But we needn't go into that," she quietly went on; "for all I get out of it is the harmless pleasure of knowing. I know, I know, I know!"— she breathed it ever so gently.

"Yes; that's what has been between us," he answered much more simply.

She could enjoy his simplicity in silence, and for a moment she did so. "If I *do* stay because you want it—and I'm rather capable of that—there are two or three things I think you ought to remember. One is, you know, that I'm there sometimes for days and weeks together without your ever coming."

"Oh, I'll come every day!" he exclaimed.

She was on the point, at this, of imitating with her hand his movement of shortly before; but she checked herself, and there was no want of effect in the tranquillising way in which she said: "How can you? How can you?" He had, too manifestly, only to look at it there, in the vulgarly animated gloom, to see that he couldn't; and at this point, by the mere action of his silence, everything they had so definitely not named, the whole presence round which they had been circling became a part of their reference, settled solidly between them. It was as if then, for a minute, they sat and saw it all in each other's eyes, saw so much that there was no need of a transition for sounding it at last. "Your danger, your danger——!" Her voice indeed trembled with it, and she could only, for the moment, again leave it so.

During this moment he leaned back on the bench, meeting her in silence and with a face that grew more strange. It grew so strange that, after a further instant, she got straight up. She stood there as if their talk were now over, and he just sat and watched her. It was as if now—owing to the third person they had brought in—they must be more careful; so that the most he could finally say was: "That's where it is!"

"That's where it is!" the girl as guardedly replied. He sat still, and she added: "I won't abandon you. Good-bye."

"Good-bye?"—he appealed, but without moving.

"I don't quite see my way, but I won't abandon you," she repeated. "There. Good-bye."

It brought him with a jerk to his feet, tossing away his cigarette. His poor face was flushed. "See here—see here!"

"No, I won't; but I must leave you now," she went on as if not hearing him.

"See here—see here!" He tried, from the bench, to take her hand again.

But that definitely settled it for her: this would, after all, be as bad as his asking her to supper. "You mustn't come with me—no, no!"

He sank back, quite blank, as if she had pushed him. "I mayn't see you home?"

"No, no; let me go." He looked almost as if she had struck him, but she didn't care; and the manner in which she spoke— it was literally as if she were angry—had the force of a command. "Stay where you are!"

"See here—see here!" he nevertheless pleaded.

"I won't abandon you!" she cried once more—this time quite with passion; on which she got away from him as fast as she could and left him staring after her.

XVIII

Mr. Mudge had lately been so occupied with their famous "plans" that he had neglected, for a while, the question of her transfer; but down at Bournemouth, which had found itself selected as the field of their recreation by a process consisting, it seemed, exclusively of innumerable pages of the neatest arithmetic in a very greasy but most orderly little pocket-book, the distracting possible melted away—the fleeting irremediable ruled the scene. The plans, hour by hour, were simply superseded, and it was much of a rest to the girl, as she sat on the pier and overlooked the sea and the company, to see them evaporate in rosy fumes and to feel that from moment to moment there was less left to cipher about. The week proved blissfully fine, and her mother, at their lodgings—partly to her embarrassment and partly to her relief— struck up with the landlady an alliance that left the younger couple a great deal of freedom. This relative took her pleasure of a week at Bournemouth in a stuffy back-kitchen and endless talks; to that degree even that Mr. Mudge himself—habitually inclined indeed to a scrutiny of all mysteries and to seeing, as he sometimes admitted, too much in things—made remarks on it as he sat on the cliff with his betrothed, or on the decks of steamers that conveyed them, close-packed items in terrific totals of enjoyment, to the Isle of Wight and the Dorset coast.

He had a lodging in another house, where he had speedily learned the importance of keeping his eyes open, and he made no secret of his suspecting that sinister mutual connivances might spring, under the roof of his companions, from unnat ural sociabilities. At the same time he fully recognised that, as a source of anxiety, not to say of expense, his future mother-in-law would have weighted them more in accompanying their steps than in giving her hostess, in the interest of the tendency they considered that they never mentioned, equivalent pledges as to the tea-caddy and the jam-pot. These were the questions—these indeed the familiar commodities—that he had now to put into the scales; and his betrothed had, in consequence, during her holiday, the odd, and yet pleasant and almost languid, sense of an anticlimax. She had become conscious of an extraordinary collapse, a surrender to stillness and to retrospect. She cared neither to walk nor to sail; it was enough for her to sit on benches and wonder at the sea and taste the air and not be at Cocker's and not see the counter-clerk. She still seemed to wait for something—something in the key of the immense discussions that had mapped out their little week of idleness on the scale of a world-atlas. Something came at last, but without perhaps appearing quite adequately to crown the monument.

Preparation and precaution were, however, the natural flow ers of Mr. Mudge's mind, and in proportion as these things declined in one quarter they inevitably bloomed elsewhere. He could always, at the worst, have on Tuesday the project of their taking the Swanage boat on Thursday, and on Thursday that of their ordering minced kidneys on Saturday. He had, moreover, a constant gift of inexorable inquiry as to where and what they should have gone and have done if they had not been exactly as they were. He had in short his resources, and his mistress had never been so conscious of them;

on the other hand they had never interfered so little with her own. She liked to be as she was—if it could only have lasted. She could accept even without bitterness a rigour of economy so great that the little fee they paid for admission to the pier had to be balanced against other delights. The people at Ladle's and at Thrupp's had *their* ways of amusing themselves, whereas she had to sit and hear Mr. Mudge talk of what he might do if he didn't take a bath, or of the bath he might take if he only hadn't taken something else. He was always with her now, of course, always beside her; she saw him more than "hourly," more than ever yet, more even than he had planned she should do at Chalk Farm. She preferred to sit at the far end, away from the band and the crowd; as to which she had frequent differences with her friend, who reminded her often that they could have only in the thick of it the sense of the money they were getting back. That had little effect on her, for she got back her money by seeing many things, the things of the past year, fall together and connect themselves, undergo the happy relegation that transforms melancholy and misery, passion and effort, into experience and knowledge.

She liked having done with them, as she assured herself she had practically done, and the strange thing was that she neither missed the procession now nor wished to keep her place for it. It had become there, in the sun and the breeze and the sea-smell, a far-away story, a picture of another life. If Mr. Mudge himself liked processions, liked them at Bournemouth and on the pier quite as much as at Chalk Farm or anywhere, she learned after a little not to be worried by his perpetual counting of the figures that made them up. There were dreadful women in particular, usually fat and in men's caps and white shoes, whom he could never let alone—not that *she* cared; it was not the great world, the world of Cocker's and Ladle's and Thrupp's, but it offered an endless field to his faculties of memory, philosophy, and frolic. She had never accepted him so much, never arranged so successfully for making him chatter while she carried on secret conversations. Her talks were with herself; and if they both practised a great thrift, she had quite mastered that of merely spending words enough to keep him imperturbably and continuously going.

He was charmed with the panorama, not knowing—or at any rate not at all showing that he knew—what far other images peopled her mind than the women in the navy caps and the shopboys in the blazers. His observations on these types, his general interpretation of the show, brought home to her the prospect of Chalk Farm. She wondered sometimes that he should have derived so little illumination, during his period, from the society at Cocker's. But one evening, as their holiday cloudlessly waned, he gave her such a proof of his quality as might have made her ashamed of her small reserves. He brought out something that, in all his overflow, he had been able to keep back till other matters were disposed of. It was the announcement that he was at last ready to marry—that he saw his way. A rise at Chalk Farm had been offered him; he was to be taken into the business, bringing with him a capital the estimation of which by other parties constituted the handsomest recognition yet made of the head on his shoulders. Therefore their waiting was over—it could be a question of a near date. They would settle this date before going back, and he meanwhile had his eye on a sweet little home. He would take her to see it on their first Sunday.

XIX

His having kept this great news for the last, having had such a card up his sleeve and not floated it out in the current of his chatter and the luxury of their leisure, was one of those incalculable strokes by which he could still affect her; the kind of thing that reminded her of the latent force that had ejected the drunken soldier—an example of the profundity of which his promotion was the proof. She listened a while in silence, on this occasion, to the wafted strains of the music; she took it in as she had not quite done before that her future was now constituted. Mr. Mudge was distinctly her fate; yet at this moment she turned her face quite away from him, showing him so long a mere quarter of her cheek that she at last again heard his voice. He couldn't see a pair of tears that were partly the reason of her delay to give him the assurance he required; but he expressed at a venture the hope that she had had her fill of Cocker's.

She was finally able to turn back. "Oh, quite. There's nothing going on. No one comes but the Americans at Thrupp's, and *they* don't do much. They don't seem to have a secret in the world."

"Then the extraordinary reason you've been giving me for holding on there has ceased to work?"

She thought a moment. "Yes, that one. I've seen the thing through—I've got them all in my pocket."

"So you're ready to come?"

For a little, again, she made no answer. "No, not yet, all the same. I've still got a reason—a different one."

He looked her all over as if it might have been something she kept in her mouth or her glove or under her jacket—something she was even sitting upon. "Well, I'll have it, please."

"I went out the other night and sat in the Park with a gentleman," she said at last.

Nothing was ever seen like his confidence in her; and she wondered a little now why it didn't irritate her. It only gave her ease and space, as she felt, for telling him the whole truth that no one knew. It had arrived at present at her really wanting to do that, and yet to do it not in the least for Mr. Mudge, but altogether and only for herself. This truth filled out for her there the whole experience she was about to relinquish, suffused and coloured it as a picture that she should keep and that, describe it as she might, no one but herself would ever really see. Moreover she had no desire whatever to make Mr. Mudge jealous; there would be no amusement in it, for the amusement she had lately known had spoiled her for lower pleasures. There were even no materials for it. The odd thing was that she never doubted that, properly handled, his passion was poisonable; what had happened was that he had cannily selected a partner with no poison to distil. She read then and there that she should never interest herself in anybody as to whom some other sentiment, some superior view, wouldn't be sure to interfere, for him, with jealousy. "And what did you get out of that?" he asked with a concern that was not in the least for his honour.

"Nothing but a good chance to promise him I wouldn't forsake him. He's one of my customers."

"Then it's for him not to forsake *you*."

"Well, he won't. It's all right. But I must just keep on as long as he may want me."

"Want you to sit with him in the Park?"

"He may want me for that—but I shan't. I rather liked it, but once, under the circumstances, is enough. I can do better for him in another manner."

"And what manner, pray?"

"Well, elsewhere."

"Elsewhere?—I *say!*"

This was an ejaculation used also by Captain Everard, but, oh, with what a different sound! "You needn't 'say'—there's nothing to be said. And yet you ought perhaps to know."

"Certainly I ought. But *what*—up to now?"

"Why, exactly what I told him. That I would do anything for him."

"What do you mean by 'anything'?"

"Everything."

Mr. Mudge's immediate comment on this statement was to draw from his pocket a crumpled paper containing the remains of half a pound of "sundries." These sundries had figured conspicuously in his prospective sketch of their tour, but it was only at the end of three days that they had defined themselves unmistakably as chocolate-creams. "Have another?—*that* one," he said. She had another, but not the one he indicated, and then he continued: "What took place afterwards?"

"Afterwards?"

"What did you do when you had told him you would do everything?"

"I simply came away."

"Out of the Park?"

"Yes, leaving him there. I didn't let him follow me."

"Then what did you let him do?"

"I didn't let him do anything."

Mr. Mudge considered an instant. "Then what did you go there for?" His tone was even slightly critical.

"I didn't quite know at the time. It was simply to be with him, I suppose—just once. He's in danger, and I wanted him to know I know it. It makes meeting him—at Cocker's, for it's that I want to stay on for—more interesting."

"It makes it mighty interesting for *me*!" Mr. Mudge freely declared. "Yet he didn't follow you?" he asked. "*I* would!"

"Yes, of course. That was the way you began, you know. You're awfully inferior to him."

"Well, my dear, you're not inferior to anybody. You've got a cheek! What is he in danger of?"

"Of being found out. He's in love with a lady—and it isn't right—and *I've* found him out."

"That'll be a look-out for *me*!" Mr. Mudge joked. "You mean she has a husband?"

"Never mind what she has! They're in awful danger, but his is the worst, because he's in danger from her too."

"Like me from you—the woman *I* love? If he's in the same funk as me——"

"He's in a worse one. He's not only afraid of the lady— he's afraid of other things."

Mr. Mudge selected another chocolate-cream. "Well, I'm only afraid of one! But how in the world can you help this party?"

"I don't know—perhaps not at all. But so long as there's a chance——"

"You won't come away?"

"No, you've got to wait for me."

Mr. Mudge enjoyed what was in his mouth. "And what will he give you?"

"Give me?"

"If you do help him."

"Nothing. Nothing in all the wide world."

"Then what will he give *me*?" Mr. Mudge inquired. "I mean for waiting."

The girl thought a moment; then she got up to walk. "He never heard of you," she replied.

"You haven't mentioned me?"

"We never mention anything. What I've told you is just what I've found out."

Mr. Mudge, who had remained on the bench, looked up at her; she often preferred to be quiet when he proposed to walk, but now that he seemed to wish to sit she had a desire to move. "But you haven't told me what *he* has found out."

She considered her lover. "He'd never find *you*, my dear!"

Her lover, still on his seat, appealed to her in something of the attitude in which she had last left Captain Everard, but the impression was not the same. "Then where do I come in?"

"You don't come in at all. That's just the beauty of it!"— and with this she turned to mingle with the multitude collected round the band. Mr. Mudge presently overtook her and drew her arm into his own with a quiet force that expressed the serenity of possession; in consonance with which it was only when they parted for the night at her door that he referred again to what she had told him.

"Have you seen him since?"

"Since the night in the Park? No, not once."

"Oh, what a cad!" said Mr. Mudge.

XX

It was not till the end of October that she saw Captain Everard again, and on that occasion—the only one of all the series on which hindrance had been so utter—no communication with him proved possible. She had made out, even from the cage, that it was a charming golden day: a patch of hazy autumn sunlight lay across the sanded floor and also, higher up, quickened into brightness a row of ruddy bottled syrups. Work was slack and the place in general empty; the town, as they said in the cage, had not waked up, and the feeling of the day likened itself to something that in happier conditions she would have thought of romantically as St. Martin's summer. The counter-clerk had gone to his dinner; she herself was busy with arrears of postal jobs, in the midst of which she became aware that Captain Everard had apparently been in the shop a minute and that Mr. Buckton had already seized him.

He had, as usual, half a dozen telegrams; and when he saw that she saw him and their eyes met, he gave, on bowing to her, an exaggerated laugh in which she read a new consciousness. It was a confession of awkwardness; it seemed to tell her that of course he knew he ought better to have kept his head, ought to have been clever enough to wait, on some pretext, till he should have found her free. Mr. Buckton was a long time with him, and her attention was soon demanded by other visitors; so that nothing passed between them but the fulness of their silence. The look she took from him was his greeting, and the other one a simple sign of the eyes sent her before going out. The only token they exchanged, therefore, was his tacit assent to her wish that, since they couldn't attempt a certain frankness, they should attempt nothing at all. This was her intense preference; she could be as still and cold as any one when that was the sole solution.

Yet, more than any contact hitherto achieved, these counted instants struck her as marking a step: they were built so—just in the mere flash—on the recognition of his now definitely knowing what it was she would do for him. The "anything, anything" she had uttered in the Park went to and fro between them and under the poked-out chins that interposed. It had all at last even put on the air of their not needing now clumsily to manœuvre to converse: their former little postal make-believes, the intense implications of questions and answers and change, had become in the light of the personal fact, of their having had their moment, a possibility comparatively poor. It was as if they had met for all time—it exerted on their being in presence again an influence so prodigious. When she watched herself, in the memory of that night, walk away from him as if she were making an end, she found something too pitiful in the primness of such a gait. Hadn't she precisely established on the part of each a consciousness that could end only with death?

It must be admitted that, in spite of this brave margin, an irritation, after he had gone, remained with her; a sense that presently became one with a still sharper hatred of Mr. Buckton, who, on her friend's withdrawal, had retired with the telegrams to the sounder and left her the other work. She knew indeed she should have a chance to see them, when she would, on file; and she was divided, as the day went on, between the two impressions of all that was lost and all that was re-asserted. What beset her above all, and as she had almost never known it before, was the desire to bound straight out, to overtake the autumn afternoon before it passed away for ever and hurry off to the Park and perhaps be with him there again on a bench. It became, for an hour, a fantastic vision with her that he might just have gone to sit and wait for her. She could almost hear him, through the tick of the sounder, scatter with his stick, in his impatience, the fallen leaves of October. Why should such a vision seize her at this particular moment with such a shake? There was a time—from four to five—when she could have cried with happiness and rage.

Business quickened, it seemed, toward five, as if the town did wake up; she had therefore more to do, and she went through it with little sharp stampings and jerkings: she made the crisp postal-orders fairly snap while she breathed to herself: "It's the last day—the last day!" The last day of what? She couldn't have told. All she knew now was that if she *were* out of the cage she wouldn't in the least have minded, this time, its not yet being dark. She would have gone straight toward Park Chambers and have hung about there till no matter when. She would have waited, stayed, rung, asked, have gone in, sat on the stairs. What the day was the last of was probably, to her strained inner sense, the group of golden ones, of any occasion for seeing the hazy sunshine slant at that angle into the smelly shop, of any range of chances for his wishing still to repeat to her the two words that, in the Park, she had scarcely let him bring out. "See here— see here!"— the sound of these two words had been with her perpetually; but it was in her ears to-day without mercy, with a loudness that grew and grew. What was it they then expressed? what was it he had wanted her to see? She seemed, whatever it was, perfectly to see it now—to see that if she should just chuck the whole thing, should have a great and beautiful courage, he would somehow make everything up to her. When the clock struck five she was on the very point of saying to Mr. Buckton that she was deadly ill and rapidly getting worse. This announcement was on her lips, and she had quite composed the pale, hard face she would offer him: "I can't stop—I must go home. If I feel better, later on, I'll come back. I'm very sorry, but I *must* go." At that instant Captain Everard once more stood there, producing in her agitated spirit, by his real presence, the strangest, quickest revolution. He stopped her

off without knowing it, and by the time he had been a minute
in the shop she felt that she was saved.

That was from the first minute what she called it to herself.
There were again other persons with whom she was occupied,
and again the situation could only be expressed by their silence. It was expressed, in fact, in a larger phrase than ever
yet, for her eyes now spoke to him with a kind of supplication.
"Be quiet, be quiet!" they pleaded; and they saw his own
reply: "I'll do whatever you say; I won't even look at you—
see, see!" They kept conveying thus, with the friendliest liberality, that they wouldn't look, quite positively wouldn't.
What she was to see was that he hovered at the other end of
the counter, Mr. Buckton's end, surrendered himself again to
that frustration. It quickly proved so great indeed that what
she was to see further was how he turned away before he was
attended to, and hung off, waiting, smoking, looking about
the shop; how he went over to Mr. Cocker's own counter and
appeared to price things, gave in fact presently two or three
orders and put down money, stood there a long time with his
back to her, considerately abstaining from any glance round
to see if she were free. It at last came to pass in this way that
he had remained in the shop longer than she had ever yet
known him to do, and that, nevertheless, when he did turn
about she could see him time himself—she was freshly taken
up—and cross straight to her postal subordinate, whom some
one else had released. He had in his hand all this while neither
letters nor telegrams, and now that he was close to her—for
she was close to the counter-clerk—it brought her heart into
her mouth merely to see him look at her neighbour and open
his lips. She was too nervous to bear it. He asked for a Post-
Office Guide, and the young man whipped out a new one;
whereupon he said that he wished not to purchase, but only
to consult one a moment; with which, the copy kept on loan
being produced, he once more wandered off.

What was he doing to her? What did he want of her? Well, it
was just the aggravation of his "See here!" She felt at this moment strangely and portentously afraid of him—had in her ears
the hum of a sense that, should it come to that kind of tension,
she must fly on the spot to Chalk Farm. Mixed with her dread
and with her reflection was the idea that, if he wanted her so

much as he seemed to show, it might be after all simply to do for him the "anything" she had promised, the "everything" she had thought it so fine to bring out to Mr. Mudge. He might want her to help him, might have some particular appeal; though, of a truth, his manner didn't denote that—denoted, on the contrary, an embarrassment, an indecision, something of a desire not so much to be helped as to be treated rather more nicely than she had treated him the other time. Yes, he considered quite probably that he had help rather to offer than to ask for. Still, none the less, when he again saw her free he continued to keep away from her; when he came back with his *Guide* it was Mr. Buckton he caught—it was from Mr. Buckton he obtained half-a-crown's-worth of stamps.

After asking for the stamps he asked, quite as a second thought, for a postal-order for ten shillings. What did he want with so many stamps when he wrote so few letters? How could he enclose a postal-order in a telegram? She expected him, the next thing, to go into the corner and make up one of his telegrams—half a dozen of them—on purpose to prolong his presence. She had so completely stopped looking at him that she could only guess his movements—guess even where his eyes rested. Finally she saw him make a dash that might have been towards the nook where the forms were hung; and at this she suddenly felt that she couldn't keep it up. The counter clerk had just taken a telegram from a slavey, and, to give herself something to cover her, she snatched it out of his hand. The gesture was so violent that he gave her an odd look, and she also perceived that Mr. Buckton noticed it. The latter personage, with a quick stare at her, appeared for an instant to wonder whether his snatching it in *his* turn mightn't be the thing she would least like, and she anticipated this practical criticism by the frankest glare she had ever given him. It sufficed: this time it paralysed him; and she sought with her trophy the refuge of the sounder.

XXI

It was repeated the next day; it went on for three days; and at the end of that time she knew what to think. When, at the beginning, she had emerged from her temporary shelter Captain Everard had quitted the shop; and he had not come again that evening, as it had struck her he possibly might—might all the more easily that there were numberless persons who came, morning and afternoon, numberless times, so that he wouldn't necessarily have attracted attention. The second day it was different and yet on the whole worse. His access to her had become possible—she felt herself even reaping the fruit of her yesterday's glare at Mr. Buckton; but transacting his business with him didn't simplify—it could, in spite of the rigour of circumstance, feed so her new conviction. The rigour was tremendous, and his telegrams—not, now, mere pretexts for getting at her—were apparently genuine; yet the conviction had taken but a night to develop. It could be simply enough expressed; she had had the glimmer of it the day before in her idea that he needed no more help than she had already given; that it was help he himself was prepared to render. He had come up to town but for three or four days; he had been absolutely obliged to be absent after the other time; yet he would, now that he was face to face with her, stay on as much longer as she liked. Little by little it was thus clarified, though from the first flash of his re-appearance she had read into it the real essence.

That was what the night before, at eight o'clock, her hour to go, had made her hang back and dawdle. She did last things or pretended to do them; to be in the cage had suddenly become her safety, and she was literally afraid of the alternate self who might be waiting outside. *He* might be waiting; it was he who was her alternate self, and of him she was afraid. The most extraordinary change had taken place in her from the moment of her catching the impression he seemed to have returned on purpose to give her. Just before she had done so, on that bewitched afternoon, she had seen herself approach, without a scruple, the porter at Park Chambers; then, as the effect of the rush of a consciousness quite altered, she had, on at last quitting Cocker's, gone straight home for the first time since her return from Bournemouth. She had passed his door every night for weeks, but nothing would have induced her to pass it now. This change was the tribute of her fear—the result of a change in himself as to which she needed no more explanation than his mere face vividly gave her; strange though it was to find an element of deterrence in the object that she regarded as the most beautiful in the world. He had taken it from her in the Park that night that she wanted him not to propose to her to sup; but he had put away the lesson by this time—he practically proposed supper every time he looked at her. This was what, for that matter, mainly filled the three days. He came in twice on each of these, and it was as if he came in to give her a chance to relent. That was, after all, she said to herself in the intervals, the most that he did. There were ways, she fully recognised, in which he spared her, and other particular ways as to which she meant that her silence should be full, to him, of exquisite pleading. The most particular of all was his not being outside, at the corner, when she quitted the place for the night. This he might so easily have been—so easily if he hadn't been so nice. She continued to recognise in his forbearance the fruit of her dumb supplication, and the only compensation he found for it was the harmless freedom of being able to appear to say: "Yes, I'm in town only for three or four days, but, you know, I *would* stay on." He struck her as calling attention each day, each hour, to the rapid ebb of time; he exaggerated to the point of putting it that there were only two days more, that there was at last, dreadfully, only one.

There were other things still that he struck her as doing with a special intention; as to the most marked of which—unless indeed it were the most obscure—she might well have marvelled that it didn't seem to her more horrid. It was either the frenzy of her imagination or the disorder of his baffled passion that gave her once or twice the vision of his putting down redundant money—sovereigns not concerned with the little payments he was perpetually making—so that she might give him some sign of helping him to slip them over to her. What was most extraordinary in this impression was the amount of excuse that, with some incoherence, she found for him. He wanted to pay her because there was nothing to pay her for. He wanted to offer her things that he knew she wouldn't take. He wanted to show her how much he respected her by giving her the supreme chance to show *him* she was respectable. Over the driest transactions, at any rate, their eyes had out these questions. On the third day he put in a telegram that had evidently something of the same point as the stray sovereigns—a message that was, in the first place, concocted, and that, on a second thought, he took back from her before she had stamped it. He had given her time to read it, and had only then bethought himself that he had better not send it. If it was not to Lady Bradeen at Twindle—where she knew her ladyship then to be—this was because an address to Doctor Buzzard at Brickwood was just as good, with the added merit of its not giving away quite so much a person whom he had still, after all, in a manner to consider. It was of course most complicated, only half lighted; but there was, discernibly enough, a scheme of communication in which Lady Bradeen at Twindle and Dr. Buzzard at Brickwood were, within limits, one and the same person. The words he had shown her and then taken back consisted, at all events, of the brief but vivid phrase: "Absolutely impossible." The point was not that she should transmit it; the point was just that she should see it. What was absolutely impossible was that before he had settled something at Cocker's he should go either to Twindle or to Brickwood.

The logic of this, in turn, for herself, was that she could lend herself to no settlement so long as she so intensely knew. What she knew was that he was, almost under peril of life, clenched in a situation: therefore how could she also know where a poor girl in the P.O. might really stand? It was more and more between them that if he might convey to her that he was free, that everything she had seen so deep into was a closed chapter, her own case might become different for her, she might understand and meet him and listen. But he could convey nothing of the sort, and he only fidgeted and floundered in his want of power. The chapter wasn't in the least closed, not for the other party; and the other party had a pull, somehow and somewhere: this his whole attitude and expression confessed, at the same time that they entreated her not to remember and not to mind. So long as she did remember and did mind he could only circle about and go and come, doing futile things of which he was ashamed. He was ashamed of his two words to Dr. Buzzard, and went out of the shop as soon as he had crumpled up the paper again and thrust it into his pocket. It had been an abject little exposure of dread-

ful, impossible passion. He appeared in fact to be too ashamed
to come back. He had left town again, and a first week
elapsed, and a second. He had had naturally to return to the
real mistress of his fate; she had insisted—she knew how, and
he couldn't put in another hour. There was always a day when
she called time. It was known to our young friend moreover
that he had now been despatching telegrams from other offices. She knew at last so much, that she had quite lost her
earlier sense of merely guessing. There were no shades of distinctness—it all bounced out.

XXII

Eighteen days elapsed, and she had begun to think it probable
she should never see him again. He too then understood now:
he had made out that she had secrets and reasons and imped-
iments, that even a poor girl at the P.O. might have her
complications. With the charm she had cast on him lightened
by distance he had suffered a final delicacy to speak to him,
had made up his mind that it would be only decent to let her
alone. Never so much as during these latter days had she felt
the precariousness of their relation—the happy, beautiful, un-
troubled original one, if it could only have been restored,—
in which the public servant and the casual public only were
concerned. It hung at the best by the merest silken thread,
which was at the mercy of any accident and might snap at any
minute. She arrived by the end of the fortnight at the highest
sense of actual fitness, never doubting that her decision was
now complete. She would just give him a few days more to
come back to her on a proper impersonal basis—for even to
an embarrassing representative of the casual public a public
servant with a conscience did owe something,—and then
would signify to Mr. Mudge that she was ready for the little
home. It had been visited, in the further talk she had had with
him at Bournemouth, from garret to cellar, and they had especially lingered, with their respectively darkened brows, before the niche into which it was to be broached to her mother
that she was to find means to fit.

He had put it to her more definitely than before that his
calculations had allowed for that dingy presence, and he had

thereby marked the greatest impression he had ever made on her. It was a stroke superior even again to his handling of the drunken soldier. What she considered that, in the face of it, she hung on at Cocker's for, was something that she could only have described as the common fairness of a last word. Her actual last word had been, till it should be superseded, that she wouldn't abandon her other friend, and it stuck to her, through thick and thin, that she was still at her post and on her honour. This other friend had shown so much beauty of conduct already that he would surely, after all, just re-appear long enough to relieve her, to give her something she could take away. She saw it, caught it, at times, his parting present; and there were moments when she felt herself sitting like a beggar with a hand held out to an almsgiver who only fumbled. She hadn't taken the sovereigns, but she *would* take the penny. She heard, in imagination, on the counter, the ring of the copper. "Don't put yourself out any longer," he would say, "for so bad a case. You've done all there is to be done. I thank and acquit and release you. Our lives take us. I don't know much—though I have really been interested—about yours; but I suppose you've got one. Mine, at any rate, will take *me*—and where it will. Heigh-ho! Good-bye." And then once more, for the sweetest, faintest flower of all: "Only, I say—see here!" She had framed the whole picture with a squareness that included also the image of how again she would decline to "see there," decline, as she might say, to see anywhere or anything. Yet it befell that just in the fury of this escape she saw more than ever.

He came back one night with a rush, near the moment of their closing, and showed her a face so different and new, so upset and anxious, that almost anything seemed to look out of it but clear recognition. He poked in a telegram very much as if the simple sense of pressure, the distress of extreme haste, had blurred the remembrance of where in particular he was. But as she met his eyes a light came; it broke indeed on the spot into a positive, conscious glare. That made up for every-thing, for it was an instant proclamation of the celebrated "danger"; it seemed to pour things out in a flood. "Oh yes, here it is—it's upon me at last! Forget, for God's sake, my having worried or bored you, and just help me, just *save* me, by getting this off without the loss of a second!" Something grave had clearly occurred, a crisis declared itself. She recognised immediately the person to whom the telegram was addressed—the Miss Dolman, of Parade Lodge, to whom Lady Bradeen had wired, at Dover, on the last occasion, and whom she had then, with her recollection of previous arrangements, fitted into a particular setting. Miss Dolman had figured before and not figured since, but she was now the subject of an imperative appeal. "Absolutely necessary to see you. Take last train Victoria if you can catch it. If not, earliest morning, and answer me direct either way."

"Reply paid?" said the girl. Mr. Buckton had just departed, and the counter-clerk was at the sounder. There was no other representative of the public, and she had never yet, as it seemed to her, not even in the street or in the Park, been so alone with him.

"Oh yes, reply paid, and as sharp as possible, please."

She affixed the stamps in a flash. "She'll catch the train!" she then declared to him breathlessly, as if she could absolutely guarantee it.

"I don't know—I hope so. It's awfully important. So kind of you. Awfully sharp, please." It was wonderfully innocent now, his oblivion of all but his danger. Anything else that had ever passed between them was utterly out of it. Well, she had wanted him to be impersonal!

There was less of the same need therefore, happily, for herself; yet she only took time, before she flew to the sounder, to gasp at him: "You're in trouble?"

"Horrid, horrid—there's a row!" But they parted, on it, in the next breath; and as she dashed at the sounder, almost pushing, in her violence, the counter-clerk off the stool, she caught the bang with which, at Cocker's door, in his further precipitation, he closed the apron of the cab into which he had leaped. As he rushed off to some other precaution suggested by his alarm, his appeal to Miss Dolman flashed straight away.

But she had not, on the morrow, been in the place five minutes before he was with her again, still more discomposed and quite, now, as she said to herself, like a frightened child coming to its mother. Her companions were there, and she felt it to be remarkable how, in the presence of his agitation, his mere scared, exposed nature, she suddenly ceased to mind. It came to her as it had never come to her before that with absolute directness and assurance they might carry almost anything off. He had nothing to send—she was sure he had been wiring all over,—and yet his business was evidently huge. There was nothing but that in his eyes—not a glimmer of reference or memory. He was almost haggard with anxiety, and had clearly not slept a wink. Her pity for him would have given her any courage, and she seemed to know at last why she had been such a fool. "She didn't come?" she panted.

"Oh yes, she came; but there has been some mistake. We want a telegram."

"A telegram?"

"One that was sent from here ever so long ago. There was something in it that has to be recovered. Something very, *very* important, please—we want it immediately."

He really spoke to her as if she had been some strange young woman at Knightsbridge or Paddington; but it had no other effect on her than to give her the measure of his tremendous flurry. Then it was that, above all, she felt how much she had missed in the gaps and blanks and absent answers—how much she had had to dispense with: it was black darkness now, save for this little wild red flare. So much as that she saw and possessed. One of the lovers was quaking somewhere out of town, and the other was quaking just where he stood. This was vivid enough, and after an instant she knew it was all she wanted. She wanted no detail, no fact—she wanted no nearer vision of discovery or shame. "When was your telegram? Do you mean you sent it from here?" She tried to do the young woman at Knightsbridge.

"Oh yes, from here—several weeks ago. Five, six, seven"— he was confused and impatient,—"don't you remember?"

"Remember?" she could scarcely keep out of her face, at the word, the strangest of smiles.

But the way he didn't catch what it meant was perhaps even stranger still. "I mean, don't you keep the old ones?"

"For a certain time."

"But how long?"

She thought; she *must* do the young woman, and she knew exactly what the young woman would say and, still more, wouldn't. "Can you give me the date?"

"Oh God, no! It was some time or other in August—toward the end. It was to the same address as the one I gave you last night."

"Oh!" said the girl, knowing at this the deepest thrill she had ever felt. It came to her there, with her eyes on his face, that she held the whole thing in her hand, held it as she held her pencil, which might have broken at that instant in her tightened grip. This made her feel like the very fountain of fate, but the emotion was such a flood that she had to press it back with all her force. That was positively the reason, again, of her flute-like Paddington tone. "You can't give us anything a little nearer?" Her "little" and her "us" came straight from Paddington. These things were no false note for him—his difficulty absorbed them all. The eyes with which he pressed her, and in the depths of which she read terror and rage and literal tears, were just the same he would have shown any other prim person.

"I don't know the date. I only know the thing went from here, and just about the time I speak of. It wasn't delivered, you see. We've got to recover it."

XXIII

She was as struck with the beauty of his plural pronoun as she had judged he might be with that of her own; but she knew now so well what she was about that she could almost play with him and with her new-born joy. "You say 'about the time you speak of.' But I don't think you speak of an exact time— *do* you?"

He looked splendidly helpless. "That's just what I want to find out. Don't you keep the old ones?—can't you look it up?"

Our young lady—still at Paddington—turned the question over. "It wasn't delivered?"

"Yes, it *was*; yet, at the same time, don't you know? it wasn't." He just hung back, but he brought it out. "I mean

906 IN THE CAGE

it was intercepted, don't you know? and there was something in it." He paused again and, as if to further his quest and woo and supplicate success and recovery, even smiled with an effort at the agreeable that was almost ghastly and that turned the knife in her tenderness. What must be the pain of it all, of the open gulf and the throbbing fever, when this was the mere hot breath? "We want to get what was in it—to know what it was."

"I see—I see." She managed just the accent they had at Paddington when they stared like dead fish. "And you have no clue?"

"Not at all—I've the clue I've just given you."

"Oh, the last of August?" If she kept it up long enough she would make him really angry.

"Yes, and the address, as I've said."

"Oh, the same as last night?"

He visibly quivered, as if with a gleam of hope; but it only poured oil on her quietude, and she was still deliberate. She ranged some papers. "Won't you look?" he went on.

"I remember your coming," she replied.

He blinked with a new uneasiness; it might have begun to come to him, through her difference, that he was somehow different himself. "You were much quicker then, you know!"

"So were you—you must do me that justice," she answered with a smile. "But let me see. Wasn't it Dover?"

"Yes, Miss Dolman——"

"Parade Lodge, Parade Terrace?"

"Exactly—thank you so awfully much!" He began to hope again. "Then you *have* it—the other one?"

She hesitated afresh; she quite dangled him. "It was brought by a lady?"

"Yes; and she put in by mistake something wrong. That's what we've got to get hold of!"

Heavens! what was he going to say?—flooding poor Paddington with wild betrayals! She couldn't too much, for her joy, dangle him, yet she couldn't either, for his dignity, warn or control or check him. What she found herself doing was just to treat herself to the middle way. "It was intercepted?"

"It fell into the wrong hands. But there's something in it," he continued to blurt out, "that *may* be all right. That is, if it's wrong, don't you know? It's all right if it's wrong," he remarkably explained.

What *was* he, on earth, going to say? Mr. Buckton and the counter-clerk were already interested; no one *would* have the decency to come in; and she was divided between her particular terror for him and her general curiosity. Yet she already saw with what brilliancy she could add, to carry the thing off, a little false knowledge to all her real. "I quite understand," she said with benevolent, with almost patronising quickness. "The lady has forgotten what she did put."

"Forgotten most wretchedly, and it's an immense inconvenience. It has only just been found that it didn't get there; so that if we could immediately have it——"

"Immediately?"

"Every minute counts. You *have*," he pleaded, "surely got them on file?"

"So that you can see it on the spot?"

"Yes, please- -this very minute." The counter rang with his knuckles, with the knob of his stick, with his panic of alarm. "Do, *do* hunt it up!" he repeated.

"I dare say we could get it for you," the girl sweetly returned.

"Get it?"—he looked aghast. "When?"

"Probably by to-morrow."

"Then it isn't here?"—his face was pitiful.

She caught only the uncovered gleams that peeped out of the blackness, and she wondered what complication, even among the most supposable, the very worst, could be bad enough to account for the degree of his terror. There were twists and turns, there were places where the screw drew blood, that she couldn't guess. She was more and more glad she didn't want to. "It has been sent on."

"But how do you know if you don't look?"

She gave him a smile that was meant to be, in the absolute irony of its propriety, quite divine. "It was August 23rd, and we have nothing later here than August 27th."

Something leaped into his face. "27th—23rd? Then you're sure? You know?"

She felt she scarce knew what—as if she might soon be pounced upon for some lurid connection with a scandal. It was the queerest of all sensations, for she had heard, she had read, of these things, and the wealth of her intimacy with them at Cocker's might be supposed to have schooled and seasoned her. This particular one that she had really quite lived with was, after all, an old story; yet what it had been before was dim and distant beside the touch under which she now winced. Scandal?—it had never been but a silly word. Now it was a great palpable surface, and the surface was, somehow, Captain Everard's wonderful face. Deep down in his eyes was a picture, the vision of a great place like a chamber of justice, where, before a watching crowd, a poor girl, exposed but heroic, swore with a quavering voice to a document, proved an *alibi*, supplied a link. In this picture she bravely took her place. "It was the 23rd."

"Then can't you get it this morning—or some time to-day?"

She considered, still holding him with her look, which she then turned on her two companions, who were by this time unreservedly enlisted. She didn't care—not a scrap, and she glanced about for a piece of paper. With this she had to recognise the rigour of official thrift—a morsel of blackened blotter was the only loose paper to be seen. "Have you got a card?" she said to her visitor. He was quite away from Paddington now, and the next instant, with a pocket-book in his hand, he had whipped a card out. She gave no glance at the name on it—only turned it to the other side. She continued to hold him, she felt at present, as she had never held him; and her command of her colleagues was, for the moment, not less marked. She wrote something on the back of the card and pushed it across to him.

He fairly glared at it. "Seven, nine, four——"

"Nine, six, one"—she obligingly completed the number. "Is it right?" she smiled.

He took the whole thing in with a flushed intensity; then there broke out in him a visibility of relief that was simply a tremendous exposure. He shone at them all like a tall lighthouse, embracing even, for sympathy, the blinking young men. "By all the powers—it's wrong!" And without another look, without a word of thanks, without time for anything or anybody, he turned on them the broad back of his great

stature, straightened his triumphant shoulders, and strode out
of the place.

She was left confronted with her habitual critics. " 'If it's
wrong it's all right!' " she extravagantly quoted to them.

The counter-clerk was really awe-stricken. "But how did
you know, dear?"

"I remembered, love!"

Mr. Buckton, on the contrary, was rude. "And what game
is that, miss?"

No happiness she had ever known came within miles of it,
and some minutes elapsed before she could recall herself sufficiently to reply that it was none of his business.

XXIV

If life at Cocker's, with the dreadful drop of August, had lost
something of its savour, she had not been slow to infer that
a heavier blight had fallen on the graceful industry of Mrs.
Jordan. With Lord Rye and Lady Ventnor and Mrs. Bubb all
out of town, with the blinds down on all the homes of luxury,
this ingenious woman might well have found her wonderful
taste left quite on her hands. She bore up, however, in a way
that began by exciting much of her young friend's esteem;
they perhaps even more frequently met as the wine of life
flowed less free from other sources, and each, in the lack of
better diversion, carried on with more mystification for the
other an intercourse that consisted not a little of peeping out
and drawing back. Each waited for the other to commit herself, each profusely curtained for the other the limits of low
horizons. Mrs. Jordan was indeed probably the more reckless
skirmisher; nothing could exceed her frequent incoherence
unless it was indeed her occasional bursts of confidence. Her
account of her private affairs rose and fell like a flame in the
wind—sometimes the bravest bonfire and sometimes a handful of ashes. This our young woman took to be an effect of
the position, at one moment and another, of the famous door
of the great world. She had been struck in one of her ha'penny
volumes with the translation of a French proverb according
to which a door had to be either open or shut; and it seemed
a part of the precariousness of Mrs. Jordan's life that hers

mostly managed to be neither. There had been occasions when it appeared to gape wide—fairly to woo her across its threshold; there had been others, of an order distinctly disconcerting, when it was all but banged in her face. On the whole, however, she had evidently not lost heart; these still belonged to the class of things in spite of which she looked well. She intimated that the profits of her trade had swollen so as to float her through any state of the tide, and she had, besides this, a hundred profundities and explanations.

She rose superior, above all, on the happy fact that there were always gentlemen in town and that gentlemen were her greatest admirers; gentlemen from the City in especial—as to whom she was full of information about the passion and pride excited in such breasts by the objects of her charming commerce. The City men *did*, in short, go in for flowers. There was a certain type of awfully smart stockbroker—Lord Rye called them Jews and "bounders," but she didn't care—whose extravagance, she more than once threw out, had really, if one had any conscience, to be forcibly restrained. It was not perhaps a pure love of beauty: it was a matter of vanity and a sign of business; they wished to crush their rivals, and that was one of their weapons. Mrs. Jordan's shrewdness was extreme; she knew, in any case, her customer—she dealt, as she said, with all sorts; and it was, at the worst, a race for her—a race even in the dull months—from one set of chambers to another. And then, after all, there were also still the ladies; the ladies of stockbroking circles were perpetually up and down. They were not quite perhaps Mrs. Bubb or Lady Ventnor; but you couldn't tell the difference unless you quarrelled with them, and then you knew it only by their making-up sooner. These ladies formed the branch of her subject on which she most swayed in the breeze; to that degree that her confidant had ended with an inference or two tending to banish regret for opportunities not embraced. There were indeed tea-gowns that Mrs. Jordan described—but tea-gowns were not the whole of respectability, and it was odd that a clergyman's widow should sometimes speak as if she almost thought so. She came back, it was true, unfailingly, to Lord Rye, never, evidently, quite losing sight of him even on the longest excursions. That he was kindness itself had become in fact the very moral it all pointed—pointed in strange flashes of the poor woman's nearsighted eyes. She launched at her young friend many portentous looks, solemn heralds of some extraordinary communication. The communication itself, from week to week, hung fire; but it was to the facts over which it hovered that she owed her power of going on. "They *are*, in one way *and* another," she often emphasised, "a tower of strength"; and as the allusion was to the aristocracy, the girl could quite wonder why, if they were so in "one" way, they should require to be so in two. She thoroughly knew, however, how many ways Mrs. Jordan counted in. It all meant simply that her fate was pressing her close. If that fate was to be sealed at the matrimonial altar it was perhaps not remarkable that she shouldn't come all at once to the scratch of overwhelming a mere telegraphist. It would necessarily present to such a person a prospect of regretful sacrifice. Lord Rye—if it *was* Lord Rye—wouldn't be "kind" to a nonentity of that sort, even though people quite as good had been.

One Sunday afternoon in November they went, by arrangement, to church together; after which—on the inspiration of the moment; the arrangement had not included it—they proceeded to Mrs. Jordan's lodging in the region of Maida Vale. She had raved to her friend about her service of predilection; she was excessively "high," and had more than once wished to introduce the girl to the same comfort and privilege. There was a thick brown fog, and Maida Vale tasted of acrid smoke; but they had been sitting among chants and incense and wonderful music, during which, though the effect of such things on her mind was great, our young lady had indulged in a series of reflections but indirectly related to them. One of these was the result of Mrs. Jordan's having said to her on the way, and with a certain fine significance, that Lord Rye had been for some time in town. She had spoken as if it were a circumstance to which little required to be added—as if the bearing of such an item on her life might easily be grasped. Perhaps it was the wonder of whether Lord Rye wished to marry her that made her guest, with thoughts straying to that quarter, quite determine that some other nuptials also should take place at St. Julian's. Mr. Mudge was still an attendant at his Wesleyan chapel, but this was the least of her worries—it had never even vexed her enough for her to so much as name it to Mrs. Jordan. Mr. Mudge's form of worship was one of several things—they made up in superiority and beauty for what they wanted in number—that she had long ago settled he should take from her, and she had now moreover for the first time definitely established her own. Its principal feature was that it was to be the same as that of Mrs. Jordan and Lord Rye; which was indeed very much what she said to her hostess as they sat together later on. The brown fog was in this hostess's little parlour, where it acted as a postponement of the question of there being, besides, anything else than the teacups and a pewter pot, and a very black little fire, and a paraffin lamp without a shade. There was at any rate no sign of a flower; it was not for herself Mrs. Jordan gathered sweets. The girl waited till they had had a cup of tea—waited for the announcement that she fairly believed her friend had, this time, possessed herself of her formally at last to make; but nothing came, after the interval, save a little poke at the fire, which was like the clearing of a throat for a speech.

XXV

"I think you must have heard me speak of Mr. Drake?" Mrs. Jordan had never looked so queer, nor her smile so suggestive of a large benevolent bite.

"Mr. Drake? Oh yes; isn't he a friend of Lord Rye?"

"A great and trusted friend. Almost—I may say—a loved friend."

Mrs. Jordan's "almost" had such an oddity that her companion was moved, rather flippantly perhaps, to take it up. "Don't people as good as love their friends when they 'trust' them?"

It pulled up a little the eulogist of Mr. Drake. "Well, my dear, I love *you*——"

"But you don't trust me?" the girl unmercifully asked.

Again Mrs. Jordan paused—still she looked queer. "Yes," she replied with a certain austerity; "that's exactly what I'm about to give you rather a remarkable proof of." The sense of its being remarkable was already so strong that, while she bridled a little, this held her auditor in a momentary muteness of submission. "Mr. Drake has rendered his lordship, for several years, services that his lordship has highly appreciated and that make it all the more—a—unexpected that they should, perhaps a little suddenly, separate."

"Separate?" Our young lady was mystified, but she tried to be interested; and she already saw that she had put the saddle on the wrong horse. She had heard something of Mr. Drake, who was a member of his lordship's circle—the member with whom, apparently, Mrs. Jordan's avocations had most happened to throw her. She was only a little puzzled at the "separation." "Well, at any rate," she smiled, "if they separate as friends——!"

"Oh, his lordship takes the greatest interest in Mr. Drake's future. He'll do anything for him; he has in fact just done a great deal. There *must*, you know, be changes——!"

"No one knows it better than I," the girl said. She wished to draw her interlocutress out. "There will be changes enough for me."

"You're leaving Cocker's?"

The ornament of that establishment waited a moment to answer, and then it was indirect. "Tell me what *you're* doing."

"Well, what will you think of it?"

"Why, that you've found the opening you were always so sure of."

Mrs. Jordan, on this, appeared to muse with embarrassed intensity. "I was always sure, yes—and yet I often wasn't!"

"Well, I hope you're sure now. Sure. I mean, of Mr. Drake."

"Yes, my dear, I think I may say I *am*. I kept him going till I was."

"Then he's yours?"

"My very own."

"How nice! And awfully rich?" our young woman went on.

Mrs. Jordan showed promptly enough that she loved for higher things "Awfully handsome—six foot two. And he *has* put by."

"Quite like Mr. Mudge, then!" that gentleman's friend rather desperately exclaimed.

"Oh, not *quite*!" Mr. Drake's was ambiguous about it, but the name of Mr. Mudge had evidently given her some sort of stimulus. "He'll have more opportunity now, at any rate. He's going to Lady Bradeen."

"To Lady Bradeen?" This was bewilderment. " 'Going—'?"

The girl had seen, from the way Mrs. Jordan looked at her, that the effect of the name had been to make her let something out. "Do you know her?"

She hesitated; then she found her feet. "Well, you'll remember I've often told you that if you have grand clients, I have them too."

"Yes," said Mrs. Jordan; "but the great difference is that you hate yours, whereas I really love mine. *Do* you know Lady Bradeen?" she pursued.

"Down to the ground! She's always in and out."

Mrs. Jordan's foolish eyes confessed, in fixing themselves on this sketch, to a degree of wonder and even of envy. But she bore up and, with a certain gaiety, "Do you hate *her?*" she demanded.

Her visitor's reply was prompt. "Dear no!—not nearly so much as some of them. She's too outrageously beautiful."

Mrs. Jordan continued to gaze. "Outrageously?"

"Well, yes; deliciously." What was really delicious was Mrs. Jordan's vagueness. "You don't know her—you've not seen her?" her guest lightly continued.

"No, but I've heard a great deal about her."

"So have I!" our young lady exclaimed.

Mrs. Jordan looked an instant as if she suspected her good faith, or at least her seriousness. "You know some friend——?"

"Of Lady Bradeen's? Oh yes—I know one."

"Only one?"

The girl laughed out. "Only one—but he's so intimate."

Mrs. Jordan just hesitated. "He's a gentleman?"

"Yes, he's not a lady."

Her interlocutress appeared to muse. "She's immensely surrounded."

"She *will* be—with Mr. Drake!"

Mrs. Jordan's gaze became strangely fixed. "Is she *very* good-looking?"

"The handsomest person I know."

Mrs. Jordan continued to contemplate. "Well, *I* know some

beauties." Then, with her odd jerkiness, "Do you think she looks *good*?" she inquired.

"Because that's not always the case with the good-looking?"—the other took it up. "No, indeed, it isn't: that's one thing Cocker's has taught me. Still, there are some people who have everything. Lady Bradeen, at any rate, has enough: eyes and a nose and a mouth, a complexion, a figure——"

"A figure?" Mrs. Jordan almost broke in.

"A figure, a head of hair!" The girl made a little conscious motion that seemed to let the hair all down, and her companion watched the wonderful show. "But Mr. Drake *is* another——?"

"Another?"—Mrs. Jordan's thoughts had to come back from a distance.

"Of her ladyship's admirers. He's 'going,' you say, to her?"

At this Mrs. Jordan really faltered. "She has engaged him."

"Engaged him?"—our young woman was quite at sea.

"In the same capacity as Lord Rye."

"And was Lord Rye engaged?"

XXVI

Mrs. Jordan looked away from her now—looked, she thought, rather injured and, as if trifled with, even a little angry. The mention of Lady Bradeen had frustrated for a while the convergence of our heroine's thoughts; but with this impression of her old friend's combined impatience and diffidence they began again to whirl round her, and continued it till one of them appeared to dart at her, out of the dance, as if with a sharp peck. It came to her with a lively shock, with a positive sting, that Mr. Drake was—could it be possible? With the idea she found herself afresh on the edge of laughter, of a sudden and strange perversity of mirth. Mr. Drake loomed, in a swift image, before her; such a figure as she had seen in open doorways of houses in Cocker's quarter—majestic, middle-aged, erect, flanked on either side by a footman and taking the name of a visitor. Mr. Drake then verily *was* a person who opened the door! Before she had time, however, to recover from the effect of her evocation, she was offered a vision which quite engulphed it. It was communicated to her some-how that the face with which she had seen it rise prompted Mrs. Jordan to dash, at a venture, at something that might attenuate criticism. "Lady Bradeen is re-arranging—she's going to be married."

"Married?" The girl echoed it ever so softly, but there it was at last.

"Didn't you know it?"

She summoned all her sturdiness. "No, she hasn't told me."

"And her friends—haven't they?"

"I haven't seen any of them lately. I'm not so fortunate as *you*."

Mrs. Jordan gathered herself. "Then you haven't even heard of Lord Bradeen's death?"

Her comrade, unable for a moment to speak, gave a slow headshake. "You know it from Mr. Drake?" It was better surely not to learn things at all than to learn them by the butler.

"She tells him everything."

"And he tells *you*—I see." Our young lady got up; re-covering her muff and her gloves, she smiled. "Well, I haven't, unfortunately, any Mr. Drake. I congratulate you with all my heart. Even without your sort of assistance, however, there's a trifle here and there that I do pick up. I gather that if she's to marry any one, it must quite necessarily be my friend."

Mrs. Jordan was now also on her feet. "Is Captain Everard your friend?"

The girl considered, drawing on a glove. "I saw, at one time, an immense deal of him."

Mrs. Jordan looked hard at the glove, but she had not, after all, waited for that to be sorry it was not cleaner. "What time was that?"

"It must have been the time you were seeing so much of Mr. Drake." She had now fairly taken it in: the distinguished person Mrs. Jordan was to marry would answer bells and put on coals and superintend, at least, the cleaning of boots for the other distinguished person whom *she* might—well, whom she might have had, if she had wished, so much more to say to. "Good-bye," she added; "good-bye."

Mrs. Jordan, however, again taking her muff from her, turned it over, brushed it off, and thoughtfully peeped into it. "Tell me this before you go. You spoke just now of your own changes. Do you mean that Mr. Mudge——?"

"Mr. Mudge has had great patience with me—he has brought me at last to the point. We're to be married next month and have a nice little home. But he's only a grocer, you know"—the girl met her friend's intent eyes—"so that I'm afraid that, with the set you've got into, you won't see your way to keep up our friendship."

Mrs. Jordan for a moment made no answer to this; she only held the muff up to her face, after which she gave it back. "You don't like it. I see, I see."

To her guest's astonishment there were tears now in her eyes. "I don't like what?" the girl asked.

"Why, my engagement. Only, with your great cleverness," the poor lady quavered out, "you put it in your own way. I mean that you'll cool off. You already *have*— !" And on this, the next instant, her tears began to flow. She succumbed to them and collapsed; she sank down again, burying her face and trying to smother her sobs.

Her young friend stood there, still in some rigour, but taken much by surprise even if not yet fully moved to pity. "I don't put anything in any 'way,' and I'm very glad you're suited. Only, you know, you did put to *me* so splendidly what, even for me, if I had listened to you, it might lead to."

Mrs. Jordan kept up a mild, thin, weak wail; then, drying her eyes, as feebly considered this reminder. "It has led to my not starving!" she faintly gasped.

Our young lady, at this, dropped into the place beside her, and now, in a rush, the small, silly misery was clear. She took her hand as a sign of pitying it, then, after another instant, confirmed this expression with a consoling kiss. They sat there together; they looked out, hand in hand, into the damp, dusky, shabby little room and into the future, of no such very different suggestion, at last accepted by each. There was no definite utterance, on either side, of Mr. Drake's position in the great world, but the temporary collapse of his prospective bride threw all further necessary light; and what our heroine saw and felt for in the whole business was the vivid reflection of her own dreams and delusions and her own return to reality. Reality, for the poor things they both were, could only be ugliness and obscurity, could never be the escape, the rise. She pressed her friend—she had tact enough for that—with no other personal question, brought on no need of further revelations, only just continued to hold and comfort her and to acknowledge by stiff little forbearances the common element in their fate. She felt indeed magnanimous in such matters; for if it was very well, for condolence or re-assurance, to suppress just then invidious shrinkings, she yet by no means saw herself sitting down, as she might say, to the same table with Mr. Drake. There would luckily, to all appearance, be little question of tables; and the circumstance that, on their peculiar lines, her friend's interests would still attach themselves to Mayfair flung over Chalk Farm the first radiance it had shown. Where was one's pride and one's passion when the real way to judge of one's luck was by making not the wrong, but the right, comparison? Before she had again gathered herself to go she felt very small and cautious and thankful. "We shall have our own house," she said, "and you must come very soon and let me show it you."

"*We* shall have our own too," Mrs. Jordan replied; "for, don't you know, he makes it a condition that he sleeps out?"

"A condition?"—the girl felt out of it.

"For any new position. It was on that he parted with Lord Rye. His lordship can't meet it; so Mr. Drake has given him up."

"And all for you?"—our young woman put it as cheerfully as possible.

"For me and Lady Bradeen. Her ladyship's too glad to get him at any price. Lord Rye, out of interest in us, has in fact quite *made* her take him. So, as I tell you, he will have his own establishment."

Mrs. Jordan, in the elation of it, had begun to revive; but there was nevertheless between them rather a conscious pause—a pause in which neither visitor nor hostess brought out a hope or an invitation. It expressed in the last resort that, in spite of submission and sympathy, they could now, after all, only look at each other across the social gulf. They remained together as if it would be indeed their last chance, still sitting, though awkwardly, quite close, and feeling also—and this most unmistakably—that there was one thing more to go into. By the time it came to the surface, moreover, our young friend had recognised the whole of the main truth, from which she even drew again a slight irritation. It was not the main truth perhaps that most signified; but after her momentary effort, her embarrassment and her tears, Mrs. Jordan had begun to sound afresh—and even without speaking—the note of a social connection. She hadn't really let go of it that she was marrying into society. Well, it was a harmless compensation, and it was all that the prospective bride of Mr. Mudge had to leave with her.

XXVII

This young lady at last rose again, but she lingered before going. "And has Captain Everard nothing to say to it?"

"To what, dear?"

"Why, to such questions—the domestic arrangements, things in the house."

"How *can* he, with any authority, when nothing in the house is his?"

"Not his?" The girl wondered, perfectly conscious of the appearance she thus conferred on Mrs. Jordan of knowing, in comparison with herself, so tremendously much about it. Well, there were things she wanted so to get at that she was willing at last, though it hurt her, to pay for them with humiliation. "Why are they not his?"

"Don't you know, dear, that he has nothing?"

"Nothing?" It was hard to see him in such a light, but Mrs. Jordan's power to answer for it had a superiority that began, on the spot, to grow. "Isn't he rich?"

Mrs. Jordan looked immensely, looked both generally and particularly, informed. "It depends upon what you call——! Not, at any rate, in the least as *she* is. What does he bring? Think what she has. And then, my love, his debts."

"His debts?" His young friend was fairly betrayed into helpless innocence. She could struggle a little, but she had to let herself go; and if she had spoken frankly she would have said: "Do tell me, for I don't know so much about him as *that*!" As she didn't speak frankly she only said: "His debts are nothing—when she so adores him."

Mrs. Jordan began to fix her again, and now she saw that she could only take it all. That was what it had come to: his having sat with her there, on the bench and under the trees, in the summer darkness, and put his hand on her, making her know what he would have said if permitted; his having returned to her afterwards, repeatedly, with supplicating eyes and a fever in his blood; and her having, on her side, hard and pedantic, helped by some miracle and with her impossible condition, only answered him, yet supplicating back, through the bars of the cage,—all simply that she might hear of him, now for ever lost, only through Mrs. Jordan, who touched him through Mr. Drake, who reached him through Lady Bradeen. "She adores him—but of course that wasn't all there was about it."

The girl met her eyes a minute, then quite surrendered. "What was there else about it?"

"Why, don't you know?"—Mrs. Jordan was almost compassionate.

Her interlocutress had, in the cage, sounded depths, but there was a suggestion here somehow of an abyss quite measureless. "Of course I know that she would never let him alone."

"How *could* she—fancy!—when he had so compromised her?"

The most artless cry they had ever uttered broke, at this, from the younger pair of lips. "*Had* he so——?"

"Why, don't you know the scandal?"

Our heroine thought, recollected; there was something, whatever it was, that she knew, after all, much more of than Mrs. Jordan. She saw him again as she had seen him come that morning to recover the telegram—she saw him as she had seen him leave the shop. She perched herself a moment on this. "Oh, there was nothing public."

"Not exactly public—no. But there was an awful scare and an awful row. It was all on the very point of coming out. Something was lost—something was found."

"Ah yes," the girl replied, smiling as if with the revival of a blurred memory; "something was found."

"It all got about—and there was a point at which Lord Bradeen had to act."

"Had to—yes. But he didn't."

Mrs. Jordan was obliged to admit it. "No, he didn't. And then, luckily for them, he died."

"I didn't know about his death," her companion said.

"It was nine weeks ago, and most sudden. It has given them a prompt chance."

"To get married"—this was a wonder—"within nine weeks?"

"Oh, not immediately, but—in all the circumstances—very quietly and, I assure you, very soon. Every preparation's made. Above all, she holds him."

"Oh yes, she holds him!" our young friend threw off. She had this before her again a minute; then she continued: "You mean through his having made her talked about?"

"Yes, but not only that. She has still another pull."

"Another?"

Mrs. Jordan hesitated. "Why, he was *in* something."

Her comrade wondered. "In what?"

"I don't know. Something bad. As I tell you, something was found."

The girl stared. "Well?"

"It would have been very bad for him. But she helped him some way—she recovered it, got hold of it. It's even said she stole it!"

Our young woman considered afresh. "Why, it was what was found that precisely saved him."

Mrs. Jordan, however, was positive. "I beg your pardon. I happen to know."

Her disciple faltered but an instant. "Do you mean through Mr. Drake? Do they tell *him* these things?"

"A good servant," said Mrs. Jordan, now thoroughly superior and proportionately sententious, "doesn't need to be told! Her ladyship saved—as a woman so often saves!—the man she loves."

This time our heroine took longer to recover herself, but she found a voice at last. "Ah well—of course I don't know! The great thing was that he got off. They seem then, in a manner," she added, "to have done a great deal for each other."

"Well, it's she that has done most. She has him tight."

"I see, I see. Good-bye." The women had already embraced, and this was not repeated; but Mrs. Jordan went down with her guest to the door of the house. Here again the younger lingered, reverting, though three or four other remarks had on the way passed between them, to Captain Everard and Lady Bradeen. "Did you mean just now that if she hadn't saved him, as you call it, she wouldn't hold him so tight?"

"Well, I daresay." Mrs. Jordan, on the doorstep, smiled with a reflection that had come to her; she took one of her big bites of the brown gloom. "Men always dislike one when they have done one an injury."

"But what injury had he done her?"

"The one I've mentioned. He *must* marry her, you know."

"And didn't he want to?"

"Not before."

"Not before she recovered the telegram?"

Mrs. Jordan was pulled up a little. "Was it a telegram?"

The girl hesitated. "I thought you said so. I mean whatever it was."

"Yes, whatever it was, I don't think she saw *that*."

"So she just nailed him?"

"She just nailed him." The departing friend was now at the bottom of the little flight of steps; the other was at the top, with a certain thickness of fog. "And when am I to think of you in your little home?—next month?" asked the voice from the top.

"At the very latest. And when am I to think of you in yours?"

"Oh, even sooner. I feel, after so much talk with you about it, as if I were already there!" Then "*Good*-bye!" came out of the fog.

"Good-*bye!*" went into it. Our young lady went into it also, in the opposed quarter, and presently, after a few sightless turns, came out on the Paddington canal. Distinguishing vaguely what the low parapet enclosed, she stopped close to it and stood a while, very intently, but perhaps still sightlessly, looking down on it. A policeman, while she remained, strolled past her; then, going his way a little further and half lost in the atmosphere, paused and watched her. But she was quite unaware—she was full of her thoughts. They were too numerous to find a place just here, but two of the number may at least be mentioned. One of these was that, decidedly, her little home must be not for next month, but for next week; the other, which came indeed as she resumed her walk and went her way, was that it was strange such a matter should be at last settled for her by Mr. Drake.

Chronology

schools and by tutors in lower Broadway and Greenwich Village. But father claims in 1848 that American schooling fails to provide "sensuous education" for his children and plans to take them to Europe.

1855–58   Family (with Aunt Kate) sails for Liverpool, June 27. James is intermittently sick with malarial fever as they travel to Paris, Lyon, and Geneva. After Swiss summer, leaves for London where Robert Thomson (later Robert Louis Stevenson's tutor) is engaged. Early summer 1856, family moves to Paris. Another tutor engaged and children attend experimental Fourierist school. Acquires fluency in French. Family goes to Boulogne-sur-mer in summer, where James contracts typhoid. Spends late October in Paris, but American crash of 1857 returns family to Boulogne where they can live more cheaply. Attends public school (fellow classmate is Coquelin, the future French actor).

1858–59   Family returns to America and settles in Newport, Rhode Island. Goes boating, fishing, and riding. Attends the Reverend W. C. Leverett's Berkeley Institute, and forms friendship with classmate Thomas Sergeant Perry. Takes long walks and sketches with the painter John La Farge.

1859–60   Father, still dissatisfied with American education, returns family to Geneva in October. James attends a pre-engineering school, Institution Rochette, because parents, with "a flattering misconception of my aptitudes," feel he might benefit from less reading and more mathematics. After a few months withdraws from all classes except French, German, and Latin, and joins William as a special student at the Academy (later the University of Geneva) where he attends lectures on literary subjects. Studies German in Bonn during summer 1860.

1860–62   Family returns to Newport in September where William studies with William Morris Hunt, and James sits in on his classes. La Farge introduces him to works of Balzac, Merimée, Musset, and Browning. Wilky and Bob attend Frank Sanborn's experimental school in Concord with children of Hawthorne and Emerson and John Brown's daughter. Early in 1861, orphaned Temple cousins come to live in Newport. Develops close friendship with cousin

Mary (Minnie) Temple. Goes on a week's walking tour in July in New Hampshire with Perry. William abandons art in autumn 1861 and enters Lawrence Scientific School at Harvard. James suffers back injury in a stable fire while serving as a volunteer fireman. Reads Hawthorne ("an American could be an artist, one of the finest").

1862–63 Enters Harvard Law School (Dane Hall). Wilky enlists in the Massachusetts 44th Regiment, and later in Colonel Robert Gould Shaw's 54th, one of the first black regiments. Summer 1863, Bob joins the Massachusetts 55th, another black regiment, under Colonel Hollowell. James withdraws from law studies to try writing. Sends unsigned stories to magazines. Wilky is badly wounded and brought home to Newport in August.

1864 Family moves from Newport to 13 Ashburton Place, Boston. First tale, "A Tragedy of Error" (unsigned), published in *Continental Monthly* (Feb. 1864). Stays in Northampton, Massachusetts, early August–November. Begins writing book reviews for *North American Review* and forms friendship with its editor, Charles Eliot Norton, and his family, including his sister Grace (with whom he maintains a long-lasting correspondence). Wilky returns to his regiment.

1865 First signed tale, "The Story of a Year," published in *Atlantic Monthly* (March 1865). Begins to write reviews for the newly founded *Nation* and publishes anonymously in it during next fifteen years. William sails on a scientific expedition with Louis Agassiz to the Amazon. During summer James vacations in the White Mountains with Minnie Temple and her family, joined by Oliver Wendell Holmes Jr. and John Chipman Gray, both recently de mobilized. Father subsidizes plantation for Wilky and Bob in Florida with black hired workers. (The idealistic but impractical venture fails in 1870.)

1866 68 Continues to publish reviews and tales in Boston and New York journals. William returns from Brazil and resumes medical education. James has recurrence of back ailment and spends summer in Swampscott, Massachusetts. Begins friendship with William Dean Howells. Family moves to 20 Quincy St., Cambridge. William, suffering from nervous ailments, goes to Germany in spring 1867. "Poor Richard," James's longest story to date, published in *Atlantic Monthly* (June–Aug. 1867). William begins intermittent criticism of Henry's story-telling and style (which will continue throughout their careers). Momentary meeting with Charles Dickens at Norton's house. Vacations in Jefferson, New Hampshire, summer 1868. William returns from Europe.

1869–70   Sails in February for European tour. Visits English towns and cathedrals. Through Nortons meets Leslie Stephen, William Morris, Dante Gabriel Rossetti, Edward Burne-Jones, John Ruskin, Charles Darwin, and George Eliot (the "one marvel" of his stay in London). Goes to Paris in May, then travels in Switzerland in summer and hikes into Italy in autumn, where he stays in Milan, Venice (Sept.), Florence, and Rome (Oct. 30–Dec. 28). Returns to England to drink the waters at Malvern health spa in Worcestershire because of digestive troubles. Stays in Paris en route and has first experience of Comédie Française. Learns that his beloved cousin, Minnie Temple, has died of tuberculosis.

1870–72   Returns to Cambridge in May. Travels to Rhode Island, Vermont, and New York to write travel sketches for *The Nation*. Spends a few days with Emerson in Concord. Meets Bret Harte at Howells' home April 1871. *Watch and Ward*, his first novel, published in *Atlantic Monthly* (Aug.–Dec. 1871). Serves as occasional art reviewer for the *Atlantic* January–March 1872.

1872–74   Accompanies Aunt Kate and sister Alice on tour of England, France, Switzerland, Italy, Austria, and Germany from May through October. Writes travel sketches for *The Nation*. Spends autumn in Paris, becoming friends with James Russell Lowell. Escorts Emerson through the Louvre. (Later, on Emerson's return from Egypt, will show him the Vatican.) Goes to Florence in December and from there to Rome, where he becomes friends with actress Fanny Kemble, her daughter Sarah Butler Wister, and William Wetmore Story and his family. In Italy sees old family friend Francis Boott and his daughter Elizabeth (Lizzie), expatriates who have lived for many years in Florentine villa on Bellosguardo. Takes up horseback riding on the Campagna. Encounters Matthew Arnold in April 1873 at Story's. Moves from Rome hotel to rooms of his own. Continues writing and now earns enough to support himself. Leaves Rome in June, spends summer in Bad Homburg. In October goes to Florence, where William joins him. They also visit Rome, William returning to America in March. In Baden-Baden June–August and returns to America September 4, with *Roderick Hudson* all but finished.

1875   *Roderick Hudson* serialized in *Atlantic Monthly* from January (published by Osgood at the end of the year). First book, *A Passionate Pilgrim and Other Tales*, published January 31. Tries living and writing in New York, in rooms at 111 E. 25th Street. Earns $200 a month from novel installments and continued reviewing, but finds New York too expensive. *Transatlantic Sketches*, published in April, sells almost 1,000 copies in three months. In Cambridge in July decides to return to Europe; arranges with John Hay, assistant to the publisher, to write Paris letters for the *New York Tribune*.

1875–76   Arriving in Paris in November, he takes rooms at 29 Rue de Luxembourg (since renamed Cambon). Becomes friend of Ivan Turgenev and is introduced by him to Gustave Flaubert's Sunday parties. Meets Edmond de Goncourt, Émile Zola, G. Charpentier (the publisher), Catulle Mendès, Alphonse Daudet, Guy de Maupassant, Ernest Renan, Gustave Doré. Makes friends with Charles Sanders Peirce, who is in Paris. Reviews (unfavorably) the early Impressionists at the Durand-Ruel gallery. By midsummer has received $400 for *Tribune* pieces, but editor asks for more Parisian gossip and James resigns. Travels in France during July, visiting Normandy and the Midi, and in September crosses to San Sebastian, Spain, to see a bullfight ("I thought the bull, in any case, a finer fellow than any of his tormentors"). Moves to London in December, taking rooms at 3 Bolton Street, Piccadilly, where he will live for the next decade.

1877   *The American* published. Meets Robert Browning and George du Maurier. Leaves London in midsummer for visit to Paris and then goes to Italy. In Rome rides again in Campagna and hears of an episode that inspires "Daisy

Miller." Back in England, spends Christmas at Stratford with Fanny Kemble.

1878   Publishes first book in England, *French Poets and Novelists* (Macmillan). Appearance of "Daisy Miller" in *Cornhill Magazine*, edited by Leslie Stephen, is international success, but by publishing it abroad loses American copyright and story is pirated in U.S. *Cornhill* also prints "An International Episode." *The Europeans* is serialized in *Atlantic*. Now a celebrity, he dines out often, visits country houses, gains weight, takes long walks, fences, and does weight-lifting to reduce. Elected to Reform Club. Meets Tennyson, George Meredith, and James McNeill Whistler. William marries Alice Howe Gibbens.

1879   Immersed in London society (". . . dined out during the past winter 107 times!"). Meets Edmund Gosse and Robert Louis Stevenson, who will later become his close friends. Sees much of Henry Adams and his wife, Marian (Clover), in London and later in Paris. Takes rooms in Paris, September–December. *Confidence* is serialized in *Scribner's* and published by Chatto & Windus. *Hawthorne* appears in Macmillan's "English Men of Letters" series.

1880–81   Stays in Florence March–May to work on *The Portrait of a Lady*. Meets Constance Fenimore Woolson, American novelist and grandniece of James Fenimore Cooper. Returns to Bolton Street in June, where William visits him. *Washington Square* serialized in *Cornhill Magazine* and published in U.S. by Harper & Brothers (Dec. 1880). *The Portrait of a Lady* serialized in *Macmillan's Magazine* (Oct. 1880–Nov. 1881) and *Atlantic Monthly*, published by Macmillan and Houghton, Mifflin (Nov. 1881). Publication both in United States and in England yields him the then-large income of $500 a month, though book sales are disappointing. Leaves London in February for Paris, the south of France, the Italian Riviera, and Venice, and returns home in July. Sister Alice comes to London with her friend Katharine Loring. James goes to Scotland in September.

1881–83   In November revisits America after absence of six years. Lionized in New York. Returns to Quincy Street for Christmas and sees ailing brother Wilky for the first time in ten years. In January visits Washington and the Henry Adamses and meets President Chester A. Arthur. Summoned to Cambridge by mother's death January 29 ("the sweetest, gentlest, most beneficent human being I have ever known"). All four brothers are together for the first time in fifteen years at her funeral. Alice and father move from Cambridge to Boston. Prepares a stage version of "Daisy Miller" and returns to England in May. William, now a Harvard professor, comes to Europe in September. Proposed by Leslie Stephen, James becomes member, without the usual red tape, of the Atheneum Club. Travels in France in October to write *A Little Tour in France* (published 1884) and has last visit with Turgenev, who is dying. Returns to England in December and learns of father's illness. Sails for America but Henry James Sr. dies December 18, 1882, before his arrival. Made executor of father's will. Visits brothers Wilky and Bob in Milwaukee in January. Quarrels with William over division of property—James wants to restore Wilky's share. Macmillan publishes a collected pocket edition of James's novels and tales in fourteen volumes. *Siege of London* and *Portraits of Places* published. Returns to Bolton Street in September. Wilky dies in November. Constance Fenimore Woolson comes to London for the winter.

1884–86   Goes to Paris in February and visits Daudet, Zola, and Goncourt. Again impressed with their intense concern with "art, form, manner" but calls them "mandarins." Misses Turgenev, who had died a few months before. Meets John Singer Sargent and persuades him to settle in London. Returns to Bolton Street. Sargent introduces him to young Paul Bourget. During country visits encounters many British political and social figures, including W. E. Gladstone, John Bright, and Charles Dilke. Alice, suffering from nervous ailment, arrives in England for visit in November but is too ill to travel and settles near her brother. *Tales of Three Cities* ("The Impressions of a Cousin," "Lady Barbarina," "A New England Winter") and "The Art of Fiction" published 1884. Alice goes to Bournemouth in late January. James joins her in May and becomes an intimate of Robert Louis Stevenson, who resides nearby. Spends August at Dover and is visited by Paul Bourget. Stays in Paris for the next two months. Moves into a flat at 34 De Vere Gardens in Kensington early in March 1886. Alice takes rooms in London. *The Bostonians* serialized in *Century* (Feb. 1885–Feb. 1886; published 1886), *The Princess Casamassima* serialized in *Atlantic Monthly* (Sept. 1885–Oct. 1886; published 1886).

1886–87   Leaves for Italy in December for extended stay, mainly in Florence and Venice. Sees much of Constance Fenimore Woolson and stays in her villa. Writes "The Aspern Papers" and other tales. Returns to De Vere Gardens in July and begins work on *The Tragic Muse*. Pays several country visits. Dines out less often ("I know it all—all that one sees by 'going out'—today, as if I had made it. But if I had, I would have made it better!").

1888   *The Reverberator*, *The Aspern Papers*, *Louisa Pallant*, *The Modern Warning*, and *Partial Portraits* published. Elizabeth Boott Duveneck dies. Robert Louis Stevenson leaves for the South Seas. Engages fencing teacher to combat "symptoms of a portentous corpulence." Goes abroad in October to Geneva (where he visits Woolson), Genoa, Monte Carlo, and Paris.

1889–90   Catharine Walsh (Aunt Kate) dies March 1889. William comes to England to visit Alice in August. James goes to Dover in September and then to Paris for five weeks. Writes account of Robert Browning's funeral in Westminster Abbey. Dramatizes *The American* for the Compton Comedy Company. Meets and becomes close friends with American journalist William Morton Fullerton and young American publisher Wolcott Balestier. Goes to Italy for the summer, staying in Venice and Florence, and takes a brief walking tour in Tuscany with W. W. Baldwin, an American physician practicing in Florence. Miss Woolson moves to Cheltenham, England, to be near James. *Atlantic Monthly* rejects his story "The Pupil," but it appears in England. Writes series of drawing-room comedies for theater. Meets Rudyard Kipling. *The Tragic Muse* serialized in *Atlantic Monthly* (Jan. 1889–May 1890; published 1890). *A London Life* (including "The Patagonia," "The Liar," "Mrs. Temperly") published 1889.

1891   *The American* produced at Southport is a success during road tour. After residence in Leamington, Alice returns to London, cared for by Katharine Loring. Doctors discover she has breast cancer. James circulates comedies (*Mrs. Vibert*, later called *Tenants*, and *Mrs. Jasper*, later named *Disengaged*) among theater managers who are cool to his work. Unimpressed at first by Ibsen, writes an appreciative review after seeing a performance of *Hedda Gabler* with Elizabeth Robins, a young Kentucky actress; persuades her to take the part of Mme. de Cintré in the London production of *The American*. Recuperates from flu in Ireland. James Russell Lowell dies. *The American* opens in London, September 26, and runs for seventy nights. Wolcott Balestier dies, and James attends his funeral in Dresden in December.

1892   Alice James dies March 6. James travels to Siena to be near the Paul Bourgets, and Venice, June–July, to visit the Daniel Curtises, then to Lausanne to meet William and his family, who have come abroad for sabbatical. Attends funeral of Tennyson at Westminster Abbey. Augustin Daly agrees to produce *Mrs. Jasper*. *The American* continues to be performed on the road by the Compton Company. *The Lesson of the Master* (with a collection of stories including "The Marriages," "The Pupil," "Brooksmith," "The Solution," and "Sir Edmund Orme") published.

1893   Fanny Kemble dies in January. Continues to write unproduced plays. In March goes to Paris for two months. Sends Edward Compton first act and scenario for *Guy Domville*. Meets William and family in Lucerne and stays a month, returning to London in June. Spends July completing *Guy Domville* in Ramsgate. George Alexander, actor-manager, agrees to produce the play. Daly stages first reading of *Mrs. Jasper*, and James withdraws it, calling the rehearsal a mockery. *The Real Thing and Other Tales* (including "The Wheel of Time," "Lord Beaupré," "The Visit") published.

1894   Constance Fenimore Woolson dies in Venice, January. Shocked and upset, James prepares to attend funeral in Rome but changes his mind on learning she is a suicide. Goes to Venice in April to help her family settle her affairs. Receives one of four copies, privately printed by Miss Loring, of Alice's diary. Finds it impressive but is concerned that so much gossip he told Alice in private has been included (later burns his copy). Robert Louis Stevenson dies in the South Pacific. *Guy Domville* goes into rehearsal. *Theatricals: Two Comedies* and *Theatricals: Second Series* published.

1895   *Guy Domville* opens January 5 at St. James's Theatre. At play's end James is greeted by a fifteen-minute roar of boos, catcalls, and applause. Horrified and depressed, abandons the theater. Play earns him $1,300 after five-week run. Feels he can salvage something useful from playwriting for his fiction ("a key that, working in the same *general* way fits the complicated chambers of *both* the dramatic and the narrative lock"). Writes scenario for *The Spoils of Poynton*. Visits Lord Wolseley and Lord Houghton in Ireland. In the summer goes to Torquay in Devonshire and stays until November while electricity is being installed in De Vere Gardens flat. Friendship with W. E. Norris, who resides at Torquay. Writes a one-act play ("Mrs. Gracedew") at request of Ellen Terry. *Terminations* (containing "The Death of the Lion," "The Coxon Fund," "The Middle Years," "The Altar of the Dead") published.

1896–97   Finishes *The Spoils of Poynton* (serialized in *Atlantic Monthly* April–Oct. 1896 as *The Old Things*; published 1897). *Embarrassments* ("The Figure in the Carpet," "Glasses," "The Next Time," "The Way It Came") published. Takes a house on Point Hill, Playden, opposite the old town of Rye, Sussex, August–September. Ford Madox Hueffer (later Ford Madox Ford) visits him. Converts play *The Other House* into novel and works on *What Maisie Knew* (published Sept. 1897). George du Maurier dies early in October. Because of increasing pain in wrist, hires stenographer William MacAlpine in February and then purchases a typewriter; soon begins direct dictation to MacAlpine at the machine. Invites Joseph Conrad to lunch at De Vere Gardens and begins their friendship. Goes to Bournemouth in July. Serves on jury in London before going to Dunwich, Suffolk, to spend time with Temple-Emmet cousins. In late September 1897 signs a twenty-one-year lease for Lamb House in Rye for £70 a year ($350). Takes on extra work to pay for setting up his house—the life of William Wetmore Story ($1,250 advance) and will furnish an "American Letter" for new magazine *Literature* (precursor of *Times Literary Supplement*) for $200 a month. Howells visits.

1898   "The Turn of the Screw" (serialized in *Collier's* Jan.–April; published with "Covering End" under the title *The Two Magics*) proves his most popular work since "Daisy Miller." Sleeps in Lamb House for first time June 28. Soon after is visited by William's son, Henry James Jr. (Harry), followed by a stream of visitors: future Justice Oliver Wendell Holmes, Mrs. J. T. Fields, Sarah Orne Jewett, the Paul Bourgets, the Edward Warrens, the Daniel Curtises, the Edmund Gosses, and Howard Sturgis. His witty friend Jonathan Sturges, a young, crippled New Yorker, stays for two months during autumn. *In the Cage* published. Meets neighbors Stephen Crane and H. G. Wells.

1899   Finishes *The Awkward Age* and plans trip to the Continent. Fire in Lamb House delays departure. To Paris in March and then visits the Paul Bourgets at Hyères. Stays with the Curtises in their Venice palazzo, where he meets and becomes friends with Jessie Allen. In Rome meets young American-Norwegian sculptor Hendrik C. Andersen; buys one of his busts. Returns to England in July and Andersen comes for three days in August. William, his wife, Alice, and daughter, Peggy, arrive at Lamb House in October. First meeting of brothers in six years. William now has confirmed heart condition. James B. Pinker becomes literary agent and for first time James's professional relations are systematically organized; he reviews copyrights, finds new publishers, and obtains better prices for work ("the germ of a new career"). Purchases Lamb House for $10,000 with an easy mortgage.

1900   Unhappy at whiteness of beard which he has worn since the Civil War, he shaves it off. Alternates between Rye and London. Works on *The Sacred Fount*. Works on and then sets aside *The Sense of the Past* (never finished). Begins *The Ambassadors*. *The Soft Side*, a collection of twelve tales, published. Niece Peggy comes to Lamb House for Christmas.

1901   Obtains permanent room at the Reform Club for London visits and spends eight weeks in town. Sees funeral of Queen Victoria. Decides to employ a typist, Mary Weld, to replace the more expensive overqualified shorthand stenographer, MacAlpine. Completes *The Ambassadors* and begins *The Wings of the Dove*. *The Sacred Fount* published.

Has meeting with George Gissing. William James, much improved, returns home after two years in Europe. Young Cambridge admirer Percy Lubbock visits. Discharges his alcoholic servants of sixteen years (the Smiths). Mrs. Paddington is new housekeeper.

1902   In London for the winter but gout and stomach disorder force him home earlier. Finishes *The Wings of the Dove* (published in August). William James Jr. (Billy) visits in October and becomes a favorite nephew. Writes "The Beast in the Jungle" and "The Birthplace."

1903   *The Ambassadors, The Better Sort* (a collection of eleven tales), and *William Wetmore Story and His Friends* published. After another spell in town, returns to Lamb House in May and begins work on *The Golden Bowl*. Meets and establishes close friendship with Dudley Jocelyn Persse, a nephew of Lady Gregory. First meeting with Edith Wharton in December.

1904–05   Completes *The Golden Bowl* (published Nov. 1904). Rents Lamb House for six months, and sails in August for America after twenty-year absence. Sees new Manhattan skyline from New Jersey on arrival and stays with Colonel George Harvey, president of Harper's, in Jersey shore house with Mark Twain as fellow guest. Goes to William's country house at Chocorua in the White Mountains, New Hampshire. Re-explores Cambridge, Boston, Salem, Newport, and Concord, where he visits brother Bob. In October stays with Edith Wharton in the Berkshires and motors with her through Massachusetts and New York. Later visits New York, Philadelphia (where he delivers lecture "The Lesson of Balzac"), and then Washington, D.C., as a guest in Henry Adams' house. Meets (and is critical of) President Theodore Roosevelt. Returns to Philadelphia to lecture at Bryn Mawr. Travels to Richmond, Charleston, Jacksonville, Palm Beach, and St. Augustine. Then lectures in St. Louis, Chicago, South Bend, Indianapolis, Los Angeles (with a short vacation at Coronado Beach near San Diego), San Francisco, Portland, and Seattle. Returns to explore New York City ("the terrible town"), May–June. Lectures on "The Question of Our Speech" at Bryn Mawr commencement. Elected to newly founded American Academy of Arts and Letters

(William declines). Returns to England in July; lectures had more than covered expenses of his trip. Begins revision of novels for the New York Edition.

1906–08   Writes "The Jolly Corner" and *The American Scene* (published 1907). Writes eighteen prefaces for the New York Edition (twenty-four volumes published 1907–09). Visits Paris and Edith Wharton in spring 1907 and motors with her in Midi. Travels to Italy for the last time, visiting Hendrik Andersen in Rome, and goes on to Florence and Venice. Engages Theodora Bosanquet as his typist in autumn. Again visits Edith Wharton in Paris, spring 1908. William comes to England to give a series of lectures at Oxford and receives an honorary Doctor of Science degree. James goes to Edinburgh in March to see a tryout by the Forbes-Robertsons of his play *The High Bid*, a rewrite in three acts of the one-act play originally written for Ellen Terry (revised earlier as the story "Covering End"). Play gets only five special matinees in London. Shocked by slim royalties from sales of the New York Edition.

1909   Growing acquaintance with young writers and artists of Bloomsbury, including Virginia and Vanessa Stephen and others. Meets and befriends young Hugh Walpole in February. Goes to Cambridge in June as guest of admiring dons and undergraduates and meets John Maynard Keynes. Feels unwell and sees doctors about what he believes may be heart trouble. They reassure him. Late in year burns forty years of his letters and papers at Rye. Suffers severe attacks of gout. *Italian Hours* published.

1910   Very ill in January ("food-loathing") and spends much time in bed. Nephew Harry comes to be with him in February. In March is examined by Sir William Osler, who finds nothing physically wrong. James begins to realize that he has had "a sort of nervous breakdown." William, in spite of now severe heart trouble, and his wife, Alice, come to England to give him support. Brothers and Alice go to Bad Nauheim for cure, then travel to Zurich, Lucerne, and Geneva, where they learn Robertson (Bob) James has died in America of heart attack. James's health begins to improve but William is failing. Sails with William and Alice for America in August. William dies at Chocorua soon after arrival, and James remains with the family for the winter. *The Finer Grain* and *The Outcry* published.

1911   Honorary degree from Harvard in spring. Visits with Howells and Grace Norton. Sails for England July 30. On return to Lamb House, decides he will be too lonely there and starts search for a London flat. Theodora Bosanquet obtains two work rooms adjoining her flat in Chelsea and he begins autobiography, *A Small Boy and Others*. Continues to reside at the Reform Club.

1912   Delivers "The Novel in *The Ring and the Book*," on the 100th anniversary of Browning's birth, to the Royal Society of Literature. Honorary Doctor of Letters from Oxford University June 26. Spends summer at Lamb House. Sees much of Edith Wharton ("the Firebird"), who spends summer in England. (She secretly arranges to have Scribner's put $8,000 into James's account.) Takes 21 Carlyle Mansions, in Cheyne Walk, Chelsea, as London quarters. Writes a long admiring letter for William Dean Howells' seventy-fifth birthday. Meets André Gide. Contracts bad case of shingles and is ill four months, much of the time not able to leave bed.

1913   Moves into Cheyne Walk flat. Two hundred and seventy friends and admirers subscribe for seventieth birthday portrait by Sargent and present also a silver-gilt Charles II porringer and dish ("golden bowl"). Sargent turns over his payment to young sculptor Derwent Wood, who does a bust of James. Autobiography *A Small Boy and Others* published. Goes with niece Peggy to Lamb House for the summer.

1914   *Notes of a Son and Brother* published. Works on "The Ivory Tower." Returns to Lamb House in July. Niece Peggy joins him. Horrified by the war ("this crash of our civilisation," "a nightmare from which there is no waking"). In London in September participates in Belgian Relief, visits wounded in St. Bartholomew's and other hospitals; feels less "finished and useless and doddering" and recalls Walt Whitman and his Civil War hospital visits. Accepts chairmanship of American Volunteer Motor Ambulance Corps in France. *Notes on Novelists* (essays on Balzac, Flaubert, Zola) published.

1915–16   Continues work with the wounded and war relief. Has
           occasional lunches with Prime Minister Asquith and fam-
           ily, and meets Winston Churchill and other war leaders.
           Discovers that he is considered an alien and has to report
           to police before going to coastal Rye. Decides to become
           a British national and asks Asquith to be one of his spon-
           sors. Receives Certificate of Naturalization on July 26.
           H. G. Wells satirizes him in *Boon* ("leviathan retrieving
           pebbles") and James, in the correspondence that follows,
           writes: "Art *makes* life, makes interest, makes importance."
           Burns more papers and photographs at Lamb House in
           autumn. Has a stroke December 2 in his flat, followed by
           another two days later. Develops pneumonia and during
           delirium gives his last confused dictation (dealing with the
           Napoleonic legend) to Theodora Bosanquet, who types it
           on the familiar typewriter. Mrs. William James arrives De-
           cember 13 to care for him. On New Year's Day, George V
           confers the Order of Merit. Dies February 28. Funeral ser-
           vices held at the Chelsea Old Church. The body is cre-
           mated and the ashes are buried in Cambridge Cemetery
           family plot.

Note on the Texts

This volume, one of five collecting the complete stories of Henry James, presents in the approximate chronological order of their completion 21 stories that were first published between 1892 and 1898. James worked on many ideas for stories during this time, usually finishing them only when he was certain that they would be published in periodicals. He considered periodical publication as an intermediate step in the composition of his stories and always revised them for book publication, making changes in wording as well as eliminating commas introduced by periodical editors; he consistently requested that publishers follow his lighter use of commas and that American publishers retain his British spellings. During this period James was living in England, and when his stories were to be published in both American and English book editions, his practice was to correct and revise the proofs of only one publisher and to have corrected proofs sent to the other publisher. He did not read the subsequent proofs for the other edition.

Collations show that the editions for which James corrected and revised proofs follow his wishes, both in punctuation and in wording, more closely than the other editions. James read proofs for the American typesetting of *The Real Thing and Other Tales*, which was published from this setting in both the United States and England in 1893. He read proofs of the English settings for *The Private Life, The Wheel of Time, Lord Beaupré, The Visits, Collaboration, Owen Wingrave* (1893; published in the United States as two separate collections: *The Private Life, Lord Beaupré, The Visits* and *The Wheel of Time, Collaboration, Owen Wingrave*); *Terminations* (1895); *Embarrassments* (1896); *The Two Magics* (1898); and *In the Cage* (1898).

The following list gives the sources of the stories included in this volume and the dates of their first periodical and first American and English book publications. (James later included 15 of the stories in the 1907–9 New York Edition of his collected works.)

"Nona Vincent" (*English Illustrated Magazine*, February–March, 1892) and "The Real Thing" (*Black and White*, April 16, 1892) appeared in *The Real Thing and Other Tales*, published in New York and London by Macmillan and Co. in March 1893. The texts printed in this volume are from the Macmillan edition.

"The Private Life" (*Atlantic Monthly*, April 1892), "Lord Beaupré" (published as "Lord Beauprey," *Macmillan's Magazine*, April–June 1892), and "The Visits" (published as "The Visit," *Black and White*, May 28, 1892) appeared in *The Private Life, The Wheel of Time, Lord Beaupré, The Visits, Collaboration, Owen Wingrave*, published in

London by James R. Osgood, McIlvaine & Co. in June 1893 and in *The Private Life, Lord Beauprè, The Visits*, published in New York by Harper and Brothers in August 1893. The texts printed in this volume are from the Osgood edition.

"Sir Dominick Ferrand" (published as "Jersey Villas," *Cosmopolitan Magazine*, July–August 1892) and "Greville Fane" (*Illustrated London News*, September 17 and 24, 1892) appeared in *The Real Thing and Other Tales*, published in New York and London by Macmillan and Co. in March 1893. The texts printed in this volume are from the Macmillan edition.

"Collaboration" (*English Illustrated Magazine*, September 1892), "Owen Wingrave" (*The Graphic, an Illustrated Weekly Newspaper*, November 28, 1892), and "The Wheel of Time" (*Cosmopolitan Magazine*, December 1892–January 1893) appeared in *The Private Life, The Wheel of Time, Lord Beauprè, The Visits, Collaboration, Owen Wingrave*, published in London by James R. Osgood, McIlvaine & Co. in June 1893, and in *The Wheel of Time, Collaboration, Owen Wingrave*, published in New York by Harper and Brothers in September 1893. The texts printed in this volume are from the Osgood edition.

"The Middle Years" (*Scribner's Magazine*, May 1893), "The Death of the Lion" (*Yellow Book*, April 1894), and "The Coxon Fund" (*Yellow Book*, July 1894) appeared in *Terminations*, published in London by William Heinemann in May 1895 and in New York by Harper and Brothers in June 1895. "The Altar of the Dead" was published for the first time in *Terminations*. The texts printed in this volume are from the Heinemann edition.

"The Next Time" (*Yellow Book*, July 1895), "Glasses" (*Atlantic Monthly*, February 1896), "The Figure in the Carpet" (*Cosmopolis*, January–February 1896), and "The Way It Came" (*Chapbook*, May 1, 1896, and *Chapman's Magazine of Fiction*, May 1896) appeared in *Embarrassments*, published in London by William Heinemann and in New York by the Macmillan Company in June 1896. The texts printed in this volume are from the Heinemann edition.

"The Turn of the Screw" (*Collier's Weekly*, January 27–April 16, 1898) appeared in *The Two Magics*, published in London by William Heinemann and in New York by the Macmillan Company in October 1898. "Covering End" was published for the first time in *The Two Magics*. The texts printed in this volume are from the Heinemann edition.

"In the Cage" appeared for the first time in *In the Cage*, published in London by Duckworth & Co. in August 1898 and in Chicago and New York by Herbert S. Stone & Co. in September 1898. The text printed in this volume is from the Duckworth edition.

This volume presents the texts of the printings chosen for inclusion here but does not attempt to reproduce features of their typographic design. Spelling, punctuation, and capitalization often are expressive features and they are not altered, even when inconsistent or irregular. The following is a list of typographical errors corrected, cited by page and line number: 30.3, Wayward; 60.33, next her; 70.34, anwered; 135.23, 'If; 162.3, never; 190.14, so see; 216.27, gentlemen; 238.10, than are; 247.27, played; 250.29, would too; 256.20, ago,; 261.27, same that; 264.19, large cold; 287.20, said me; 330.16, 'I; 385.28, arrives?"; 385.33, him.' "; 386.21, lookd; 399.31, worst.'; 434.38, Why; 443.26, Mr.; 471.36, you; 474.36, restrospect; 485.16, on more."; 570.39, don't how; 579.9, dont!; 599.1, bride a; 612.20, were he; 626.30, you chair.; 633.24, Release; 654.8, matters.; 826.14, man.'; 833.34, "Who'; 847.16, love" s.

Notes

In the notes below, the reference numbers denote page and line of this volume (the line count includes titles and headings). No note is made for material included in standard desk-reference books such as Webster's *Collegiate*, *Biographical*, and *Geographical* dictionaries. Quotations from Shakespeare are keyed to *The Riverside Shakespeare*, ed. G. Blakemore Evans (Boston: Houghton Mifflin, 1974). For further background than is provided in the notes, see *Henry James Letters*, ed. Leon Edel (Cambridge: The Belknap Press of Harvard University Press, Vol. I—1843–1875 [1974]; Vol. II—1875–1883 [1975]; Vol. III—1883–1895 [1980]; Vol. IV—1895–1916 [1984]); and *The Complete Notebooks of Henry James*, ed. Leon Edel and Lyall H. Powers (New York and Oxford: Oxford University Press, 1987).

1.30   inedited] Unedited.

4.11   *intraitable*] Inflexible, unyielding.

29.10   Hyperion . . . satyr!] Cf. Shakespeare, *Hamlet*, I.ii.140.

32.37   "sunk" . . . painting] One on which the colors have spread or sunk into the paper, losing their effect.

46.2   *bêtement*] Stupidly.

46.17–18   *profils perdus*] Three-quarter views.

49.1   *sentiment de la pose*] Feel for posing.

49.20   lazzarone] Neapolitan usage for a vagabond, beggar.

52.23   *"Ce sont . . . porte."*] "These are people you have to throw out of the house."

52.34   *coloro che sanno*] Cf. *Inferno*, IV.131: "'l maestro di color che sanno" ("the master of those who know"), Dante's epithet for Aristotle.

58.18   *fleur des pois*] The pick of the bunch.

66.32   *cher maître*] Dear master.

67.12   *haricots verts*] Green beans.

67.14   *régal*] Pleasure, treat.

68.11   *débit*] Oral delivery.

68.12   Comédie-Française] The French national theater in Paris.

75.6   *Où . . . venir?*] Where do you want to go from here? (i.e., "What are you getting at?")

89.19   Manfred]   The tortured, rhetorically extravagant hero, "half-dust, half-deity," who lives in the Bernese Alps in Byron's *Manfred* (1817).

94.35   *moi qui vous parle*]   I who speak to you.

95.30   *parti*]   Eligible marriage partner.

164.20   cottage piano]   Low upright piano.

172.38–39   barley-sugar]   A boiled candy.

191.20   *suivante*]   Attendant.

194.7   fly]   A one-horse covered carriage.

203.17   *repaire*]   Den of thieves.

221.2   Lucien de Rubempré . . . Vidame de Pamiers]   Characters in Balzac's *Human Comedy* stories, including *Lost Illusions* and *The History of the Thirteen*.

224.40–225.1   Desdemona . . . man.]   Shakespeare, *Othello*, I.iii.162–63.

225.13   *gagne-pain*]   Livelihood, means of subsistence.

227.22   *premiers frais*]   Initial outlay.

231.5   *vieux jeu*]   Old hat.

232.23   *trouvailles*]   Finds.

234.37   *les jeunes*]   The young (i.e., usually young, often stridently bohemian, practitioners of a new school of art).

238.16   of race]   Of a thoroughbred.

238.23   *convenances*]   Propriety, social conventions.

238.32   *jeune mees*]   Young "miss."

241.16   *bout de causerie*]   Round of chat.

241.31   *il faut opter*]   You have to choose.

241.39   *C'est à se tordre!*]   That breaks me up!

242.6   *Pas davantage*]   No more.

242.30   *le roman russe*]   The Russian novel.

242.32   *là-bas*]   Over there.

243.24   '*Chère madame, voyons!*']   "Dear Madam, we see that!"

243.31   *vous . . . l'art!*']   " . . . you know that for me there's nothing but art!"

244.14–15   *Cela . . . nerfs.*]   That got on my nerves.

245.2 *Abendlied*] Evening song.

245.12 *à la maison*] At home.

246.4 *ces gens-là.*] Those people.

246.35 *"Was . . . dazu?"*] "What do you say to that?"

247.9 *Foilà*] Voilà, "There you are!" "Behold!"

247.14–15 *"Dieu, . . . beau!"*] "God, how beautiful it is!"

247.35 *pis que pendre*] (He deserves) worse than hanging.

248.3 *"Et moi donc!"*] "And so me!"

248.5 *des bêtises*] Nonsense.

248.14 *C'est juste!*] That's right!

248.35 *il n'y a que ça!*] That's all there is!

249.14 *Ça y est*] There it is! That's it.

249.20 *C'est . . . esprit.*] This is a very great mind.

249.22 *C'est . . . génie.*] This is a very fine genius.

249.22–23 *nous . . . espaces!*] We are in infinite space!

250.10 *douanes*] Customhouses; customs.

250.39 needle-gun] Single-shot breech loading rifle, so-called because of its needlelike firing pin.

251.18 *quatrième*] Fourth-floor apartment.

252.6 *visages de bois*] Wooden, lifeless, faces.

252.15 *jusqu'au . . . l'âme*] To the depths of her soul.

252.36 *vous autres!*] You people!

258.3 crammer] One who prepares persons for examinations.

259.22 Sandhurst] Village in Berkshire, England, site of the Royal Military Academy.

266.19 Bayswater] A middle-class neighborhood along the north side of Hyde Park.

280.27 Paul and Virginia] "Paul et Virginie" (1787), a romance by Bernardin de Saint-Pierre about a pair of orphans in love since childhood.

294.15 Bradshaw] *Bradshaw's Monthly Railway Guide*, a series of timetables begun in 1839 by George Bradshaw.

303.1 want of drawing.] Something out of perspective.

304.39   the Row]   Rotten Row, fashionable bridle path in London's Hyde
Park.

309.39   *coup de foudre*]   Great love (literally, "thunderbolt").

339.31   *Qui dort dîne!*]   Whoever sleeps forgets his hunger!

340.25   *bergère*]   Shepherdess.

357.6   "Under the fifth rib!"]   "To the heart!"

362.23   *passe encore*]   Well and good; okay.

383.21–22   Flaubert's . . . literature?]   In a review of *Correspondance de
Flaubert* (1893) published in *Macmillan's Magazine*, March 1893, James wrote
of "the charge perpetually on Flaubert's lips in regard to his contemporaries,
the accusation of malignantly hating it," i.e., literature.

383.25   *valet de place*]   Guide who seeks employment from travelers.

386.31   'If . . . love?']   Cf. *The Pannel* (1788), I.i, John Philip Kemble's
adaptation of Isaac Bickerstaffe's *'Tis Well it's no Worse* (1770): "When first I
attempted your pity to move, / You seemed deaf to my sighs and my prayers;
/ Perhaps it was right to dissemble your love, / But why did you kick me
downstairs?"

389.31   *inédit*]   Unpublished.

391.30   the Abbey]   The remains of a number of celebrated writers, including Chaucer, Dickens, and Browning, are interred in Westminster Abbey;
it was sometimes referred to as England's "temple of fame."

396.39   *for intérieur*]   Innermost heart.

421.8   *"Moi pas comprendre!"*]   "I don't understand!"

427.7   *Werden*]   Development, evolution.

495.36   *"Je . . . malheur."*]   "I bring you bad luck."

504.19   Board-school]   Elementary school administered by a locally
elected board.

514.12–13   *Aux . . . remèdes.*]   For desperate diseases, desperate remedies.

516.37   *"Que voulez-vous?"*]   "What do you expect?"

525.10   a blow.]   A bit of recreation.

526.1   out of drawing]   Out of perspective.

539.13–14   on the straw]   Destitute.

540.20–21   phrase . . . inclinations.]   Edward Gibbon on Gordianus II (d.
A.D. 238) in *The History of the Decline and Fall of the Roman Empire* (1776–
88), chap. 7: "Twenty-two acknowledged concubines, and a library of sixty-

two thousand volumes, attested the variety of his inclinations, and from the productions which he left behind him, it appears that the former as well as the latter were designed for use rather than ostentation."

540.24   dished]   Defeated, utterly ruined, cheated.

554.20   *Que voulez-vous?*]   What do you want?

560.4   *"Vous-en-êtes là?"*]   "So you've come to that?"

564.31   "Lohengrin,"]   Opera (1850) by Richard Wagner.

592.25   *Vera . . . dea!*]   Virgil, *Aeneid*, I.405: " . . . in her gait she was revealed to be a very goddess," describing Aeneas' recognition of Venus.

593.5   *secousse*]   Shock, jolt.

594.14–15   *"Tellement . . . tête!"*]   "I'd so love to see your face!"

598.32   *trouvaille*]   Find.

611.26   the "Long."]   The summer vacation at the universities.

614.24   Bond Street]   Area of fashionable shops and picture-galleries.

616.9   *entêtement*]   Obstinacy.

626.34   *soit*]   Granted.

638.8   *Raison de plus*]   All the more reason.

655.1   Udolpho]   In Ann Radcliffe's *The Mysteries of Udolpho* (1794), a castle where the orphaned heroine is terrorized by seemingly supernatural occurrences.

685.31   Mrs. Marcet]   Jane Haldimand Marcet (1785–1858), author of grammar texts, children's stories, and popular books on science and political economy.

768.18   'simple . . . flower']   Alfred Tennyson, "Lady Clara Vere de Vere," line 15.

775.30–31   puss-in-the-corner]   Game in which four players occupy the corners of a room and a fifth attempts to gain one when they change positions.

786.28   Dead Sea fruit.]   In legend, beautiful apples that taste of ashes.

787.34   Aldus]   Italian editor and scholar Aldus Manutius (1449–1515) founded the Aldine Press that produced the earliest printed editions of many Greek and Latin classics, including in his lifetime the works of Aristotle and Aristophanes.

801.31   as Chicago]   In 1871, half the city was destroyed by fire.

835.12   "sounder,"]   Device that transmits messages in audible code.

835.33   "Court Guide"] Directory of names and addresses of nobility, gentry, and members of "society."

836.33   Chalk Farm] An area of London north of Regent's Park.

839.28   *Picciola*] Story (1836) by Xavier Saintine about a prisoner solaced by nurturing a plant that suddenly appears outside his cell.

CATALOGING INFORMATION

James, Henry, 1843–1916.
    Complete stories 1892–1898/Henry James.
        p.   cm. — (The Library of America ; 82)
1. Manners and customs—Fiction.   I. Title.   II. Series.
PS 2112   1996   95–23463
813'.4—dc20
ISBN 1-883011-09-4

This book is set in 10 point Linotron Galliard,
a face designed for photocomposition by Matthew Carter
and based on the sixteenth-century face Granjon. The paper is
acid-free Ecusta Nyalite and meets the requirements for permanence
of the American National Standards Institute. The binding
material is Brillianta, a woven rayon cloth made by
Van Heek-Scholco Textielfabrieken, Holland.
The composition is by The Clarinda
Company. Printing and binding by
R.R.Donnelley & Sons Company.
Designed by Bruce Campbell.

X

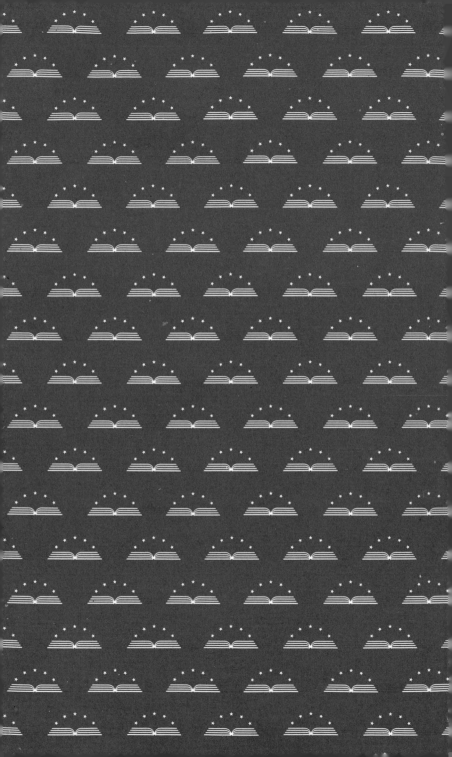